Beowulf and Beyond

STUDIES IN ENGLISH MEDIEVAL LANGUAGE AND LITERATURE

Edited by Jacek Fisiak

Vol. 18

PETER LANG

Frankfurt am Main · Berlin · Bern · Bruxelles · New York · Oxford · Wien

Hans Sauer/Renate Bauer (eds.)

Beowulf and Beyond

PETER LANG
Europäischer Verlag der Wissenschaften

Bibliographic Information published by the Deutsche Nationalbibliothek

The Deutsche Nationalbibliothek lists this publication in the Deutsche Nationalbibliografie; detailed bibliographic data is available in the internet at <http://www.d-nb.de>.

ISSN 1436-7521
ISBN 3-631-55925-9
US-ISBN 0-8204-8751-1

Printed in Germany 1 2 3 4 5 6 7

www.peterlang.de

Contents

Abbreviations

a) General abbreviations

acc.	accusative
adj.	adjective
AmE	American English
AN	Anglo-Norman
arch.	archaic
Aux	auxiliary verb
Bk.	book
BL	British Library
CCCC	Corpus Christi College Cambridge
dat.	dative
dm	determinatum
dt	determinant (determiner)
EETS	Early English Text Society
EM	East Midlands
EME	early Middle English
f.	feminine
G	German
gen.	genitive
Gk	Greek
Gmc	Germanic
IE	Indo-European
imp.	imperative
imperf.	imperfect
ind.	indicative
inf.	infinitive
Lat	Latin
lit.	literally
m.	masculine
ME	Middle English
MS/MSS	manuscript/manuscripts
N	noun
n.	neuter
NME	northern Middle English
nom.	nominative
OE	Old English
OF	Old French
OHG	Old High German

OI	Old Irish
OLG	Old Low German
P	free-morph prefix or adverb
p.	page
part.	participle
partic.	particle or adverbial element
pass.	passive
PDE	Present-day English (~ Modern English)
pl.	plural
Prep	preposition
Prep + N	prepositional phrase
pres.	present
pret.	preterite
S	subject
sg.	singular
stz.	stanza
subj.	subjunctive
subst.	substantive
trans.	translator/translation
V	verb
WGmc	West Germanic
WM	West Midlands
WRY	West Riding of Yorkshire

b) Authors and texts

Ad[1]	British Library, London, MS Additional 5140		
ÆCHom	Peter Clemoes (ed.)		
		1997	*Ælfric's Catholic homilies: The first series.* (EETS s.s. 17.) London: Oxford University Press.
	Malcolm Godden (ed.)		
		1979	*Ælfric's Catholic homilies: The second series.* (EETS s.s. 5.) London: Oxford University Press.
ÆGram	Julius Zupitza (ed.)		
		1880	*Ælfrics Grammatik und Glossar.* Berlin: Weidmann.
		2001	(3rd edition.) With a preface by Helmut Gneuss.

ASPR	The Anglo-Saxon Poetic Records: A Collective Edition. New York: Columbia University Press.		
	vol. 1: George Philip Krapp (ed.)		
		1931	*The Junius manuscript.*
	vol. 2: George Philipp Krapp (ed.)		
		1932	*The Vercelli book.*
	vol. 3: George Philipp Krapp -- Elliott van Kirk Dobbie (eds.)		
		1936	*The Exeter book.*
	vol. 4: Elliott van Kirk Dobbie (ed.)		
		1953	*Beowulf and Judith.*
	vol. 5: George Phillip Krapp (ed.)		
		1932	*The Paris Psalter and the Meters of Boethius.*
	vol. 6: Elliott van Kirk Dobbie (ed.)		
		1942	*The Anglo-Saxon minor poems.*
AV	*Authorised Version*, or King James Bible (1611)		
BlHom	Richard Morris (ed.)		
		1874	*The Blickling homilies.* (EETS o.s. 58, 63, 73.) London: Oxford University Press.
Chron	Charles Plummer (ed.)		
		1892-99	*Two of the Saxon chronicles parallel.* 2 vols. Oxford: Clarendon.
CT	Chaucer's *Canterbury tales*		
Ddi	*De die iudicii*		
El	Huntington Library, San Marino, MS Ellesmere 26 C 9		
ELV	Early and later version (of the Wyclif Bible)		
Ép	Bibliothéque municipale, Épinal, MS 72 (2)		
ÉpErf	the *Épinal-Erfurt glossary*		
Erf	Wissenschaftliche Allgemeinbibliothek, Erfurt, Codex Amplonianus F. 42		
EV	Early version (of the Wyclif Bible)		
Hg	National Library of Wales, Aberystwyth, MS Hengwrt 154 (Peniarth 392D)		
JDay II	*Judgement Day II* (cf. ASPR 6)		
Li	*Lindisfarne Gospels*, ed. Skeat (see below *Ru 2*)		
LV	Later version (of the Wyclif Bible)		

Or	Janet Bately (ed.)		
		1980	*The Old English Orosius*. (EETS s.s. 6.) London: Oxford University Press.
Riverside	Larry D. Benson (ed.)		
		1987	*The Riverside Chaucer*. (3rd edition.) Boston: Houghton Mifflin.
Ru 1	*Rushworth 1* (i.e. Mt.; Mk. 1-2,15; Jn. 18,1-3), ed. Skeat (see *Ru 2*)		
Ru 2	*Rushworth 2* (except Mt.; Mk. 1-2,15, Jn. 18,1-3), ed. Skeat		
	Walter W. Skeat (ed.)		
		1871-87	*The Holy Gospels in Anglo-Saxon, Northumbrian, and Old Mercian Versions*. Cambridge: Cambridge University Press.
VercHom	Donald G. Scragg (ed.)		
		1992	*The Vercelli Homilies and related texts*. (EETS o.s. 300.) Oxford: Oxford University Press.
WSCp	*West Saxon Gospels* (MS CCCC 140), ed. Liuzza		
	R.M. Liuzza (ed.)		
		1994-2000	*The Old English Version of the Gospels*. 2 vols. (EETS o.s. 304 & 314.) Oxford: Oxford University Press.

c) Books of the bible and apocrypha

Apoc.	Apocalypsis
Bar.	Baruch
D.A.	Deeds of the Apostles
Dan.	Daniel
Deut.	Deuteronomy
Ecclus.	Ecclesiasticus = Jesus Sirach
1, 2 Esd.	Esdras
Est.	Ester
Ezek.	Ezekiel
Gen.	Genesis
Is.	Isajah
Jer.	Jeremiah
Jgs.	Judges

Jn.	John
Kgs.	Kings
Lev.	Leviticus
Lk.	Luke
1,2 Macc.	Maccabees
Mk.	Mark
Mt.	Matthew
Num.	Numbers
Prov.	Proverbs
Pss.	Psalms
Rom.	St. Paul's letter to the Romans
Tob.	Tobit
Wisd.	Wisdom
Zeph.	Zephaniah

d) Dictionaries and reference works

AND	William Rothwell *et al.* (eds.)		
		1992	*Anglo-Norman dictionary*, London: Modern Humanities Research Association.
BEASE	Michael Lapidge *et al.* (eds.)		
		1999	*The Blackwell encyclopedia of Anglo-Saxon England.* Oxford: Blackwell.
BT	Joseph Bosworth -- T.Northcote Toller		
		1882-1898	*An Anglo-Saxon dictionary.* Oxford: Oxford University Press.
BTS	T. Northcote Toller		
		1908-1921	*An Anglo-Saxon dictionary: Supplement.* Oxford: Oxford University Press.
ClH	John R. Clark Hall		
		1960	*A concise Anglo-Saxon dictionary.* (4th edition with a supplement by Herbert D. Meritt.) Cambridge: Cambridge University Press.
CHEL	Richard M. Hogg (gen. ed.)		
		1992-2001	*The Cambridge history of the English language.* Cambridge: Cambridge University Press.

vol. 1: Richard M. Hogg (ed.)
1992 *The beginnings to 1066.*
vol. 2: Norman Blake (ed.)
1992 *1066-1476.*
vol. 3: Roger Lass (ed.)
1998 *1476-1776.*
vol. 4: Suzanne Romaine (ed.)
1998 *1776 to present day.*
vol. 5: R.W. Burchfield (ed.)
1994 *English in Britain and overseas.*
vol. 6: John Algeo (ed.)
2001 *English in North America.*

DMLBS	R.E. Latham -- D.R. Howlett		
		1975-97	*Dictionary of medieval Latin from British sources.* Vol 1: A-L. Oxford: Oxford University Press, for the British Academy.
DOE	Angus Cameron *et al.*		
		2003	*The dictionary of Old English.* Fascicles A-F on CD-ROM, version 1.0. Toronto: Pontifical Institute of Medieval Studies.
DOEC	Antonette di Paolo Healey (ed.)		
		2004	*The dictionary of Old English corpus in electronic form*, Toronto, <http://ets.umdl.umich.ed/o/oec>.
EWDS	Friedrich Kluge		
		1995	*Etymologisches Wörterbuch der deutschen Sprache*. (23. Aufl. bearbeitet von Elmar Seebold *et al.*) Berlin: de Gruyter.
IMEPC		2004	*The Innsbruck Middle English prose corpus on CD-Rom* (2nd edition.) Innsbruck: University of Innsbruck, English Department.
IMEV	Carleton Brown -- Rossell Hope Robbins (eds.)		
		1943	*The index of Middle English verse.* New York: Columbia University Press.

LALME	Angus McIntosh *et al.*		
		1986	*A Linguistic Atlas of Late Medieval English*. 4 vols. Aberdeen: Aberdeen University Press.
Lewis&Short	Charlton D. Lewis		
		1879	*A Latin dictionary*. Oxford: Oxford University Press.
LexMA	R.-H. Bautier *et al.* (eds.)		
		1977-1999	*Lexikon des Mittelalters*. 9 vols. (& register). Munich: Artemis, Stuttgart: Metzler.
MED	H. Kurath *et al.* (eds.)		
		1952-2001	*Middle English dictionary*. 17 vols. Ann Arbor, Michigan: Michigan University Press.
ManualME	J. Burke Severs -- A.E. Hartung -- P.G. Beidler (gen. eds.)		
		1967-	*A manual of the writings in Middle English 1050-1500*. 11 vols. (The Connecticut Academy of Arts and Sciences.) Hamden: Archon Books.
ODEE	C.T. Onions		
		1966	*The Oxford dictionary of English etymology*. Oxford: Oxford University Press.
OED	J.A.H. Murray *et al.* (ed.)		
		1884-1928 1989	*The Oxford English dictionary*. (2nd edition.) Prepared by J.A. Simpson, E.S.C. Weiner. 20 vols. Oxford: Oxford University Press.
STC	Alfred W. Pollard -- Gilbert R. Redgrave (eds.)		
		1976-1986	*A short-title catalogue of books printed in England, Scotland, and Ireland and of English books printed abroad 1475-1640*. (2nd edition.) 2 vols. London: Bibliographical Society.
ThLL		1900-	*Thesaurus Linguae Latinae*. Leipzig: Teubner.

Introduction

Hans Sauer (Munich, Germany)

IAUPE, the International Association of University Professors of English, was founded in 1950/51 and has held triennial conferences since 1950. Since 1977, a Medieval Symposium has been held immediately before (or sometimes after) the main IAUPE conference, usually in a city not far from the venue of the main conference. The venues and the organisers of the ten IAUPE Medieval Symposia so far have been:[1]

1977	Cracow	Przemyslaw J. Mroczkowski
1980	York	Jacques Berthoud & Derek Pearsall
1983	Aachen	Wolf-Dietrich Bald & Horst Weinstock
1986	Newcastle	Richard N. Bailey
1989	Zurich	Andreas Fischer & Udo Fries
1992	Ottawa	Douglas Wurtele
1995	Roskilde	Bent Preisler
1998	Sheffield	Norman Blake
2001	Munich	Hans Sauer
2004	Vancouver	Stephen Partridge

So far, proceedings have only been edited for the 1983 Aachen symposium.[2] The present volume contains a selection of papers from the Medieval Symposium held at the University of Munich in 2001 (25-28 July, to accompany the main conference in Bamberg) as well as from the Medieval Symposium held in Vancouver in 2004 (St. John's College, 6-7 August); they are supplemented by some papers from the Middle English Section (section 6) of the main 2004 IAUPE conference, also held in Vancouver (University of British Columbia, 8-14 August).[3]

The speakers at the Munich Medieval Symposium were: Alfred Bammesberger, Andrew Breeze, George Clark, Ian Kirby, Patrizia Lendinara, Conrad Lindberg, Manfred Malzahn, Manfred Markus, Saara Nevanlinna, Michiko Ogura, Saburo Oka, Hans Sauer, A.C. Spearing, Horst Weinstock. The speakers at the Vancouver Medieval Symposium were: Andrew Breeze, George Clark, Monika Fludernik, Carol Kaske, Ian Kirby, Conrad Lindberg, Hans Sauer, Michael W. Twomey, Horst Weinstock, Gernot Wieland. The speakers at the Middle English section of the Vancouver IAUPE conference were Claire Fennell, Sangsup Lee, Manfred Markus, Michiko Ogura, Liliana Sikorska, Michael W. Twomey.

The papers collected in this volume are mainly concerned with aspects of Old and Middle English language, literature, and culture. They are arranged in rough chronological order, first those dealing with Old English, then those dealing with Middle English; the more literary papers preceding the linguistic papers. Some of the best-known literary authors and texts are represented (*Beowulf*, Margery Kempe, and Malory with one paper each, Chaucer with two papers), but also runic inscriptions (two papers) and a legal document (*The assize of bread* of 1256).

There is also no strict separation between linguistics, literature, and culture: Alfred Bammesberger's analysis of some of the runes on the Ruthwell Cross has also necessarily to take the poem *Dream of the rood* into account; Saara Nevanlinna uses late Middle English rhymes and rhyme words for a linguistic analysis. Nor is there a strict division between past and present, between research and teaching: While most of the papers deal with the literary or linguistic interpretation of their material, two are more concerned with how to teach the medieval texts to university students in our time: Manfred Malzahn and Muhammad Abu al-Fadl Badran show that *Beowulf* can be made interesting to Arab students of English; Carol Kaske asks which moral lessons the warlike and continuously fighting Arthurian society depicted in Malory's *Morte Darthur* and related texts can teach to students in the USA. I give a brief overview of the contributions:

(1) **Manfred Malzahn & Muhammad Abu al-Fadl Badran** ("*Beowulf* in Arabia: Teaching heroic poetry in a post-heroic age") deal with a pedagogical and cultural question: They show that *Beowulf* can today be successfully taught to Arab students, especially in the United Arab Emirates (UAE), because in these countries a traditional heroic society with many parallels to the one depicted in *Beowulf* persisted well into the 20th century.

(2) **Patrizia Lendinara** ("Translating Doomsday: *De die iudicii* and its Old English translation, *Judgement Day II*") takes a close look at the Old English poem *Judgement Day II*, and compares it in great detail with its Latin source, the poem *De die iudicii*. *Judgement Day II* is interesting for a number of reasons: Whereas most Old English poems (including *Beowulf*) are difficult to date (though some may be early) and are presumed to be ultimately of Anglian origin, *Judgement Day II* is generally regarded as a late Old English poem (10th century) and of West-Saxon origin. Moreover, it is one of the few Old English poems where a Latin source is extant, namely the anonymous (Pseudo-Bedan?) *De die iudicii*. Lendinara also attempts to re-evaluate *Judgement Day II*: Whereas this poem has sometimes been viewed as a slavish translation, she sees it on the whole as a successful rendering, a literal translation that nevertheless "finds room for imaginative variations".

(3) The meaning of some of the Old English runic inscriptions is discussed by **Alfred Bammesberger** ("Old English runic inscriptions: Textual criticism and historical grammar"); in particular, he analyses the inscription on the Harford Farm Brooch (7th century; "A wish for the person who wore or carried the brooch"), the Brandon Antler Runic Inscription ("Grew on a wild animal"), the Overchurch Stone ("For the people we erected this monument: Pray for Æthelmund"), and the much-discussed Ruthwell Cross Inscription. Bammesberger supports recent attempts to look at the latter (the *Ruthwell crucifixion poem*) as a poem in its own right rather than just a short version of the poem *Dream of the rood* transmitted in the Vercelli Book.

(4) Different kinds of runes are dealt with by **Ian Kirby** ("The Narragansett Runic Inscription, Rhode Island"). These are connected with the question of whether Norsemen (Vikings) sailed to North America and if so, how far they got. Whereas it now seems to be clear that they certainly reached Newfoundland in the 11th century, it is unclear whether their explorations led them any further. Runic inscriptions found further to the south have often been regarded as later forgeries, e.g. the Kensington inscription. Kirby, however, argues that it is possible that the Narragansett Runic inscription found in Rhode Island, although difficult to decipher and to interpret, may be genuine and may be a further testimony to Norse explorations in America.

(5) **Michiko Ogura** ("Old English preverbal elements with adverbial counterparts") assembles the Old English verbs of motion (e.g. *gan, gangan, cuman, feran, astigan* etc.) and their Latin counterparts (*ire, abire, exire, introire, transire, uenire, ascendere, descendere* etc.), and investigates under which conditions particles (adverbial elements) are prefixed to the verbs (e.g. *ingan, utgan*) and under which conditions particles are placed after the verb (*gan in, gan ut*). On the whole, the historical development has been away from pre-position (*ingan*) to post-position (*go in*), i.e. phrasal verbs and prepositional verbs.

(6) The Épinal-Erfurt glossary (archetype ca. 680-690) is the oldest English text of any length that we have. Among other things it provides information on early English word-formation. **Hans Sauer** ("Old English names for people in the Épinal-Erfurt glossary") tries to define the word-field 'people', and he counts more than 60 Latin and more than 60 Old English words referring to 'people' in *ÉpErf.* He analyses their etymology, their word-formation patterns (mainly compounding, prefixation, suffixation, and derivation with a change of the stem vowel), as well as their semantic structure (agent, experiencer and patient nouns); he also pays attention to the relation between the Latin lemmata and their Old English renderings and to the question of Old English loan formations modelled on Latin words.

(7) *The assize of bread* (1256) is a statute issued under Henry III (1216-72). It attempts to regulate the size and weight of the loaves of bread and what they cost; the reconstruction of size and price involves a certain amount of mathematics for us. *The assize of bread* exists in several manuscripts: some contain a Latin version, some a French one, and some an English one. **Claire Fennell** describes this text and edits the versions from four manuscripts:
J = Oxford, Jesus College, MS 29 (II) (Latin)
P = Peterborough, MS 1 (Latin)
S = London & Oslo, The Schøyen Collection, MS 563 (Latin and French)
R = Oxford, Bodleian Library, Rawlinson, MS B 520 (Middle English).

(8) The Wyclif Bible (2nd half of the 14th century) exists in two versions, the earlier is more literal, the revised later version is more idiomatic. **Conrad Lindberg**, who has devoted much of his life's work to a new edition of the Wyclif Bible, edits a kind of conflated version of Baruch 3 in his paper "Revising the Wyclif Bible" in order to show the revision procedure and the different stages in the development of the text.

(9) One of the less well studied aspects of Chaucers poetry, namely his use of Latin words, phrases and sentences, is investigated by **Michael W. Twomey** ("Chaucer's Latinity"). Twomey distinguishes between intra-textual Latinisms, i.e. those spoken by the narrators and the characters (e.g. the Prioress's *Amor vincit omnia* and the boy's *Alma redemptoris mater*, or the Summoner's *questio quid iuris*), and extra-textual Latinisms, e.g. textual markers such as explicits and incipits between sections of works, furthermore marginal glosses – whereas the former (intra-textual) are usually Chaucer's, some of the latter (extra-textual) may have been inserted by later scribes. Twomey concludes that Chaucer used quotations and formulae from Latin but, unlike his contemporary Gower, did not attempt to create his own Latin phrases and sentences. Twomey furthermore discusses the Latin pronunciation which Chaucer might have used.

(10) **Saburo Oka** ("Chaucer's *Troilus* in a new comparative context") interprets Chaucer's description of the appearance and character of Troilus. First, he compares it with earlier versions of the Troy story where Troilus appears (e.g. Dictys Cretensis, Benoît de Sainte-Maure, Guido delle Colonne, Joseph of Exeter); then, he looks at some passages in Chaucer's *Troilus and Criseyde* which are central for the description of Troilus.

(11) The genre of the *Book of Margery Kempe* is difficult to pinpoint. It combines the elements of a mystical treatise, of an autobiography (the first, or at least the first extended one in English), and of a travel account. Margery Kempe's (c. 1373-c. 1439) character and motivation have also caused a lot of debate. **Liliana Sikorska** ("Between penance and purgatory: Margery Kempe's

'Pélerinage de la vie humaine' and the idea of salvaging journeys") interprets Margery Kempe's role as that of a 'fool of Christ', who endures dislike and slander for the love of God.

(12) **Carol Kaske** deals with Sir Thomas Malory's (c. 1410-c. 1471) great collection of Arthurian stories (*Le Morte Darthur*) and their frequent depiction of violence. She argues that Malory sometimes criticises this violence, e.g. in *The tales of Balin*. This criticism can appear in different forms: for example, sometimes fighters who kill their opponents are rebuked, and sometimes restraint in knights is praised. Kaske also looks at the numerous scenes where knights rehorse fallen comrades by unhorsing an enemy, and she proposes that "Malory is trying to portray battle as a matter of helping your friends more than hurting your foes" in these scenes.

(13) **Saara Nevanlinna** ("Observations on the loss of final plosive consonants in late Middle English rhyme-words") uses the Helsinki Corpus in order to find out more details about the deletion of final plosives in Middle English poetry (c. 1350-1500), mainly in rhyming pairs such as ... *wirschip/... Egipt*, or ... *óf/... sóft*, where apparently the final *-t* was dropped in the pronunciation of *Egip(t)* and *sof(t)*. She stresses that this must have been an oral phenomenon (poetry was usually recited) and she establishes different types and contexts of deletion or assimilation. She also stresses the regional aspect and concludes that the deletion of final plosives occurred most frequently in areas that had earlier been under Scandinavian influence, i.e. mainly the northern and eastern areas.

(14) Hyphens have not been studied much either synchronically or diachronically. **Manfred Markus** ("Hyphens and hyper-hyphens in Middle English [corpus-based]") tries to fill this gap in our knowledge – at least partly. He distinguishes between link hyphens (used within words), and break hyphens (used for breaking the line), and he arrives at a number of interesting conclusions, e.g. that until c. 1400, prefixes were often hyphenated, whereas after 1400, compounds were often hyphenated, or, that the native prefix *a-* and the prefix *de-* (borrowed from French) were often hyphenated in Middle English, whereas others were almost never hyphenated.

(15) English and German are both West-Germanic languages and thus closely related; but subsequently, they developed quite a number of differences, in their vocabulary as well as in their phonological, morphological and syntactic structure. **Horst Weinstock** ("Medieval English and German: A guide to Modern similarities and dissimilarities") looks at some of these differences, from the pronunciation of the letters of the alphabet (German /a:, be:, tse:/ etc. but English /ei, bi:, si:/ etc.), to syntax: Whereas German still has variant patterns of

word-order (SVO, but also SOV, OVS etc.), English almost exclusively employs the pattern SVO.

This volume thus shows at least some of the many aspects of Medieval English language, literature, and culture as well as of the history of English, and it also exhibits some of the various possible approaches to these areas.

My thanks are due to my co-editor **Renate Bauer**, who formatted this volume and produced the electronic version for the publisher. Both of us have to thank Jacek Fisiak for his constant encouragement, our contributors for their patience while this volume was in the making, and Susan Bollinger, Eva Gachstetter, Julia Hartmann, Ursula Lenker and Judith Rodrigues for checking the final version of the manuscript.

Notes

[1] The next main conference will be in Lund, 6-10 August 2007; the 2007 Medieval Symposium will be in Ystad (3-4 August 2007), see <iaupe.academic@englund.lu.se>. In order to reconstruct the dates and venues of the earlier Medieval Symposia, I had to ask several colleagues; my thanks are especially due to Andreas Fischer, Ian Kirby and Horst Weinstock.

[2] Wolf-Dietrich Bald -- Horst Weinstock (ed.). 1984. *Medieval Studies Conference Aachen 1983: Language and Literature.* (Bamberger Beiträge zur Englischen Sprachwissenschaft 15.) Frankfurt am Main: Lang.

[3] A selection of the papers given at the Bamberg IAUPE Conference (2001) has just been prublished: Herbert Grabes -- W. Viereck (ed.). 2006. *The wider scope of English.* (Bamberger Beiträge zur Englischen Sprachwissenschaft 51.) Frankfurt am Main: Lang.

Beowulf in Arabia: Teaching heroic poetry in a post-heroic age

Manfred Malzahn, Muhammad Abu al-Fadl Badran (Al-Ain, United Arab Emirates)

1. Purpose and scope of this paper

Within the framework of the present collection, it seems no more than fair to admit right at the outset of this contribution that it cannot lay claim to any original discoveries in either Anglo-Saxon or Classical Arabic scholarship. It is rather intended to demonstrate the fact that the two literatures concerned can be studied and taught comparatively, and to underpin the contention that works such as *Beowulf* should be seen as having their rightful place in English curricula especially in Arab countries, where the discussion of Old English literature can be integrated very well into a contemporary cultural debate.

2. OE literature in a United Arab Emirates (UAE) context

For anyone who teaches English literary texts in an entirely different setting from that in which they originated, questions of canon will of course have an added poignancy. Today, Old English writings occupy at best a marginal position within the framework of English studies in anglophone countries. Even in England itself, many curriculum planners would agree with the verdict that "a nodding acquaintance with the language and literature of the Anglo-Saxons is all that it is reasonable to demand" (Bateson -- Meserole 1976: 14). One might thus be tempted to bypass it completely wherever the temporal distance between author and reader is matched by spatial, linguistic, and cultural removes that would seem to make understanding, let alone enjoyment, highly unlikely indeed.

The United Arab Emirates can certainly be counted as one of those locations that fit the above description. Of the students majoring in English here, only few bring with them a command of the language that makes them see the prospect of reading literature in English as holding a promise of pleasure rather than of pain. For most of them, Britain is an island of which they have no first-hand experience, and often no more than some vague and general ideas. As in many other regions, the image of anglophone culture is nowadays clearly dominated by the overwhelming presence of the USA, particularly on various kinds of screens. In spite of Britain's past role as a colonial power on the Arabian peninsula, its inhabitants have become more and more inclined to regard the United States of America, for better or worse, as the representative norm not only of the English-speaking world, but of the entire occident.

If a fairly undifferentiated perception of Western culture is common among UAE students, then the young female English majors who outnumber their male counterparts at a ratio of about 18 to 1, and who lead their lives within relatively narrow geographical and social boundaries, can hardly be expected to represent too much of an exception. Among them as among other members of their society, the West tends to be perceived as appealing and appalling at the same time. From a typical Arab viewpoint, the allure of the commercial and cultural artifacts that epitomise the Western way of life masks a lack of what Arab-Islamic culture preserves: namely, traditional values and forms of social organisation based primarily on the bonds of kinship, and on the notion of the family or clan as the all-important social unit.

To students with such expectations in mind, the encounter with the world of *Beowulf* at the outset of their obligatory historical survey course can come as an eye-opener. The version of the text used will obviously be a modern translation, but this is really all it takes to facilitate the engagement with a tale that is bound to strike UAE students as surprisingly familiar, because of the very recent past of their own country as well as because of their indigenous literary heritage. Neither heroic ideals and lifestyles, nor the heroic poetry that describes them, are as remote to young Arabs at the beginning of the 21st century as they are to their English contemporaries, in whose eyes medieval epic heroes would likely belong to the virtual world of fantasy role-playing, an "ephemeral art" which is mainly "sheer entertainment", with only the feeblest connection to practical modern reality (Schick 1991: 15).

In the United Arab Emirates, on the other hand, the post-heroic age has only just arrived. From the very top right down to the bottom of the social pyramid, relationships between a sheikh and his followers can still be said to resemble those between Hrothgar and his retainers more than those between any elected president and his voters in the western world. Clan loyalties and boundaries are well-marked, and blood-money, locally known as *diya*, is paid to the victims of accidental and deliberate killings, in the manner of the Anglo-Saxon *wergild*. Gift-giving is still important in expressing and cementing personal relations between rulers and ruled, even if it may often be symbolic rather than substantial: public holidays, for instance, are decreed at short notice, rather than fixed in advance and hence taken as a matter of employees' rights. In exchange for material and ritual tokens of goodwill, the populace in turn publicly show corresponding signs of gratitude and of loyalty to the leadership on every suitable occasion.

But while the political organisation of the state thus still bears many of the ancient hallmarks, much else has changed so radically that the air-conditioned country in which the present-day generation of students dwells, looks almost totally alien to the environment that their grandfathers and grandmothers knew, while their fathers and mothers lived to see the whirlwind transition from near-medieval to futuristic. The following extract from the 40th-anniversary brochure of Oasis Hospital in Al-Ain, at about 300,000 inhabitants the second largest city in the Emirate of Abu Dhabi and likewise the seat of UAE University with its about 17,000 students, may serve in lieu of a lengthy documentation:

> In 1960, the population of Al-Ain and its related villages was approximately 2000. Population growth was totally stagnant. The infant mortality rate was estimated at 50%, and the maternal mortality rate was around 35%. … The 'home remedies' practiced by the people seemed to have done more damage than good. But the doctors were obviously a great help, and the local population was thrilled to have live, happy, bouncing babies, and to have mothers who would care for the family a day after delivery. It was also a joy for the hospital staff, to see the people's excitement– often expressed by shooting holes into the roof of the hospital. The practice at the time was to fire seven rifle shots for the birth of a boy, and three for a girl. Thus the staff always knew how many babies were born and their sexes, by simply counting the rifle shots. (Anonymus 2000: 4)

Such was the custom only four decades ago: today, men in the UAE are no longer in the habit of carrying guns around, and they do not even wear the *khanjar*, the ornamental dagger which still adorns some of their Omani neighbours. To see fully armed tribal warriors, one would have to venture as far as Yemen. The memory of a heroic past, however, is kept alive not only in the official image of its history which the country proudly preserves and promotes, but also in the popular imagination.

By way of evidence, we would once again like to cite just one significant example: namely, the legends surrounding a burial site just outside Dubai. The copse marking the site is now enclosed by a roundabout, one of whose exits leads onto the broad and brightly lit Al-Ain motorway. A newspaper report published in March 2001 quotes the great-great-grandson of Saeed Bu Khadra, after whom the spot was named, telling the story of his ancestor who died there in a battle against an invading tribe around the year 1900. According to the descendant Ali Bu Khadra, Saeed Bu Khadra had continued to fight even after one of his legs was severed from his body. Today, the location is credited with miraculous happenings, which Ali Bu Khadra was ostensibly doing his best to discredit in front of the interviewer.[1] The article closes, however, with the following:

> Yet strangely, when asked if he would pose for a photograph in the shaded glade, Bu Khadra resisted, giving no clear reason for his reticence. Visibly uncomfortable at the thought, he shivered: 'I just wouldn't want to go in there...' (Langley -- Idris 2001: 3)

What transpires here is the survival of archaic patterns of thought and behaviour beneath a relatively thin layer of modernity, and this is more or less typical not only of the Arabian peninsula, but of large parts of the Arab world. In today's UAE, the nomadic freedom of the *bedu* lifestyle belongs to the recent past, but nevertheless to the past, and the life-experience of the present generation is that of a largely regulated and sedentary existence among an abundance of modern conveniences. At the same time, however, families try to maintain traditional forms of social organisation, and to keep close control especially over their female members. For young males, the scope for thrill-seeking is thus severely limited on two fronts. The result is one which a criminologist might well identify as anomy, with reckless driving or drug-taking supplanting the martial raids or amorous visits celebrated in that ancient poetry which most of the young would still be familiar with.

A high degree of acquaintance with classic poems can indeed be found not only in the Gulf countries, but throughout the Arab world. In a study of an Egyptian village, for example, Dwight Fletcher Reynolds notes that quoting from time-honoured texts is part of a widespread communicational pattern there, with social status to be gained from or manifested in "the deployment of memorized classical Arabic poetry" (Reynolds 1995: 33). However, the question regarding the relevance or the precise role of heroic poetry in contemporary Arab society is a potential bone of contention. A recent survey by John Renard contrasts the perpetuation of "a rather distant and idealistic" heroism in some modern Arabic literature with the contemporary criticism voiced by other authors such as Nizar Qabbani from Syria:

> In my land,
> In the land of the simple,
> Where we slowly chew on our unending songs –
> A form of consumption destroying the east –
> Our east is chewing on its history.
> Its lethargic dreams,
> Its empty legends (Renard 1999: 10)

3. Heroic parallels and peculiarities

Whether it perceives ancient texts as supplying an inspirational counter-image to actual reality, or rather as affording an easy escape route into fantasy and hence an easy excuse for reality's deficiencies, the reception of early heroic poetry in Arabic cannot but highlight the fact that its poetic heroes are made such by non-heroes who receive, remember, and reiterate their epic narratives. Unlike in *Beowulf* with its third-person narration, the poet in Classical Arabic texts tends to be the singer of his own deeds, *scop* and skirmisher blended into one figure reminiscent of the Celtic Ossian, or indeed of the Germanic Odin, the god of poetry and "actor of diverse roles" who speaks in the *Hávamál* (Edwards -- Pálsson 1998: 12).

Because of the method of narration, the voice of the heroic-poetic speaker in early Arabic poetry often carries a greater immediacy than that of the *Beowulf* poet, who talks of past events which he did not personally witness. The boasting of Beowulf is commented on by the narrator and other characters; the boasting of the heroes in the *Mu'allaqat*, the classic ten long poems of the pre-Islamic period, is bound to reverberate without either mediation or retort. The egocentric or narcissistic nature of the poetic statement shows clearly enough in the opening motif, the lament for the departure of the beloved as her tribe or clan break up their camp, leaving only fading traces in the sand behind them. As in Renaissance sonnets, the speaker is prone to profess himself not only deserted, but cruelly wronged, like Imru'ul-Qais, who addresses his lady with the following words: "When you shed tears, those were only your arrows, / plunged into the depth of a slain heart."[2]

This is clearly not a sentiment that Beowulf or the *Beowulf* poet would express or share, but the *Mu'allaqat* do thematise, as palpably as does the Beowulf tale, the contrast and possible contradiction between individual-heroic desires and aspirations on the one hand, and social-communal obligations and restraints on the other. When Imru'ul-Qais speaks the famous words "Today I'll have wine, tomorrow I'll have revenge", he signals a turn from the extravagant and hedonistic life of a Prince Hal to the single-minded pursuit of retribution for the killing of his father: this makes him the true leader of his tribe, through a metamorphosis not unlike that of the "sluggard" and "feeble princeling" Beowulf into giant-crusher and monster-slayer (Crossley-Holland 1999: 72-3).

Another type of hero in ancient Arabic poetry may even openly turn against his community: the prime example here is Antara Ibn Shaddad. As the illegitimate child of a high-born leader of the Banu Abs tribe and a black slave woman, Antara rebels against his unfree status by demonstrating excellence in the aristocratic pursuits of martial arts and poetry. When Antara's heroic prowess is needed to help fend off an attack on his people, this opens the road to reconciliation with his tribe, recognition by his father, and union with his beloved, his cousin Abla whose praise he sings in his verse. The image of the hero as a lover stands in a marked contrast to the *Beowulf* poem, where the main character seems to have no special interest in women. In the case of Antara, images of the warlike and the amorous qualities of a champion are fused in lines such as the following:

> When the battle began I would fain kiss the swords,
> For their gleam looked like that of your smiling teeth.

With regard to feats of superhuman physical strength, on the other hand, the speaker of these verses does resemble "the megalomaniac hero who can swim for eight days and eight nights over the Baltic Sea in full armor slaying whales all the way". Cedric H. Whitman (1982: 20) thus sums up the character of Beowulf, by way of contrast with the all-embracing humanity which he perceives in the heroes of the Greeks. If, for the sake of the present argument, we accept the view of Beowulf as cutting an essentially catalectic figure, and hence the view of the Anglo-Saxon heroic ideal as restrictive, we would have to ask whether Antara comes any closer to that all-round perfection which makes Whitman and others see the Greek heroic notion as a link between the human and the divine. Whitman (1982: 20) formulates what he calls the heroic paradox as follows:

> The hero is ourself, expanded for our inspection and understanding … and pushed to logical – or illogical – extremes. And, as the Greek tradition presents him to us, we see him motivated by two simultaneous, opposite needs: the need for absolute status, and the need for human context, commitment; or, as the Greeks would put it, the urge toward divinity, and the necessity of remaining mortal.

In spite of his double identity as warrior and lover, and thus of his apparently richer humanity, the application of the above-mentioned formula to the case of Antara would encounter major obstacles in the form of many grave weaknesses. He is shown as having a lack of self-control that results in drunkenness, rape, and even gratuitous killing. Antara thus stands as the very opposite to the Stoic ideal of keeping the passions at bay; he indulges even the noblest of his emotions to an extent at which they have unethical consequences, as for instance the execution of many hundreds of prisoners, ordered by Antara because he is "unrestrained in grief" for a dead friend or a dead son (Lyons 1995: 95). A parallel to this incident can indeed be found in *Beowulf*, but given only in the form of a warning to the hero, with the bad king Heremod named as perpetrator:

> In mad rage he murdered his table-companions,
> his most loyal followers; it came about
> that the great prince cut himself off
> from all earthly pleasures, though God had endowed him
> with strength and power above all other men,
> and had sustained him. For all that his heart
> was filled with savage blood-lust. He never gave
> gifts to the Danes, to gain glory. He lived joyless,
> agony racked him; he was long an affliction
> to his people. Be warned, Beowulf,
> learn the nature of nobility. (Crossley -- Holland 1999: 57)

It would appear that Antara learns the treacherous nature of nobility when he loses his restraint,[3] and that his union of the lover's and the fighter's passion yet leaves him a less accomplished human being than Beowulf. After all, as Hrothgar remarks to Beowulf at the outset of his mission, the young Geat embodies the unlikely union of youth and wisdom. To find exemplary wisdom in dealings with women in the Old English epic, however, one would have to go to a minor character: namely, the dauntless Offa who tames and reforms the evil queen Thryth by means which are so mysteriously unspecified that they might once again recall the divine Odin and his spells, culminating in an infallible, but ultimately secret recipe for patriarchal bliss. As is hinted earlier in *Hávamál*, such happiness is beyond the ken and hence beyond the scope of mere mortals, who err when they think themselves the masters of their households and their possessions:

> The man's a born fool
> who boasts he can rule
> either women or wealth:
> his pride is so dense,
> it defies commonsense,
> and inflates his wild fancies. (Edwards -- Pálsson 1998: 57)

But not even Odin gets it right all the time,[4] and the many shortcomings of the immortals in the polytheistic universes of the Hellenic and the Germanic peoples stand in a marked contrast to stories which show a belief in the perfectibility or near-perfectibility of men. Like the greatest of the Greek heroes, Beowulf is made to look morally superior to some of those whom he would have worshipped, and of whom the extant version of his story is conspicuously silent. The Christianisation of Beowulf's tale has a parallel in the Islamisation of hero figures such as Antara, but while the coexistence of pagan and Christian elements in *Beowulf* has given rise to widely divergent theories about the composition and the original audience, the editorial process is slightly more obvious in Antara's case. Here, existing texts contain explicit references to the fact that he was not a Muslim, but likewise reassure the reader that he would certainly have been one if he had not been born before the revelation of Islam.

In both cultural traditions, literary texts document the need or the desire to adopt or adapt a pagan heroic ideal in the transition to a new monotheistic religion with a different ethic. In the case of *Beowulf*, the adaptation appears most clearly in the association of Grendel and his mother, through their being simultaneously "under God's curse and the instrument of God's justice", not only with the race of Cain but also with the arch-ambivalent Satan (Fajardo-Acosta 1989: 69).[5] The hero's foes are thus the enemies of God and Man; this identification, however, cannot change the fundamental tone of the tale, which not only J.R.R. Tolkien quite rightly calls elegiac. Man's struggle may be heroic and bring temporary victory over the forces of doom, but even as we celebrate such short-lived triumphs, "we approach slowly and reluctantly the inevitable victory of death" (Tolkien 1963: 84).

The Arabic as well as the Anglo-Saxon hero distinguishes himself by the unflinching acceptance of his ultimate fate. "Death is a well I must drink from", says Antara; but although he has no hesitation to risk his life in combat, he does not hold life's pleasures in disregard either. As Muraqqash Al-Akbar puts it: "We sell our life cheap in battle, but we don't trifle with it in time of peace." Anglo-Saxon heroes would appear inclined to agree that a man's time is well spent not only on the battlefield, but likewise on occasions of ceremonial splendour and conviviality. Beowulf himself reports the goings-on in Heorot with admiration:

> Then there was revelry; never in my life,
> under heaven's vault, have I seen men
> happier in the mead-hall. (Crossley -- Holland 1999: 67)

However, while telling the story of his victory over Grendel and complimenting his audience on their festive spirit, the hero suddenly switches to dark forebodings of discord and bloodshed between rival parties of revellers. The moment at which he relishes and, as today's talk-show hosts would say, shares the memories of past triumph with others, is thus fraught with foreknowledge of coming evil, and Beowulf, though called "unfated", cannot help bearing the burden of the one who sees ahead, instead of merely living out the moment in the blissful hæcceity of the young. The last words of the dying Abu Firas al-Hamdani can serve as a fit comment on this predicament:

When you call me and I can't reply, say:
'The best of young men, Abu Firas, never had youth.'

It is worth noting that in Beowulf's prophecy, it is an old man who incites a young warrior to break the peace of the festivities. The burden of the past is thus borne by the young, and the defeat of evil never complete: consequently, feasting and fighting follow each other in the endless cycle of heroic life, where periods of peace and happiness must be bought by heroic action. This suggests that the ideal leader would possess a dual nature, showing the same degree of excellence both in the field and in the hall. In *Beowulf*, it is possible to see the different virtues as divided between different characters, such as the "wise, generous, and legislative" Hrothgar, and the "fierce, terrifying, and hugely strong" Beowulf (Hill 1995: 75). It has likewise been claimed, however, that Beowulf himself has a dual nature, and that the darker of his two sides is a downright monstrous one. Fidel Fajardo-Acosta (1989: 3) asserts the following:

> The monsters are embodiments of the temptations with which Beowulf is confronted – to all of which he succumbs – and also mirror-images of Beowulf, of what he slowly becomes as he moves up the ladder of heroic achievement.

For those who are reluctant to see a hero-monster or monster-hero in Beowulf, Classical Arabic poetry has some more clearly marked specimens to offer. Above all, there is Shanfara of Azd:[6]

In the cold night so bitter that men will burn
Their most precious bow and arrow to warm them,
I wandered alone through the rainy dark,
No fellows but fog, horror, hunger and danger;
I slew fathers of children and grooms of brides,
And as I had left, returned before daybreak.
In the morning, I sat safely back at Qumaisa,
Leaving two pale-faced crowds to ask,
'In truth, we did hear the dogs howl last night:
Is a wolf passing by, we said, or hyenas?'
'No, it was muffled growling; they sleep now;
They were surely disturbed by some errant bird.'
'If a jinn was here, he did much evil work;
If a man–but this cruelty was not human.'

4. Conclusions and perspectives

At this point, it should be evident that a critical reading of heroic poetry in the 21st century calls for a critical examination of heroic concepts and their possible place in a civic society. What Old English and Arabic texts offer us is a window into the lives and thoughts of "face-to-face, non-centralized people" (Hill 1995: 150), whose social organisation is designed to give any two members of a tribe "some reason why the two should not attempt to kill each other" (Diamond 1998: 272), while making it rather more difficult to find such reasons for any two members of different tribes. Tribal identity and allegiance is as central a motif in ancient Arab poems as it is in Anglo-Saxon ones. When the egocentric 'I' is displaced by a phylocentric 'We', the boasting becomes communal, but the underlying ethic remains the same, as in the following example by Amr Ibn Kulthum of the Taghlib:[7]

> The earth, all its people, belong to us;
> And when we seize, we seize with might.
> The firm dry land we flood with our men;
> The back of the sea is filled with our ships.

Comparable passages can easily be found in Anglo-Saxon texts, and a comparative discussion may serve as an apt reminder of the fatal tendency of human beings to see the world's inhabitants as divided, whether it be along tribal, racial, religious or other lines, into two groups thought of as 'we' and 'they', while regarding the first of those as naturally favoured. Classical Arabic and Old English literature show extreme forms of behaviour resulting from such thought, as well as narrative or poetic attempts to rationalise the claim to a privileged status for a particular 'we-ness' in view of the fact that it must seem no more than one among many 'they-nesses' to others. Especially in *Beowulf*, we find hints at a possible squaring of the circle through a moral dimension: the vindication of the just through association with others who are just, in a manner that shows virtue to be consistent with self-interest. This is the gist of Robert Frank's theory of moral sentiments, as summed up in the following:

> The virtuous are virtuous for no other reason than that it enables them to join forces with others who are virtuous, to mutual benefit. And once cooperators segregate themselves off from the rest of a society a wholly new force of evolution can come into play: one that pits groups against each other, rather than individuals. (Ridley 1997: 147)

One problem is, of course, that in order to achieve cooperation among groups, the process must be repeated on the collective level. The other is that, in order to tell both the cooperative or virtuous individuals and the cooperative or virtuous groups from the unjust or selfish, virtues must not only be claimed, but unequivocally seen as being practised by the claimants. An extended walk through the streets of Belfast or Al-Quds[8] would certainly provide more evidence of mutually exclusive claims to righteousness than of any collective moral superiority. However, no group – whether it claims to defend the true faith against infidels, or the civilised world against terrorism – should be exempted from the need to vindicate its self-definition as 'good' through measuring its own actions by the most rigorous moral standards. The critical evaluation of the values proclaimed or embodied in heroic poetry can provide a useful means of testing moral principles and their practical application, for in heroic tales, justice is always a subject, whether given implicitly or explicitly, as here by Labid Ibn Rabiah:

> When our glorious tribe gathers, it never lacks
> One who dares to act high as honour demands,
> Nor a judge with wisdom to weigh each clan's claims,
> And stay calm in the clamour till all are content.

Apart from thus encouraging ventures onto the ground of moral philosophy and practical ethics or gender issues,[9] the teaching of *Beowulf* in Arabia can finally help to foster a debate that treats evil not only as a metaphysical datum, but more importantly, as a type of behaviour whose every instance asks for an individual explanation. In the case of Grendel and his mother, their fiendish nature furnishes only one half of the reason, and it is surely no less important to note that the crimes begin when the monsters have to suffer the inadvertent addition of insult to injury, in form of a daily reminder of the abjectness of their condition:

> Then the brutish demon who lived in darkness
> impatiently endured a time of frustration:
> day after day he heard the din of merry-making
> inside the hall, and the sound of the harp
> and the bard's clear song. (Crossley -- Holland 1999: 4-5)

Not only for the citizens of oil-rich Gulf states, would it make sense to try an alternative way of thinking of Grendel and his mother, as representing those underprivileged who live within earshot of the wealthy. In our global village, this definition would include urban slum-dwellers and starving peasants virtually anywhere. If we think of the story of Beowulf in terms of social psychology, we can read it as a nightmare in which the ugly forms of the have-nots surface from the stinking swamps to which they have been relegated, to haunt those who would love to have their enjoyment untainted by such unsightly spectacles. We feel that such a reading may set off a train of thought which it is perhaps as useful to pursue in Derby as in Dubai, and in Cambridge as in Cairo.

Notes

[1] Such miracles are popularly credited to the *awliya'Allah* or 'Friends of God'; the singular term for a saintly miracle-worker or religious hero is *wehli*.

[2] Here as well as in the following, English versions of Arabic texts are offered by the authors of this paper, unless marked otherwise. The aim is not philological accuracy, but a rendering that approximates the poetic power of the original.

[3] The figure of Alexander the Great, whose royal blood infused with alcohol boiled hot enough to cause the murder of his friend Cleitus, furnishes another parallel in the occidental tradition.

[4] He confesses, for instance, his improper timing of social calls, and reports an instance of unrequited love or lust that brought him "nothing but shame" (Edwards -- Pálsson 1998: 62).

[5] The line that Fajardo-Acosta cites in support of his reading, "Grendel gongan, Godes yrre baer", seems to be in itself ambivalent (cf. Fajardo -- Acosta 1989: 69).

[6] This version follows the German translation by Reuss (1853).

[7] This version follows the German translation by Landau (1968).

[8] The Arabic name for the city which is otherwise known as Jerusalem.

[9] For suggestions concerning a feminist approach to literary heroism, we would recommend Daly (1993).

References

Anonymus (ed.)
2000 *In touch with you... for 40 years.* Al-Ain: Oasis Hospital.

Bateson, F.W. -- Harrison T. Meserole
1976 *A guide to English and American literature.* (3rd edition.) London: Longman.

Crossley-Holland, Kevin (trans.)
1999 *Beowulf.* (Oxford World's Classics.) Oxford: Oxford University Press.

Daly, Pierrette
1993 *Heroic tropes: Gender and intertext.* Detroit: Wayne State University Press.

Diamond, Jared
1998 *Guns, germs and steel: A short history of everybody for the last 13,000 years.* London: Vintage.

Edwards, Paul -- Hermann Pálsson (trans.)
1998 *The words of Odin: Hávamál.* Edinburgh: Lockharton Press.

Fajardo-Acosta, Fidel
1989 *The condemnation of heroism in the tragedy of Beowulf: A study in the characterization of the epic.* (Studies in Epic and Romance Literature 2.) Lewiston: Edwin Mellen Pess.

Hill, John M.
1995 *The cultural world in Beowulf.* Toronto: University of Toronto Press.

Landau, Jacob
1968 *Arabische Literaturgeschichte.* Stuttgart: Kroener.

Langley, Joanna -- Abdullah Idris
2001 "Remains of a hero under gaff trees", *Gulf news* 27 May: 3.

Lyons, M.C.
1995 *The Arabian epic: Heroic and oral story-telling*. Vol. I: *Introduction*. (University of Cambridge Oriental Publications 49.) Cambridge: Cambridge University Press.

Nicholson, Lewis E. (ed.)
1963 *An anthology of Beowulf criticism*. Notre Dame: University of Notre Dame Press.

Renard, John
1999 *Islam and the heroic image: Themes in literature and the visual arts*. Macon: Mercer University Press.

Reuss, Ed.
1853 "Schanfara: Übersetzt von Prof. Ed. Reuss", *Zeitschrift der Deutschen Morgenländischen Gesellschaft* 7: 97-100.

Reynolds, Dwight Fletcher
1995 *Heroic poets, poetic heroes: The ethnography of performance in an Arabic oral epic tradition*. Ithaca: Cornell University Press.

Ridley, Matt
1997 *The origins of virtue*. Harmondsworth: Penguin.

Schick, Lawrence
1991 *Heroic worlds: A history and guide to role-playing games*. Buffalo: Prometheus Books.

Tolkien, J.R.R.
1936 "*Beowulf*: The Monsters and the Critics", *Proceedings of the British Academy* 22: 245-95.
1963 Reprinted in: Nicholson (ed.), 51-103.

Whitman, Cedric H.
1982 *The heroic paradox: Essays on Homer, Sophocles, and Aristophanes*. Ithaca: Cornell University Press.

Translating Doomsday: *De die iudicii* and its Old English translation (*Judgement Day II*)

Patrizia Lendinara (Palermo, Italy)

1. *De die iudicii (Ddi)*

The Latin poem beginning with the words "Inter florigeras fecundi cespitis herbas" is currently known as *De die iudicii* (*Ddi*); this title is not authorial, but was drawn by the poem's modern editors from line 8.[1] The poem enjoyed a large circulation both in England[2] and on the Continent (cf. Lendinara 2001b), and such a wide diffusion weighs negatively on the possibility to ascertain the name of the author and the country of origin of the poem.[3] The success of *Ddi* in England is witnessed also by an Old English translation, which is datable to the second half of the tenth century (*Judgement Day II*).[4] This vernacular version is likewise anonymous; it is more than three hundred lines long and is uniquely preserved in MS Cambridge, Corpus Christi College 201, at pp. 161-167. This manuscript was copied by several hands in the last part of the eleventh century (Gneuss 2001: nos. 65, 65.6) and contains a number of late Anglo-Saxon poems, as well as homilies, juridical and ecclesiastical material, a translation of the *Pater Noster* (the so called *LPr II*) and of the *Gloria* (*Glor I*).[5]

After a short *Natureingang*, *Ddi* introduces the "iudiciique diem" (l. 8) and, in the following sections, lingers on the theme of the imminent end of the world and the subsequent Day of Judgment. The poem offers models of conduct and stresses the need of penitence – which is indeed the main theme of *Ddi*. A few signs of the impending Doom are mentioned (l. 50-56 and 72-77), followed by a description of the Last Judgment itself (l. 57-71 and 78-86), the terror of Hell (l. 93-123), and the happiness of Heaven awaiting the blessed (l. 124-154). Though not entirely devoted to Judgement Day, as announced in the prologue, the poem has a balanced structure: the initial description of a windy grove is echoed by the flowery description of Heaven, and the list of the torments of Hell is matched by that of the joys of Heaven. The warning to repent while one has still got time is repeated twice in lines 43ff. and 87ff.[6]

As far as style is concerned, *Ddi* is characterized by a remarkable accumulation of words, a stylistic feature cherished by Dracontius and Venantius Fortunatus (cf. Clerici 1973). The poem borrows *iuncturae* and entire lines from Vergil and Venantius Fortunatus and displays a sufficient prosodic competence.[7] Notwithstanding the lack of originality – the poem is a cento of common themes and images – it enjoyed a considerable fortune, which is witnessed also by the translation into Old English.

2. *Ddi* and *JDay II*

The Old English poem has been defined as "a close expanded translation" of the Latin original (Greenfield -- Calder 1986: 238). This short and effective definition needs some adjustment, and a careful analysis of *JDay II* will enable us to assess not only the procedure of this translation, but also to reach a better understanding of the translation techniques in use in Anglo-Saxon England.

The rendering of the first lines is quite free (*Ddi* l. 1-12 = *JDay II* l. 1-25), and greatly expands on the Latin source. In the following lines the translation strives to provide a literal rendering of the Latin antecedent. The opening lines of the Old English poem, although quite imaginative, contain themes and formulas which occur elsewhere in vernacular poetry, such as the *hwæt*-formula, and the insistence on the seclusion of the narrating voice (for *ic ana*, cf. *The Wife's Lament* l. 35 and *The Wanderer* l. 8). The leafy grove described in the opening passage – at variance with the gloomy scene of the Latin version – suggests a sense of security and protection (for a similar use of *bearu*, cf. *Phoen* l. 71, 80, 122, and *Gen* l. 902). The translation adds the detail of the water running across the garden where the first scene is set (cf. *Phoen* l. 62-63).[8]

The first penitential note occurs at the beginning of the poem, when the focus shifts from the problems of an unnamed individual, brooding on his troubles, to a general homiletic address concerning the future afterlife of the sinful (*synfulra gehwam* l. 18a). *Ddi* employs the familiar penitential imagery and so does the Old English translation; the distressed man beats his breast, cries and prostrates himself in the dust. The theme of the Old English poem is made clear in line 56, where it is said that man should look for *seo soðe hreow* 'the true repentance', a phrase which repeats but, at the same time, transforms the Latin antecedent, which instead reads *confessio vera* (l. 28).[9] The poem outlines the stages of penance, from the injunction to confess the individual's sins to a general address to all mankind (the first shift from personal to homiletic occurs in *Ddi* l. 9-10 = *JDay II* l. 17-20).[10] Weeping for one's guilt is one of the ways by which to reach true repentance and the recourse to penitential tears (foreshadowed by the very first image of the flowing water) will be mentioned again later. Crying will also betray the fear of each man when he stands waiting for judgement before God's throne; however, weeping is, above all, the means by which man may cleanse his soul from sins. The passage on the purifying function of tears prepares for the image of the divine Physician healing the wounds of sin (*Ddi* l. 22-46 = *JDay II* l. 43-91), which introduces the exemplum of the penitent thief, Dismas (*Ddi* l. 27-32 = *JDay II* l. 53-64). The need for repentance is stressed and the audience is reminded that, on Judgement Day, every deed performed in life will be revealed.

The poem describes a few eschatological events, such as the *parousia*, the resurrection of mankind, the end of the world and the Last Judgement. The *Ddi* betrays knowledge of the Sibylline acrostic in its insistence on the role of Christ as judge,[11] the account of his arrival and the signs preceding it, which are accumulated rather than listed in a few central lines of the poem (*Ddi* l. 50-57 = *JDay II* l. 97-114a, and lines *Ddi* l. 72-76 = *JDay II* l. 145-154). The description of the Last Judgement (*Ddi* l. 60-86 = *JDay II* l. 119-175) is followed by a brief allusion to the soul and body theme (*Ddi* l. 87-91 = *JDay II* l. 176-184). Hell, with all sorts of terrors and fire everywhere, is beyond description, but the poet tries his best for many lines (*Ddi* l. 92-122 = *JDay II* l. 185-246). On Doomsday, all the wicked pleasures of this world, which the damned used to be devoted to in life, will vanish one by one. The transitory nature of this world is stressed and the poet bitterly comments that the damned will discover the truth all too late.

The poem reverts to the happy destiny of the blessed (*Ddi* l. 124-125 = *JDay II* l. 247-250). The description of Heaven with the joy of the blessed (*Ddi* l. 128-152 = *JDay II* l. 254-301) contrasts with the picture of Hell and is concluded by the beatific vision of Mary, who leads the white-clad band through the kingdom of God. The poem ends with a homiletic exclamation commenting on the fact that no hardship of this life is too hard to bear, as it earns us the bliss of Heaven (*Ddi* l. 153-154 = *JDay II* l. 303-306).

3. The translation technique

As far as the rendition of Latin poetry into Old English is concerned, it is generally argued that it follows a rigid and mechanic technique of "two-for-one", insofar as two Old English lines translate one Latin hexameter. In fact, this is not the rule and the Old English version of the *Ddi* features several variants which are worth investigating. Moreover, being one of the few translations of a known Latin source into the vernacular, its analysis will yield more general and relevant data. If we compare the *Ddi* (which, excluding the address to Acca, is 154 lines long), to the Old English poem in CCCC 201 (306 lines in all), it is evident that the method of translating each hexameter with two alliterative lines is followed half of the time, that is precisely in ninety-seven instances.[12]

There are also instances when a hexameter is translated with one line of Old English (ratio 1:1). This is the case with seventeen lines of *Ddi*: for example, "Et reserate nefas Christo cum voce gementi" (l. 18) is translated with "and geopeniað man ecum drihtne" (l. 37). This kind of translation is the same as the one used for the Latin proverbs in MSS London, BL, Cotton Faustina A. x and Royal 2. B. v. (ASPR 6, 108). Also, two lines of the *De actibus apostolorum* by Aratus (I, 226-227) are translated by two alliterative lines in Byrhtferth's *Enchiridion.*[13] In other instances, a hexameter is matched by three or four lines of Old English, but there are also examples of a ratio 1:1 and ½ or 1:2 and ½. It is as if the translator was trying his hand at always new solutions, and also within the most common scheme of 1:2 a number of variants are possible.

The procedure followed in the "two-for-one" translation of the *JDay II* needs a careful examination. Indeed, the commonplace rule that the translator of this poem, as well as the authors of other translations from Latin poetry into Old English, would fit a hexameter into a pair of first half-lines, filling out the second halves with alliterating synonyms, is not consistently followed. The addition of a word or phrase is needed either to round off the line or to meet the alliteration's requirements. These half-line fillers usually – but not always – occupy the b-lines. There are also instances where the words which translate the Latin text are concentrated in the b-line, e.g., in "þonne stedelease steorran hreosað" (l. 107), where the b-line faithfully translates the Latin *astra cadunt* (l. 54), and *stedelease* of the a-line alliterates with *steorran.*

The use of a high number of fillers is evident also in the Old English riddles which were translated, *in toto* or in part, from a Latin *enigma* (cf. Whitman 1973: 81-86); the same technique was used when the *Metres of Boethius* were changed from prose to poetry. The a-line fillers of *JDay II* are mainly additions, consisting, for example, of the subject and verb which were implicit in the source; rarely are they mere fillers.[14] By contrast, the b-line additions are, in several instances, mere fillers, which vary or repeat a concept already expressed, and do not contribute anything to the meaning of the translated material. They provide further details of destination, space, time, colour, and effect.[15] The Latin "cum voce gementi" (*Ddi* l. 18) is not translated in the corresponding Old English line (*JDay* II l. 37), and to fill the second half-line the adjective *ece* 'eternal' is added. The same kind of translation technique is applied a few lines ahead, when "Pectoris et linguae, carnis vel crimina saeva" (*Ddi* l. 21) is translated as "breostes and tungan, and flæsces swa some" (*JDay II* l. 42). The first half-line of the Old English is a literal translation of the first part of the Latin hexameter, while the translator, once again struggling with the second part of the Latin hexameter, chose not to translate *crimina saeva* and to add *swa some* 'at the same time' instead. The latter phrase does not contribute anything as far as the meaning is concerned, but fills out the b-line.

Several additions have a Scriptural background, such as *þæt þu beo hrædra* 'be ready' (*JDay II* l. 75; cf. Mk. 8.32), and *weana to leane* 'as a rewards for sins' (*JDay II* l. 184; cf. Rom 6.23). Entirely orthodox, the Old English poem highlights the importance of God, by changing the phrase *gaudia sanctorum* into *mærðe drihtnes / and þara haligra* (*JDay II* l. 21b-22a); a number of fillers, for example, *æt lifes frean* (*JDay II* l. 81b) or *drihtne to willan* (*JDay II* l. 85b) are meant to stress the role of God in the absolution of sins.

4. Holonomastic lines

It is interesting to see how the holonomastic lines of the Latin version, which were not easy to fit into the metrical patterns of Old English poetry, were recast. Holonomastic lines consisted entirely of either nouns or adjectives and were a stylistic feature cherished by Venantius Fortunatus, whose works are among the sources of the *Ddi* (cf. Lendinara 2001b: 320-323). The holonomastic lines are concentrated in the central parts of the poem (*Ddi* l. 115, 118-120, 130-137, 140), and the Old English translation seems to experiment with always new and different solutions.

Faced with these thirteen compressed holonomastic lines, the Anglo-Saxon translator generally resorts to the familiar solution of the "two-for-one" translation,[16] although trying out different degrees of freedom in the rendering of the elements of each holonomastic line. The craftsmanship in handling these lines demonstrates his talent in a wide range of styles. For example, *Ddi* (l. 118) "Ebrietas, epulae, risus, petulantia, iocus" ('Drunkenness, banquets, laughter, wantonness, play') is translated as "þonne druncennes gedwineð mid wistum, / and hleahter and plega hleapað ætsomne" (*JDay II* l. 234-235). Both lines are provided with a verb, the former with *gedwinan* 'disappear' and the latter with *hleapan* 'leap'. In the two-fold restructuring of the hexameter, with *druncennes* 'drunkenness' and *wist* 'feasting' in one line and *hleahter* 'laughter' and *plega* 'play' in the other, the fourth word of the Latin version, *petulantia*, is irremediably lost. In the other instances, too, the translation is unable to reproduce the overall sequence of the nouns in the Latin original, and often, at least one of them is omitted. In lines 240-241 three synonyms, *somnus*, *torpor* and *desidia*, are reduced to one. In line 265 the Latin pair *nix* and *grando* (*Ddi* l. 133) is felicitously translated as "hagulscuras hearde mid snawe".

A different solution was tried out before, where one Latin verse is reworked into four lines of Old English, which are, nonetheless, insufficient to provide a complete translation of the Latin ("Dira cupido, tenax luxus, scelerata libido", *Ddi* l. 119):

and wrænnes eac gewiteð heonone,
and fæsthafolnes feor gewiteð,
uncyst onweg and ælc gælsa
scyldig scyndan on sceade þonne. (*JDay II* l. 236-239)

In the Old English version, the three Latin adjectives, *dirus*, *tenax* and *sceleratus*, are not translated. The numerous verbs employed in the translation succeed in creating an impressive progression in which the earthly lusts glide away, one by one. This image was already anticipated by *gedwinað heonone* in l. 232b and by *gewitað mid ealle* in l. 233b, followed by *gedwineð* and *hleapað* (*JDay II* l. 234 and 235), and, further down, by *gewiteð heonone*, *feor gewiteð* and *scyndan* (*JDay II* l. 236, 237, and 239, respectively). All these Old English verbs are verbs of motion combined with an adverb of motion (see also *onweg* in *JDay II* l. 238), which replace the static *cessabunt* of the Latin version (*Ddi* l. 117). The translation "and hleahter and plega hleapað ætsomne" (*JDay II* l. 235) is remarkably felicitous.

When dealing with another holonomastic line ("Taedia, tristititiae, curae, tormenta, ruinae", *Ddi* l. 132, that is 'weariness, sadness, anxieties, torments, disasters'), the Anglo-Saxon translator is, once again, compelled to move away from its model by the different practice of vernacular versification and translates: "Nis þær unrotnes ne þær æmelnys,/ ne hryre ne caru ne hreoh tintrega" (*JDay II* l. 261-262). The translation cannot follow the asyndetic series of nouns and hence reshapes them into either word-doublets or three-word combinations, as well as altering the order in which the five dreads are listed. To meet the metrical and alliterative requirements of Old English verse, the adjective *hreoh* is added in order to alliterate with *hryre* of the first half-line. The use of the anaphoric *ne* is typical of Old English poetry where it occurs quite frequently, both in positive and negative descriptions, such as those of Heaven and Hell (cf. Tristram 1978: 102-113).

5. Omissions and additions

The translation is faithful to the original and preserves as much as possible of the Latin text. Even when a number of adjectives and adverbs of the Latin original are apparently omitted, they are in fact replaced, at short distance, by an Old English equivalent. For example, four occurrences of the adjective *cunctus* are omitted in the Old English version, but OE *eall* figures among the most frequent additions; the same can be said of the Latin adverb *nunc*. It is not possible to establish the principles guiding the omission of passages of the Latin version: among the largest omissions are *commissa meorum* (*Ddi* l. 6), *cum voce gementi*

(*Ddi* l. 18, reproduced later in *JDay II* l. 35 as *dreccað mid wope*), *vel crimina saeva* (*Ddi* l. 21), and the pair *ab arce polorum* (*Ddi* l. 48) and *in sede polorum* (*Ddi* l. 141). Holonomastic lines undergo a great reshuffling as we have seen. As to the rest, there are a few simplifications, such as *fetor praeingenti* [...] *putredine* (*Ddi* l. 103) rendered with *unstenc* 'stench' (*JDay II* l. 208), or *nix* and *grando* (*Ddi* l. 133), which are condensed into a remarkable compound, *hagulscur* 'hailshower' (*JDay II* l. 265).

As is customary in the Old English translations from Latin, the major changes are aimed at amplification, expanding on the Latin phrases and applying, in some instances, the technique of variation. If one compares the Old English poem with the Latin one, the introduction of lines, phrases, and words with no counterpart in the original is evident. This is not simply a device to cope with the structural difference between Germanic and Latin metrics, but, at least as far as *JDay II* is concerned, the additions originate from a desire to expand on the source with a swarm of vivid details, comments, personal asides, and addresses to the audience. Many of the additions are indeed connective comments. There are entire lines without a counterpart in the Latin version: lines 3, 4, 16, 98 (an explanation), 106, 110, 151 (an enlarged repetition of "impletur", *Ddi* l. 72), 153, 165 (an explanation), 182 (a digression), 193, 244, 246, 279 (which adds the subject), 293 (a variation), and 302. Some of the new lines are mere repetitions; other lines restate the idea in a different syntactic form.

The most common single fillers are Old English adjectives and adverbs. Quite regular is the addition of adverbs of place and time: *æghwær* (l. 228), *aweg* (l. 223), *embutan* (l. 114), *forð* (l. 306), *her* (l. 45, 84, 95, 157, 179, 301), *hider* (l. 111), *in* (l. 63), *inne* (l. 38, 205), *nu* (l. 82, 178, 243), *sona* (l. 36, 108), *swa lange* (l. 66), *swa some* (l. 42), *þa* (l. 10), *þær* (l. 5, 38, 162, 164, 174, 194, 196, 209, 220, 223, 226, 228, 230, 256, 257, 259, 261, 261, 263, 265, 266, 268, 274, 284, 287, 289, 290), *þær inne* (l. 198), *þider* (l. 129), *þonne* (l. 111, 117, 135, 158, 234, 252), *ufon* (l. 111).[17] Both poems underscore, at every step, the difference between life and afterlife, Heaven and Hell. Emphasis is also put on the difference between the time for forgiveness and the time for either suffering or joy. The contrast between this world and the next is intensified by the use of locative and temporal adverbs, which, abundant though they may be in the *Ddi* (*ibi, ubi, illic, tum, tunc*), are exponentially multiplied in the Old English translation. The other Old English adverbs, mainly added for alliteration's sake, have little semantic content: *ætsomne* (l. 143, 172), *eac* (l. 5, 17, 104, 145, 230, 236), *fægere* (l. 277), *færinga* (l. 119), *forhte* (l. 161), *freolice* (l. 277), *glædlice* (l. 273), *horxlice* (l. 168), *hwæne* (l. 141), *miclum* (l. 103), *recene* (l. 48), *samod* (l. 268), *symle* (l. 289), *swiðe* (l. 29, 49), *swiðlice* (l. 160), and *wel* (l. 27, 250, 276).[18]

There are several Old English adjectives without a counterpart in the Latin version: *ænlic* (l. 282), *ana* (l. 46, 72), *atol* (l. 218), *biter* (l. 242), *breme* (l. 297), *ece* (l. 37, 76, 269, 272, 299), *eall* (l. 9, 26, 32, 99, 103, 104, 115, 128, 137, 141, 145, 146, 149, 163, 172, 175, 213, 233, 292, 297),[19] *earm* (l. 9, 43, 65, 213), *færlic* (l. 259), *fela* (l. 159), *gearu* (l. 68), *glæd* (l. 179), *halig* (l. 285), *hean* (l. 39), *heanlic* (l. 258), *heard* (l. 265), *hreoh* (l. 262), *hreowlic* (l. 75), *laðlic* (l. 260, 263), *lytel* (l. 219), *mihtig* (l. 19), *read* (l. 288), *reðe* (l. 166), *rice* (l. 300), *scearplic* (l. 53), *scene* (l. 296), *synnig* (l. 67), *sweart* (l. 199), *swiðlic* (l. 227), *torn* (l. 79), *unbleoh* (l. 304), *ungeryd* (l. 102, referred to the tossing sea), *uplic* (l. 146), *wac* (l. 51), *wælgrim* (l. 211, referred to the worms of Hell), *wælhreow* (l. 228), *werig* (l. 245), and a pres. part. *weallend* (l. 200).

Of the additional Old English adjectives, many convey a negative connotation: for example, *biter* 'dire', *earm* 'wretched' (with this meaning in l. 43 and 240), *hean* 'abject', *heanlic* 'abject', *laðlic* 'loathsome', *synnig* 'sinful', *torn* 'distressing', *swiðlic* 'excessive'. There are also a few adjectives with a positive connotation – though the lexical variety is limited: *ece* 'eternal', *ænlic* 'incomparable', and *halig* 'holy'. The adjectives occurring in the frame of larger fillers also have either a negative connotation, such as *atol* (l. 218), *biter* (l. 173), *digol* (l. 20, see also l. 40), *deorc* (l. 106), *dimhiw* (l. 106), *dimm* (l. 14), *earh* (l. 125), *hearm* (l. 137), *heortleas* (l. 125), *lað* (l. 244), *laðlic* (l. 206, 210), *mihtleas* (l. 126), *read* (l. 150, 153), *reaðe* (for *reðe* 'fierce' l. 153), *stedeleas* (l. 107, referring to the stars falling from the firmament), *sweart* (l. 106), or a positive one. The latter generally refer to the divinity, *ælmihtig* (l. 287), *bliðe* (l. 279), *ece* (l. 115), *freolic* (l. 298), *mihtig* (l. 19), *rice* (l. 74), *micel* (l. 129), *healic* (l. 281), *scyppend* (l. 73), *waldend* (l. 52). Many adjectives are in the comparative or superlative, *mære* (l. 55), *beorhtost* (l. 291), *leofest* (l. 244), *gesæligost* (l. 248), *mæst* (l. 125, 253), and *selast* (l. 295).

Several additions in the Old English version of the poem form the first or second member of a word pair; they are nouns or verbs or, in a few instances, adjectives: for example, Lat *mordebunt* is rendered as *ceorfað and slitað* (l. 169b), Lat *fletus* as *wop and wanung* (l. 202), and Lat *impius* as *scyldig and manful* (l. 57b). Half-line fillers supply the indirect object: for example, *þissere worulde* (l. 178), *ænegum on eorðan* (l. 188) and other complements, such as the genitive of specification: *ænigre wihte* (l. 203). The additions fill metrical and alliterative patterns, but, at the same time, add details lacking in the source: for example, *of hleorum* (l. 28), *mid lustum* (l. 70), *on mode* (l. 92), *manes* (l. 139b), *on worulde* (l. 141b), *on grunde* (l. 189), *on sceade* (l. 239), *þeostrum* (l. 254). Among the new spatial indications are *on eorðan* (l. 14b, 16b, 31b, 87b, 98b), *on heofonan rice* (l. 22b), *on gebedstowe* (l. 30b), *on grunde* (l. 189b). The addition of *on ecnesse* (l. 304b) contributes a specification of time.

An evident effort to bind the sentences of the Anglo-Saxon poem brings about the accumulation of OE conjunctions: *ac* (l. 61, 71), *and* (l. 7, 9, 18, 22, 25, 31, 36, 76, 91, 158, 167, 179, 180, 192, 206 [twice], 229, 229, 235, 235, 236, 237, 238, 247, 248, 250, 252, 269, 269, 270, 271, 275, 275, 276, 277), *oþþe* (l. 138, 139, 156, 258), *ne* (l. 221, 222, 259, 259, 261, 262, 262, 262, 263, 263, 264, 264, 265, 266, 266, 266, 267, 267, 267), and *swylce* (l. 271).[20]

6. Word pairs

Among the fillers of *JDay II*, there is a large number of word pairs, that is two nearly synonymous words linked by a conjunction (cf. Malkiel 1959). Word pairs, which are typical of all Germanic traditions,[21] are a recurrent feature of the Old English translations from Latin – and *JDay II* is no exception. Several word pairs replace a single word: OE *synna and gylta* (l. 56b) for Lat *peccata*; OE *scyldig and manful* (l. 57b) for Lat *impius*; OE *beþunga and plaster* (l. 80b) for Lat *fomenta*; OE *henða and gyltas* (l. 88b) for Lat *crimina*; OE *dreosað and hreosað* (l. 100a) for Lat *ruent*; OE *ceorfað and slitað* (l. 169b) for Lat *mordebunt*; OE *wop and wanung* (l. 202a) for Lat *fletus*; OE *(bið) breged and swenced* (l. 214b) for Lat *torquetur*. In some word pairs, or rather word-doublings, it is the first member that repeats the Latin, for example in OE *wop and wanung* (l. 202a), which translates the single *fletus*. In other instances the first member is independent from the Latin text, for example, OE *wagedon and swegdon* (l. 7b) for Lat *resonantis*, OE *bugað and myltað* (l. 101b) for Lat *liquescent*, and OE *wean and þrosme* (l. 200b) for Lat *caligine*. There are also several instances where the entire word pair is an addition by the Anglo-Saxon translator, such as *swegdon and urnon* (l. 3b), *weoxon and blowon* (l. 5b), *todæleð and todemeð* (l. 20a), *heaf and wopas* (l. 90b), *sweart and gesworcen* (l. 105a), *deorc and dimhiw* (*and dwolma sweart*) (l. 106), *mihte and þrymme* (l. 116b), *heortleas and earh* (l. 125b), *amasod and amarod* (l. 126a), *read and reaðe*, *ræsct and efesteð* (l. 153); finally Lat *salsis* [...] *guttis* (l. 17) are translated with *mid wope and sealtum dropum* (l. 35b-36a). It is remarkable how literally *earm and eadig* (l. 163) render the Latin *miser et dives* (l. 81), whereas OE *lig and cyle* (l. 206) switch the asyndetic *frigora, flammae* (l. 102).

Most of the word pairs are exclusive of *JDay II* and are to be reckoned among the peculiar features of this translation; only a few have a limited number of occurrences elsewhere, mainly in the homilies. The pair *heaf and wopas* (l. 90) occurs in the form *wop and hof* both in poetry (*Genesis* l. 924, *Guthlac* l. 1047) and prose (*BlHom* no. 7, p. 85, 28 and no. 11, p. 115, 15), while the phrase *in heaf ond in wop* occurs only once in the Preface to the translation of Gregory's *Dialogi*.[22]

7. Incorrect renderings and variant readings

There are a few instances where the translation is quite awkward, if not plainly wrong. The Latin line "Membra solo sternam, meritosque ciebo dolores" (*Ddi* l. 15) is translated too slavishly as "and minne lichaman lecge on eorðan / and geernade sar ealle ic gecige" (*JDay II* l. 31-32). The same is the case with *bonum cunctis Deus* [...] *ministrant* translated as "ece drihten / him ealra goda gehwylc [...] ðenað" (*JDay II* l. 272b-273), owing to a mistake or a voluntary change. Similarly – but more felicitously – *laetitiae facies* [...] *nulla* is transformed into "ansyn [...] ænigre blisse" (*JDay II* l. 225). A consecutive Latin clause, introduced by *quin*, is transformed into a final Old English clause introduced by *þæt* (*JDay II* l. 40). The translation of *insuper* with "ufenan eall ðis" (*JDay II* l. 145, 213, 272) is quite clumsy. The rendering of *inamabile* with *langan* (*JDay II* l. 13) is debatable, although the latter could possibly be emended into *laðan*; Lat *errantes* is taken to mean 'guilty' and therefore translated as *synnge* (*JDay II* l. 230).

There are instances where the Latin text was misunderstood, as if the copy on which the translation was based was in a bad condition or hastily read. Some errors seem to be the product of an oral performance of the Latin poem: "qui solet" (*Ddi* l. 24) was mistaken for *qui solus* and translated "se ana mæg" (*JDay II* l. 46); Lat *solio fulget* was read as *sol fulget* (see "sicut sol" of Mt. 13.43 and Apoc. I.16) and translated as *sigelbeorht* 'as bright as the sun' (cf. *JDay II* l. 117).[23] By the same token Lat *turmis* 'throng, swarm' was mistaken for Lat *turris* 'tower' and translated *hleo* 'defence' (*JDay II* l. 127); the meaning of Lat *scelerum* (gen. pl. 'mischiefs') was misunderstood and rendered with *synnful* 'guilty' (*JDay II* l. 154); Lat *parvo tempore* was translated with OE *frecnan tid*, owing to a misreading of *parvo* as *pavido* (*JDay II* l. 215); Lat *laetatur* was rendered with OE *bliðe* possibly because of a misreading of the verbal form as *laetus* or *laetatus* (*JDay II* l. 251); Lat *pia* was mistaken for *pura* and translated as *clæne* (*JDay II* l. 294); *benedicta* ("per benedicta regna" *Ddi* l. 149) was taken for an apposition to *Maria* and translated *gebletsodost (ealra)* (*JDay II* l. 297). The translation of "flebilis hora" (*Ddi* l. 87) is "(hwæt miht þu on þa tid) þearfe gewepan" 'cry in distress' (*JDay II* l. 177), which is possibly based on a variant reading *flebis*. However, the Old English rendering may also have originated from a misreading.

There are a number of errors which undoubtedly stem from corruptions of the text underlying the Old English translation. In line 32 of *Ddi* there occurs *apertas* 'open' which, if written *ap'tas*, could easily be taken for *aptas* 'proper' as the OE translation *ænlican* 'incomparable, unique' suggests. *Ddi* changed the Biblical phrase *linum fumigans* (Is. 42.3, a prophecy applied to Christ in Mt.

12.20) into *lini tepidos*, which the Old English translator in turn rendered with *waces *fle(a)xes* 'of soft linen'. When copying down *JDay II*, the CCCC 201 scribe unravelled the metaphor, producing a vivid though mistaken image, *waces flæsces* 'of the week flesh', which cannot be maintained because of impossible accord with *wlacan smocan* (*JDay II* l. 51). In the sentence "Ne mæg þær æni man bearnum gewyrhtum" (*JDay II* l. 170) *bearnum* is clearly an error for *be agnum (gewyrhtum)* (= Lat *meritis*). Lat *flentibus* is rendered with OE *wera* (*JDay II* l. 222), but in the original Old English version there probably was *wependra*. The original translation of Lat *signa minantia mortem* was "deaðbeacnigende tacn", and the last word, omitted in CCCC 201, has been restored by the editors (*JDay II* l. 112). The manuscript's *fule stowa* has been emended by some of the editors to "fulle stowa" (*JDay II* l. 189) on the basis of the Latin text which has *loca plena ignibus*, and that might indeed be the original reading.

The Old English poem reproduces the variant readings of a manuscript or a group of manuscripts of the English Benedictine Reform: "quassatos animos" (*Ddi* l. 25, instead of *calamos*) is rendered with "wanhydige mod" (*JDay II* l. 50), with substitution of the plural with a singular (as it happens throughout the poem); Lat *dabat* (instead of the future *dabit*) is translated with *gesceop*, a preterite (*JDay II* l. 53); Lat *mercedem* (*reddere*) (instead of *rationem reddere*): *deman* (*JDay II* l. 95); Lat *timidus* (instead of *tumidus*): *afæred* (*JDay II* l. 163); Lat *virorum* (instead of *vivorum*): *manna* (*JDay II* l. 186); Lat *durus* (instead of *dirus*): *stearcheard* (*JDay II* l. 201); Lat *felix o nimium* (instead of *felix omnium*): *ofersælig* (*JDay II* l. 247); Lat *laetatus* (instead of *laetatur*): *bliðe* (*JDay II* l. 251); Lat *fulmina* (instead of *flumina*): *liget* (*JDay II* l. 263); Lat *regnant* (instead of *regnum*): *ricxað* (*JDay II* l. 268); finally, *þæt analyfed is nu* (*JDay II* l. 243) is not the translation of *illicitat* ('allures' of line 121) but of the adjective *illicita* 'forbidden' which occurs in some manuscripts of the *Ddi*. As to the variant readings *turma / turba* of *Ddi* l. 86, the translation *heap* (*JDay II* l. 175) suggests that the manuscript which was used by the transaltor had *turma* (as in l. 283; but at l. 288, *heap* renders 'triumphis'). The pret.ind. *beseah* (*JDay II* l. 242) might well translate the two attested variants *merget* and *mergit*. Moreover, the translation of lines 86-87 fits perfectly the reading *vindice iudice* of line 44 of the *Ddi*, as attested by CCCC 139, where this variant reading is written in the left margin of the folio.

Finally, lines 121-123 of the Latin poem need a reshuffling: although it is not witnessed by any manuscript, the original order must have consisted of lines 123-121-122, as it was reproduced as such by the Old English poem.

8. The grammatical treatment of the original

A series of changes and additions were made necessary by the differences in the morphology of Latin and Old English, such as the introduction of the OE prepositions *be* (l. 122, 170), *for* (l. 34, 195, 196), *mid* (l. 29, 49, 58, 61, 75, 78, 79, 161, 180, 214),[24] *on* + dat. (l. 6, 31, 179, 217, 230), *þurh* (l. 8), *wið* + acc. (l. 224). The Old English text is marked by the presence of demonstrative pronouns used as articles: *se* nom. sg. m. (l. 53, 86, 102, 123, 155, 192, 192, 240, 260), *seo* nom. sg. f. (l. 56, 108, 137, 138, 294), *þæt* nom. sg. n. (l. 92, 166, 213), *þæt* acc. sg. n. (l. 17, 76, 245), *þone* acc. sg. m. (l. 15, 51, 116), *þa* acc. sg. f. (l. 13), *þæs* gen. sg. m. (l. 14, 180, 195, 255, 297), *þam* dat. sg. m. (l. 44, 74, 282, 303), *þære* dat. sg. f. (l. 136, 299), *þa* nom. pl. (l. 7, 99, 196, 209, 245, 287), *þa* acc. pl. (l. 63, 167, 224, 296), *þara* gen. pl. (l. 22, 93, 204, 222), *þæra* gen. pl. (l. 283, 290), and *þas* acc. sg. f. (l. 215).

Several additions stem from the effort to clarify the Latin text by repeatedly specifying the subject. Hence the recurrent Old English pronouns: *ic* (l. 1, 10, 24, 25, 26, 32, 33, 65, 75), *þu* (l. 66, 66, 67, 68, 78, 80, 82, 123, 176, 177, 178, 181), *he* (l. 45, 59, 61, 157), *hit* (l. 40, 217), *se* (l. 247), *we* (l. 119), and noun phrases: "þæt man lange hæl" (l. 144), "His sunu bliðe, sigores brytta" (l. 279). The main verb is provided in many occasions: *bið* (l. 226, 228, 247, 259, 263, 266), *is* (l. 92), *nis* (l. 261), *sy* (l. 157), *synt* (l. 191), as well as *wyle* (l. 52), *byrnað and yrnað* (l. 231), *gedwineð* (l. 234), *hleapað* (l. 235), *gewiteð* (l. 236, 237), *scyndan* (l. 239), *flyhð* (l. 240), *gelimpeð* (l. 257), *hwyrfð* (l. 290). In some instances both OE subject and verb are added: *heo let* (l. 296), *ic ondræde me* (l. 15, 17), *ic gemunde* (l. 21). Sometimes the addition concerns the direct object: *eow* (l. 26), *wiht* (l. 34), *hy* (l. 211), and the indirect object *drihtene* (l. 59), *þe* (l. 65, 178), *anra gehwam* (l. 280). The proliferation of possessive adjectives is meant to identify the person referred to: *min* (l. 9, 16, 30, 31), *his* (l. 20, 49, 60, 62, 252), *heora* (l. 160, 168, 212), the same can be said of *agen* (l. 170), and *sylf* (l. 18, 122, 182).

As far as the verbs are concerned, the translator had to face abrupt changes of both person (from the first to the third) and tense (from the past tense to the present and future), which, however, were all successfully coped with. There are several differences which stem from the different verbal system of the two languages.[25] Usually, the Latin future is rendered with the OE present; Latin simple future passive is translated with the present of *beon* + pass. part.: for example, *cogentur adesse*: *bið aboden* (*JDay II* l. 129); *implebitur*: *beoð gefylde* (*JDay II* l. 209); *videbitur*: *bið gemet* (*JDay II* l. 225). The future passive, such as in *homines cogentur (adesse)* is rendered with *Adames cnosl (bið) aboden* (*JDay*

II l. 128-129), and the subj. passive *reddantur luci* with *sy abœred* (*JDay II* l. 40-41).

Also, the future perfect of Lat *venerit* is rendered with the OE present, *demeð* (*JDay II* l. 71). Latin future is also translated with a periphrasis employing modal verbs: *praestabit*: *mæge fremman* (*JDay II* l. 224); *effugiet*: *mæg forbugon* (*JDay II* l. 250); *tenebit*: *mot habban* (*JDay II* l. 252-253). Modal verbs are also used in periphrasis with decorative function: pres. ind. *confidit* is translated with *mæg gedyrstig wesan* (*JDay II* l. 170-171); pres. ind. *valet* with *mæg beon* (*JDay II* l. 187); *flebis* with *miht gewepan* (*JDay II* l. 177). Latin pres. ind. is rendered with *wile* + inf.: *vindicat*: *wrecan wile* (*JDay II* l. 89), and when passive, it is once translated with *mæg* + inf., *censetur*: *mæg beon* (*JDay II* l. 301). The OE verb *sceal*, as elsewhere, expresses both future and obligation (*JDay II* l. 72). Once, the Latin pres. subj. *valeat* is translated with an OE pres. ind. *forstent* (*JDay II* l. 55).

Active forms are translated as passive ones: for example, the Latin future *patebunt* is rendered with *beoð gesweotolude* (*JDay II* l. 135), and *timebunt* with *beoð afœred* (*JDay II* l. 163). The same happens with the impersonal future *licebit scire*: *bið alyfed* (*JDay II* l. 143-144), the pres. ind. *diffundit*: *bið gefylled* (*JDay II* l. 151), and the past perfect subj. *meruisset (poenas)*: *wurde cwylmed* (*JDay II* l. 217). Vice versa, once, the perfect pass. *fuerunt parata* is changed into active pret. *drihten geteode* (*JDay II* l. 183).

The rendering of Latin participial phrases with an OE clause is a common practice in the translations from classical languages. In *JDay II*, pres. participles are replaced by finite verbs and verb phrases: *ramis resonantis* with *þa wudubeamas swegdon* (*JDay II* l. 7); *commemorans* with *(ic) gemunde* (*JDay II* l. 12); *memorans* with *ic gemunde* (*JDay II* l. 24); *sedens* with *swegles brytta sitt* (*JDay II* l. 117); *oculos* [...] *flentes* with *eagan wepað* (*JDay II* l. 194); *stridentes* [...] *dentes* with *teþ* [...] *gryrrað* (*JDay II* l. 196); *tradens* with *his sunu* [...] *sylð* (*JDay II* l. 279-280); *splendentia* with *þœr* [...] *scinað* (*JDay II* l. 289).[26] In a few instances, the pres. part. is translated with an adjective *calentes: hate* (*JDay II* l. 28), *praesens: gehende* (*JDay II* l. 171), *horrens*: *angryslic* (*JDay II* l. 226), *praesens: andweard* (*JDay II* l. 274). Vice versa, *sub murmure* become *murcnigende* (*JDay II* l. 25), *salubre*: *halwende* (*JDay II* l. 84), *vindex: wrecenda* (*JDay II* l. 155), and *noxia*: *deriende* (*JDay II* l. 232). Passive participles are replaced by sentences with finite and infinite verbs: for example, *turbatus* is rendered with "and min earme mod eal wæs gedrefed" (*JDay II* l. 9); *discretis* with *frea* [...] *todœleð* (*JDay II* l. 19-20); *stipata* with *stillað* [...] *werod* (*JDay II* l. 114-115); *comitata* [...] *agmina* with *werod ymtrymmað* (*JDay II* l. 128); *ablutus* with *he* [...] *sy* [...] *afeormod* (*JDay II* l. 157); *coniunctus Christo* with *his þeodne geþeon* (*JDay II* l. 252); *iunctos* with *hy beoð geþeode*

(*JDay II* l. 284). Vice versa, once, *mixta* is translated with *gemenged* (*JDay II* l. 191). The gerundive *metuendus* is correctly rendered with the adjective *egeslic* (*JDay II* l. 94), and the gerund *flendi* with an OE noun, *wop* (*JDay II* l. 83).

Lat *suadeo* + subj. is rendered with a *þæt* clause with subj.: *suadeo praevenias*: *Ic lære þæt þu beo* [...] *forfoh* (*JDay II* l. 75-76), *rogo* + imp. is rendered with a *þæt* clause with subj. *rogo* [...] *aperite*: *bidde þæt* [...] *ontynan* (l. 26-27); *precor* + imp. is translated with a *þæt* clause with either subj. or ind.: *precor* [...] *non parcite*: *Ic bidde* [...] *þæt* [...] *ne wandian* (*JDay II* l. 33-34) *dreccað* (*JDay II* l. 35) *ofergeotaþ* (*JDay II* l. 36) *geopeniað* (*JDay II* l. 37); *sis memor*: *Ic bidde* [...] *þæt þu gemune* (*JDay II* l. 123). Several infinitive constructions are translated as finite *þæt* clauses: *est* [...] *salus* [...] *reserare*: *is* [...] *hæl* [...] *he* [...] *gecyðe* (*JDay II* l. 43-45); *tardas* [...] *pandere*: *latast* [...] *þæt* [...] (*JDay II* l. 66); *pænituisse iuvat tibi* [...] *flere salubre est*: *is halwende þæt man* [...] *wepe* (*JDay II* l. 84); *and dædbote do* (*JDay II* l. 85); *verebar scire*: *þæt* [...] *sceamode* [...] *þæt he* [...] *ypte* (*JDay II* l. 141-142); on the other hand, *gaudes servire* is rendered with a couple of correlated sentences *þu þeowast* [...] *and* [...] *leofast* (*JDay II* l. 178-179).

The constant switch of personal and impersonal in the Latin poem is not always reproduced in the Old English. Impersonal phrases are translated as personal: *nec lateat quicquam*: *owiht* [...] *ne belife* (*JDay II* l. 38); *fletibus assiduis*: *þu scealt greotan* (*JDay II* l. 82-83); *liceat*: *þu mote* (*JDay II* l. 303). On the other hand, personal utterances are rendered as impersonal in at least three occasions: *pænituisse iuvat tibi*: *is halwende þæt man* [...] (*JDay II* l. 84); *sis memor*: *Ic bidde, man, þæt þu* [...] (*JDay II* l. 123); *quod* [...] *aliquem* [...] *scire verebar*: *eal þæt* [...] *sceamode* [...] *þæt he* [...] *ypte* (*JDay II* l. 142). In two occasions, the subject changes: the Lat passive *miseri* [...] *volvuntur* is rendered with *þis atul gewrixl earmsceapene men* [...] *wendað* (*JDay II* l. 197-198), and Lat *fetor* [...] *complet* [...] *nares* with a longer clause *hy mid nosan ne magon naht geswæccan* (*JDay II* l. 207).

Genitive constructions are recurrent in Old English translations. *JDay II* is no exception to this and introduces several instances of noun + gen. partitive (pl. or sg.): *genus humanum*: *manna cynn* (*JDay II* l. 19); *spes certa*: *selest hihta* (*JDay II* l. 44); *lacrimis* [...] *profusis*: *teara gyte* (*JDay II* l. 79); *Deus aetherius*: *heofenes god* (*JDay II* l. 88); *coetibus angelicis*: *engla werod* (*JDay II* l. 115); *cælestibus* [...] *turmis*: *of swegles hleo* (*JDay II* l. 127); *angelica* [...] *agmina*: *engla werod* (*JDay II* l. 128); *cunctorum* [...] *virorum*: *manna gehwylces* (*JDay II* l. 186); *picea caligine*: *pices* [...] *þrosme* (*JDay II* l. 200); *fetor praeingenti*: *unstences ormætnesse* (*JDay II* l. 208); *angelicas* [...] *turmas*: *engla werode* (*JDay II* l. 282); *sanctas* [...] *cohortes*: *haligra heapum* (*JDay II* l. 283); *roseis* [...] *triumphis*: *rosena* [...] *heapas* (*JDay II* l. 288); *candida* [...] *agmina*: *þæra hwittra* [...] *mædenheap* (*JDay II* l. 290); *aetherium* [...] *senatum*: *rædwitan rodera* (*JDay II* l. 300). In one instance, the first noun is in the instrumental case: *celsithronus* [...] *iudex*: *heahþrymme cyningc* (*JDay II* l. 95). All in all, the partitive genitives proliferate: *synfulra gehwam* (*JDay II* l. 18, for *reis*), *on heofonan rice* (*JDay II* l. 22), *anra gehwylcum* (*JDay II* l. 96), *goda gehwylc* (*JDay II* l. 273), *anra gehwam* (*JDay II* l. 280); *populi* is translated as *folca unrim* (*JDay II* l. 159).

Adj. + subst. is thrice translated with a compound: *florigeras* [...] *herbas* is rendered with *wynnwyrta* (*JDay II* l. 5); *solio* [...] *alto*: *heahsetle* (*JDay II* l. 118); *cælestia regna*: *heofonrice* (*JDay II* l. 253). Partitive genitives are also translated with a compound: *cordis in antro*: *on heortscræfe* (*JDay II* l. 39), or with a word pair: *spes* [...] *quietis*: *ne hopa ne swige* (*JDay II* l. 221); *poenarum* [...] *clades*: *cwyldas and witu* (*JDay II* l. 249b-250a); *solo* [...] *fidei sermone*: *mid lyt wordum ac geleaffullum* (*JDay II* l. 61); and *scelerum* [...] *piaclis*: *leahtrum* [...] *mid synnum* (*JDay II* l. 77b-78a).

The change of Lat pl. nouns or adjectives into the OE sg. has a stylistic function and it deliberately aims at avoiding abstract images. Such a shift occurs so often as to become one of the most relevant features of the entire translation.[27] The abstract images are transformed into simpler terms, *allisos* is rendered with *aglidene mod* (*JDay II* l. 47); *Titan*: *sunne* (*JDay II* l. 108); *in ortu*: *on morgen* (*JDay II* l. 108); *arcana*: *digle geþancas* (*JDay II* l. 136); *ultricibus*: *ættrenum* (*JDay II* . 146); *ditione*: *lage* (*JDay II* l. 164); *loca* [...] *gehennae*: *on helle* (*JDay II* l. 190); *frigora*: *gicela* (*JDay II* l. 192); *ferventibus* [...] *flammis*: *þrosma lig* (*JDay II* l. 192); *dolor*: *sari mod* (*JDay II* l. 227); *delectatio carnis* [...] *cæca scelerum mergit vertigine mentem*: *þæt werige mod wendað þa gyltas* (*JDay II* l. 245); *virgineo flore*: *blostmum (behagen)* (*JDay II* l. 291);[28] *senatum*: *rædwitan* 'counsellors' (*JDay II* l. 300).

A series of passages which might be hard to grasp, are either clarified, such as *qui* translated with *se sceaþa* (*JDay II* l. 57); or implemented, as *gessit* rendered with *manes gefremede* (*JDay II* l. 139); or simplified as *Iudiciique diem* translated as *dom* (*JDay II* l. 15); *usque crucem*: *on rode* (*JDay II* l. 57); *iudex* [...] *venerit*: *demeð god* (*JDay II* l. 71); and *mortis in articulo*: *deaðe gehende* (*JDay II* l. 59). Further simplifications include *sceleratis* [...] *actis*: *undædum* (*JDay II* l. 58), *verba precantia*: *bena* (*JDay II* l. 60), and *est* [...] *data gratia flendi*: *tima sy* (*JDay II* l. 83). The references to the final Judgement are carefully reworked into a coherent description: *mercedem reddere* becomes *deman* (*JDay II* l. 95), *gestus*: *dæd* (*JDay II* l. 122), and *tribunal*: *domsetl drihtnes* (*JDay II* l. 124).[29]

Another process of simplification, which is perhaps intended to provide more clarity, is that by which the Latin verbs *censeri* (*Ddi* l. 301), *manere* (*Ddi* l.

93), *praestare* (*Ddi* l. 223), *stare* (*Ddi* l. 162), and *valere* (*Ddi* l. 55, 187) are rendered with OE *beon*. Similarly, OE *ænlic* renders a series of Latin words with a wide range of meanings: *fecundus* (l. 6), *aptus* (for *apertus*) (l. 63), *almus* (l. 292); in l. 282 it is also referred to the angels' throngs; *eall* renders both *omnis* (l. 143) and *cunctis* (l. 135 [twice], 273, 274), *synn* translates *scelus* (l. 12), *peccatum* (l. 56, 79), and *piaclum* (l. 78). The same words are repeated over and over, such as *afæran* (*JDay II* l. 126 and 163, in both cases as a free rendering), *feormian* (*JDay II* l. 78) and *afeormian* (*JDay II* l. 157), *ansyn* (*JDay II* l. 120 – a variation –, 204, 225), *astyrian* (*JDay II* l. 114, 180), *atol* (*JDay II* l. 198, 218), *laðlic* (*JDay II* l. 206, 210, 260, 263), and *dæd* and its compounds (*JDay II* l. 16, 58, 93, 96, 122).

9. The vocabulary of *JDay II*

The Old English poem contains a large number of *hapax legomena*: *abæran* (l. 41), *amarian* (l. 126), *beweorþian* (l. 118), *braslian* (l. 152), *brynig* (l. 212), *dægcuð* (l. 40), *deaðbeacnigende* (l. 112), *dimhiw* (l. 106), *drut* (l. 292), *eahgemearc* (l. 149), *eoredheap* (l. 113), *flecgan* (l. 110, if not emended into *fleogan*), *frowe* (l. 293), *geþuxian* (l. 105), *gryrran* (l. 196), *heofonsetl* (l. 278), *heortleas* (l. 125), *heortscræf* (l. 39), *mædenheap* (l. 290), *ofersælig* (l. 247), *scad* (l. 73), *stearcheard* (l. 201), *stiþmægen* (l. 114), *synscyldig* (l. 169), *uncræftig* (l. 240), *unstenc* (l. 208), *wæterburne* (l. 3), *wynwyrt* (l. 5).[30] The verb *geswæccan* (l. 207) is employed in the transitive form (for the intransitive use of this verb, see *Vitellius*, *Royal*, and *Arundel Psalter*, Pss. 113.14 and *ÆGram*, p. 221, 5).

A few lexemes of the poem belong to the poetic lexicon, where they have a limited number of occurrences, such as *behlænan* (l. 115 and *Seasons* l. 112, *Jul* l. 577, and *Christ* l. 870), *breostgehygd* (l. 60, 173 and *Gen* l. 1289, 2318, *And* l. 997, *Christ* l. 262, *Prec* l. 22, and *Beo* l. 2819), *hagulscur* (l. 265 and *Men* l. 35, *And* l. 1257), *heahþrym* (l. 95 and *Guth* l. 1324), and *sigelbeorht* (l. 117 and *Men* l. 89, 203). In many instances, these lexical choices betray the effort to create *ad hoc* compounds, capable to render the Latin counterpart, such as *heortscræf* 'hearth' (literally 'cave of the hearth', *JDay II* l. 39) translating the Latin *cordis in antro* (l. 19). Some compounds, though based on traditional models, are the Anglo-Saxon translator's own coinage: for example, *wæterburne* is modelled on other *wæter*-compounds such as *wæterædre* 'source' or *wætergefeall* 'waterfall'.

However, the contrary is much more frequently true, that is, the Old English poem employs words which otherwise occur prevalently or exclusively in prose. There are several words in *JDay II* which are never used elsewhere in poetry.[31] Some of them have only a limited number of occurrences in the Old English corpus,[32] such as *æmelnes, -nys* (l. 229, 261), *ærdæd* (l. 93, 96), *afeormian* (l. 157), *amasian* (l. 126, the word also occurs once in a gloss to Canticle 5, 16, in the same MS of the *Lambeth Psalter*), *beþung* (l. 80), *brysan* (l. 49, the only other occurrence in a gloss to the *Liber scintillarum* 20, 20), *cwelre* (l. 204), *emnes* (l. 151), *fæsthafolnes* (l. 237), *fleax* (l. 51), *foresteal* (l. 147), *gebrasl* (l. 260 and *VercHom* no. 21, p. 359, 191), *gedwæscan* (l. 52), *gedwinan* (l. 232, 234), *gehæge* (l. 4), *gehreran* (l. 8), *gemang* (preposition, l. 282, 303), *gesyman* (l. 58), *gewepan* (l. 177), *gicel* (l. 192), *gnagan* (l. 212), *ligspiwel* (l. 210 and a gloss to Prudentius I, 207), *mihtleas* (l. 126), *murcnian* (l. 25), *ofergeotan* (l. 36), *ormætnes* (l. 208), *plaster* (l. 80), *rædwita* (l. 300 and a gloss to a Calendar Prognostic for New Year's Day, p. 297, 31), *ræscettan* (l. 153, 166), *sargung* (l. 246 and a gloss to the *Liber scintillarum* 6, 27), *slincan* (l. 241), *smoca* (l. 51), *stedeleas* (l. 107), *todeman* (l. 20 and a gloss to the *Lambeth Psalter*, Pss. 81.1), *towearde* (adverb, l. 134), *tuxl* (l. 212), *þrece* (l. 192 and a gloss to *Lambeth Psalter*, Pss. 118.28), *þunerrad* (l. 264), *ufenan / ufenon* (preposition, l. 145, 213, 272), *unbleoh* (l. 304 and in the prose part of the *Paris Psalter* 15.6), *undæd* (l. 58), *ungeryde* (l. 102 and in the *Visio Leofrici* 45), *unhyrlic* (l. 11 and *Alexander's Letter to Aristotle* 30), *wlacu* (l. 51), and *wylspring* (l. 27). The Middle English continuations of *sluma* (which occurs only at l. 241 and in *Guth* l. 243) make its classification as a poetic word highly improbable.

In *JDay* II, there occur prose words with a larger diffusion in Old English, such as *æmtig* (l. 149), *astifian* (l. 174), *biterlice* (l. 167), *cweartern* (l. 217), *dædbot* (l. 85), *færlic* (l. 259), *fefer* (l. 259), *fers* (l. 11), *gælnes* (l. 179), *geclypian* (l. 138), *gehende* (l. 59, 171), *geþwærnes* (l. 271), *gyte* (l. 79), *lagu* (l. 164), *oga* (l. 172), *pic* (l. 200), *scearplic* (l. 53), *sticel* (l. 180), *swegan* (l. 3, 7), *unalyfed* (l. 243), *underfon* (l. 121), *wanung* (l. 202), and *ymtrymman* (l. 128).[33]

This striking presence of many prose words may be due to the fact that *JDay II* is much younger than most of the surviving Old English poetry (which is, however, often preserved in late manuscripts).[34] In the literary production of the late Anglo-Saxon period the distinction between prose and poetry is blurred as far as content and style, as well as language are concerned. The use in poetry of words typical of prose is one of the features of late poems,[35] but, even so, in its high number of prose words *JDay II* is exceptional and may be compared only to *An Exhortation to Christian Living*.

Much poetry of the late tenth and early eleventh century draws on Latin and vernacular sources. In fact, another version of *JDay II* is represented by a section of a homily in Oxford, Bodleian Library, Hatton 113, ff. 66-73.[36] The manuscript contains twenty-seven homilies in Latin and Old English. The homily in question is generally known as Napier no. 29. It is an anonymous piece on Judgement Day and includes a passage overlapping with lines 92-285 of *JDay II* (the section based on the poem begins in line 10 of fol. 68ʳ, with no indication of source). Napier no. 29 does not provide a parallel for several words and short phrases of the poem, and lines 166-175, 213-218, 232-243 and 271b-284 of *JDay II* have no counterpart in the homily. The presence in Napier no. 29 of such an overlap with *JDay II* may be compared to the overlap between *Exhort* and two anonymous homilies, namely *VercHom* no. 21 and Napier no. 20 (Whitbread 1963: 347-364). Napier no. 29 provides evidence that there was either a prose version of *Ddi* in circulation or that a vernacular prose version and the extant verse version, namely *JDay II*, were a double product, the prose having precedence (Stanley 1971: 389-390). Since the extant prose version is less extensive than the poem it is likely that the compiler of the homily used only part of the prose text that underlies or went with *JDay II*.[37] The copy of this original prose version used by the homilist was less corrupted than that used by the author of *JDay II*, and in some instances Napier no. 29 may indeed be used to emend *JDay II*. According to Eric Stanley an Old English prose translation *Ddi* pre-dates the poetic one[38] and both extant vernacular works (that is *JDay II* and Napier no. 29) had a lost prose version in Old English as their source. However, as Roberta Frank (1994: 106) warily remarks, the question of priority between the poem and the homily is still unanswered.

Dialectal difference may have played a role in the word choices of the poem, because *JDay II* was probably first composed in West Saxon (Menner 1947: 583-597; Wenisch 1979: 328). Therefore, it did not undergo the process of adaptation from Anglian which characterizes almost the entire Old English poetic corpus. The content of the poem should also be taken into account, because words such as *plaster* 'plaster' (l. 80), *fleax* 'flax' (l. 51) or *fers* 'verse' (l. 11), which have no counterpart in Old English poetry, were introduced to translate the words of the Latin poem verbatim.

Finally, the vocabulary of *JDay II* is characterized by idiosyncratic choices, for example, a penchant for adjectives with the *-ig* suffix,[39] such as *ælmihtig* (l. 69, 287), *æmtig* (l. 149), *ænig* (l. 170), *brynig* (l. 212), *dreorig* (l. 35), *eadig* (l. 163, 305), *gedyrstig* (l. 171), *gesælig* (l. 247, 248), *halig* (l. 22, 283, 285), *mihtig* (l. 19), *ofersælig* (l. 247), *sarig* (l. 227), *scyldig* (l. 57, 239), *synnig* (l. 67, 160, 230), *synscyldig* (l. 169), *uncræftig* (l. 240), *wanhydig* (l. 50), *weleg* (l. 164), and *werig* (l. 245).[40]

10. The features of the translation

A comparison between *De die iudicii* and *Judgement Day II* can shed light on the techniques of translation in Anglo-Saxon England, but, at the same time, it reveals the translator's idiosyncrasies and his personal interpretation of the Latin poem.

There are lines where the translation is deliberately literal and almost overlaps with the Latin original. One can compare *Ddi* l. 39 and *JDay II* lines 77-78a, as well as l. 40 and lines 78b-79; l. 41 and 80-81a; l. 50 and 97; l. 61 and 121-122b; l. 89 and 180: l. 92 and 185-186a; l. 97 and 196; l. 126 and 251. But even in the lines where the translation is apparently closer, the Latin and the Old English version are hardly ever identical.

Remarkable is the balanced and regular translation of some lines, such as l. 100 of *Ddi* = l. 201-202a of *JDay II*; l. 109 = l. 219-220a, which is particularly felicitous; l. 113 = 225; l. 116 = l. 230-231a; l. 117 = l. 232-232a; l. 120 = l. 240-241a; l. 127 = l. 252-253a; l. 128 = l. 254-255; l. 138 = l. 272-273; l. 139 = l. 274-275. There are examples of quite mechanic translations at short distance: *JDay II*, lines 136, 137, 138, 140, 142, and 144 (each with a b-line filler). From line 290 onwards the translation is very free.

At times the Old English translation is independent from the Latin source: l. 63 of *Ddi* = l. 125-126 of *JDay II*, l. 67 = 131-134, l. 73 = 147-148, l. 76 = 154. The same can be said of l. 190 of the *JDay II* (replacing *gehennae* of the original), l. 216 (translating *sibimet*), l. 218 (rendering *perpetuas* [...] *poenas*), l. 244 is very felicitous in Old English, but independent of the original. Entirely free but effective is the translation of l. 55 (= l. 109-110), but so different to allow the supposition that it might have been drawn from a different source. Totally autonomous but felicitous is the translation of *solo* [...] *fidei sermone* with *mid lyt wordum ac geleafullum* (l. 61). Quite successful is the translation of *bis* with *ofer ænne siþ* (l. 89), of *minantia mortem* with *deaðbeacnigende* (l. 112), and of *potestas* with *stiþmægen* (l. 114).

A few simple sentences of *Ddi* receive an over-elaborate translation, for example, l. 66 (= l. 129). The same is true with lines 107-108 (= l. 215-218). In some instances one word of the source is translated with an entire line of Old English: one Latin adjective, *apostolicus* (*Inter apostolicas animis laetantibus arces Ddi* l. 145) is expanded into a whole Old English line, *þær þa ærendracan synd ælmihtiges godes* (*JDay II* l. 287). Also *turbatus* (l. 9), and *genitrix* (l. 293) are expanded into an entire clause; the same happens with *sis memor* [...] *pavor* (l. 123); *tortorum* is rendered with *þara cwelra þe cwylmað ða earman* (*JDay II* l. 204), and *illicita* with *þæt unalyfed is nu* (*JDay II* l. 243).

The translation is at times redundant: details and specifications are added by means of different strategies: *sub tegmine* is translated as *mid helme beþeht* (*JDay II* l. 2), *ramis*: *wudubeamas* (*JDay II* l. 7); *mortis* [...] *tempus*: *tid þæs dimman cyme deaðes* (*JDay II* l. 13-14); *signum*: *forebeacn* (*JDay II* l. 97); *medelae*: *lifes læcedomes* (*JDay II* l. 81); *memento*: *gemyne* [...] *on mode* (*JDay II* l. 92); *montes*: *beorga hliðu* (*JDay II* l. 101); *mentes*: *manna mod* (*JDay II* l. 103); *caelum*: *upheofon* (*JDay II* l. 104); *manus*: *mannes hand* (*JDay II* l. 139); *scelerum*: *synscyldigra* (*JDay II* l. 169); *dentes*: *teþ* [...] *manna* (*JDay II* l. 196); *flentibus*: *wependra worn* (*JDay II* l. 222); *stridor*: *gristbitung* (l. 227); *flammae*: *liges gebrasl* (*JDay II* l. 259); *mors*: *deaðes gryre* (*JDay II* l. 266, rhyming with *lyre*, "ne lyre ne deaðes gryre"); *altithrona*: *heofonsetle hean* (*JDay II* l. 278). Similarly, *ulli* is translated with *ænigum men* (l. 89); *aliquem*: *ænigum men* (*JDay II* l. 142); and *nullus*: *æni man* (*JDay II* l. 170). Some adjectives used as nouns are replaced by OE adj. + subst.: *miseros* is rendered by *earman saula* (*JDay II* l. 167); *miseri*: *earmsceapene men* (*JDay II* l. 197); *malignis*: *awyrgendum gastum* (*JDay II* l. 184). Both for metrical reasons and the natural tendency of Old English poetry to slow down the pace of narration, *cecini* is translated with *onhefde mid sange* (*JDay II* l. 11); *precor*: *ic bidde* [...] *benum* (*JDay II* l. 33); *sanare*: *gode gehælan* (*JDay II* l. 47); *solvere*: *recen onbindan* (*JDay II* l. 48); *reddere rationem*: *gyldan scad wordum* (*JDay II* l. 73); *penituisse*: *dædbote do* (*JDay II* l. 85); *praecurrunt*: *feran onginnað* (*JDay II* l. 97); *gessit*: *manes gefremede* (*JDay II* l. 139); *stupet*: *stænt astifad* (*JDay II* l. 174); *gaudes*: *glæd leofast* (*JDay II* l. 179); *edicere*: *spellum areccan* (*JDay II* l. 187); *gaudere*: *brucan bliðnesse* (*JDay II* l. 306).

There is a recherché use of parallelism, e.g. between the two fillers *for ærdædum* (*JDay II* l. 93) and *be ærdædum* (*JDay II* l. 96).[41] The translation introduces a parallel between the anguish of the nature, *wolcn wæs gehrered* (*JDay II* l. 8) and the state of mind of the guilty man, *mod* [...] *wæs gedrefed* (*JDay II* l. 9), with a repetition in l. 25: "mode gedrefed". With an envelope pattern, *winda gryre* (*JDay II* l. 8a) is echoed by *deaðes gryre* (*JDay II* l. 266, where *gryre* is unparalleled in the Latin text). A number of parallels may stem from lack of ingenuity, and the recourse to stereotyped phrases, which are common late Old English poetry, brings along the homologation of unrelated Latin phrases, such as *eall engla werod* (*JDay II* l. 115a and 128a) translating both *coetibus angelicis* and *angelica* [...] *agmina* respectively. The same happens with *hu micel is þæt wite* (*JDay II* l. 92), translating *quanta* [...] *tormenta*, and *hu micel bið se broga* (*JDay II* l. 123), translating *pavor*, as well as with *ne bið þær ansyn* (*JDay II* l. 203 and 225) translating both *non* [...] *facies ibi cernitur ulla* and *facies* [...] *nulla videbitur illic*.

The poem makes consistent use of a number of different stylistic figures such as plain repetition, which has an unquestionable structural function.[42] There are six cases of *figura etymologica*, *mearn* / *murcnigende* (*JDay II* l. 24-25), *tima* / *tid* (*JDay II* l. 83), *geþancas* / *geþohte* (*JDay II* l. 136-137), *leohtes* / *leoht* (*JDay II* l. 219), *lof* / *leoflic* (*JDay II* l. 271), *unalyfed* / *leofest* (*JDay II* l. 244-245), and six of paronomasia: *rican* / *riht* (*JDay II* l. 74), *sweart* / *gesworcen* (*JDay II* l. 105), *amasod* / *amarod* (*JDay II* l. 126), *mannes* / *manes* (*JDay II* l. 139), *leofest* / *life* (*JDay II* l. 244), *lof* / *lif* / *leoflic* (*JDay II* l. 271). They are all quite effective.

Echoic repetition is a stylistic feature of Old English poetry, but the repetition of the same words and phrases, to the detriment of variation, such as occurs in *JDay II*, is typical of the late poetic compositions.[43] There is a core of words that recur repeatedly, such as the adjectives *eall*, *ece*, and *earm*.[44] Greenfield (1966: 149-151) has remarked that *eall* is a key word in the second half of the *Wanderer*, lending "its collective semantic weight to the observations reported". When compared to the remaining corpus of Old English poetry, *JDay II* is characterized by repetitions of all sorts[45] while it avoids both variation and synonymy. A remarkable exception is represented by the epithets for God and Christ, which present a number of variations. *Christus* is translated by *drihten* (l. 37), *nerigend* (l. 64), *þeoden* (l. 252), and, when unparalleled in the Latin version, he is referred to as *waldend Crist* (l. 52), *Crist* (l. 54), as well as two widespread epithets, *swegles brytta* (l. 117) and *sigores brytta* (l. 279); *se godes sunu* (l. 86) is also used. *Deus* is translated by *drihten* (l. 272), and *god* (l. 88, 292). *Drihten* (l. 21, 59, 85, 122, 124, 183) is also used independently of the Latin, as well as *fæder* (l. 275), *frea* (l. 19, 74), *lifes frea* (l. 81), *god* (l. 287), *scyppend god* (l. 73), *wealdend engla* (l. 50), and the traditional epithet *heofonrices weard* (l. 70).

Apart from the restrictions imposed by the faithfulness to the original, *JDay II* has a place within the tradition of Old English poetry. It shares its incipit, *hwæt*, with several other Old English poems such as *Beowulf*, *Exodus*, *Andreas*, and the *Dream of the Rood*. There are a few concessions to widespread poetic clichés, such as *eorðan ymbhwyrft* (l. 72) translating *orbis*; *homines* is translated by *Adames cnosl eorðbuendra* (l. 130); and *pectus*: *breostgehygd* (l. 60, 173). Finally, the phrase *wanhydige mod* (l. 50) also occurs in *The Wanderer* (l. 67).

11. *JDay II* and the Old English prose versions

The technique of translating from Latin into the vernacular which was in use in Anglo-Saxon England – if there ever was one which was somehow codified and generalized –, has never been examined in detail.[46] Yet, a number of studies have been devoted to single works or authors.[47] Although it is common knowledge that bilingualism, such as that existing in Anglo-Saxon England, fosters the practice of translation, the number of translations from Latin poetry into Old English is small, and in general, the works which were translated were not so much by Classical or late antique poets, as by Insular writers,[48] such as riddles nos. XXXIII (*De lorica*)[49] and C (*De creatura*) by Aldhelm.[50] The first part of the *Phoenix*[51] (up to l. 296) is translated from the *De ave phoenice*, once attributed to Lactantius.[52] The translation of the *De die iudicii* may be compared to the three poems mentioned above, but also to other apparently quite different compositions, that is, prose versions of Latin works.

The prose versions of the Latin texts provide interesting parallels for some of the translation procedures of *JDay II*. There are three examples of prose versions from Anglo-Saxon England: that of the third book of the *Bella Parisiacae urbis* by Abbo of Saint-Germain-des-Prés (cf. Lendinara 1999: 73-89), the *Expositio hymnorum* in London, BL, Cotton Julius A. vi and Cotton Vespasian D. xii (a prose paraphrase of 95 hymns accompanied by a continuous gloss), and the prose recast of 24 monastic canticles in the latter manuscript, where each paraphrase follows the hymn or canticle it belongs to. All three prose versions are accompanied by Old English interlinear glosses.[53]

Analysis of these prose versions yields very similar results to those reached by analysis of syntactical glosses.[54] There are several common features: in the prose versions the vocative, preceded by *o*, always opens the phrase. Otherwise it was the verb to open the sentence, displaced only by conjunctions or adverbs like *haud*, *minime* or *ne*, and followed, in that order, by the subject, the direct object, the indirect object and the other complements. The genitive case always follows its referent. The adjective precedes the substantive it refers to, but this rule does not apply to the possessive adjective, which is often put after the noun.

In the translation of l. 33 of *Ddi*: "Cur, rogo, mens, tardas medico te pandere totam?" which is rendered with "Ic acsige þe, la, earme geþanc / hwi latast þu swa lange, þæt þu ðe læce ne cyþst" (*JDay II* l.65-66) there are a number of additions: the subject *ic* and the interjection *la* are added to point out that the Latin *mens* is a vocative, a grammatical case which is not formally distinguished from the nom. in Old English. *þe* (acc. of *þu*) was also added to specify that the question is addressed to the mind (*geþanc*), which is further connotated by the adjective *earm*, alliterating with *acsige* of the first half-line.

The addition of pronouns (either as subject or complement) and of *la* (or *eala*) has a counterpart in interlinear glosses,[55] where such additions are dictated by pedagogic aims and not by stylistic preoccupations. In the latter of the two

Old English lines discussed above, *cur* is translated by *hwi* and *tardas* by *latast*; the verb is followed by the subject, *þu* and by the filler *swa lange* 'for such a long time' which completes the a-line, providing another allitterant (l). The Latin infinitive, *te pandere* is rendered with a *þæt*-clause with explicit subject, *þu*. Similar choices are evident in the translation of l. 124 of *Ddi* ("Felix o nimium, semperque in saecula felix"), which reads:

> Eala, se bið gesælig and ofersælig
> and on worulda woruld wihta geseligost (*JDay II*, ll. 247-248)

The two long lines render faithfully and symmetrically the first and the second part of the Latin hexameter respectively. In l. 247 *eala* translates the Latin exclamation *o*; once again subject (*se*) and verb (*bið*) are provided. The translation of the adverb *nimium* with the adjective *ofersælig* is felicitous, since this adjective repeats but, at the same time, varies the former *gesælig*, corresponding to the Latin *felix*. The phrase *semper in saecula* is translated, as is common practice in both Old English poetry and prose, with *worulda woruld*, which elsewhere renders the Latin *in saecula saeculorum*. The redundancy of the line, which is modelled, as far as the first part is concerned, on Vergil and other poets, is not shunned by the translator. By contrast he has emphasized it by using a compound, the second member of which is *sælig*; the same adjective (*gesælig*) is used, once more, in the superlative, at the end of line 248.

12. A successful translation

The importance of the translation of the *Ddi* lies in the fact that it represents one of the few instances in which it is possible to compare an Old English poetic text with its Latin source. If one takes into account the entire translation of the poem, the assessment can only be positive. Its redundancy is dictated by the unavoidable devices employed to match the Germanic long line to the Latin original. The translation is literal but finds room for imaginative variations. The diction and style of the poem are occasionally marred by infelicities and awkwardness, but these are compensated by felicitous choices of words and phrases. The translation is, at times, very successful. For example, the rendering of "Et solo meruit fidei sermone salutem" (*Ddi* l. 31) with "He mid lyt wordum ac geleaffullum / his hæle begeat and help recene" (*JDay II* l. 61-62) is excellent, and so is that of "lucis ubi miseris nulla scintilla relucet" (*Ddi* l. 109) with "þær leohtes ne leoht lytel sperca / earmum ænig" (*JDay II* l. 219-220a).

The translation is accurate, but not slavish: the indebtedness to the Latin source is not avoided by the translator, but the manner in which the source is employed affords ample evidence that he was a lettered man well steeped in Anglo-Saxon poetic technique and conventions. It is this technique that conditions and determines both the grammatical and the literary adaptation of the Latin source. *JDay II* was evidently written with a certain target in mind, as its location within CCCC 201 proves. The penitential and educational potentiality of the *Ddi* was understood and it fostered a brilliant recast which was meant to be enjoyed as well as studied and meditated.

Notes

[1] The most recent edition of the poem, henceforth *Ddi*, is that by Fraipont (1955: 439-444).

[2] A number of manuscripts of the *Ddi* were written in England: CCCC 139, ff. 57^{r}-58^{v} (s. XII^{med}, Durham), Cambridge, Trinity College O. 2. 31, ff. 41^{r}-43^{v} and 45^{r} (s. X/XI, Christ Church, Canterbury), Cambridge, University Library, Gg. 5. 35, ff. 416^{r}-418^{v} (s. XI^{med}, St Augustine, Canterbury), London, BL, Additional 11034, f. 2 (X, ?England), London, BL, Cotton Domitian i, ff. 51^{r}-54^{v} (s. X^{2}-X^{med}, St Augustine, Canterbury), Paris, Bibliothèque Nationale, lat. 8092, ff. 42^{v}-45^{r} (s. XI$^{2/4}$, England), Salisbury, Cathedral Library, 168, ff. 85^{v}-87^{r} (s. XI^{ex}, Salisbury), Worcester, Cathedral Library F. 57, ff. 70^{r}-70^{v} (s. XIII, Worcester), and York, Chapter Library XVI Q. 14, ff. 48^{v}-49^{r} (s. XII/XIII, ?England).

[3] The attribution of the poem to Bede is still a matter of scholarly debate; in the past the *Ddi* has been attributed, among others, to Alcuin: see Whitbread (1944: 198-199).

[4] The first editors of *JDay II* coined a neologism and gave the poem the title of *Be domes dæge*, see Lumby (1876) and Löhe (1907). The most recent edition of the Old English poem is that by Caie (2000). The edition of Dobbie (cf. ASPR 6, 58-67) is still useful. All quotations are from this edition, as well as references to line numbers.

[5] All short titles of OE texts are given according to the *DOEC*.

[6] In l. 156 a personal epilogue begins where the narrator of *Ddi* takes leave from Acca and his brethrens in Hexham, saying that the poem was written at the request of this bishop. These lines are attested only in a few manuscripts; they may well have been added to the poem at a later date and were not translated into Old English.

[7] See Whitbread (1944: 198-206 and 1966: 635-656).

[8] Huppé (1959: 80-94), Hoffman (1968: 170-178) and Caie (2000: 58-64), suggest an allegorical interpretation for the garden image, see also Whitbread (1966: 645-646).

[9] The penitential theme is accentuated, for example, in *JDay II* l. 86-89; cf. *Ddi* l. 44-45.

[10] In these first lines the translation tries to ease the transition by introducing a correlation between the penitent and mankind ("ic eac [...] ondræde me / and synfulra gehwam" lines 17-18), after several additions have made clear the first-person speaker ("Ic ondræde me" l. 15, "for mandædum minum" l. 16). Elsewhere the shift from personal to general and homiletic is only in the Old English text: one can compare "Paenituisse iuvat tibi" (l. 43) with "nu is halwende þæt man her wepe / and dædbote do" (l. 84-85a).

[11] Knowledge of the acrostic is suggested, not only by the title given to the poem in several manuscripts, but also by lines 9, 36, 38, 44, 49, 61, and 84, cf. Lendinara (2003: 100-101).

[12] These data are conveniently summarized in Appendix I and II.

[13] Baker -- Lapidge (1995), cf. Whitbread (1948: 476), and the comment by Stubbs (1874: xx).

[14] There are 17 a-verse fillers: see l. 12a, 14a, 15a, 21a, 52a, 54a, 70a, 74a, 107a, 119a, 129a, 188a, 191a, 218a, 238a, 240a, 294a.

[15] There are 83 b-verse fillers: see l. 1b, 2b, 8b, 5b, 20b, 22b, 24b, 25b, 28b, 30b, 33b, 40b, 55b, 58b, 60b, 62b, 73b, 74b, 81b, 82b, 85b, 87b, 90b, 93b, 94b, 96b, 105b, 112b, 113b, 115b, 116b, 117b, 118b, 120b, 122b, 136b, 137b, 138b, 139b, 141b, 144b, 147b, 149b, 150b, 156b, 158b, 161b, 164b, 173b, 174b, 175b, 176b, 178b, 184b, 186b, 195b, 202b, 203b,. 204b, 206b, 210b, 222b, 224b, 228b, 231b, 233b, 235b, 236b, 237b, 239b, 241b, 248b, 253b, 254b, 257b, 264b (? if not a mistaken translation of *procellae*), 275b, 281b, 284b, 291b 295b, 298b, 304b.

[16] This is how l. 115, 118, 120, 130, 131, 132, 134, 135, and 137 of the Latin were translated. Line 136 of *Ddi* was not translated and was probably missing either in the Latin source or in the translation owing to an eye-skip.

[17] This list includes only the additions which are not part of half-line fillers, of lines without a counterpart in the Latin or of lines with a free translation.

[18] Some may be intensifying. The following adverbs occur in half-line fillers or lines with a free translation: *æfre* (l. 257), *ætsomne* (l. 165, 235, 275), *eac* (l. 15, 21), *elles* (l. 202), *emnes* (l. 151), *feor* (l. 237), *heonone* (l. 236), *næfre* (l. 254), *nu* (l. 33), *on hinder* (l. 241),

onweg (l. 238), *recene* (l. 28, 62), *swiðe* (l. 24, 105, 246), *þa* (l. 33), *þænne* (l. 129, 244), *þær* (l. 191, 218), *þearle* (l. 158), *þonne* (l. 107, 239), and *wihte* (l. 222).

[19] The adjective *eall* occurs 35 times (24 times without a counterpart in the Latin); *ece* occurs 10 times (7 times without a counterpart in the Latin); *earm* occurs 13 times (9 of which without a counterpart in the Latin); in some occurrences this adjective is used as a noun.

[20] The connectives of word pairs (cf. section 6 of this paper), as well as those occurring in the larger fillers, are not listed.

[21] A number of these doublets are common in several Indo-European traditions, cf. Krause (1922) and, as far as other Germanic languages are concerned, Bremmer Jr. (1983). On Old English word pairs cf. Kail (1889), Koskenniemi (1968), and Guerrieri (1982).

[22] The word pairs which occur elsewhere are *ypte oððe cyðde* (l. 143), *earm and eadig* (l. 163), *wop and wanung* (l. 202), *ege and fyrhtu* (l. 226), *hleahter and plega* (l. 235) – which occurs once in the *Liber scintillarum* 55, 22 – *sorh ne sar* (l. 256), *hunger oþþe þurst* (l. 258), *wuldor and wurðmynt* (l. 270), and *lof and life* (l. 271).

[23] It was Whitbread (1966: 640) who pointed out this kind of mistake.

[24] The conjunction *mid* is also used to bind asyndetic sequences of words (l. 234, 241, 265, 268).

[25] Latin passive ind. pres. was translated with the OE present of *beon* + passive participle: *obducitur*: *bið gesworcen* (l. 104-105), *rapimur*: *beoð brohte* (l. 119), *impletur*: *bið gefylled* (l. 145), *cernitur*: *bið gesewen* (l. 203), *sentitur*: *bið gemeted* (l. 205), *torquetur*: *bið breged* (l. 213-214).

[26] An active pres. participle is rendered with a passive relative sentence: *pendens* [...] *latro* with "sescaþa [...] þe mid Criste wæs cwyldmed" (*JDay II* l. 53-54).

[27] See *gaudia*: *mærðe* (l. 21), *rea*: *synful* (l. 29), *pectora*: *breost* (l. 29), *pugnis*: *fyste* (l. 29), *membra*: *lichaman* (l. 31), *lacrimis*: *wope* (l. 45), *allisos*: *aglidene mod* (l. 47), *quassatos*: *wanhydige* (l. 50), *animos*: *mod* (l. 50), *tepidos*: *wlacan* (l. 51), *fumos*: *smocan* (l. 51), *undis*: *wætere* (l. 52), *exempla*: *bysne* (l. 53), *certa*: *gearugne* (l. 91), *tempora*: *timan* (l. 91), *tormenta*: *wite* (l. 92), *mentes*: *mod* (l. 103), *turris*: *hleo* (l. 127), *ultricibus*: *ættrenum* (l. 146), *flammis*: *lige* (l. 146), *pectora*: *breost* (l. 160), *pugnis*: *mid fyste* (l. 161), *dicta*: *spræce* (l. 185), *ignibus*: *fyres* (l. 189), *flammis*: *lig* (l. 192), *facies*: *ansyn* (l. 203), *frigora*: *cyle* (l. 206), *flammae*: *lig* (l. 206), *curis*: *care* (l. 214), *solatia*: *frofor* (l. 223), *tristitiae*: *unrotnes* (l. 228), *tedia*: *adl* (l. 229), *flammis*: *on lige* (l. 230), *caelestia*

regna: *heofonrice* (l. 253), *febres*: *fefur* (l. 259), *morbi*: *adl* (l. 259), *clades*: *cwyld* (l. 259), *flammae*: *liges gebrasl* (l. 260), *frigora*: *cyle* (l. 260), *tristitiae*: *unrotnes* (l. 261), *taedia*: *æmelnys* (l. 261), *ruinae*: *hryre* (l. 262), *curae*: *caru* (l. 262), *tormenta*: *tintrega* (l. 262), *fulmina*: *liget* (l. 263), *perpetuis*: *ece* (l. 280), *donis*: *mede* (l. 280), *turmas*: *werode* (l. 282), *agmina*: *mædenheap* (l. 290), *patres*: *fæder* (l. 298), *natos*: *sunu* (l. 298), *cohortes*: *werode* (l. 303). The opposite occurs only six times: *sermone*: *wordum* (l. 61), *pauper*: *þearfan* (l. 162), *potens*. *þeodcyningas* (l. 162), *grando*: *hagulscuras* (l. 265), *flore*: *blostmum* (l. 291).

[28]At the same time, Latin *candida agmina* is rendered with "þæra hwittra [...] mædenheap" (*JDay II* l. 290) owing to the influence of *virgineo flore*.

[29] The word *iudex* is translated with *dema* at lines 76 and 171, with a specification, "eces deman", at l. 76, otherwise, it is rendered with *god* (*JDay II* l. 18, 71), *cyningc* (*JDay II* l. 95), and "se godes sunu" (*JDay II* l. 86).

[30] The homily Napier no. 29 features a further occurrence of *amarian*, *braslian*, *dæþbeacnigende* (written as two words), *dimhiw*, *geþuxian* (*geþuhsian*), *heortleas*, *ofersælig*, *þrece*, and *unstenc*.

[31] These words are in part listed by Stanley (1971).

[32] The homily Napier no. 29 features a further occurrence of *amasian*, *æmelnes*, *ærdæd*, *afeormian*, *biterlice*, *færlic*, *gebrasl*, *gewepan*, *gycel*, *gnagan*, *ligspiwel*, *mihtleas*, *ormætness*, *towearde*, *þrece*, and *ungeryde*.

[33] Another group of prose words in *JDay II* occur at least once in other poems: *ærendraca* (l. 287 and *Creed* l. 12), *angryslic* (l. 226 and *PPs* CII.33, 3), *arfæstnes* (l. 220, 269 and *KtHy* l. 24), *cwylman* (l. 54, 204, 217 and *El* l. 688), *drunceness* (l. 234 and *Exhort* l. 44), *dwolma* (l. 106 and *Met* 5, 43), *forgifnes* (in the meaning "forgiveness", l. 68, 91 and *Christ* l. 427), *forsweorcan* (l. 108, 199 and *Beo* l. 1767), *fyrenian* (ms. *fyrgende*) (l. 215 and *Soul I* l. 103, *Sat* l. 619, *Rid* 20, 34), *gebedstow* (l. 30 and *Jul* l. 376), *gegladian* (l. 221 and *Seasons* l. 191), *gristbitung* (l. 227 and *Sat* l. 333), *halwende* (l. 84 and *PPs* CXVIII.103, 3), *hopa* (l. 221 and *Exhort* 10, *Inc* l. 253), *horh* (l. 77, 157 and *El* l. 297), *horxlice* (l. 168 and *Soul* 2 l. 109), *hreowlic* (l. 75 and *PPs* CVIII.9, 2), *micelnys* (l. 186 and *PPs* LXVI.1, 4), *nosu* (l. 207 and *PPs* CXIII.14, 1, CXXXII.17, 3), *ræpling* (l. 48, and *Rid* 52, 1; it has only another occurrence in the *Stowe Psalter* Ps LXVIII.34), *swiðlic* (l. 182, 227 and *Christ* l. 954, *Jul* l. 55, *Jud* l. 240), *upcund* (l. 307 and *Christ* l. 268 and *OrW* l. 34), and *wrænnes* (l. 236 and *Met* 25, 41).

[34] The phrase *lifes frea* (l. 81), instead of the more common compound *liffrea*, is also found in *Creed* l. 5 and *Seasons* l. 3.

[35] Literature of the late Anglo-Saxon period is marked by bilingualism, and, as far as poetry is concerned, by the decay of metrics, the use of rhyme, the introduction of new stylistic features instead of those typical of the previous productions (such as variation), and the use of prose words. As far as the content is concerned, late Old English poetry is characterized by the frequency of eschatological motifs as well as homiletic, penitential and didactic themes (cf. Lendinara 2001a).

[36] Napier (1967: 136, 27-140, 2). The manuscript is a companion volume to Hatton 114 and Oxford, Bodleian Library, Junius 121 (cf. Gneuss 2001: nos. 637, 638 and 644).

[37] The former view that the prose passage of the homily Napier no. 29 is "eine sehr verderbte widergabe" of the poem (Napier [1967]: viii) has been questioned both by Stanley (1971: 389-390), and Frank (1994: 106-107).

[38] Stanley (1971: 389) quoted by Caie (2000: 23).

[39] On this suffix see Ahlsson (1991: 80-85).

[40] Frequent are also the adjectives ending in *–lic*: *ænlic* (l. 6, 63, 282, 292), *angryslic* (l. 226), *earmlic* (l. 188), *egeslic* (l. 102 and the adverb *egeslice* l. 94), *færlic* (l. 259), *freolic* (l. 298), *gelic* (l. 174), *healic* (l. 281), *heanlic* (l. 258), *heofenlic* (l. 255, 281), *hreowlic* (l. 75), *laðlic* (l. 206, 210, 260), *leoflic* (l. 271), *scearplic* (l. 53), *swiðlic* (l. 182, 227), *unhyrlic* (l. 11), *uplic*, *upplic* (l. 46, 113, 146, 299) and the *-lice* adverbs: *biterlice* (l. 167), *freolice* (l. 277), *gelice* (l. 144), *glædlice* (l. 273), *horxlice* (l. 168), and *swiðlice* (l. 160).

[41] See also "eal swa ic secge" (*JDay II* l. 4) and "eall swylce þu cwæde" (*JDay II* l. 12), "ic gemunde" (*JDay II* l. 21 and 24), *swegdon* is said of the water and the trees (*JDay II* l. 3 and 7).

[42] Several Old English poems feature the repetition of key words or phrases. Beaty (1934) has studied instances of identical words or root-syllables, which are repeated with a different meaning, connotation or association. For the structural function of repetition in Anglo-Saxon poetry, cf. Huppé (1943), Greenfield (1954), Hieatt (1971), Kintgen (1974), and Gardner (1975: 18-32).

[43] See, for example, *Mald*: *sendon* l. 29 and *sendan* l. 32, *Seasons*: *lar* and *læran* at l. 2, 3, 8, 9 and 11, *Creed*: *giftum* and *handgyft*, *earðbuendum* and *foldbuendum*, *engla* and *englas*; *uplic* is repeated thrice (l. 11, 32, and 37).

[44] On the semantic value of the adjective *earm*, see Coppola (1988-1989).

[45] Several repetitions should be added to those already noted above: *gyldan* / *agyldan* (l. 73-74), *lifes* / *lifes* (l. 81), *sweart* / *sweart* (l. 105-106), *wæron* / *wæron* (l. 133-134), *eall* / *eall* (l. 145-146), *earm* / *earm* (l. 163-164), *gewiteð* / *gewiteð* (l. 236-237), *nawih* / *wihte* (l. 202-203), *gesælig* / *ofersælig* (l. 247), *worulda* / *woruld* (l. 198, 248), *fæder* / *fæder* (l. 297-298), see also "ne se mona næfð nanre mihte wiht" (l. 109).

[46] See the remarks by Bodden (1987: 24-39). As far as the whole Germanic tradition is concerned, see Luiselli Fadda (1991) and the essays in the volume published by Contamine in 1989. As to the Old English tradition, the book by Gonser (1909) is still valuable.

[47] Several examinations have been devoted to the translation techniques of Alfred and Ælfric, including studies of the prefaces to their works, which both reflect on the value and the aims of translation, see Minkoff (1976), St-Jacques (1983), and Marsden (1991), see also the two volumes published by Szarmach in 1978 and 1986.

[48] Two prose works by Alcuin were translated into Old English: the *Liber de virtutibus et vitiis* and the *Interrogationes Sigewulfi in Genesin*.

[49] A translation into Northumbrian dialect is preserved in Leiden, Bibliotheek der Rijksuniversiteit, Vossianus lat. 4° 106, see Smith [1990] and, for the edited text, ASPR (6, 109), for the West Saxon version, see ASPR (3, 198).

[50] ASPR (3, 200-203), cf. O'Brien O'Keeffe (1980) and (1985).

[51] See Blake (1990: 24-35). According to the estimate of Emerson (1926), the translator used only 107 lines of the Latin poem, which correspond to 380 lines of the OE *Phoenix*, the entire poem is 677 lines long.

[52] The text of the *De ave phoenice* (which is 170 lines long) is printed in Blake (1990: 88-92).

[53] See, respectively, Zupitza (1887), Gneuss (1968: 91-101, 135-155, 194-206), and Korhammer (1976: 128-138).

[54] Syntactic patterns analogous to those of prose versions are shown by syntactical glosses, see Robinson (1973) and O'Neill (1992).

[55] For similar instances, see the Old English glosses to Ælfric's *Colloquy* (ed. Garmonsway 1978) and to the third book of the *Bella Parisiacae urbis*.

References

Ahlsson, Lars-Erik
1991 "Untersuchungen zum suffigierten Adjektiv im Altniederdeutschen und Altfriesischen unter Berücksichtigung des Altenglischen", *Niederdeutsches Wort* 31: 77-122.

Baker, Peter -- Michael Lapidge (eds.)
1995 *Byrhtferth's Enchiridion*. (EETS s.s. 15.) Oxford: Oxford University Press.

Beaty, John O.
1934 "The echo-word in *Beowulf* with a note on the *Finnsburg Fragment*", *PMLA* 49: 365-73.

Blake, Norman F. (ed.)
1964 *The Phoenix.* Manchester: Manchester University Press.
1990 Revised edition. Exeter: University of Exeter Press.

Bodden, Mary Catherine
1987 "Anglo-Saxon self-consciousness in language", *English studies* 68: 24-39.

Bremmer Jr., Rolf H.
1983 "Old English *feoh and feorh*, Old Norse *fé ok fjọr*, ergo: Old Frisian *fiā and ferech* 'money and life'", *Us Wurk* 32: 55-62.

Caie, Graham D. (ed.)
2000 *The Old English poem* Judgement Day II*: A critical edition with editions of* De die iudicii *and the Hatton 113 Homily* Be domes dæge. (Anglo-Saxon Texts 2.) Cambridge: Brewer.

Clerici, Ergisto
1973 "Due poeti: Emilio Blossio Draconzio e Venanzio Fortunato", *Rendiconti dell'Istituto Lombardo, Cl. di lettere e scienze morali e storiche* 107: 108-50.

Contamine, Geneviève (ed.)
1989 *Traduction et traducteurs au moyen âge: Actes du colloque international du CNRS organisé à Paris, Institut de Recherche et d'Histoire des Textes, les 26-28 mai 1986*. Paris: CNRS.

Coppola, Maria Augusta
1988-1989 "*... gebleod wundrum, eadgum ond earmum ungelice.* La parusia nel *Cristo III*", *Romanobarbarica* 10: 31-63.

Emerson, Oliver F.
1926 "Originality in Old English Poetry", *Review of English studies* 2: 18-31.

Fraipont, John (ed.)
1955 *Bedae venerabilis liber hymnorum, rhythmi, variae preces. Bedae opera* IV. (Corpus Christianorum, Ser. lat. 122.) Turnhout: Brepols.

Frank, Roberta
1994 "Poetic words in Late Old English prose", in: Godden -- Gray -- Hoad (eds.), 87-107.

Gardner, John
1975 *The construction of christian poetry in Old English.* Carbondale-Edwardsville: Southern Illinois University Press.

Garmonsway, George N. (ed.)
1939 *Ælfric's Colloquy.* (Methuen's Old English Library). London: Methuen.

1978 Revised edition. Exeter: University of Exeter Press.

Gneuss, Helmut
1968 *Hymnar und Hymnen im englischen Mittelalter.* (Buchreihe der Anglia 12.) Tübingen, Winter.

2001 *Handlist of Anglo-Saxon manuscripts.* Tempe: Center for Medieval and Renaissance Studies.

Godden, Malcolm -- Douglas Gray -- Terry Hoad (eds.)
1994 *From Anglo-Saxon to Early Middle English: Studies presented to E. G. Stanley.* Oxford: Clarendon.

Gonser, Paul (ed.)
1909 *Das angelsächsische Prosa-Leben des Heiligen Guthlac.* (Anglistische Forschungen 27.) Heidelberg: Winter
1966 Reprinted edition. Amsterdam: Swets-Zeitlinger.

Greenfield, Stanley B.
1954 "Attitudes and values in *The seafarer*", *Studies in philology* 51: 15-20.

1996 "The Old English Elegies", in: Stanley (ed.), 149-51.

Greenfield, Stanley B. -- Daniel G. Calder
1986 *A new critical history of Old English literature.* New York: New York University Press.

Guerrieri, Anna Maria
1982 "La congiunzione *ond* nel *Beowulf*: problemi di dizione, di sintassi e di stile", *AION, fil. germ.* 25: 7-55.

Hieatt, Constance B.
1971 "Dream frame and verbal echo in the *Dream of the rood*", *Neuphilologische Mitteilungen* 72: 251-63.

Hoffman, Richard L.
1968 "Structure and symbolism in the *Judgement Day II*", *Neophilologus* 52: 170-78.

Huppé, Bernard F.
1943 "*The Wanderer*: Themes and structure", *Journal of English and Germanic philology* 42: 516-38.

1959 *Doctrine and poetry: Augustine's influence on Old English poetry*. New York: State University of New York.

Kail, J.
1889 "Über die Parallelstellen in der ags Poesie", *Anglia* 12: 17-47.

Kintgen, Eugene R.
1974 "Echoic repetition in Old English poetry, especially the *Dream of the rood*", *Neuphilologische Miteilungen* 75: 202-23.

Korhammer, Michael
1976 *Die monastischen Cantica im Mittelalter und ihre altenglischen Interlinearversionen: Studien und Textausgabe*. (TUEPh 6.) Munich: Fink.

Koskenniemi, Inna
1968 *Repetitive word pairs in Old and Early Middle English prose*. (Annales Universitatis Turkuensis, ser. B, 107.) Turku: Turun Yliopisto.

Krause, Wolfgang
1922 "Die Wortstellung in den zweigliedrigen Wortverbindungen, untersucht für das Altindische, Awestische, Litauische und Altnordische", *Zeitschrift für vergleichende Sprachforschung* 50: 74-129.

Lendinara, Patrizia
1986 "The third book of the *Bella parisiacae urbis* by Abbo of Saint-Germain-des-Prés and its Old English gloss", *Anglo-Saxon England* 15: 73-89
1999 Revised reprint, in: Lendinara 1999, 157-75.

1999 *Anglo-Saxon glosses and glossaries.* (Variorum Collected Studies Series CS622.) Aldershot: Ashgate.

2001a "La poesia anglosassone alla fine del X secolo e oltre", *AION, sez. studi tedeschi, fil. germ.* n. s. 11: 7-46.

2001b "Alcuino e il *De die iudicii*", *Pan* 18-19 (= *Miscellanea di studi in memoria di Cataldo Roccaro*): 303-24.

2003 "The *Versus sibyllae de die iudicii* in England", in: Powell -- Scragg (eds.): 85-101.

Löhe, Hans
1907 *Be domes dæge*. (Bonner Beiträge 22.) Bonn: Hanstein.

Lumby, J. Rawson (ed.)
1876 *Be domes dæge: De die iudicii.* (EETS o.s. 65.) London: Trübner.

Luiselli Fadda, Anna Maria
1991 "La traduzione nel Medioevo germanico: condizioni culturali e linguistiche e procedimenti operativi", *Romanobarbarica* 11: 257-90.

Malkiel, Yakov
1959 "Studies in irreversible binomials", *Lingua* 8: 113-60.

Marsden, Richard
1991 "Ælfric as translator: The Old English prose 'Genesis'", *Anglia* 109: 319-56.

Menner, Robert J.
1947 "The vocabulary of the Old English poems on Judgement Day", *PMLA* 62: 583-97.

Minkoff, Harvey
1976 "Some stylistic consequences of Ælfric's theory of translation", *Studies in philology* 73: 29-41.

Napier, Arthur (ed.)
1883 *Wulfstan: Sammlung der ihm zugeschriebenen Homilien nebst Untersuchungen über ihre Echtheit.* Berlin: Weidmann
1967 Reprinted edition with an app. by Klaus Ostheeren. Dublin: Weidmann.

O'Brien O'Keeffe, Katherine
1980 "Exeter riddle 40: The art of an Old English translator", *Proceedings of the patristics, medieval, and Renaissance conference* 5: 107-17.

1985 "The text of Aldhelm's 'Enigma' no. C in Oxford, Bodleian Library, Rawlinson C. 697 and Exeter riddle 40", *Anglo-Saxon England* 14: 61-73.

O'Neill, Patrick P.
1992 "Syntactical glosses in the Lambeth Psalter and the reading of the Old English interlinear translation as sentences", *Speculum* 46: 250-56.

Powell, Kathryn -- Donald Scragg (eds.)
2003 *Apocryphal texts and traditions in Anglo-Saxon England.* (Publications of the Manchester Centre for Anglo-Saxon Studies 2.) Cambridge: Brewer.

Robinson, Fred C.
1973 "Syntactical glosses in Latin manuscripts of Anglo-Saxon provenance", *Speculum* 48: 443-75.

Smith, Albert H. (ed.)
1933 *Three Northumbrian poems.* London: Methuen.
1978 Revised edition. Exeter: University of Exeter Press.
1990 Reprinted edition.

Stanley, Eric G. (ed.)
1966 *Continuations and beginnings.* London: Nelson.

1971 "Studies in the prosaic vocabulary of Old English verse", *Neuphilologische Mitteilungen* 72: 385-418.

St-Jacques, Raymond
1983 "*Hwilum word be worde, hwilum andgit of andgiete*? Bede's 'Ecclesiastical history' and its Old English translator", *Florilegium* 5: 85-104.

Stubbs, William (ed.)
1874 *Memorials of Saint Dunstan Archbishop of Canterbury.* (Rolls Series 63.) London: Longman.

Szarmach, Paul E. (ed.)
1978 *The Old English homily and its background.* Albany: University of New York Press.

1986 *Studies in earlier Old English prose*. Albany: University of New York Press.

Tristram, Hildegard L. C.
1978 "Stock descriptions of heaven and hell in Old English poetry", *Neuphilologische Mitteilungen* 79: 102-13.

Wenisch, Franz
1979 *Spezifisch anglisches Wortgut in den nordhumbrischen Interlinearglossierungen des Lukasevangeliums.* (Anglistische Forschungen 132.) Heidelberg: Winter.

Whitbread, Leslie
1944 "A study of Bede's 'Versus de die iudicii'", *Philological quarterly* 23: 193-221.

1948 "Byrhtferth's hexameters", *Notes & queries* 193: 476.

1963 "Wulfstan' homilies XXIX, XXX and some related texts", *Anglia* 81: 347-64.

1966 "The Old English poem *Judgement day II* and its Latin source", *Philological quarterly* 45: 635-56.

Whitman, Frank H.
1973 "A major compositional technique in Old English verse", *English language notes* 11: 81-86.

Zupitza, Julius
1887 "Altenglische Glossen zu Abbos Clericorum Decus", *Zeitschrift für deutsches Altertum und deutsche Literatur* 31: 1-27.

Appendix I

In Appendix I, fillers (+a) are distinguished from the additions (+*a*) which were compelled by the different linguistic systems, for example, the articoloids or the auxiliary verb for the passive forms. Half-line fillers are not preceded by +. An asterisk marks the single half-lines of the *JDay II*.

Ddi	*JD II*	*a*-verse	*b*-verse	ratio
v. 3	v. 1	+2a+ *sæt* (= *sedi* v. 4)	2a	1:2
	v. 2	+1a	2a (variation)	
+	v. 3	descriptive addition (including a word pair)		0:1
+	v. 4	3a	personal aside	0:1
v. 1	v. 5	+2a	3a (a word pair)	1:2
	v. 6	+*1a*+1a	+1a	
v. 2	v. 7	+1a+*1a*	+2a (second member of a word pair)	1:2
	v. 8	+*1a*	3a (aside comment)	
v. 4	v. 9	free transl. of *turbatus*		1:1
v. 5	v. 10	+2a+ *færinga* (= *subito* v. 4)	2a+ *unrot* (=*maestus* v. 3) (forming a word pair)	1:2
	v. 11		+2a	
+	v. 12a	personal remark		0:½
v. 6	v. 12b			1:½
v. 7	v. 13		+*1a*	1:2
	v. 14	3a	+2a	
+	v. 15a	connective addition		0:½
v. 8	v. 15b		+*1a*	1: ½
+	v. 16	explanatory addition		0:1
v. 9	v. 17	+*1a*+2a	+2a	1:2
	v. 18	+2a	+2a	
v. 10	v. 19	+3a		1:2
	v. 20	+2a (second member of a word pair)	4a	
+	v. 21a	addition (anticipation of v. 24a)		0:½

v. 11	v. 21b		+1a	**1:2 and ½**
	v. 22	+1a+*1a*	3a	
	v. 23		+2a (first member of a word pair)	
v. 12	v. 24	+1a+*1a*	4a (anticipation of v. 25a)	**1:2**
	v. 25	+2a	2a	
v. 13	v. 26	+2a	+1a	**1:3**
	v. 27	+2a (*þæt* clause)	+1a	
	v. 28	+2a	3a (variation)	
v. 14	v. 29		+1a+*1a*	**1:2**
	v. 30	+2a	2a	
v. 15	v. 31	+2a	+*1a*	**1:2**
	v. 32		+2a	
v. 16	v. 33	+1a	3a	**1:2**
	v. 34	+2a (*þæt* clause)	+1a+*1a*	
v. 17	v. 35		3a (incl. *mid wope*= *cum voce gementi* v. 18)	**1:2**
	v. 36	+1a	+1a	
v. 18	v. 37		+1a	**1:1**
v. 19	v. 38	+1a	+2a	**1:2**
	v. 39		+1a	
v. 20	v. 40	+1a+*1a*	4a (explanatory addition)	**1:2**
	v. 41		+1a (variation)	
v. 21	v. 42		+2a	**1:1**
v. 22	v. 43		+1a	**1:2**
	v. 44	+*1a*		
v. 23	v. 45	+3a (*þæt* clause)		**1:1 and ½**
	v. 46a			
v. 24	v. 46b		+1a	**1:2 and ½**
	v. 47	+1a	+1a	
	v. 48		+1a	

v. 25	v. 49	+1a+*1a*+1a	+1a	**1:2**
	v. 50		2a (subject)	
v. 26	v. 51	+*1a*	+1a	**1:2**
	v. 52	3a (including a further transl. of *vult* v. 25)		
v. 27	v. 53	+*2a*	+1a	**1:2**
	v. 54	4a (relative clause)		
v. 28	v. 55	+*1a*	4a (variation)	**1:2**
	v. 56	+*1a*	+2a (second member of a word pair)	
v. 29	v. 57	+1a	+2a (second member of a word pair)	**1:2**
	v. 58	+*1a*	2a	
v. 30	v. 59	+2a+*1a*		**1:2**
	v. 60	+1a	1a	
v. 31	v. 61	+1a+*1a*	+1a	**1:2**
	v. 62	+1a	3a	
v. 32	v. 63	+1a	+*1a*	**1:2**
	v. 64			
v. 33	v. 65	+3a	+1a	**1:2**
	v. 66	+3a	+3a (*þæt* clause)	
v. 34	v. 67	+1a	+1a	**1:2**
	v. 68	+1a	+1a	
v. 35	v. 69			**1:2**
	v. 70a	2a (variation)	+2a	
v. 36	v. 71	+1a		**1:1**
	v. 72a	+1a		**and ½**
v. 37	v. 72b		+1a	
	v. 73	+1a	3a	**1:2**
	v. 74	4a (variation of v. 73b)	2a (variation of v. 73a)	**and ½**
v. 38	v. 75	+5a (*þæt* clause)	+*1a*+1a	**1:2**
	v. 76	+1a+*1a*	+1a	
v. 39	v. 77			**1:1**
	v. 78a	+*1a*		**and ½**

v. 40	v. 78b		+1a	**1:1 and ½**
	v. 79	+*1a*	+1a	
v. 41	v. 80	+2a	+2a (second member of a word pair)	**1:2**
	v. 81	+1a	3a	
v. 42	v. 82	+2a+*1a*	2a (variation)	**1:2**
	v. 83	+*1a*	+2a (second member of a word pair)	
v. 43	v. 84		+3a (*þæt* clause)	**1:2**
	v. 85	+1a	3a	
v. 44	v. 86	+*1a*+1a	free transl. of *te vindice*	**1:2**
	v. 87	? free transl. of *te iudice*	4a	
v. 45	v. 88		+2a (second member of a word pair)	**1:2**
	v. 89	free transl. of *bis vindicat*	+1a	
v. 46	v. 90	+*1a*	3a (a word pair)	**1:2**
	v. 91	+1a		
v. 47	v. 92	+2a	+*1a*+1a+*1a*	**1:2**
	v. 93	+1a+*1a*	2a	
v. 48	v. 94		3a (variation)	**1:1 and ½**
	v. 95a	+1a		
v. 49	v. 95b		+1a	**1:1 and ½**
	v. 96	+1a	2a	
v. 50	v. 97		+1a	**1:1**
+	v. 98	explanatory addition		**0:1**
v. 51	v. 99	+1a	+*2a*	**1:3**
	v. 100*	+2a (second member of a word pair)		
	v. 101	+1a	+2a (second member of a word pair)	
v. 52	v. 102	+*1a*	+1a	**1:2**
	v. 103	+2a	+1a	

v. 53	v. 104*	+1a+*1a*+1a		1:3
	v. 105	+2a (second member of a word pair)	2a (variation)	
	v. 106	variation (including a three words cluster)		
v. 54	v. 107	2a		1:2
	v. 108	+*1a*	+1a	
v. 55	v. 109	free transl.		**1:1**
+	v. 110	addition (*þæt* clause)		**0:1**
v. 56	v. 111	+2a	+1a	**1:2**
	v. 112		3a	
v. 57	v. 113		1a (variation)	**1:1 and ½**
	v. 114a			
v. 58	v. 114b		+1a	**1:2 and ½**
	v. 115	+1a	2a (variation)	
	v. 116	+*1a*	3a (a word pair)	
v. 59	v. 117	+1a	2a (explicit subject)	**1:2**
	v. 118		2a	
v. 60	v. 119	+1a+*1a*+1a		**1:2**
	v. 120		3a (variation)	
v. 61	v. 121*			**1:2**
	v. 122	+1a	3a	
v. 62	v. 123	free transl. of *sis memor*	free transl. of *pavor* (*þæt* clause)	**1:2**
	v. 124		+1a	
v. 63	v. 125	free transl. (including a word pair)		**1:2**
	v. 126	free transl. (including a word pair)		
vv. 64-65	v. 127		+1a	**2:2**
	v. 128	+1a		
+	v. 129a	4a (addition)		**0: ½**
v. 66	v. 129b		+1a	**1:1 and ½**
	v. 130	redundant transl. of *omnes homines*		

v. 67	v. 131	free and redundant transl.		1:4
	v. 132	free and redundant transl.		
	v. 133	free and redundant transl.		
	v. 134	free and redundant transl.		
v. 68	v. 135	+1a+*1a*		**1:2**
	v. 136	+1a	3a	
v. 69	v. 137	+1a+*1a*	2a	**1:4**
	v. 138	+1a+*1a*	3a	
	v. 139	+2a	+1a	
	v. 140		3a	
v. 70	v. 141	+2a	3a	**1:2**
	v. 142	+3a (*þæt* clause)	3a (a word pair)	
v. 71	v. 143	+*1a*	+1a	**1:2**
	v. 144		4a (explicit subject)	
v. 72	v. 145	+1a+*1a*	+1a+*1a*	**1:2**
	v. 146	+2a		
v. 73	v. 147	+*1a*	5a (commenting remark)	**1:2**
	v. 148	free transl. of *ruptis habenis*		
v. 74	v. 149	free transl. of *inane*	1a	**1:1 and ½**
	v. 150a	3a		
+	v. 150b		enlarged repetition of v. 146b	**0:½**
+	v. 151	enlarged repetition of v. 145b		**0:1**
v. 75	v. 152		+2a (second member of a word pair)	**1:2**
	v. 153	3a (a word pair)	3a (variation: a word pair)	
v. 76	v. 154	free transl.		**1:1**
v. 77	v. 155	+*1a*		**1:2**
	v. 156	+1a	2a (variation)	

v. 78	v. 157	+2a	+1a	**1:2**
	v. 158	+2a	2a (variation)	
v. 79	v. 159	+1a	+1a	**1:3**
	v. 160	+1a	+1a	
	v. 161	+1a+*1a*	2a	
v. 80	v. 162	+1a		**1:1**
v. 81	v. 163		+1a+*1a*	**1:3**
	v. 164	+2a	4a (variation)	
	v. 165	explanatory addition and variation		
v. 82	v. 166	+1a+*1a*	+1a	**1:2**
	v. 167	+1a	+*1a*+1a	
v. 83	v. 168	+1a	+1a	**1:2**
	v. 169		+2a (second member of a word pair)	
v. 84	v. 170	+*1a*+1a+*1a*	+*1a*+1a	**1:2**
	v. 171	+1a		
v. 85	v. 172	+1a	+1a	**1:2**
	v. 173		4a	
v. 86	v. 174	+2a	2a (a simile)	**1:2**
	v. 175	+1a	3a (variation)	
v. 87	v. 176	+2a	3a (repetition of v. 176a)	**1:2**
	v. 177	+2a+*1a*	+1a	
v. 88	v. 178	+4a	2a	**1:2**
	v. 179	+3a	+1a	
v. 89	v. 180	+1a+*1a*	+*1a*	**1:1**
v. 90	v. 181	+1a		**1:2**
	v. 182	repetition of v. 181		
v. 91	v. 183		+1a	**1:2**
	v. 184	+1a (variation)	3a	
v. 92	v. 185			**1:2**
	v. 186		2a	
v. 93	v. 187	+1a	+1a	**1:2**
	v. 188	3a		
v. 94	v. 189		+2a	**1:2**
	v. 190	free transl. of *gehennae*		

v. 95	v. 191	4a		1:3
	v. 192	*+1a*	+1a+*1a*	
	v. 193	variation		
v. 96	v. 194	+1a		**1:1 and ½**
	v. 195a	*+2a*		
+	v. 195b		5a (aside)	**0:½**
v. 97	v. 196	*+2a*	+2a	**1:1**
v. 98	v. 197		+1a	**1:2**
	v. 198	*+1a*	+2a	
v. 99	v. 199		+1a	**1:2**
	v. 200	+2a	+2a (first member of a word pair)	
v. 100	v. 201			**1:2**
	v. 202	+2a (second member of a word pair)	2a	
v. 101	v. 203	*+1a*	2a	**1:2**
	v. 204	*+1a*	4a (relative clause)	
v. 102	v. 205	*+1a*+1a		**1:1 and ½**
	v. 206a	+1a		
v. 103	v. 206b		3a (anticipation of *fetor*)	**1:2 and ½**
	v. 207	+4a	+1a	
	v. 208	+1a (second transl. of *fetor*)		
v. 104	v. 209	+1a+*2a*		**1:2**
	v. 210		2a	
v. 105	v. 211	+2a		**1:2**
	v. 212	+1a+*1a*+1a (variation)		
v. 106	v. 213	+1a+*1a*	*+2a*+1a	**1:2**
	v. 214	*+1a*	+2a (second member of a word pair)	
v. 107	v. 215	*+1a*	*+1a*	**1:2**
	v. 216	free transl. of *sibimet*		

v. 108	v. 217	+2a+*1a*	+*1a*	**1:2**
	v. 218	+1a+*1a*+2a (relative clause)		
v. 109	v. 219	+*1a*	+1a	**1:1 and ½**
	v. 220a			
v. 110	v. 220b		+1a	**1:1**
	v. 221a		+1a	
v. 111 (*flentibus arridet)*	v. 221b	+1a		**½:1 and ½**
	v. 222	+1a+*1a*	2a	
v. 111 (*Fugiunt...*)	v. 223a	+1a		**½:½**
v. 112	v. 223b		+*1a*+1a	**1:1 and ½**
	v. 224	+1a+*2a* (relative clause)	3a (variation)	
v. 113	v. 225	+*2a*		**1:1**
v. 114	v. 226	+2a		**1:2**
	v. 227	+1a	+1a	
v. 115	v. 228	+2a	2a	**1:2**
	v. 229	+1a	+1a	
v. 116	v. 230	+2a	+*1a*	**1:2**
	v. 231		3a (a word pair)	
v. 117	v. 232		+1a	**1:2**
	v. 233		3a (variation)	
v. 118	v. 234	+1a	+2a	**1:2**
	v. 235	+2a	2a (variation)	
v. 119	v. 236	+2a	2a (variation)	**1:4**
	v. 237	+1a	2a (repetition)	
	v. 238	2a	+2a	
	v. 239	+1a	3a	
v. 120	v. 240	4a		**1:2**
	v. 241	+1a	3a (variation)	

v. 123	v. 242		+1a	**1:1 and ½**
	v. 243a			
v. 121	v. 243b		+3a	**1:½**
+	v. 244	further remark without a counterpart in the Latin		**0:1**
v. 122	v. 245	+*1a*+1a	+*1a*	**1:1**
+	v. 246	additional remark (including a word pair)		**0:1**
v. 124	v. 247	+2a	+1a (*ofersælig* = *nimium*)	**1:2**
	v. 248	+1a+*1a*	2a	
v. 125	v. 249	+*1a*+1a		**1:2**
	v. 250	+2a	+1a	
v. 126	v. 251			**1:1**
v. 127	v. 252	+1a	+2a	**1:1 and ½**
	v. 253a	+1a		
+	v. 253b		4a (exclamatory aside)	**0:½**
v. 128	v. 254		2a	**1:2**
	v. 255	+*1a*		
v. 129	v. 256	+1a		**1:1**
v. 130 (*non labor ullus*)	v. 257	+1a	2a	**½:1**
v. 130 (*Non … somnus*	v. 258	+1a	+1a	**½:1**
v. 131	v. 259	+3a	+2a	**1:2**
	v. 260	+2a	+*1a*+1a	
v. 132	v. 261	+2a	+2a	**1:2**
	v. 262	+2a	+2a	
v. 133	v. 263	+3a	+2a	**1:3**
	v. 264	+1a	3a (? a wrong transl. of *procellae*)	
	v. 265	+2a	+2a	

v. 134	v. 266	+4a	+2a	**1:2**
	v. 267	+2a	+2a	
v. 135	v. 268	+2a	+1a	**1:2**
	v. 269	+1a	+2a	
v. 136	-	the Latin verse is not translated		**1:0**
v. 137	v. 270*	+1a		**1:2**
	v. 271	+2a+ *lif* (= *vita* v. 136)		
v. 138	v. 272	+*1a*	+1a	**1:2**
	v. 273	+2a	+1a	
v. 139	v. 274	+1a		**1:2**
	v. 275	+2a	2a	
v. 140	v. 276*	+2a		**1:2**
	v. 277	+1a	+2a	
v. 141	v. 278			**1:1**
v. 142	v. 279	3a (explicit subject)	2a (variation)	**1:2 and ½**
	v. 280	+2a		
	v. 281a			
+	v. 281b		4a (exclamatory aside)	**0:½**
v. 143	v. 282	+*1a*+1a		**1:2**
	v. 283	+*1a*	+2a (second member of a word pair)	
v. 144	v. 284	+2a+*1a*	3a	**1:2**
	v. 285	+1a	+1a	
v. 145	v. 286			**1:2**
	v. 287	expanded transl. of *apostolicas*		
v. 146	v. 288		+1a	**1:2**
	v. 289*	+2a		
v. 147	v. 290	+1a+*1a*	+1a	**1:2**
	v. 291	+1a	2a (variation)	
v. 148	v. 292	+1a	+1a	**1:4**
	v. 293	expanded transl. of *genitrix*		
	v. 294	3a (variation)	+*1a*	
	v. 295	+2a	2a	
v. 149	v. 296	+2a+*1a*+1a		**1:2**
	v. 297	+1a	+*1a*+1a	

v. 150	v. 298		2a	**1:1**
v. 151	v. 299	+*1a*+1a		**1:2**
	v. 300	+1a	+1a (variation)	
v. 152	v. 301	+*1a*	+1a	**1:1**
+	v. 302	addition		**0:1**
v. 153	v. 303	+*1a*+1a	+*1a*	**1:2**
	v. 304	+1a	2a	
v. 154	v. 305	+1a		**1:2**
	v. 306	+1a	+*1a*+1a	

Appendix II

Additions
ratio 0:½: vv. 12a; 15a; 21a; 129a; 149b; 195b; 253b; 281b.
ratio 0:1: vv. 3; 4; 16; 98; 110; 151; 244; 246; 302.

Omissions
ratio 1:0: v. **136** is omitted in the OE translation.

Translation
ratio 1:½ : v. **6**: 12b; v. **8**: 15b; **121**: 243b.
ratio ½:½: v. **111** (2nd part): 223a.
ratio 1:1: v. **4**: 9; v. **18**: 37; v. **21**: 42; v. **50**: 97; v. **55**: 109; v. **76**: 154; v. **80**: 162; v. **89**: 180; v. **97**: 196; v. **110**: 220b-221a; v. **113**: 225; v. **122**: 245; v. **126**: 251; v. **129**: 256; v. **141**: 278; v. **150**: 298; v. **152**: 301.
ratio 2:2: vv. **64-65**: 127-128.
ratio ½:1: v. **130** (2nd part): 257; v. **130** (1st part): 258.
ratio ½:1 and ½: v. **111** (1st part): vv. 221b-222.
ratio 1:1 and ½: v. **23**: 45-46a; v. **36**: 71-72a; v. **39**: 77-78a; v. **40**: 78b-79; v. **48**: 94-95a; v. **49**: 95b-96; v. **57**: 113-114a; v. **66**: 129b-130; v. **74**: 149-150a; v. **96**: 194-195a; v. **102**: 205-206a; v. **109**: 219-220a; v. **112**: 223b-224; v. **123**: 242-243a; v. **127**: 252-253a.
ratio 1:2: v. **1**: 5-6; v. **2**: 7-8; v. **3**: 1-2; v. **5**: 10-11; v. **7**:13-14; v. **9**: 17-18; v. **10**: 19-20; v. **12**: 24-25; v. **14**: 29-30; v. **15**: 31-32; v. **16**: 33-34; v. **17**: 35-36; v. **19**: 38-39; v. **20**: 40-41; v. **22**: 43-44; v. **25**: 49-50; v. **26**: 51-52; v. **27**: 53-54; v. **28**: 55-56; v. **29**: 57-58; v. **30**: 59-60; v. **31**: 61-62; v. **32**: 63-64; v. **33**: 65-66; v. **34**: 67-68; v. **35**: 69-70; v. **38**: 75-76; v. **41**: 80-81; v. **42**: 82-83; v. **43**: 84-85; v. **44**:

86-87; v. **45**: 88-89; v. **46**: 90-91; v. **47**: 92-93; v. **52**: 102-103; v. **54**: 107-108; v. **56**: 111-112; v. **59**: 117-118; v. **60**: 119-120; v. **61**: 121-122; v. **62**: 123-124; v. **63**: 125-126; v. **68**: 135-136; v. **70**: 141-142; v. **71**: 143-144; v. **72**: 145-146; v. **73**: 147-148; v. **75**: 152-153; v. **77**: 155-156; v. **78**: 157-158; v. **82**: 166-167; v. **83**: 168-169; v. **84**: 170-171; v. **85**: 172-173; v. **86**: 174-175; v. **87**: 176-177; v. **88**: 178-179; v. **90**: 181-182; v. **91**: 183-184; v. **92**: 185-186; v. **93**: 187-188; v. **94**: 189-190; v. **98**: 197-198; v. **99**: 199-200; v. **100**: 201-202; v. **101**: 203-204; v. **104**: 209-210; v. **105**: 211-212; v. **106**: 213-214; v. **107**: 215-216; v. **108**: 217-218; v. **114**: 226-227; v. **115**: 228-229; v. **116**: 230-231; v. **117**: 232-233; v. **118**: 234-235; v. **120**: 240-241; v. **124**: 247-248; v. **125**: 249-250; v. **128**: 254-255; v. **131**: 259-260; v. **132**: 261-262; v. **134**: 266-267; v. **135**: 268-269; v. **137**: 270-271; v. **138**: 272-273; v. **139**: 274-275; v. **140**: 276-277; v. **143**: 282-283; v. **144**: 284-285; v. **145**: 286-287; **146**: 288-289; v. **147**: 290-291; v. **149**: 296-297; v. **151**: 299-300; v. **153**: 303-304; v. **154**: 305-306.

ratio 1: 2 and ½ : v. **11**: 21b-23; v. **24**: 46b-48; v. **37**: 72b-74; v. **58**: 114b-116; v. **103**: 206b-208; v. **142**: 279-281a.

ratio 1:3: v. **13**: 26-28; v. **51**: 99-101; v. **53**: 104-106; v. **79**: 159-161; v. **81**: 163-165; v. **95**: 191-193; v. **133**: 263-265.

ratio 1:4: v. **67**: 131-134; **69**: 137-140; v. **119**: 236-239; v. **148**: 292-295.

Summary

Additions

Lat: OE		**Lat lines**	**OE lines**
ratio 0:1	(x 9)	0	9
ratio 0:½	(x 8)	0	4
		——	——
	Sub-total	0	13

Omissions

Lat: OE		**Lat lines**	**OE lines**
ratio 1:0		1	0
		——	——
	Sub-total	1	0

Translation

Lat: OE		**Lat lines**	**OE lines**
ratio 1:½	(x 3)	3	1 and ½
ratio ½:½	(x 1)	½	½
ratio 1:1	(x 17)	17	17
ratio 2:2	(x 1)	2	2
ratio ½:1	(x 2)	1	2
ratio ½:1 and ½	(x 1)	½	1 and ½
ratio 1:1 and ½	(x 15)	15	22 and ½
ratio 1:2	(x 97)	97	194
ratio 1:2 and ½	(x 6)	6	15
ratio 1:3	(x 7)	7	21
ratio 1:4	(x 4)	4	16
		——	——
	Sub-total	**152**	293
	Total lines	**154**	**306**

Old English runic inscriptions: Textual criticism and historical grammar

Alfred Bammesberger (Eichstätt, Germany)

The editorial problems[1] presented by runic epigraphical material are in some ways similar to those presented by texts preserved in manuscripts employing the Latin script,[2] but in some ways they are notably different.[3] Whereas modern technology allows us to read certain faded and almost erased passages from manuscripts, epigraphical material has often suffered damage beyond repair. If a stone monument has been impaired by the inclemency of the weather or by human barbarism we have in most cases little hope of restoring the pristine shape of an inscription. But taking into account details of comparative linguistics and the history of the language may be of help in interpreting fragmentary inscriptions.

The following lines will deal with philological problems presented by four selected Old English runic inscriptions. Two of these inscriptions were found recently, the remaining two have been known from the beginning of serious runic studies. The emphasis in my account will lie on questions of historical grammar.

1. The *Harford Farm Brooch*

The *Harford Farm Brooch* was published by John Hines in 1991, who introduced his account as follows: "A seventh-century runic inscription has been found on an Anglo-Saxon brooch excavated from a cemetery site at Harford Farm, Caistor-by-Norwich, Norfolk" (Hines 1991: 6). A somewhat more detailed account of the inscription is available in Parsons's monograph (Parsons 1999: 53-4); figure 1 is taken from Parsons (1999: 54).

The inscription is partly legible without any trouble, but some runes are less clear.
The inscription can be transcribed as follows:

l	**u**	**d**	**a**	**:**	**g**	**i**	**b**	**œ**	**t**	**æ**	**s**	**i**	**g**	**i**	**l**	**æ**
1	2	3	4		5	6	7	8	9	10	11	12	13	14	15	16

At least part of the text seems to make sense immediately. If we take the points following the runes for **luda** (1-4) as a word divider, then it is likely that **luda** represents a name, which is actually what all specialists who dealt with the inscription find acceptable. The remaining sequence readily splits up as **gibœtæ sigilæ**, and the second of these words is likely to refer somehow to the brooch, so that what precedes may be considered as a finite verbal form belonging to the verb OE *ge-bētan* 'to improve, repair, make amends'.

Hines thinks the inscription means 'manifestly': 'Luda repaired the brooch'. He appends the following note:

> *Luda* is a recorded Old English masculine personal name, and *gibœtæ* is the predictable form in a runic inscription of this date of the 3rd person singular preterite of the verb recorded in later Old English as *gebētan* 'to repair'. The form *sigilæ* is just slightly unusual in its ending *-æ*, which as an accusative singular inflection is that of a strong feminine noun, but a strong feminine *sigel* is recorded in Toller's *Supplement* to Bosworth and Toller's *An Anglo-Saxon Dictionary* beside the more familiar neuters *sigel* and *sigle*. (Hines 1991: 7)

The interpretation outlined so far is certainly possible. Some misgivings remain, however. The preterite of *gibœ̄tan* is to be expected in Old English as *gibœ̄ttæ* in the seventh century, the period to which the brooch has usually been assigned. It is perhaps conceivable that the geminate *-tt-* was simplified in the runic inscription, but the preterite of *gebē̆tan* is regularly *gebē̆tte* in Old English. We may therefore wonder whether **gibœtæ** should morphologically be accounted for in a different way.

The ending **-æ** functioned in Old English as the marker for singular of the present subjunctive (see now my 2003 paper), a form that at a later stage appeared regularly as *-e*.[4] It is therefore readily possible to interpret **gibœtæ** as third person singular of the present subjunctive of **gibœtan**. The form can be assumed to mean 'may (he) improve, may (he) get better', possibly also 'may he repair'.

We now turn to the following word, which according to Hines is mostly found as a neuter. The ending **-æ** can represent the dative, and the dative had also taken over the function of the instrumental. If we allow **sigil** to mean 'brooch', then a dative instrumental **sigilæ** can readily mean 'by means of the brooch'.

In the final analysis, I suggest that the whole inscription should be interpreted as a wish for the person who wore or carried the brooch. Theoretically the precise syntactic analysis of the inscription allows two possibilities: **luda** can be the nominative, then we would translate 'may Luda make amends by means of the brooch'. Alternatively **luda** could be a vocative, but then the finite verb would be expected as a second person imperative. Since

gibœtæ cannot be analysed as an imperative, this alternative is unconvincing. Even if uncertainties remain with regard to the interpretation of the complete inscription, I think that **gibœtæ** should definitely be parsed as a third person singular of the present subjunctive.

2. The *Brandon Antler* runic inscription

The so-called *Brandon Antler* was published by David Parsons in 1991, but had already been referred to in a slightly earlier publication by R.I. Page (1991: 39): "The runes run along the length of the artefact, with some twelve letters visible and traces of others." Parsons offered a detailed description of the piece together with a drawing of it and a special drawing and transliteration of the runes. The inscription[5] consists of fifteen runic units, which will be numbered consecutively. Runes 1-12 can be identified without major difficulty. Only runes 13 and 14 are unclear, therefore question marks will be put in their places. Rune 15 is a ligature, of which we can readily identify an **a** and an **n**. The inscription may be transliterated as follows (see also Mitchell 1994; Flowers 1999: 6):

w	**o**	**h**	**s**	**w**	**i**	**l**	**d**	**u**	**m**	**d**	**e**	**?**	**?**	**$\widehat{\text{an}}$**
1	2	3	4	5	6	7	8	9	10	11	12	13	14	15

Parsons interpreted runes 1-4 as OE *wōhs* 'grew' (preterite of *weaxan* 'grow') and 5-10 as *wildum* 'wild' (dative singular of the adjective *wilde*), which is likely to be correct. The remaining five runic units pose some problems, however, although runes 11 and 12 are likely to be read as **d** and **e**. It would certainly seem plausible to read runes 13 and 14 as **o** and **r** respectively, since what is visible in the drawing may well represent traces of these letters. Parsons (1991: 10) concluded: "The text is clearly: *wōhs wildum dēoran* 'grew on a wild animal'."

But the form *dēoran* is unexpected in the paradigm of the *a*-stem *dēor* (neuter) 'animal', as Parsons noted. The assumption of "a weak masculine *dēora* (otherwise found only as a possible personal name element in place names) beside the familiar strong neuter *dēor*" (Parsons 1991: 10) cannot really be supported by further evidence and is therefore very doubtful indeed. Theoretically, one could perhaps assume that *deoran* as dative plural (with *-um* appearing as *-an*) would be in congruence with a dative plural *wildum*, but the resulting translation 'grew on wild animals' does not make sense in the given context, since the tine certainly grew on one animal. The reading *wildum deoran* does not lead to a viable analysis of the text.

In the year following Parsons's edition, the Belgian runologist René Derolez published a brief note on the *Brandon Antler* inscription, in which he gave the following interpretation:

> *wōhs wildum dēor an* (or *on*, if that reading is possible), with the preposition in postposition. The grammar would be different than in David Parsons' suggestion in *Nytt om Runer* 6 (1991), pp. 9-10: *wōhs wildum dēoran*, with an anomalous inflection of *deor*. The translation, however, would be the same: 'grew on a wild animal'. (Derolez 1992: 8)

Derolez's analysis has been accepted by Page (1999: 170).

Derolez's approach seems correct, but the analysis of the unit given as rune 15 allows some further discussion. If runes 13 and 14 are indeed to be read as **o** and **r**, then the resulting form *deor* (nominative or accusative) is not congruent with the dative *wildum*. We expect a dative *deore*. One could suggest that *-e* was left out before the vocalic initial of the following word. But this is possibly too facile.

If we take into consideration that **wohs** (= OE *wōx*) represents the historically correct preterite of a strong verb of class VI with the vowel *ō*, which was then replaced by the diphthong *ēo* taken over from class VII (see Campbell 1959: 318), we may assume that the inscription belongs to an early stage of Old English. Since Mitchell (1994) dates the inscription to "late 7th to early 9th century", we may assume that the distinction of the final vowels *-æ* and *-i*, which later fell together under *-e*, was still preserved (Campbell 1959: 153). For an early period of Old English the dative singular of *dēor* could be postulated as *dēoræ* (Campbell 1959: 224).

The final phoneme *-æ* of *dēoræ* may perhaps be contained in the ligatured rune 15. Rune 15 has so far been interpreted as a ligature of **a** + **n**, which is plausible. But if the ligature was originally intended to represent **æ** + **a** + **n**, it would probably not have had a different shape. One may even surmise that **o** as the second member of the sequence would not have caused a modification in the shape of the ligature either, so that Derolez's reading of the postposition as *on* seems acceptable: The preposition appears as *on* in the majority of its occurrences, but *an* is also found.

The sequence of runes on the *Brandon Antler* can therefore be transliterated as either *wōhs wildum dēoræ an* or *wōhs wildum dēoræ on*. The text meaning 'grew on a wild animal' suggests "a link with Anglo-Saxon riddle tradition" (Parsons 1991: 11).

3. The *Overchurch Stone*

The so-called *Overchurch Stone* was found in 1887 when a small church at Upton (Wirral) was dismantled. Formerly the stone was in the Grosvenor Museum in Chester, now it is on permanent loan to the Williamson Art Gallery, Birkenhead, near Liverpool. The runic text in two lines can be transcribed as follows:[6]

f	**o**	**l**	**c**	**æ**	**a**	**r**	**æ**	**r**	**d**	**o**	**n**	**b**	**e**	**c**
1	2	3	4	5	6	7	8	9	10	11	12	13	14	15

b	**i**	**d**	**d**	**a**	**þ**	**f**	**o**	**t**	**e**	**æ**	**þ**	**e**	**l**	**m**	**u**	**n**
16	17	18	19	20	21	22	23	24	25	26	27	28	29	30	31	32

Although the inscription is not complete, certain elements can be distinguished without major difficulty. The sequence **arærdon** (runes 6-12) is likely to represent the preterite of *aræran* 'raise', and **biddaþ** (runes 16-21) can be interpreted as the imperative of *biddan* 'pray'. It may be assumed that two runes were lost preceding **biddaþ**, and **gebiddaþ** will certainly fill the space. The last three runes **bec** (runes 13-15) of line one may represent the beginning of the word **becun** 'sign'. Furthermore, it is probable that **fote** (runes 22-25) is miswritten for **fore**. The preposition is likely to have been followed by a name, and the incomplete sequence **æþelmun** (runes 26-32) may be assumed to stand for the name **æþelmundæ**. The second line can therefore be translated as 'pray for Æthelmund', which is what may be expected in this context.

Problematic is the first line. The usual assumption is that the line means 'the people erected this monument' (Elliott 1959: 71; 1989: 95). The translation is meaningful, but the initial five runes are not compatible with it. The subject of a clause with this meaning could only be expected as **folc**, since the neuter *folc* would remain unchanged in the plural. It is unlikely that **æ** was inserted by accident, therefore we have to inquire whether a form **folcæ** can reasonably be interpreted in the given context. Grammatically, **folcæ** is the regularly shaped dative singular of **folc**, and we have to examine whether a dative singular 'for the people' makes sense in the given context.

If we assume that **folcæ** is the dative object and **becun** the accusative object of **rærdon**, then the clause would be without an expressed subject. This is by no means unheard of in Old English. The beginning of Cædmon's Hymn *Nu scylun hergian* (Smith 1933: 38) is rendered in the Latin version as 'nunc laudare debemus', which shows that a plural form like *scylun* could be analysed by speakers of Old English as first person plural even if no personal pronoun was added.[7] If we assume that in a similar way **arærdon** means 'we erected', then the inscription can be interpreted in a meaningful way: Æthelmund was evidently an important and wealthy person, and his heirs set up a monument in his honour. On the monument they inscribed a text which means: 'For the people (i.e. so that the people can see it) we erected this monument: Pray for Æthelmund.'

4. The *Ruthwell Cross* inscription

Howlett (1993: 71) characterised the *Ruthwell Cross* (Dumfriesshire, Scotland) and its inscriptions as follows:

> The Ruthwell Cross, one of the most glorious relics of Anglo-Saxon culture, exhibits an extensive program of sculpture, the longest extant series of Anglo-Latin inscriptions, the longest Old English runic inscription, and the most beautiful poem in the Old Northumbrian dialect.

Although the interpretation of the runic inscription on the *Ruthwell Cross* has always benefitted from the Vercelli Book version of the poem entitled *The dream of the rood*, there are certainly also some respects in which the parallelism was detrimental. With some 260 runes still clear on the cross the runic inscription is certainly "the most sustained piece of runic carving in Anglo-Saxon England, and so gives us the clearest opportunity for seeing English runes in action in formal expression" (Page 1973: 151; 1999: 148).[8]

Only in the seventies and eighties of the twentieth century did a completely new approach to the *Ruthwell Cross* inscription develop. The main innovation was provided by David Howlett's 1978 paper. This short paper represents the first serious attempt to reconstruct the text of what has since been called the *Ruthwell Crucifixion poem* as a poem in its own right. Previously, the Ruthwell text had been viewed as a minor version of the Vercelli Book *Dream of the rood*. The interpretation of the *Ruthwell Crucifixion poem* was further advanced in a long paper by Ó Carragáin (1987-8).[9]

I wish to deal mainly with four separate textual problems: The first word **]geredæ** on the east panel is only partly preserved, so that the restoration of the original reading presents problems (4.1.). In the cases of **fusæ** (4.2.) and **strelum** (4.3.), the grammatical analysis of well preserved forms is at issue. And finally the form **gastæ**, which Howlett (1978) posits, is no longer legible at all; we can therefore only examine whether the reconstruction is linguistically tenable (4.4.). Finally, a speculation concerning the inscription on the top of the cross is submitted (4.5.).

4.1. -geredæ

The first word on the east panel can be read as **geredæ** nowadays; the preceding part of the word was destroyed when the Cross was toppled down. There is an early drawing (see Page 1959a) which allows us to read the word as **+ondgeredæ**, although the identification of the first rune remains doubtful, because in early drawings the runes for **o**, **a**, and **æ** were not consistently distinguished. But the reconstruction **+ondgeredæ**, accepted also by Howlett (1978), is probably correct.

The point I want to make is not affected by this question, however. I am mainly concerned with Howlett's *Anglia* paper, in which he offers a totally new interpretation of this form: "one might translate *ondgeredæ hinæ god almeȝttig* not 'God almighty stripped himself', nor even 'God almighty girded himself', but 'God almighty prepared himself for conflict' or 'girded himself as an adversary'" (Howlett 1998: 235). Since *ond-* and its far more frequent form *on-* in verbal compounds regularly have the meaning of 'off, away', I would certainly maintain that **ondgeredæ** must mean 'he stripped himself', namely Christ took off his clothes, and of course in iconography he normally wears just a loincloth.[10]

4.2. fusæ

The runic inscription on the west face of the *Ruthwell Cross* clearly corresponds to the following lines in the *Dream of the rood*:

Crist wæs on rode.
Hwæðere þær fuse feorran cwoman
to þam æðelinge. Ic þæt eall beheold. (*Dream of the rood*, 56b-58)

Although not all runes can be read nowadays and the lower part of the inscription is completely destroyed, a considerable number of individual runes can be deciphered without major trouble. If we split up the sequence of runes into sixteen words we can distinguish three main clauses in five half-lines:[11]

krist wæs on rodi;
hweþræ þer fusæ fearran kwomu
æþþilæ til anum; ic þæt al biheald;

Page (1973: 151; 1999: 148) translated the runic sequence as follows: "'Christ was on the cross. Yet to this solitary one there came men from afar, eager and noble. I beheld it all.'"

There is no doubt that the translation of the first and the third clause is correct. With regard to the second clause some uncertainty remains, however. Part of the problem lies in the fact that the Vercelli Book version diverges to a certain extent from the epigraphical one. Since the *Dream* version can be translated as 'however there came from afar eager ones to the noble one' it has often been assumed that **til anum** means something like 'to the solitary one' and refers to Christ. It is somewhat strange that **æþþilæ** on the *Ruthwell Cross*, most likely to be an adjective used as the subject of its clause and meaning 'noble ones', should appear as *æðelinge*, evidently dative singular of *æðeling* 'noble one', in the Vercelli Book version.

In a detailed study Rissanen (1967) showed that **til anum** cannot refer to Christ. That **anum** should in any way indicate 'solitariness' seems quite unlikely because neither the epigraphical document nor the manuscript tradition mentions Christ's loneliness. But the strongest indication that **til anum** cannot mean 'to this solitary one' is provided by the fact that a construction in this sense cannot be evidenced from our Old English documentation. If anything like 'noble ones came to him, namely Christ' had been intended, we would certainly expect the anaphoric pronoun ***him** to have been used.

With regard to **til anum** Rissanen is likely to have found the right solution. Rissanen also raises the question who **fusæ** and **æþþilæ** in the clause **hweþræ þer fusæ fearran kwomu æþþilæ til anum** may refer to. A definitive answer does not seem possible, and Rissanen (1967: 287) concludes: "... it is evident, in any case, that **fusæ** and **æþþilæ** refer to two or more persons".

As far as I can see, **fusæ** and **æþþilæ** have always been interpreted as grammatically identical, namely as forms for the nominative plural of the strong adjective. For **æþþilæ** this interpretation is evidently correct. For **fusæ** an alternative can be suggested, however. Since adverbs derived from adjectival stems regularly end in *-e* in Old English and this ending points back to earlier *-æ* we may well ask whether **fusæ** represents an adverb. Corresponding adverbs in **-æ** occur as **hweþræ** 'however' and **saræ** 'sorely, painfully' in the *Ruthwell Cross* inscription. The rendering 'noble persons came eagerly together' avoids the otherwise most difficult question what precisely the meaning of an adjective **fusæ** would be in the given context, since 'eager nobles' or the like does not seem meaningful.[12]

4.3. miþ strelum giwundad

The left margin of the west face of the *Ruthwell Cross* contains in eight rows of mostly two runes a sequence that can be split up into three words: **miþ strelum giwundad**. These three words scan metrically as a half-line and call to mind line 62b of the *Dream of the rood*:

Forleton me þa hilderincas
standan steame bedrifenne; eall ic wæs mid strælum forwundod
(*Dream of the rood*, 61b-62)

Whereas in the Vercelli Book *wæs mid strælum forwundod* clearly functions as the predicate of the Cross speaking to the first person narrator in his dream, it is likely that **miþ strelum giwundad** on the *Ruthwell Cross* refers to Christ. The half-line is mostly translated as 'wounded by arrows', but Swanton (1970: 122) added the following remark: "Alternatively *stræl* might refer to the soldier's spear which pierced the side of Christ (19-20, 48-9) were it not for the plural form of the noun supported by the sense of *eall*." Ó Carragáin (1987-8) also considers a translation 'wounded by the lance', which seems reasonable.

The main question to be dealt with here is the precise analysis of **strelum**. With regard to Swanton's comment it may be pointed out that the adverbial *eall* 'completely' does not tell us anything at all about the number of *strælum* because we can say 'I was completely wounded by an arrow' or 'by arrows'. But the main problem is the analysis of **strelum**, which definitely is not a singular form. It should be mentioned, however, that words for weapons in particular do occur in non-singular form although clearly a singular is meant. This applies to forms like *mecum*, *sweordum*, *hiltum*, which mean 'by the sword'. The reason for this at first sight surprising usage of a form in *-um* certainly is that we are here concerned with fossilised dual forms, so that *mecum* originally meant 'by means of the two edges of the sword'. Therefore, we should not hesitate to interpret **strelum** as meaning 'by the lance', which is of course perfectly meaningful theologically, because Christ's body was opened by one wound inflicted by a soldier, and from this wound his blood gushed forth; later theologians considered Christ's wound as the source for the church. Rendering **strelum** by 'arrows' in the plural would destroy the whole theological context of the poem.[13]

4.4. gastæ

The left border of the east panel is incomplete towards the bottom. Howlett (1978) gave a probable reconstruction of what the original reading may have been. The last half-line is reconstructed as follows: **siþþan He His gastæ sendæ.**[14] There is hardly any doubt that originally the inscription was similar to what Howlett reconstructed, but one detail definitely requires a correction.

With regard to the form **gastæ** Howlett refers to *Bede's death song*, in which this form certainly occurs (Smith 1933: 42). But in the sequence *huaet his gastae ... doemid uueorthae* the form *gastae* is no doubt a dative of the singular, as is regularly to be expected in this syntactic context. A dative singular would make no sense whatsoever in the reconstructed passage of the *Ruthwell Crucifixion poem.* Since the half-line should mean 'after he sent forth his spirit', the form for 'spirit' must be in the accusative; we therefore need **gast**. Furthermore the simplex verb *sendan* would probably not mean 'send forth', therefore a prefix is likely to have occurred. I suggest that Howlett's reconstruction should be corrected as follows: **siþþan he his gast ondsendæ**,[15] but the precise shape of the verbal prefix can hardly be determined.

4.5.][.]æ f a u œ þ o [

By way of conclusion to an inconclusive paper, I wish to add a short remark on the panel on top of the cross. This panel now depicts a bird perched on a branch bearing fruit. What is left of the runic inscription has been given by Page (1999: 146) as follows: **][.]æ f a u œ þ o [** "standing amidst other, unidentifiable, runes". With regard to explaining this inscription Page icily comments: "Attempts at interpreting this sequence have shown more ingenuity than judgement." The assessment is fully justified.

Since all previous suggestions are certainly not convincing, I wish to point out that this could be simply a representation of the futhark, with the new Old English runes inserted between the regular futhark signs: **f - u - þ - o** would represent the regular sequence of the runic "alphabet" in Anglo-Saxon times, whereas **æ - a - œ** would draw attention to the innovations that occurred in prehistoric Old English times. But this is of course also only a speculation.

Notes

[1]This revised text of my paper read at the Munich 2001 Medieval Symposium incorporates suggestions made in the discussion following its presentation. Basically, the text of

the oral delivery has been preserved, but footnotes referring to further investigations and providing bibliographical details have been added.

[2]On editing manuscript material see above all Gneuss (1998) with many references to further literature on the question.

[3]Runes are transliterated in **boldface**. Some preliminary indications towards an edition of the Old English runic material are given in Bammesberger (1994).

[4]The Germanic subjunctive goes back to the optative of Indo-European. In thematic presents the optative was characterized by IE **-o-i-* preceding the person markers, IE **-oi-* yielded **-ai-* in Germanic (cf. Go. *bairai* 'he may carry'), and final **-ai* led to *-æ* in early Old English, which was weakened to *-e*. On the history of the subjunctive paradigm see Brunner (1965: 277), Campbell (1959: 298), and Bammesberger (1984: 70).

[5]Figure 2 gives illustrative material made available by Robert Carr, Archaeological Service, Conservation Team, Environment & Transport department, Suffolk County Council, Archaeological Unit, Shire Hall, Bury St Edmunds, Suffolk.

[6]Figure 3 gives a drawing of the inscription. A photograph provided by the museum is available in Bammesberger (1991, plate 2).

[7]The beginning of *Cædmon's hymn* can be analysed in different ways however; see above all Ball (1985: 40).

[8]A very detailed account of the runes is available in Page (1959a).

[9]For readily accessible editions of both the *Ruthwell crucifixion poem* and *The Dream of the rood* see ASPR 2, Dickins -- Ross (1934), Bütow (1935), Swanton (1970), Schwab (1978), and Kelly -- Quinn (1999).

[10]I argue this point at greater length in Bammesberger (2002a).

[11]The semicolon is used to mark off three syntactic units.

[12]A somewhat more detailed account of this problem will be found in Bammesberger (2003a).

[13]Ultimately in most cases of this type we are probably concerned with dual forms. Klaeber (1950: 151) briefly comments on these forms, which he terms 'generic plural'. I have collected some relevant material in my 2001 paper.

[14]Howlett (1978) uses capitals in **He** and **His**, but since the runic script would not distinguish capitals from lower case letters, no distinction is made in the following discussion.

[15]I deal with this part of the inscription in more detail in my paper Bammesberger (2002a).

References

Baker, Peter S. -- Nicholas Howe (eds.)
1998 *Words and works: Studies in medieval English language and literature in honour of Fred C. Robinson.* (Toronto Old English Series 10.) Toronto: University of Toronto Press.

Ball, C. J. E.
1985 "Homonymy and polysemy in Old English: A problem for lexicographers", in: Bammesberger (ed.), 39-46.

Bammesberger, Alfred
1984 *A sketch of diachronic English morphology.* Regensburg: Pustet.

1994 "Editing Old English runic inscriptions", G. Blaicher -- B. Glaser (eds.), *Anglistentag 1993 Eichstätt*, Tübingen: Niemeyer, 503-15.

2001 "Altenglisch *æt hēafdum* und der elliptische Dual", in: Fritz -- Zeilfelder (eds.), 25-34.

2002a "A doubtful reconstruction in the Old English *Ruthwell Crucifixion poem*", *Studia Neophilologica* 74: 143-45.

2002b "The *Brandon Antler* runic inscription", *Neophilologus* 86: 129-31.

2003a "Das erste Wort der altenglischen Runeninschrift auf dem *Ruthwellkreuz*", *Anglia* 121: 265-73.

2003b "The Harford Farm Brooch runic inscription", *Neophilologus* 87: 133-35.

2003c "Zu **fusæ** in der Runeninschrift auf dem Ruthwell-Kreuz", in: Heizmann -- van Nahl (eds.), 28-34.

Bammesberger, Alfred (ed.)
1985 *Problems of Old English lexicography: Studies in memory of Angus Cameron*. Regensburg: Pustet.

1991 *Old English runes and their continental background*. Heidelberg: Winter.

Brunner, Karl
1965 *Altenglische Grammatik nach der Angelsächsischen Grammatik von Eduard Sievers*. (3rd edition.) Tübingen: Niemeyer.

Bütow, Hans
1935 *Das altenglische 'Traumgesicht vom Kreuz', Textkritisches, Literaturgeschichtliches, Kunstgeschichtliches*. Heidelberg: Winter.

Campbell, A[listair]
1959 *Old English grammar*. Oxford: Clarendon.

Cassidy, Brendan (ed.)
1993 *The Ruthwell cross: Papers from the colloquium sponsored by the Index of Christian Art, Princeton University, 8 December 1989*. Princeton: Princeton University Press.

Derolez, René
1992 "Comment on the deer's antler from Brandon, Suffolk", *Nytt om Runer* 7: 8.

Dickins, Bruce -- Alan S. C. Ross (eds.)
1934 *The Dream of the rood.* London: Methuen.

Elliott, R. W. V.
1959 *Runes: An introduction.* Manchester: Manchester University Press.
1989 2nd edition.

Flowers, Stephen
1999 *A concise edition of the Old English runic inscriptions.* Smithville, Texas: Rûna-Raven Press.

Fritz, Matthias -- Susanne Zeilfelder (eds.)
2001 *Novalis Indogermanica: Festschrift für Günter Neumann zum 80. Geburtstag.* Graz: Leykam.

Gneuss, Helmut
1998 "Old English texts and modern readers: Notes on editing and textual criticism", in: Baker -- Howe (eds.), 127-41.

Heizmann, Wilhelm -- Astrid van Nahl (eds.)
2003 *Runica – Germanica – Mediaevalia.* Berlin: de Gruyter.

Hines, John
1991 "A new runic inscription from Norfolk", *Nytt om Runer* 6: 6-7.

Howlett, David
1978 "A reconstruction of the Ruthwell Crucifixion Poem", *Studia neophilologica* 50: 54-58.

1992 "Inscriptions and design of the Ruthwell Cross", in: Cassidy (ed.), 71-93.

1998 "English *ondgierwan, ongierwan, ungierwan*", *Anglia* 116: 223-26.

Kelly, Richard J. -- Ciarán L. Quinn (eds.)
1999 *Stone, skin, and silver: A translation of the Dream of the rood.* Middleton: Litho.

Klaeber, Frederick
1950 *Beowulf and The fight at Finnsburg.* (3rd edition.) Boston: D.C. Heath.

Mitchell, M.
1994 *Corpus of English runes.* Basle: [no publisher given].

Ó Carragáin, Éamonn
1987-1988 "The Ruthwell Crucifixion Poem in its iconographic and liturgical contexts", *Peritia* 6-7: 1-71.

Page, Raymond I.
1959a "An early drawing of the Ruthwell Cross", *Medieval archaeology* 3: 285-88.

1959b *The inscriptions of the Anglo-Saxon rune-stones.* Unpublished Ph.D. dissertation, University of Nottingham.

1973 *An introduction to English runes.* London: Methuen.

1991 "Anglo-Saxon runic studies: The way ahead?", in: Bammesberger (ed.), 15-39.

1999 *An introduction to English runes.* (2nd edition.) Woodbridge: Boydell.

Parsons, David
1991 "New runic finds from Brandon, Suffolk", *Nytt om Runer* 6: 8-11.

1999 *Recasting the runes: The reform of the Anglo-Saxon futhorc.* (Runrön. Runologiska bidrag utgivna av Institutionen för nordiska språk vid Uppsala universitet 14.) Uppsala: Institutionen för nordiska språk.

Rissanen, Matti
1967 "Two notes on Old English poetic texts", *Neuphilologische Mitteilungen* 68: 276-88.

Schwab, Ute
1978 "Das Traumsgesicht vom Kreuzesbaum: Ein ikonologischer Interpretationsansatz zu dem ags. *Dream of the rood*", in: Schwab -- Stutz (eds.), 131-92.

Schwab, Ute -- Elfriede Stutz (eds.)
1978 *Philologische Studien, Gedenkschrift für Richard Kienast*. Heidelberg: Winter.

Smith, A. H. (ed.)
1933 *Three Northumbrian poems.* London: Methuen.

Swanton, Michael (ed.)
1970 *The Dream of the rood.* Manchester: Manchester University Press.

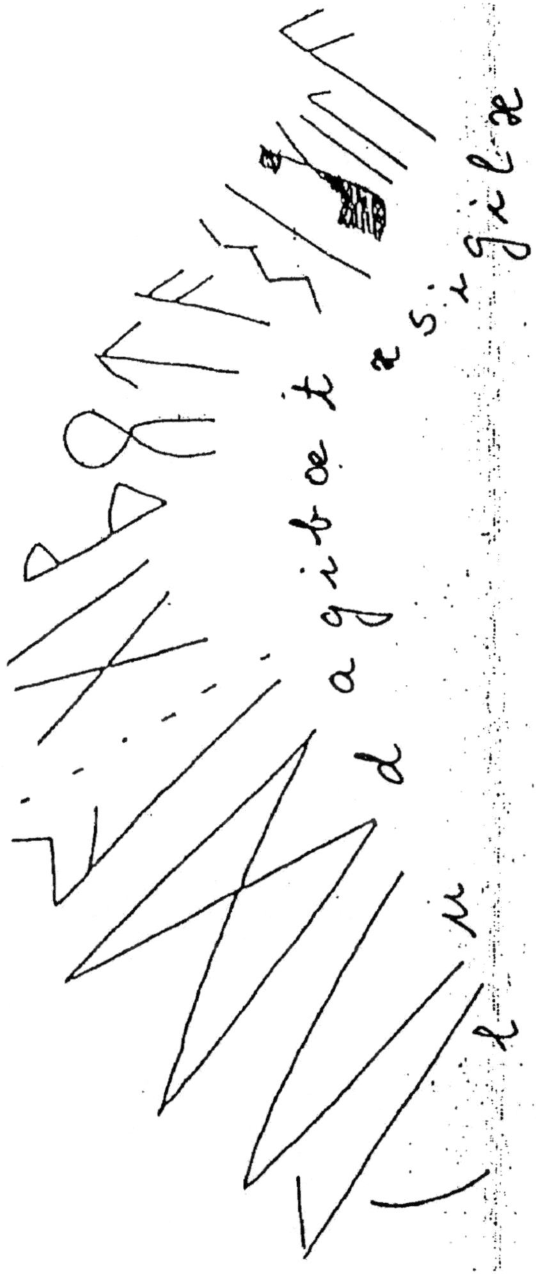

Figure 1: The *Harford Farm Brooch* inscription

Figure 2: The *Brandon Antler*

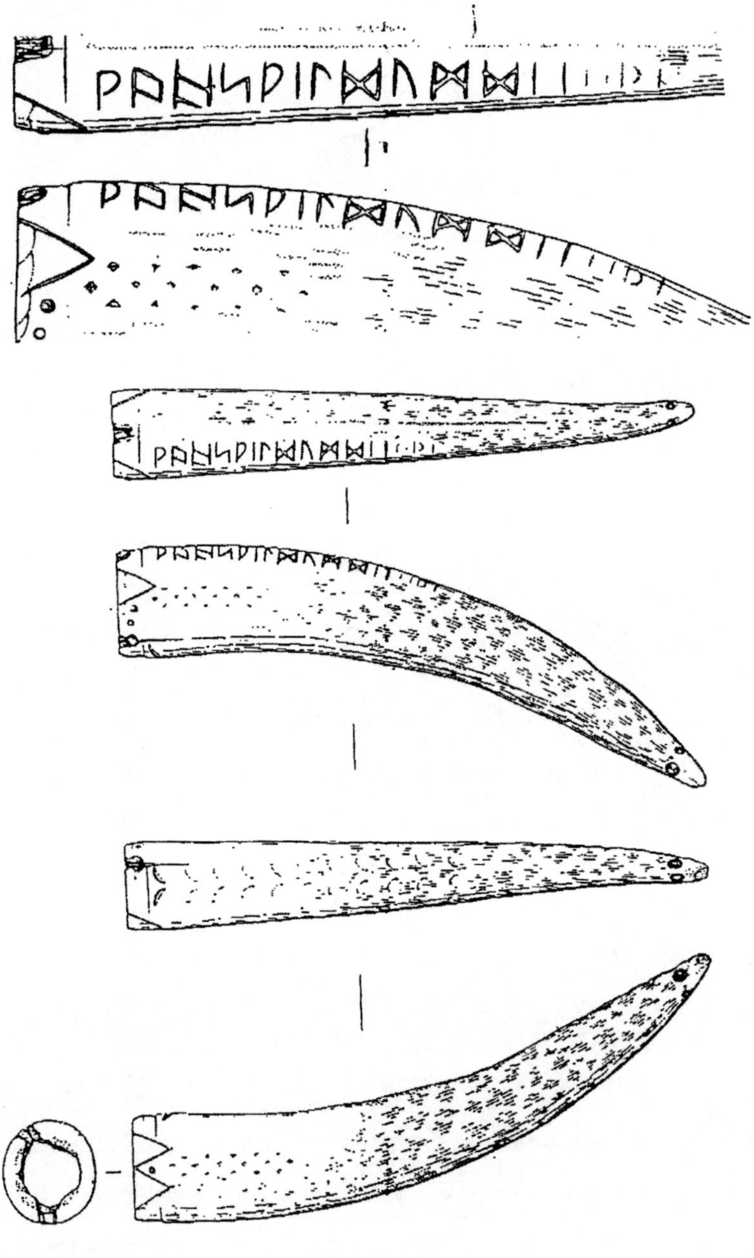

Figure 3: The *Overchurch Stone* inscription

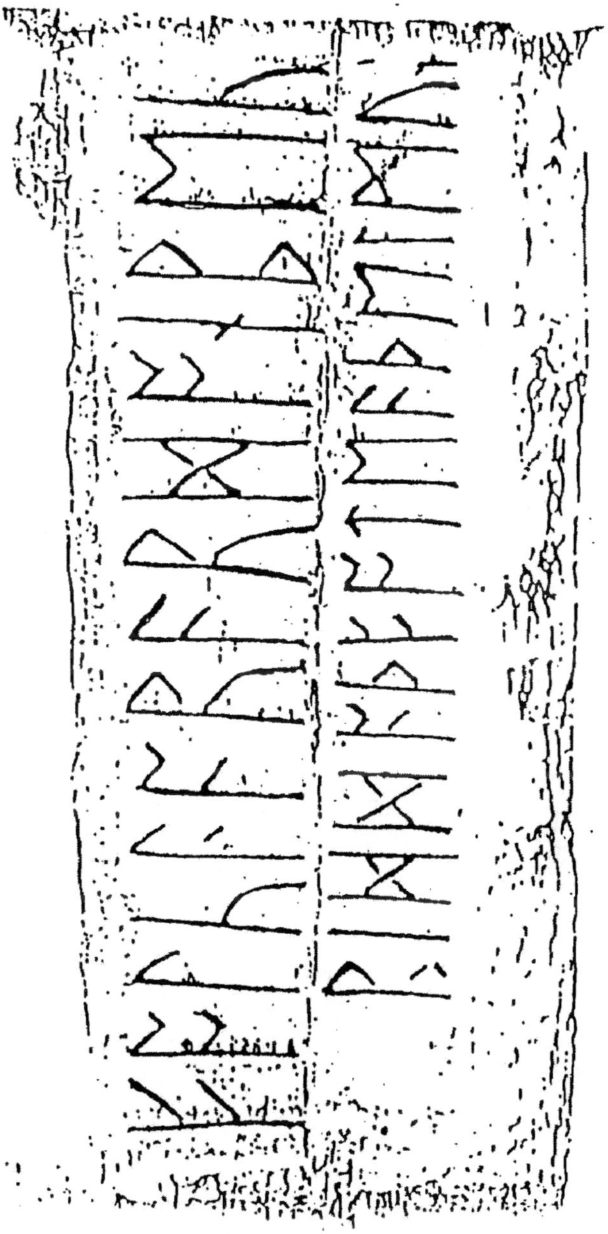

The Narragansett runic inscription, Rhode Island[1]

Ian Kirby (Lausanne, Switzerland)

Half a century ago it was the common view, held even by some scholars in the field of Scandinavian studies, that Norsemen got no further west than Greenland, and this in spite of the accounts in the Norse sagas of the Greenlanders and of Erik the Red. This view ceased to be widely held in the nineteen-sixties as a result of the identification of the L'Anse aux Meadows site close to the north-western tip of Newfoundland as a Norse settlement, or way station, inhabited briefly early in the 11th century. But it seems to me that another kind of invisible barrier has subsequently come into being, this time an east-west line just to the south of L'Anse aux Meadows: for it appears to be the common view among Scandinavian scholars today that the Norse explorations did not extend significantly southwards from this site. Even the discovery in the New England state of Maine of a late 11th-century Norwegian penny has not modified this view, for the common scholarly opinion is that the coin came into the possession of the Native Americans much further north and made its way more than a thousand miles southwards to Penobscot Bay via their coastal trade routes – a valid explanation, certainly, but not, of course, the only possible one. In this paper I shall examine another potential source of evidence that the Norsemen did in fact extend their exploration of the North American continent much further south than Newfoundland.

Runic inscriptions in North America have been a scholarly problem for more than a century, though there is no *a priori* reason to rule out the possibility that a genuine medieval one might some day be identified. After all: the L'Anse aux Meadows discovery demonstrated beyond reasonable doubt the presence of Norsemen in Newfoundland; wherever the Norsemen went, from northern Greenland to Piraeus and Istanbul, they carved runes; we must therefore allow that they could have done so in North America. This possibility was admitted by the archeologists who worked on the Newfoundland site, and who looked unsuccessfully for an inscription in the neighbourhood of L'Anse aux Meadows.

As is well known, the nature of the problem is not that there are no runic or might-be-runic inscriptions in North America, but that there are rather too many of them. The best known is the Kensington inscription, which has been almost unanimously rejected by runologists as a late 19th-century fake; but this is only one of fifty or so inscriptions which have at one time or another been considered genuine by some investigators. In the early nineteen-sixties the German scholar Hertha Marquardt published a substantial list containing most of these, and concluded that not one of them was a genuine medieval runic inscription: they were either plough marks, the result of natural weathering, man-made but not runic symbols, or runic but modern. Her views have been generally accepted by runologists, though in at least one case, that of the Bourne stone on Cape Cod, some uncertainty may remain. Since then, we have had the discovery of the Spirit Pond stones, now in the Augusta, Maine, museum, which can most certainly be regarded as fakes: the ultra-violet fluorescence test demonstrates this beyond reasonable doubt, and confirms the views of runologists. However, there is one inscription, which came to scholarly attention in 1985, which is not so readily dismissed: the Narragansett inscription.

This inscription is found on a rock currently situated at a point between high and low tide on the west side of Narragansett Bay, in the community of North Kingstown, Rhode Island State. It is a few hundred yards from the Potowomut river mouth, which separates North Kingstown from the township of Warwick. The inscription is covered by the tide for about nine hours in every twelve. It is one of a fair number of inscriptions in the Bay area, some of which have been claimed to be runic; but to the best of my knowledge it is the only one that is.

The rock is a relatively hard quartzite. It is of uneven shape, the maximum measurements being about 2.4 m long, 1.6 m wide at the seaward side but tapering land-wards, and 65 cm above the sand. It would appear that not much of the rock is hidden under the sand. The relatively flat side on which the inscription is carved faces skywards. It is partly covered by green weed and small white barnacles, which latter tend to cluster in the inscription cuts and thus help to render it visible.

The inscription is close to the seaward, wider side of the rock, and is read from the landward side; it may well have been cut by someone sitting close to the landward edge, if the rock was in its current position when the inscription was carved. It is carefully cut with hammer and chisel-type implements, though it seems likely that the surface disturbance in front of the first symbol was caused by an initial attempt which caused the surface to shear off, and the same thing may have happened at the end of the first line. The first four symbols of the first line are very distinct, as are the two of the second line; the fifth and sixth are uncertain, while the seventh vertical does not show clear traces of human intervention, and may be no more than a natural line. The symbols are some 5 to 6 cm in height, and are quite smooth.

The inscription first came to the notice of scholars in 1985. It was reported by a clam-digger, locally known as a *quahogger*, whose attention was drawn to it in December 1984 by the white barnacles in the cuts. It was then examined by local members of the New England Antiquities Research

Association (NEARA), and several articles and comments on it have subsequently been written.

In 1993, I was informed about the inscription by the State Archeologist of Massachusetts, the late Mr James Whittall, and made a brief and superficial initial examination of it in difficult circumstances – the tide was out at the beginning and end of each day, and weather conditions were poor. But enough was visible to make it clear that this is quite definitely a runic inscription: not plough marks, not natural weathering, not in a non-runic script. The problem, however, is (and for the moment remains) the date it was cut: on first inspection it seemed that it could have been done any time between about AD 600 and 1984.

In August 1999, in virtually perfect climatic conditions, I returned to Narragansett Bay together with Dr Peter Pieper, a forensic scientist from the University of Düsseldorf, who had worked with me on an earlier investigation. He made a detailed scientific documentation of the inscription, while I concerned myself more particularly with the historical information which might be gleaned about it from different sources.

First, however, a provisional analysis of the individual symbols of the inscription, since it does not yield an obvious meaning (see figure 1). The first symbol is clearly runic; in most runic alphabets it corresponds to the letter *s*. Other possibilities include *j*, and *a* (on the Istaby stone from southern Sweden, see Moltke 1985: 145). The second symbol is uncertain. One possibility is that it represents a later *h*-rune, but in this the *x*-shape arms are not normally as long. Another is that it is a bind-rune, representing *ig* or *gi*, or *an* or *na*; but I have not seen an instance of the former elsewhere, and only one of the second (on the Føvling stone in Jutland, see Moltke 1985: 409). The third symbol seems to represent the runic *r*. Although the runic form does not usually have the angled lines meet the vertical in the middle, there are numerous instances where they do, including, for example, the Kingiktorsoak stone from northern Greenland. The fourth symbol is runic and appears in the older Germanic alphabet and some others: it normally stands for *o*. The fifth symbol is uncertain, partly because it was not possible to determine whether or not there is an angled cut to the right of the vertical, as the spacing between the runes might seem to indicate. If there was, it may be the final *R*-rune, or the later *m*-rune; if not, we may have the later *k* in reverse. The sixth symbol is very uncertain. The vertical is clear; the cut rising diagonally from the bottom is very probable; if this is a complete rune we may have an upside-down *l*. On the other hand, these two lines might be part of another rune, perhaps a *d*, not completed because of shearing off.

The first symbol of the second line is a major problem. Without the nick on the higher right-hand stave the symbol is a normal older runic *g*; but close examination suggests that the nick was cut at the same time as the rest of the inscription. This gives us a symbol which is otherwise solidly attested only in North America, and only on the Kensington Stone, usually regarded as a late-19th-century forgery, and the Spirit Pond stones, which as indicated earlier we regard as 20th-century forgeries: in all cases it is used to represent *a*. The second symbol is runic, almost always *a*. So one problem with the previous identification is that we seemingly have two different symbols representing the same sound or closely similar ones. The final dot is usually a word division, indicating that the inscription was to be continued. There is, however, no sign of a continuation.

The interpretation of this inscription is thus, for the moment, highly uncertain. The symbols do not seem to fit exactly with any of the known runic alphabets. Though there is a high degree of correspondence with the early Germanic and the transitional Norse futhark of the 7th and 8th centuries, not to mention the Anglo-Saxon one, no obvious meaning results in any case. One approach might be to take the first three symbols of the first line as indicating the Norse word *sigr* 'victory'; even more speculatively, the first five symbols might represent *sigrom* 'we conquer'. But this does not cover the whole of the first line, and can at the very most be the best available guess – assuming, of course, that this is an ancient rather than modern inscription. As to the second line, *ga* (if indeed that is what it is) is reminiscent of the mysterious bind-runes on a Danish spear-shaft (Kragehul) and an English bracteate (Undley: see Moltke 1985: 101, 104f), and the Norse verb in this form has the meaning 'pay attention (to)'; but the problem of the nick, or hook, remains.

In view of all this uncertainty, it was necessary to consider other kinds of information which might lead to an answer to the question whether the inscription is ancient or modern. The first that I shall examine is historical.

Two kinds of information can be adduced under this heading: that resulting from conversations with present and past residents of the immediate neighbourhood, and that available from historical records of various kinds. As already mentioned, the rock is at the present time on the beach between high and low tide: it is completely exposed at low tide, completely covered at high tide. But this has not always been the case. In conversation with Mr James McMahon, owner of the immediately adjacent property for the 30 years between 1947/48 and 1978, we learned that he had known of the inscription since before he acquired the land, and that, when he first saw it, it was not covered by the tide nor, in consequence, by the barnacles etc. which are there today; he and his children had often sat by the rock and wondered what the inscription meant.

That it was not covered by the tide at that time was confirmed by Mr David Brusby, owner of the Mobil station a few miles from the rock. Furthermore, about a hundred metres from the rock, at the same relative position between high and low tide, there is a partly-calcified tree stump. It would thus seem that the beach was much more substantial in the earlier part of the 20th century, and that it was severely damaged by the devastating hurricanes of 1954 and, perhaps, 1938. It follows from this that water erosion and smoothing of the inscription has only been operating for some fifty years, not for centuries.

I was also able to obtain, from books and records in the North Kingstown Public Library, further information about the early history of this spot and its immediate neighbourhood, known as Pojac Point. It was apparently deeded by the local Native American sachem Coquinoquant on June 11, 1659 to a company associated with the English Major Atherton; and in the following centuries it has been owned by different persons, all except the most recent being of English, or at any rate British, stock, to judge by their names. In 1686, it came into the hands of a family named Green; and it remained in their possession until 1848, when it was given to the Welling family as part of a dowry – Mr Bert Welling, greatgrandson of the first Welling owner, still lives in a house near Pojac Point proper, and gave us this information. In 1947, the piece of land closest to the rock was sold to Mr McMahon, who in turn sold it in 1978 to the present owner and builder of the house on it, Mr John Di Giulio. Our thanks are due to these gentlemen for sharing their knowledge with us, and to Mr Di Giulio for allowing us access to the beach through his property.

The rock is about 100 yards northwards from another, much larger, parcel of land giving on to the Bay which has a somewhat different history. The site was acquired in or about 1872 by John Carter Brown, best known perhaps through his association with Brown University at Providence, who in that year constructed the first of several buildings now on the site. In 1907 it became a hospital for tubercular and/or crippled children; and since 1957 it has been a Catholic nursing home for aged Americans of Italian origin. There would seem to be no reason to assume that any of the persons associated with this property would have had either the knowledge or the inclination to have produced the inscription.

It seems then that the inhabitants of the immediate area up to about a century ago were either of Native American or British origin; and it would appear safe to assume that none of them were responsible for the cutting of the inscription. Indeed, with the exception of Mr Di Giulio and Mr McMahon and their families, the inscription was apparently unknown to any of the residents in the area until very recently: Mr Brusby, for example, only got to know of it a few years before our visit, probably as a result of the investigation by the

NEARA people. This may seem surprising: but the beach is remote and adjacent to private land, and only normally visited by persons such as quahoggers who make their way along the Bay. Furthermore, there is now little beach space: and bathing is not attractive since the water contains tiny mites which bite, as we discovered to our very painful cost. The quahoggers, and the nuns from the Catholic home, go into the water fully dressed!

What of the 20th century? From the census information available in the North Kingstown Public Library it would seem that by the beginning of the century Scandinavians and Germans had begun to move into the district in some numbers; and the Scandinavians were overwhelmingly Swedish. Furthermore, Mr Brusby told me that his grandfather employed a stonemason of Swedish origin in or about 1880 to build a stone wall in the adjacent community of Warwick, some three miles from the rock. And the records show that at least two families of Swedish origin have lived on the Point from the 1940s onwards, and in one of these cases to the present day. To summarise the information we obtained on this: a G. Elmer Lindberg is first mentioned as being in the area in 1926, as having owned land on the Pojac Point road, and as having built a house there around 1956; he died soon after, but his widow was still living there in 1964. However, this family is no longer traceable. On the other hand: a certain Gustav Viktor Carlson was in the area in the early 1940s, did a number of different jobs, married, and settled down close to the entrance to the Catholic rest home. I telephoned his daughter, who told me that she and her mother had not known of the inscription until very recently, her father had never mentioned it, and they thought it unlikely in the highest degree that it had been made by him, a statement echoed by Mr Welling. From all of this it can be seen that, while there have in the 20th century been people living in the Pojac Point area who could have had the knowledge and ability to carve the inscription, we have no solid evidence that any one of them did so.

However, the position of the rock makes it necessary to consider a second possibility; that the inscription was carved, not by someone living in the immediate vicinity, but by someone who came along the beach, or by boat from an adjacent area. From the historical perspective, one might certainly build up a case for the possibility that the above-mentioned stonemason or one of his fellow-countrymen made his way along the beach from Warwick to Pojac Point and cut the inscription, which he could have done in, say, two or three hours. On the beach Dr Pieper found a metal railway spike which is the kind of implement which might have been used for the purpose; alternatively, a stonemason could have had suitable tools with him. The existence of the hooked symbol suggests the possibility that the cutter knew of the Kensington controversy, though this would push the date of cutting well into the first decade of the 20th century. Be that as it may: the most probable conclusion from this is that if the inscription should prove to be modern it was carved by a person of Swedish origin some time from around 1880 to the 1940s.

The final possibility, and by no means the weakest, is that the inscription was carved by someone who had come from a greater distance one or many centuries ago, had sailed into Narragansett Bay and stopped at Pojac Point for a shorter or longer time, leaving only the inscription as evidence of his passage. But we have no further evidence for this possibility.

Thus much for the historical evidence. I turn next to the scientific evidence of different kinds which Dr Pieper examined, and which I shall summarise for the purposes of the present paper. The first relates to the degree of weathering of the inscription. Several factors have to be taken into account here. As mentioned, the Narragansett inscription is very smooth: it shows no signs of recent cutting. However, some of the runes are still fairly deep; and at this stage in our investigation we cannot be sure whether this is because they were cut early in the 20th century or very much earlier. Other rock inscriptions in the Narragansett Bay area still clearly show dates in the 19th century; and some of the carvings on the Dighton Rock, which is a softer rock than Narragansett, were first seen as long ago as 1680 but are still clearly visible. Dighton Rock, on the east side of the Taunton river some thirty miles north-eastwards from North Kingstown, seems to have a similar history to the Narragansett rock, though it was between high and low tide when Delabarre wrote about it in 1928, and has been in an on-site museum since 1973.

Secondly, Dr Pieper used a hand-held ultra-violet lamp in an examination of the Narragansett and other rock inscriptions in the Bay area, to see which inscriptions showed fluorescence and which did not. Particularly fruitful was the examination of the Dighton Rock, which has a large number of inscriptions dating from before 1680 until well into the 20th century. It transpired that, in general terms, inscriptions of 20th-century date showed a degree of fluorescence on the inscription cuts, while pre-20th century inscriptions did not. On the Narragansett rock, which we examined at night, there was a degree of generalised fluorescence, which we think is likely to have been caused by the cleaning of the inscription in 1985 by the first investigators. But there was no separate evidence of fluorescence on the inscription cuts. This test, therefore, though unfortunately not definitive for the dating of the Narragansett inscription, would seem to suggest that the inscription was not made after the early decades of the 20th century.[2]

Finally, for the present, on the beach near the Narragansett rock Dr Pieper found a piece of iron slag. From the North Kingstown records it transpires that in the 18th century there was a forge in the near vicinity of Pojac

Point where wrought iron was made out of bog iron. But it is well known that there was a smithy at the Norse settlement at L'Anse aux Meadows where bog iron was smelted: and it thus seemed appropriate to take a piece of this slag and have it tested by the C14-AMS processes. I submitted it to Professor Bonani of the ETH Zurich for this purpose. Unfortunately, his report was that there was so little carbon in the sample that no date could be given. At the time of writing it is our hope that it may prove possible to date the slag by other methods. Of course, the probability is that the slag is 18th century: but we do not propose to leave any stone unturned.

What highly provisional conclusions may be drawn from the investigation to date concerning the interpretation and the date of the Narragansett inscription? No normal reading of the inscription according to the Germanic, early Norse or Anglo-Saxon futharks gives a clearly discernible meaning: the *sigrom ga* suggestion is no more than that, and begs a number of questions, notably the significance of the Kensingtonian-style hooked *a*.

However, reading it as a Kensingtonian-type inscription is highly problematic as well. Of the six certain letters, only the *s* and *r* (and of course the hooked *a*) correspond closely to Kensington: Narragansett's *o* and *a* are not found in Kensington, and the second letter of the first line is the later *h*-rune in Kensington, and its form corresponds there to the norm. The Narragansett runes are all cut in straight lines: many of Kensington's are rounded. Also, the word-division in Kensington is a colon-type, not a single central dot as in Narragansett. There is no reason, apart from the hooked *a*, to surmise that Narragansett is dependent on Kensington; and certainly no reason to suppose that the carver of Narragansett ever saw Kensington, or a reproduction of it. At most he may have got his information second or third hand.[3]

I have tested the Narragansett runes against certain hidden systems known to have been in use in Scandinavia, without coming to any conclusion. They do not, for instance, seem to relate to the *orklaski* type, where to obtain the name one must substitute the immediately preceding rune in the shorter futhark (Moltke 1985: 132). The names of the runic letters do not seem to be significant. On the other hand, Dr Pieper noticed that the symbols, if interpreted suitably, can be re-ordered to form the initials and surname of G. V. Carlson, which may or may not be a coincidence. And when I presented a similar paper to a runologists' conference last year, my attention was drawn to a certain Professor Dag Sandström who could have carved the symbols as a hoax in the early 20th century. But this presents problems too. For me at least, the question is still wide open.

As to the date of the inscription: neither the scientific nor the historical tests have enabled us, so far, to say whether the cutting was done in the medieval period or early in the 20th century. A case can be made out for the latter possibility, but not a strong one. What can be said about the possibility that it is medieval? Here again, the evidence is circumstantial. That the Norsemen could have come this far southwards does not in itself seem to be a major problem. We know that they got to Newfoundland; we know that a Norse coin was found in Maine, and one possible explanation of this is that it came thus far south with them. We know that bog iron was smelted at L'Anse aux Meadows; it is an interesting coincidence that in the vicinity of both Bourne and Pojac Point there is also bog iron. All these places are close to, or on, the sea shore.

To this may be added the following points. Like many genuine runic inscriptions, Narragansett is not easily interpreted; it could not therefore have been made primarily for financial profit, as the Spirit Pond stones most probably were. It is remote from the normal land routes, and remained unknown until very recently: if a modern carver did it for fame, he has had to wait a long time for recognition. The purpose of such a carving, if modern, thus remains very obscure. The best guesses are that it is somehow connected with the Kensington controversy, and that its lettering largely coincides with the name of a Swede who lived on Pojac Point; but as we have seen we have limited evidence for these guesses, and some information which argues against them.

All in all, I am of the opinion that unless and until further scientific or historical evidence comes to light, and until the above-mentioned objections are disposed of, the Narragansett inscription needs to be regarded as potentially a most important piece of evidence in regard to Norse explorations in America.

Notes

[1] This paper is an interim report on work in progress.

[2] It may be added that we subsequently tested the Bourne stone on Cape Cod, which we studied in 1993, in the same way, and the inscriptions on it showed no sign whatever of fluorescence. Since this stone has been in the Aptucxet Trading Post museum since the 1930s, we can confidently affirm that whatever the inscriptions are, they are not from the 20th-century, and most probably not from the late 19th-century either. But this is another story.

[3] If the Narragansett runes are to be compared with any other inscriptions in North America, three come to mind: the Bourne stone on Cape Cod, and the Heavener and Poteau inscriptions, all of which are short and in the same general style. Unlike Kensington and the Spirit Pond stones, but like Narragansett, they have no obvious meaning; two of the Bourne symbols, and the Heavener/Poteau runes, are also largely in

accord with the older Germanic futhark, and the letters they have in common with Narragansett are similar to that inscription - in particular, they all have the *o*-rune. This may, of course, be coincidence.

References

Delabarre, E. B.
1928 *Dighton Rock: A study of the written rocks of New England.* New York: Walter Neale.

Marquardt, Hertha
1961 *Die Runeninschriften der Britischen Inseln.* Göttingen: Vandenhoeck und Ruprecht.

Moltke, Erik
1985 *Runes and their origin: Denmark and elsewhere.* Peter G. Foote (trans.). Copenhagen: Nationalmuseets Forlag.

Figure 1: The Narragansett runic inscription

Old English preverbal elements with adverbial counterparts

Michiko Ogura (Chiba, Japan)

A growing tendency to prefer verb-adverb combinations to prefixed verbs from the late tenth century onwards has been reported in Hiltunen (1983) and Niwa (1991 and 1995). It is true that, when a preverbal element is a free morpheme (or, more precisely, when it has an adverbial counterpart), it shows a tendency to move to a postverbal position, unless the element order should involve a semantic change (like PDE *overcome* and *come over*). On the other hand, when the preverbal element is a bound morpheme, what matters is not a postposition but the interchangeability of the preverbal element under semantic (e.g. PDE *come* and *become*) or dialectal/scribal (e.g. *onsacan* and *ætsacan*) condition.

Since I have already reported on the case of bound-morph prefixes in Ogura (1995), I focus on the free-morph prefixes here in this paper. My aim is to propose some patterns of the basic element order in Old English and then to examine Old English renderings in the three versions of the Gospels in comparison with Old High German renderings on the use of verbs with free-morph prefixes in order to see if Old English renderings follow the basic patterns or if they faithfully follow the Latin order.

1. Basic element orders in Old English

I propose the following patterns of element order, not as rules but as strong preferences.

(a) V_{imp} + Partic.
(b) (⁊/ac +) Partic. + V (+ {Prep + N})
(⁊/ac +) V + Partic. (+ {Prep + N})
(⁊/ac +) Partic. + {Prep + N} + V
N.B.{Prep + N}+ V + Partic. and {Prep + N} + Partic. + V are less frequent and V + {Prep + N} + Partic. is unattested
(c) gif/ þe + Partic. + V (+ Aux)
(d) Partic. + to + V_{-enne}

Pattern (a) means that, when a verb is in the imperative (or optative or hortative), a particle or an adverbial element is to be postposed. Example (1) illustrates an imperative and (2) a hortative.

(1) *BlHom* 15 187.35 Rǽre *up* þín heafod & geseoh þis þæt Simon deþ
'Raise up thy head and see this that Simon does'

(2) *BlHom* 15 181.19 *Cuman* nu myccle hundas *forþ* & hine abitan beforan þyssum casere
'Let great dogs now come forth and bite him before this emperor'

Exceptions to this pattern are found with the verbs with bound-morph prefixes, as in

(3) *ÆCHom* I,39 523.98 *Ymbscrydað eow*
'Clothe yourselves'.

Pattern (b) shows the possible choice of the element order in the principal or *ך/ac/ne* clauses. In the first type a particle is preposed to the verb and in the second type it is postposed, which means that a tendency towards the postposition is not notable at all in these clauses. At times, however, as illustrated by example (4), the preposition and the postposition can tell a semantic difference: the postposed *of* 'off' should be stressed so as to emphasize the action of striking something, while the preposed *of-* may focus on the completed action of killing.[1]

(4) *Or* 4 5.90.14-15 ærest hiene mon swong, þa sticode him mon þa eagan ut, ך siþþan him mon *slog* þa handa *of*, þa þæt heafod, ך eall his cynn mon *ofslog*
'first they scourged him, then put his eyes out, and afterwards struck off his hands, then his head, and slew all his kin'

A preposed element and a postposed element can be different even if they denote much the same. In example (5) *onfeng* and *feng to* can be compared (since there is no instance of **feng on* or **tofeng*).[2]

(5) *Chron* A 560(18.1-2) Her Ceawlin *feng to* rice to Wesseaxum, ך Ælle *feng to* Norþanhymbra rice
'In this year Ceawlin succeeded to the kingdom in Wessex and Ælle succeeded to the kingdom of the Northumbrians'
Chron E 560(19.1-2) Her Ceawlin rice *onfeng* on Weast Seaxum, ך Ælle *feng to* Norðhymbra rice

In example (6) we find a combination of an adverbial element and a verb in different orders with the same sense.

(6) *Chron* A 734(44.14) Her wæs se mona swelce he wære mid blode begoten; ך *ferdon forþ* Tatwine ך Bieda
'In this year the moon was as if it were covered with blood and Tatwin and Bede died'

Chron E 734(45.14) Her wæs se mona swilce he wære mid blode begoten. ⁊ Tatwine *forðferde* erceƀ. ⁊ eac Beda.

When a prepositional phrase with a close connection to both the verb and the particle is involved, it is more often postposed than preposed to the combination of the other two elements. But it may also follow a particle and, as a result, come between the particle and the verb. In example (7) the two verbs show two different orders; the first one is also an example of pattern (a).

(7) *ÆCHom* II,12 114.132-3 *Astih* ðu eft *up to me*, and aaron samod; Moyses ða godes hǽse gefylde. and *eft up to him astah*
'Come again up to me, and Aaron as well; then Moses fulfilled God's command and again went up to him'

Thus, such element orders as *astigan up to him*, *up to him astigan*, *upastigan to him*, *to him upastigan* and *to him astigan up* can be found, but **astigan to him up* is not attested.[3]

Pattern (c) illustrates the order in the subordinate clause, as in examples (8) and (9); when an auxiliary cooccurs, it comes at the end of the clause, as in (8).

(8) *Or* 2 5.48.19 Morþonius, Xersis þegn, forlet þa scipa þe hie *on farende wæron*
'Mardonius, Xerxes' general, left the ships in which they had been sailing'

(9) *ÆCHom* I,37 500.111 swa þ ða cristenan bealdlice *ineodon*
'so that the Christians boldly went in'

Pattern (d) is an order with inflected infinitives. A particle, if a free morpheme, stands before *to*, as in example (10).

(10) *Chron* A 669 (34.10) (=B, C, F) Her Ecgbryht cyning salde Basse mæsseprioste Reculf mynster *on to timbranne*
'In this year king Egbert gave Reculver to Bass the priest to build a monastery'

Cf. *Chron* E 669 (35.11) Her Egbriht cining sealde Basse preost Raculf, mynster *to tymbrianne*.

If a prepositional phrase cooccurs, it can be a strong cause of the postposition of a particle, as in

(11) *ÆCHom* II,22 207.38 He geceas him timan to acennenne on menniscnysse. to ðrowigenne. to arisenne of deaðe. *to astigenne up to heofenan*. mid þam lichaman ðe he middanearde gefette

'He chose time to bring forth in incarnation, to suffer, to rise from death, to ascend up to heaven,with the body which he obtained in the world'

2. A comparison between Old English and Old High German versions of the Gospels

Are the basic patterns found in original prose in the previous section relevant to Old English versions of the Gospels? It is obvious that interlinear glosses are materials improper to an investigation of syntax. The *Lindisfarne* version is expected to represent Latin element orders, even though it sometimes violates the element-for-element translation. The *Rushworth 1* version appears more independent than *Rushworth 2*, a closer copy of *Lindisfarne*, in addition to the dialectal difference, though the latter does not always follow the model. The *West Saxon* version (here I use MS CCCC 140)[4] is much freer and similar to the contemporary prose and more proper to a syntactic investigation. The reason for the comparison between these three Anglo-Saxon versions and the Old High German Tatian is that, in order to examine linguistic development and find a clue to an earlier form of Anglo-Saxon, this ninth-century version is the most reliable material among the related languages and, if the basic element order patterns are similar in both languages, we may tell the difference between a native grammar and a Latin-based syntax in a more convincing way than we have done with Anglo-Saxon versions alone. The comparison between the three Anglo-Saxon versions is useful for making dialectal and stylistic differences clear and, adding an Old High German version, we may see which Anglo-Saxon version is closer to the Old High German one in syntax and translation style and whether the similarity and/or the difference is thoroughgoing or not.

As an appendix, I give two tables. Table 1 illustrates the lexical comparison of the renderings of Latin verbs of motion. All types of verbs are investigated, then the Old English verbs with free-morph prefixes are chosen, and finally, the verbs whose preposed elements (i.e. apparent prefixes) can be postposed so as to prove their independence are left for illustration. Mt., Mk., Lk. and Jn. in brackets mean that the lexeme is found especially (if not exclusively) in the Gospel of Matthew, Mark, Luke or John. Only the major counterparts are cited in the table, which means that the one-to-one lexical correspondence is rather rare. Among the Latin prefixes, *in-* (and *intro-*) seems to be translated faithfully with the exception of *WSCp*, but *ex-* and *ad-* are not always rendered *ut-* and *to-* respectively. *Trans-* is rendered *ofer-* and *de-*, *ofdune-*, in *Li* and *Ru1 & 2*, but *WSCp* prefers simple verbs. The lexical choice is more strict in Tatian than in Old English versions, but still three to five counterparts are regularly found in rendering one particular Latin verb.

Table 2 shows the number of occurrences of the preposition and the postposition of a free-morph prefix or an adverbial element. *Intrare* and *introire* are likely to be rendered with a preposed element except *WSCp*, a fact that is also attested in Table 1. The choice of a simple verb (sometimes with a bound-morph prefix, as in *astigan*) is preferred in most instances. Tatian shows a preference for the preposition in rendering *exire* (*ûzgangan*), *intrare* and *introire* (*ingangan*), *descendere* (*nidarstigan*) and *accedere* (*zuogangan*). The post-position of the adverbial element is not so frequent, but in translating *exire*, *intrare*, *descendere* and *egredi* (and *abire*, especially in *Ru*), each version tries the syntax. (Asterisks on some of the numbers in *Li* denote the translations of Latin adverbs: * means *foras* and ** *intro*.)

Examples (12) and (13) are chosen to illustrate the basic pattern (a). In the optative construction in (12), *Li* and *WSCp* use an obvious preposition, while *Ru1* alone has the postposed *to*. Since *cuman* and *becuman* are synonymous, the choice between the two (including cognates in other languages) does not matter much. Imperative forms in (13) show postposition except *Li*.

(12) Mt. 6.10 [*adueniat* regnum tuum]
Gothic: *qimai* þiudinassus þeins
Li: to-cymeð ríc ðin
Ru1: *cume to* þin rice
WSCp: *to-becume* þin ríce
Heliand: *Cuma* thîn craftag rîki
Tatian: *queme* thín rihhi
Otfrid: *Biquéme* uns thinaz ríchi
(*AV*: Thy kingdome come)

(13) Mt. 7.13 [*Intrate* per angustam portam quia lata porta et spatiosa uia quæ ducit ad perditionem et multi sunt qui intrant per eam]
Li: *inngeonges* ðerh nearuo port ł dure ł gæt forðon ðiu wide geat ⁊ rumwelle weg ðiu lædas to lose ł losing ⁊ monigo sint ða ðe inngeongas ðerh ða ilco
Ru1: *gaþ inn* þurh naarwe geate for þon wíd geatte ⁊ rúm weg þe lǽdeþ to for-wyrde ł forlore ⁊ monige sindun þa þe in-gan þurh þære ł þæne
WSCp: *Gangað inn* þurh ꝥ nearwe geat. forþon þe ꝥ geat is swyþe wíd. ⁊ se weg is swiþe rum þe to for-spillednesse gelæt ⁊ swyþe manega synt þe þurh þone weg farað
Tatian: *Gét ín* thuruh enga phorta, uuanta breit phorta inti uúit uúeg thie thar leitit zi furlore, inti manage sint thie thuruh thie gangent
(*AV*: Enter ye in at the strait gate, for wide is the gate, and broad is the way that leadeth to destruction, and many there be which goe in thereat)

Examples (14) and (15) contain negation. Since the negative particle *ne* is regularly put immediately before the verb, an adverbial element may occupy the position that either precedes or follows '*ne* + V'. The order '*ne*+ P + V' can be, when P is a free-morph prefix, a slavish translation of Latin. In (14), *Li* has '*ne* + P + V' and *WSCp* 'P+ *ne* + V', while *Ru1* and Tatian have '*ne*/*ni* +V + P'. We cannot say the same thing for (15); *Li* has '*ne* + P + V' and *Ru2* follows it, while *WSCp* shows '*ne* + V + {Prep + N}' and Tatian 'P + *ni* + V'. In the latter example, two prepositional phrases following are involved in the choice of element order in *WSCp*.

(14) Mt. 23.13 [quia clauditis regnum caelorum ante homines uos enim *non intratis* nec intro-euntes sinitis intrare]
Li: forðon gie tyndon ríc heofna before ł aer monnum gie forðon *ne inn-eadege* ne ða inngeongende gíe letas inn-geonga
Ru1: þe gelucaþ rice heofona beforan monnum ge þonne *ne gǽþ* ínn* ne þa ingangende letaþ ingangen (**gangǽþ*, alt. to *gǽþ*)
WSCp: forþam ge belucað heofona rice. beforan mannum; Ne gé *in ne gaþ* ne ge ne geþafiað ꝥ oðre ingan
Tatian: inti bisliozet himilo richi fora mannon: ir *ni get in* noh thie ingangenton ni lazet ingangan
(*AV*: for yee shut vp the kingdom of heauen against men: For yee neither goe in your selues, neither suffer ye them that are entring, to goe in)

(15) Jn. 10.1 [qui *non intrat* per ostium in ouile ouium sed ascendit aliunde ille fur est et latro]
Li: seðe *ne Inn-gaas* ł ðerh duru in scipa plett ł locc ah astiged ofer on oðre halfe ł ðe ðeaf is ⁊ settere ł sceacere
Ru2: seðe *ne ingæð* ðerh dura hiorde is (*sic*) scipa ah astigeð oðre hwoena he scead ł ðæf is ⁊ sceaðo
WSCp: se þe *ne gæð* æt þam gete *into* sceapa falde. ac styhþ elles ofer he is þeof ⁊ sceaða
Tatian: thie thar *in ni gét* thurah duri in then euuist thero scapho, oh gistigit allesuuanan, ther ist thíob inti scaheri
(*AV*: He that entreth not by ye doore into the sheepefold, but climeth vp some other way, the same is a theefe, and a robber)

In (16) the case ending is reconfirmed by a preposition, except the slavish *Li*.[5]

(16) Mk. 5.18 [Cum *ascenderunt nauem* coepit illum depræcari qui dæmonio uexatus fuerat ut esset cum illo]
Li: ⁊ miððy *astigon ðæt scip* ongann hine gebidda seðe from diowle auæled ł gebered wæs ꝥte were mið him

Ru2: ⁊ miððy *astigun in ꝥ scip* ongan hine gibidda seðe from diowle awæled wæs ꝥte were mið him
WSCp: Þa he *on scip eode* hine ongan biddan se ðe ǽr mid deofle gedreht wæs. ꝥ he mid him wære
Tatian: Mit thiu her tho *arsteig in skef*, ...
(*AV*: And when hee was come into the ship, he that had bene possessed with the deuill prayed him that hee might bee with him)

When the Latin version has a prefixed verb and a prepositional phrase following, it is rendered either 'P + V + {Prep + N}' or 'V + P + {Prep + V}', as in

(17) Jn. 4.30 [*exierunt* de ciuitate et ueniebant ad eum]
Li: *út eadon* of ðær byrig ⁊ ge-cuomon to him
Ru2: ⁊ *ut-eodun* of ðær byrig ⁊ gicomon to him
WSCp: Ða *eodon* hi *ut* of ðære byrig ⁊ comon to him
Tatian: Tho *giengun* sie *uz* fon dero burgi inti quamun zi imo
(*AV*: Then they went out of the citie, and came vnto him)

When the Latin version has *foras* (Mt. 10.14, 21.17 and 26.75 (= Lk. 22.62)) or *intro* (Mt. 26.58) that follows a verb, even *Li* can show postposition in faithfully translating Latin adverbs.

(18) Mt. 10.14 [Et quicumque non receperit uos neque audierit sermones uestros *exeuntes foras* de domo uel de ciuitate excuitite puluerem de pedibus uestris in testimonium eorum]
Li: ⁊ suæ hua ne onfoas iuh ne héres worda Iuera *geongas úut* of hus ł of ceastræ sceaccas ða asca of fotum Iurum in cyðnisse ł in gewitnisse hiora ł ðara
Ru1: ⁊ swa hwilce swa nyle onfo eow ne heran wordum eowrum *gáð ut* of þæm huse oþþe þære cæstre ascákeþ dust of fotum eowrum in cyþnisse heora
WSCp: And swa hwa swa eow ne under-fehð ne eowre spræca ne gehyrð. þonne ge *út-gan* of ðam huse oððe of ðære ceastre asceacaþ ꝥ dust of eowrum fotum
Tatian: Inti so uúer iuuih ni inphahit noh ni horit iuuaru uuort, *úzgangante* fon themo hús odo fon theru burgi árscutet then melm fon iuuaren fuozin ín zi giuuiznesse
(*AV*: And whosoeuer shall not receiue you, nor heare your wordes: when yee depart out of that house, or city, shake off the dust of your feete)

(19) Mt. 21.17 [Et Relictis illis *abiit foras* extra ciuitatem in bethaniam ibique mansit]
Li: ⁊ forletno weron ða *ge-eade uta* buta ceastra in bethania ⁊ ðer wunade
Ru1: ⁊ forletende hiæ *eode ut* of þara ceastræ in bethaniæ ⁊ þær wunade
WSCp: ⁊ he forlet hi þa ⁊ *ferde* of þære byrig to bethania. ⁊ lærde hi þar be godes rice

Tatian: Inti in tho forlazenen, ..., *gieng uz* fon thera burgi in stat thiu Bethania heizit, inti thar uuoneta
(*AV*: And he left them, and went out of the citie into Bethany, and he lodged there)

(20) Lk. 22.62 [et *egressus foras* petrus fleuit ámare]
Li: ⁊ *foerde uta* petrus geweap bitterlice
Ru2: ⁊ *foerde utt* petrus weop biterlice
WSCp: Ða *eode* petrus *út* ⁊ biterlice weop
Tatian: Inti *uzgangenti* Petrus uuiof bittaro
(*AV*: And Peter went out, and wept bitterly)

(21) Mt. 26.58 [et *ingressus intro* sedebat cum ministris ut uideret finem]
Li: ⁊ *eode Inn* gesætt mið ðæm ðegnum ꝥte he gesege ðone ende
Ru1: ⁊ *ingangende* gesæt betwih mið þæm þægnum ꝥ he gesæge endunge
WSCp: ⁊ he *in-eode* ⁊ sæt mid þam þenum ꝥ he ge-sawe þone ende
(*AV*: and went in, and sate with the seruants to see the end)

In (18) and (20) Tatian uses *uzgangan* and in (21) *Ru1 ingangan*, ignoring Latin order. In (19) *WSCp* chooses a simple verb *feran*. In (20) *WSCp* has '*þa* V S P' order, in contrast with *Li* and *Ru2*. *Þa* 'then' + VS order is also found in (17), where Tatian takes the same order, and later in (27), where Tatian has 'V *tho* P S'; in these two examples a prepositional phrase follows the particle.[6] There are two dubious instances in which *Li* shows postposition. One is Jn. 10.1 in (15), where *aliunde* 'from some other direction' may correspond not to one word but to *ofer on oðre halfe*. The other is (22), where *contra* corresponds to *togægnas*, and *ofer* might have been a prefixed element, as *transire* is often rendered *oferfaran*, but is postposed owing to the hortative construction (see the basic pattern (a), though *WSCp* free translation chooses '*uton* + infinitive').

(22) Mk. 4.35 [Et ait illis illa die cum sero esset factum *transeamus contra*]
Li: ⁊ cwæ[ð] to him on ðæm dæge miððy efern ł smyltnis were awordæn *fære wæ ofer togægnas*
Ru2: ⁊ cwæð to him on ðæm dæge miððy efern wæs giworden *fære we ofer togægnes*
WSCp: ⁊ sæde him þonne æfen bið *uton faran agen*
(*AV*: And the same day, when the Euen was come, he saith vnto them, Let vs passe ouer vnto the other side)

Let us look at some more examples of Latin verbs whose Old English counterparts may, if not translated as simple verbs, show either preposition or postposition of the adverbial element. Both *ascendere* and *descendere* can be rendered *astigan*; the downward movement, however, is often emphasised by *ofdune* or *niþer*, while the upward movement can be expressed without *up*. Thus in (23), '*astigan* + *of*-phrase' is enough to denote the upward movement but *ofdune* or *niþer* is used for the downward movement. Tatian uses prefixed verbs for either direction. In (24) *descendere* occurs twice; *Li* tries to avoid choosing the same lexeme and uses a double gloss, in which *foerde in* should be considered an unexpression of the prepostional object rather than postposition. *Ru2* does not follow *Li* faithfully but alters the syntax. Instead of *feran*, *WSCp* uses *cuman* and makes full use of prepositional phrases. Tatian uses two different prefixes. In (25), postposition is chosen except *Li*, probably owing to the command to the third person.

(23) Mt. 3.16 [Baptizatus autem confestim *ascendit* de aqua et ecce aperti sunt ei caeli et uidit spiritum die *descendentem* sicut columbam uenientem super sé]
Li: mið ðy wæs gefulwad ueototlice hraðe ł sona *astag ł aras* of wætre ⁊ heonu untyned weron him heofnas ⁊ gesæh gast godes *of-dune stigende* suelce culfre cymmende ofer him
Ru1: þa gedeped [wæs] se hælend hræþe *ástág* of þæm wættre ⁊ henu him weron ontynde heofunas ⁊ he gesæg godes gast *niþer-stigendne* swa culfre cumende ofer hine
WSCp: Soþlice þa se hælend gefullod wæs. hrædlice he *astah* of ðam wætere. ⁊ him wurdon þærrihte heofonas ontynede ⁊ he ge-seah godes gast *niþer-stigende* [*WSH*: *niþer-astigende*] swa swa culfran. ⁊ wunigende ofer hine
Tatian: ... inti themo heilante gitoufitemo inti betontemo, sliumo *úfarsteig* fon themo uuazzare. Senu thô aroffonota uuarun imo himila, inti gisah gotes geist *nidarstigantan* lichamlichero gisiuni samaso tubun, quementan ubar sih
(*AV*: And Iesus, when hee was baptized, went vp straightway out of the water: and loe, the heauens were opened vnto him, and he saw the Spirit of God descending like a doue, and lighting vpon him)

(24) Jn. 5.4 [angelus autem domini secundum tempus *descendebat* in piscinam et mouebat aquam qui ergo primus *descendisset* post motum aquae sanus fiebat á quo-cumque languore tenebatur]
Li: engel uutudlice drihtnes æfter tid *of-dune astag* in ꝥ uoel ł in ꝥ fisc-pol ⁊ ymbcerde ł ꝥ uæter seðe forðon ærist *ofdune stagade ł foerde in* æfter styrenise ł uætres hal son uere ł from suæ–huælc un-hælo ł adle uere ahaldan ł
Ru2: engel wutudlice drihtnes æfter tide ꝥ ymb-cerde ðæt wæter swa hwælc swa forðon ærist *of-dune astag ł foerde of-dune astag* in ða burg æfter styrenisse wætres hale wosa from adle swa hwelc were gihalden
WSCp: Drihtenes engel *com* to his timan on þone mere ⁊ ꝥ wæter wæs astyred. ⁊ se þe raþust. *com* on þone mere æfter þæs wæteres styrunge weraþ gehæled fram swa hwylcere untrumnysse swa he on wæs

Tatian: Gotes engil after ziti *nidarsteig* in den uuiuuari inti ruorta thaz uuazzar. Der dar erist *ingisteig* aftter giruornisse thes uuasseres, heil uuas uon so uuelichero suhti uuas bihabet.
(*AV*: For an Angel went downe at a certaine season into the poole, and troubled the water: whosoeuer then first after the troubling of the water stepped in, was made whole of whatsoeuer disease he had)

(25) Mt. 24.17 [et qui in tecto non *descendat* tollere aliquid de domo sua]
Li: ⁊ seðe in hrof ł in hus ne *ofstiges* genioma huot-hwoego of hus hiora
Ru1: ⁊ seþe on þæce siæ ne *stigað* he *niðer* to genimanne owiht of hi huse
WSCp: ⁊ seþe ys uppan hys huse ne *gá* he *nyþyr* ꝥ he ænig þing on his huse fecce
Tatian: Thanne ther der in theki ist ni *stigit nidar* zi nemanne uuaz fon sinemo huse
(*AV*: Let him which is on the house top, not come downe, to take any thing out of his house)

Three examples are given for *ingredi* and *egredi*. In (26) a pair of inward and outward movement is represented by the alteration of preposed elements in all versions except *WSCp*, which uses *gan* once and postposes the pair *in ⁊ út*. (For *introire* that precedes these verbs, *WSCp* alone use *gan* without *in*, while the other versions use prefixed verbs, as is basic for *gif*-clauses.) In (27) postposition is found in *WSCp* and Tatian, a prefixed *utgangan* in *Ru1*, and *geferan* in *Li*.[7] In (28) Tatian alone chooses postposition.

(26) Jn. 10.9 [ego sum ostium per me si quis introierit saluabitur et *ingredietur et egredietur* et pascua inuenieet]
Li: ic am duru ðerh mec gif huælc inngaeð ł gehæled bið ⁊ *inn-fœreð* ⁊ *ut-fœreð* ł ⁊ lesua ł gemoetað
Ru2: ic am duru-word ðerh mec gif hwelc in-gæð gi-hæled bið ⁊ *in-fœreð ⁊ utt-fœreð* ⁊ leswe gemoeteð
WSCp: ic eom geat swa hwylc swa þurh me gæð byþ hal. ⁊ *gæð in ⁊ út* ⁊ fint læse
Tatian: Ih bim duri. Thurah mih oba uuer ingengit, ther ist giheilit, inti *inget inti úzget* inti findit fuotrunga
(*AV*: I am the doore; by me if any man enter in, he shall be saued, and shall goe in and out, and find pasture)

(27) Mt. 22.10 [et *egressi* serui eius in uias congregauerunt omnes quos inuenerunt malos et bonos]
Li: ⁊ *gefoerdon* ða ðegnas his on wegum gesomnadon alle ðaðe onfundon yfelra ⁊ godra

Ru1: ⁊ þa ***utgangende*** þa eesnas on weogas somnadun alle þa þe hi gemettun gode ⁊ yfle
WSCp: Ða ***eodon*** þa þeowas ***út*** on þa wegas ⁊ gegaderedon ealle ða þe hig gemetton góde ⁊ yfele
Tatian: ***Giengun*** thô ***ûz*** sine scalca in uuega inti samanotun alle thie sie fundun, ubile inti guote
(*AV*: So those seruants went out into the high wayes, and gathered together all as many as they found, both bad and good)

(28) Mk. 5.40 [ipse uero eiectis omnibus adsumit patrem et matrem puellae et qui secum erant et ***ingreditur*** ubi erat puella iacens]
Li: he hueðre miððy fordrifenum allum ł miððy alle ute fordraf genom ðone fader ⁊ moder ðæra maedne ⁊ ðaðe mið him weron ⁊ ***infoerde*** ðer wæs ðæt mæden licende
Ru2: he hweðre mið fordrifnum allum ginom ðone fæder ⁊ moder ðæs mægdnes ⁊ ða ðe mið him weron ⁊ ***in-foerde*** ðer wæs ðæt mægden licgende
WSCp: He þa eallum út adrifenum. nam petrum ⁊ þæs mædenes modor. ⁊ þa ðe mid him wæron. ⁊ ***inn-eodon*** suwiende þar ꝥ mæden wæs
Tatian: Hér thó allen úzaruuorphanen, ginomanemo fater inti muoter thes magatines inti then mit imo uuarun, ***gieng in*** thar thaz magatin lág
(*AV*: But when he had put them all out, he taketh the father and the mother of the damosell, and them that were with him, and entreth in where the damosell was lying.)

(29) is an example of *introire* with negation; postposition is chosen in *WSCp* and Tatian, in contrast with the slavish order of *Li* and *Ru2*.

(29) Jn. 20.5 [et cum sé inclinasset uidet posita linteamina non tamen *introiuit*]
Li: ⁊ miððy hine gebég gesæh gesettedo ða linnin hræglo nó huoeðre ł suæðæh ***inn-eode***
Ru2: ⁊ miððy hine gibeg gisæh gisette ða lineno hrægl ne hweðre ***in-eode***
WSCp: ⁊ þa he nyðer-abeah he geseah þa linwæda licgan; ⁊ ne ***eode*** þeah ***in***
Tatian: Inti mittiu her sih nidarheldita, gisah thiu lininun lachan gilegitíu, ni ***gieng*** thoh uuidoro ***ín***
(*AV*: And he stouping downe and looking in, saw the linnen clothes lying, yet went he not in)

(30) and (31) are given for *abire*. In (30), though preposed elements differ, *Li* and *Ru1* prefer preposition, while *WSCp* and Tatian use simple verbs. (In Tatian, *thana* 'from there' can be an alternative of a prefixed element.) In (31), *Ru1* and *WSCp* show postposition, while *Li* and Tatian use simple verbs.

(30) Mt. 27.66 [illi autem *abeuntes* munierunt sepulchrum signantes lapidem cum custodibus]
Li: ða ilco uutedlice *from eodon* gefæstnadon þ byrgenn mercande ł gemercadon ðone stán mið haldendum
Ru1: hiæ þa *awœg gangende* mid heordum geoldun (*sic*) þa byrgenne gemerkade þon stan mid heordum
WSCp: Soþlice hig *ferdon* ⁊ ymbe-trymedon þa byrgene ⁊ inn-seglodon þone stan mid þam weardum
Tatian: Sie tho thana *gangenti* festinotun thaz grab biinsigilenti then stéin mit bihalterin
(*AV*: So they went, and made the sepulchre sure, sealing the stone, and setting a watch)

(31) Mt. 22.22 [et audientes mirati sunt et relicto eo *abierunt*]
Li: ⁊ gehercnadon ł miððy geherdon wundrigendo sint ł ge-uundradon ⁊ miððy forleorton hine *ge-eadon*
Ru1: ⁊ hiæ geherende wundradun ⁊ forleten hine *eodun awœg*
WSCp: Þa hig þ ge-hyrdon þa wundrodon hig ⁊ forleton hyne ⁊ *ferdon onweg*
Tatian: Thaz thô gihorente vvuntorotun, inti imo furlâzanemo *fuorun*
(*AV*: When they had heard *these wordes*, they marueiled, and left him, and went their way)

In (32) *accedere* is rendered by a simple verb in all versions except Tatian.[8]

(32) Mt. 25.20 [et *accedens* qui quinque talenta acceperat optulit alia quinque talenta dicens]
Li: ⁊ *geneolecde* seðe ða fif cræfto onfeng gebrohte oðero fif cræfto cuoeð
Ru1: ⁊ þa *cumende* seþe fif ... onfeng brohte oþre fif cweþende
WSCp: Ða *com* seþe ða fif pund underfeng ⁊ brohte oþre fife ⁊ cwæð
Tatian: Inti *gieng zuo* therde fimf talenta intfieng, brahta andero fimf talenta quedenti
(*AV*: And so hee that had receiued fiue talents, came and brought other fiue talents, saying)

3. Conclusion

To sum up, *Li* is most faithful to the Latin and most reluctant in accepting postposition, and *Ru2* follows it, though they do not always translate Latin prefixes but at times use simple verbs (or *ge-*/*a*-verbs). *Ru1*, on the other hand, shows independent renderings with occasional choice of postposition. *WSCp* in its free translation either shows postposition or uses a simple verb with a prepositional phrase. Tatian is somewhere in between *Ru1* and *WSCp*, and the basic patterns of element order are nearly the same as those of Old English. The increasing use of prepositional phrases after late Old English has given English a new way of syntactic development besides the alternative set of preposition and postposition of the adverbial element. The threshold of the verb-adverb combination found in *WSCp* might be, at the same time, the departing point of English from German in their linguistic history.

Notes

[1] This is not a rendering faithful to Latin. See the commentary of Bately's edition, p. 276: "90/13-15.ærest ... heafod. Hanno's end was in fact much more unpleasant: see OH IV. vi. 19 'primo uirgis caesus, deinde effossis oculis et manibus cruribusque fractis, uelut a singulis membris poena exigeretur, in conspectu populi necatus est'."

[2] *On-* in *onfon* is a bound-morph prefix and cannot be postposed, and *tofæncge*, a noun with a bound-morph prefix found in a double gloss in the *Lambeth Psalter* 123.6, should be read as *to fæncge* (rendering *captionem*). Three examples of *onfeng to rice* are found in *Chronicles* (*Chron* A II (6.3); *Chron* E 39 (7.15), 784 (53.33-34) but only one example of *on rice feng* (*Chron* D (cf. Classen 1926) 972.1).

[3] I have gone through the examples in the *Microfiche Concordance* for the constructions with *astigan*, *up* and *to*-phrase (both *to* a person and *to* a place) and got this result.

[4] For the other manuscripts of the West Saxon version and their differences, see Liuzza 1994: Introduction.

[5] In Mt. 26.42 *from me* is written independently in *Ru1*:

> [pater mi si non potest hic calix *transire* nisi bibam illum fiat uoluntas tua]
> *Li* : fader min gif ne mæge ðes cælc oferliora nymðe ic drinca hine ł đene sie willo ðin
> *Ru1*: fæder min gif ne mæge þeos cælic *leoran from me* nymþe þ ic of him drince beo hit þin willæ
> *WSCp*: Min fæder gyf þes calic ne mæge *gewitan* [*WSH: witen*] buton ic hyne drince gewurþe þin willa
> Tatian: min fater, oba bi mag these kelih *furifaran* nibih in trinke, uuese thin uuillo
> (*AV*: O my father, if this cup may not passe away from me, except I drinke it, thy will be done)

[6] Cf. Example (4), *Or* 4 5.90.14 *þa sticode him mon þa eagan ut*, which is not an example of the postposition but *ut* occurs independently at the end of the clause.

[7] In sixteen instances of *egredi*, *(ge)feran* is chosen eight times, i.e. 50%.

[8] *Therde* is a compound relative (i.e. *ther* + *the*), which corresponds to Anglo-Saxon *seþe*.

References

Editions

Behaghel, Otto (ed.)
1948 *Heliand und Genesis.* (6th edition.) Halle: Niemeyer.

Classen, Ernest *et al.* (eds.)
1926 *An Anglo-Saxon chronicle, from British Museum, Cotton MS, Tiberius B. IV.* (Modern language texts: English series.) Manchester: Manchester University Press.

Sievers, Eduard (ed.)
1962 *Tatian*. Paderborn: Schöningh.

Studies

Hiltunen, Risto
1983 *The decline of the prefixes and the beginnings of the English phrasal verb.*Turku: Yliopisto.

Lucas, Peter (ed.)
2002 *Middle English from tongue to text.* Dublin: Dublin University Press.

Niwa, Yoshinobu
1991, 1995 *The function and development of prefixes and particles in three Early English texts.* (vols. I & II) Tokyo: Kinseido.

Ogura, Michiko
1995 "The interchangeability of Old English verbal prefixes", *Anglo-Saxon England* 24: 67-93.

2002 "*On the way*, *on way* and *away* in Old and Middle English", in: Lucas (ed.): 71-82.

Robinson, Orrin W.
1992 *Old English and its closest relatives*. London: Routledge.

Venezky, Richard L. -- Antonette diPaolo Healey (ed.)
1980 *A microfiche concordance to Old English.* Toronto: Pontifical Institute of Medieval Studies.

Table 1: Renderings of Latin words in each version

	Li	*Ru*	*WSCp*	Tatian
uenire	cuman gecuman	cuman	cuman gan	quëman biquëman
ire	gan gangan	gan gangan	faran gan feran (Lk.)	faran gangan
abire	gan gangan (Mt.) feran	gan feran (Lk., Jn.)	feran faran (Jn.) gan	gangan faran
exire	gan gangan (Mt.) feran (Lk.)	gan feran (Lk.) utgan (Mt.)	gan utgan (Mt.) feran	angan
transire	oferferan oferfaran	gelioran (Mt., Mk.) oferferan	faran feran gewitan	faran furifaran
introire	in(n)gan in(n)gangan	ingan inferan	gan	ingangan
intrare	in(n)gan in(n)gangan	ingan ingangan	gan ingan	ingangan
ambulare	gangan gan	gangan gan	gan gangan	gangan
vadere	gan gangan	gan gangan	faran (Mt., Jn.) gan	faran
ascendere	astigan	astigan	astigan faran (Jn) feran	arstigan stigan
descendere	ofdune astigan (Lk.) ofdune stigan (Jn.) ofstigan	astigan ofdune astigan (Jn.)	cuman (Jn.) faran feran (Lk.)	nidarstigan
accedere	geneolecan	geneolecan gan (Mt.) cuman (Mt.)	genealæcan cuman (Mt.)	gangan zuogangan

Table 2: Positions between the verb and the free-morph prefix or an adverbial element

	Li	*Ru*	*WSCp*	Tatian
Partic. + V	6	7	2	
abire V	77	67	76	54
V + Partic.	1*	5	2	1
Partic. + V	18	26	33	44
exire V	101	70	70	11
V + Partic.	1*	8	17	9
Partic. + V	72	35	21	30
intrare V	5	21	44	14
V + Partic.		5	6	3
Partic. + V	46	39	10	16
introire V	3	8	35	7
V + Partic.			3	
Partic. + V	3	2	3	5
ascendere V	54	49	50	25
V + Partic.	1	1	3	2
Partic. + V	39	17	7	18
descendere V	6	11	28	3
V + Partic.		4	4	3
Partic. + V	19	16	19	8
ingredi V	1	2	10	
V + Partic.	1**			
Partic. + V	1	2	9	9
egredi V	25	16	12	
V + Partic.	2*	2	4	1
Partic. + V	8	4	1	14
accedere V	57	58	61	21
V + Partic.		1		4
Partic. + V	28	16	2	4
transire V	13	23	40	19
V + Partic.	1	1		

N.B. V simple verb with or without a bound-morph prefix

Old English words for people in the *Épinal-Erfurt glossary*

Hans Sauer (Munich, Germany)

1. Introduction

If we can call a glossary a text – this is what, for example, Henry Sweet did in his edition[1] – then the *Épinal-Erfurt glossary* (*ÉpErf*) is certainly the oldest English text of any length that we have. Therefore, it is invaluable for studying the earliest stage of the English language, especially its spelling, phonology, morphology, in particular word-formation, and its vocabulary.[2]

In the present paper, I shall look more closely at the Old English names for people (persons) which *ÉpErf* contains; of course, their Latin lemmata will also be taken into account. There are c. 64 such Old English names in *ÉpErf*. This is not a very large number, especially when compared with the number of plant names in *ÉpErf* (more than 120) and the names for animals (more than 110).[3] Moreover, for several reasons no precise number of names for people can be given (see 3. below), but this is true of the animal and plant names as well. Nevertheless, the names for people offer several interesting aspects. In particular, I am going to analyse their etymology (see 5. below), their morphology (with a special view to word-formation, see 6. below) and their meaning (see 7. below). This is the centre of the investigation. To start with, however, I shall briefly present the manuscripts (see 2. below), discuss the question of words to be included and to be excluded (see 3. below), and sketch the nature of the Latin lemmata and the problems they posed to the Old English glossator(s) (see 4. below). To conclude, I shall look at the question of survival (see 8. below) and, in the ninth section, add a few final remarks. The basis of the investigation, the list of the Old English names for people in *ÉpErf* is given in section 10 (section 10 also provides a list of Latin lemmata plus their Old English glosses), and a bibliography (see References).[4]

2. The *Épinal-Erfurt glossary*

2.1. The manuscripts

ÉpErf is transmitted in two manuscripts, which are obviously derived from a common ancestor. Strangely enough, one of the extant manuscripts of the oldest English text was written on the continent, and both are now located on the continent. These manuscripts are:

(1) Épinal, Bibliothèque municipale 72 (2), fols. 94-107, written in England by an English scribe in the late 7th or early 8th century (Ép);
(2) Erfurt, Wissenschaftliche Allgemeinbibliothek, Codex Amplonianus F.42, fols. 1a1-14va33, written in Cologne by a German scribe in the late 8th or early 9th century (Erf).

The common ancestor of *ÉpErf* has been dated c. 670-690, i.e. the time when Theodore of Tarsus (602-690) and Hadrian (c. 636-709/710) taught at Canterbury (i.e. from 669 onwards), and it may be connected with Theodore's school at Canterbury.[5]

ÉpErf has been described and edited several times.[6] The most recent edition is Pheifer (1974), which I have used for the present article, and all line references are to Pheifer's edition. The most recent facsimile edition is the one by Bischoff *et al.* (1988).[7]

2.2. The structure of *Épinal-Erfurt*

Épinal-Erfurt is a Latin glossary in a rough alphabetical order, mostly in a-order, i.e. with the Latin lemmata arranged only according to their first letter, with some parts in ab-order. It contains more than 3280 Latin lemmata. Most of them have Latin glosses, but c. 1100, roughly a third, are glossed in Old English.[8] Many of the Latin words are common words, but some are relatively rare (see also 4.1. below). The nouns are often given in the nom. sg., but sometimes in inflected cases, e.g. *adsaeculam* 101 (acc. sg.), *coniurati* 201 (nom. pl.), *censores* 197 and *gladiatores* 481 (both nom. and acc. pl.), *gregariorum* 479 (gen. pl.), *stipatoribus* 929 (dat. pl.), *foederatas* 436 (acc. pl.), etc. This probably reflects the fact that originally the lemmata were taken from texts and were only arranged alphabetically later. The inflected cases are often imitated in the Old English glosses, as far as this is possible in the Old English inflexional system, e.g. *gimodae* 201, *giroefan* 197 and *caempan* 481 (nom. and acc. pl.),[9] *aedilra* 479 (gen. pl.), *ymbhringendum* 929 (dat. pl.), etc.

Compounds are often written as two words in *ÉpErf* (on word-division in the manuscripts, cf. Pheifer 1974: xxiii = § 4); in the present study, I have often inserted a hyphen between the elements of compounds in order to make the morphological structure clear. In the list in section 10, the spellings of both Ép and Erf are given if they differ; otherwise, the spelling of Ép is normally quoted, unless Erf has the better (i.e. more original) spelling or is the only witness.

3. The word-field 'people': Its delimitation and its subdivisions

3.1. Inclusions and exclusions

As stated in section 1, a precise number of the names for people attested in *ÉpErf* cannot be given. There are several reasons for this, in particular:

(1) Names for people/persons can be regarded as a semantic field (word-field), but semantic fields are often difficult to define and to delimit, and there are different ways of doing this. With many semantic fields there is a group of words which belong to the core of the field, whereas others belong to the margin.[10] The words collected here as representing the concept 'people, person' are listed in different sections of Roberts -- Kay (1995), to give just a few examples: *burgleod* 'citizen(s)', *dweorg* 'dwarf', *fostorcild* 'foster-child', *steopfæder* 'stepfather' and others are presented under 'Humankind' (02.03), whereas *cempa* 'warrior, fighter, man' is listed under 'War' (13.02.10.01), and *gerefa* is listed several times, once also under 'War' (section 13.02.10.01.01) and once under 'Social Interaction' (e.g. 12.01.01. 05) – polysemous words obviously often have to appear in different sections. *Grima* 'spectre, ghost' and *orc* 'demon' at best belong to the margin of the field 'people', but I have still included them here; Roberts -- Kay list them under 'Religion: the extrasensorial world' (16.01.03). Strite (1989) has a different division: among other fields, he distinguishes between terms for 'Deity', for 'Kinship', for 'Male and Female', for 'Monster' and for 'Nobility'. Some words in the *ÈpErf* refer to attributes of people rather than to people themselves, e.g. *sceol(h)egi* 'squinting' 981 or *felospraeci* 1009 'talkative'; I have excluded those. For my tentative subdivision of the semantic field, see 3.2. below.

(2) The borderline between present participles (normally ending in *-ende* in the nom. sg.) and agent nouns (normally ending in *-end* in the nom. sg.) is also not always easy to draw.[11] As a rule, I have included forms which translate Latin agent nouns (esp. in *-or*, *-ator*), e.g. *baedendrae* for *inpulsore* 539, *bisuicend* for *impostorem* 545 or *ymbhringendum* for *stipatoribus* 929 (see further section 6.6.1. below), but I have mostly excluded Old English forms that translate Latin participles, e.g. *tilgendum* 78 (for *tiliendum*) for *adnitentibus*. A dictionary such as ClH seems to follow the same principle: it lists *bǣdend*, *beswicend* etc. as a separate words (in addition to their bases *bǣdan*, *beswican*), but not *tiliend*.

(3) Some words are ambiguous or polysemous and might or might not refer to persons. Thus, *actuaris* 87 (probably a form of *actuarius*) might refer to a ship or to a person ('scribe');[12] the same applies to its Old English gloss

uuraec: it could refer to a ship or to a person ('persecutor'), cf. Pheifer (1974: 64). *Uuildae* 'wild ones' 99, glossing *agrestes*, could refer to 'wild people', i.e. 'inhabitants of the countryside'. According to Pheifer (1974: 65) it rather refers to 'wild plants'; a decision seems, however, difficult.

(4) Occasionally a Latin lemma containing no personal name is rendered with an Old English gloss containing a personal name (*uia secta – iringaes uueg*, 1050), and conversely, occasionally a Latin lemma containing a personal name is not rendered with a personal name in the Old English gloss (*pliadas – sifunsterri*, 762).

3.2. Semantic subgroups

I have tentatively subdivided the Old English names for people into five subgroups. Although female terms are included in groups 1-2 and 4-5, I have in addition also set up a subgroup 6 'women'. The number of clearly marked names for women (circa six) is much smaller than that of the names for men, although some names are perhaps really neutral and might include men as well as women (e.g. *burg-leod, cneorissa, fostor-bearn, grima, scin, uuildae* etc.). It is also striking that relatively many of the names for women have a negative denotation or connotation (*cebisae, haegtis, mera*). Some of the groups seem relatively self-evident (1 and 2), whereas others are more mixed (4 and 5). Moreover, there will always be words which are difficult to assign: for example, the distinction between occupation and profession on the one hand and status on the other is not always certain. Thus, I have put *mundbora* into the status-group (4), but *raedbora* into the occupation group (2); see further section 7.3 below. The lists also show that *ÉpErf* is not a systematic guide to the (Latin or Old English) vocabulary and its semantic structure in our sense of a dictionary: among the kinship terms, for example, basic terms such as 'father, mother, brother, sister, husband, wife' etc. are missing, whereas more marginal terms such as 'stepfather' and 'concubine' are included.

(1) Kinship: (i) general and neutral: *cneorissa, fosturbearn, meeg*; (ii) men: *steup-faeder, sueor* (2x), *gesuirgion*; (iii) women: *cebisae, nift*.

(2) Profession and occupation: *byrgere, edisc-ueard, egdere, flitere in ebhatis, gibuur, haetend, hors-thegn, hrof-uuyrcta, lecea, ledir-uyrcta, leuuis, orit-mon, roedra, red-bora, giroefa, scinlaeca, scinnere, scyend, teblere.* Among these *red-bora* and *giroefa* could be singled out as having a political and administrative function.

(3) Warlike or destructive occupation: *caempa, ferhergaend, strael-bora, uuicing-sceadan.*

(4) Status, social relation and interaction: *aedil, aeldor (ealdor), baedend, bisuicend, burg-leod, byrgea, ceap-cnext, dweorg, fultumend, gimodae, gidopta, mundbora, sigiras, gitreeudae, thegan, tyctaend uuildae, uuoda, uuoedendi, uuraec, ymbhringend(um).*
(5) Mythology, extrasensorial and extraterrestrial world:[13] (i) Gods: *tiig, orc*; female: *burg-runae, uuyrdae*; (ii) demons, spectres, witches etc.: *grima, egisi-grima, scina*; women: *haegtis, mera, uuydu-mer*; (iii) stars: *iringaes uueg*; *sifun-sterri*.
(6) Women, females: (i) kinship: *cebisae* (for *pelices*); *nift* (for *priuigna*); (ii) Gods, mythology: *burg-runae* and *uuyrdae* (for *parcae*); (iii) demons, witches: *haegtis* (*striga*), *incuba* (*mera*); (iv) stars: *sifunsterri* (*pliadas*), i.e. the woman's name is only expressed in the Latin lexeme, but has not been translated into the Old English one.

4. The nature of the Latin vocabulary and the problem of how to render it into Old English

4.1. The origin of the Latin lemmata

Most of the Latin words in *ÉpErf* referring to persons were inherited from classical Latin (about three quarters);[14] a quarter (c. 18), however, seem to be post-classical. Many of the latter are also rare, and some seem to be corrupt. Moreover, sometimes the original gender and inflexional class were changed.[15] Postclassical are: *arcister* 'archer' (according to Pheifer [1974: 5] a corruption of *arcites*, and used instead of the more common *sagittarius*; cf. *DMLBS*); *broel(l)arius* 'park-keeper' (derived from *broilus* 'park', a Late Latin [Gallo-Latin] loan from continental Celtic); *byrseus* 'tanner' (from Greek); *commentariensis* 'clerk of a law-court, registrar of public documents'; *contribulus* 'of the same tribus' (for *contribulis*); *dromedarius* 'camel or camel-driver' (from Greek); *ephilenticus* 'epileptic' (probably for *epilepticus* from Greek); *erpicarius* 'harrower'; *incuba* 'female incubus'; *inpostor(em)* 'impostor'; *larbula* (first recorded in Aldhelm), *mascus* 'ghost, spectre' (normally *masca*; chronologically one of the latest elements: ultimately from Arabic, borrowed into Medieval Latin in the 7th century; the origin of PDE *mask*, G *Maske* etc.); *maulistis* 'seducer, pimp' (from Greek); *nitatio* 'shining, ghost' (perhaps from *niteo* 'shine' or rather **nitito* / **nititare* 'shine repeatedly'); *phisillos* (perhaps for *physicus* or for *physiologus*, originally 'natural philosopher' etc.; the meaning 'physician' of *physicus* is late); *via secta* 'milky way' (rare); *vispell(i)o* 'a thief who robbed corpses of their grave-clothes', and, at least with a post-classical meaning, *vetellus* (for *vitellus*) 'father-in-law'.[16]

4.2. The character of the Latin lemmata

What is more important and interesting, however, is the character of the Latin words for people or persons used in *ÉpErf.* Predominantly they refer to men, females occur much more rarely (see section 3.2). Perhaps even more surprisingly, no specifically Christian terms occur, although *ÉpErf* obviously originated in the context of a Christian school in Anglo-Saxon England (perhaps Theodore's school at Canterbury). On the other hand, many of the Latin words (and especially some of the classical ones) specifically refer to Roman or late antique culture, institutions, occupations and professions, mythology etc., e.g. *actuaris* 87 (if for *actuarius* 'a short-hand writer'); *censores* 197 'Roman magistrates responsible for the citizens' morals'; *commentariensis* 223 'registrar of public documents'; *contribulus* 164 'a member of the same tribe'; *dromidarius* 320 'dromedary, dromedary-driver'(from Greek); *gladiator* 481'gladiator, fighter in a public circus'; *iurisperiti* 557 'the learned in the law, legal expert'; *Mars* 663; *mulio* 658 'mule-keeper, muleteer'; *orcus* 698; *parcae* 761 and 764 'goddesses of fate'; *pleiades* 762 'the seven stars' (from Greek); *rabulus* 854 'a brawling advocate, pettifogger'; *scaenicus* (*scienicis*; from Greek) 952 'player, actor on the stage'; *vispellones* 760 'thieves who robbed corpses of their grave-clothes'.

4.3. The problem of how to render them into Old English

Due to their partly culture-specific character it is not surprising that the glossator(s) sometimes had difficulties in translating these and similar terms, and they applied different strategies to cope with the task.

(1) On the whole the Old English renderings are quite adequate, e.g. *burg-leod* for *municeps* 'citizen'; *ceap-cnext* for *empticius* 'bought' (i.e. 'bought slave)'; *dweorg* 'dwarf' for *nanus uel pumilio*; *fer-hergend* for *grassator*; *fostur-bearn* for *alumnae*, etc. How far these renderings are native words and how far they represent loan-formations or loan-meanings (semantic loans) is sometimes difficult to decide and will be discussed later (see section 5.6.).

(2) In three or four instances the renderings are even quite ingenious and represent a kind of cultural transposition or substitution: a Latin word or phrase is rendered by an Old English word or phrase that replaces the classical concept with a native concept. (i) *uuicing-sceadan* for *piraticum, piraticam* 736; (ii) *iringaes uueg* for *uia secta* 1050, (iii) *tiig* 'Tiw, Germanic god of war' for *Mars* 663;[17] for an explanation of *uuicing-sceadan* and *iringaes uueg* see 6.5.4. below. (iv) *Parcae* was apparently a

little more difficult. It occurs twice within a few lines (761, 764) and is translated differently on those two occasions (*burg-runae* and *uuyrdae*). Whether the use of *uuyrdae* for *parcae* suggests that there may have been goddesses of fate in Germanic mythology, or whether this is just an attempt at translating an unfamiliar Latin term (and is basically integrated into the Christian world-picture), has been hotly disputed.[18] The fact that *uuy[r]d* is also used in *ÉpErf* to translate *sortem, condicionem* (980) seems to speak against a 'Germanic' interpretation of *wyrd*; apparently it was semantically relatively open and could translate various Latin words – *wyrd* also renders *fatum, fortuna* etc. in Old English literature, see, e.g., BT s.v. 'wyrd',[19] so there does not seem to be a connection to Germanic godesses of fate. The literal meaning of *burg-runae* for *parcae*[20] seems to be something like 'counsellors in a town'. The second element *–rune* 'one who knows or tells secrets' is related to *rūn* 'counsel, mystery, secret, letter, runic letter', but apparently it does not occur independently in Old English, only as a second element of combinations (compounds), see BT and BTS s.v. '-rune'.

(3) In at least one instance, the Old English glossator even tried to paraphrase a Latin term, namely *flitere in ebhatis* (*ebhat(is)* is a form of *eofot* 'crime, sin, guilt') 'a disputer, quarreller in lawsuits' for *rabulus* 'cheap lawyer, pettifogger, demagogue' (854); see Pheifer (1974: 116).

(4) Occasionally the Old English translation is more general and less specific than the Latin term, e.g. *giroefa* (*gerēfa* > PDE *reeve*) 'high official' for *censores* as well as for *commentariensis* – apparently *(ge)refa* was often used for translating titles of non-English officials (see Pheifer 1974: 73; *BTS*, s.v. 'gerefa II'); less specific translation equivalents are also *byrgeras* 'corpse-bearers, lit. 'buriers' for *uispellones* (see section 4.2.); *oritman* (for *eored-mon*) 'horse-man, rider' for *dromidarius* 'camel-driver'; *thegan* 'servants, warriors, noblemen' for *adsaeculam* 'follower, attendant' (according to Lewis & Short, s.v. 'assecla', the latter was often used contemptuously; thus *thegan* was probably more positive). More negative than its Latin lemma is probably *scinneras* 'magicians, illusionists' for *scienicis* (prob. for *scaenicis*) 'players, actors'.[21]

(5) Not quite correct is *hors-thegn* 'ostler, groom, lit. horse-servant' for *mulio* 'mule-keeper, muleteer' (658); as with *dromidarius* (rendered more vaguely as *oritman*, see above), the Old English glossator apparently had problems in rendering names of animals that he did not really know. *Dromedarius* is actually attested in the Bible (e.g. Is. 60.6), but much more rarely than *camelus*; *mulus*, *mula* is also attested, e.g. 2Kgs. 18.9; 1Prov. 12.40. By glossing *gregarius* (*gregariorum* 479) 'belonging to a flock or herd, of the common sort' with *aedil(ra)* 'noble, aristocratic', the glossator apparently

changed the meaning presented by the Latin lemma into its contrary (antonym); perhaps he thought of the contrast between common soldiers and noblemen presented in some of the apparent sources and chose the wrong member of the pair (cf. Pheifer 1974: 91).[22] *Mund-bora* 'protector, guardian etc.' also is rather the opposite of *suffragator* 'supporter' (934).[23]

5. Etymology and loan-influence

With regard to etymology, one basic distinction is between native words and loan-words, another is according to chronological layers. The distinction between native words and loan-words is, however, blurred by hybrid formations, loan-formations and semantic loans. Both hybrid formations and loan-formations are English formations, but hybrid formations use loan-words as their basis, whereas loan-formations imitate a foreign, in our case usually a Latin model with native material. Semantic loans are also native words, but their meaning has been taken over from a foreign, in our case also usually a Latin word, e.g. PDE *hell*, G *Hölle* < Gmc **xaljō*, originally probably 'a hidden place', the later, Christian meaning taken from Lat (*loca*) *inferna*. Loan-formations, of course, usually also entail a loan-meaning. With loan-words, a distinction also has to be made between immediate origin and ultimate origin: *byrseus*, e.g., is a Latin word in the context of *ÉpErf*, but ultimately it comes from Greek.

Chronologically, several layers can be distinguished: layers usually recognized are Indo-European (IE), Germanic (Gmc), West-Germanic (WGmc) and Old English (OE); sometimes still finer distinctions are made. Etymological dictionaries and studies do not always agree on the chronological labelling, however, and they often use different conventions for rendering the reconstructed Indo-European and Germanic forms. Another complication is that sometimes a root or base or word goes back to an earlier stage, but the derivation from it was coined at a later stage: this is the case, for example, with many of the agent nouns in *-end* and *-ere*: they were formed in Old English, but the underlying verb (or noun) is often older (see section 6.6.1.-2.).

Words can usually be labelled as IE or Gmc or WGmc because they have cognates in related languages; conversely, words are labelled as OE when they have no cognates. But even here, problematic cases occur: Carr (1939: 129) for example, regards a number of compounds which have related forms in Old English, Old High German etc. as independent parallels and not as going back to Germanic or to West-Germanic – I am not sure whether his reasons are always convincing, but I follow his classification here. In the following, I shall deal first with the native words and then with loan-words, hybrid formations, loan-formations and semantic loans. Although the compounds dealt with here are usually nouns, they are listed separately from the simple nouns.

5.1. Indo-European

Of the c. 64 words for people in *ÉpErf*, only c. four can be traced back to Indo-European; all of them are simple nouns, namely (i) *dweorg* 'DWARF' < Gmc **dwerg-az* (cf. G *Zwerg*) < IE **dwergwk-os* 'dwarf'; (ii) *lecea(s)*, *lǣce* < Gmc **lǣkjaz* < IE **legios*; (iii) *nift* 'niece' < Gmc **nefti-* (cf. G *Nichte*) < IE **nepti*; (iv) *sweor* 'father-in-law' < Gmc **swehura-* (cf. G arch. *Schwäher*) < IE **swekura* (Lat *socer*). No compounds can be traced back to Indo-European.

5.2. Germanic

Among the c. 14 words inherited from Germanic, there are eight nouns, two adjectives and three verbs, furthermore one compound and one prefix-formation which was perhaps originally a compound.

(1) Nouns: (i) possibly *geswirgion* (*geswiria*) 'cousin'; (ii) *grima* 'ghost, spectre'; (iii) *mare* (written *mera* in *ÉpErf* 558) < Gmc **maron*, *maron* 'female incubus', which survives in PDE *nightmare* < possibly even IE, cf. OI *mor*, *morrigain* 'queen of nightmares'; (iv), *mǣg* 'relative, kinsman' < Gmc **mǣga-*; (v) *tiig* 'Germanic god of war'; (vi) *þegn* < Gmc **þegna-*, which survives in PDE arch. *thane* (cf. arch. G *Degen*); (vii) *wyrd* < **wurð-i-* (see further section 6.7.); (viii) *wrǣc* 'ship' or 'persecutor'.

(2) Adjectives: (i) *wild* < Gmc **swelþija-*; (ii) *wod* < Gmc **wōda-*.

(3) Verbs: (i) *bǣdan* 'to urge, incite'; (ii) *hǣtan* (weak 1) 'to heat, to make (or be or become) hot' < **hait-jan* (> OE **hāt-jan* > *hǣtan*; cf. G *heizen*); (iii) *treowian* (wk. 2) 'trust', derived from *treow* (cf. G *trauen*).

(4) Compound nouns: Whereas apparently no compounds were inherited from Indo-European (at least not among the names for persons), one clear and one questionable compound go back to Germanic: (i) *burg-lēod* 'inhabitants'; cf. Toth (1980: 271-273; Carr 1939: 129); (ii) *steop-fæder* < Gmc **stiup-faðer* (> PDE *stepfather*; cf. G *Stiefvater*); see Carr (1939: 52). It was perhaps originally a compound, but is here regarded as a prefix-formation, because *steop-* existed not even in Old English any longer as an independent word (see section 6.5.4.).

5.3. West-Germanic

The West-Germanic layer is apparently slightly smaller than the Germanic layer; it consists of c. ten words, c. six nouns, one adjective, two verbs, and one compound nouns.

(1) Nouns: (i) *gebūr* < WGmc **ga-būr-*, *gi-būr-*, which survives in PDE *neighbour* (cf. G *Bauer*, *Nachbar*); (ii) *byrgea* 'one who gives bail' < WGmc **burg-jōn* (cf. G *Bürge*); (iii) *cebisae* 'concubine' < WGmc **kabiso* (cf. G *Kebse*); (iv) *gidopta*: perhaps a variant of *ge-dohta*, formed on the adj. *dohtig* > PDE *doughty* (cf. G *tüchtig*) or its basis *dugan* (*dohte*) (cf. G *taugen*); (v) *haegtis* 'witch' (G *Hexe*), see section 6.6. (3); (vi) *roedra* (ClH *rēðra*) < WGmc **rōþr-i*, derived from *rōðor* 'rudder' (cf. G *Ruder*).

(2) Adjectives: (i) *aeðele* (*ÉpErf aedilra* 479) < WGmc **aþl-ja-* (cf. G *edel*, related to *Adel*).

(3) Verbs: Possibly (i) *forhergian* (cf. G *verheeren*) and (ii) *ymbhringan* (cf. G *umringen*), since both also occur in German.

(4) Compound nouns: (i) *mund-bora* 'protector, lit. protection-bearer' 934, see Carr (1939: 102, no. 77).

5.4. Old English

The majority of the native names for persons attested in *ÉpErf* are Old English formations (c. 27); most of them apparently arose through word-formation processes. Some are possibly loan-formations, see section 5.5.

(1) Nouns: (i) c. nine derivations in *-end*, see section 6.6.1. The underlying verbs are usually older; (ii) c. five derivations in *-ere* (see section 6.6.2.): *byrgere*, *egderi* (possibly WGmc), *flitere*, *scinnere*, *teblere*; (iii) c. five others: *ealdor*, *giroefa*, *leuuis*, *scina*, *scinnlæca*.

(2) Adjectives used as nouns: *gemod* (*ÉpErf gimodae*).

(3) Compound nouns: These form the largest group (c. 15); in the *ÉpErf* spelling they are: *burg-leod*, *burg-runae*, *edisc-ueard*, *egisi-grima*, *fostur-bearn*, *hors-thegn*, *hrof-uuyrcta*, *ledir-uuyrcta*, *orit-mon* (for *eored-mon* according to Pheifer 1974: 80), *red-bora*, *sifun-sterri*, *strel-bora*, *uuicing-sceadan*, *uuydu-mer*, *Iringaes uueg*. For their subdivision see section 7.1.

5.5. Loan-words and hybrid formations

There is just one simple loan-word among the names for persons in *ÉpErf*, that is *orc* (borrowed into Old English from Lat *orcus* originally 'underworld', then also 'God of the underworld'),[24] but there are a few hybrid formations, namely

(i) *caempa* 'warrior, fighter' (< WGmc **kamp-jon*), a West-Germanic formation (cf. G *Kämpe*) based on the Latin loan-word OE *camp* (G *Kampf* < Lat *campus*); (ii) *teblere* 'gambler', based on the Latin loan-word *teblae/tefil* < Lat *tabula* (in the meaning 'game of dice') – Lat *tabularius* also existed, but it had a different meaning, 'registrar'; thus it is unlikely that *teblere* is an immediate borrowing from Latin and more likely that it was newly formed in Old English from *teblae*; (iii) the OE compound *ceap-cnext*, the first element of which is *cēap* 'bargain' < Lat *caupo* (cf. G *Kauf*), > PDE *cheap*.

5.6. Loan-formations and semantic loans

Old English adopted not only loan-words from Latin, but also created a number of loan-formations based on Latin models,[25] as well as some semantic loans (loan meanings). The number of loan-formations was probably even higher than the number of loan-words.[26]

5.6.1. Subgroups within loan-formations

Within the loan-formations ('Lehnbildungen') a threefold subdivision is often made between loan-translations ('Lehnübersetzungen'), loan-renditions ('Lehnübertragungen') and loan-creations ('Lehnschöpfungen').

(1) Loan-translations are usually complex words (compounds or prefix- or suffix-formations) and they follow their Latin model most closely by rendering it morpheme by morpheme, e.g. *hǣlend* – *salvator*, where the stem of *salvare* is rendered by the stem of *hǣlan* 'HEAL', and the agent suffix *-(a)tor* is rendered by the agent suffix *-end*.[27]
(2) In loan-renditions only one element of the Latin model is translated literally and one is rendered more freely. For example, in *ceap-cnext* 'bought slave', perhaps modelled on *empticius*, the first element *emere, emptus* is translated relatively literally by *ceap*, but whereas in Latin the second element *-icius* is a suffix, in the Old English the second element (*cnext*) is a word.
(3) Loan-creations are still freer: They show no formal correspondence with their Latin model. This is also the reason why loan-translations are easiest and loan-creations are most difficult to recognise. But even loan-creations normally use the same word-formation processes as native words and therefore cannot always be distinguished from native formations at first sight (and sometimes not at all).

(4) Loan-formations can also be hybrid, i.e. they can contain a loan-word. This is the case with *ceap-cnext* and probably also with *teblere*, see sections 5.5. and 6.4.2. (2).

5.6.2. Criteria for loan-formations and semantic loans

In order to classify an Old English word as a loan-formation, it should be certain or at least likely that this word did not exist before as a parallel but independent Old English formation; in order to classify it as a semantic loan (loan meaning), it should be certain that it had another meaning before it took over its new meaning from Latin. A number of criteria have been suggested for the distinction between loan-formations and semantic loans on the one hand and parallel but independent native words or native meanings on the other.[28] But none of the criteria proposed so far is sufficient to decide all problematic cases, and even if they are combined they are not always decisive. Some of these criteria are:

(1) The concept or thing was not known to the Anglo-Saxons before they came into contact with the Christian missionaries, nor to their Germanic ancestors before they came into contact with the Romans. This is generally likely for most of the specifically Christian concepts (e.g. *almighty*, *gospel*, *hell*, *sin*). As we noted above, some words for 'people' attested in *ÉpErf* are quite general and the concepts probably also existed in Anglo-Saxon England, but a number of the Latin words for persons in *ÉpErf* also stand for specifically Roman or late Antique concepts and the glossators sometimes had difficulties in translating them (cf. section 4). This does not mean, however, that all of the Old English words used to render them are loan-formations or have a loan-meaning;[29] as we pointed out above (see section 4.3), in a number of cases we may simply have to do with imprecise translations that give only a very rough Old English equivalent of the Latin word or transpose it into the Anglo-Saxon world, e.g. *censores* and *commentariensis* – *giroefa(n)* 'REEVE'. We also do not know whether the Anglo-Saxons had separate professions for all the kinds of workers and artisans that are referred to in the Latin lemmata and that are given Old English equivalents (*byrgere*, *egderi*, *hors-thegn*, *hrof-uuyrcta*, *ledir-uuyrcta* etc.): Harrowing (*egðan*) was certainly done by the farmers, but probably just as one of many things a farmer had to do (cf. also section 7.3.).

(2) There is a close morphological correspondence between the Latin model and its Old English counterpart; this applies in particular to loan-translations and partly also to loan-renditions. This does not mean,

however, that all Old English words which are morphologically similar to corresponding Latin words are loan-translations or loan-renditions based on these Latin words; the parallels might be accidental.

(3) The Old English word is rare or even a hapax legomenon, and/or it occurs only in glossaries. But some words which in Old English are attested only in glossaries must have been common, as is clear from their later use.

(4) The glossators apparently had no fixed Old English equivalent for a certain Latin word and therefore they had to experiment, using different Old English formations for the same Latin word.[30]

It has also to be kept in mind that, once they are created, loan-formations lead an independent life and do not necessarily gloss or translate the Latin word which triggered off their coinage; see, e.g. the remarks on *strel-bora* and *hrof-wyrcta* below.

5.6.3. The status of the Old English names from *ÉpErf*

Taking these points into consideration, I would very tentatively suggest the following classification:

(1) Native words are certainly or probably: *æðele* (*aedilra*), *byrgea*, *cebisae*, *dweorg*, *ealdor*, *flitere*, *gidopta*, *fostur-bearn* (although attested only in glossaries), *grima*, *haegtes*, *hors-thegn*, *leceas*, *meeg*, *mera* (for *mare*), *mund-bora*, *nift*, *red-bora*, *roedra*, *scina*, *seofon-sterri*, *sigiras*, *steop-faeder* (*steup-faedaer*; orthographic variants), *sueor(as)*, *gesuirgion*, *teblere* (a hybrid formation), *tiig*, *wild(ae)*, *wod(a)*, *wraec*.

(2) The following are imprecise translations for persons and offices connected with the Roman or Late Antique world, but they are also native words or formations: *cempa – gladiator* 481 (hybrid, i.e. a native formation based on a loan-word); *flitere* (*in ebhatis*) – *rabulus* 854; *gebur* – *colonus* 163; *giroefa(n)* – *censores* 197, *commentariensis* 223; *red-bora(n)* – *iurisperiti* 552; *thegn* – *adsaeculam* 101 etc.

(3) The following might be semantic loans (i.e. have a loan-meaning): *Gimodae* 'of one mind' for *coniurati* (cf. BT, BTS s. v. 'gemōd', adj.). *Uuyrdae* for *parcae* (764) can also be regarded as having a loan-meaning. *Burg-leod* (see above) is a Germanic compound; according to Toth (1980: 271-3) it has a loan-meaning when translating *civis*; this probably also applies to Ép 620, where it glosses *municeps*.

(4) Loan translations: (i) The eight agent nouns in *-end* attested in *ÉpErf* (see also section 6.6.1.) are based on native verbs, but as agent nouns they could be loan-translations, rendering Latin agent nouns in *-(a)(t)or* (and sometimes also Latin (present) participles): *baedend(rae)* – *inpulsor(e)* 539;

bisuicend – inpostor(em) 545; *ferhergaend – grassator* 467; *fultumend(i) – adstipulatus* 95; *hætendae – calentes* 206; *scyhend – maulistis* 654; *uuoedend(i)* – Lat *lymphatico*; *ymb-hringend(um) – stipator(ibus)* 929. According to Kärre (1915: 229) most Old English agent nouns in *-end* were "exclusively literary words"; they were occasional formations and are attested very rarely.[31] This is also true of the formations attested in *ÉpErf*. (ii) Apart from the group consisting of agent nouns in *-end*, there are relatively few examples among the names for persons in *ÉpErf* which could be regarded as loan-translation. A possible case is *egderi* (*egðere*) 'harrower' for *erpicarius* (normally *herpicarius*) 396, which occurs only in glossaries (but is a WGmc formation, attested also in OHG & OLG).

(5) Loan renditions: To this group belong perhaps: (i) *ceap-cnext* for *empticius* 349, which is rare and mainly attested in glossaries, apart from an occurrence of *cype-cniht* in Ælfric; (ii) *edisc-uueard* (hapax legomenon) for *broelarius* 'park-keeper' 148, which was perhaps not a profession or occupation in Anglo-Saxon England; (iii) *hrofwyrcta* (literally, 'roofmaker') for *tignarius* ('carpenter, builder' cf. Klump 1908: 120); according to Pheifer (1974: 127) it is, however, modelled on *sarcitector* rather than on *tignarius*. *Ledir-wyrcta* (for *byrseus*), on the other hand, might be native; (iv) *strel-bora* (hap. leg.) 'archer', lit. 'arrowbearer' for *arcister* 114 – if this is a loan rendition, it is, however, modelled on *sagittarius* rather than on *arcister* (cf. Pheifer 1974: 65); (v) *uuicing-sceadan* for *piraticum/piraticam* 736: *uuicing* is a name for persons (see further section 6.6.4.), but whereas Lat *piraticum* (*piraticam*) is originally an adj. (*piraticus* 'pertaining too pirates', the agent noun is *pirata*), in OE *sceaða(n)* there may have been a confusion between the action noun *sceaðe* and the agent noun *sceaða*, with the glossator substituting the more frequent *sceaða* 'enemy, warrior' etc. for the rarer *sceaðe*, *sceaða*, *sceþþu* 'crime'. In all the cases mentioned so far, the Latin lemma is a suffix-formation, whereas its Old English rendering is a compound; (vi) *gitreeude – foederatas* is perhaps also a loan-formation; here, both the Latin and the Old English word are suffix-formations.

(6) Loan creations: To this group belong perhaps: (i) *burg-runae* for *parcas* 761 – *burg-runae* is a hapax legomenon; moreover, the *glossator(s)* apparently experimented and within a few lines used once *uuyrdae* 764 and once *burg-runae* 761 for *parcae*, *parcas*; see also section 4.3.2.; (ii) *byrgeras* for *uispellones* 760 is rare and only occurs in glossaries; (iii) *egisi-grima* 'ghost', lit. prob. 'terror mask' – *larbula*; (iv) *orit-mon* for *dromidarius* is a hapax legomenon (prob. for *eored-mon*) – camel-drivers were certainly not a usual feature in Anglo-Saxon England (but see section

4.3.5.); (v) *scinneras* for *scienicis* (prob. for *sc[ae]nicis*) is rare and occurs in glossaries only. (vi) *uuydu-mer – Echo*.

6. Morphology, especially word-formation

6.1. Theoretical and methodological questions

6.1.1. The area of word-formation

Within morphology, inflexion can be regarded as the creation of different forms of the same word (lexeme), whereas word-formation can be regarded as the creation of new words. This distinction is fairly straightforward in many cases, but there are also areas where word-formation is not so easy to separate from inflexion. We mentioned the sometimes problematic distinction of agent nouns and present participles (see section 3.1.2 and also 6.6.1.); another unclear area is the substantivization of adjectives (see section 6.8.). The latter is often regarded as an inflexional or syntactic phenomenon, but since the word-class changes in the process, it could also be mentioned in the context of word-formation. With other patterns, such as the bahuvrihi nouns and zero-derivation (conversion) it has been disputed whether we have to do with word-formation or with a purely semantic process.

6.1.2. Simplexes, complex words and their distinction

Apart from the distinction between word-formation and inflexion it is, of course, also important to separate complex words (consisting of two or more morphemes), from simplexes (monomorphemic words). The former belong to the field of word-formation, whereas the latter do not.[32] Thus, *burg-leod, teblere* and *ceap-cnext* are clearly complex words, whereas *dweorg, meeg* (*mæg*), *grima, sweor, þegn* etc. are simplexes, at least from an Old English point of view. On the whole, there are relatively few simplexes among the names for persons in *ÉpErf*.

The structure of words can change in the course of time, however. A number of words were originally complex (i.e. in Indo-European or in Germanic or even in very early Old English), but, mainly due to phonetic and phonological processes were later obscured into simplexes. To give a few modern examples: *lord, lady, gospel, sheriff, woman* are simplexes (monomorphemic words) in Modern English, but they were compounds in Old English (*hlāf-weard, hlǣf-dige, gōd-spel, scīr-gerefa, wīf-man*). This is, of course, connected with the question of whether one should attempt a diachronic analysis (in our case reaching back into reconstructed Germanic or even Indo-European forms) or a strictly synchronic analysis (taking only Old English forms into account that are motivated in Old English), and it is also connected with the question of productivity and analysability. Basically, I shall attempt a synchronic classification of the complex words although it is often difficult not to get involved in etymological considerations. I shall also sketch the history of the compounding patterns and the etymology of the prefixes and suffixes. Since there are many borderline cases, a strict division of synchrony and diachrony is not always possible. Thus, there are many formations showing i-mutation in their stem-vowel, such as *byrgea* (ClH *byrga*), *caempa*, *giroefa*, *roedra*, *wyrd* (to take just the examples from *ÉpErf*). These are monomorphemic forms from a strictly synchronic point of view (even at the time of *ÉpErf*), but they were originally formed with a suffix **-i*, *-j* etc.; they form a relatively large and conspicuous group, therefore they are included here and dealt with in section 6.7. See further Kastovsky (1992: 357-61).

6.1.3. A model for describing word-formation

There is no commonly accepted model for describing word-formation processes and complex words which have been created through such processes. Consequently, schemes of classification vary. One of the most elaborate models was developed by Marchand (1969: esp. chapters 1-2). Basically, it still seems useful although it has to be modified and supplemented. Here, I can sketch the model only very briefly, although there are problems of analysis on all levels and, accordingly, all levels have been the subject of extensive discussion.[33]

(1) Morphological shape describes the word-class and the morphological status of the elements: *burg-leod* consists of two nouns; *teblere* consists of a noun (*tebl*) and a suffix (*-ere*). The word-class and the morphological status are not always clear, however.

(2) Morphological structure: Here it is assumed that complex words as a rule consist of two immediate constituents, the determinant (dt) and the determinatum (dm); in other terminologies: the modifier and the head. The determinant (modifier) specifies the determinatum and restricts its range of reference (semantically speaking, the compound is a hyponym of its determinatum); the determinatum (head) dominates grammatically, i.e. it indicates the word-class and the semantic category. Thus, *burg* is the determinant in *burg-leod* and *leod* is the determinatum; in *teblere*, *tebl* is the determinant and the suffix *-ere* is the determinatum, indicating the agent in this case – but there are also cases where the dt and the dm are more difficult to establish. The combination of morphologic shape and

morphologic structure yields the the types and subtypes of word-formation as dealt with here; see sections 6.2ff.

(3) The syntactic paraphrase[34] provides a sentence which contains the elements (constituents) of the complex word and explains their relation: *burg-leod* 'people [leod] who inhabit, live in a town [burg]'; *teblere* 'someone who [-ere] gambles or has to do with gambling [tebl]'. The syntactic paraphrase thus also is a kind of semantic analysis. One problem of the syntactic analysis is that in compounds without a verbal element sometimes different verbs can be inserted (see above: 'inhabit' or 'live in'); another, that for us it is, of course, difficult if not impossible to form correct Old English sentences. If it is not possible to paraphrase a complex word with the help of its elements, then this word is probably idiomatized or lexicalized; see under 5.iv below.

(4) The type of reference forms a bridge between morphological structure and syntactic paraphrase; it states which part of the sentence (subject, object, adverbial, verb or rather the verbal action indicated by the verb) has been topicalized and becomes or corresponds to the determinatum of the complex word. Thus, both *burgleod* and *teblere* are subject-types ('people live in a town'; 'someone is connected with gambling'); *ceap-cnext* is an object-type ('someone has bought the slave' or 'someone has acquired the slave through buying', see section 6.2.2.(4)). As these examples show, in order to allow comparison, the type of reference must be established from a full, declarative sentence in the active voice, which is still open as to the types of reference – a relative clause (as given in section 3) or a passive clause has already been topicalized and the type of reference has been fixed.

(5) Semantic structure (meaning): This is probably the most complex level and thus also most difficult to describe in a systematic and satisfactory way. In the case of complex words, at least a threefold distinction can be made, that is between reference, sense (meaning) and the internal relation of the constituents. In addition to this, the question of idiomatization and lexicalization comes into play. (i) Reference: Most of the words discussed here refer to persons/people (often to quite specific kinds of people); (ii) Sense: One distinction is according to broad semantic categories such as agent nouns, experiencer nouns and patient (passive) nouns. Thus, *teblere* is an agent noun, because it implies an activity; *burg-leod* is an experiencer noun, because living somewhere is not really an activity; *ceap-cnext* is a patient noun, because its meaning is 'slave or servant who has been bought'; see further section 7.1. Another distinction is between several semantic fields (word-fields), such as names of relation, occupational names etc.; see section 3.2.; (iii) Internal structure: Complex words are

morphologically motivated, i.e. dt (A) and dm (B) stand in a relation to each other; most generally this can be described as 'B has something to do with A', or 'B is somehow connected with A'. The precise connection must then be specified. This can be done with the help of a syntactic paraphrase of the kind mentioned above under (3) and (4); it can also be done by assigning semantic roles to the constituents, e.g. *burg-leod* [PLACE/INHABITANT]; *teblere* [ACTIVITY/AGENT]; *ceap-cnext* [ACTIVITY/ PATIENT];[35] (iv) Idiomatization and lexicalization: What has been said so far refers to complex words with regular semantic structures, which can be paraphrased with the help of their elements relatively easily or can be assigned semantic roles. If a paraphrase with the help of the elements is unsatisfactory or impossible, then the complex word is probably idiomatized or lexicalized. In cases of idiomatization or lexicalization the meaning of the entire word is different from the sum of the meanings of its constituents; often semantic features have been added, or sometimes also lost. Thus, *iringaes uueg* refers to the Milky Way, which is not apparent from *iring* plus *way*. If a distinction between idiomatization and lexicalization is made, then lexicalization refers to a later, diachronic change of meaning (and sometimes also of form), whereas idiomatization refers to a synchronic process, to complex words which had semantic peculiarities from the moment of being coined. Sometimes the distinction is difficult to make. *Iringaes uueg*, however, seems to be a clear case of idiomatization: probably, it did not have an earlier meaning, but was coined with the meaning 'Milky Way'.

6.1.4. Recursivity of word-formation processes

Word-formation can be recursive, that is a word can undergo a sequence of several word-formational processes (occasionally, processes also seem to work simultaneously). To give a Modern English example, *friend* (noun) can be suffixed to yield *friendly* (adj.); this can be prefixed to yield *unfriendly* (adj.), this can be suffixed again to yield *unfriendliness* (noun). Words which have undergone two (or more) processes are accordingly listed twice (or several times). Thus, for example, *bisuicend* is discussed under the prefix *be-*, *bi-* and under the suffix *-end*; *iringaes uueg* is discussed under the noun + *s* + noun compounds and under the suffix *-ing*.

6.1.5. The structure of the entries

With compounding types, the following information is given: (a) definition; (b) attestation in *ÉpErf*; (c) problems, e.g. distinction from other types; (d) history (prehistory and later development) and productivity; (e) syntactic-semantic subclassification; (f) literature. Similarly, with prefixes and suffixes, the following information is given: (a) form, i.e. first the 'normal' Old English form (i.e. form in Late West Saxon), then the form in *ÉpErf*, followed by the PDE form (if the prefix or suffix survives) and the basic meaning; (b) attestation in *ÉpErf*; (c) problems, e.g. distinction from other affixes, question of affix family; (d) history (etymology and later development) and productivity; (e) gender and inflexional class; (f) function, derivation, meaning(s) and semantic subgroups; (g) literature.

6.2. Compounds (compound nouns)

6.2.1. The range of compounds

Compounds are sometimes difficult to distinguish from syntactic groups on the one hand and from affix (prefix and suffix) formations on the other, but we need not discuss this question here (cf., e.g., Sauer (1992: 57-124, 221-41, 298-309).

6.2.2. The types of compounds

Among the compound nouns, several subtypes can be distinguished. The following are certainly or possibly attested among the names for people in *ÉpErf*: noun + noun; noun in the genitive + noun; numeral + noun; verb + noun; noun + deverbal (agent) noun without a suffix; noun + deverbal (agent) noun with suffix *-t*. Others are missing, such adjective + noun, but this is probably due to the limited scope of the material in *ÉpErf*. The productivity of these types varies: Noun + noun is the strongest type in *ÉpErf* (see further below). Noun + deverbal agent noun is also well attested, whereas the others are rare in *ÉpErf* and generally rarer than noun + noun.
Literature: See, e.g., Kastovsky (1992: 362-76); Sauer (1992: 125-48).

(1) **Noun + noun**:

(a) In noun + noun compounds, both elements are primary nouns, i.e. there is no verbal element on the surface; compounds where one element is deverbal are here assigned to other types, see especially (4)-(6) below.

(b) About nine noun + noun compounds are attested among the names for people in *ÉpErf*: *burg-leod*, *burg-runae*, *edisc-ueard*, *egisi-grima*, *fostor-bearn*, *hors-thegn*, *orit-mon* (for *eored-mon*), *uuicing-sceada*(*n*), *uudyumer*.

(c) Of course, it is not always easy to be certain whether an element should be labelled as primary or as deverbal. (i) For a discussion of *ceap-cnext*, see (4) below; (ii) Kastovsky (1968: 235-8) apparently regards *weardian* as primary and *weard* as derived (deverbal), but here *weard* is regarded as primary and *weardian* as derived, following the rule of thumb that strong verbs are primary and related nouns are derived, whereas weak verbs are secondary and in their turn derived from nouns, adjectives or other verbs; (iii) Moreover, sometimes a noun is originally deverbal but functions as primary in the compound, e.g. *sceada* (*sceaða*)'criminal, robber etc.' (or *sceadu* etc. 'crime, robbery', see section 5.6.3. (5)) is derived from the verb *scieððan*, *sceaððan* (strong VI),[36] but *uuicing-sceada* 'pirate' is a copula compound meaning something like 'the criminal is a viking';[37] (iv) *Haegtis* is re-garded as an obscured compound by some, but it is here classified as a suffix formation, see section 6.6 (3); (v) *-runae* (< **rūno*) 'the woman who knows/tells secrets', connected with *rūn* 'mystery, secret etc.', apparently is not attested independently (but cf. *gerūna*).

(d) The type noun + noun is an old composition type, going back to Indo-European.[38] The earliest formation in our corpus goes back to Germanic, namely *burg-leod.*[39] The others are apparently Old English formations. Throughout the history of English, noun + noun has apparently always been the most productive composition type.[40]

(e) Noun + noun has many syntactic-semantic subgroups. As far as the sense is concerned: Among the names for people there are three subgroups (from the point of view of semantic roles): agent nouns (e.g. *hors-thegn*), experiencer nouns (e.g. *burg-leod*), and patient (passive) nouns (e.g. *fostur-bearn*); see further section 7.1. As far as the relation of the elements is concerned: A basic distinction is between copula compounds (where a form of 'to be' has to be supplied) and rectional compounds (where another verb has to be supplied). The only possible copula compound is *uuicing-sceada(n)*, if *sceada* is regarded as an agent noun: 'a viking is a criminal'.[41] The others are rectional compounds. Syntactically, both the agent and experiencer nouns are subject-types, e.g. *hors-thegn* 'B looks after A', *burg-leod* 'B inhabits A' (subject – object in the paraphrase sentence; object – subject in the compound), whereas the patient nouns are object types, e.g. *fostur-bearn* 'someone gives A (food, maintenance

[fostor]) to B (bearn)' (i.e. subject – direct object – indirect object in the paraphrase sentence; direct object – indirect object in the compound).
(f) Literature: Marchand (1969: 45-53 and 60-3); Koziol (1972: 48-58 = §§ 69-97); Kastovsky (1992: 365-9); Sauer (1992: 148-51 and 389-420).

(2) **Noun in the genitive + noun** (genitival compounds):
(a) Both elements are also primary nouns, but the first noun is in the genitive.
(b) There is just one example of a noun in the genitive + noun compound among the names for persons in *ÉpErf*, i.e. *iringaes uueg*, lit. 'Iring's way', i.e. 'the Milky Way' (which contains a personal name as first element, but does not refer to a person as a whole; for *iring*, see section 6.6.4.).
(c) Genitival compounds are not always easy to distinguish from syntactic genitive groups; see, e.g., the discusssion in Sauer (1992: 152-5). Basically, a syntactic genitival group has a very specific (specifying) reference, e.g. PDE *my father's car* is only my father's car if my father actually owns it, whereas a genitival compound has a more general (classifying) reference, e.g. PDE *the driver's seat* refers to the seat behind the steering wheel where the driver habitually sits, even if this seat is empty at the moment, or if it is occupied, e.g., by a child that cannot drive.
(d) Genitival compounds are apparently a relatively young type; sometimes they are also called "secondary compounds", see Carr (1939: 309ff.). Perhaps originally they coalesced from the corresponding syntactic genitival groups (in German, they are therefore sometimes called 'Zusammenrückungen'). At least, the names of the days of the week, however (e.g. *Tuesday*, *Wednesday*, *Thursday*), go back to West-Germanic, and they are usually regarded as loan-translations from Latin. *Iringaes uueg* may even be Germanic, because *Irings vegr* is also attested in Old Norse. Genitival compounds have always been of limited productivity in the history of English.
(e) Literally, *iringaes uueg* can probably be explained as 'This way has been named after Iring' (perhaps more specifically because according to legend he was the first to walk on it [metaphorically]). This compound is certainly idiomatized, because it refers to the 'Milky Way'.[42]
(f) Literature: Carr (1939: 309-18); Marchand (1969: 65-9); Koziol (1972: 60-2 = §§101-3); Kastovsky (1992: 369-70); Sauer (1992: 152-63).

(3) **Numeral + noun**:
(a) The first element is a numeral, the second a noun.
(b) There is just one example, *sifunsterri*, which is not a personal name, but glosses (translates) a Latin name (*pliadas* < Gk *pleiades*) in *ÉpErf*.

(c) *Sifunsterri* is actually quite complex because it also has the suffix *-i* (< *-ja*) which indicates collectivity (cf. G *Berg* – *Gebirge*; *Schwester* – *Geschwister*; *Stern* – *Gestirn(e)*); the normal OE form is *steorra*. *Sifunsterri* thus belongs to a type which combines compounding with suffixation. Whereas compounds with a numeral as a first element are here set up as a separate type, they are sometimes subsumed among other types in the literature, e.g. among adjective + noun compounds; formations such as OE *seofonleaf* rather belong to the bahuvrihi compounds (cf. Carr 1939: 164-70; Sauer 1992: 241-6).
(d) The type has apparently always been rare.
(e) Syntactically-semantically, *sifun-sterri* could be analysed as a copula compound, 'the(se) stars are seven'.
(f) Literature: Kluge (1926: 35 = § 66); Marchand (1969: --); Koziol (1972: 63f. = § 108); Kastovsky (1992: --); Sauer (1992: 171-4, 241-6).

(4) **Verb + noun** (verbal stem + noun):
(a) The first element is a verb or, in Old English (as well as in Modern German), rather the stem of a verb; the second element is a noun.
(b) There is also just one possible example, namely *ceap-cnext* 'bought servant or slave' (349).
(c) It is sometimes difficult to decide whether a given compound should be analysed as noun + noun or as verb + noun. This is also true of *ceap-cnext*, which could be analysed as noun *cēap* (a loan-word from Lat *caupo*, cf. G *Kauf*) + noun *cnext* 'servant [cnext] who has been acquired by bargain [ceap]', or as *cēap-*, stem of *cēapian*, (weak 2; in its turn derived from *cēap* noun), + noun cnext 'servant [cnext] who has been bought [ceap-]'. The fact that the verb was derived from the noun suggests that *ceap-* in *ceap-cnext* should perhaps rather be analysed as a noun; on the other hand, the more natural syntactic paraphrase (at least in Modern English) would be 'a slave who has been bought' rather than 'a slave who has been acquired by trading, purchase'. The formation is here listed as an example of the verb + noun compounds mainly to show that this type existed in Old English.
(d) This type was perhaps developed in West Germanic. It arose from formations where the first element "was a deverbal noun which was formally identical with the verb stem" (Kastovsky 1992: 370f.); the deverbal noun could then be interpreted as the verb stem. The type has been moderately productive from Old English to Modern English.
(e) Semantically, *ceap-cnext* represents a patient noun, and syntactically, an object type, 'servant, slave [cnext] who has been bought' < 'Someone has bought the slave'.

(f) Literature: Carr (1939: 175-96); Marchand (1969: 72-4); Koziol (1972: 65f. = § 113); Kastovsky (1992: 370-1); Sauer (1992: 185-94).

(5) **Noun + deverbal noun with suffix *-t*:**
(a) The first element (dt) is a noun, the second (dm) is a deverbal noun with the suffix *-t*.
(b) The element *-wyrhta* (see Klump 1908: 42-9), which contains the suffix *-t*, is attested as second element in two compounds in *ÉpErf*, namely *hrof-uuyrcta* 996 (for Lat *tignarius*) and *ledir-uuyrcta* 155 (for Lat < Gk *byrseus*) – both occur in glossaries only, see Klump (1908: 64 & 119-20).
(c) Compounds with a second element (dm) containing the suffix *-t* are here set up as a separate type of compounds. *-wyrcta*/*-wyrhta* is derived from the present stem of the weak verb (class 1) ***wyrcan*** – *worhte* – *geworht* (see also under section d); *wyrhta* was also commonly used as an independent noun.
(d) In the suffix *-t*, several Gmc suffixes fell together, e.g. *-ti*, *-tjo*. *Wyrhta* is a Gmc formation (< **wurh-tjo* < weak verb 1 **wurk-jan* or immediately from the stem Gmc **wurk-* < **werk-am*, > OE *weorc* > PDE *work*). Some compounds of the type noun + deverbal noun with suffix *-t* also seem to go back to Germanic, e.g. *neawist* (cf. Carr 1939: 58, no. 4), or to WGmc, e.g. *man-sli(e)ht* (cf. Carr 1939: 101, no. 70). *Hrof-uuyrcta* and *ledir-uuyrcta* are OE formations. The suffix *-t* lost its productivity in Middle English.
(e) The suffix *-t* derived deverbal nouns.
(f) The suffix *-t* derived mainly names of things, e.g. *ǣht* 'property', *gift* 'GIFT' – *wyrhta* is thus a bit unusual in being a name for persons and an agent noun 'B works [i.e. makes] A (e.g. a roof, leather)'; in both compounds (*hrof-uuyrcta*, *ledir-uuyrcta*) the object is an effected object.
(g) Literature: Klump (1908: esp. on *-wyrhta*); Kluge (1926: 66 f. = § 127 f.); Marchand (1969: --)[43]; Koziol (1972: 207f. = § 485f.); Kastovsky (1992: 358-60 & 384); Sauer (1992: 207-10).

(6) **Noun + deverbal (agent) noun (without a suffix)** = noun + verb$_{\varnothing\ \mathrm{noun}}$
(a) The first element is a noun, the second is a deverbal agent noun without a suffix. The word class of the second element changes from verb to noun.
(b) There are c. four compounds referring to persons the second element of which is clearly deverbal: in three, the second element is *-bora*, in one, *-laecea*: *mund-bora*, *red-bora*, *strel-bora*; *scinn-laecea(n)*.
(c) Although the handbooks do not always clearly separate noun + deverbal noun compounds from noun + noun compounds (often subsuming the former among the latter), both should be kept apart. The deverbal agent nouns can be derived from strong and from weak verbs: *-bora* is derived

from the past participle stem of *beran* (strong IV; OE *beran – bœr – bǣron – (ge)**boren***).[44] The basis of *laecea-* is doubtful. Possible candidates are *lǣcan* 'spring up', *gelǣcan* 'emulate, join with' (or even the noun *gelǣca* 'rival'), but all of these words were rare; moreover, the semantic connection with *laecea* is unclear. As the form *-bora* shows, derivation from strong verbs was not always made from the present stem, but often from one of the past stems or the past participle stem. Derivation from a "low ablaut grade" even seems to have been the original pattern (Carr 1939: 216), which also suggests that derivation from strong verbs was older than derivation from weak verbs. The deverbal noun is often also used as an independent word, but it does not have to be; *-bora* and *-(ge)laeca* almost always occur as second elements of compounds. But even elements such as *-bora* and *(ge)laeca* should not be regarded as suffixes, but rather as potential words, derived from another word (cf. Kastovsky 1992: 365).

(d) The composition type noun + deverbal agent noun is an old pattern and goes back at least to Germanic (see Carr 1939: 216). *Mundbora* 'guardian' is a West-Germanic formation (Carr 1939: 102, no. 77), the others seem to be Old English. As the examples show, the type was fairly productive in early Old English; later, its productivity diminished. Many of the Old English formations died out in Middle English, but there were also some new formations; Sauer (1992: 202-5), still has more than 40 noun + deverbal agent nouns attested in Early Middle English. Competing types were formations in *-end* and *-ere*, see section 6.6.

(e) The deverbal noun normally is a weak (consonantal) masculine (n-stem; cf., e.g., Campbell 1959: 249 = § 618). All of these formations are agent nouns; a rough general paraphrase would be 'B performs the action indicated by the underlying verb on A', e.g. 'B bears [i.e. gives] rǣd [counsil]'; 'B bears [i.e. carries] stræl [an arrow]' (idiomatized or lexicalized for 'archer'). Syntactically they are subject types, i.e. the second element (dm) corresponds to the subject of the sentence. The first element corresponds to the object; in *strel-bora* it is an affected object. In *mund-bora* and *red-bora*, literally and syntactically the object is an affected object ('B bears, i.e. carries protection, advice'), but semantically the object is an effected object ('B gives protection, advice'). Whereas in *-bora* the original meaning of the verb can still be seen ('someone who bears = carries something'), the connection of *-laecean* with *lǣcan* 'to spring up, rise, flare up' or *gelǣcan* 'to emulate' is more difficult to establish, see above. Possibly *scinn-laecea* was formed in Old English in analogy to the noun OE *scīn-lac* 'magic', a West-Germanic formation (Carr 1939: 107, no. 23; cf. also Sauer 1992: 235-7).

(f) Literature: Kärre (1915: --); Carr (1939: 5f. & 216-9); Koo (1946: 16-8); Marchand (1969: 79-80); Koziol (1972: 58f. = § 98); Kastovsky (1992: 365 & 367-9); Sauer (1992: 198-207).

6.3. Combinations with locative particles

6.3.1. General remarks

The first element is a locative particle; the second element is a noun. Locative particles can be used as prepositions (e.g. OE *ymbe*) or adverbs (e.g. OE *ūt* > PDE *out*) or both (e.g. OE *ofer* > PDE *over*). They are sometimes also used in transferred meanings, e.g. temporal; *over* and *under* are often used in the meaning 'too much, more than should be', resp. 'too little, less than should be'; this is a meaning which they do not have in independent use. In the literature on word-formation, locative particles are often silently subsumed under the prefixes (e.g. by Koziol 1972: 89-127), but since particles also occur as independent words, combinations with them should be kept separate and classified as compounds. Nevertheless there seems to be a widespread feeling that locative particles are more like prefixes than like words.[45] Perhaps this has to do with the fact that they are function words belonging to the closed word-classes, and not content-words belonging to the open word-classes (cf. Sauer 2000: 112 & 132).
Literature: Carr (1939: --); Marchand (1969: 108-21); Koziol (1972: 89-127); Kastovsky (1992: --); Sauer (1992: 176-85).

6.3.2. The particles

There is only one example in our material.
(1) ***ymb(e)-***
(a) *ymb(e)* occurs independently as a preposition and as an adverb meaning 'around, about' (cf. G *um*); in compounds, the *-e* is often omitted.
(b) *ymbhringendum* (Ép 929) or *ymbdringendum* (Erf 929), lit. 'surrounders', for Lat *stipatoribus* 'attendants'; (possibly a loan translation, see section 5.6.3.4.).
(c) The Ép form *ymbhringend(um)* and the Erf form *ymbdringend(um)* probably represent different verbs, *ymbhringan* and *ymbdringan* – not quite consistently, ClH lists the verbs and the agent noun *ymbhringend* as separate words, but the agent noun *ymbdringend* only as a variant of *ymb-hringend*. The forms *ymbhringend(um)* and *ymbdringend(um)* are here

regarded as agent nouns formed from the verbs (theoretically, they could also be present participles), see section 3.1.(2).

(d) *Ymb(e)* developed from Gmc **umbi-* (cf. G *um*). Combinations with *ymbe-* were quite frequent in Old English; judging from ClH, there were c. 130 different formations. There were far fewer even in Early Middle English.[46] In the course of Middle English, *ymb(e)* changed into *umb(e)*, *emb(e)*, but then it died out as well as all the combinations formed with it. It survives in German as *um-* (*um das Haus herum*, *umgeben*, *umringen* etc.).

(e) *Ymb(e)-* has the meaning 'around'. It is combined with verbs.

(f) Literature: *MED* s.v. 'umbe', adj, adv, prep, pref; *OED* s.v. 'umbe-'; Marchand (1969: --); Koziol (1972: 126f. = § 289); Kastovsky (1992: --); Sauer (1992: 182).

6.4. Prefix- and suffix-formations (affix formations)

6.4.1. General considerations

(1) Definition: Affixes, i.e. prefixes and suffixes are defined as bound morphemes, as elements that do not occur independently. Prefixes are attached in front of a word; suffixes are attached at the end of a word.

(2) Distinction from words: The distinction between words and affixes (prefixes and suffixes) is not always clearcut, especially since a number of prefixes and suffixes developed from words.[47] As stated above, locative particles are here not regarded as prefixes, nor are deverbal agent nouns such as *-bora*, *-wyrhta* regarded as suffixes (even if they rarely occur independently); members of both groups are regarded as words (or at least as potential words).

(3) Variation, its reasons and its classification: Some prefixes and suffixes occur in a number of spellings in Old English as well as in Middle English (e.g. *be-* and *bi-*; *for-* and *fer-* etc.). There can be several reasons for such variation, in particular: (i) There was no standardized spelling in Old English yet (nor in Middle English); (ii) There were stressed and unstressed variants; see, e.g. Campbell (1959: 30-5 = §§ 71-92), and the remarks on *be-*, *bi-* below; (iii) The prefixes and suffixes in question go back to Germanic or even Indo-European prefixes or suffixes which occurred in variant forms (see, e.g., below on *for-*, *fer-*). The question arises whether such variant forms should be regarded as variants (spelling variants, pronunciation variants, allomorphs) of the same prefix or suffix or as different prefixes or suffixes. This question has to be considered for each

group of variants separately. Sometimes it is useful to regard such a group as a prefix- or suffix-family (following Kastovsky 1992: 384).

6.4.2. Prefixes

(1) ***be-. bi-***

(a) *ÉpErf* still has the earlier form *bi-*, see (d) below; in later Old English as well as in Modern English (and in Modern German), the usual form is *be-* (PDE *be-* /bɪ/). The meaning is basically 'by, around, about, near etc.'.

(b) The only form attested in *ÉpErf* (among the names for persons) is *bisuicend* 'deceiver, impostor' for Lat *inpostor(em)* (545), the agent noun formed from the verb (strong I) *bisuican* (*beswican*) 'deceive'.

(c) The prefix *bi-* is related to the particle (preposition, adverb) *be* (> PDE *by*; cf. G *bei*), but is nevertheless treated as a prefix here, because it often has a different meaning, and partly also a different form. On the question of stress, see the following section.

(d) *bi-* comes from the Germanic prefix **bi-*, which is the unstressed form of the particle Gmc **bi*, the latter in its turn was often lengthened: OE *bi* > PDE *by* /baɪ/, OHG *bi* > G *bei*. In Old English, however, unstressed (*be-*) and stressed (*bi-*) forms of the prefix apparently also co-existed. According to Campbell (1959: § 73), the stressed (and lengthened) form was used with nouns, the unstressed with verbs. Since in *ÉpErf bi-* precedes a noun derived from a verb, however, it seems more likely to me that the *bi-* in *ÉpErf* simply represents the older form. The unstressed form of the prefix *bi-* was weakened/lowered to *be-* in the course of Old English (and also in the course of German: *be-*, e.g. *betrügen*), but raised again in PDE *be-* /bɪ/. *Be-* was productive in Old English (see ClH). *Beswican* is an Old English formation, which, however, died out later. *Be-* still exists in Modern English.

(e) --

(f) *be-* is basically a verbal prefix, which then also occurs in nouns and adjectives derived from verbs with *be-*. *Be-* has basically the meaning 'by, around, about, near etc.', but since in *bisuican* the basic verb *swican* also means (among other things) 'abandon, deceive', the *bi-* (*be-*) in *bisuican* (*beswican*) probably just has an intensifying meaning 'to deceive (thoroughly)'. According to ClH (s.v. 'be-'), one of the functions of *be-* is to make intransitive verbs transitive (including *beswican*), but since the simplex *swīcan* could also be used transitively, this function does not seem to apply here.

(g) Literature: *EWDS*, s.v. 'be-, bei'; *ODEE*, s.v. 'be-, by'; Lenze (1909); Campbell (1959: 31 =§ 73 f.); Marchand (1969: 146-8); Koziol (1972: 95-7 = §§209-16); Kastovsky (1992: 379).

(2) ***for-*, (*fer-*)**

(a) The normal Old English form is *for-* (which is still the Modern English form: *for-* /fɔ:/, /fə/), but *ÉpErf* also has the variant form *fer-* (cf. G *ver-*), cf. (d) below.

(b) The only form attested among the names of persons in *ÉpErf* is *ferhergaend* 'ravager' for Lat *grassator* (467), the agent noun formed from the weak verb 2 *forhergian* (*ferhergian*) 'to ravage, plunder, destroy'.

(c) The prefix *for-*, (*fer-*) is different from the particle *fore-*, which is also often used in word-formation.

(d) The prefix OE *for-*, *fer-* can ultimately be traced back to IE **pro-*, **per-* (cf., e.g., Lat *por-*, *pro*, *per*), i.e. there have always been variant forms, which can be regarded as members of a prefix family. The corresponding German prefix is *ver-* (as in *verbieten*, *verlassen* etc.). *For-* was productive in Old English (see ClH) and formations with *for-* still exist in PDE (*forbid*), but *for-* does not seem to be productive any longer. *Ferhergian* is possibly a West-Germanic formation, cf. G *verheeren* (OHG *firherion*).

(e) *For-*, *fer-* was mainly a verbal prefix, but it was also used with adjectives and adverbs and, of course, it occurs in nouns derived from verbs with *for-* (as in *ferhergaend*).

(f) *For-*, *fer-* had several meanings; in *ferhergian*, there is the sense of 'destruction', but since the underlying verb *hergian* (OHG *herion*) had the same meaning ('ravage, plunder', originally 'to ravage, destroy with an army [here]'), the function may be intensifying.

(g) Literature: *EWDS*, s.v. 'ver-'; *ODEE*, s.v. 'for-1'; Marchand (1969: --) (Marchand deals only with *fore-*); Koziol (1972: 99f. = §§ 221-2); Kastovsky (1992: 379-80).

(3) ***ge-*, *gi-*** (and **ge-* + *-ja*)

(a) The usual Old English form was *ge-*, but *ÉpErf* uses mainly *gi-* (Ép has *ge-* just once, 214; Erf has *ge-* slightly more frequently). The prefix no longer exists in English.

(b) Six formations with *ge-*, *gi-* are attested among the names for persons in *ÉpErf*: *gibuur* 'farmer' for Lat *colonus* (163); *gidopta* (*gidogta*) 'comrade' for Lat *contubernalis* (189); *gimodae* 'of one mind' for Lat *coniurati* (201); *giroefa(n)/geroefa(n)* 'high officials, REEVES' for Lat *censores* and *commentariensis*; *gisuirgion* 'cousin (nephew, sister's son)' for Lat *consubrinus*; *gitreeudae* 'federates' for Lat *foederatas*.

(c) For problematic aspects, see section (f) below.

(d) *ge-*, *gi-* goes back to a Germanic prefix **ga-*. It was very productive in Old English; but in Middle English, it was weakened to *y-*, *i-* and died out in Late Middle English / Early Modern English, leaving few traces (see, e.g. *ODEE*, s.v. 'y-'), which suggests that it had lost all its original functions in English. It lives on in German as *ge-* (*Gebirge*, *Gebrüder*, *Geschwister* etc.) and was grammaticalized for the past participle (*gearbeitet*, *gegangen*).

(e) --

(f) *ge-*, *gi-* had two main functions: a) It was a verbal prefix expressing perfectivity and was accordingly frequently used for the past participle (but often also for the present forms); b) it was a nominal prefix expressing collectivity. Here we are concerned with the nominal prefix which expresses collectivity and associativity. All the formations listed above under (b) have this meaning, at least originally. (i) *gibuur* (which is preserved in PDE *neighbour*, cf. G *Nachbar*; the basic word lives on in PDE *bower*) is a West-Germanic formation **gi-bur* or **ga-bura* (cf. G *Bauer*), originally meaning 'the fellow occupier of a dwelling' (*ODEE*). Whether it was still transparent in Old English is another question. The other formations are morphologically a bit more complex; (ii) *giroefa(n)* (ClH *(ge)refa*) and *gisuirgion* (ClH *geswigra*) show a combination of the prefix *ge-* and an original suffix *-ja*, which caused i-umlaut before disappearing (cf. Kluge 1926: 35 = § 66 *ga-* – *-ja*): *giroefa* (< **gi-rōf-ja*) is doubly lexicalized: a) because the underlying noun *rōf* 'number, enumeration' is no longer attested independently in Old English (but cf. *secg-rof*, *stæf-rof* and OHG *ruova*, *ruoba*), and b) because its meaning 'high official' is no longer connected with the meaning 'number'; (iii) *Gisuirgion* is derived (with metathesis) from *sweger* 'mother-in-law' (Gmc **swegro* < IE **swekru*, cf. Lat *socer*, *socrus*; G arch. *Schwieger*, later expanded to *Schwiegermutter* (and *Schwiegervater*)), which in its turn is related to OE *sweor* (< Gmc **swehura-* < IE **swekuro*; G arch. *Schwäher*); (iv) *Gimodae* seems to be a bahuvrihi-adjective, i.e. a noun used as an adjective (in this case as nom. pl. m. of the strong adjective declension): *gi-* + *mod* 'having one mind, being of one mind'; (v) *gitreeudae* was probably derived from the past part. of the weak verb *treow(i)an* 'to trust in, confederate with', or it could be an extended bahuvrihi-adjective formed from the noun *treow* 'truth, promise, treaty'; (vi) *gidogta* (Erf) seems to be the more original form than *gidopta* (Ép); *gidogta* (nom. sg. m. of the weak adjectival declension) could be derived from the adj. *dohtig* 'valiant', which in its turn goes back to the pret. pres. verb (II) OE *dugan, dēag, dugon, **dohte*** (cf. G *taugen* and the adj. *tüchtig*).

(g) Literature: *EWDS*, s.v. 'ge-'; *ODEE*, s.v. 'y-'; Kluge (1926: 35 = § 66, *ga- – -ja*); Marchand (1969: --) ; Koziol (1972: 102-4 = § 227); Kastovsky (1992: 380).

(4) ***steop-, steup-***

(a) The usual Old English form was *steop-*, but Ép has the earlier form *steup-* and Erf has *staup-*; the PDE form is *step-* as in *stepfather* (G *Stief-* as in *Stiefvater*).

(b) Attested in *ÉpErf* is *steup-faedaer* 'STEPFATHER' for Lat *uitricius* 1070.

(c) Status of *steop-*: The status of *steop-* has been disputed. For example, the *ODEE* s.v. 'step-' calls it an element prefixed to terms of relationship, the *EWDS* s.v. 'Stief-' calls it a prefixoid (Präfixoid), whereas Carr (1939: 52) lists combinations with *step-* among the compounds. In my opinion, for Old English (as well as for PDE), *step-* should be labelled as a prefix because it does not occur independently in Old English. The related verb OE *astiepan, astypan* etc. 'to deprive, bereave', which is adduced by the proponents of the word-status of *steop-* was apparently derived from *steop-* before the latter died out in independent use; in any case *astiepan* does not prove the word-status of *steop-* in Old English.

(d) *steop-* is apparently a Germanic prefix (Gmc **steup-*; not attested in Gothic); it is attested, for example, in German (G *Stief-* < OHG *stiof-*) and Old Norse (*stjup-*); to judge from OE *steop-*, Ép *steup-* has preserved the original Germanic form. Many combinations (including *stepfather*) are also Germanic, see Carr (1939: 52). The prefix lives on as *step-* in PDE (and as *Stief-* in G), but, due to its function and meaning, is of limited productivity. OE forms are *steop-bearn* and *steop-cild* 'step-child' (also 'orphan'), *steop-fæder* 'stepfather', *steop-moder* 'stepmother', *steop-sunu* 'stepson' and *steop-dohtor* 'stepdaughter'. Late Middle English formations are *step-brother*, *stepsister* and *stepdame*.

(e) *steop-* is prefixed to nouns, more precisely to nouns of relationship.

(f) *steop-* has a clearly defined meaning, which is, however, not easy to paraphrase: according to the *ODEE*, s.v. 'step-', it "designate[s] a degree of affinity resulting from the remarriage of a widowed parent", i.e. the relation is no blood-relation, but acquired through remarriage of a parent. Marchand (1969: 193) explains stepfather as 'father to a bereaved child' (perhaps this should be rather 'someone who acts like a father to a bereaved child').

(g) Literature: *EWDS*, s.v. 'Stief-'; *ODEE* s.v. 'step-'; Carr (1939: 52, nos. 62-5); Marchand (1969: 193); Koziol (1972: 114 = § 252); Kastovsky (1992: --).

6.5. Suffixes

(1) ***-end***

(a) The usual Old English form of this suffix, which formed agent nouns, was *-end*; this is also the normal form in *ÉpErf*. Ép once has *-aend* (*ferhergaend*, 467). The suffix no longer exists in English.

(b) About nine agent nouns with the suffix *-end* are attested in *ÉpErf*:[48] (i) *baedend(rae)* 'inciter, one who urges' from *bǣdan* for Lat *inpulsore* 539; (ii) *bisuicend* 'deceiver' from *beswican* for Lat *inpostor(em)* 545 (on *be-*, see above); (iii) *ferhergaend* 'ravager' from *forhergian* for Lat *grassator* 467 (on *for-*, see above); (iv) *fultemend* (2x) 'helper' from *fultumian* for Lat *adstipulatus* and Lat *adsessor(e)* 95; (v) *haetend(ae)* 'those who heat' from *hǣtan* for Lat *calentes* 206; (vi) *scyhend* 'seducer, pimp' from *scȳan* 'to persuade, incite, tempt' for Lat (< Gk) *maulistis*; (vii) *tyhtend* from *tyhtan* 'invite, incite etc.' for Lat *inlex* 509; (viii) *uuoedend(i)* (= *wēdend*) from *wēdan* 'to rave, be mad' for Lat *lymphatico* (*wēdan* in its turn is derived from *wōd*, cf. *wōda* 383 for *ephilenticus*, probably an error for *epilepticus*); (ix) *ymb-hringend(um)* 'surrounder(s)' from *ymbhringan* (with the variant *ymbdringendum* from *ymbðringan*) for Lat *stipator(ibus)* 929.

(c) As stated above (cf. 3.1.2.), agent nouns with the suffix *-end* and present participles with the ending *-ende* are not always easy to separate. Here, I have included among the agent nouns mainly those forms which translate a Latin agent noun in *-or*, *-(a)tor*.[49] Although there were also compounds with the deverbal agent nouns in *-end* as second element, *ÉpErf* has only uncompounded forms.

(d) The suffix *-end(e)*, used for the present participle of verbs and then also for agent nouns, goes back to Germanic (and ultimately to Indo-European); as the examples show, it was quite productive in Old English (it is preserved in German as *-end* for the present participle, e.g. *gehend*, *stehend*, and – no longer productive – as *-and* for the agent noun, e.g. *Heiland* or names such as *Weigand*). All the forms listed under (b) above seem to be Old English formations, and all of them may be loan-translations (see section 5.6.3.4). In connection with the loss of the present participle ending *-end(e)* and its substitution by *-ing* in the course of Middle English, however, the agent noun-suffix *-end* also died out and with it also most of the words formed with it (with the exception of *fiend*, *friend*, which were no longer transparent). As Koziol (1972: 188) points out, *-ing* could not be used as a suffix for agent nouns because it was (and still is) used for action nouns. *-end* was replaced by other agent noun suffixes, in particular by *-er(e)*.

(e) *-end* formed agent nouns from verbs. Whereas the present participle in *-ende* was mainly inflected according to the adjectival declension, agent nouns in *-end* were mainly inflected according to the Gmc a-stems (strong masculines), but there was some overlap in inflexion.

(f) *-end* had a competitor in *-er(e)*, which eventually supplanted it; on *-er(e)*, see below. *-end(e)* apparently always derived present participles and agent nouns from verbs, whereas *-ere* apparently initially derived nouns from nouns, but then increasingly also derived nouns from verbs; this may have been an additional reason why *-er(e)* ousted *-end(e)*.

(g) Literature: Kärre (1915: 77-233); Kluge (1926: --); Koo (1946: 44-63); Marchand (1969: --); Koziol (1972: 188 = § 446); Pheifer (1974: lxxvii = § 65.1); Kastovsky (1992: 385).

(2) ***-ere***

(a) The usual Old English form of this suffix, which forms agent nouns, was *-ere*; this is also the usual form in *ÉpErf*. Ép once has the older form *-eri* (*egderi* 396). The suffix lives on as PDE *-er* and is still very productive.

(b) Five derivations in *-ere* are attested in *ÉpErf*: (i) *byrgere* (*byrgeras*) 'burier, corpse-bearer' for Lat *uispellones* 760; (ii) *egderi* 'harrower' for Lat *erpicarius* 396, cf. also *egdae – erpica* 395; (iii) *flitere* (*in ebhatis*) 'quarreler (in lawcourts)' for Lat *rabulus* 854; (iv) *scinneras* 'magicians' for Lat *sc[ae]nicis*; (v) *teblere* 'gambler' for Lat *aleator* 7, cf. also *teblae*, *tefil – alea* 6. On *sigiras* see section 6.8.

(c) --

(d) The suffix *-ere* is an early loan-suffix; it was probably borrowed into Germanic from the Latin suffix *-arius* (or rather from loan-words containing this suffix).[50] The Germanic form **-arjaz*, **-ærjaz* developed into the OE form *-eri* (see above) and the into *-ere*. As can be seen from the attestations in *ÉpErf*, it was productive even in early Old English and is still productive today in its PDE form *-er* /ə/.

(e) *-ere* derived masculine nouns inflected according to the Gmc (strong) a-declension (cf. Brunner 1965: 202 = § 248.1).

(f) *-ere* (> PDE *-er*) derived and still derives mainly agent nouns; to a smaller extent, also instrument nouns; all the formations in *ÉpErf* belong to the agent nouns. Marchand (1969: 273) gives the basic meaning as 'someone or something connected with what the basis denotes'. In Latin, *-arius* derived agent nouns from nouns (i.e. denominal nouns), as can also be seen from several Latin lemmata in *ÉpErf*, where the basic noun more or less immediately precedes the derived noun in *-arius*: *broel* 147 – *broelarius* 148; *dromidus* – *dromidarius* 320; *erpica* 395 – *erpicarius* 396 (for *herpica* and *herpicarius*); cf. further *gregarius* (*gregariorum*, 479) from *grex*; *tignarius* 996 from *tignum* (and *alea* 6 – *aleator* 7). Derivation from nouns also seems to have been the original function in Germanic and early Old English; later, derivation from verbs became more frequent. Apparently, when the first element (the basic word) could be regarded as a primary noun or as a verb (stem of a verb) or a deverbal noun, it was later connected with the verb. In *ÉpErf*, too, several formations allow of a double explanation. All examples can be explained as denominal nouns, but most could also be deverbal nouns: *byrgere* could be derived from *byrgen* (noun) or *byr(i)an* (verb; cf. also *byrgend* 'gravedigger'); *egdere* (ClH *egðere*) from *egðe* (noun) or *(ge)egðan* (verb); *flitere* from *(ge)flit* (noun) or from *(ge)flitan* (strong verb I); *taeflere* from *taefl* (*tebil*) (noun) or from *tæflian* (verb). Only *scinnere* can apparently just be derived from the noun *scinn* (the verb *scīnan* has long *i* and a different meaning). *Taeflere* could be a loan-word from Lat *tabularius*, but in Classical Latin *tabularius* meant 'registrar, keeper of archives etc.' and not 'gambler', whereas Lat *tabula* 'table' among other meanings also had the meaning 'a board to play on'; thus, OE *teblere* should probably be regarded as a hybrid Old English formation, i.e. as an Old English formation which used a loan-word from Latin as its basis.[51] On the question of how far the *-ere* formations attested in *ÉpErf* could be loan-formations (possibly *egderi*), see section 5.6.3 (4). Since both *-end* and *-ere* formed agent nouns, they became competing suffixes (cf. also formations such as *-bora* and *-wyrhta*). Originally, however, they had different bases for derivation, see above. Occasionally there were formations from the same basic word with both suffixes, e.g. *byrgere* (*ÉpErf* 760) and *byrgend* (both of which were rare, however). There are, however, no directly competing formations attested in *ÉpErf*; see further Koo (1946: 354-62).

(g) Literature: *EWDS* s.v. '-er'; *ODEE* s.v. '-er[1]'; Kärre (1915: --); Kluge (1926: 6f. = §§ 8-11); Koo (1946: 64-82 and 354-62); Marchand (1969: 273-81); Kastovsky (1971: 285-325); Koziol (1972: 188-91 = §§ 447-52); Kastovsky (1992: 385-6).

(3) ***-es(s)*** etc.

(a) This suffix appears in Old English in several forms: *-es(s)*, *-is(s)*, *-ys(s)*, *-isn* etc. Apparently, *-is(s)* is the earlier form, whereas *-es(s)* is the later weakened form. *ÉpErf* has the earlier form *-is* (Ép *-isae* and *-issa*, Erf *-issae* are probably inflected forms), see below.

(b) Three words certainly or possibly containing this suffix are attested among the names for persons in *ÉpErf*: (i) *cebisae* (probably pl.) 'concubine(s), kept mistress(es)' (G *Kebse*) for Lat *pelices*; (ii) *cneorissa* 'generation, family, tribe' etc. for Lat *sanguinis*; (iii) *haegtis* 'witch' for Lat *strig(i)a*.

(c) The different forms can probably be regarded as variants of the same suffix (or as a suffix family). The suffix, however, seems to have been rare in Old English, and many formations with it are problematic from a morphologic or semantic point of view (or both); see (f) below. It has nothing to do with the PDE suffix *-ess* (as in *actress*, *heiress*, *stewardess* etc.), which was borrowed from French into English in the 13th century. Handbooks of English word-formation often ignore it, whereas some Old English grammars mention it.

(d) The suffix goes back to a West-Germanic suffix **-isjō-* (or **-isi* according to Campbell 1959: 238 = § 592.d). *Cebisae* is a West-Germanic formation (**kabisō*) and exists in German as *Kebse* (archaic); *haegtis* is also a West-Germanic formation and exists in German as *Hexe* (cf. Carr 1939: 99, no. 38 and *EWDS* s.v. 'Hexe'). *Cneorissa* seems to be an Old English formation which was frequently used. Campbell (1959) and Brunner (1965) list just eight formations between them, apart from *cebisae* (*ciefes*, *cefes*), *cneoriss* and *haegtess* also *byres* 'chisel', *forleges* 'adulteress, harlot', *ides* 'female', *Lindis* (the county of Lincoln) and *lynis* 'linchpin' (G *Lünse*). The suffix probably lost its productivity even in Old English. With it, practically all formations died out as well.

(e) *-is* apparently derived mainly strong feminine nouns (Gmc *jō*-stems) from nouns, i.e. denominal nouns. Ép *cebisae* probably is the nom. pl. (Érf *caebis* seems to have lost the ending), *cneorisae* Erf reflects the gen. sg., and *cneorissa* Ép is the old gen. sg. ending (Brunner 1965: 205 f. = § 252).

(f) The suffix appears to have had the basic meaning 'belonging to, pertaining to'. Four of the eight formations refer to women, three of which have a negative connotation or denotation (*cebisae*, *forleges*, *haegtess*; *ides*), two to instruments (*byres*, *lynis*), one to a place or rather area (*Lindis*), and one to an abstract, *cneoris* (which is, however, here listed among the names for people). All three formations attested in *ÉpErf* are problematic from an Old English point of view: (i) The noun underlying *cebis(ae)* apparently no longer existed even in Old English; thus *cebisae* is an obscured formation (the underlying noun seems to have been a loan-word meaning 'bed', taken from Lat *cavea*; *cebisae* thus originally seems to have meant something like 'one who shares the bed'); (ii) *Cneorissa* 'generation' was perhaps formed from *cneo(w)* 'KNEE' in its meaning 'generation, step in a pedigree'. But if this is the case, it seems to be tautological semantically, whereas formally the <r> is difficult to explain (a case of dissimilation?);[52] (iii) The first element of *hægtis* is OE *hæg*, *haga* 'hedge, enclosure' (cf. G *Hag*), but the second element *-tis* poses a problem. It has been reconstructed as a word **tusjo* which, however, is not attested independently in Old English nor in Old High German (and the meaning of which also seems to be unclear) – this would make *haegtis* an obscured compound. Here, however, it has been classified as a derivation with the suffix *-ess*, *-iss* (following the Old English grammars) – but if this is the case, then the inserted <t> is difficult to explain. The original meaning seems to have been something like 'someone/a female who is active in hedges'.[53] For a survey of opinions, see Jente (1921: 295-9 = § 168).

(g) Literature: *EWDS* s.v. 'Hexe', 'Kebse'; Kärre (1915: 40-1); Jente (1921: 295-9 = § 168); Kluge (1926: 25 = § 46); Marchand (1969: --); Koziol (1972: --); Kastovsky (1992: --); Campbell (1959: 238 = § 592.d); Brunner (1965: 209 = § 258(c), note 6).

(4) ***-ing***[1]

(a) The normal Old English form of this suffix was *-ing*, more rarely *-ung*; *-ing* is also used in *ÉpErf.*

(b) Two formations are attested among the names for people, both as parts of compounds (which do not refer to people as a whole), see section 6.2.2. (1–2): (i) *iring* (personal name) in *iringaes uueg* 1050 for Lat *uia secta*; (ii) *uuicing* 'VIKING' in *uuicing-sceada(n)* 736 for Lat *piraticum, piraticam.*

(c) Here we have to do with the denominal suffix *-ing*, not with the deverbal suffix *-ing*.

(d) The suffix goes back to a Gmc **-inga*, **-unga* > OE *-ing* (*-ung*); for its ultimate origin, see, e.g., Kluge (1926: 12 = § 23). It was fairly productive in Old English; later, its productivity was largely lost (in contrast to the deverbal suffix *-ing*) – very few new formations seem to have been coined in the Modern English period, and none in the 20th century.

(e) *-ing*[1] typically derives masculine nouns (Gmc a-stems) for persons from nouns (or adjectives), i.e. denominal nouns; cf. Campbell (1959: 228 = § 574.6).

(f) One basic meaning of *-ing* is 'belonging to, coming from, descending from'. This was orginally apparently also true of the two words attested in *ÉpErf.* Both are, however, difficult to explain: (i) *Iring* is perhaps a West-Germanic patronymic 'son or descendant of Ir-'; *Ir-* however, is probably an obscured form of the underlying noun (apparently not mentioned by

Munske 1964); (ii) The etymology of *wicing* has been disputed: By some it has been regarded as a loan-word from Old Norse (< *vikingr*). Since, however, the first attestation of *uuicing* in *ÉpErf* precedes the first Viking raids on the English coast (from 793 onwards) by c. hundred years, the explanation as a native English formation seems more likely (see, e.g. *ODEE*, s.v. 'Viking'): *wic* 'camp' + *-ing*, i.e. originally meaning 'someone who lives in/comes from a (temporary) camp'.[54]

(g) Literature: *EWDS*, s.v. '-ing'; *ODEE*, s.v. '-ing[3]' and 'Viking'; Kluge (1926: 11-6 = § 22-7); Munske (1964); Marchand (1969: 305); Koziol (1972: 195 = § 463, -ing[1]); Kastovsky (1992: 386).

(5) ***-or***

(a) *-or* forming masculine names of persons is a rare suffix in Old English.

(b) The only attestation in *ÉpErf* is *aeldor* (ClH *ealdor*) in: *bituicn aeldrum* for *inter primores* 546.

(c) The *-or* discussed here is not identical with the suffix *-or* as in *actor*, *inventor* etc., nor with the comparative suffix OE *-ra* (> PDE *-er*). In the *ÉpErf* form *aeldrum* (dat. pl.) the vowel of the suffix has been syncopated.

(d) The suffix seems to go back to an IE **-ter* (Kluge **-tr̥*). According to Kluge it was widespread in the Indo-European languages, but apparently it was rare even in Germanic and also in Old English. *Baldor* 'prince' is the only other formation mentioned by Kluge for Old English. *Aeldor* (*ealdor*) goes at least back to WGmc, it is derived from the adj. *ald* (*eald*); the compound *ealdorman* (> PDE *alderman*) has corresponding forms in other West-Germanic languages, but Carr regards these as independent parallels. *-or* apparently became unproductive even in the Old English period.

(e) *-or* apparently derived weak masculines (n-declension).

(f) *-or* derived names of persons (masculines), originally apparently agent nouns.

(g) Literature: Kluge (1926: 17 = § 30); Carr (1939: 149); Marchand (1969: --); Koziol (1972: --); Kastovsky (1992: --).

6.6. Derivation with change of stem-vowel

(a) Many words do not have a suffix in their attested Old English form, but they have i-umlaut in the stem, which shows that originally (i.e. in Germanic or in West-Germanic or in preliterary Old English) they were derived with a suffix that consisted of or contained an *-i-* or *-j-* (Gmc **-i-* or **-ja-* or **-jan-* or **-jōn*).

(b) About six nouns from our *ÉpErf* material belong to this group: (i) *byrgea* 921 'one who gives bail, trustee' (G *Bürge*) for Lat *sequester*; (ii) *caempa(n)* 481 'fighter(s), warrior(s)' for Lat *gladiator(es)*; (iii) *giroefa(n)* (ClH *gerefa*) 223 'high official(s), REEVE(S)' for Lat *censor(es)* and *commentariensis* (see section 4.3.4.); (iv) *roedra* (ClH *reðra*) 875 'rower (sailor)' for Lat *remex*; (v) *gisuirgion*; (vi) *uuyrd*. On **ge-…-ja* (*giroefa* and *gisuirgion*), see section 6.5.3.; on *uuyrd*, see 5.2.

(c) These formations cannot be explained strictly synchronically, but because they form a relatively large and conspicuous group, they are dealt with here.

(d) This pattern goes back to Germanic and was still productive in (early) Old English, but died out later. *Cempa* is probably a Germanic formation (**kamp-jan*) from the Latin loan-word OE *camp*, G *Kampf* (< Lat *campus*), cf., e.g. G *Kämpe* (and *Kämpfer*). *Wyrd* (*uuyrd*) is probably also a Germanic formation from an ablaut grade (preterite pl. stem) of the strong verb of class III OE *weorþan* – *wearþ* – ***wurdon*** – *geworden* (see Seebold 1970: 559-61). *Byrgea* is a West-Germanic formation (< **burg-jōn*; cf. G *Bürge*), probably derived from the strong verb of class III OE *beorgan* – *bearg* – ***burgon*** – *(ge)borgen*.[55] As pointed out in 6.5. (3) above, *giroefa(n)* was formed in Old English from the combination prefix *ge-* plus suffix *-ja*. *Rēðra* was apparently also formed in Old English, from *rōðor* 'oar, scull, RUDDER' + **-ja*.

(e) The derivations in **-ja(n)* belong to the weak masculines (n-stems). In our material, there are derivations from nouns (denominal derivations), i.e. *caempa*, *giroefa*, *roedra*, *giswirgion*, and derivations from verbs, i.e. *byrgea*, *wyrd*. Derivation from verbs was not always from the present stem, but often from a past stem (cf. above (d) and 6.2.2.5.).

(f) Most of the formations listed here are agent nouns; whether *wyrd* was originally also an agent noun or rather an action noun ('that which happens') is unclear (see 4.3. (2) above).

(g) Literature: Kluge (1926: 4ff. = §§ 5,7,12-14); Campbell (1959: 250 = § 619(2)); Kastovsky (1968); Marchand (1969: --); Koziol (1972: --); Kastovsky (1992: 360-1, 382-3, 392ff.).

6.7. Adjectives used as nouns

(a) Most adjectives could be used as nouns in Old English.

(b) The examples from *ÉpErf* among the material relevant here are (i) *uuildae* 99 for Lat *agrestes*; (ii) *uuoda* (ClH *woda*) 'madman' 383 for Lat *ephilenticus* (probably for *e[p]ile[p]ticus* < Gk); (iii) possibly *aedil(ra)* for *gregariorum*.

(c) Whether the substantivization of adjectives should be regarded as an inflexional, a syntactic, or as a word-formational phenomenon is open to dispute. It is often regarded as an inflexional (grammatical) phenomenon because it was a fairly regular process in Old English and because it is often connected with a change of inflectional class; it could, however, also be regarded as a word-formational phenomenon (a case of conversion or zero-derivation) because a change of word-class is involved.[56] For the latter reason it is mentioned here.
(d) The use of adjectives as nouns was inherited from Germanic; it was common in Old English and is still common in German. This use has become rather restricted in Modern English (*the blacks*, *the whites* with plural *-s*; *the poor*, *the rich*, *the beautiful*, *the ugly* without plural *-s*); often, prop-words such as *one* or *-man* have to be added (*the good ones*).
(e) When adjectives are used as nouns, they are inflected according to the weak or consonantal (n-)declension if they are preceded by a demonstrative pronoun (definite article), and according to the strong (vocalic) declension if they are used on their own.
(f) --
(g) Literature: Brunner (1962: 73-8 = § 14); Marchand (1969: --); Koziol (1972: 282f. = § 666).

6.8. Difficult and unclear cases

We have several times pointed out that a number of apparently complex words are difficult to analyse for a number of reasons; see, e.g., *ceap-cneht*, *haegtis* etc. Two words have not been assigned to a specific word-formation type here: (i) *leauuis* for Lat *scurra*. A number of explanations have been put forward, see Pheifer (1974: 125). Pheifer himself suggests to analyse it as a compound adj. **lea-wis* 'scurrilous'. This would explain it as a bahuvrihi adjective with *-wis* 'having a certain way' as second element (cf. *riht-wis* 'RIGHTEOUS' and see Sauer 1992: 308-9), but an OE **lea* 'glad, scurrilous' does not seem to be attested; (ii) *sigir(as)* 'glutton(s)' for Lat *lurcones auidi*: *sigir* might be a derivation with the suffix *-ere* (see above), but the form *-ire* (nom. acc. pl. *-iras*) would be very unusual. Moreover, the underlying verb is unclear: Pheifer (1974: 96) posits an unattested weak verb 1 **sigirjan*; the attested verb *sigan* (strong I) 'sink' does not seem to fit semantically.

6.9. Morphological variants and peculiarities

6.9.1. Formations with blocked (unique) morphemes

In some compounds one constituent does not (or no longer) occur independently; also, in some prefix- and suffix-formations the basic word no longer exists independently even in Old English. Examples from our material are: Compounds: (i) *burg-runae* (*-runae* does not occur independently); prefix-formations: (ii) *giroefa* (ClHall *gerēfa*), see sections 6.4.2 (3) and 6.7; suffix-formations: (iii) *cebis(ae)*, *Iring*, see sections 6.5. (3) & (4).

6.9.2 Obscured compounds

In obscured compounds, one or both constituents have developed differently in the compound than in independent use; usually one or both have been weakened, shortened, and assimilated, so that they can no longer be recognized. There is a scale from slight to heavy obscuration; heavily obscured compounds have become monomorphemic (e.g. PDE *gospel*, *lammas*, *lord*, *lady*, *sheriff*, *woman* etc.). Since there was no standardized spelling in Old English, it is sometimes difficult to tell whether a given form is just a spelling variant or an obscured form. Obscuration can be regarded as an advanced form of lexicalization (see 6.1.2.5 above). An example is *orit-mon*: *orit* seems to be a variant of *eored*, see Pheifer (1974: 80) and 6.2.2.(1) above; another example may be *leuuis* 977a, see section 6.9.

7. Semantic structure

As indicated in sections 3. and 6.1.2 (5), there are several ways of looking at and classifying the meaning of words. Unfortunately for the analyst, there is no one to one correspondence between word-formation types and semantic patterns: A given word-formation pattern can exhibit several semantic patterns (see, e.g. section 6.2.2.(1) on noun + noun compounds); conversely, a given semantic pattern can be expressed by several word-formation patterns. Here, I concentrate on the distinction between agent nouns, experiencer nouns and patient (passive) nouns. The agent nouns are by far the largest group.

7.1. Agent nouns, experiencer nouns, patient nouns

7.1.1. Agent nouns

In agent nouns, the second element (dm) indicates a person who performs some activity with respect to the first element (dt). Syntactically, agent nouns represent a subject type, i.e. the second element (dm) is the subject in the underlying or paraphrase sentence; the first element (dt) often is the object. The object can be the affected object or the effected object. Agent nouns occur among: (i) The noun + noun compounds: *edisc-uueard*, *hors-thegn* (both with affected object) 'B deals with, takes care of, guards A'; *egisi-grima* 'B causes A'; (ii) The noun + deverbal noun compounds, e.g. *mund-bora*, *hrof-wyrcta*, *scinn-laeca*, see further section 6.2.2.(5). The first element in *hrof-wyrcta* is an effected object; whether the first element in *mund-bora* and *scinn-laeca* is affected or effected, is more difficult to tell; (iii) The suffix formations in *-end*, e.g. *ferhergaend*, see further 6.6.(1) above; (iv) The suffix formations in *-ere* listed under 6.6.(2) above, e.g., *flitere*. Actually, all formations of the types mentioned under (ii), (iii) and (iv) are agent nouns (or were at least originally agent nouns); (v) Some of the derivations with change of stem-vowel, e.g. *caempa*, *roedra*, see section 6.7. Here, the original meaning may have been 'someone who has to do with a camp [combat, battle]', 'someone who has to do with a *roðor* [oar]', but the actual meaning 'warrior, fighter' and 'oarsman' (cf. G *Ruderer*) is that of an agent noun.

7.1.2. Experiencer nouns

Experiencer nouns are rarer; they indicate persons who do not really perform an activity, but are rather in a (often permanent) state. Syntactically, they also represent a subject type, e.g. *burg-leod* 'B inhabits, lives in A'. Experiencer nouns, too, occur within several morphological types, in particular: (i) Noun + noun compounds, e.g. *burg-leod*, *burg-runae* and *uuydu-mer* 'B lives in A, inhabits A', perhaps also 'B is active in A', which would, however, make them an agent noun; *orit-mon* 'B belongs to, is a member of A'; (ii) formations with the prefix *steop-*: *steop-faeder* 'B is not the real father, but the mother's second husband'; (iii) formations with the suffix *-ing*^{1}, e.g. *iring*, *uuicing*, which indicate descent or origin ('B comes from A') – later, *wicing* was probably rather seen as an agent noun; (iv) bahuvrihi adjectives, e.g. *gimodae* 'those who have the same mind [mod]'; (v) simplexes such as *dweorg*.

7.1.3. Patient (passive) nouns

Nouns expressing a passive relationship are still rarer (which is also the case in PDE). They indicate a person on which a certain action is or has been performed, e.g. among the verb + noun compounds *ceap-cnext* 'servant, slave [cneht] who has been bought, has been acquired through trade [ceap]'; *fostur-bearn* 'child [bearn] that is given or receives food, sustenance [fostor]'. The passive sentence has, however, already been topicalized. To ensure comparability the basic syntactic paraphrase has to start from an active sentence, too; this reveals the patient nouns from a syntactic point of view as object types (with a direct or a prepositional object): 'Someone buys /has bought this servant/slave'; 'someone gives sustenance to this child (or 'someone provides this child with sustenance').

7.2. Other structures

The complex words which do not refer to a person (although some of them contain a word for a person) cannot be analysed in terms of agent or experiencer nouns. Thus, *iringaes uueg* probably has to be paraphrased as 'the way which Iring has gone/has taken'; *sifun-sterri* as 'the stars are seven' (a copula compound); *uuicing-sceaðe* as 'harm, damage which is/has been done by vikings' (but possibly also as a copula compound 'a viking is a harmful person', see section 6.2.2.1.).

7.3. Idiomatized and lexicalized formations

Some formations cannot be (or can only partly be) explained with their elements; they are idiomatized or lexicalized (see section 6.1.2.5). Idiomatization and lexicalization can be seen as a scale: there is a cline from formations which are not idiomatized or lexicalized, formations which are just slightly idiomatized or lexicalized (see on *hors-thegn* below), formations which are more strongly idiomatized or lexicalized (e.g. *fostur-bearn*; see below) and formations which are heavily or totally idomatized or lexicalized (e.g. *Iringaes uueg*). It has often been said that the addition of fairly general semantic features (such as [+habitual], [+professional]) leads to slight idiomatization or lexicalization, whereas the addition of more specific features (such as [+not one's own child]) leads to stronger lexicalization. Where exactly idiomatization begins, however, is not easy to tell; thus *sifun-sterri* can still be paraphrased as 'seven stars'; it does not refer to any seven stars, however, but to a specific constellation; thus it is perhaps slightly idiomatized. The names for occupations or professions attested in *ÉpErf* do not always reveal how far these occupations were done professionally or habitually, or just occasionally, or, to put it differently, whether the person in question did this activity as his (or her) main or only occupation or just occasionally as one of several occupations; this applies, e.g., to *hors-thegn*, *hrof-uuyrcta*, *bisuicend*, *ferhergaend*. From a cognitive point of view it could be said that these formations conceptualize a typical occupation or activity of the person concerned. Compounds with blocked morphemes, i.e. where one element does not (or no longer) occur independently, can also be regarded as lexicalized; the same applies to prefix- and suffix-formations where the underlying word (basic word) no longer occurs independently: *cebisae*, *giroefa*. Other clearly idiomatized or lexicalized complex words are: (i) Noun + noun: *fostor-bearn* can still be explained as 'child [bearn] that is given sustenance [fostor]' (see above), but the implication is that it is not one's own child, but an adopted child; (ii) Noun + *s* + noun: *iringaes uueg* is clearly idiomatized , see above; (iii) Numeral + noun: on *sifun-sterri*, see above; (iv) Verb + noun: *Ceap-cnext* is interesting because it implies tense. Normally, tense is neutralized in compounds, but *ceap-cnext* apparently refers to a 'servant/slave who has been bought' (and not to a servant who is being bought or who will be bought); (v) Prefix formations: *gebur* 'farmer' etc. was probably no longer associated with its underlying noun *bur* 'dwelling, cottage, BOWER'.

8. Survival, or: Looking ahead

Just as it is interesting to look at the origin (etymology) of the words (see section 5.), it is also interesting to look at their survival. But the further fate of the words is also not easy to classify. Apart from words which clearly died out (see 8.1.) and words which clearly survive (see 8.2.), there are also complex words which do not survive as such but where one or both elements survive (see 8.3); more rarely, there are words which survive only as parts of compounds or complex words (see 8.4). Moreover, some words survive formally, but have clearly changed their meaning (8.5); in other cases, one form was substituted by a related, but morphologically distinct form; e.g. *wyrhta* (< *wyrcan*) has been replaced by *worker* (< *work*), or the basic word survives, but not the derivation (e.g. *bear* < *beran*, but not *-bora*) – but I did not want to set up too many subdivisions here. In any case it is striking that among the words for people attested in *ÉpErf*, the large majority has died out, i.e. c. 52 (if 8.1 and 8.3 are taken together), whereas only c. 14 survive (if 8.2 and 8.4-5 are taken together) – even if 8.2-5 are taken together, only c. 29 survive, whereas c. 37 (see 8.1) have died out.

8.1. Words which have died out (c. 37)

aedil, baedend, bisuicend, byrgea, cebisae, caempa, cneorissa, egdere, egisigrima, flitere, fultemend, gibuur, gidogta, grima, haegtes, meeg (ClH *mǣg*), *leuuis, mundbora, nift, orc, redbora, roedra* (ClH *rēðra*), *scyhend, scinn, scinnlaeca, scinnere, sigir(as), strelbora, sueor(as), gesuirgion, gitreuudae, uuoda, uuoedendi* (*wēdend*), *uuraec, uuyrd, ymbhringend, ymbdringend.*

8.2. Words which have survived (c. 8)

dweorg (> *dwarf*); *ealdor* (> *elder*); *giroefa* (> *reeve*); *haetendae* (> *to heat*); *steup-faedaer* (> *stepfather*); *thegn* (> *thane*; archaic); *uuicing* (> *Viking*); *wilde* (> *wild*).

8.3. Complex words which have died out but where one or both constitutents survive (c. 15)

burg-leod and *burg-runae* (but *borough, -burgh*); *byrgere* (but *to bury*; as a possible word: *burier*); *ceap-cnext* (but *cheap* and *knight*, see 8.5.); *ediscuueard* (but cf. *warden*, a later loan word); *ferhergian* (but *to harrow*); *fosturbearn* (but *to foster*); *gimodae* (> *mood*, see 8.5.); *hors-thegn* (but *horse* and archaic *thane*); *hrof-uuyrcta* (but *roof*); *Iringaes uueg* (but *Iring* and *way*); *oritmon* (but *man*); *sifun-sterri* (but *seven* and *star(s)*); *teblere* (but *table*); *uuydumer* (cf. *nightmare*).

8.4. Words which have survived as parts of compounds or complex words (c. 3)

mera (*mare*) in *nightmare*; *gebur* in *neighbour*; *Tiig* in *Tuesday* (*Tues-* is a blocked morpheme in Modern English).

8.5. Words which have survived but have clearly changed their meaning (c. 3)

ceap (noun) (> *cheap* adj.); *cnext* 'servant, slave' (> *knight*); *gimodae* (cf. *mood*).

8.6. Latin lemmata which were borrowed into English after the Old English period

In c. seven cases, the Old English gloss died out, but the Latin lemma was taken over into English after the Old English period:
Bisuicend – *inpostorem* (PDE *impostor*); *caempan* – *gladiatores* (PDE *gladiator*); *cneorissa* – *sanguinis* (cf. PDE *consanguinuity*); *fostur-bearn* – *alumnae*; cf. PDE *alumni*; *mascus* – *grima* (cf. PDE *mask*); *mera* – *satyrus*, *saturnus* (cf. PDE *nightMARE*, but also *satyr*, *Saturn*); *orit-mon* – *dromidarius* (cf. PDE *dromedary*); *gitreeudae* – *foederatas* (cf. PDE *federates*); *uuoda* – *ephilenticus* (prob. for *epilepticus*; cf. PDE *epileptic*).

9. Conclusion

I hope to have shown that all the aspects of the names for people we have looked at, especially the questions of word-field, etymology, word-formation, semantics, and survival show a rich internal structure and subdivision. Clearly, some patterns were more productive and prominent than others, e.g. as regards word-formation compounds consisting of noun + noun and of noun + deverbal agent noun without a suffix as well as agent nouns in *-end*; as regards semantics agent nouns (as opposed to experiencer and patient nouns). Eventually, this study could be expanded into a more comprehensive survey of the areas mentioned as attested in *Épinal-Erfurt*, but especially as far as word-formation is concerned. It has become clear that the word-formation processes and the prefixes and suffixes dealt with here are unevenly represented in the handbooks on English word-formation. Those that were productive in Old English and are still productive (such as noun + noun, *be-*, *-ere*, *-ing*[1]) are usually discussed in the handbooks; those that were rare in Old English or have a doubtful status and died out later or even in the Old English period (such as *-ess*/*-iss*) are often ignored in the handbooks, but sometimes information on them can be found in the grammars and dictionaries.

10. Word-lists

10.1 List of the Old English names for people in *Épinal-Erfurt*

The entries are arranged as follows:

(a) Late West-Saxon spelling of the word or of its first element according to ClH (the question marks at *gidopta* and *leuuis* indicate that there does not seem to be an entry in ClH).
(b) *ÉpErf* spelling. If the spellings of Ép and Erf differ, usually both spellings are listed, first the spelling of Ép, then the spelling of Erf.
(c) Meaning in ' '; if the Modern English equivalent is the more or less regular descendant of the Old English word, it is given in capitals. If there is an etymologically (and semantically) related German word, this is also given.
(d) Indication, if it is a rare word.
(e) Latin lemma in *ÉpErf*.
(f) Entry number in *ÉpErf* (ed. Pheifer 1974).

For the words beginning with A-F, the entries in the *DOE* were checked.

1. *æðele*: *aedilra* (gen.pl.) 'noble, aristocratic' (cf. G *edel*) – *gregariorum* 'common (soldiers)' (gen.pl.), *ÉpErf* 479; cf. *DOE* s.v. 'æþele 1.e.ii'.
1a. *aeldor* > *ealdor*
2. *bǣdan*, *bǣdend*: *baedendrae* (Ép), *bedændræ* (Erf) 'inciter, instigator, one who urges' – *inpulsore*, *ÉpErf* 539; only under the vb. *bǣdan* in *DOE*
3. *beswīcan*, *beswicend*: *bisuicend* (Ép), *bisuiccend* (Erf) 'deceiver, impostor' – *inpostorem* Ép, *inposterem*, Erf 545; cf. *DOE* 'be-swīcend'
3a. *-bur*: see *gebur*
4. *burg*, *burh*: *burg-leod* (*a mu[ni]cipio*) 'citizen, inhabitant' (lit. 'town-people') – *municeps*, Ép 620 (Erf 00)
5. *burg*, *burh*: *burg-runae* (Ép; nom. and acc. pl.), *burg-runæ* (Erf) 'fates, furies, wise women, sybils' (only in glossaries and glosses) – *parcas* (acc.pl.), *ÉpErf* 761 (Jente 1921: 329)
6. *byrga*: a) *byrgea* 'one who gives bail, guarantor' (cf. G *Bürge*) – *sequester* 'depositary, trustee' *ÉpErf* 921; b) *byrgea* – *pres et uas* (*Ép*), *praes et uas* (*Erf*) 'surety, bondsman' *ÉpErf* 776.
7. *byrgere*: (*þorh*) *byrgeras* (Ép; pl.), (*dorh*) *buyrgenas* (Erf, probably for *b[y]rge[r]as*) 'corpse-bearer', lit. 'burier' (rare; only in glossaries) – *(per) uispellones* 'thieves who robbed corpses of their grave-clothes', *ÉpErf* 760

8. *ceap*: (> PDE *CHEAP*; cf. G *Kauf*): *ceap-cnext* 'bought servant, slave' – *empticius*, Erf 349 (Ép 00); *DOE* has one entry *cēap-cniht*, *cȳpe-cniht*
9. *cempa*: *caempan* (Ép; nom. and acc. pl. etc.), *cempan* (Erf) 'warriors, champions' (cf. G *Kämpe*, *Kämpfer*) – *gladiatores* 'gladiators, fighters in the public games', *ÉpErf* 481
10. *cifes*: *cebisae* (Ép), *caebis* (Erf) 'concubine, kept mistress, harlot' (cf. G *Kebse*) – *pelices* (sg. *pelex*, *paelex*), *ÉpErf* 745
11. *cneoris(n)*: *cneorissa* (Ép), *cneorissae* (Erf) 'generation, family, tribe, line of descendants etc.' – *sanguinis* (gen. sg.) 'blood, blood-relation, consanguinity', *ÉpErf* 903; *DOE* has two different entries, *cnēoris* and *cnēorisn*
11a. *-dopta*, *-dohta*: see *gedopta*, *gidopta*
12. *dweorg*: *duerg* 'DWARF' – *nanus uel pumilio* (*punilio* Erf), *ÉpErf* 686
13. *ealdor*: *bituicn aeldrum* (Ép), *bituichn ældrum* (Erf) 'ELDER, chief, leader etc.' – *inter primores* (sg. *primoris*), *ÉpErf* 546
14. *edisc*: *edisc-ueard* (Ép), *edisc-uard* (Erf) (in glossaries only) 'park-keeper' – *broelarius* (Ép), *broellearius* (Erf), *ÉpErf* 148
15. *eges-grima*: *egisi-grima* 'ghost', lit. 'terror mask' etc. – *larbula ÉpErf* 569; cf. *grima*
16. *egðere*: *egderi* (Erf; Ép 00) 'harrower' (in glosses only) (cf. G *Egge*, *eggen*) – *erpicarius* Erf 396 (Ép 00) (for *herpicarius*); cf. *egdae* – *erpica* 395 (for *herpica*; not in Lewis & Short); *DOE* s.v. 'egeþere'
16a. *eored-*: see *orit-mon*
17. *flītere*: *flitere in ebhatis* 'quarreler in lawcourts'– *rabulus* 'petty advocate', *ÉpErf* 854
18. *for-*, *forhergian*, *forhergend*: *ferhergænd* (Ép), *ferhergend* (Erf) 'ravager' (rare; only in glossaries) – *grassator* 'rioter, street robber', *ÉpErf* 467
19. *fostor* (> PDE *FOSTER*): *fostur-bearn* (Ép), *foetri-barn* (Erf, for *foe[s]tri-barn*) (probably pl.) (rare; in glosses & glossaries) 'foster-child(ren), fosterling(s)' – *alumn(a)e* 'foster-daughters', *ÉpErf* 108[57]
20. *fultum(i)an*, *fultum(i)end*: a) *fultemendi* (dat. sg.) 'helper' – *adstipulatus* (for *adstipulator* 'one who joins another in a stipulation, an assistant in a trial') *ÉpErf* 74; b) *fultemendum* (dat. pl.) 'helpers' – *adsessore* (Ép), *adsessores* (Erf) 'he that sits by one, assessor, assistant of a judge' 95
21. *gebur*: *gibuur* (Ép) 'freeholder, farmer', *uicinus* (Erf) – *colonus* 'tiller of the soil etc.', *ÉpErf* 163
22. ?: *gidopta* (Ép), *gidogta* (Erf) 'comrade' (?) – *contubernalis* 'comrade', literally 'tent-companion', *ÉpErf* 189
23. *gemōd*: *gimodae* (Ép), *gimode* (Erf) (nom. pl.), lit. 'of one mind' – *coniurati* 'conspirators', *ÉpErf* 201

24. *gerēfa*: a) *giroefan* (pl.) (Ép), *geroefan* (Erf) 'high official(s), REEVE(S)' – *censores* 'censors', *ÉpErf* 197; b) *giroefa* (Ép), *geroefa* (Erf) – *commentariensis* 'recorder, the clerk of a law court', *ÉpErf* 223
24a. *ge-*: see further *sweor*, *treowan*
25. *grima*: a) *grima* 'mask, ghost, spectre' – *mascus*, Ép 646; *marcus* (probably for *ma[s]cus*) Erf 638a; b) *grima* (*ÉpErf*) – *scina*, *ÉpErf* 904; c) *nitatio uel grima* (*ÉpErf*) – *scina*, *ÉpErf* 953[58] (cf. also *egisi-grima*, no. 15 above)
26. *hægtes(se)*, *hægtis*: *haegtis* (Ép), *hegtis* (Erf) 'fury, witch' (G *Hexe*) – *strigia* Ép, *striga* Erf 'witch (screech-owl)' (< Gk *strix*), *ÉpErf* 913 (Jente 1921: 295–299 = § 168)
27. *hǣtan* (> PDE *HEAT*): *haetendae* (pres. part. pl.) (Ép), *hattendae* (Erf) 'those who heat' – *calentes*, *ÉpErf* 206
28. *hors*: *hors-thegn* 'ostler, groom', lit. 'horse-servant' – *mulio* 'mule-keeper, mule-driver etc.', Ép 658 (Erf 00)
29. *hrōf*: *hrof-uuyrcta* (Ép), *hrof-huyrihta* (Erf) 'roofmaker' – *tignarius* (Ép), *trigrarius* (Erf, for *t[i]g[n]arius* 'carpenter, builder'), *ÉpErf* 996
30. *Iring*: *iringaes uueg* (Ép) – *iuuuringes uueg* (Erf) 'Milky Way', lit. 'Iring's Way' – *uia secta* (apparently not in Lewis & Short), *ÉpErf* 1050
31. *lǣce*: *leceas* (*ÉpErf*, nom. and acc. pl.) 'physician, doctor, LEECH' – *phisillos* (for *physiologos* or *physicos*? < Gk) 'people with a knowledge of nature', *ÉpErf* 746
32. *leðer-*: *ledir-uuyrcta* (Ép), *ledir-uyrhta* (Erf) (hapax legomenon) 'tanner', literally 'LEATHERmaker' – *byrseus* (Ép), *byrreus* (Erf) (< Gk, not in Lewis & Short), *ÉpErf* 155
33. ?: *leuuis* (*ÉpErf*) – *scurra* originally 'elegant man', later 'city buffoon, jester', *ÉpErf* 977a – the interpretation of *leuuis* is difficult, see (Pheifer 1974: 125): suggestions include *leas* 'false, deceitful'; *lews(a)* 'misery' (less convincing); **leawis* 'scurrilous'
34. *mǣg*: *meeg* (Ép 164 – Erf has *consanguinis*) 'kinsman, relative' – *contribulus* 'of the same tribus' (rare according to Lewis & Short), *ÉpErf* 164
35. *mare*, *mera*: *mera* (*uel satyrus*) (Ép), *merae* (*uel saturnus*) (Erf, probably for *sat[y]r[u]s*) 'female incubus', cf. PDE *nightMARE* – *incuba*, *ÉpErf* 558 (cf. *uuydu-mer*, no. 62 below)
35a. *-mod*: see *gemod*
36. *mund* 'protection': *mund-bora* 'protector, guardian, prefect, advocate' – *suffragator* 'supporter', *ÉpErf* 934; cf. *mundbyrd* 'protection, help' – *suffragium* Ép, *subfragium* Erf 935 'voting tablet, vote, favorable decision'

37. *nift*: *nift* (*ÉpErf*) 'niece, stepdaughter, granddaughter' (cf. G *Nichte*) – *priuigna filia sororis idest nift*, *ÉpErf* 734 (Lat *priuigna* strictly speaking means only 'stepdaughter'; 'granddaughter' is *neptis*; 'niece' is *filia fratris* or *filia sororis*)
38. *orc*: *orc* (*ÉpErf*) 'God of the underworld, demon' – *orcus* 'abode of the dead, god of the infernal region, death' Ép, *orci* Erf 698. *Orc* is probably a loan-word from Lat *orcus* (see section 5.5.; Jente 1921: 137 = § 97)
39. ?: *se orit-mon* (probably for *eored-mon*, ClH *ēoredmann*) 'horse-man, member of a troop of riders' – *dromidarius* 'camel-driver', Erf 320 (Ép 00)
40. *rǣd*: *red-boran* (nom. and acc. pl.) 'advisers, counsellors' – *iurisperiti* 'those skilled in the law', *ÉpErf* 552
41. *rēðra*: *roedra* 'rower, sailor' – *remex*, *ÉpErf* 875
41a. *-rēfa*: see *gerefa*
42. *scīn*, *scinn*, *scina* 'spectre, illusion, evil spirit', *ÉpErf* 904, 953: see *grima*, 25 above with footnote 58 (Jente 1921: 155 = § 108; cf. § 169)
43. *scinnere*: *scinneras* (Ép), *scineras* (Erf) 'magicians' – *scienicis* (probably for *sc[ae]nicis* < Gk), *ÉpErf* 952 (Jente 1921: 157 = § 108; cf. § 169)
44. *scinnlǣca*: *scinlaecean* (Ép; gen. sg.), *scinlecan* (Erf) 'wizard, magician' – *nebulonis* (gen. sg. of *nebulo* 'worthless fellow, rascal'), *ÉpErf* 681 (Jente 1921: 160 = § 108; cf. § 169)
45. *scȳan* (?) 'persuade, tempt': *scyhend* (Ép; 00 Erf) 'seducer, pimp' (hapax legomenon) – *maulistis* (< Gk *maulistes*), Ép 654 (not in Lewis & Short)
46. *seofon*: *sifunsterri* (Ép), *funsterri* (Erf, for *[si]funsterri*) 'the seven stars' – *pliadas* (for *Pleiades* < Gk), *ÉpErf* 762
47. *siger*: *sigiras* 'gluttons' – *lurcones auidi uel sigiras* (Ép), *lurcones sigiras uel auidi* (Erf), 568
48. *steop-*: *steup-faedaer* (Ép), *staup-fotar* (Erf) 'STEPFATHER' (G *Stiefvater*) – *uitricius*, *ÉpErf* 1070 (for *vitricus*)
49. *strǣl*: *strel-bora* (hapax legomenon) 'archer, bowman', literally 'arrow-bearer' – *arcister* (probably for *arcites*), *ÉpErf* 114
50. *swēor*: a) *suehoras* (Ép), *sueoras* (Erf) 'fathers-in-law' (G *Schwiegerväter*) – *uitelli*, *ÉpErf* 1062; b) *sueor* 'father in law' – *uetellus* (probably for *u[i]tellus*, literally 'little calf'), Erf 1099 (Ép 00)
51. *geswiria*: *gesuirgion* (Ép), *gisuirgian* (Erf) 'cousin (father-in-law)' – *consubrinus* (for *cons[o]brinus* 'cousin'), *ÉpErf* 214
52. *tǣfl*: *teblere* (Ép), *tebl.re* (Erf) 'gambler' – *aleator*, *ÉpErf* 7 (cf. also *teblae*, *tefil* – *alea*, *ÉpErf* 6)
53. *Tīw*: *tiig* (*ÉpErf*) 'Tiw, Germanic god of war' (cf. OE *Tiwesdæg* > PDE *TUESDAY* for Lat *Martis dies*) – *mars martis*, *ÉpErf* 663 (Jente 1921: 86 ff. = § 59)

54. *treowian*: *gitreeudae* (nom. and acc. pl.) (Ép), *getreudœ* (Erf) 'federates' – *foederatas*, *ÉpErf* 436
55. *tyhtan*: *tyctaend anb* [for *ab*] *inliciendi* (Ép), *tychtend ab inliciendo* (Erf) 'inciter, instigator' – *inlex*, *ÉpErf* 509
56. *þegn*: *thegn* (Ép), *degn* (Erf) 'servant, vassal, warrior, nobleman, THANE' – *adsaeculam* (Ép), *adsexulam* (Erf) 'follower, attendant', *ÉpErf* 101 (see also *hors-þegn*)
57. *wicing*: *uuicing-sceadan* (Ép), *uuicing-scadae* (Erf) 'pirate' or 'piracy' (?) – *piraticum* (Ép), *piraticam* (Erf) 'piracy', *ÉpErf* 736
58. *wilde*: *uuildae* (*ÉpErf*) 'wild' (could refer to wild people or to wild plants) – *agrestes*, *ÉpErf* 99
59. *wēdend* (from *wēdan*): *uuoedendi* (Ép), *uuodenti* (Erf) 'raving, mad' – *lymphatico* 'distracted, panic-struck', 575; cf. *wōda*, no. 60.
60. *wǭda*: *uuoda* (Erf; 00 Ép) 'madman' – *ephilenticus* (probably for *e[p]ile[p]ticus* < Gk), Erf 383
61. *wræc*: *uuraec* (Ép), *uraec* (Erf) 'ship' or 'persecutor' (normally in OE 'misery, persecution') – *actuaris* (for *actuari[u]s*?) 'swift sailer' or 'scribe', *ÉpErf* 87 (*uuraec* 90 for *aegit* is a form of *wrecan* 'drive' etc., also *uuraec* 1002 for *torquetur*)
62. *wudu-mǣr*: *uuydu-mer* 'wood-sprite' ('wood-nymph') – *Echo*, *ÉpErf* 347; cf. *mare*, *mera*, no. 35 above
63. *wyrd*: a) *uuyrdae* (*ÉpErf*; nom. pl.) 'the Fates' – *parcae* Ép, *parce* Erf 764 b) *condicionem id uuyd* (Ép; probably for *uuy[r]d*), *conditionem id uyrd* (Erf) 'fate, fortune, chance, event etc.'– *sortem*, *ÉpErf* 980 (Jente 1921: 199–208 = § 128)
64. *ymbe-*: *ymb-hringendum* (dat. pl.) (Ép), *ymb-dringendum* (Erf), literally 'surrounders' – *stipatoribus* 'attendants, members of a retinue', *ÉpErf* 929

10.2. The Latin names for people in the *Épinal-Erfurt* Glossary

(1) List of the Latin names:
This list of Latin lemmata is mainly given to provide cross-references to the Old English glosses; not all the spelling variants are therefore given.

1) actuaris (for actuarius?) – uuraec
2) adsaecula(m) (assecla) – thegan
3) adsessor(e) – fultemend(um)
4) adstipulatus (for adstipulator?) – fultemend(i)
5) agrestes – uuildae
6) aleator – teblere
7) alumn(a)e (alumna, alumnus) – fostur-bearn

8) arcister (not in Lewis & Short; late?) – strel-bora
9) broel(l)arius (not in Lewis & Short; late) – edisc-u(e)ard
10) byrseus, byrreus (not in Lewis & Short; not in *DMLBS*; late?) – ledir-uuyrcta
11) calentes (from caleo) – haetend(ae)
12) censor(es) – giroefa(n)
13) colonus Ép (Erf: uicinus) – gibuur
14) commentariensis – giroefa
15) coniurati – gimodae
16) consubrinus (probably for consobrinus) – gesuirgion
17) contribulus – meeg
18) contubernalis – gidopta
19) dromedarius, dromidarius – orit-mon
20) Echo – uuydu-mer
21) empticius – ceap-cnext
22) ephilenticus (probably for epilepticus < Gk) – uuoda
23) erpicarius (for herpicarius) – egderi
24) foederatas (from foederatus, foederata) – gitreeudae
25) gladiator(es) – caempa(n)
26) grassator – ferhergaend
27) gregariorum (gregarius) – aedilra
28) incuba – mera (uel satyrus Ép, uel saturnus Erf)
29) inlex – tyctaend
30) inpulsor(e) – baedend(rae)
31) inpostor(em) – bisuicend
32) iurisperiti (juris-peritus) – red-bora(n)
33) larbula (not in Lewis & Short; late: first recorded in Aldhelm) – egisi-grima
34) lurco(nes) – sigiras
35) lymphatico – uuoedendi
36) Mars martis – tiig
37) mascus (7th century) – grima
38) maulistis (< Gk; post-classical) – scyhend
39) mulio – hors-thegn
40) municeps – burgleod
41) nanus (classical but vulgar according to Lewis&Short), pumilio (classical) – duerg
42) nebulo(nis) – scin-laecea(n)
43) orcus – orc (Latin loanword into Old English)
44) a) parca(s) – burg-runae; b) parca(e) – uuyrdae

45) pelices (pelex, paelex) – cebisae
46) phisillos (for physiologos or physicos?; < Gk) – lece(as)
47) piraticum, piraticam – uuicing-sceada(n)
48) pliadas (for Pleiades; < Gk) – sifunsterri
49) primor(es) – aeldrum
50) priuigna – nift
51) pumilio: see nanus
52) rabulus – flitere in ebhatis
53) remex – roedra
54) sanguinis (sanguis) – cneorissa
55) scienicis (probably for sc[ae]nicis from scaenicus) – scinneras
56) scina (possibly an Old English word) – a) grima; b) nitatio uel grima
57) scurra – leuuis
58) sequester – byrg(e)a
59) stipator(ibus) – ymbhringend(um), ymbdringend(um)
60) strig(i)a (cf. strix) – haegtis
61) suffragator – mund-bora
62) tignarius – hrof-uuyrcta
63) uia secta (post-classical?) – Iringaes uueg
64) uispello(nes) – byrgeras
65) a) uitelli (uitellus) – sue(h)or(as); b) uetellus (probably for uitellus) – sueor
66) uitric(i)us – steup-faedaer

(2) A few etymological notes:
(a) The following ultimately go back to Greek:
byrseus < βύρσευς
dromedarius < δρομεδάριος
Echo < ἠχώ
ephilenticus (probably for epilepticus) < ἐπιλέπτικος
lymphaticus: cf. νυμφολεπτός
maulistis < μαυλίστης
phisillos (for physiologos or physicos?) < φυσιόλογος
piraticum, piraticam < πειράτικος
pliadas (for Pleiades) < πλειάδες
satyrus (see incuba) < σάτυρος
scienicis (probably for scaenicis from scaenicus) < σκηνικός
strig(i)a (cf. strix, strigis) < στρίγζ

(b) Of Celtic origin is:
broelarius

(c) Of Arab origin is:
mascus

(3) The following suffixes occur among the Latin lemmata (cf. Leumann 1963):
-alis: contubernalis
-ans, -ens (present participles): calentes
-arius: actuaris (if for actuarius); broel(l)arius; dromedarius; erpicarius; gregariorum; tignarius
-atus, -itus (past participle): adstipulatus (perhaps for adstipulator); coniurati; foederatas; iurisperiti
-estis: agrestes
-ensis, -iensis: commentariensis
-ester: sequester
-ex: remex
-icius: empticius; uitric(i)us
-icus: ephilenticus (probably for epilepticus); piraticum, piraticam; scienicis (probably for scaenicis from scaenicus)
-inus: consubrinus
-ister: arcister
-istis (from Gk): maulistis
-o, -io, -ilio: mulio; nebulo(nis); pumilio; uispello(nes)
-or, -tor, -ator: adsessor(e); aleator; censor(es); gladiator(es); grassator; inpulsor(e); inpostor(em); primor(es); stipator(ibus); suffragator
-ulus, -ellus: contribulus; rabulus; uitelli (from uitellus or uetellus?)

(4) Spelling:
Strikingly, with prefix-formations usually the original non-assimilated form is given in *ÉpErf*: *adsaecula(am)* (cf. *assecla*); *adsessor(e)* (cf. *assessore*); *adstipulatus* (cf. *astipulatus*); *inlex* (cf. *illex*); *inpulsor(e)* (cf. *impulsor*); *inpostor(em)* (cf. *impostor*) – but *suffragator* (however, *suffragium* Ép, *subfragium* Erf 935); cf. further, e.g., *adnitentibus* (78).

Notes

[1] Cf. Sweet (1885). Greenfield -- Robinson (1980), on the other hand, do not regard glossaries as literature and accordingly (and unfortunately), exclude them from their *Bibliography of publications on Old English literature*. For brief surveys of the Old English glossaries, see, e.g. Gneuss (1987-1989); Lendinara (1999).

[2] The evidence of *ÉpErf* for inflexional morphology is limited (but see 2.2. below), and there is hardly any evidence for syntax.

[3] On these, see Sauer (1999a) and (1999b).

[4] For help with the present article and critical comments, my thanks are due to Christian Heimerl, Wilhelm Heizmann, Michael Herren and Ursula Lenker.

[5] Cf. Pheifer (1995: 329-333); see also Lapidge (1996: esp. 154). By some, it has also been connected with the school of Aldhelm (c. 640-709/710) at Malmesbury – Aldhelm was a student of Theodore and Hadrian. On the sources of *ÉpErf*, see Lindsay (1921).

[6] For descriptions see, e.g., Ker (1957: no. 114 and App. no. 10); Pheifer (1974, xxi-xxviii, §§ 1-13)

[7] Earlier facsimiles are Sweet (1885) and Schlutter (1912). One of the earlier editions is Sweet (1885).

[8] Pheifer (1974) edits only those Latin lemmata which have Old English glosses, but the facsimile by Sweet (1883), for example, has a transcription of all the lemmata and glosses, including the Latin – Latin ones. See also Goetz (1881-1923: 5, 337-401).

[9] Theoretically, *caempan* and *giroefan* could also represent other inflected cases, but not the nom. sg.

[10] Cf. Sauer (2001: 254-255).

[11] See, e.g., Brunner (1965: §§ 286, 305); Campbell (1959, § 632).

[12] More probably to a ship, if *wraec* is derived from *wrecan* 'drive, impel'.

[13] On this aspect of *ÉpErf*, see Herren (1998: esp. 97-99).

[14] Strikingly, with prefix-formations the original non-assimilated forms are often given; see section 10.2 (4).

[15] To start with, I checked Lewis&Short and labelled as post-classical those words which are not listed there. A further check of the *ThLL* usually confirmed this. Among the classical as well as among the post-classical Latin words, several directly or ultimately go back to Greek; see section 10.2 (2).

[16] The bases from which *vispell(i)o* and *vetellus/vitellus* are derived are unclear: *Vetellus* (Erf) literally is 'a little old man'; possibly, this is a misspelling of *vitellus* (Ép), lit. 'little calf' (from *vitulus*) – a connection with the Roman emperor Vitellius seems doubtful. The normal Latin word for 'father-in-law' was *socer, socrus*.

[17] The replacement of the Roman gods by their Germanic equivalents was common practice in the days of the week (e.g. *dies martis* – *tiwesdaeg* > *Tuesday*), which are loan-translations going back to the 2nd or 3rd century A.D., i.e. to the West-Germanic period.

[18] On the meaning of OE *wyrd*, see, e.g. Weber (1969) and Stanley (1975) with reference to earlier discussions; see also Strite (1989: 70f.) for references.

[19] On the etymology of *wyrd*, see section 6.7.

[20] Thus the same Latin word is rendered by two different Old English words (*parcae*: *uuyrdae*, *burgrunae*); conversely, the same Old English word renders two (or three) different Latin words: *uuyrd*: *parcae*, *condicio(nem)*, *sort(em)*. Cf. also *giroefa*: *censor(es)*, *commentariensis*.

[21] Perhaps a reflex of the fact that the church had never liked the Roman theatre and its plays.

[22] Another possible explanation would be that the glossator read *egregius*.

[23] Outside the word-field 'people', a nice case of translating a Latin word with its Old English antonym (and simultaneously a case of cultural adaptation/substitution) is: *res puplica* – *cynidom* 859.

[24] Cf. also *orcneas* 'monsters', *Beowulf* 112. *Orc* 'pitcher, cup, flagon', a loan-word from Lat *orca, urceus* is less likely, but cf. Pheifer (1974: 106).

[25] Usually through word-formation processes, especially compounding, and, probably to a lesser degree, derivation. Although most histories of the English language stress this fact, the only extensive study of this phenomenon (at least as far as Old English is concerned) is still Gneuss (1955). Cf. also, e.g., Kastovsky (1992: 300, 309-317).

[26] See Gneuss (1955).

[27] Irrelevant features are, e.g., the position of the elements and their inflection: whereas Lat *liber evangelii* is a genitival phrase with the noun in the genitive following the noun

in the nominative, the Old English loan-translation *godspellboc* has changed the order of elements as well as substituted the genitive by a nominative.

[28] See, e.g., Gneuss (1955); Toth (1980: 23-28).

[29] This is what Kastovsky (1992: 310) seems to suggest.

[30] See footnote 18 above.

[31] Apart from a few which were used frequently, in particular *hǣlend*, *scieppend*, *wealdend* and a few others. But even those which then became popular were probably originally loan-translations (*hǣlend* < *salvator*, *scieppend* < *creator*).

[32] For the purpose of distinguishing complex words from simplexes, we disregard inflexional endings. Simplexes can, of course, be useful for the semantic analysis.

[33] See, e.g., Sauer (1992); Stekauer (2000). For a recent introduction to English word-formation, see Schmid (2005). I disregard the question of accent here.

[34] In transformational terms, one could speak of an underlying sentence. For our purpose, we can disregard the question whether the sentence is just a paraphrase or whether it actually underlies the complex word and whether the complex word was derived from it.

[35] For a relatively consistent attempt to analyse English word-formation with the help of semantic roles, see Hansen *et al.* (1982).

[36] See Seebold (1970: 408); Kastovsky (1968: 144-145).

[37] A problem here is that *sceada* refers to a person, whereas the Latin lemmata in *ÉpErf* *piraticum*, *piraticam* rather refer to an action – perhaps the glossator confused *sceaða* with *sceaðe*, see further section 5.6.3. (5).

[38] In Indo-European, compounding consisted of a combination of stems rather than of a combination of words, however.

[39] See Carr (1939: 129 no. 13). In this as in other cases, Carr regards the OE, OHG and OLG parallels as "parallel and independent formations in the West Germanic languages", and not as inherited from West-Germanic – whether he is right here is another question.

[40] If other types, such as noun + deverbal noun, are subsumed under it, it obviously becomes an even stronger type.

[41] It is a rectional compound, however, if *sceade* is regarded as an action noun: 'damage done by vikings' < 'vikings do damage, commit crimes'.

[42] According to Pheifer (1974: 131; quoting earlier sources), Iring was a Germanic hero who slew Theoderic the Frank and escaped with the help of his sword; *Iringaes uueg* seems to imply (by way of exaggeration) that he escaped via or to the Milky Way. See now Heizmann, forthcoming.

[43] Marchand (1969: --) etc. indicates that there is no information on the pattern or affix in question.

[44] Cf. Seebold (1970: 104-106); Kastovsky (1968: 148f).

[45] Carr (1939) does not include compounds with locative particles in his treatment.

[46] See Sauer (1992: 182), who lists three formations, two of which, however, were newly formed in Early Middle English.

[47] For example, PDE *-hood* developed from the noun OE *hǣd*, which died out in ME; OE *dōm* split up into the PDE noun *doom* /du:m/ and the PDE suffix *-dom* /dəm/.

[48] My list differs slightly from the one in Kärre (1915: 228), probably due to the difficulty of separating agent nouns from present participles.

[49] Of the ten Latin nouns ending in *-or, -tor, -ator* (cf. section 10.2.3.), five have been glossed with Old English nouns in *-end(e)*: *adsessor(e) – fultemend(um)*; *grassator – ferhergaend*; *impulsor(e) – baedend(rae)*; *inpostor(em) – bisuicend*; *stipator(ibus) – ymbhringend(um)*; four have been glossed with Old English nouns ending in other suffixes or with Old English compounds: *aleator – teblere*; *censor(es) – giroefa(n)*; *gladiator(es) – caempa(n)*; *suffragator – mund-bora*. On the other hand, some Old English formations in *-end* render Latin words not ending in *-(a)(t)or*.

[50] Among the Latin lemmata in our material, the following five or six nouns in *-arius* occur:
actuaris (for *actuarius*?) – *uuraec*; *broelarius – edisc-u(e)ard*; *dromedarius – orit-mon*; *erpicarius* (for *herpicarius*) – *egderi*; *gregariorum – aedilra*; *tignarius – hrof-uuyrcta* – only one of them (*erpicarius*) has been glossed with an Old English noun ending in the suffix *-ere*.

[51] See section 5.6.1. An alternative, but less convincing explanation would be to regard *teblere* as a loan-word with a change of meaning, influenced by one of the meanings of *tabula*.

[52] According to Campbell (1959: 238 = § 592.d) *cneoriss* is “of uncertain formation”, whereas Pheifer (1974: lxxvii, fn. 3) explains the second element as *rysi* < **runsiz* (without giving a meaning), which would exclude it from the derivations in *-ess*, *-iss*.

[53] Herren (1998: 99) explains *haehtisse* (glossing *Eumenides*) as a corrupt form of *Hecates* ‘of Hecate’ (< **Hecatissa*).

[54] Munske (1964: 125), however, does not believe this explanation.

[55] *Byrgea* ‘trustee’ (G *Bürge*) is probably homonymous with (but not directly related to the stem of) *byrg(e)an* ‘to bury’ and *byrgere* ‘burier’.

[56] Similar considerations apply to the question of whether the formation of adverbs (with *-lice* > *-ly*) belongs to grammar or to word-formation.

[57] *Alumnis* Ép 115a, glossed by *aelifnae*, is a different word, see Pheifer (1974: 65f.: *alum*).

[58] Although given as a Latin lemma twice in *ÉpErf* (904, 953), *scina* is possibly not a Latin word, but OE *scīn*, *scinn*, *scinna* ‘spectre, illusion, evil spirit’, see Pheifer (1974: 123f.) and no. 42 in section 10.1.

References

(Many of the dictionaries, handbooks and editions have often been reprinted; of the *LexMA* there is also a CD-ROM edition.)

Bischoff, Bernhard *et al.* (eds.)
1988 *The Épinal, Erfurt, Werden, and Corpus glossaries.* (Early English Manuscripts in Facsimile 22.) Copenhagen: Rosenkilde and Bagger.

Brunner, Karl
1960-62 *Die englische Sprache: Ihre geschichtliche Entwicklung.* 2 vols. (2nd edition.) Tübingen: Niemeyer.

1965 *Altenglische Grammatik nach der Angelsächsischen Grammatik von Eduard Sievers.* (3rd edition.) Tübingen: Niemeyer.

Campbell, A[listair]
1959 *Old English grammar.* Oxford: Oxford University Press.

Carr, Charles T.
1939 *Nominal compounds in Germanic.* (St Andrews University Publications 41.) Oxford: Oxford University Press.

Conrad O'Briain, Helen *et al.* (eds.)
1999 *Text and gloss: Studies in insular learning and literature presented to Joseph Donovan Pheifer.* Dublin: Four Courts.

Falkner Wolfgang -- Hans-Jörg Schmid (eds.)
1999 *Words, lexemes, concepts: Approaches to the lexicon: Studies in honour of Leonhard Lipka.* Tübingen: Narr.

Gneuss, Helmut
1955 *Lehnbildungen und Lehnbedeutungen im Altenglischen.* Berlin: Schmidt.

1987-1989 s.v. 'Glossen, Glossare: IV', in: *LexMA.*

Goetz, Georg
1881-1923 *Corpus Glossariorum Latinorum.* 7 vols. Leipzig: Teuber.

Greenfield, Stanley B. -- Fred C. Robinson
1980 *A bibliography of publications on Old English literature to the end of 1972.* Toronto: University of Toronto Press.

Hansen, Barbara *et al.*
1982 *Englische Lexikologie.* Leipzig: VEB Verlag Enzyklopädie.

Heizmann, Wilhelm
(forthcoming) s.v. 'Thüringische Heldensagen', in: Hoops (ed.).

Herren, Michael W.
1998 "The transmission and reception of Graeco-Roman mythology in Anglo-Saxon England, 670-800", *Anglo-Saxon England* 27: 87-103.

Holthausen, Ferdinand
1934 *Altenglisches etymologisches Wörterbuch*. Heidelberg: Winter.
1974 3rd edition.

Hoops, Johannes (ed.)
1973- *Reallexikon der germanischen Altertumskunde*. (2nd edition.) Berlin: de Gruyter.

Jente, Richard
1921 *Die mythologischen Ausdrücke im altenglischen Wortschatz*. (Anglistische Forschungen 56.) Heidelberg: Winter.

Kärre, Karl
1915 *Nomina agentis in Old English*. Part I. Doctoral dissertation. Upsala [only part I published]: University Press.

Kastovsky, Dieter
1968 *Old English deverbal substantives derived by means of a zero morpheme*. Unpublished doctoral dissertation. University of Tübingen.

1971 "The Old English suffix *-ER(E)*", *Anglia* 89: 285-325.

1992 "Semantics and vocabulary ", in: *CHEL* 1, 290-408.

Ker, N.R

1957 *Catalogue of manuscripts containing Anglo-Saxon.* Oxford: Oxford University Press.

1990 Reprinted edition with supplement.

Kluge, Friedrich

1886 *Nominale Stammbildungslehre der altgermanischen Dialekte*. Halle: Niemeyer.

1926 3rd edition. Ed. Ludwig Sütterlin -- E. Ochs.

Klump, Wilhelm

1908 *Die altenglischen Handwerkernamen*. (Anglistische Forschungen 24.) Heidelberg: Winter.

Koo, Zung-Fung Wei

1946 *Old English living noun-suffixes exclusive of personal and place-names*. Unpublished doctoral dissertation. Radcliffe College, Cambridge, Mass.

Koziol, Herbert

1937 *Handbuch der englischen Wortbildungslehre*. Heidelberg: Winter.

1972 2nd edition.

Lapidge, Michael (ed.)

1995 *Archbishop Theodore: Commemorative studies on his life and influence*. (CSASE 11.) Cambridge: Cambridge University Press.

1996 *Anglo-Latin literature 600-899*. London: The Hambledon Press.

Lendinara, Patrizia

1999a s.v. 'Glossaries', in: *BEASE*.

1999b *Anglo-Saxon glosses and glossaries*. (Variorum collected studies series.) Aldershot: Ashgate.

Lenze, Josef
1909 *Das Präfix bi- in der altenglischen Nominal- und Verbalkomposition.* Doctoral dissertation. University of Kiel.

Leumann, Manu
1963 *Lateinische Laut- und Formenlehre.* (= Leumann -- Hofmann -- Szantyr, *Lateinische Grammatik* I.) München: Beck.

Lewandowska-Tomaszczyk, Barbara -- Irena Czwenar (eds.)
1999 *A new curriculum for English studies.* Piotrków Trybunalski: Naukowe Wydawnictwo Piotrkowskie przy Filii Akademii Swietokrzyskiej.

Lindsay, W.M
1921 *The Corpus, Épinal, Erfurt and Leyden glossaries.* (Publications of the Philological Society 8.) Oxford: Oxford University Press.

Marchand, Hans
1960 *The categories and types of Present-Day English word-formation.* Wiesbaden: Otto Harrassowitz.
1969 2nd edition. München: Beck.

Munske, Horst Haider
1964 *Das Suffix *-inga/-unga in den germanischen Sprachen.* Marburg: Elwert.

Pheifer, Joseph Donovan (ed.)
1974 *Old English glosses in the Épinal-Erfurt glossary.* Oxford: Oxford University Press.

1995 "The Canterbury bible glosses: Facts and problems", in: Lapidge (ed.), 281-333.

Roberts, Jane -- Christian Kay
1995 *A thesaurus of Old English.* 2 vols. London: King's College.

2000 2nd edition. Amsterdam: Rodopi.

Ryder, Mary Ellen
1994 *Ordered chaos: The interpretation of English noun-noun compounds.* Berkeley: University of California Press.

Sauer, Hans
1992 *Nominalkomposita im Frühmittelenglischen.* (Buchreihe der Anglia 30.) Tübingen: Niemeyer.

1999a "Old English plant names in the Épinal-Erfurt glossary: Etymology, word-formation and semantics", in: Falkner -- Schmid (eds.), 23-38.

1999b "Animal Names in the Épinal-Erfurt Glossary", in: Conrad O'Briain *et al.* (eds.), 128-58.

2000 "Time words and time concepts in Anglo-Saxon prose: The *Theodulfi Capitula*", in: Lewandowska-Tomaszczyk -- Czwenar (eds.), 251-74.
2003 Revised reprint, in: *Prospero: Rivista di culture anglo-germaniche* 10: 247-71.

Schlutter, Otto Bernhard
1912 *Das Epinaler und Erfurter Glossar:* Vol. 1: *Faksimile und Transliteration des Epinaler Glossars.* (Bibliothek der angelsächsischen Prosa 8.) Hamburg: Grand.

Schmid, Hans-Jörg
2005 *Englische Morphologie und Wortbildung.* (Grundlagen der Anglistik und Amerikanistik 25.) Berlin: Schmidt.

Seebold, Elmar
1970 *Vergleichendes und etymologisches Wörterbuch der germanischen starken Verben.* (Janua Linguarum ser. pract. 85.) The Hague: Mouton.

Stanley, Eric G
1975 *The search for Anglo-Saxon paganism.* Cambridge: Brewer.

Stekauer, Pavol
1998 *An onomasiological theory of English word-formation.* Amsterdam: Benjamins.

2000 *English word-formation: A history of research (1960-1995).* Tübingen: Narr.

Strite, Vic
1989 *Old English semantic field studies.* (American University Studies. IV.100.) New York: Lang.

Sweet, Henry (ed.)
1883 *The Épinal glossary, Latin and Old-English.* (EETS o.s. 79b) Photo-Lithographed from the original MS by W. Griggs. London: Humphrey Milford, Oxford University Press.
1936 Reprinted edition.

1885 *The oldest English texts.* (EETS o.s. 83.) London: Oxford University Press.

Toth, Karl
1980 *Der Lehnwortschatz der althochdeutschen Tatian-Übersetzung.* Würzburg: Königshausen & Neumann.

Tournier, Jean
1985 *Introduction descriptive à la lexicogénétique de l'anglais contemporain.* Paris: Champion-Slatkine.

Weber, Gerd Wolfgang
1969 *Wyrd: Studien zum Schicksalsbegriff der altenglischen und altnordischen Literatur.* Bad Homburg: Gehlen.

The assize of bread (1256)

Claire Fennell (Trieste, Italy)

1. Introduction

In their Introduction to Book I (1235-1377) of the *Statutes of the realm*, printed in 1810, the editors found that the extant statutes of Henry III (1216-72) were written almost entirely in Latin, whereas the statutes of Edward I (1272-1307) and Edward II (1307-27) were written in both Latin and French. The editors wrote:

> It seems on the whole to be highly probable that for a long Period of Time, Charters, Statutes and other Public Instruments were drawn up indiscriminately in French or Latin, and generally translated from one of those Languages into the other, before the Promulgation of them, which in many Instances appears to have been made at the same Time in both Languages. (Record Commission 1831: xlii)

The editors merely took note, *en passant*, of a "very ancient [English] Translation of some of the Statutes of the Time of Henry III and Edward I" (Record Commission 1831: xlii).

One of these statutes, known as the *assisa panis et ceruisie*, laid down the "method by which the price of ale and bread was to be fixed" (Salter 1921: 130), and also established the profit and reimbursement to which the baker was entitled, known as the *lucrum pistoris*. The *assisa panis et ceruisie* is extant in many manuscripts; I can mention only five here (cf. 4. Edition: list of manuscripts). In a footnote placed at the beginning of their text, based on Cotton Claudius, MS D II (C), the editors of the *Statutes of the realm* observed that "[t]he Printed Copies give this as a Statute of 51 Hen. III" (Record Commission 1831: 199), but prudently write *Temp. Incert.* above it (Record Commission 1831: 200). Nevertheless, until recently the statute was generally assigned by scholars to the 51st year of Henry III's reign (1266/7). In his introduction to the records of courts held in Oxford in connection with the assize of bread and ale between 1309 and 1351, Salter took issue with the dating of the statute to 1267, for, he maintained,

> [t]he Statute [...] is really of uncertain date; and in any case it is certain that the assize was much older [... it] was nothing more than recognizing what existed already, and ordaining that the same scale should be used throughout the realm (Salter 1921: 130).

It is certainly true that few of the many extant versions of the Assize are provided with a dating clause, and that the assize *per se* was nothing new (Cunningham 1910: 567-9). What is new, however, is the price-weight relationship of wheat and bread which is the basis for the calculations in C. This arithmetical relation is not applied in an incomplete *assisa panis*, contained in MS Peterborough 1 (P), fol. 85v, preceded by the dating clause "die Mart*is* p*roximo* t*re*s sept*imanas* pasch*e* Anno d*o*m*ini* m°. cc° .L.iij. [iij] yd*us* Maii" (Tuesday 13th May 1253) – but is applied in an undated version of the statute written out on the page facing the 1253 assize, virtually identical to the text in C. In 1963 Betty Hill was able to show that under the year 1256 the annals of Burton Abbey (Staffordshire), having stated that "justices were sent throughout the country to reform the measures, *qui etiam per loca assisam panis, vini et cervisiae sub forma tradiderunt subsequenti*" (Hill 1963: 204), gave a text using the method adopted in C. An Anglo-Norman assize, Huntingdon, 31911, fol. 264, using the same calculations, is followed by the date clause, "anno regni regis henrici filii Regis Iohannis xlv°" – that is, 45 Henry III 1(261/2). So I think the promulgation of the assize can be assigned with a fair degree of certainty to 1256.

The meaning of *assize* (Latin *assisa*, Anglo-Norman *assise*, Middle English *assise*) as it is used in the *assize of bread and ale* is 'ordinance…regulating quality, weight, size, price, etc., of commodities' (*MED*, s.v. 'assise' 3 [a]). From the regulation of size to the (statutory, or standard) size itself the step was evidently short, and today the aphetic form of the word, *size*, is there to remind us of an ordinance that "as a control on the charges of bakers…would presumably have been useful to virtually any consumer" (Cartlidge 1997: 259), and would remain unrepealed until 1836. In truth, although the word *assise* exists in Old French, with various meanings deriving from the fundamental one of 'session', I have found the meaning given to it in the *Assize of bread* only in the *AND*, not in the Old French ones I consulted. The *OED* (s.v. 'assize'), takes note of a suggestion made by Stubbs that the meaning 'ordinance' assumed by *assisa/assise* in trilingual England might have come about by the word being used to render Old English *ʒesetnes*, Middle English *isetnesse* 'statute, ordinance'. At this point, it is perhaps worth quoting Plucknett (1922: 12) on the non-technical uses of such terms as *statute*, *ordinance* and so forth in the period to which our assize belongs: "[certain] passages […] suggest that the word 'statute' means the provision made rather than the instrument embodying it […]" … "there is no contrast expressed or distinction visible between statutes and ordinances. Neither of these words was as yet a technical term, and neither had any special meaning" (Plucknett 1922: 33).

I should like now to consider four versions of the assize, or rather, of a part of it (the *Assize of bread*), none of which, as far as I know, has been printed before, and which I print in section 4 of this paper. Two are written in Latin, in P, fol. 86^r, and Oxford, Jesus College, MS 29 II (J), fol. 195^r; one in Anglo-Norman, in London & Oslo, The Schøyen Collection, MS 563 (S), fol. 76; and one in Middle English, in Oxford, Rawlinson, MS B 520 (R), fols. 43^v-44^r. The manuscripts that contain them were all compiled around the turn of the thirteenth century, that is, during the reign of that "great legislator [...] great administrator [...] great organizer" (Maitland 1908: 20), Edward I, when collections of the statutes begin to appear.

The weights and measures we shall find in the Latin versions of the assize of bread are *quarterium. libra, solidus, denarius, obolus* and *quadrans*, in the Anglo-Norman version *quartier, liuere, sou, dener, obole, ferlink/quadrant*, and in the English *quarter, pound, silling, peni, halpeni* and *furþing*. Before outlining the arithmetic involved in the assize of bread, I shall briefly refer to part of a constitution of weights and measures that is contained in both S (fol. 76^r) and R (fol. 42^v), which I also print in section 2. The basic unit of weight (and price) is the silver penny. Thirty-two average grains of wheat make a penny, 20 pence an ounce, 12 ounces or 20 shillings a pound, 8 pounds a gallon, 8 gallons a bushel, and 8 bushels a quarter. Although to our way of thinking we have here a mixture of weights, measures and prices, it is not hard to calculate that the weight of a quarter of wheat, on which the price of bread is based, is 512 lb. Our two lists do not spell out how many pence make a shilling, but given that there are 20 pence to the ounce, and 12 ounces to the pound, it follows that there are 240 pence to the pound; and since the pound weighs 20 shillings, there are, indeed, 12 pence to the shilling. Prices in the *Assize of bread* are in terms of weight – starting with the pennyworth of silver – but the weight will be expressed in pounds, shillings, pence, halfpence and farthings (with 12 pence to the shilling and 20 shillings to the pound).

Now for a brief summary of the mathematics involved in the assize of bread. The assize started by establishing the relation between the price of a quarter of wheat (512 lbs.) and the price of a loaf of bread, or rather, between the price of a quarter of wheat and the weight of the standard farthing loaf, the wastel (the same lexeme as modern French *gâteau*). The price of the loaf remained constant, but its weight decreased or increased as the price of wheat rose or fell. Alan Ross has investigated the "arithmetical relation between the price per quarter of corn (p) and the weight of the unit, the farthing-wastel-loaf (w)" (Ross 1956: 340). In the earlier assizes, according to his calculations, for every increase of a penny in p, there was a decrease of a shilling in w, expressed in the relation w=12 (7-p) (and this method was still being applied in the 1256 version of the assize to prices of corn ranging from 3 s. to 4 s. 6 d. So it is in all our versions of the assize: for instance when p=12d., w=12 (7-3)=12 x 4=48s., or 2 lb. 8 s.). In the 1256 assize, however, the relation of w to p was calculated according to the principle of inverse proportion, expressed in wp=136 (Ross 1956: 340). In all our versions, except R, which omits the "16 shillings", when p=12 d., w=136 s., that is, 6 lbs. 16 s., and so on.

Space does not allow me to go through each and every variation in the price of a quarter of wheat from one to twelve shillings to see how our four versions agree with each other and with the correct weight of the farthing-loaf according to Ross's calculations. What does seem to emerge, however, is that the mistakes, of which there are several, usually involve either an omission, or the addition or subtraction of a unit, which given the use of the minim to express one, and four minims to express number four, is a fairly easy slip to make.

Having set the lowest price for the quarter of wheat (12 d., or 1 s.), and the heaviest weight for the standard, or wastel, loaf (6 lb. 16 s.), the assize went on to establish the relative weights of six other qualities of bread from which a farthing loaf might be made. These were listed in descending order of quality, with one apparent exception. After the wastel came the cocket (two qualities), the simnel, whole wheat bread, treat bread and meal bread. The poorer the quality of the bread, obviously, the heavier the loaf. The first type of cocket weighed 2 s. more than the wastel, the second type 5 s. more; the simnel weighed 2 s. less (this is the exception), the whole wheat loaf one and a half cockets, the treat loaf two wastels, and the meal loaf two cockets.

We can make out a list of the weight in the 1256 assize of a farthing loaf of the various types of bread when a quarter of wheat cost 12 d.:

12 d.	*wastel*		6 lb 16s.
12 d.	*first cocket*	[wastel + 2 s.]	6 lb. 18 s.
12 d.	*second cocket*	[wastel + 5 s.]	7 lb. 1 s.
12 d.	*simnel*	[wastel – 2 s.]	6 lb. 14 s.
12 d.	*whole wheat*	[1.5 cockets]	10 lb. 11 s. 6 d.
12 d.	*treat*	[2 wastels]	13 lb 12 s.
12 d.	*meal*	[2 cockets]	14 lb. 2 s.

It is apparent from this list that I have calculated the weights of the *panis integer* and the *panis de omni blado* on the basis of the weight of the second, heavier, inferior cocket loaf. None of the texts considered in this paper tells us which of the two cockets is meant, but an assize of bread contained in the roughly contemporary *Oak Book of Southampton* calls the second cocket *cocketus maior* and stipulates that the *panis integer* should weigh "cocketum et dimidium maioris ponderis" (Studer 1910-11: 29) and the *panis de omni blado* "ij cocketos maioris ponderis" (Studer 1910-11: 31). Since the prices in general coincide with those of our assizes, I think we can follow the *Oak Book* on this.

After establishing the weight of the standard farthing loaf and of the other six types of bread when a quarter of wheat cost twelve pence (or *denarii* or *deners*), that is, a shilling (or *solidus* or *sou*), the assize went on to calculate the weights of the wastel farthing loaf for wheat prices ranging from 1 s. 6. d. to 12 s. a quarter, going up by 6 d. a time. In our assizes, these are written out consecutively, that is, they are not entered as tables, and in each assize the exact words used to express the relationship vary somewhat before the most economical formula is found and then kept to, generally at the point in which a quarter of wheat costs 2 s. 6 d. I have stopped printing each text when this happens. As a matter of fact, the English version never does hit on a single formula, so I have reproduced it in full. Since the English version, unlike the Anglo-Norman and especially the Latin versions, also hardly ever resorts to abbreviations, and indeed sometimes writes out numbers in full, it appears to be quite a bit longer than the others.

2. The manuscripts and their versions

Each of our four versions of the *Assize of bread* is different as regards the part or parts of the *Assize of bread and ale* that appear(s) in the manuscript, and the order in which they are set out. Of the Latin versions, P has no rubric, and contains the *assisa panis* and the *lucrum pistoris*, but not the *assisa ceruisie*; J, which is not complete, contains only the assize of bread, under a centred heading "Ass[isa] panis Anglie". The English and Anglo-Norman versions both contain all three parts of the statute. The English version has first a general heading, "Here biginnez þe Assise of bred ant of Ale", and ends with "Here hendez þe assise of bred ant of ale". However, whereas the assize of bread is followed by the *lucrum pistoris* without a break, the assize of ale begins a new line, and space is made at the end of that line to write, in red, "Assise of ale". In the Anglo-Norman version, in which the *lucrum pistoris* follows the assize of ale, the three parts of the assize are each given as separate instruments, with a separate rubric, respectively "Incipit assisa panis", "Incipit assisa Ceruisie", and "Incipit lucrum pistoris".

I shall now take a brief look at the manuscripts in which our four assizes appear. P is a cartulary of the Abbey of Peterborough, written mainly in Latin, with some Anglo-Norman texts, at present housed in Cambridge University Library. The manuscript originally belonged to Robert Swapham, successively pittancer and cellarer of the Abbey, who died in 1273. The first 350 leaves (which incidentally include the best Latin version of the story of Hereward the

Exile – later to be known as the *Wake* – on fols. 320-339) were "compiled in the end of the thirteenth and beginning of the fourteenth centuries" (Hardy -- Martin 1888: xlvii). It is immediately preceded by the imperfect 1253 version of the statute we noticed earlier; this is written in a rather cramped hand below the closing lines of a constitution, in Anglo-Norman, of weights and measures, which lacks the beginning, the very part that concerns the *Assize of bread* (fols. 85); before that by an Anglo-Norman glossary of English legal terms (fol. 84), and a list in Latin of the counties and bishoprics of England (fol. 83^{v}-84^{r}). Our assize, which is written out in a rather informal hand, is followed by three blank pages (fols. 86^{v}. and 87), then by a list of *Privilegia apostolica* (fol. 88).

The second Latin assize is the only piece of Latin in J (the *The owl and the nightingale*-MS), presently housed in the Bodleian Library, which otherwise contains virtually nothing but literary works, written in English before the *Assiza* and in Anglo-Norman after it. The *Assize* occupies sixteen and a half lines, with seven lines left blank at the end of the page. It is preceded on the same page by the closing lines of a description, in English, of the shires and bishoprics of England – the only other work "of general reference" in the manuscript (Cartlidge 1997: 259) – and before that by a verse homily on "soþe luue" (fols. 193^{r}-194^{r}), an "orison of our lord" (fols. 192^{r}-193^{r}) – each headed "Tractatus quidam", and the *Proverbs of Alfred* (fols. 189^{r}-192^{r}) headed "Incipiunt documenta Regis Aluredi". It is followed on folio 195^{v} by an Anglo-Norman poetic work entitled "Ici comence de Tobye". It is the date of our *assisa* which provides the date *post quem* for the manuscript.

S is at present in Oslo, in the custody of its owner, Martin Schøyen. This codex, like R, is a collection of statutes. Of these collections Woodbine (1990: 9) observed that

> one of the most interesting of the many types of manuscript volumes from the thirteenth and fourteenth centuries is that which was compiled for the use of English lawyers during the period of the first three Edwards... it contained, if not the whole, at least a large part, of the library of the lawyer who owned it. The volume usually begins with a collection of the Statutes which goes down to about the time the book was written. Following this come a number of tracts and treatises... [o]ften a Register of Writs complete the volume [...].

The first of the Statutes was considered to be Magna Carta. S begins with an early *inspeximus*, dating back to 1225, the ninth year of Henry's reign; the latest dateable statute goes back to 1293. The assize is preceded by that part of a long description of weights and measures (fol. 76^{r}) which is to be found in section 2 below, and before that by a statute known by its first words as "Circumspecte agatis" (fols. 75^{v}-76^{r}), promulgated in 1285. It is followed on fol. 76^{v}, after the *assisa ceruisie* and the *lucrum pistoris*, by an *extenta manerii* (fol. 76^{v}-77^{r}), a series of instructions, formulated in 1276, on making a correct survey of manors.

R is the collection of statutes noted by the editors of the *Statutes of the realm*. It also begins with Magna Carta, in this case Edward I's *inspeximus* of 1297 or 1300 (all but the first folio of the charter is missing, so we have no dating clause). The latest dateable statute is from 1299. The *Assize of bread and ale* is preceded on fols. 42^{v}-43^{r} by a complete constitution of weights and measures, before that by instructions on the "maner to maken homage ant feoutee"; it is followed by the 1276 Statute of Exeter (fols. 44r-45r), erroneously entitled "Here...biginnez þe statut of Oxeneforde".

3. The description of the types of bread

I would now like to make a comparison of the way in which our four versions indicate and describe the various types of bread, to see if this suggests anything about the relationships between the four texts as regards content and language. P tells us that the *wastell[us]* is "bene coctus", J that the *wastellus* is "albus et bene coctus"; S that the *wastel* is "bien buletee e bien quyt"; R that the standard loaf is "þe furþing of wite bred ant alse þe wastel". The wastel was obviously a well baked loaf made of white, finely boulted wheat flour. Each of our texts concentrates on different characteristics of the loaf, its whiteness, the length of its baking, the fineness of the flour. The English text actually pairs the wastel with "wite bred", as if they were two different types of loaf, of equal value. Whether the wastel was actually what we would call bread, or rather something more similar to a brioche, with the addition of eggs, butter, milk and/or sugar, is one of the many questions I have not the time to pursue in this paper.

Of the next type of bread, which was only slightly heavier than the wastel – 138 shillings as against 136 – three texts give us the same information. P and J inform us that the *koket[us]* was made "de eodem blado et de eodem bultello" as the wastel, S that the *coket* was "de meme le blee e de meme le buletel" (The grain was of the same quality, and the sifting as fine; could it have been slightly less well done, and therefore heavier?). In R we read that the *coket* is "of þilke sulue corne ant bussel". Evidently, the scribe either misread or misunderstood the word *bul(e)tel(lus)* in some exemplar – <lt> in some scripts does look very similar to <ss>. In the context, at any rate, the word *bussel* makes some sort of sense, because we could take the relative phrase to mean "of the same grain and of the same batch". What is not certain, of course, is what language the potential exemplar was written in, since *bultel* is one of those words that were lifted straight from one language into the other.

As for the second kind of cocket, the assize in P specifies that it is "de blado minoris precii", and the *Assisa panis anglie* in J adds "& de grossiori bultello", than the wastel. In S we read that it is "de blee de mendre pris", and in R "of corne of lasse pris". The words might be construed to mean that the flour was not wheaten – each version uses its indigenous word for corn, which can mean any type of grain, not only wheat – but I am inclined to think that the grain was in fact wheat, albeit from an inferior batch, and was less finely sifted than the wastel and cocket 1, which meant that more bran was left in.

We now come to the apparent exception in our list, the simnel – (P *simenell[us]*, J *symenel*, S *simenel*, R *siminel*), which is listed after the two cockets but weighs two shillings less than the wastel. None of the texts I have selected gives any description of the simnel, or the reason for this apparent anomaly. However, the assize in C (fol. 252^{v}) explains that simnel bread weighs less than the wastel "quia bis coctus est". In other words, it is lighter because having been baked twice it contains a lower percentage of humidity.

The last type of bread for which the same lexeme appears in all the versions is treat bread, (*tret* in P and S, *trait* in R; there is a line missing here in J). *Trait/tret* was the name given in Anglo-Norman to the second, middling coarse quality of bran, so treat bread – which is worth half the wastel – would be made of middling coarse wheat bran. It is worth 25% less than whole-wheat bread, so maybe there was virtually no flour in it at all.

We do have two kinds of bread that are described by each language in its own words, the third to last and the last quality. Like treat bread, they are only described, not given a name. The first is described as *integer de frumento* in P and J, *enteer de furment* in S, *al hol* in R. This is pretty clearly 'whole-wheat', made, that is, of wheat flour together with the bran, perhaps the finer bran, since it is worth 25% more than treat bread. The second, which is the cheapest bread of all, is described as being made *de omni blado* in P and J, *de tuz blez* in S, *of alle kunne corne* in R, that is, from any type of meal: rye, barley, oats or even peas (in later English versions of the assize we find it being called *horse bread*!).

I think we may now make a few observations about the assize of bread as it appears in our four selected versions. Our assizes represent something like 4 % of all the extant versions we know of, but there are probably many more we are not aware of. Even as far as these four versions are concerned, given the space at my disposal, I have been able to take only a most cursory look at their content, context, and language. As regards the content, we have seen that the assizes show a great deal of freedom in the way they are written down, the way they describe certain types of bread, the order in which they present their information, even their formulation of the relationship between the price of corn and the weight of the farthing loaf. Before drawing any serious conclusions from these data, we should have to examine most if not all of the extant assizes. It might be argued by some, for instance, that the various forms of the assize we have here, as well as others we have not considered, might fall into some recognizable pattern; or that all the Latin versions might turn out to share certain characteristics as against the Anglo-Norman ones – of the English versions, I know only of the existence of R.

What we have said about the content of the assizes is true of the context in which we find them. Two manuscripts (R and S) are collections of statutes: R is written entirely in English, S is written almost indiscriminately in Anglo-Norman and Latin, though the rubrics are all in Latin. One manuscript is a cartulary (P), written mainly in Latin, with some Anglo-Norman, but contains an explanation in Anglo-Norman of some English legal terms. And finally, J is an almost exclusively poetic compilation, in which there is "little to suggest a subordinate status for any of the three languages" (Scahill 2003: 29). We have seen that the *assisa* is preceded by a list, in English, of the shires and bishoprics of England, a useful guide for lawyers when planning eyries. The list, this time in Latin, also precedes the assize in P, though not immediately, while it is absent from the two collections of statutes. We saw that three of our assizes are immediately preceded by a description of weights and measures, of which the one in P, without a heading, lacks the begininning, the very part that would have been useful for the assize; R is complete, and is headed "composicion of mesures", S has the beginning only, the part that concerns the assize of bread, under the rubric "composicio monete & mensure". Each of our assizes is followed by a different text, and we may note that there is no chronological order to be perceived in the arrangement of the datable texts within the codices. The grouping of the texts seem rather to reflect a similarity of subject – for instance, in our case, numbers and lists – whereas the choice of what statute or tract to include in the collections of statutes seems to be dictated rather by the interests of a given individual.

Finally, as regards the linguistic aspect of the assizes, we have seen how some terms are lifted straight from one language to another, for instance the designations of certain types of bread. The language most often borrowed from seems to be Anglo-Norman, and for our assizes we may well appropriate Studer's comments on an entry in a roughly contemporary collection of municipal ordinances, the *Oak book of Southampton*: "the language [...] is Norman French (or, as it is now often called, Anglo-French); other entries are in mediaeval Latin, which often is but thinly disguised French or English" (Studer 1910-11: I, vii), and again "some of the words have not even been translated into Latin, but appear in their French form, though occasionally the scribe has adorned them with a Latin termination" (Studer 1910-11: II, vi). In P, in fact, not once are the endings for *wastell*, *simenell* or *koket* written out in full, though they are for other words, and the form of the word *treat*, that is, *tret*, reflects Anglo-Norman phonology. We have noticed that some of these words are peculiar to the French of England, and that the extension of the possible meanings of *assisa/assise* to include regulation of the price of bread and ale might have been influenced by English usage. Furthermore, our Anglo-Norman assize (though not the two Latin ones!) actually adopts the English lexeme *furþing*, for it refers to the wastel farthing loaf as *le wastel de ferlink*, whereas when giving the weight of the loaf it always uses the abbreviation *q.* (Anglo-Norman or Latin?) for the farthing. Apart from these cases, the names of the weights are Latin in the Latin texts, romance in the Anglo-Norman texts, and English in the English text. In other words: each language seems to have gone its own way as far as expressing the meaning of the statutes was concerned, each borrowing from the other whenever convenient. Finally, what are we to make of R, the – as far as I know – solitary extant English collection of statutes dating from the time of Edward I? Were the editors of the *Statutes of the realm* wrong to consider only Anglo-Norman and Latin as the languages in which the statutes were promulgated during his reign? If not, then the existence of this English collection of statutes, compiled for the use of an English lawyer so soon after the promulgation of the statutes themselves, might still be one more instance of some "higher local status of written English" (Scahill 2003: 31).

4. Edition

In printing the texts below I have expanded all the abbreviations (which appear in italics), in order to facilitate the reader. Sometimes I have had to guess at the intentions of the scribe; I feel sure that on more than one occasion he had no particular idea in his own mind as to what the expanded version of his abbreviations might be.

I have maintained the punctuation of the scribe, though I have sometimes had to make my own decisions. Where he placed full stops at various distances from the words that preceded and followed them, especially when writing numbers, I have made a choice and applied it throughout. In the case of certain letters, such as <w>, it is virtually impossible to distinguish upper from lower case.

The symbol { represents the paragraph mark in P, R and S. Words placed between square brackets are my own proposed additions or emendations.

List of manuscripts mentioned or edited here:

1. C: London, British Library, MS Cotton Claudius D ii (Middle English; not edited here; edition: Record Commission, *The Statutes of the Realm*, I)
2. J: Oxford, Jesus College, MS 29 (II) (Latin; edited below)
3. P: Peterborough, MS 1; housed in Cambridge, University Library (Latin; edited below)
4. R: Oxford, Bodleian Library, MS Rawlinson B 520 (Middle English; edited below)
5. S: London & Oslo, The Schøyen Collection, MS 563 (Latin and French [Anglo-Norman]; edited below)

P: Peterborough, MS 1

[fol. 86^r] {Quando quart*erium* fr*umenti* vendit*ur* p*ro* .xij. d*enarios*. tunc Panis Wastell*i* pond*erabit* .vj. Li*bras* .xvj. Panis aut*em* de koket de eod*em* blado & de eod*em* bultell*o* pond*erabit* plus q*ua*m Wastell*o* .ij. s*olidos*. et de blado minor*is* p*re*cii pond*erabit* plus q*ua*m Wastell*o* .v. s*olidos*. Panis v*ero* Simenell*i*. pond*erabit* minus Wastello .ij. s*olidos* & pan*is* integ*er* de q*uadrante* de fr*umento* pond*erabit*. Coket & dim*idium*. Panis v*ero* de Tret pond*erabit* .ij. Wastell*os*. Panis v*ero* de om*n*i Blado pond*erabit* .ij. Cok*etos*. {Quando q*uarterium* fr*umenti* vend*itur* p*ro* .xviij. d*enariis*. Tunc panis de wastell*o* bene coctus pond*erabit* .iiij. Li*bras* .x. s*olidos* .viij. d*enarios*. {Qu*ando* vendit*ur* p*ro* .ij. s*olidis*. Tunc pan*is* de q*uadrante* pond*erabit* .Lxviij. s*olidos*. {Quand*o* vendit*ur* p*ro* .ij. s*olidis* .vj. d*enariis*. Tunc pan*is*. q*uadrantis*. pond*erabit* .Liiij. s*olidos* .iiij. d*enarios*. ob*olum*. q*uadrantem* [...]

J: Oxford, Jesus College, MS 29 (II)

[fol. 195^r] Ass*isa* panis Anglie

Qvando frum*en*tum vendit*ur* p*ro* .xij. denar*iis*. tu*n*c wastellus de q*uad*ran*te*. alb*us* & ben*e* coctus. po*n*d*er*abit sex libr*as*. & sexdecim solid*os*. Panis aut*em* de koket. de eode*m* blado & de eode*m* Bultello. pond*er*ab*it* pl*us* wa[s]tello .ij. s*olidos*. & blado minor*is* p*re*cii & de grossiori bultello plus q*uam* wastello [.v. s*olidos*]. Panis de symenel min*us* de wastello ponderabit .ij. s*olidos*. Panis integer [de q*uadrante* de fr*umento* pond*erabit*. Coket & dim*idium*. Panis v*ero* de Tret] ponderabit .ij. wastellos. & panis de o*mn*i blado .ij. kokes.

Qvando q*uarterium* de frum*en*to vend*itur*. p*ro* .ij. s*olidis*. tu*n*c pond*er*abit wastell*us* .lxviij. sol*idos*. Qv*a*ndo p*ro* .ij. s*olidis*. & .vi. denar*iis*: tu*n*c po*n*d*er*ab*it* .Liij. sol*idos* .iiij. denar*ios*. & .iij. quadr*antes*.

S: London & Oslo, The Schøyen Collection, MS 563

[fol. 76r] *Incipit Composicio monete & mensure.*

Per discrecionem totius Regni Anglie fuit mensura d*omi*ni Reg*is* co*m*posita videlicet quod denarius anglican*us* qui vocat*ur* sterlingus rotundus sit & sine tonsura et ponderabit .xxxij. grana frum*en*ti rubei in medio spice. {Et .xx. denar*ii* faciunt vnciam Et .xij. vncie faciunt libram. scil*ice*t .xx. solid*os*. Et .viij. libre faciunt gallonem vini & octo gallones vini faciunt bussellum london*iensem* Hoc est octauam p*ar*tem q*ua*rterii. {*Explicit Composicio monete & mensure. Incipit assisa panis*

Qaunt le quarter de furment se vend pur .xij. den*er*s donc peysera le Wastel de ferlink bien buletee e bien quyt. vj liueres e .xvj. souz. Payn Coket de meme le blee e de meme le buletel peysera plus ke le Wastel de deus souz. E de blee de mendre pris peysera plus ke le Wastel de. iiij Souz. le Simenel peysera meyns du wastel de deuz souz le Payn enteer de furment peysera Coket e demy. payn de tret peysera deus Wasteus. {E payn de tuz blez peysera deus Cokes. {Qaunt pur .xviij. deners donk peysera le wastel de ferlink .iiij. liueres .x souz. e viij. deners. {Qaunt pur. deus souz donk peysera. lxviij. souz. {Qaunt pur .ij. souz e .vj. den*er*s donk liiij. souz. iiij. d*eners*. ob*ole*. q*uadrant*......

R: Oxford, Bodleian Library, Rawlinson, MS B 520

[fol. 42v] Here...biginnez þe composicion of Mesures

Þoru þe discrecion of al þe reaume of yngelonde was þe king-ges mesures imade. þat is to wite þat te Englisse peni. þat is cleoped sterling round ant biþoute clippinge sal pisen tuuo ant þritti greines of wete. amidde þe pis. {Ant .xx. panes makez an vnze. ant tuuelfe vnzene makiez a pound .xx. sillinges. ant Eȝtte pound makez a galon. ant Eȝtte galons makez a bussel of Londone þe Etteþe del a quarter...

[fols. 43v-44r] Here biginnez þe Assise of bred ant of Ale.

Wan me sullez þe quarter of ȝwete for .xii. panes. þanne sal þe furþing worth bred. weie .vj. pond [ant xvj sillinges] ase of wastel. þe furþing worth bred of Coket. of þilke sulue corne. ant bussel. sal weie more þan þe wastel. bi .ij. sillinges. ant of corne of lasse pris. þe coket sal weien more þan þe wastel bi .v. sillinges. þe bred of siminel sal weie lasse þan þe wastel bi .ij. sillinges. Of al hol bred þe furþingwort sal weie a Coket ant an half. Bred of trait sal weie tuuei wasteles. Bred of alle kunne corne. sal weie. tuuei cokettes. {Wan þe quarter of wete is isold for .xviij. panes. þanne sal. þe furþing of wite bred ant alse þe wastel. weien .þre [iiij] pond. ant .x. sillinges. ant .viij. panes. Wan þe quarter wete. is at .ij. silling. þanne sal þe furþingworth weie eȝtte ant sixti sillinges. Ant wan. þe quarter is at tuuei sillinges ant .vj. panes. þanne sal þe furþingworth. weie .iiij. ant vifti sillinges. ant .iiij. panes ant halfpeni. ant a furþing. Ant wan he is at. þre sillinges. þanne þe bred of a furþing. sal weien .viij. ant .xl. sillinges. Wan he is at þreo sillinges ant .vj. panes. þanne sal þe furþingworth weie tuuo ant forti sillinges. Wan he is at .iiij. sillinges. þanne sal þe furþing weie .vj. ant. þritti sillinges. Wan he is for .iiij. sillinges ant .vj. panes. þanne sal þe furþingworth weie. þritti sillinges . Wan he is for vif sillinges. þanne sal þe furþing bred weie .vif. ant .xx sillinges ant .ij. panes ant an half peni. Wan for .vif. sillinges. ant .vj. panes. þanne sal þe furþing bred weie .iiij. ant .xx. sillinges ant .viij. panes ant a furþing. Wan for .vj. sillinges. þanne is a furþing bred .xxij. sillinges. ant viij. panes. Wan for .vj. sillinges ant .vj. panes. þanne þe furþing bred sal weie .xx. sillinges ant .xi. panes. Wan for .vij. sillinges. þanne þe furþing bred sal weie .xix. sillinges ant .v. panes. Wan for .vij. sillinges. ant .vj. panes. þanne sal þe furþing bred weie .xviij sillinges ant a peni ant halpeni. Wan for .viij. sillinges. þanne þe furþing bred sal weie xvij sillinges ant vj panes. Wan for .viij. sillinges ant .vj. panes. þanne sal þe furþing bred weie .xvij. sillinges. Wan for nine sillinges. þanne sal þe furþing bred weie viftene sillinges ant a furþing. Wan for nine sillinges ant .vj. panes. þanne sal þe furþing bred weie .xiiij. sillinges ant .iiij. panes ant an halpeni. ant. a furþing. Wan for .x. sillinges. þanne sal þe furþing bred weie .xii. sillinges ant .vij. panes ant a furþing. Wan for .x. sillinges ant .vj. panes. þanne þe furþing bred sal weie .xi. sillinges ant .iiij. panes ant a furþing. Wan for .xj. silling. [fol. 44^r] ant .vj. panes. þanne þe furþing bred sal weie .xii. sillinges ant x. panes. Wan for tuuelf sillinges. þanne þe furþing bred sal weie .xi. sillinges ant .iiij. panes ant an halpeni.

References

Cartlidge, Neil
1997 "The composition and social context of Oxford, Jesus College, MS 29(II) and London, British Library MS Cotton Caligula A.ix", *Medium Ævum* 66: 250-69.

Cunningham, W.
1910 *The growth of English industry and commerce*. (5th edition.) Cambridge: Cambridge University Press.

Hill, Betty
1963 "The history of Jesus College, Oxford, MS. 29", *Medium Ævum* 32: 203-13.

Hardy, Thomas Duffus -- Charles Trice Martin (eds.)
1888 *Lestoire des Engles solum la translacion Maistre Geffrei Gaimar.* (Rolls Series 91) Vol. I. London.

Maitland, Frederic W.
1908 *The constitutional history of England.* Cambridge: Cambridge University Press. [many reprints]

Plucknett, T.F.T.
1922 *Statutes and their interpretation in the first half of the fourteenth century.* Cambridge: Cambridge University Press.

Record Commission (ed.)
1831 *The statutes of the realm: Printed by command of His Majesty King George the Third in pursuance of an address of the House of Commons of Great Britain from original records and authentic manuscripts.* Vol I. n.p.: Record Commission.

Ross, Alan S.C.
1956 "The assize of bread", *Economic history review* (2nd series.) 9: 332-42.

Salter, Herbert Edward (ed.)
1921 *Mediaeval archives of the University of Oxford.* Vol. II. Oxford: Clarendon.

Scahill, John
2003 "Trilingualism in Early Middle English miscellanies. Languages and literature", *The year book of English studies* 33: 18-32.

Studer, Paul (ed.)
1910-11 *The Oak Book of Southampton of c. A.D. 1300.* 2 vols. Southampton: Cox and Sharland.

Woodbine, George Edward
1910 *Four thirteenth century law tracts.* Oxford: Oxford University Press.

Revising the Wyclif Bible

Conrad Lindberg (Linköping, Sweden)

1. Introduction

The Wyclif Bible exists in two versions, one more literal, one more idiomatic. Forshall -- Madden printed them in 1850 in parallel columns; in the present article, I have combined the two (see below), using the first text as a base and marking deviations from the second text by underlinings for additions, square brackets for omissions, a double apostrophe " for transpositions, numbered in footnotes in complex cases, and raised Arabic numerals for substitutions explained in footnotes. By thus giving the two texts together, I hope to make the changes from one version to the other more visible.

The process of translating the Bible is set out in the so-called *General Prologue* to the versions. The author, probably John Purvey, mentions four steps taken by someone he refers to as *he*, not improbably Wyclif himself: first to make a Latin bible sufficiently true, then to examine the text by using commentaries etc., thirdly, to consult others as to hard words and passages, and fourthly, the translation, that is the final version, not the preliminaries. A fifth step is suggested by his using competent men to correct, or revise the translation.

What we have now is a revised text of an original version. We can see how literal Latinisms were gradually eliminated in favour of more English phrasing. This process probably started from the very beginning, perhaps first by glossing the Latin text established, then extracting the first English rendering and making the literal text readable. The final step, or steps, meant a virtual re-translation of the earlier text, using guidelines set out in the *Prologue*: to translate after the sense and not only after the words, to resolve Latin constructions as the ablative absolute and participial constructions, also relative pronouns, to add (or omit) things understood in the text, to change the order of words, and to use connecting words freely.

2. Baruch 3.20: "risen. The ȝunge"

At this point (Bar. 3.20), two manuscripts of the earlier version break off abruptly, one (MS Bodley 959) at the end of a recto, and the other (MS Bodley Douce 369 1st part) with a note following: "here ends the translation of Nicholas of Hereford". A third manuscript (MS CUL Ee. Is. 10) says here: "here ends the translation of N and begins the translation of J".

Forshall -- Madden (1850) believed the first manuscript to be the original copy of the translator and the second to be a later copy. They do not mention the note in the third manuscript. They even went so far as to date the making of the first text to 1382 when Hereford was called away to the Blackfriars' synod in Rome. Fristedt (1953) showed in his thesis that Forshall -- Madden (1850) were wrong in thinking the break to be the end of the original translation, since the manuscript shows signs of having been copied from an even earlier text.

And yet, the agreement of the three manuscripts at this point must have a significance. It is reasonable to assume that the archetype behind these manuscripts was an unfinished original which was revised in the copying out of MS Bodley 959, which has many instances of original corrections and revisions. The date 1382 may not be far wrong, as Hereford was one of Wyclif's closest disciples in Oxford in the 1370s.

The J. mentioned in the Cambridge manuscript has been diversely interpreted: Margaret Deanesly might have thought it meant John Purvey; Forshall -- Madden (1850), who do not mention the note, may have thought it meant John Wycliffe; I, myself have thought of John Ashton, another close disciple of Wyclif's. The crucial question in this connection is how to interpret the word *translation*: is it meant to signify a version or can it stand for a revision? Let us consider the rest of the chapter.

There is a difference between the two halves of the third chapter of Baruch. Although mainly translated in the same fashion, the two versions tend to converge more, the number of changes are smaller as can be seen from the number of footnotes and notes. Is this the result of a change of translators or of a change of revisers? A change of translators would rather increase the differences, a change of revisers would be noticeable more in details, such as personal preferences.

This tendency in the two versions to converge is even more apparent in books coming after Baruch, sometimes, as in the Book of Jonah, so predominant that one may think of just one translation with minor modifications. I think this is the result of extensive revision undertaken with the aim of producing a uniform text, which was probably the ultimate aim from the very beginning. The preliminary steps taken were inevitable: first the gloss-like Latin-based turning of the Bible text, then the smoothing out of this crude version in a literal type of text, revised and approved before the final translation, using the earlier efforts, could be undertaken. This late version was copied extensively (there are more than 150 MSS extant of it, whereas the early version exists in less than 50 MSS), and in this process further revision was introduced, taking into account both of the existing texts.

Revising the Wyclif Bible then meant a scrupulous refinement of the text, constantly referring back to the Latin original and comparing variants of translation in order to arrive at a satisfactory version of the Bible. To be satisfactory, it had to be true to the Word and yet easy to read. We can understand the various attempts from this double aim.

A modern researcher should proceed in much the same fashion: always consult the Latin Vulgate, test the literal possibility and draw on the idiomatic resources of the language. Thus, a study of revision becomes a clue to understanding this monumental bible.

3. The text: Baruch 3

And now, Lord [almiʒti] God of Irael, the[1] soule in anguysshes,
2 and the[1] spirit tormentid[2] crieth to thee. 'Heere [thou] " Lord,
and haue mercy; for God " thou art merciful'. And haue [thou]
3 mercy of[3] vs, for wee han synned bifor thee, that sittist 'in to
euermor[4], and wee shul not pershe 'in to the spirituel during[4].
4 Lord God al myʒti, God of Irael, here [thou] now the orisoun[5]
of the deade men of Irael, and of the sonus of hem, 'for thei
han synned[6] bifor thee, and thei herden not the vois of the Lord
" ther
5 God, and ioyned[7] " ben " to vs " euelis. 'Wile thou not[8] han
mynde of[3] the wickenesse of oure fadris, but haue [thou]
mynde of[3] thin
6 hond and of[3] thi name in this tyme; for thou art Lord " oure
God,
7 and 'wee shul preise[9] the " Lord. 'For that[10] thou hast ʒoue thi
drede in oure hertes, that wee inwardli[11] " clepe thi name', and
preise[9] thee in oure caitifte; for wee shul be turned[12] fro the
8 wickenesse of oure fadris, that synneden in[13] thee. And lo! wee
'in oure caitifte " ben to dai, 'that vs thou hast scatered[14], in to
repref[15], and in to cursing, and in to synne, after[16] alle the
wickidnessis[17] of oure fadris, that wenten[18] awei fro thee,
9 [thou] Lord " oure God. 'Here thou " Irael, the
[co]maundemens of lif; ' with eres " parceyue [thou]', that thou
wite[19] prudence.
10 'What is [it] " Irael, that 'in the lond of the enemys " thou
11 art'? Thou 'hast eldid[20] in an alien lond, thou art defoulid with
deade men, thou art set[21] with men goende[22] doun in to helle?

12, 13 Thou hast forsake the welle of wisdam; for [whi] if ‘in the
weies of God " thou haddest go’, ‘thou ‘shuldist han[23] dwellid "
for-
14 sothe[24] in pes vp on erthe. Lerne [thou], wher be[25] prudence[26],
wher be[25] vertue, wher be[25] vnderstonding, that thou wite
togidere, wher be[25] long abiding[27] of lyf and of liflode, wher
be[25]
15 liȝt of eȝen, and pes. Who fond ‘his place[28]? [and] who entride
in
16 to ‘his tresores[29]? Wher ben the princes of Jentilys[30], and that
17 lordshipen[31] of[32] [the] bestes, that ben vpon erthe? That[33] ‘in[34]
18 the briddis of heuene " pleien; that[33] siluer " tresoren and gold,
in whiche trosten " men, and ther is " noon ende’ of the
purchasing of hem? That[33] siluer " forgen[35], and ben besy, ne[36]
ther is "
19 finding of ‘the werkus of hem[37]? Thei ben outlawid[38], and ‘to
helle[39] " thei wente[18] doun’; and othyr men ‘in the place of
hem"
20 risen. The ȝunge
men of hem sawen liȝt, and dwelten on erth. Sothely[40] thei
knewen
21 not the wei of disciplyne[41], nether vndirstoden the pathis ‘of
it[42]; nether the sones of hem resceyueden it. ‘Fro the face of
hem
22 " it is[43] maad fer’; it is not herd in the lond of Canaan, nether
23 it is seen in Theman. And[44] the sones of Agar, that souȝten out
prudence that[33] is of erth, the marchauntis of erth, and [of]
Theman, and the ‘fablers, or ianglers[45], and seekers out of
prudence, and of vnderstondinge; sothely[40] thei knewen not the
weie of
24 wysdam, nether hadden mynde of[3] the paathis therof. O! Yrael,
‘hou[46] grete " is " the hous of God[47], and ‘hou grete " [is] " the
25 place of his possessioun[47]; [it is] gret and ‘not hauynge[48] eende,
26 heeȝ and ‘with outen mesure " grete. ‘Ther " weren " named
gyauntis[49]; tho[50] that ‘fro[51] the bigynnynge " weren in[52] grete
stature’,
27 witynge[53] bataile. The Lord chese not these, nether thei
founden
28 the weie of discipline[41]; therfor thei pershiden. And for thei

29 hadde not wijsdam, thei pershiden for her vnwijsdam. Who
steiȝede in to heuen, and toke it[54], and ledde[55] it doun fro [the]
cloudis?
30 Who passide ouer the se, and foonde it, and brouȝt it to, vpon[56]
31 chosen gold? Ther is " not[57], that may wite[58] the waies therof,
32 nether that sekith out the pathes therof; bot he that wote[59] alle
thingis, knewȝ it, and foond it by his prudence. The whiche
maade redy the erth in euerlastynge tyme, and fulfilled it with
feeld[60]
33 bestes, and four footid bestis. The whiche sendith out liȝt, and
it goth; and he clepid it, and it obeischide[61] to hym in tremb-
34 lynge. Forsoth sterris ȝauen liȝt in her keepyngus, and
gladiden[62];
35 thei[63] ben[64] clepid, and thei[63] seiden, We ‘cumen to[65]; and thei[63]
36 shyneden to hym with mirth, that maad hem[63]. This is our God,
and
37 ‘other shal not[66] ben gessid aȝenis hym. He this foonde al[67]
weie of disciplyne[41], and bitoke[68] it to Jacob, his child, and to
Yrael,
38 his derworth[69]. After these thingus he was seen in erthis[70], and
lyued with men.

Notes on the Middle English text (variants in the versions)

[1]a [2]anoied [3]on [4]withouten ende [5]preier [6]that synneden [7]fastned; 4+2+1+3 [8]Nyle thou [9]herie [10]For whi for this thing [11]to help [12]conuertid [13]aȝens [14]whidur thou scateridist vs [15]schenschipe [16]bi [17]wickidnesse [18]ȝeden [19]kunne [20]wexidist eld [21]arettid [22]hem that goon [23]haddist [24]sotheli [25]is [26]wisdom where is prudence [27]duryng [28]the place therof [29]the tresouris therof [30]hethene men [31]ben lordis [32]ouer [33]which/e [34]with [35]maken [36]and no [37]her werkis [38]distried [39]hellis [40]But [41]wisdom [42]therof [43]was [44]Also [45]tale telleris [46]ful [47]3+2+1 [48]hath noon [49]3+2+1 [50]thei [51]at [52]of [53]and knewen [54]that wisdom [55]brouȝte [56]more than [57]noon [58]knowe [59]kan (han) [60]twei footid [61]obeieth [62]weren glad [63]tho [64]weren [65]ben present [66]noon other schal [67]ech [68]ȝaf [69]derlyng [70]londis

Notes on the underlying Latin text

1 Domine /omnipotens/ [2]anxius 2 Audi Domine quia Deus es misericors [3]miserere nostri 3 [4]in sempiternum; in aevum 4 [5]orationem [6]qui/a/ peccaverunt Domini Dei sui [7]agglutinata sunt nobis mala 5 [8]Noli meminisse iniquitatis, memento manus tuae et nominis tui 6 Dominus Deus noster [9]laudabimus te Domine 7 [10]quia propter hoc [11]ut invocemus nomen tuum [9]et laudemus [12]quia convertemur [13]in te 8 nos in captivitate nostra sumus [14]quo (qu/i?/a) nos dispersisti [15]in improperium [16, 17]secundum omnes iniquitates [18]qui recesserunt Domine Deus noster 9 Audi Israel mandata auribus percipe [19]ut scias prudentiam 10 Quid est Israel quod in terra inimicorum es 11 [20]inveterasti [21, 22]deputatus es cum descendentibus 13 [23, 24]Nam si in via Dei ambulasses habitasses utique in pace super terram 14 [25, 26]Disce ubi sit prudentia, ubi sit virtus, ubi sit intellectus [27]ubi sit longiturnitas 15 [28, 29]locum eius; in thesauros eius 16 [30]gentium [31, 32]dominantur super bestias 17 [33, 34]Qui in avibus caeli ludunt 18 [34]qui argentum thesaurizant in quo confidunt homines et non est finis [33, 35]qui argentum fabricant [36, 37]nec est inventio operum illorum 19 [38]Exterminati [39, 8]et ad inferos descenderunt et alii loco eorum surrexerunt
20 [40]autem [41]disciplinae 21 [43]a facie ipsorum longe facta est 23 [44]quoque [45]fabulatores [40]autem [3]commemorati sunt semitas eius 24 [46, 47]quam magna est domus Dei et ingens locus 25 [48]Magnus /est/ et non habet finem excelsus et immensus 26 [49]Ibi fuerunt gigantes nominati [50, 51]illi qui ab initio fuerunt [52]statura magna [53]scientes 27 [41]disciplinae 29 [54]accepit eam [55]et deduxit eam 30 attulit illam [56]super aurum electum 31 [57, 58]Non est qui possit scire vias eius exquirat 32 [59]scit [60]replevit eam pecudibus 33 [61]obaud/iv/it 34 [62]laetatae sunt 35 [63, 64]/et/ vocatae sunt et dixerunt [65]Adsumus [63]qui fecit illas 36 [66]/et/ non aestimabitur alius 37 Hic [67]omnem viam disciplinae [68]tradidit [69]dilecto suo 38 [70]in terris

Notes on vocabulary items

Bar. 3.1	tormentid[2] - [2]anoied: anxius; 'tormented' Pss.101.1 EV, 'anguished' LV, ELV Ecclus.5.10, 'annoyed' LV Bar.3.1
Bar. 3.3	'in to euermor[4] - [4]withouten ende: in sempiternum; '/for/ evermore' EV Gen.13.15; I Kgs.27.12, '/into/ without end' LV Gen.13.15, ELV Deut.5.29
Bar. 3.3	'in to the spirituel during[4] - [4]withouten ende: in aevum; LV 'without end' Ecclus.41.16 - EV 'spiritual world' Ecclus.18.8, 'spiritual time' 38.39

Bar. 3.4	orisoun[5] - [5]preier: orationem; 'orison' EV III Kgs.8.28, LV 'prayer', ELV Tob.6.18
Bar. 3.4	ioyned[7] - [7]fastned; agglutinata; 'join /fast/' ELV Ecclus.25.16, Jer.13.11, EV Bar.3.4, 'fasten' LV Bar.3.4, 'glue /tog./' ELV Ezek.29.4
Bar. 3.6	preise[9] - [9]herie: laudabimus; 'praise' EV I Pss.29.13, ELV II Pss.5.13, 'hery' LV I Pss.29.13, ELV Dan.2.23
Bar. 3.7	inwardli[11] - [11]to help: in-voc.; 'inwardly clepe' ELV Gen.4.26, EV 48.16, LV Rom.10.12, 'cl. inw.' Zeph.3.9 LV, 'clepe' LV Gen.48.16, 'clepe /in/to help' LV Ecclus.36.14, 46.6, 'in-clepe' Dan.9.18 EV
Bar. 3.7	turned[12] - [12]conuertid: convertemur; 'convert' EV Lev.19.4, 'turn' LV, v.v. III Kgs.8.47
Bar. 3.8	repref[15] - [15]schenschipe: inproperium; 'reproof' EV Wisd.5.3, ELV Rom.15.3, 'shendship' LV Tob.3.4, Ecclus.22.27 ('despite' EV)
Bar. 3.11	'hast eldid[20] - [20]wexidist eld: inveterasti; 'eeld' EV II Esd.9.21, 'wax old' LV, 'inw. eeld' Pss.6.8., 'be old' LV Is.65.22
Bar. 3.11	set[21] - [21]arettid: deputatus; 'set' EV Bar.3.11, 'aret' LV Est.14.8, 'ordain' ELV II Macc.4.19
Bar. 3.14	prudence[26] - [26]wisdom (prudence): prudentia; 'wisdom' EV Deut.32.28, 'prudence' LV, ELV Prov.2.3
Bar. 3.14	abiding[27] - [27]duryng: longiturnitas; cf. longiturnus: 'long during' EV Bar.4.35, 'full long' LV
Bar. 3.16	Jentilys[30] - [30]hethene men: gentium; 'Gentiles' Gen.10.5 EV, ELV III Esd.1.49, 'heathen /men, folk/' LV Gen.10.5, ELV IV Kgs.16.3, EV Dan.3.37
Bar. 3.16	lordshipen[31] - [31]ben lordis: dominantur; 'have lordship' EV Gen.1.28, 'be lord/s' LV, ELV both III Esd.4.3 and Gen.45.26, 'lordship' EV Num.24.19, ELV III Esd.2.27
Bar. 3.18	forgen[35] - [35]maken: fabricant; 'forge' EV II Esd.4.11, 'make' LV, ELV Num.32.16
Bar. 3.19	outlawid[38] - [38]distried: exterminati; 'destroy' LV Esd.30.33 ('put out' EV), ELV Judith 5.22, 'outlaw' ELV III Esd.4.8, Judith 3.13 EV
Bar. 3.20	disciplyne[41] - [41]wisdom: disciplinae; 'discipline' EV Lev.26.23 ('doctrine' LV), 'wisdom' LV Wisd.1.5, 'prudence' LV Job 33.16

Bar. 3.23	'fablers, or ianglers[45] - [45]tale telleris: fabulatores; no other instance indexed
Bar. 3.24	hou[46] - [46]ful: quam; 'how' ELV Gen.28.17, EV T.7.2, 'full' LV III Esd.3.18, ELV D.A.17.15
Bar. 3.29	ledde[55] - [55]brouȝte: de]duxit; 'lead down' EV Gen.42.38, LV Tob.13.2, ELV Jer.14.17, 'bring down' EV I Kgs.2.6, LV Jer.9.18
Bar. 3.35	'cumen to[65] - [65]ben present: adsumus; 'be present' LV Gen.4.7, ELV D.A.10.33, 'come' LV Jgs.14.15, ELV II Kgs.24.8
Bar. 3.37	bitoke[68] - [68]ȝaf: tradidit; 'give' LV Gen.9.2, ELV 29.29, 'betake' LV Gen.14.20, ELV 21.14
Bar. 3.37	derworth[69] - [69]derlyng: dilecto; 'dearworth' EV II Esd.13.26 ('loved' LV), 'darling' LV Pss.28.6, ELV both Mt.17.5 and 12.18
Bar. 3.38	erthis[70] - [70]londis: terris; 'earth' EV Gen.2.11, 'land' LV, v.v. I Kgs.14.32

References

Deanesly, Margaret
1920 *The Lollard Bible.* Cambridge: Cambridge University Press.

Forshall, Josiah -- Madden, Frederic (eds.)
1850 *The Holy Bible.* (Wycliffite Versions.) Oxford: Oxford University Press.

Fristedt, Sven
1953 *The Wycliffe Bible.* (Part I.) Stockholm: Stockholm Studies in English.

Chaucer's Latinity

Michael W. Twomey (Ithaca/NY, USA)

The English word *Latinity* of course derives from the Latin third-declension noun *Latinitas*, referring to Latin style. It is a Classical Latin word that was not anglicized until after the Middle Ages. Its earliest attestation in the *OED* is from the seventeenth century, and in its traditional sense, it refers almost exclusively to 'pure' Latin – classical Latin as opposed to Vulgar Latin or Medieval Latin.[1]

Whereas virtually every other aspect of Chaucer has been discovered, covered, and recovered, the Latin in Chaucer's works has received only passing scholarly attention. Nevertheless, students must learn to read Chaucer's Middle English aloud, and Chaucer's texts include words, phrases, even entire sentences in Latin.[2] The first bit of Latin in the *Canterbury tales* is the inscription on the Prioress's brooch: *Amor vincit omnia.* Should we use classical, ecclesiastical, or some other pronunciation?[3] The question of how to pronounce Chaucer's Latin leads to questions about the nature and significance of Chaucer's use of Latin. As we know, unlike his friend John Gower, who appealed to posterity in French and Latin as well as in English, Chaucer left behind works only in English; and yet we know that Chaucer was at least comfortable reading and translating Latin, French, and Italian. His grasp of scientific Latin was secure enough to enable him to translate the *Treatise on the astrolabe*, and he probably read the Roman authors Virgil, Ovid and Statius in Latin; but in composing works such as the *Clerk's tale* and *Boece*, Chaucer seems to have used a French translation, which he checked against the Latin when necessary.[4] Ultimately, for as much as has been written about Chaucer's Latin sources, we still lack a systematic study of the kinds of Latin that Chaucer knew, and the role that Latin plays in Chaucer's works.

In this essay, I want to outline some of the main questions such a study might address:

- Which Latin is Chaucer's?
- What are the registers of Chaucer's Latin?
- How was Chaucer's Latin pronounced?
- And of course, what does Chaucer's usage of Latin 'say' about his literary aims and the expectations he might have held of his reader, and how his use of Latin might illustrate the state of late Anglo-Latin before humanism and the state of English before its final adoption as the prestige language of Britain?

To begin, we have to ascertain when Chaucer is 'speaking' to us in Latin. A lot of what Chaucer does with Latin falls under the heading of ' Latinism' – words that are morphologically Latin rather than English or French – but the italicized Latinisms in the *Riverside Chaucer* tend to be the ones signaled by Chaucer as such, and Chaucer's Latinisms are not equal in status. There are broadly speaking two kinds of Latinisms in Chaucer. The first kind are words and phrases spoken by Chaucer's narrators and characters, such as the Prioress's "Alma redemptoris mater" (VII, 641). I call these intra-textual Latinisms. The other kind are those written into the manuscripts as textual markers: explicits and incipits between sections of works like the *Knight's tale* and *Troilus and Criseyde*, epigraphs, and glosses. I call these extra-textual Latinisms. We can safely assume that intra-textual Latinisms are from Chaucer's own pen; but we cannot assume the same of extra-textual Latinisms, which at least sometimes must be scribal, unless they were done at Chaucer's instruction in some lost manuscript predating Hengwrt and repeated by subsequent scribes.

Intra-textual Latinisms are superficially the easiest to identify. Most if not all of them can be described as what Chaucer himself called *terms*, which are given a very useful general treatment in Burnley (1983: chapter 7). As Burnley shows, the Middle English word *term,* which refers to the specialized vocabulary and style of a defined sphere of usage, such as law, hunting, or war, closely approximates the modern linguistic concept of register. In the years before the rise of an English standard, an English-speaker would display both copiousness and propriety by using terms correctly. In the *Canterbury tales,* Chaucer refers often to the use of *terms.*[5] The word *term* came to English via French, but it can refer to specialized language in Latin. Examples of terms would be the Friar's pleasant "in principio" (*CT* I.254) from the gospel of John, a term that was used apotropaically even after the Reformation (cf. Bloomfield 1955), and the term *Fortuna Major*, the name of the constellation that rises on the morning after Troilus and Criseyde make love for the first time (*Troilus and Criseyde* III, 1420). The Summoner had a few terms, "two or three / That he had learned out of some decree" (*CT* I, 639-40), one of which was "questio quid iuris" (*CT* I, 646). Except for the Wife of Bath and the Canon's Yeoman, the secular members of the Canterbury pilgrimage generally profess not to know any terms. The Franklin feigns ignorance of astrological terms (*CT* V, 1266), which would have been in Latin. After hearing the *Physician's tale*, Harry Bailly avers that he cannot speak "in terme" (*CT* VI, 311), and he enjoins the Clerk to avoid terms, colors, and figures of rhetoric (*CT* IV, 16) in his tale. But Chaucer's Latin goes beyond terms to oaths and ejaculations, such as the many *benedicites* and the many variations on God's *corpus* (e.g. *CT* I, 3743) that color the speech of the Canterbury pilgrims. And let us not forget the Wife of

Bath's infamous "quoniam" (III, 608). One part of a study of Chaucer's Latinity will be to classify the varieties of Latin reflected in these Latinisms.

With one exception, none of Chaucer's intra-textual Latin is longer than a phrase. The exception is the twelve-line Latin summary of Statius's *Thebaid*, book by book, that follows line 1498 in Book V of *Troilus and Criseyde* in all but two of its sixteen manuscripts.[6] The lines are in randomly mixed unrhymed hexameters and pentameters,[7] they come at the beginning of Cassandra's rehearsal of Theban history, and they are echoed in a general way by the English text that follows them. Skeat is the only modern editor who treats the lines as part of Chaucer's text. Some of the lines have been traced to prefaces in manuscripts of the *Thebaid*,[8] and scholars tend to regard them as notes from which Chaucer translated Cassandra's speech, but ultimately we do not know whether the lines are Chaucer's or not. If they are Chaucer's, why did Chaucer leave them in the text? If they are not Chaucer's, then why did scribes so faithfully reproduce them?

Extra-textual Latinisms occur as epigraphs, textual links, and glosses. Unlike intra-textual Latinisms, they are unprotected by the surrounding English text, and in Chaucer manuscripts and incunabula they are sometimes changed and sometimes omitted entirely, which casts some doubt on their authorial status – although it is well to remember that scribes did not always copy Chaucer's English texts accurately or completely, either.

The epigraphs are most likely to be Chaucer's. In *Riverside*, the *Knight's tale* is prefaced with a heading and an epigraph, both italicized. First, in English, "Heere bigynneth the Knyghtes Tale", and after that, an abbreviated quotation in Latin from Statius's *Thebaid*. *Riverside's* italics separate these statements from Chaucer's text. Now *Riverside*, like Robinson's 2nd edition before it, is based on the Ellesmere manuscript (El) with supplementary readings provided from Hengwrt (Hg), both widely regarded as the two earliest surviving manuscripts of the *Canterbury tales*, as well as from other manuscripts.[9] The English incipit, "Heere bigynneth the Knyghtes Tale", seems to function as a textual boundary that keeps the Statian epigraph inside the text of the *Knight's tale*. And yet, the incipit is not enough of a boundary to protect the epigraph fully, since the epigraph is missing from three of the nine manuscripts used in *Riverside*.[10] Caxton's 1483 edition (*STC*, no. 5094) of the *Canterbury tales* leaves it out, and some of the major modern editions, such as Baugh's, relegate it to the notes. In contrast, the Latin epigraph from Jeremiah 6.16 that begins the *Parson's tale* is successfully protected by an English heading in all nine manuscripts used in *Riverside*, as well as in Caxton.

Chaucer was among the first English writers whose works were formally divided with Latin textual markers in the manuscripts (Butterfield

1996: 60-61). This so-called *ordinatio* had long been used for authoritative texts in Latin, and so the use of these textual markers in fifteenth-century manuscripts of Chaucer is one sign of Chaucer's status as an *auctor*. But are these textual markers scribal or authorial? The Latin incipits and explicits that divide sections of some of the *Canterbury tales* and works like the *House of fame* [three books], *Troilus and Criseyde* [five books], and the *Legend of good women* are also unprotected in the manuscripts. Consequently, they are reproduced erratically both in manuscripts and in print. Once again, Hg and El often agree on these, but because textual markers are formulaic, and because they are a standard part of the *ordinatio* of a manuscript, the scribes observe neither the same word order nor the same vocabulary.[11] Even if in fact they were authorial, the textual markers in the manuscript would have been regarded as instructions from the author, but not as part of the author's text. They were optional and malleable. This is true even of the colophon for the *Canterbury tales*, which follows Chaucer's Retraction. Some manuscripts (e.g. El) give an English colophon reading, "Heere is ended the book of the tales of Caunterbury, compiled by Geffrey Chaucer, of whos soule Jhesu Crist have mercy. Amen." Others (e.g. Ad^1) have a Latin colophon with some variation of *Hic capit Auctor licenciam* – "Here the author takes his leave".[12]

Another kind of extra-textual Latin comes in the form of marginal glosses. There are glosses from the *Thebaid* in the *Knight's tale*, from Petrarch in the *Clerk's tale*, from Jerome's *Adversus Jovinianum* in the *Wife of Bath's prologue* and the *Franklin's tale*, and from Innocent III's *De miseria humanae conditionis* in the *Man of law's tale* and the *Pardoner's prologue and tale*. The few scholars who have worked on these glosses consider them to be Chaucer's, inserted either as reminders about source-materials to be used in revising the English text, or as source-acknowledgments.[13] I see no reason to argue against this hypothesis. However, in the transmission history of Chaucer manuscripts, the glosses, like the rubrics, were textually unprotected, and therefore they were not systematically copied, when they were copied at all. Although Chaucer's English text too was subject to scribal change, the glosses were even more so, because they are not part of a systematic program anchored to the English text, such as the program of Latin verses, commentaries, glosses, and colophons in manuscripts of Gower's *Confessio amantis* (Pearsall 1989: 14-15). A problem similar to that of the glosses is the phrase "radix Chaucer", referring to the beginning point for astrological calculations about (or perhaps by) Chaucer, which was written in a fourteenth- or early fifteenth-century hand into a set of tables in Cambridge MS Peterhouse 75. I, fol. 5^v. John North (1988: chapter 4, esp. 170-80) has argued that the phrase was written into the manuscript by Chaucer himself, while I have counter-argued that it is not possible to know.

The Latin in Chaucer's Retraction might be considered both intra- and extra-textual. The Retraction ends with an English prayer to Christ "that I may been oon of hem at the day of doom that shulle be saved", to which is attached the liturgical Latin colophon *Qui cum patre et spiritu sancto vivit et regnat Deus per omnia secula*, which lacks the final word *seculorum*. The Retraction occurs in only 28 of the 82 or 83 manuscripts of the *CT*,[14] and in some manuscripts only the first few words of the Latin prayer are given. Again, the Latin prayer may be Chaucer's, but it could just as easily be scribal.

One striking fact that emerges from this brief survey of Chaucer's Latin is that unlike Gower and other contemporaries and followers, Chaucer did not compose an original text in Latin. His Latin occurs either as single Latin words, as quotations, or as formulas. Chaucer uses Latin *as* Latin, but he does not seem to have attempted to speak in his own voice in Latin. Assuming that the Retraction is meant to be his literary farewell, Chaucer's last words are a formulaic Latin prayer. Chaucer's voice, so seemingly modern and individual, merges in the end with all the other voices that have ever spoken or written that prayer. What is more, Latinisms are much rarer outside the *Canterbury tales*. *Troilus and Criseyde* has perhaps three, which is one less than the number in just the *General prologue*.[15] The only other work in which there is more than one or two Latinisms is the *Treatise on the astrolabe*, where Chaucer uses the imperative *nota* to call attention to important points and where he uses several terms in Latin rather than translate them into English. As if we needed any more confirmation of the achievement of the *Canterbury tales*, Chaucer's Latinisms in the *Canterbury tales* imply an audience far more learned than even the sophisticated court audience that we presume for *Troilus and Criseyde*, or the scientific audience that we presume for the *Treatise on the Astrolabe*. The presumed audience of the *Canterbury tales* would have to be familiar with both French and Latin and know a number of registers of each.

One question is whether to consider **loanwords and Latin names** as Latinisms, or whether these should be regarded as English words. The problem with loanwords is that it is not always possible to tell whether the word is morphologically English or Latin. A famous example is the word *ambages* from *Troilus and Criseyde* (V, 897).[16] As a Latin word, *ambages* would be a third-declension noun with singular and plural in *-es*, like *vulpes* 'fox'. As an English word, it would be the plural of a presumed French loan, *ambage*. Chaucer immediately glosses the word, which suggests that *ambages* is a term he does not expect his reader to know: "That is to sayn, with double wordes slye". However, this gloss does not tell us anything about the origin of the word. Likewise, with names whose morphology is Latin, we cannot be sure whether the name counts as English or Latin, since so many classical names retained their original forms – as witness the name of the goddess Venus in Modern English.

The problem of loanwords and names is complicated by **pronunciation**, which helped to blur the lines between English and Latin. Whereas the picture of Chaucer's Latinity that I have been drawing emphasizes the compartmentalization and specialization of Latin that characterizes Latinity in England at the end of the Middle Ages, Chaucer's Latin pronunciation, as I have reconstructed it, suggests the extent to which the English language had assimilated Latin, and it forecasts the increased borrowing from Latin into English that was to take place after the Reformation. The explanation for this assimilation is, simply stated, that by the fourteenth century, Latin pronunciation reflected the norms of Middle English.

By all accounts, the pronunciation of medieval Latin in England was always influenced by the pronunciation of the vernacular – Anglo-Saxon before the Norman Conquest, Middle English and Anglo-Norman French after the Conquest, and Middle English after the fourteenth century, when English superseded French as the dominant vernacular.[17] The situation seems simple, but it is complicated by the presence, late into the Middle Ages, of Latin verse composed according to the classical rules of scansion – such as John Gower's Latin verses in the *Confessio Amantis* – which indicates a knowledge of quantitative distinctions and possibly of other features of classical pronunciation.[18] It seems safer to suppose two styles of Latin pronunciation – one, more formal, that aspired to classical norms, and the other, less formal, that was pulled into the orbit of vernacular norms. However, the distinction between the two styles is chiefly vowel quantity, which is important for composing verse in classical meters (Rigg 1996: 80-1).

The problem lies in determining just what the influence of the vernacular would have been. Because of the Norman Conquest, England lay along the fault line that divided northern and southern pronunciation of Latin – that is, Germanic-speaking countries vs. Romance-speaking countries. Before the Norman Conquest, England was in the Germanic camp. Under the apparent influence of the Germanic Stress Rule, the Anglo-Saxons would lengthen vowels in the initial syllable of disyllabic words such as *pater* whose classical pronunciation calls for a short vowel. Under the influence of their own vernacular practices, the Anglo-Saxons would pronounce *g* before a front vowel as a semi-vowel [y] and they would voice intervocalic *s* to [z].[19] After the Conquest, when Latin was taught by French schoolmasters, French pronunciations began to be introduced. For example, *g* before a front vowel now became the affricate [ʤ] as in Modern English *gem* and *gin* (Allen 1978: 102, Fowler 1937: 100, 104). Despite this French influence on Anglo-Latin, for the twelfth and thirteenth centuries, it is not always clear whether to use Middle English or Anglo-Norman pronunciation for Anglo-Latin. For example, the Latin relative pronoun *qui* might be French [ki:] or English/classical Latin [kwi:].

From the fifteenth century through the Reformation, the situation is also complex. During the period of the Great Vowel Shift, which was underway by the mid fifteenth century, Latin long vowels must have kept pace with English long vowels, since at the end of the shift the Latin long vowels are pronounced as English long vowels, i.e., as in 'old Latin' and legal Latin. For example, after the Great Vowel Shift, "Deus hic" in the *Summoner's tale* (*CT* III, 1770) would be pronounced [di:ʊs haik]. But the Great Vowel Shift is only one of several influences on English pronunciation of Latin in this period. In the sixteenth-century, the Reformation dispersed English Catholics to various Continental lands where they would have acquired Continental Latin pronunciation, including the reformed classical pronunciation promoted by Erasmus.[20] When these Catholics brought their Continental Latin back to England under Queen Mary, there would have been a number of competing systems in play.

The fourteenth century, in contrast, poses fewer problems, and so we can ascertain the Latin pronunciation of fourteenth-century England with a little more confidence than we can ascertain the Latin pronunciation of the periods before or afterwards. The end of the fourteenth century, the period of Chaucer's literary career, is the period of greatest certainty for Anglo-Latin pronunciation. At around 1400, the Great Vowel Shift had not yet begun – or at least we are fairly sure that Chaucer's conservative pronunciation does not give evidence of it (cf. Smith 1996: 86-111). Hence, as a general rule, we can probably pronounce Chaucer's Latin as if it were Chaucer's Middle English – i.e., the two languages are allophonic. Here are some examples of Latinisms cited earlier in this essay:

- The Prioress' brooch: *Amor vincit omnia* [ˈɑmɔr ˈvɪnsɪt ˈɔmnɪa] (*CT* I, 162).
- The Summoner's cry: *Questio quid iuris* [ˈkwɛsti·ɔ: kwɪd ˈʤyrɪs] (*CT* I, 646).
- Nicholas's song: *Angelus ad virginem* [ˈɑnʤɛlʊs ɑt ˈvɪrʤɪnɛm] (*CT* I, 3216).
- The Wife of Bath's prized bodily part: her *quoniam* [ˈkɔnɪ·am] (*CT* III, 608).

The question of how to pronounce Chaucer's Latin is in effect a synecdoche of the whole problem of Chaucer's Latinity. In the fourteenth century, Latin was being absorbed into English, a process that accelerated into the early modern period. As A. G. Rigg argues in his *History of Anglo-Latin literature*, fourteenth-century Latin in England was a language that increasingly was acquiring a strong English 'flavour'. If in the fifteenth century it would undergo the influence of humanism and "the establishment of Classical Latin Standards" (Rigg 1992: 242), in the fourteenth century Anglo-Latin was becoming fragmented into numerous specialized varieties.[21] This is the condition represented by Chaucer's use of what I earlier referred to as *terms*.

And yet, despite this absorption of Latin into English, histories of English language and literature often see English as a language struggling against French and Latin for authority. Most recently, in the Introduction to part one of the *Cambridge history of medieval English literature*, the editor, David Wallace, calls "Latinitas" a "hegemonic force" of such power that, together with French, it "rendered the native population mute" in the years after the Norman Conquest, and in the prefaces to later sections of the *Cambridge History*, Wallace extends the hegemony of Latinity down through the end of the Middle Ages.[22] Wallace is not alone in characterizing Latinity as an oppressor, nor am I singling him out, since there has long been a tendency to see the career of English in the fourteenth century in chauvinistic terms. To some extent, this is due to a misreading of the chronicle record. As Thorlac Turville-Petre and Steven Justice have separately observed, accounts of English and English literature from the Norman Conquest through the English Rising of 1381 fail to realize the element of nationalist polemic in medieval chronicles, and they erroneously pit English against Latin in a struggle for political power.[23] Postcolonialism and cultural studies ironically seem to be the new home for a very old form of linguistic chauvinism in which the English language rises up against its oppressors, French and Latin.

Chaucer is often enlisted in this struggle via his still-popular role as the putative originator of English poetry, but as Christopher Baswell has argued in *The making of Chaucer's English*, Chaucer's English may be a good deal less original than we might think. What we consider 'English' is so because of our regard for his poetry, not because Chaucer single-handedly forged the English language out of ruder – or nobler, as the case may be – elements. Middle English scholarship's concern with 'vernacularity' too often emphasizes the political at the expense of the literary and linguistic. In narrating the rise of English, it is well for us to remember that in the Middle Ages and through the Reformation, Britain was a polyglot island where one could hear Latin, English, French, Scots, Welsh, and Cornish. Not only were there many voices speaking in many languages, but within each language there were various registers, and this is as true of Latin as it is of the other languages of Britain. In the *Cambridge history* itself, this point is made by Baswell, whose fittingly-titled essay "Latinitas" neatly summarizes the view taken in Rigg's *History of Anglo-Latin literature*: that in England, Latin is "a language regularly contested by other languages of real or putative authority", and that ultimately Latin itself devolved into "an array of increasingly disparate, specialized language practices" (Baswell 1999: 123).[24] In his paper at the 19th Triennial Conference of IAUPE (12 August 2004), Richard Bailey, reporting about a book in progress, made a case for considering English in Britain as part of a multilingual environment, and I would suggest that a study of Chaucer's Latinity would help to fill in our understanding of that environment from a perspective that avoids linguistic chauvinism. Terms such as triglossia or even polyglossia seem more accurate for describing Chaucer's linguistic environment than metaphors of struggle against a Latin hegemony that for Chaucer almost certainly did not exist.

In this essay, I have outlined some issues regarding Chaucer's use of Latin, in hopes of making a start towards an understanding of the place that Latin occupies in Chaucer's vocabulary, in his literary language, and in manuscripts of his work. I have suggested that Chaucer's Latin occurs both intra-textually and extra-textually, in the form of Latinisms, formulas, and quotations – but not as Latin that is original to Chaucer. The question of the Latin in Chaucer manuscripts that occurs as textual markers and glosses remains open, but even if these are also Chaucerian, they too are Latinisms, formulas, and quotations from sources, thus they too are not original to Chaucer. Chaucer's Latin is less a *langue* than a set of pre-existing *paroles*, less a system from which new Latin utterances are produced than a closed set of utterances that have always already been produced. This Latin was often highly specialized terms. Chaucer's Latin illustrates the changes taking place both in Anglo-Latin and in English that culminated in what linguistic chauvinists call "the triumph of English". But I would like to suggest that teleological and political models are inadequate for describing the day-to-day understanding of usage that guided Chaucer in his linguistic choices. If, as Rigg says, Anglo-Latin was fragmenting into diverse areas of specialized use, far from being a "hegemonic force", Anglo-Latin in Chaucer's time is being absorbed into English. If there is a hegemony, it must be the hegemony of English.

Notes

[1] *OED*, s.v. 'Latinity': "1. The manner of speaking or writing Latin; Latin (with reference to its construction or style). In the first quot. the sense of the word is doubtful, and the text insecure. 1619 in Crt. & Times Jas. I (1848) II. 172 One Shingleton..who preaching in Pauls..glanced, they say, scandalously at him [Bacon], and his Latinities, as

he called them. a1656 HALL Rem. Wks. (1660) 241 The Romans expressed the womans marriage by, nubere, which signifies to vail... Neither doubt I but before all Latinity was hatched this was alluded to by Abimelech, Genes. 20. 16. 1661 BOYLE Style of Script. (1675) 148 That cardinal..that said, that once indeed he had read the Bible, but if he were to do it again, 'twould lose him all his Latinity. 1781 GIBBON Decl. & F. xlvii. II. 738 His Latinity is pure. 1826 MISS MITFORD Village Ser. III. (1863) 519 [He] used to..growl as he compounded the medicines over the bad Latinity of the prescriptions. 1831 CARLYLE Sart. Res. (1858) 81, I undertook to compose his Epitaph..which, however, for an alleged defect of Latinity..still remains unengraven. 1865 MERIVALE Rom. Emp. VIII. lxiv. 100 The last remains we possess of classical Latinity are the biographies of the later emperors."

2 My essay, "Reading Chaucer's Latin aloud" (Twomey 2005), describes phonetic rules for Chaucer's late fourteenth-century Anglo-Latin.

3 From the *General prologue* (I, 162). All citations from Chaucer are according to *Riverside*.

4 For summaries of scholarship, see *Riverside's* "Explanatory notes", pp. 1092 (*Treatise on the astrolabe*), 1003 (*Boece*), and 880 (*Clerk's tale*).

5 Among other examples, Burnley cites: "termes of astrologye" (*CT* V, 1266), "scole-termes" (*CT* IV, 1569), "termes queinte of lawe" (in some MSS.; *CT* II, 1189), "termes of phisik" (*Troilus and Criseyde* II, 1038), "termes of philosophie" (*House of fame*, 857).

6 According to both *Riverside*, p. 1177, and Robinson (1957: 921).

7 For a summary of medieval Latin forms, see Rigg (1992: 316). The metres of the 12-line epitome of the *Thebaid* are randomly mixed, not elegiac couplets.

8 See Magoun (1955), Clogan (1964), and more generally, Windeatt (1992: 123).

9 MS Ellesmere 26 C 9, ca. 1400, formerly in the possession of Lord Ellesmere, now at the Henry E. Huntington Library, San Marino, California; MS Hengwrt 154 (Peniarth 392D), ca. 1400.

10 See textual notes to the *Knight's tale* in *Riverside*, p. 1122.

11 For example, *Clerk's tale* after IV, 448: "Incipit pars tercia" (Hg) vs. "Incipit tercia pars" (El); *Clerk's tale* after IV, 784: "Incipit pars quinta" (Hg) vs. "Sequitur pars quinta" (El). Text: Ruggiers (1979).

[12] Cf. Textual notes in Robinson (1957: 898).

[13] Cf. Dempster (1943-4), Silvia (1965), Lewis (1967), Caie (1975-6). These glosses were first noticed in Manly -- Rickert (1940: 3, 483-527).

[14] My count of the MSS is from *Riverside*, pp. 1118 and 1135.

[15] In *Troilus and Criseyde*: "bendiste" (I, 780), "mea culpa" (II, 525), "Fortuna Major" (III, 1420). In the *General prologue*: "Amor vincit omnia" (I, 162), "in principio" (I, 254), "Questio quid iuris" (I, 646), "Significavit" (I, 662).

[16] [Diomede to Criseyde]: "'And if but Calkas lede us with ambages – / That is to seyn, with double wordes slye, / Swich as men clepen a word with two visages –'." Burnley (1983: 137) locates the Latin term *ambages*, meaning a deliberate ambiguity, in medieval Latin sources.

[17] The scheme of Latin pronunciation in England that is used in the present essay is based on the following: Allen (1978: Appendix B, 102-10), Fowler (1937), (Rigg 1992: "Appendix: Metre", 313-29; 1996a; 1996b). Rigg (1996a: 47-56) discusses several forms of evidence that we can use to reconstruct the pronunciation of Latin in England: rhyme, alliteration, spelling, loan-words, comparative analysis, post-Reformation authorities, and modern legal Latin (which reflects post-Reformation, post-Great Vowel Shift pronunciation).

[18] Latin scansion is summarized in Rigg (1992: 313-29). An excellent study of Gower's verses in particular is Echard -- Fanger (1991).

[19] The Germanic Stress Rule describes the tendency in Germanic languages to stress the initial syllable in polysyllabic words (cf. Lass 1992: 85-90). On Anglo-Saxon pronunciation of Latin, see Allen (1978: 102) and Fowler (1937: 104).

[20] Erasmus, *De recta latini graecique sermonis pronuntiatione* (1528). Erasmus was responding not to the Counter-Reformation but to the linguistic confusion resulting from the plethora of Latin pronunciations in use on the Continent by the early sixteenth century. On the rise and fall of Erasmus's reformed pronunciation at Cambridge University in the sixteenth century via John Cheke, the first Regius Professor of Greek, and Thomas Smith, the first Regius Professor of Civil Law, see Allen (1978: 103-05).

[21] Without counting literary Latin, no less than three dozen kinds of Latinity are listed in Mantello --- Rigg (1996: "Varieties of medieval Latin", part two, section D-E-F).

[22] Wallace (1999: 5, 4); specific instances from the prefaces (Wallace 1999: 314, 485, 486, 637) are critiqued by Somerset (2001: 489-90). As counter-examples, Somerset cites the essays by Christopher Baswell, Winthrop Wetherbee, Glending Olson, and Andrew Galloway in Wallace (1999), to which I would add Galloway's forthcoming essay, "Latin England". As a group, the essays in the *Cambridge history* share the view that Latinity was a linguistically and culturally unifying influence that remained associated with power and authority throughout the Middle English period. A good example is Winthrop Wetherbee's essay on Gower, which calls the *Vox clamantis* "a clear expression of a class-based anxiety" about the uprising in 1381 (Wetherbee 1999: 594). Outside of the *Cambridge history*, another example would be Gellrich (1995: esp. chapters 2, 3, 5).

[23] Turville-Petre (1996: 181, 227), Justice (1994: 17, 225). Among histories of the language, I list Cottle (1969) and the mass-market *Story of English*, by Robert McCrum, William Cran, and Robert MacNeil. On the English Rising of 1381, see Gellrich (1995: chapter 5).

[24] Cf. Rigg (1992: e.g., 242).

References

Allen, W. Sidney
1978 *Vox latina: The pronunciation of classical Latin.* (2nd edition.) Cambridge: Cambridge University Press.
1999 Reprinted edition.

Baswell, Christopher
1999 "Latinitas", in: Wallace (ed.), 122-51.

Bloomfield, Morton W.
1955 "The magic of *In principio*", *Modern language notes* 70: 559-65.

Burnley, David
1983 *A guide to Chaucer's language*. Norman: University of Oklahoma Press.

Burton, T.L. -- John F. Plummer (eds.)
2005 *'Seyd in forme and reverence': Essays on Chaucer and Chaucerians in memory of Emerson Brown, Jr.* Provo: Chaucer Studio Press.

Butterfield, Ardis
1996 "*Mise-en-page* in the *Troilus* manuscripts: Chaucer and French manuscript culture", in: Lerer (ed.), 49-80.

Caie, Graham D.
1975-6 "The significance of the early Chaucer manuscript glosses (with special reference to the *Wife of Bath's prologue)*", *Chaucer Review* 10: 350-60.

Clogan, Paul M.
1964 "Chaucer and the *Thebaid* scholia", *Studies in philology* 61: 599-614.

Cottle, Basil
1969 *The triumph of English 1350-1400.* London: Blandford.

Dempster, Germaine
1943-4 "Chaucer's manuscripts of Petrarch's version of Griselda's story", *Modern Philology* 41: 6-16.

Echard, Siân -- Claire Fanger
1991 *The Latin verses in the* Confessio amantis*: An annotated translation.* With a preface by A.G. Rigg. East Lansing: Colleagues Press.

Fowler, G. Herbert
1937 "Notes on the pronunciation of medieval Latin in England", *History*, new series 22: 97-109.

Galloway, Andrew
n.d. "Latin England", in: Lavezzo (ed.), 39-95.

Gellrich, Jesse M.
1995 *Discourse and dominion in the fourteenth century: Oral contexts of writing in philosophy, politics, and poetry*. Princeton: Princeton University Press.

Justice, Steven
1994 *Writing and rebellion: England in 1381*. (The new historicism 27.) Berkeley: University of California Press.

Lass, Roger
1992 "Phonology and morphology", in: *CHEL* 2, 25-155.

Lavezzo, Kathy (ed.)
n.d. *Medieval English nation*. Minneapolis: University of Minnesota Press.

Lewis, Robert E.
1967 "Glosses to the *Man of law's tale* from Pope Innocent III's *De miseria humane conditionis*", *Studies in philology* 64: 1-16.

Lerer, Seth (ed.)
1996 *Reading from the margins: Textual studies, Chaucer, and medieval literature*. San Marino: Huntington Library.

Magoun, F.P.
1955 "Chaucer's summary of Statius' *Thebaid* II-XII", *Traditio* 11: 409-20.

Manly, John M. -- Edith Rickert
1940 *The text of the Canterbury tales, studied on the basis of all known manuscripts*. 8 vols. Chicago: University of Chicago Press.

Mantello, F.A.C. -- A. G. Rigg (eds.)
1996 *Medieval Latin: An introduction and bibliographical guide*. Washington, D.C.: Catholic University of America Press.

McCrum, Robert -- William Cran -- Robert MacNeil
1992 *Story of English*. (Revised edition.) London: Faber and Faber.

McGee, Timothy J. -- A.G. Rigg -- David N. Klausner (eds.)
1996 *Singing early music: The pronunciation of European languages in the late Middle Ages and the Renaissance*. Bloomington: Indiana University Press.

Minnis, A.J. (ed.)
1989 *Latin and vernacular: Studies in late-medieval texts and manuscripts*. Wolfeboro: Brewer.

North, John
1988 *Chaucer's universe*. Oxford: Oxford University Press.

Pearsall, Derek
1989 "Gower's Latin in the *Confessio amantis*", in: Minnis (ed.), 13-25.

Rigg, A.G.
1992 *A history of Anglo-Latin 1066-1422*. Cambridge: Cambridge University Press.

1996a "Anglo-Latin"; in: McGee -- Rigg -- Klausner (eds.), 46-61.

1996b "Orthography and pronunciation", in: Mantello -- Rigg (eds.), 79-82.

Robinson, F.N. (ed.)
1957 *The works of Geoffrey Chaucer*. (2nd edition.) Boston: Houghton Mifflin.

Ruggiers, Paul G. (ed.)
1979 *A facsmile and transcriptions of the Hengwrt manuscript, with variants from the Ellesmere manuscript.* (Variorum Chaucer 1.) Norman: University of Oklahoma Press: Wm. Dawson & Sons.

Silvia, Daniel S.
1965 "Glosses to the *Canterbury tales* from St. Jerome's *Epistola adversus Jovinianum*", *Studies in philology* 62: 28-39.

Smith, Jeremy
1996 *An historical study of English: Function, form, and change.* London: Routledge.

Somerset, Fiona
2001 "*The Cambridge history of medieval English literature on* 'Latinitas'", *Studies in the age of Chaucer* 23: 489-93.

Turville-Petre, Thorlac
1996 *England the nation: Language, literature, and national identity, 1290-1340.* Oxford: Clarendon.

Twomey, Michael W.
1991 Review of John North, *Chaucer's universe. Anglia* 109: 186-90.

2005 "Reading Chaucer's Latin aloud", in: Burton -- Plummer (eds.), 181-90.

Wallace, David (ed.)
1999 *The Cambridge history of medieval English literature.* Cambridge: Cambridge University Press.

Wetherbee, Winthrop
1999 "John Gower", in: Wallace (ed.), 589-609.

Windeatt, Barry
1992 *Troilus and Criseyde*. (Oxford Guides to Chaucer.) Oxford: Clarendon.

Chaucer's *Troilus* in a new comparative context

Saburo Oka (Tokyo, Japan)

1. Introduction

It is certain that Chaucer's *Troilus* as well as his *Canterbury Tales* are the subject of such a flood of print that a justification is needed by anyone who adds to it. To complete my topic, I should need a whole book; the most important previous attempt in almost the same line of research is, without doubt, *The European tragedy of Troilus*, edited by Piero Boitani in 1989, which is a collection of thirteen articles on the topic by distinguished Chaucerian scholars. All big and significant topics, however, leave room for further extension or more detailed exploration. Chaucer criticism has, if we count the contemporary fourteenth century, a history of seven centuries, and we can say that each of these centuries has a remarkably distinctive characteristic. At the beginning of the new century, therefore, we must have an expectation of something new in Chaucerian studies.

In the so-called 'whetstone stanza' in Book One of *Troilus*, Chaucer's Pandarus gives his proverbial advice to his young friend Troilus, saying "By his contraire is every thynge declared." (637)[1] In fact, the comparative method is one of the most efficient ways of human thinking. And in the last two centuries the comparative method has produced many monumental achievements in almost all fields of science and scholarship. As for Chaucerian studies in the 20th century, we can certainly say that remarkable research has been done in a broader perspective, that is to say, extending the perspective from English to European. Now, after the European perspective, which should come next?

2. Chaucer's portrait of Troilus in European classical and medieval contexts

Story-telling is, indeed, a human characteristic. In other words, a human being can be defined as *homo narrans* and it has always two tasks: first, how to preserve the preceding stories and presentations, which makes him *homo conservans*, and secondly, how to transform the accumulated materials, by which he can be *homo ludens*. Many methods of such transformations have been tried, including focalization, simplification, or amplification.

As an example of these conservations and transformations, we can mention Chaucer's portrait of *Troilus* in Book Five, which was made according to the medieval formulaic phrase, "as bokes us declare" (V, 799).

> And Troilus wel woxen was in highte,
> And complet formed by proporcioun
> So wel that kynde it nought amenden myghte;
> Yong, flessh, strong, and hardy as lyoun;
> Trewe as stiel in ech condicioun;
> Oon of the beste entecched creature
> That is or shal whil that the world may dure.
>
> And certeynly in storye it is yfounde
> That Troilus was nevere unto no wight,
> As in his tyme, in no degree secounde
> In durryng don that longeth to a knyght.
> Al myghte a geant passen hym of myght,
> His herte ay with the first and with the beste
> Stood paregal, to durre don that hym leste. (827-840)

We can hardly get any vivid portrait of Troilus in Classical Literature: Homer has left us only one epithet ἱππιοχάρμης ('one who fights from a chariot', or simply, 'a horseman') in the *Iliad*, Bk. 24, l. 257; Sophocles' *Troilus* is extant in a very fragmentary state, in which Troilus is described as ἀνδρόπαις, 'a youth near manhood' (Lloyd-Jones 1996: 306-7). The first medieval author who gave us a somewhat detailed portrait of Troilus was Dares the Phrygian. In his influential *De Exidio Trojae Historia*, cap. 12, Dares says, "Troilum magnum, pulcherrimum, pro aetate valentem, fortem, cupidum virtutis." ('Troilus, a large and handsome boy, was strong for his age, brave, and eager for glory.')[2]

A slightly different way of representation was adopted by Dictys of Crete in his *Ephemeris Belli Troiani*, Book Four, Section 9:

> Capti etiam Lycaon et Troilus Priamidae, quos in medium productos Achilles iugulari iubet indignatus nondum sibi a Priamo super his, quae secum tractaverat, mandatum. quae ubi animadvertere Troiani, tollunt gemitus et clamore lugubri Troili casum miserandum in modum deflent recordati aetatem eius admodum immaturam, qui in primis pueritiae annis cum verecundia ac probitate, tum praecipue forma corporis amabilis atque acceptus popularibus adolescebat.
>
> (And two of Priam's sons were captured, Lycaon and Troilus, the throats of whom, when they had been brought forth into the center, were cut, by order of Achilles, who was angry with Priam for not having seen to that business they had discussed. The Trojans raised a cry of grief and, mourning loudly, bewailed the fact that Troilus had met so grievous a death, for they remembered how young he was, who, being in the early years of his manhood, was the people's favorite, their

> daring, not only because of his modesty and honesty, but more especially because of his handsome appearance.)[3]

Dictys does depict Troilus from the perspective of the Trojan people. Thus, we can confirm that Dares, Dictys and Chaucer share almost the same references about Troilus: young, strong, brave, and handsome.

On the other hand, in his *Roman de Troie*, Benoît de Sainte-Maure amplifies his portrait of Troilus extensively, beginning from his handsome appearance as follows:

> Troïlus fu beaus a merveille;
> Chiere ot rient, face vermeille,
> Cler vis apert, le front plenier:
> Mout covint bien a chevalier.
> (Troïlus était extrêmement beau. Sa physionomie souriante, son teint vermeil, son visage clair et ouvert, son front haut, tout en lui était digne d'un chevalier.)[4]

Due to the restrictions of space, let us quote the following lines (5397-5446) only in Modern French prose translation by Baumgartner.

> Sa chevelure blonde et naturellement brillante lui seyait particulièrement. Ses yeux pers étincelaient de gaieté: leur beauté était incomparable. Lorsqu'il était de bonne humeur, son regard était si doux que c'était un plaisir de le voir. Mais je peux vous dire en toute vérité qu'il offrait à ses ennemis un tout autre visage! Son nez était long et bien proportionné. L'armure convenait bien à sa stature. Sa bouche était bien faite, ses belles dents plus blanches qu'ivoire ou argent. Son menton carré, son cou, élancé et droit, allaient très bien avec sa cuirasse. Les épaules, d'une belle carrure, allaient en s'affinant. La poitrine était bien formée sous les lacets du haubert. Ses mains étaient bien faites et beaux ses bras. Sa taille était bien prise et ses hanches larges. Ses vêtements lui allaient fort bien. C'était un très beau chevalier. Il avait les jambes droites, la voûte plantaire bien formée, tous ses membres étaient bien faits et son assiette à cheval très solide. Il était très grand mais sa haute stature allait de pair avec les proportions de son corps.
> Je ne pense pas qu'il y ait à l'heure actuelle de par le vaste monde d'homme qui le vaille, qui aime autant la joie et les plaisirs, qui tienne moins de propos désagréables et qui soit aussi valeureux et épris de gloire et de hauts faits. Il n'était ni insolent ni porté aux excès mais joyeux, rieur et enclin à aimer. Il fut aimé et il aima avec passion, et il en éprouva bien des tourments. C'était encore un tout jeune homme, mais il était le plus beau et le plus preux des Troyens, à l'exception de son frère Hector dont la suprématie à la guerre ne fut jamais contestée. Darès nous en est ici garant: Hector fut vraiment la fleur de toute chevalerie et Troïlus fut sur ce point bien digne de son frère. Oui, il était vraiment son frère pour la prouesse, la courtoisie et la générosité. (pp. 106-7)

In his *Historia Destructionis Troiae*, Guido delle Colonne has transformed Benoît's Old French romance style into the historical narrative style in Latin; he has condensed Benoît's detailed description about Troilus as follows:

> Troylus uero, licet fuerit corpore magnus, magis fuit tamen corde magnanimus, animosus multum sed multam habuit in sua animositate temperiem, dilectus plurimum a puellis, cum ipse aliqualem seruando modestiam delectaretur in illis. In viribus uero et strennuitate bellandi uel fuit alius Hector uel secundus ab ipso. In toto eciam regno Troye iuuenis nullus fuit tantis uiribus nec tanta audacia gloriosus. (liber VIII)
>
> (Troilus, although he was large of body, was even larger of heart; he was very bold but he had moderation in his boldness. He endeared himself to young girls, since he was pleased to maintain a certain reserve toward them. In strength and valor for fighting he was another Hector, or second to him. Moreover, in the whole kingdom of Troy, no young man was celebrated for such great strength and such great daring.)[5]

It is noteworthy that Guido refers to Troilus's inclination toward young girls in addition to his famous bravery.

Lastly, let us quote from Joseph of Exeter's *Bellum Troianum*, which is said to be 'Chaucer's Dares' by Robert K. Root (1917):

> Troilus in spacium surgentes explicat artus, mente gigas, etate puer, nullique secundus audendo uirtutis opus, mixtoque uigore gratior illustres insignit gloria uultus.
>
> (Troilus was broad and tall. In spirit he was a giant, but in age he was a boy. He was second to none in venturing upon brave deeds. Pride graced his noble feature, more pleasing because it was blended with manly vigour.)[6]

Nevertheless, it is difficult to say that Chaucer's main source of his portrait of Troilus in this passage is Joseph of Exeter's paragraph quoted above. As a matter of fact, Chaucer does not accept Joseph's "mente gigas", but says "Al myghte a geant passen hym of myght".

In the last century Comparative Literature made a large contribution to literary studies by source hunting, but sometimes failed in finding the undeniable definite source of the literary work, or of its plot, or of some particular passages. That is because any author in any age is always both *homo conservans* and *homo ludens*; it is in extremely rare cases that the author dares to expose his raw materials in his work. In Chaucer's portrait of Troilus, we can confirm his way of mixing materials and adding his own, eventually preserving the fundamental elements.

3. Towards a global perspective

Now if we want to have Chaucer's genuine and unique portrait of Troilus, we must examine *Troilus and Criseyde* as a whole, line by line, or word by word. But we can choose here, at least, a few basic or fundamental problems out of so many textual cruxes and difficulties in the interpretation of the work.

First of all, I would like to confirm the correct and proper title of this work. Among all the editors and critics who call it *Troilus and Criseyde*, Robert K. Root (1926: xi) alone says that "by what title Chaucer wished his book to be known is not clear" in the Introduction to his edition. But it is an indisputable piece of evidence that Chaucer's narrator declares in the opening lines, "My purpos is / The double sorwe of Troilus to tellen". And once more the narrator confirms his *purpos* as follows:

> But for to tellen forth in special
> Of this kynges sone of which I tolde,
> And leten other thing collateral,
> Of hym thenke I my tale forth to holde,
> Both of his joie and of his cares colde,
> And al his werk, as touching this matere,
> For I it gan, I wol therto refere. (260-266)

Certainly, some misleading titles can be found in the colophons of some manuscripts: "Liber Troili et Criseydis" in London, British Library, MS Harley 2280; Morgan Library MS 817; Oxford, Bodleian Library, MS Selden Supra 56; Cambridge, St. John's College L. 1, or "the book of Troilus and of Cresseyde" in Oxford, Bodleian Library, MS Rawlinson Poet. 163. Fortunately, we can find some proper titles in other manuscripts: "the book of Troylus of double sorwe in loving of Cri[seyde]" in Oxford, Bodleian Library, MS Selden B. 24, which is too long as the title, although it certainly echoes faithfully the opening lines of the work; "Liber Troili" in London, British Library, MS Harley 2392, and Cambridge, Corpus Christi College 61; "Troylus" in Cheltenham, Huntington Library, MS Phillips 8250, and London, British Library, MS Harley 3943. Therefore, the correct and proper title of this work must be *The Book of Troilus* or simply *Troilus*.

Before we proceed to the problem of the narrative structure of the work, it may be convenient for us to enter into the problem of whether the work is a tragedy or a comedy. Every human narrative consists of some eventful sequences, which naturally narrate some kinds of changes in the situation or the relationship among the participants in the particular narrative, either from *concordia* to *discordia*, or from *discordia* to *concordia*. Every narrative has its own substantial middle part between the beginning and the ending. The narrator is able to begin his or her narrative either from *concordia* or from *discordia*, and to include many kinds of *concordia* and *discordia* in the middle part, making his or her story more interesting and more thrilling. Whether it is a tragedy or a comedy, or whether the narrative is tragic or comic solely depends upon the ending in either *concordia* or *discordia*.

Therefore, if Chaucer's narrator stops his narrative at line 1785 of Book Five, his *Troilus* is undoubtedly tragic, and there should be no problem when the narrator says in the next stanza, "Go, litel bok, go, litel myn tragedye" (1786). At the same time, it must be noted that the selfsame narrator prays that "Ther God thi makere yet, er that he dye, / So sende myght to make in som comedye!" (1787-8) We can understand that "er that he dye" is almost equivalent to "er that I parte fro ye" (5) in the opening stanza in Book One of the work, because Chaucer's narrator continues his ending not in *discordia* but in *concordia* in a new and significant dimension of Being. Thus, his *Troilus* becomes a comedy finally, or a divine comedy in a sense. It is true that Chaucer's narrator certainly tells us Troilus's "double sorwe" in the substantial middle part of the work, just as he promised to his audience in the opening lines, but in the final stanzas Chaucer's narrator begins to tell us about Troilus after his death, who "ful blisfully is went / Up to the holughnesse of the eighthe spere" (V, 1808-1809). The first sorrow of Troilus was dispersed by the happy consummation of love, which is narrated in Book Three, and now his second sorrow after the departure of Criseyde to the Greek camp has been overcome by his blissful ascending to heaven after his tragic death by Achilles. Therefore, the vector of the narrator's narrative is not how the hero became sorrowful, but how his "double sorwe" has been overcome. Then the extremely important narrative is about the actions of the deceased Troilus in the ending of the work. Indeed, Chaucer's Pandarus said already in Book Two:

> How so it be that som men hem delite
> With subtyl art hire tales for to endite,
> Yet for al that, in hire entencioun
> Hire tale is al for som conclusioun.
> And sithe th'ende is every tales strengthe (256-260)

It is not a mere proverbial wisdom, but offers us a key for the structural interpretation of the work. The ending of any narrative has always a cardinal importance to both the narrator and the audience or the reader. The following twenty one lines tell us all actions and movements of Troilus after death:

And whan that he was slayn in this manere,
His lighte goost ful blisfully *is went*
Up to the holughnesse of the eighthe spere,
In convers letyng everich element;
And ther he *saugh* with ful avysement
The erratik sterres, *herkenyng* armonye
With sownes ful of hevenyssh melodie.

And down from thennes faste he *gan avyse*
This litel spot of erthe that with the se
Embraced is, and fully *gan despise*
This wrecched world, and *held* al vanite
To respect of the pleyn felicite
That is in hevene above; and at the laste,
There he was slayn *his lokyng down he caste*,

And in hymself he *lough* right at the wo
Of hem that wepten for his deth so faste,
And *dampned* al oure werk that foloweth so
The blynde lust, the which that may nat laste,
And sholden al oure herte on heven caste;
And forth he *wente*, shortly for to telle,
Ther as Mercurye sorted hym to dwelle. (1807-1827)[7]

When we find in these stanzas such a set of verbs, especially *despise*, *lough* and *dampned*, we cannot help remembering the several stanzas in Book One which describe the young Troilus when he appears in the narrative for the first time:

This Troilus, as he was wont to gide
His yonge knyghtes, lad hem up and down
In thilke large temple on every side,
Byholding ay the ladies of the town,
Now here, now there; for no devocioun
Hadde he to non, to reven hym his reste,
But *gan to preise and lakken* whom hym leste.

And in his walk ful faste he *gan to wayten* –
If knyght or squyer of his compaignie
Gan for to syke, or lete his eighen baiten
On any womman that he koude espye.
He wolde *smyle and holden it folye*,
And seye hym thus, 'God woot, she slepeth softe
For love of the, whan thow turnest full ofte!' (183-196)[8]

Then, the narrator, after severely criticizing "this fierse and proude knyght" Troilus, just like a "proude Bayard" (211-266), continues to follow this Troilus, who "leet hymselven so konnynge, / And scorned hem that Loves peynes dryen" (302-303), or "Repentynge hym that he hadde evere ijaped / Of Loves folk" (318-319). And finally,

Right with hire look thorugh-shoten and thorugh-darted,
Al feyneth he in lust that he sojorneth,
And al his chere and speche also he borneth,
And ay of Loves servantz every while,
Hymself to wrye, at hem *he gan to smyle*. (325-329)[9]

As a matter of fact, the narrator says clearly in the opening lines that his *purpos* in this work is to tell 'The double sorwe of Troilus / In lovynge", that is to say, "how his aventures fellen / Fro wo to wele, and after out of joie" (1-5); in later lines that the narrator's tale should be "Both of his joie and of his cares colde; / And al his werk" (264-265). However, we can subsume, according to Troilus's first appearance and his last in heaven, that the narrator tells us the *double smile and despise*, that is to say, how his proud smile and contempt for the men and women in love transform to a new smile and contempt for the mortal world in general from the higher dimension of human knowledge.

Of course, the opening of the work conveys the most important message of the narrator. But it is sometimes necessary to paraphrase it as a result of our interpretation of the work. For instance, Homer begins his *Iliad*, saying: Μῆνιν ἄειδε, Θεά, Πηληϊάδεω 'Αχιλῆος ('The wrath dost thou sing, o goddess, of Peleus' son, Achilles.'). As a matter of fact, during his long narratives Homer's narrator focalizes on the wrath of Achilles. But in the last Book of the *Iliad*, we can certainly confirm that a sense of pity has been produced from his fierce wrath against the old Trojan King Priam, as Jinyo Kim argued recently in his *The pity of Achilles* (2000). Likewise, in the *Odyssey*, Homer's narrator says in the first line: 'Ἄνδρα μοι ἔννεπε, Μοῦσα, πολύτροπον... ('Tell me, Muse, of the man of many devices, ...') It is certain that the main parts of the work are occupied by the narrative about the adventures of Odysseus, "the man of many devices". But at the same time, we can say that the subject of the work is the story of the family reunion as a result of our interpretations of the whole work.

Returning to Chaucer's *Troilus*, we must not forget the significance of the contrast between the young Troilus in the opening and the deceased Troilus in the end, because the narrator tells us carefully in detail how the young Troilus is maturing as a person by his love experience. Already at the end of Book One, the narrator says as follows:

> And in the town his manere tho forth ay
> So goodly was, and gat hym so in grace,
> That ecch hym loved that loked on his face.
>
> For he bicom the frendlieste wight,
> The gentilest, and ek the mooste fre,
> The thriftiest, and oon the beste knyght
> That in his tyme was or myghte be;
> Dede were his japes and his cruelte,
> His heighe port and his manere estraunge,
> And ecch of tho gan for a vertu chaunge. (1076-1085)

In the soliloquy in the temple in Book Four, the young Troilus, who is now three years older since his first appearance, develops his Boethian meditations on Providence and Free Will. Thus, through "his joie" and "his cares colde", his mind has been prepared to be ascended high up to the heavens.

From the famous opening lines of the work, one may easily suggest the capital letter *W* as the pattern of the narrative structure of the work. But we would like to propose the vertical structure of the narrative, at the bottom of which the young proud Troilus appears, and on the top of which the deceased Troilus peacefully sits; all other substantial narratives on his love affair are included between the bottom and the top.

In order to establish such a vertical narrative structure, the idea of ascending to heaven is indispensable. If we confine our perspective within the European context, we can easily refer to Plato's *Timaeus*, or Plotinus' *Enneades*, or other medieval Platonic authors, or Dante's *Divine Comedy* and Boccaccio's *Teseida*. But, all over the world, there are the countless myths, tales, and legends concerning human and superhuman beings who fly away into Heaven; such a universal diffusion of the symbolism of ascension is based upon the essential longing of human beings for absolute freedom from the inevitable human conditions. The symbolism of ascension has been explored extensively by Mircea Eliade in his monumental writings, and especially in his article, "Symbolisms of Ascension and 'Walking Dreams'" which was included in his

Myths, dreams and mysteries: The encounter between contemporary faiths and archaic realities (1960).

Finally, we can say that, although Chaucer's narrator is undoubtedly Christian, his imagination about Troilus's ascension to heaven is deeply rooted in the human longings since our archaic culture. Troilus's laughing at the grief of those who weep for his death or his despising of this wretched world when he is in heaven must be interpreted as his absolute freedom and transcendence from the inevitable human condition.

Notes

[1] All quotations from Chaucer are from *Riverside*.

[2] The original Latin quotation is from Meister (1873); the English translation from Frazer (1966).

[3] The original Latin quotation is from Eisenhut (1973); the English translation from Frazer (1966).

[4] The original Old French quotation is from Costans (1907); the Modern French translation from Baumgartner (1987).

[5] The original Latin quotation is from Griffin (1936); the English translation from Meek (1974).

[6] The original Latin quotation is from Riddehough (1951); the English translation from Roberts (1970).

[7] Italics are mine.

[8] Italics are mine.

[9] Italics are mine.

References

Baumgartner, Emmanuèle (trans.)
1987 *Le Roman de Troie de Benoît de Sainte-Maure*. Paris: Union Générale d'Editions.

Boitani, Piero (ed.)
1989 *The European tragedy of Troilus*. Oxford: Clarendon.

Costans, Leopold (ed.)
1907 *Roman de Troie*. (SATF.) Paris: Libraire de Firmin-Didot.

Eisenhut, Werner (ed.)
1973 *Ephemeridos Belli Troiani libri*. (2nd, revised and enlarged edition.) Leipzig: Teubner.

Eliade, Mircea
1960 *Myths, dreams and mysteries: The encounter between contemporary faiths and archaic realities*. New York: Harper & Row.

Frazer, R.M., Jr. (trans.)
1966 *The Trojan War: The chronicles of Dictys of Crete and Dares the Phrygian*. Bloomington, Ind.: Indiana University Press.

Griffin, N.E. (ed.)
1936 *Historia Destructionis Troiae*. (Medieval Academy of America, Publication 26.) Cambridge, Mass.: Medieval Academy of America.

Kim, Jinyo
2000 *The pity of Achilles: Oral style and the unity of the Iliad*. Lanham, Maryland: Rowman & Littlefield.

Lloyd-Jones, Hugh (ed. & trans.)
1996 *Sophocles Fragments*. (The Loeb Classical Library.) London *et al.*: Heinemann *et al.*

Meek, Mary E. (trans.)
1974 *Historia Destructinis Troiæ [by] J. Guido delle Colonne*. Bloomington, Ind.: Indiana University Press.

Meister, Ferdinand (ed.)
1873 *Daretis Phrygii de Excidio Troiæ Historia*. Leipzig: Teubner.

Riddehough, G.B. (ed.)
1951 *Bellum Troianum*. PhD dissertation. Harvard University.

Roberts, G. (trans.)
1970 *Joseph of Exeter: The Iliad of Dares Phrygius*. Cape Town: Balkema.

Root, Robert K.
1917 "Chaucer's Dares". *Modern Philology* 15: 1-22.

Root, Robert K. (ed.)
1926 *The book of Troilus and Criseyde by Geoffrey Chaucer*. Princeton: Princeton University Press.

Between penance and purgatory: Margery Kempe's *Pélerinage de la vie humaine* and the idea of salvaging journeys

Liliana Sikorska (Poznan, Poland)

Pilgrims and pilgrimages were one of the most characteristic sights of the medieval world. Treated both literally as a form of penance and metaphorically as life's journey, pilgrimage/travel becomes a literary trope which still continues to occupy the minds of scholars as a psychological as well as sociological phenomenon.

In Catholic Poland, masses of people travel on foot (or even wheelchairs) to the Marian shrine and monastery in Częstochowa, the central place of pilgrimage in Poland, to meet on 15th August, the feast of Assumption. In August, pilgrims and pilgrimages appear in the various news media. The language of the news is that of information; where the pilgrims leave from; how long they will walk and who organized the pilgrimage. Locations and numbers, sometimes short interviews with the participants who verbalize their particular intentions as to what they want to achieve through their 'pilgrimaging' (some are clearly there to have some form of holiday and meet other people). But while August pilgrimages make the news, the spiritual context of the travel apart from singing and loud prayers is by and large neglected from the point of view of the reportage. Still, in some ways, the pilgrims' motives and drive are similar to those of medieval pilgrims, namely to atone for one's sins, to be given the grace of God in particular matters, to pray for themselves and others and, finally, to cleanse themselves of sin.

Called by Clarissa Atkinson (1983) a mystic and a pilgrim, Margery Kempe is one of the most famous medieval pilgrims.[1] The entire Book One of *The book of Margery Kempe* (1438)[2] is permeated with narratives of various journeys, the reasons for which are not always stated; mostly she undertakes various trips abiding by the inner imperative, the voice of Jesus. As Roland Maissonneuve (1982) argued persuasively, her character is akin to the figure of the fool of God, or a perfect fool, always following the will of God while patiently bearing abuse and shame. Yet, in the much less discussed Book Two, Margery becomes concerned with various aspects of her travels besides the spiritual one. She becomes painfully aware of the clash between the spirituality of pilgrimage and the physicality of travelling.

This paper is an attempt to revise Maissonneuve's views and contrast the idea of the fool of God which Margery resembles in Book One with the character of Margery Kempe from Book Two where she becomes a more conscious, or one could even say, archetypal traveler (despite the fact that she herself always feels to be the chosen one, Christ's singular love), whose inner voice compels her to leave her dwelling place and undertake the penitential but at the same time 'purgatorial' journey for the sake of another human being and not herself. Rewriting the pilgrimage of the life of man, she does not pose as an Everyman, although her *Book* is to be an example for others to follow. In Book Two, her trips testify to her 'singular' grace but create the image of Margery Kempe, the textual character, a wandering saint. Early in the *Book*, Kempe abandons the Old Testament ideal of a large family and devotion to family life and embarks on her *iter asceticum*, following the New Testament model of solitary, spiritual life ('life on the road' one almost wants to say), propagated by Jesus and his followers.

St. Paul urged Christians to think about themselves as *peregrini* 'pilgrims'. Christianity perceived pilgrimage as the symbol of an individual life's journey. The motif of a journey-pilgrimage is reiterated in secular and religious literature with its two 'extremes' Chaucer's 'realistic' pilgrims and Lydgate's allegorical Pilgrim. These texts make up the mosaic of medieval *peregrine*, detailing the voyages of the one who wanders the land for his/her penance and edification. In Chaucer's version, we see the micro scale of human life, the penitential journey becomes a pretext to show the panorama of medieval society, whereas in Lydgate's *Pilgrimage of the life of man* (1426) we see pilgrimage on a macro scale: it is life's journey from birth to death, a journey inadvertently leading each and every human being to the last things. After all, even the funeral procession brings to mind, literally and metaphorically, a journey – the final one. The eschatological thinking is present in both Chaucer's and Lydgate's works as both portray pilgrimage as a spiritual and devotional obligation. Both encourage the readers/participants to see pilgrimage as an active ascetic practice in the name of atonement for human weakness. Chaucer supports the view that during such a journey each and every participant is a humble pilgrim whose earthly belongings and status are of no importance for spiritual matters. Lydgate, using personifications of sins and virtues, offers his readers an allegorical representation of life. And it is the allegory that helps to look at one's life from a distance and be ready for a change of heart, while going *per pedes apostolorum*. Lydgate reminds his readers of the necessity to learn the highest truth, namely the fleeting passage of time and the inevitability of death: "Pylgrymes schal the verray trouthe lerne" (Lydgate, l. 82). There are two prologues in *The pilgrimage of the life of man*. Lydgate's translation of Deguileville's prologue is directed to the reader. In his own prologue, Lydgate recounts how he wrote the first version to his prologue and lost it afterwards, and how he writes another. He tells the readers of his dream of the glorious Jerusalem and promises to take them to the heavenly city. The spirit of penitence occasions a mass pilgrimage in search of Truth in Langland's *Piers Plowman*, but the pilgrims get lost and because of their own ignorance cannot find/see Truth. They meet a professional Pilgrim, whose lack of knowledge of where Truth is expresses Langland's criticism of pilgrims, their motives and the significance of such penitential journeying.

Margery Kempe is never referred to as a pilgrim in the *Book*. She goes on pilgrimages as a penitent with tears of contrition "for hir owyn synnes and sumtyme for oþer mennys synnes also" (*The book*, 61). Although she is frequently drawn towards heavenly things, as Christ promises her bliss in heaven,[3] she is not immune to falling from grace. Her life, just like the allegorical journey of Lydgate's Pilgrim's, is to provide a model. Through its roots in reality of everyday life of late medieval England, it is much more plausible than those of the early Christian saints. In allegorical literature, Man is a pilgrim on earth traveling through the land of exile towards his celestial home. The pilgrimage of the life of Margery Kempe is also to end in heaven as Christ declares in their numerous conversations. Margery's *peregrinatio vitae* is on the one hand reminiscent of the journey each and every fool of God undertakes, a slow progression from one humiliation to another. On the other hand, her pilgrimages are evocative of the purgatorial mortifications, and strengthen her argument about *discretio spirituum*, God's voice inside her consequently reinforcing her claims to holiness. Kempe's motives are akin to the motives of those whose life was devoted to *peregrinatio pro Christi amore*, those specific pilgrimages which link the allegorical and literal dimensions of traveling.

In Book One, Margery travels with her husband a number of times: firstly, to secure for herself the vows of chastity, to which both John and herself have to agree and for which both have to be present in front of the bishop; secondly, to meet various religious people and ecclesiastical authorities including the famous Julian of Norwich and other well recognized persons. Naturally, as a devout woman, she

> had a desyr to se þo placys wher he was born & wher he sufferyd hys Passyon & wher he deyd, wyth oþer holy placys wher he was in hys lyue & also aftyr hys Ressurrexyon (*The book*, 32)

and Christ promises her pilgrimages to Rome and Jerusalem. The pilgrimage to Jerusalem seems to be a particular instance of devotional travel

> [a]lthough the sterner moralists such as Gregory of Nyssa and Anthony the hermit warned against the frivolities of pilgrimage, which easily degenerated into the

> love of travel for its own sake, the Christians journeying to Jerusalem increased steadily in numbers. (Barber 1991: 15)

Margery never wants to go on her own account but is fulfilling Christ's will, at the same time satisfying her curiosity to see holy places in foreign lands. Her faith travel responds to the deeply ingrained motifs, impulses, which according to Webb (2002: xv) were older and wider than Christianity. As Margaret Wade Labarge says:

> The desire for pilgrimage was obviously strong among the great as among the simple and continued with quite astonishing force until the end of the Middle Ages and beyond. Pilgrimage in some shape or form has been a constant human passion. By the end of the Middle Ages it seems to have had a strong admixture of wanderlust and curiosity as well. (Labarge 1983: 95)

For some pilgrims, as Langland demonstrated, holy thoughts and penitence could well be balanced by the love of adventures, and the search for Truth is never completed.

While insisting on spiritual marriage, Margery wants to rid herself of conjugal debt but first and foremost her prerogative is to be able to travel without restraint. This is why she wants to be given the ring and the mantle, the symbols of her separation from her husband. Apart from legal there were also financial considerations, which run ever present throughout the entire *Book*. Margery pays the debts of her husband, she also pays her own debts:

> ...sche preyd þe parysch preste of þe town þer sche was dwellyng to sey for hir in þe pulpyt þat, yf any man er woman þat cleymyd any dette of hir husbond or of hir þei xuld come & speke with hir er sche went, & sche, wyth þe help of God, xulde makyn a-seth to ech of hem þat þei schuldyn heldyn hem content. (*The book*, 60)

Paying her and her husband's debts before leaving town is not only an act of Christian justice but first and foremost reveals Margery as an honest businesswoman, who, at the onset of her penitential journey, wants to have a clean account both with God as well as with people (cf. Ellis 1990). Margery willingly gives herself to the care of Christ's mercy, but she is never deprived of financial worries. Such material factors are present in Book Two when she tries to excuse herself from carrying out God's plan and going on a trip with her daughter-in-law:

'I am not purueyd of gold ne of syluer sufficiently for to gon wyth as I awt to be, and, þow I wer & wolde gon, I wote wel my dowtyr had leuar I wer at hom, & perauentur þe schip-maistrys xulde not receyuyn me in-to her vessel for to gon wyth hem' (*The book*, 227)

This, in fact, calls in question Margery's absolute and utter adherence to her inner voice. Although she does show the necessary simplicity of heart, and places the love of Christ above all earthly love, she is also quite a skillful manipulator in creating her self-image or better, the image projected onto the text. As Lynn Staley (1994: 11) asserts:

One of Kempe's most important means of achieving her scrutiny of contemporary institutions is her deployment of the individual, Margery, as both a foil for and a representative of the community that she adumbrates in the numerous episodes that compose the Book.

Practical as ever, Margery takes care of her daughter-in-law who, after the death of her husband (Margery's unnamed son), lives with her for a year and a half before her friends want her to come back to Germany. She has a child in care of some friends in Prussia, no husband in England, and simply wants to return home. Margery cares for her daughter-in-law's well-being, and shows necessary Christian altruism. Still, she deliberates:

'Lord, ȝyf it wer þi wille I wolde takyn leue of my confessowr & gon wyth hir ouyr þe see.' Owr Lord answeryd to hyr thowt, seying, 'Dowtyr, I wote wel, yf I bode þe gon, þu woldist gon al redy. Þerfor I wyl þat þu speke no word to hym of þis mater'. (*The book*, 225-226)

Christ is not anxious for her to go, and she herself begins to feel her age (66), after all, she is now an elderly lady, for whom such trips might be dangerous. Still, she decides to accompany her daughter-in-law to Ipswich as the necessary sacrifice of a wandering saint who exchanges the comforts of home with the inconveniences of exile. Margery does not seem particularly eager to go, perhaps remembering that she was in great peril before. Thus, she is reluctant to put her life in jeopardy once again. And moreover, she has hurt her foot, about which her confessor reminds her. But as a true good Christian, fool of God, she trusts the Lord again, and as the two women walk out of Lynne and stop at a church

þe forseyd creatur, desiryng teerys of deuocyon, not myth purchasyn at þat tyme but euyr was comawndyd in hir hert for to gon ouyr þe see wyth hir dowtyr. Sche wolde a putt it owt of hir mende, & euyr it cam a-geyn so fast þat sche myth not

> rest ne qwiet han in hir mende but euyr was labowryd & comawndyd to gon ouyr þe see. (*The book*, 226)

Margery is tormented by various worries but she is a true *peregrinus* (or perhaps *peregrina*), whose life is to carry the aura of holiness, because of her ceaseless wandering. Like the knights in chivalric tales, who have to leave Camelot in order to seek adventures and undergo constant testing, Margery puts her body and general well-being in danger in order to save, or rather keep saving, her soul. Such quests never promise the return from wilderness, but always entail the never-ending, self-imposed exile similar to that of medieval monks.[4] Her last pilgrimage, more than any other before, just like for Lydgate's Pilgrim, is a quest for herself.

Kempe's attempts at accomplishing what Christ sets out for her strengthen Maissonneuve's arguments about Margery's holy simplicity. For some theologians, like the fifteenth-century scholar Nicholas of Cusa (1977: 667), the mysteries of faith were to be attained through "not knowing". Nicholas represents the conviction of learned ignorance where faith always takes precedence over knowledge. The medieval idea of the holy fool or the fool of God promoted an image of a human being who gave himself/herself entirely to God's commands. S/he was "to proclaim and live, through his word and daily life, the gospel of the beatitudes, to participate in Christ's *kenosis*, passion and divine folly of infinite love" (Maisonneuve 1982: 1). Maissonneuve stresses the spirit endorsed by Pauline writings, as in some way Christ was a fool of God, the puppet in the hands of the Almighty. One finds similar arguments, although framed in a much more extended medieval context, in Karma Lochrie's work (1991: 156-163). Lochrie concentrates on the spiritual aspect of the idea of excess of love and intensity of religious experience, while Maissonneuve highlights the physical aspects of being a fool of God, such as poverty, peregrinations and withstanding abuse and derision. Holy fools are Christ's chosen people, the choice is not theirs but His. The motto of such behavior is that of *imitatio Christi*. "They do all they can to conform themselves to his total self-surrender. They want to live his mystery of self-emptying and nakedness. They even search for all possible humiliations." (Maissonneuve 1982: 2) In some ways, perfect fools transform themselves into sacred jesters, clowns – not hesitating to perform bizarre or strange actions, if they are convinced God required them to do so. "The fool of God lives as a child, in its simplicity and purity, being the soul of compassion for those less fortunate in the world." (Maissonneuve 1982: 5) Maissonneuve proceeds with presenting Margery as a fool of God, perfect in her blind following of the voice of Christ inside her. Lochrie (1991: 157) maintains that the fool's folly begins with the excess of love, an element common to all mystical texts, which in some way attempt to channel such excess through visions and, consequently, writing.

Kempe's love for Christ, one of the pre-requisites for the fools of God, is contained in her need to experience Him. This in fact, provides yet another form of journeying, that of the mind. In many medieval sources, reading is presented as a journey of the mind. Medieval monks were urged to undertake salvaging peregrinations in their daily contemplations. The spiritual effect of such journeys was that of inward illumination. Margery's contemplations usually take the form of dialogues with Christ. Her inner life as well as her visions evince her literal perception of spiritual matters; still each and every one of her meditations resembles a journey of the mind. The excessive tears remind one of the doctrine of compunction, the pain of the spirit, a suffering resulting simultaneously from two causes: the existence of sin and our own tendency toward sin – *compunctio paenitentiae*, *timoris*, *firmidinis* – and the existence of our desire for God and even, our very possession of God. Leclercq (1988: 30) claims that it was St. Gregory who laid stress on this aspect of religious life. If the soul is hardened (*durata*) by sin and egoism, compunction is the process that softens it (*emollitur*), enabling the soul to be cleansed from rust (Leclercq 1988: 31).

> The soul illuminated by God's light, the soul which knows God, perceives in itself all that is impure and contrary to God. Thus, it is confirmed in humility, in the same attitude which had been the point of departure and the fundamental reason for its initial flight toward God. (Leclercq 1988: 33)

Kempe might not be aware of the sophisticated theological doctrine but she is familiar with the existing models of affective piety, as she has various works read to her. Richard Rolle, Bridget of Sweden and Elizabeth of Hungary are her models, undoubtedly emulated only to an extent to which she could follow the teaching of a hermit and imitate the life of aristocratic women. Although she is "not lettyrd", she understands the importance of the written word (sacred biographies that recount the lives of saints were after all passed down in written form). The insistence on textual culture or rather the awareness of the existence and the strength of textual culture is never undervalued in the *Book*. Clumsy as it may seem, Kempe repeatedly asserts her knowledge of the Bible and uses dialogue to dramatize her encounters with Christ. She also mentions a number of female models, out of which only one, Marie de Oigny, is brought up by her scribe.

> Margery seeks to emulate a written tradition which will be accepted by those in her society whom she perceives will be her audience. The purpose of hagiography is to instruct, and, according to the Church fathers, the aesthetic dimensions of hagiographic narratives were less important than the devotion it prompted. (Akel 2001: 11)

The events selected from her daily life even though not presented chronologically, express Kempe's metadesign for Margery's holy living (Akel 2001: 10). Her particular understanding of *imitatio Christi*, as many scholars noticed, is an attempt to balance the personal with the public aspects of her life. At the same time Margery's *imitatio Christi* is shaped by textual tradition of various devotional texts.[5] In a way, she chooses *vita mixta*, the life in the world with the spiritual aim in mind, so aptly summarized by Lucifer in *Wisdom* as the ideal life established by Christ himself:

> And all hys lyff was informacyon
> Ande example to man.
> Sumtyme with sinners he had conversacyon;
> sumtyme with holy also comunycayon;
> Sumtyme he laboryde, preyed; sumtyme tribulacyon;
> Thys was vita mixta þat Gode here began. (*Wisdom*, 1.425-428)

Reporting problems and hesitations about writing her *Book*, Margery is strikingly exact in her account of who wrote what, and how this whole thing came about. In Book Two, she establishes the exact temporal frame of the text. Her second scribe copied the previous manuscript of Book One and began to write Book Two beginning "in þe fest of Seynt Vital Martyr sweche grace as owr Lord wrowt in hys sympyl creatur ȝerys þat sche leuyd aftyr..." (*The book*, 221). No doubt, she is in control of the process of creation and writing. In Book Two, authority and self-definition are of less importance, as Margery feels quite confident in her role of the wandering saint. Lynn Staley notices that Margery's book is less an autobiography,[6] and more of, as Heffernan terms it, a "sacred biography":

> ...[a] form increasingly translated into vernacular languages throughout the late Middle Ages. The work of Kempe's fellow East Anglians Osbern Bokenham and John Capgrave provides strong evidence of the growing public for such vernacular lives. By using Margery's life as means of scrutinizing not only the foundations of English society but also the nature of ecclesiastical and political authority, Kempe develops what was nascent in the traditions of sacred biography she would have inherited from Latin and Continental models. She also reveals her shrewd grasp of

> the ways in which the issues and the language of her day could be used to signify more fundamental truths about societies; like Chaucer and Langland, she is able to convey a world whose immediacy only appears a reflection of reality. ... Written in English about an English "saint" *The book of Margery Kempe* dramatizes the weaknesses of the social and ecclesiastical institutions of an age whose need for such sanctity is acute. (Staley 1994: 37-38)

The idea of travel, of leaving home and giving herself to the mercy of others, is one of Kempe's assumptions about sainthood, which she consequently accomplishes despite the clerical and secular opposition she encounters everywhere she goes. Her piety frequently earns her people's dislike and she is left alone and exposed to slander. All such instances are patiently endured *pro amore Dei*. Spared the tribulations of early Christian saints, her form of martyrdom, thus, is that "by slander" as Gail McMurray Gibson (1989: 47) observes. I would add that Margery's martyrdom is that "by exclusion" from the various groups and communities she tries to belong to, both at home and indeed the communities of pilgrims. It is Christ's holy word:

> [s]wech holy dalyawns & spechys in hir sowle cawsyd hir to sobbyn ryth boistowsly & wepyn ful plentyuowsly. Þe mor sche wept, þe yrkar was hir man of hir cumpany & þe raþar besyd hym to gon fro hir & leeuyn hir a-lone. He went so fast þat sche myth not folwyn wyth-owtyn gret labowr & gret disese. He seyd þat he was a-ferd of enmyis & theuys þat þei xulde takyn hir a-way fro hym perauentur & betyn hym & robbyn þer-to." (*The book*, 233-234)

That was in Stralsund (Strawissownd as the *Book* names the place). Concurrently, the insults she has to endure provide the necessary amount of suffering on Earth, also indispensable in hagiography. In Book Two, although Kempe is spared the drastic accusations of being a Lollard and other such slanderous remarks, she is nevertheless not spared harsh words:

> Sum seyd it was a womanys witte & a gret foly for þe lofe of hir dowtyr-in-lawe to putte hir-self, a woman in gret age, to perellys of þe see & for to gon in-to a strawnge cuntre wher sche had not ben be-forn ne not wist how sche xulde come a-geyn. (*The book*, 228-229)

This, far from being a particularly harsh opinion, is countered by another view of those who treat the trip as an act of charity:

> Summe heldyn it was a dede of gret charite for-as-meche as hir dowtyr had be-forn-tyme left hir frendys & hir cuntre & cam with hir husbond to visityn hir in þis cuntre þat sche wolde now halpyn hir dowtyr hom a-geyn in-to þe cuntre þat sche cam fro. (*The book*, 229)

The balance of suffering, however, has to be preserved and going back from Germany to England, in Aachen Margery is left alone and is called a hypocrite:

> owr Lord ʒaf hir so mech swetnes & deuocyon þat sche wept and sobbyd wondyr sor & not myth restreyn hir-self þerfro. Þe monke was wroth & al hir felaschip for sche wept so sor, &, whan þei wer comyn a-geyn to her waynys, þei chedyn hir & rebukyd hir, clepyng hir ypocrite & seyd many an euyl worde vn-to hir. (*The book*, 235)[7]

Thus, like in Book One, Margery is frequently exiled from her company. The rule for such exile is clear, the more she receives from Christ, the more she is despised by her fellow Christians. What more should a true saint want?

After all, she is called by Christ to the holy life; the rejection suffered from fellow human beings, at least those who do not believe in her, is part of the struggle of the pilgrimage of life of Margery Kempe. But it is Christ himself who strengthens her in her vocation. In Book Two, Margery, a woman past her prime, is still a beloved daughter of God and during her ultimate journey to and from Germany she is repeatedly reassured by Christ:

> 'Dowtyr, þu wist wel a woman þat hath a fayr man & a semly to hir husbonde, ʒyf sche loue hym, sche wyl gon wyth hym wher-euyr he wil. And, dowtyr, þer is non so fayr & so semly ne so good as I. Þerfor, yf þu loue me, þu xalt not dredyn to gon wyth me wher-þat-euyr I wil hauyn þe. Dowtyr, I browte the hedyr, & I xal bryngyn þe hom a-geyn in-to Inglond in saf-warde. Dowte it not, but leue it ryth wel.' (*The book*, 233)

Such is the representation of Christ's love, "give yourself to me and I will make everything alright for you"; which woman can refuse such a declaration from a man she loves? On a serious level, though, these assertions are reminiscent of the idea of the discernment of spirits, *discretio spirituum,* a medieval ecclesiastical doctrine which validated visionary experience and aimed at distinguishing between true and false visionaries.[8] Hence, the stress Margery places on Christ's voice and will rather than on her own. Rosalynn Voaden (1999: 110) recalls that conflict and controversy surrounded the life of Margery Kempe and as such it is inscribed in the text.[9] In Book Two, Margery fulfills yet another role, that of an intermediary between God and the world, which is the role saints frequently play. In order to become a recognized holy woman, she must almost blindly obey the Church while at the same time obey the voice within her. It seems that Book One never achieves such resolution and Margery is constantly entangled in a conflict between orthodoxy and heresy. Similar to the fashionable *Lives*, such as later John Capgrave's *Life of St. Augustine*, *The book of Margery Kempe* encompasses the two archetypal extremes, a sinner and a saint, thus giving its subject a more life-like dimension of character. While her life's story can be seen as comparable to the story of Lydgate's Pilgrim, the insistence on *discretio spirituum* and Margery's numerous 'good works' maintain equilibrium between rights and wrongs suffered in the hands of others. Even though Margery thrives on expiating on the wrongs done to her by others:

> for les þan sche had an had sweche gostly comfortys it had ben vnpossybyl hir to a boryn þe schamys & wonderyngys þe whech sche suffyrd pacyently & mekely for þe grace þat God schewyd in hyr. (*The book*, 99)

After the death of her son and husband, Kempe devotes herself entirely to the well-being of her daughter-in-law. Her trip to Germany (one should call it a trip rather than a pilgrimage) is not commenced upon because of her own spiritual needs, but for more practical reasons: Her daughter-in-law, which she refers to as "daughter", being in a foreign country, and "[i]t is not goodly þat sche xulde gon so fer with a ȝong man a-lone in strawnge cuntre wher her neiþyr is knowyn" (*The book*, 226). What is voiced here are the real dangers of traveling in the Middle Ages, so aptly outlined by Jean Verdon (2003) and by Diana Webb (1999), the latter being a collection of documents on traveling and pilgrimage, and travelers' and pilgrims' experiences. Natural conditions, the weather, bad roads, thieves on land and pirates at sea provided tangible threats to the well-being of pilgrims. Margery herself articulated such fears frequently:

> many tymes, as sche went be þe wey & in þe feldys, þer fel gret leuenys wyth hedows thunderys, gresely & greuows, þat sche feryd hir þat it xulde a smet hir to deth, & many gret reynes, whech cawsyd in hir gret drede & heuynes. (*The book*, 101)

In Book Two, she is not spared the fear of dying at sea either: "þe tempestys weryn so greuows & hedows þat þei myth not rewlyn ne gouerne her schip" (*The book,* 229). Margery's adventures overseas, her meeting dishonest and evil wishing people are generally similar to what one finds in the accounts of so many of her earlier pilgrimages.[10] Her incessant penance is recognized by those "... which knewe mor of þe creaturys leuyng supposyd & trustyd þat it was þe wille & þe werkyng of al-mythy God to þe magnifying of hys own name" (*The *book*, 229). Margery fulfills the will of God but she is not spared human fears and doubts. In Book Two, Christ reproves Margery for losing faith in his power:

> Owr mercyful Lord, spekyng in hir mende, blamyd hir of hyr feerdnes, seying, "Why dredist þe Why art þu so aferd? I am as mythy her in þe see as on þe londe. Why wilt þu mistrostyn me? Al þat I haue hite þe I xal trewly fulfillyn, & I xal neuyr deceyuyn þe. Suffyr paciently a while & haue trost in my mercy. (*The book*, 230)

The idea that Kempe is being chastised by God himself and suffers physical discomfort patiently clearly points to the purgatorial character of her trip. In a rather overlooked episode of a six-week stay in Gdańsk (Danzig), most probably at the end of April/beginning of May 1433, nothing is mentioned of the imminent war between the Teutonic Order Knights and Poland. Throughout the 15th century, Prussia was a tumultuous and dangerous place;[11] notwithstanding the lack of traveling company, Christ "monischyd hir to gon owt of þe cuntre" (*The book*, 231). Left to her own devices, Margery cannot choose with whom to go but simply accepts offers from, sometimes, very suspicious people, who cheat and rob her. In Aachen, she is once again "forsaken" and has to spend a night alone.

> Þe nyght fel up-on [hyr], & sche was ryth heuy, for sche was a-lone. Sche wist not wyth whom sche myth reston þat nyght ne wyth whom sche xulde gon þe next day. Þer cam preistys to hir, þer sche was at oste, of þat cuntre. Þei clepyd hir Englisch sterte & spokyn many lewyd wordys vn-to hir, schewyng vn-clenly cher & cuntenawns, proferyng to ledyn hir a-bowtyn yf sche wolde. Sche had mech drede for hir chastite & was in gret heuynes. (*The book*, 236)

While Margery has finally found lodgings with a "good wife", this was certainly one of her most frightening adventures, *locus horridus*, the sum of all of Margery's fears. Here, the *sacrum* of the pilgrimage is reduced to the *profanum* of the life on the road. In Lydgate's text, the readers become *peregrini*, and pilgrims assuredly are brothers to one another:

> … a-mong pylgrymes, thys a lawe,
> That, as brother vu-to brother
> Euerych sholde a-byden other. (Lydgate, l. 298-301)

In Margery's case, the brotherhood or even simple Christian charity fails other people too frequently to describe all such instances here. Early medieval literature abounds in stories of expulsions. Various 'wanderers' roam medieval poetic texts lamenting their unjust lot. From the stories of Anglo-Saxon poetry to the medieval Irish Mad-Sweeney legend, exclusion, loneliness and wandering evince the harshness of human destiny of those left unprotected. Having found oneself in an environment hostile to human beings, the chances of survival for a single person in the wilderness were slim, as Margery herself learns many times in the course of her wanderings. After all, a *peregrinus*, was "...literally and originally a foreigner or stranger, and artists represented the stranger with the instantly recognizable attributes of the pilgrim" (Webb 2002: 1661).

If we treat pilgrimages as geared towards contrition and penitence, Margery's sea voyage to the North of Europe is more purgatorial in its character. In Lydgate's works as well as many other medieval works such as morality plays, sins are portrayed as thieves and rascals.[12] Setting aside inconveniences of travel, lack of hygiene and sickness, in the literal as well as metaphorical meaning, pilgrimages were beset with peril. And most commonly, hell, or in this case purgatory was other people. Margery never treats her trips as in any way 'purgatorial', although the doctrine of purgatory is known to her. Until the 12th century, the idea of purgation, *purgatories ignis* was known to the Church fathers, who contributed to the development of the purgatorial imagery. Since the 12th century, purgatory had been understood as a separate place, whose origin was traced by Jacques le Goff (1986). One of the chief issues here is that purgatory exists in time as well as in space, not unlike penitential trips, wherein the primary purpose of a soul was purgation. Grave as the metaphorical baptism in fire is, purgatory afforded temporary suffering. In order to shorten the time one would spend in purgatory, one had to atone for one's sins while still on earth by means of penance. Penance was expressed in terms of pilgrimages both far and near, and indulgences which were also articulated in terms of days, weeks and years (Webb 2002: 21), hence one of the forms of atonement was pilgrimage. Davidson (1994: 10) talks about the widespread belief in the presence of saints and apostles in heaven, as they were the ones who passed through death to bliss, without suffering the fires of purgatory. Margery Kempe is continually assured that Jesus will forgive her sins and she is promised:

> þow schalt neuyr com in Helle ne in Purgatorye, but, whan þow schalt passyn owt of þis world, wyth-in þe twynkelyng of an eye þow schalt haue þe blysse of Heuyn, for I am þe same God þat haue browt þi synnes to þi mend & mad þe to be schreve þerof. And I grawnt þe contrysyon in-to þi lyues ende. (*The book*, 17)

What is more, it is Christ who assures her that the slander she endures on Earth is sufficient purgatorial fire and atonement:

> …þu xuldyst noon oþer Purgatory han þan slawndyr & speche of þe world, for I haue chastysed the my-self as I wolde be many gret dredys & turmentrijs þat þu hast had wyth euyl spyritys boþin slepyng & wakyng many ȝerys. & þerfor I schal preseruyn þe at þin ende thorw my mercy þat þei schal no powyr haue ouyr þe neyþyr in body ne in sowle; it is gret grace & myracle þat þu hast thy bodyly wyttys for þe vexacyon þat þu hast had wyth hem a-for-tyme. (*The book*, 51)

All the storms and sicknesses that Margery has to endure constitute part of God's grand plan as to her person which can be summarized with the words of Julian of Norwich that in the end "all shall be well".

Here, the confessional pattern which dominated mystical literature is used to stress the interconnection between the life of a(n) (erring) sinner and the life of a (forgiven and blessed) saint, an interconnection which, on a large scale, provided models of moral living by paradoxically creating a model sinner and penitent. A scribe of a holy (recognized) woman whose life was ordinary and extraordinary at the same time must have been aware of the necessary tensions between the sinful and saintly behavior of an individual. Both earlier as well as later 'lives' tend to idealize their subjects in order to grant them unquestionable sainthood.[13] Hence, *exemplar* (the exemplary) takes precedence over *historia* (the factual). The question of historical truth is yet another issue. Most of the early saints' lives blended the historical with the exemplary, offering texts in which legends are most commonly presented as verifiable sources.[14] Leclercq (1988: 162) argues that "[t]he desire to praise God in His saints is conducive to exaggeration: everything becomes admirable, and the narrative turns into a panegyric". As the saint is treated as a model Christian, it was understood that less edifying facts should be "passed over in silence – or altered" (Leclercq 1988: 162). At the time of the great upsurge of female mysticism, the Church acknowledged that the audience sought different, more plausible models.[15] The Christian community then was different from that of the early Christian times, although the demand for edifying books was still great enough to comply with what Duffy (1992: 4) calls "a voracious lay appetite for religious literature".[16]

The pattern of the saint's life includes good works and the conversion of sinners. Throughout her 'career', Margery represents herself as having the gift of foresight which was used for predicting the future and telling people what their deceased spouses do, or in the case of erring religious people, it was used to tell them their sins and call for their reform. In Book Two, Margery performs the ultimate act, that of converting a sinner by praying for (and receiving grace) in the name of her straying son. The words to describe his sin of lechery are not those of spiritual degeneration but rather those of physical ugliness: "… hys colowr chawngyd, hys face wex ful of whelys & bloberys as it had ben a lepyr"

(*The book*, 222). The mysterious sickness "for whech men fleddyn hys company & hys felaschep as for a lepyr" (*The book*, 222) disappears under the strength of Margery's prayer; her son changes. He is reformed and goes on pilgrimages. Then, as we learn, he is forgiven by God and becomes a God-fearing Christian "þe mor reuerent to-owr-Lord-ward" (*The book*, 224). The language of the passages describing his conversion does not concentrate on the son, however, but on Margery's force of prayer and the grace the Lord shows her by fulfilling her desire to change him:

> ...sche openyd hir hert to hym [her son], schewyng hym & enformyng how owr Lord had drawyn hir thorw hys mercy& be what menys, also how meche grace he had schewyd for hir, þe whech he seyd he was vnworthy to heryn. (*The book*, 224)

Again, Margery becomes the intermediary between God and her son, consulting God's will in relation to her son and of course, he "trustyd meche in hys moderys cownsel" (*The book*, 224). Here she achieves two goals: "[s]he thus audaciously promotes herself as a holy woman who is, at once, the mediator of God's mercy, the emblem of his parenthood, and the leading player in His drama of salvation" (Winstead 1994: 12). Margery represents herself as an extraordinary and ordinary person at the same time, someone who is not spared the pains of everyday life, and yet, she is Christ's chosen spouse, as if she was 'the chosen Everyman'. Unfortunately, Margery's blissful relationship with her son does not last long, even though he decides to come back home with his wife. When they arrive in England, Margery's son is overcome by a mysterious sickness and dies a day after their arrival, most probably in 1431 (*The book*, 225).[17] So in literal and symbolic terms, her son comes home. Margery does not show excessive grief, but simply notes that soon after his father followed him to the land of "wher deth xal neuyr aperyn" (*The book,* 225).

Conclusion

Life, as St. Columbán pointed out, is a road to eternity (Bitel 1993: 222). The road is infused with traps in the form of various temptations and transgressions, but at its end there is the promise of redemption and paradise. The pilgrimage of the life of man is an educative and penitential journey of metaphorical Manhood. The trope re-iterates the dramatization of Christian repentance and in a way, rephrases Lydgate's invitation to a journey; an enlightening journey of the mind. The journey itself becomes a metaphor of a change, the transformation of the sinner into the saint, or more commonly the condemned into the saved. Various difficulties awaiting the penitent on the road are chastising hardships s/he has to endure, temptations s/he has to resist and sins s/he has to avoid. Both in Book One as well as in Book Two, Kempe's narrative abounds in edifying examples of penitential voyages and purgatorial adventures. Here, the topos of life's journey is seen through the pattern of pilgrimage, being part of her 'saintly' life. In a way, her journeys are quests of Christ in the world and tests of His unending love for her. Concurrently, they are also journeys of self-discovery despite her rather self-absorbing introspection. Undertaking her pilgrimages in Book One, Margery wants to learn about God through the utmost experience of passion, and visit the places related to Christ's life and death and the places connected with the saints. Resuming her travels in Book Two, Margery Kempe becomes a wandering saint, compelled to fulfill the will of God, to complete her sacred biography. The trips articulate the need of salvation and can be related both to the vision of the medieval world of the fools of God, simpletons, eternal wanderers purging themselves through their 'pilgrimaging' as well as to the vision of the modern secular world in which a non-conforming individual can be an outcast, one who is perpetually trying to find a place in society or the community and for whom travelling/moving is the constant quest and the only form of salvation[18].

Notes

[1] Most of the critical sources on Margery's life and times discuss her pilgrimages in detail, cf. Collis (1983), Gallyon (1995), Goodman (2002).

[2] Hereafter referred to as *The book*.

[3] For the images of bliss, see Sikorska (2004).

[4] Wandering is a particular trait of many Irish saints. Many medieval Irish monks left their home in search of sanctity in foreign lands. They believed that "their deaths in the wasteland would demonstrate God's judgment on a sinner, but that their survival would bring spiritual rewards beyond anything they could find at home" (Bitel 1993: 223). Some historians attribute "the fervor of Irish exiles to genetically inspired wanderlust that drove them to row restlessly away from their rainy island" (Bitel 1993: 223). Yet, Bitel argues that forced exile was a sentence for the crimes against society: aristocratic and ecclesiastical power (1993: 223). The self-imposed exile of the monks functioned as a penitential practice. While criminals were punished by the authorities for their crimes, the monks punished themselves for their sins. The voluntary rejection of civilized life with its entitled protection by the community rendered the exiles vulnerable; but they were convinced of the righteousness of their behavior as the will of God. Such is the meaning of the self-imposed exile of the saint-traveler St. Brendan.

[5] Cf. Lochrie (2001), Staley (1994), Dinshaw (2003) and others.

[6] Because *The book of Margery Kempe* was one of the first of its kind where apart from religious and devotional content one finds a number of details of Kempe's private life, the Book was customarily presented as "spiritual autobiography" in a number of works (cf. Ross 1991 and Dinshaw 2003) to name just a few. Maissonneuve (1982: 14) also sees the text as an autobiography, whose generic specifications strengthen the argument about the depth of Margery's mystical life.

[7] The group of people with whom Margery travels to Aachen can be referred to as God's poor, as they beg their way and "before entering a city deloused themselves, a detail which suggests the appropriateness of the bequest made in 1474 by a widow of Hildesheim for the provision of two 'soul-baths' for pilgrims on their way to and from Aachen" (Webb 1999: 91).

[8] Voaden (1999: 112) argues that "scribes, editors and translators were the church's first line of defense in the battle against promulgation of false revelations".

[9] Voaden (1999: 109-10) presents the critical appraisal of Kempe's text as controversial also in contemporary literary criticism, in which mutually exclusive opinions are not infrequent.

[10] Labarge claims that pilgrimages were great undertakings even for the well-to-do, the greatest of all pilgrimages being the one to the Holy Land. Here, as in any other travel, a pilgrims' "wealth could usually provide rather minor improvements on the general conditions, since it was unwise to appear too wealthy in Moslem territory" (Labarge 1983: 72).

[11] For more on 15th century Prussia, see Carsten (1954: 73-148).

[12] In Book One, Margery was cheated and robbed several times. Once she was robbed by a priest: "…a preste wech was in her cumpany toke a-wey a schete fro þe forseyd creatur & seyd it was hys. Sche toke God to wytnesse þat it was hire schete. Than þe preste swor a gret othe, & be þe boke in hys hand, þat sche was as fals as sche mygth & dispysed hir & alto-rebuked hir" (*The book*, 67).

[13] Early Christianity devised hagiography as a dominant mode of educational literature. The lives of the saints offered supposedly real models and were pillars of the new Christian community. In the later Middle Ages, Christianity was no longer struggling with outside forces (the Roman Empire). Instead, as it spread throughout Europe, Asia and North Africa, it had to contend with infidels as well as various heresies (Cathars, Waldensians, Free Spirits and many others) within its own population. The *Omnis*

utriusque sexus decree was a device in that incessant struggle, yet the confessional manuals or sin manuals, practical as they were, aided the birth of yet another hero of medieval literature, the sinner. Such manuals provided their audience with values and forms of behavior that ecclesiastical authorities considered normative. The Church, which affirmed its authority and gained control over an individual conscience, used confession manuals and works like John Mirk's *Instructions for parish priests* to educate a self-conscious penitent, a penitent who was not only willing to change but first and foremost was aware of his transgressions, as only then was his confession valid.

[14] "The sacred biographers of the Middle Ages considered their work historical insofar as they developed categories which they reserved exclusively for this type of writing. History was a category of writing under the general aegis of grammar and had always been considered as part of the study of rhetoric. Cicero, while commenting on the difference between the annalist and the historian, remarked that the annalist was a mere recorder whose guiding principle was 'brevity without obscurity', while the historian was involved in a literary endeavor. His rhetorical skills were necessary since historical writing was either read or listened to." (Heffernan 1988: 66)

[15] Still, the importance of the biblical paradigm of Christ's life on earth, although here seeming to function in the background, is the prism through which saints' lives are seen and told. "Christ's behavior in the Gospels was the single authenticating norm for all action. For actions (*res*) narrated in the lives of the saints to be binding for the community, they had to be an *imitatio Christi*" (Heffernan 1988: 5). The particular *imitatio Christi* also dominated the reception of any of such lives.

[16] "There are two additional reasons for the primacy of the dramatic deed in medieval saints' lives: the paradigmatic actions of Christ in the New Testament and the illiteracy of the audiences for whom these texts were intended. The lives of the saints were sacred stories designated to teach the faithful to imitate actions which the community had decided were paradigmatic." (Heffernan 1988: 5)

[17] Dates quoted according to Emily Hope Allen's "Introduction" to *The book of Margery Kempe.*

[18] Interestingly, the motif of the pilgrimage as self-discovery but also quite literally as healing was used by David Lodge in the novel ominously called *Therapy*.

References

Akel, Catherine S.
2001 "'... A schort tretys and a comfortybl ..': Perception and purpose of Margery Kempe's narrative", *English Studies* 1: 1-13.

Atkinson, Clarissa W.
1983 *Mystic and pilgrim: The book and the world of Margery Kempe*. Ithaca and London: Cornell University Press.

Barber, Richard
1991 *Pilgrimages*. Woodbridge: Brewer.

Bitel, Lisa M.
1990 *Isle of the saints: Monastic settlement and Christian community in early Ireland*. Ithaca: Cornell University Press.
1993 Paperback edition.

Carsten, Francis L.
1954 *The origins of Prussia*. Oxford: Clarendon.

Cusa, Nicholas, of
1977 "On learned ignorance", in: Ross -- McLaughlin (eds.), 667-75.

Collis, Louise
1983 *The life and times of Margery Kempe*. New York: Harper and Row.

Dinshaw, Carolyn -- David Wallace (eds.)
2003 *Medieval women's writing*. Cambridge: Cambridge University Press.

Dinshaw, Carolyn
2003 "Margery Kempe", in: Dinshaw -- Wallace (eds.), 222-40.

Dyas, Dee
2001 *Pilgrimage in medieval English literature 700-1500.* Woodbridge: Brewer.

Eccles, Mark (ed)
1969 *The macro plays: The castle of perseverance, Wisdom, Mankind.* (EETS o.s. 262.) Oxford: Oxford University Press.

Ellis, Deborah
1990 "The merchant's wife's tale: Language, sex and commerce in Margery Kempe and in Chaucer", *Exemplaria* 2: 295-627.

Gallyon, Margaret
1995 *Margery Kempe of Lynn and medieval England.* Norwich: The Canterbury Press.

Gibson, Gail McMurray
1989 *The theatre of devotion: East Anglian drama and society in the late Middle Ages.* Chicago: The University of Chicago Press.

Glasscoe, Marion (ed.)
1982 *The medieval mystical tradition in England.* Exeter: University of Exeter Press.

Goodman, Anthony
2002 *Margery Kempe and her world.* London: Longman.

Heffernan, Thomas J.
1988 *Sacred biography: Saints and their biographers in the Middle Ages.* Oxford: Oxford University Press.

Kempe, Margery
1940 *The book of Margery Kempe.* Stanford N. Meech -- Hope Emily Allen (eds). (EETS, o.s. 212.) Oxford: Oxford University Press.
1993 Reprinted edition.

Krygier, Marcin -- Liliana Sikorska (eds.)
2004 *For the loue of Inglis*. (Medieval English Mirror 1.) Frankfurt/M.: Lang.

Labarge, Margaret Wade
1983 *Medieval travellers*. New York: W.W. Norton & Co.

Leclercq, Jean O.S.B.
1961 *The love of learning and the desire for God: A study of monastic culture*. New York: Fordham University Press.
1988 Reprinted edition.

Le Goff, Jacques
1981 *The birth of purgatory*. Arthur Goldhammer (trans.). Chicago: University of Chicago Press.
1986 Paperback edition.

Lochrie, Karma
1991 *Margery Kempe and translations of the flesh*. Philadelphia: University of Pennsylvania Press.

Lydgate, John
1899 *The pilgrimage of the life of man*. F.J. Furnivall (ed.), with introduction, notes, glossary and indexes by Katherine B. Locock. (EETS, e.s. 77, 83, 92.) Woodbridge: Boydell and Brewer.
1996 Reprinted edition.

Maissonneuve, Roland
1982 "Margery Kempe and the Eastern and Western tradition of the 'perfect fool'", in: Glasscoe (ed.), 1-17.

Ross, Ellen, M.
1991 "Spiritual experience and women's autobiography: The rhetoric and selfhood in *The book of Margery Kempe*", *Journal of the American Academy of Religion* 3: 527-46.

Ross, James Bruce -- Mary Martin McLaughlin (eds.)
1977 *The medieval reader*. Harmondsworth: Penguin.

Sikorska, Liliana
2004 "Imagining heaven: Visions of bliss in medieval mystical discourse", in: Krygier -- Sikorska (eds.), 97-132.

Staley, Lynn
1994 *Margery Kempe's dissenting fictions*. University Park: The Pennsylvania State University Press.

Turner, Victor -- Edith Turner
1978 *Image and pilgrimage in Christian culture*. New York: Columbia University Press.

Verdon, Jean
2002 *Travel in the Middle Ages*. George Holoch (trans.). Notre Dame: University of Notre Dame Press.

Voaden, Rosalynn
1999 *God's words, women's voices: The discernment of spirits in the writing of late medieval visionaries*. York: York Medieval Press

Voragine, Jacobus de
1993 *The golden legend: Readings on the saints*. William Grynger Ryan (trans.). 2 vols. Princeton: Princeton University Press.

Webb, Diana
1999 *Pilgrims and pilgrimage in the Medieval West*. (International library of historical studies 12.) London: I.B. Tauris.

2002 *Medieval European pilgrimage*. Houndmills: Palgrave.

Winstead, Karen A.
1994 "The conversion of Margery Kempe's son", *English Language Notes* 2: 9-13.

Malory's critique of violence before and just after the oath of the Round Table

Carol Kaske (Ithaca/NY, USA)

1. Introduction

Violence in the Middle Ages at large is a huge and complex topic. It is a sometimes contested commonplace that, in life and in literature, chivalry served to circumscribe a violence that had previously ruled almost unchecked.[1] The relation of chivalry and violence in Malory in particular has been much discussed. I will address recent work by Lynch, Whetter, and Kennedy. Kennedy strives for moral closure and hence is more suitable for teaching undergraduates; Lynch and Whetter problematize Malory's attitude toward violence, finding it to be a "strangely double view of war" (cf. Whetter 2004: 181, and n. 43; Lynch 1997: 35) and hence they are better for teaching graduate students; both projects unearth evidence that illuminates Malory's work. All would agree that Malory occasionally expresses criticism of the violence of a particular source-passage by changing it, or of the bloodlust of a particular character by having him rebuked for it or praised for restraining it. Whetter and Lynch scorn these approaches, but obviously sometimes Malory does this, and undergraduates need to cut their teeth on these approaches before proceeding to the high mysteries. My first two examples – *The Tales of Balin* and of Arthur's Roman war – are more or less acknowledged to contain some such critiques of violence, and I have found new and at times peculiar examples of them. My two final examples – Sir Brian of the Isles and horse-replacements – have not to the best of my knowledge been recognized as critiques of violence, and they critique violence in an exaggerated way, thus illustrating what Lynch calls Malory's "split consciousness". Looking for this theme in all four passages can explain peculiar actions on the part of the characters and deviations from the source on the part of the author. The pious tone of the Grail Quest renders restraints on violence less remarkable there, hence I will not talk about it; my examples all occur prior to the Grail Quest; indeed, they come from Caxton's first five books, that is, the Winchester MS's first two.[2] Arthur and Sir Brian of the Isles illustrate long-range character development; and Arthur and Balin bear some relation to the Oath of the Round Table (3.15) – an oath which reads in part:

> never to do outrageousity nor murder, and always to flee treason; also, by no mean to be cruel, but to give mercy unto him that asketh mercy, upon pain of forfeiture of their worship and lordship of King Arthur for evermore; and always to do ladies, damosels, and gentlewomen succour, upon pain of death.

The Winchester MS adds "strengthe hem in their rightes, and never to enforce them", that is "rape them".

2. Balin and the Roman war

The above mentioned part of the oath can be seen as belatedly rebuking Balin and altering the character of Arthur and so bringing to these episodes a degree of moral closure that undergraduate readers need in order to find their moral compass in this complex work. It is obvious that the moral, insofar as there is one, of Caxton Book II, the Book of Balin, is 'don't be too quick to act' and 'don't put too much force into your blows'. In Chapter 5, in a fair fight, Balin kills Sir Lanceor, who has been sent from Arthur to bring him back to court; in the process, he occasions the suicide of Lanceor's lover Colombe. It is to highlight these pacifistic morals, I propose, that Malory drags in the seemingly digressive prophecy that Lancelot and Tristram will fight on this very spot, "and yet none of them shall slay other" (Caxton 2.7-8). On the simplest and most moralistic level, they are dragged in because they exhibit more restraint than does Balin, thus functioning as a rebuke to him. In the source, which for Balin is the *Merlin continuation* in the *Post-Vulgate*, the prophecy occurs but it ends with "neither will die" – which lacks the moral point.[3] The rebuke of fighters who kill their opponents and the praise of fighters (including one of the same fighters, Lancelot) who manage not to come up again explicitly in the Grail Quest. So far, the moral is clear. But it is hard to see what Balin could have done differently in this instance, except snatch the sword from the lady while she was in a swoon. A tragic fate also dogs Balin and renders his best-laid plans destructive; Balin is not only sword happy but sword unhappy: almost everyone he strikes, he kills; and to this extent there is no moral and the prophet is just telling us that there are luckier people than Balin who live in a more benevolent universe.

Before the oath, in Book One, in the battle with the eleven kings, Merlin rebukes Arthur as follows:

> Thou hast never done, hast thou not done enough? Of three score thousand this day has thou left alive but fifteen thousand, and it is time to say 'Ho!' For God is wroth with thee, that thou wilt never have done... (Caxton 1.17)

In the French source – "The story of Merlin" in the Vulgate cycle – the condemnation is there, but it is milder and shorter: "King Arthur, what are you trying to do? Isn't it enough that you have thoroughly beaten your enemies? Go back to your land" (cf. Pickens 1993: 233). This is criticism by overt condemnation.

Another vehicle of criticism is praise of restraint. Even Arthur's enemies praise Arthur's restraint in one instance: "Let us put our foot-men from us ... for the noble Arthur will not tarry on the foot-men, for they may save themselves" (Caxton 1.16). Then at the end of Book III, comes the oath, administered by Arthur, but obviously devised by a greater mind than his or at least by a nobler part of himself. Then in Caxton Book V, the account of Arthur's Roman war, after Arthur has been crowned at Rome, he assents to his men's request to go home, saying, "for to tempt God it is no wisdom" even adding temperately in the Winchester MS "enough is as good as a feast". Malory added this to the source, in which Arthur does exactly the opposite. In the *Alliterative Morte Darthur*, Arthur says in effect, "That was fun. Now let's go on a crusade" (Hamel 1984: l. 3206-3217).[4] Malory's Arthur exhibits that restraint which Merlin and the oath enjoined upon him.

Arthur develops chivalry towards women too, and I submit that this also comes about because of the oath. Back in Caxton Book III, chapter 5 before the oath, Arthur shrugged off a damsel who came to court to complain of an injury, only to suffer a graver injury, and Merlin rebuked him for doing so. Then came the oath. Then in Caxton Book V in the Roman war, as Vinaver and Hamel note, Arthur shows kindness to enemy women and Malory makes their pleas for mercy more philosophically compelling than in the source. The women are trying to dissuade Arthur from razing their city and slaughtering all its inhabitants. They appeal to the rights of innocent bystanders; as they say in the Winchester MS: "for then shal dye many a soule that grevid thee never". In line with the Oath, which of course is not in the source, Arthur consents to receive the keys of the city in peace, assures them that neither they nor the women of their households will be sexually molested, and commands his men accordingly. Even though this book has a different source from the rest, Malory portrays Arthur's character as becoming a bit more pacifistic than he was, and he modifies the source to do so. Incidentally, this gradual development in his character supports Lumiansky's thesis of unity across the boundaries of the tales as against Vinaver's claim that "Arthur and Lucius" is a tale separate unto itself.

Of course, I must admit that Malory harbors another motive for these revisions besides a simple critique of violence. The source shows Arthur degenerating and becoming a warmonger who is recalled from embarking on another war (as mentioned above) only by a premonitory dream (Hamel 1984: l.

3206-3217) and by news that his caretaker Mordred has taken over his kingdom and his wife. If Malory really wanted to limit violence, someone might object, he could have just have gone along with "the anti-war spirit"[5] of his source. At the end of the *Morte Darthur*, Malory does show some "anti-war spirit" – a spirit deriving indirectly and in part from this source; there his Arthur too will degenerate into a warmonger (in this case under Gawain's influence) and be called home too late by just this turn of events, and as in the *Alliterative Morte Darthur*, he will die attempting to recover his realm and his wife. But Malory does not want to have the catastrophe just yet and he does want to retain the forceful Arthur of the *Alliterative Morte Darthur* without his taint of bloodthirstiness. This is another reason why he chooses to portray Arthur in the Roman war as not too bloodthirsty, occasionally merciful, and knowing when to stop. As we have seen, this Arthur has already manifested the flaw attributed to him by the *Alliterative Morte Darthur* in 1.11, and he has evidently corrected it, I suggest, because of the Oath which he has promulgated and therefore must uphold. Malory made this paragon more interesting by having him start as a potential berserker (1.11) and an insensitive boor about women (3.5) and be educated into restraint by the oath.

If these instances of an Arthur who was selfish before the oath and raising his moral standards after the oath have been convincing, readers might perceive the same selfish Arthur destined to reform in his cruel exposure of the so-called May-day children (1.27), leading to the deaths of all but Mordred. As Kennedy (2003: 164) says, Malory does not mention this act again, let alone present the Fall of the Round Table as its punishment. I suggest that this is so because after the oath's prohibition of cruelty, Arthur learns to rein in such violent tendencies.

3. Sir Brian of the Isles and musical horses

Now let us look at two neighbouring incidents which place limitations on violence even though they occur before the oath and independently of it. They do so in morally complex ways.

In Caxton Book III, chapter 13, right before the oath, Malory portrays a virtual pacifist, someone who not only proleptically agrees with the oath but goes beyond it – an anomaly in Malory's chivalric economy. "There is no trace of this long dialogue in French", notes Vinaver (cf. Malory 1973: 117, MS 43^{r}). A knight describes the pacifist as follows in the Winchester MS: "my sworne brother, a passynge good knyght, and hys name is Bryan of the Ilis, and he ys full lothe to do ony wronge or to fyght with ony man but if he be sore sought on", and Caxton adds, "so that for shame he may not leave it". Brian's pacifism implies that most chivalric combat is 'wrong'. Yet, the interlocutor does not scorn him as a milksop, but says with modern-sounding casualness, "Bring him to the court ... one of these days". This indicates that Malory adds Sir Brian's pacifism to the French source of Caxton 3.13 in order to make a pacifistic point, and thus was of two minds about knightly combat. This peculiar knight, especially in Caxton where he never recurs and never fights, represents a metapoetic moment, a critique of chivalry itself from a viewpoint so high minded as to be alien to all of Malory's *Morte* except the Grail Quest. He functions as a silent rebuke to the other characters just as Sir Lancelot and Sir Tristram do to Balin. Edmund Spenser inserts such a moment in his chivalric romance *The Faerie Queene* when his Hermit Contemplation says to a young knight, "And [in old age, after a successful chivalric career] wash thy hands from guilt of bloudy field, / For bloud can nought but sin, and wars but sorrow yield" (Spenser 1977: I.x.60). Both virtual pacifists are too good for this world, but their message may be what their authors really believed, at least in some moods. Note that Malory's pacifistic sentiments here are not dictated by Christianity as Spenser's are, and as Malory's will be later in the Grail Quest; Brian's is just another point of view.

In the Winchester MS only, in another part of the work, the Roman war (MS 81^{v}), Malory provides an interesting development that somewhat reconciles Sir Brian's pacifism with the values of those around him and thus offers the puzzled undergraduate reader some moral closure. He includes an uncharacterized Sir Brian without a toponym in a roll-call of Arthur's knights in his Roman war. He had found this Sir Brian in the source for this part of the work, the *Alliterative Morte Darthur*.[6] This fighter's character is enriched by Malory's having characterized him as a pacifist in Caxton 3.13. The brief mention here indicates what circumstances would drive this pacifist to fight – an international war in a national emergency, triggered by a foreign king's supposedly unjust demand for tribute, backed by threats. Thus, in the Winchester MS, Brian's rejection of chivalry proves to be not so categorical.

For my final example, let us go back to the beginning, to the war with the eleven kings treated in Section I (Caxton 1.14-17): We have seen Arthur's violence overtly criticized and his forbearance overtly praised there. Now let us look at exemplary actions of other knights through which Malory laboriously strives to cast a rosy haze over violence. We are asked to believe that a large proportion of the battle is taken up with a lengthy series of actions so bizarrely repetitive that they sound like something out of *Monty Python and the Holy Grail*: it is the game of musical horses, or rehorsing fallen comrades by unhorsing an enemy. An attacker's first goal is to get a horse for his unhorsed friend. I propose that Malory is trying to portray battle as a matter of helping your friends more than hurting your foes. Indeed, in real life, loyalty, camaraderie, or male bonding is often said to be a principal motive for fighting once men get into any battle.

The first four rehorsings are identical in both the French and Malory's version (see my Appendix, numbers 1-4, and so are both of the numbers 9). But in number 7, Griflet smites an anonymous knight and gives the victim's horse to Sir Lucan, and Caxton's version of Malory adds, departing from the sources (and also as it happens, from the Winchester MS): "For Brastias had slain a knight tofore and horsed Griflet". Malory's number 7 illustrates that you do not have to rehorse the person who rehorsed you; if that is not possible, you should rehorse anybody just to keep the favors circulating. The Winchester MS just says "because Brastias had slain a knight tofore" which makes no sense as a motive; many knights slew other knights. Malory or Caxton must have introduced Brastias's previous rehorsing of Griflet to emphasize that one rescues people because one has oneself been rescued, especially if like Griflet one has been rescued twice, the last time without passing on the favor. Also in a tournament a few pages earlier, Lucan had rehorsed Griflet (1.11) without being rehorsed by him in return. A skeptic would say that Malory mistakenly wrote Brastias here when he meant Lucan; if we were to emend "Brastias" to "Lucan", the pattern of reciprocation would be complete. But there is some evidence of a different sort of pattern subtending the text as we have it. The point is that Griflet has had to be rescued twice in this battle and once in the preceding tournament, never mind by whom. This is because he is portrayed as young and hence not so great a warrior as are his rescuers – Kay, Lucan, and Brastias. This point will be confirmed retrospectively when Griflet will subsequently be involved in a patent youth-age contrast in his fight with Pellenore: Pellenore tries to dissuade him from the unequal contest; once Griflet forces Pellenore to fight him and receives the inevitable defeat, Pellenore does not finish him off but helps him back onto his horse and points him in the direction of home (1.22-23) – another act of charity to the young expressed partly in terms of rehorsing.

Dante said that charity is a good undiminished by sharing, and the same is true of camaraderie. Malory dramatizes that it is in fact increased by it, for Lucan in his turn immediately proceeds to slay two anonymous young knights and rehorse two of his downed comrades, thus showing the productivity of such mutual assistance in the chivalric economy. (Malory, number 8). This is not in the source, where the rehorsed Lucan (French version, number 8) goes on to rescue someone else but nothing is said about horses; then Lucan merely *helps* two comrades hoisting two other comrades back onto their own horses (cf. Pickens 1993: 230-31). This is messy and barely counts as a horse replacement at all, and Malory condenses it meaningfully: he attributes the double rehorsing to Lucan and Lucan alone and makes him in the process kill two of the enemies.

What sounded ridiculous is now emerging as a repetition with significant moral variations on the themes of youth and altruism.

Even Malory's enemies play the horse-replacement game – three of them in one terse and original paragraph (1.14). In the French, only one of the enemies rehorses another (event number 2). Malory adds three other horse-replacements – the King with the Hundred Knights again and King Lot twice – for a total of four (1.16). These horse-replacements on the part of the enemy seem to be one more instance of their general *esprit de corps* which is praised in moving terms throughout this particular war. As Lynch (1997 and 2000) says, the bad guys must not be portrayed as too bad because this is a civil war and all the combatants will live together side by side as one nation later in the book. A contrast proves Malory's purpose. In the next great battle – the Roman war – no horse replacements occur. One reason is that Malory is certainly not eager to praise the *esprit de corps* of the Romans and their Saracen allies. But not even the good guys do it. In the War with the Eleven Kings, Malory was not narrating history but making a point about the possibility of infusing violence with altruism. A similarly rosy view of war was projected in the film *Forrest Gump* with Tom Hanks in the title role. Forrest Gump never attacked an enemy; we only saw him running to the field hospital carrying wounded friends.

Most of these horse-replacements are more or less modeled on the French source (see my Appendix); but Malory not only adds three on the part of the bad guys, as we have seen, and sharpens the double one on our side, but also by his characteristic pruning subtracts so much of the other action that they all stand in high relief.[7] In the French source, Kay snags a stray horse and gives it to his fallen father Ector (whom the French version calls Antor, cf. number 5; see Vinaver's notes to pages 29.23-30 in Malory 1973). The rehorsed Antor smites down Morganor and gives his horse to Brastias (whom the French version calls Bretel, cf. number 6). Malory's Kay obtains a horse for his fallen father Ector in the martial way by smiting down Morganor and taking his (Malory, number 5). Malory even paid a price for this change: because he has already used up Morganor in this way, he has to invent a new enemy, Lardans, whose horse can be given to Brastias (Malory, number 6). Considered in isolation, using a stray horse seems more pacifistic, so am I wrong about the meaning of Malory's changes? Malory dislikes using a stray horse, apparently because it earns no glory. Evidently he is not advocating pacifism here, he is imbricating an altruistic motive with warfare's two selfish motives: winning glory and conquering the enemy. These competitive purposes Malory wants not to eliminate but to gild and temper with his third and somewhat contradictory value, loyalty, camaraderie or fellowship, so he emphasizes and even adds horse-replacements. He is trying here to moderate competitiveness, not eliminate it, much as he did with Arthur's acts of mercy at the siege. With an awkwardness betraying a split consciousness, Malory works some degree of altruism into a violent code which he is unwilling to condemn categorically.

4. Conclusion

Both Malory's tempering of Arthur's violence in the Roman war and his imbrication of violence with fellowship in the musical-horses game illustrates the truth of the conventional wisdom that chivalry in general and Malory in particular tempered violence by attributing to it some social benefits. But the contrast between the intrinsic violence of chivalry and the almost total pacifism of Sir Brian of the Isles indicates that on violence as on love Malory is not consistent. Like Whetter (2004) and Lynch (1997 and 2000), I feel that Malory wanted his work to be somewhat dialogic because this corresponded to his ambivalent view of this topic. Perhaps dialogism also was prized by his audience as an occasion for courtly debates after the nightly reading in the great hall. As Richard Kaeuper (2000: 29, cf. also 33) says in his fine article on violence in the Vulgate cycle: there may well be "an internal debate … on the causes, scale, and consequences of the knightly prowess so highly prized in high society" analogous to the recognized internal debate about love.

5. Appendix: Horse-replacements in Caxton 1.14-16

Events between ** are not in the French source. Events with the same numbers correspond, sometimes with changes.

5.1. Horses in the French source[8]

1 p. 230: Kay smites King Neutres and rehorses Girflet.
2 King with Hundred Knights smites Kay and rehorses King Lot.
3 Girflet and Lucan smite two anonymous enemies and give one of the horses to Kay. (Who gets the other? We never hear. It is messy.)
4 Arthur smites King Tradelment and rehorses Ulfin.
5 p. 231: Kay captures a riderless horse and rehorses his father Antor (=Ector).
6 Antor smites Morganor and rehorses Bretel (=Brastias).
7 Girflet smites an anonymous enemy and rehorses Lucan.
8 Lucan rescues Malruc of the Rock. Malruc helps two companions helping two other companions back onto their horses. (It is messy, and it hardly counts as a horse-replacement.)

9 p. 233: Arthur kills an anonymous enemy and rehorses Ban.

5.2. Horses in Malory

1 1.14: Kay smites King Nentres and rehorses Griflet, also smites King Lot.
2 1.14: King with Hundred Knights smites Kay and rehorses Lot.
3 1.14: Griflet smites Pinel and rehorses Kay.
Enemies (King with Hundred Knights again, and Lot twice) rehorse three of their men.
4 1.14: Arthur smites King Cradelment and rehorses Ulfius.
1.14: *King with a Hundred Knights smites Sir Ector, Kay's father, and rehorses King Cradelment.*
5 1.14: Kay smites Morganor and rehorses his father Ector.
6 1.14: Ector smites *Lardans* and rehorses Brastias.
7 1.14: Griflet smites an anonymous enemy and rehorses Lucan *because Brastias had rehorsed him at some time in the past [this is not in the Winchester MS either].*
8 1.14: Lucan slays two anonymous bachelors and rehorses Bellias of Flanders and Gwinas.
9 1.16: Arthur kills an anonymous enemy and rehorses Ban.

Notes

1 Contested, for instance, by Kaeuper (2000: 34-5) and Lynch (2000: 24-41; 1997, passim).

2 For ease of reference, I will cite Caxton unless the Winchester MS presents significant differences; for Caxton quotations, I employ the modernized spelling of Malory (1969). For the Winchester MS, I will cite Malory (1973), with the page of the MS for the benefit of those who are using other editions.

3 Chapter 9 of Asher (1993: 185-91).

4 Malory's significant departures from the *Alliterative Morte* include the addition of "Malorian dialogs and name-catalogs"; also "the criticism of Arthur's imperialism is removed and that of his arrogance of character much softened", according to Hamel (1984: 6).

5 Vinaver's phrase, 1369, quoted from William Matthews (1966).

[6] A Sir Bryane appears as a fighter in the *Alliterative Morte Darthur*, (cf. Hamel 1984: l. 1606 and 1744), again without toponym or characterization. At l. 1606, Hamel's note identifies the Sir Bryane of the *Alliterative Morte Darthur* with the fighter "Sir Bryan de les ylyes" in the Winchester MS's version of the Roman war (Malory 1973, MS 81^{v}). Furthermore, Vinaver's note to this Sir Bryan who fights (Malory 1973: note to p. 212) suggests that he is the same as Sir Bryan of the Isles in the "story of Merlin" (i.e. Caxton 3.13). Vinaver does not comment on the implied qualification of Bryan's principles (cf. Malory 1973).

[7] Cf. "The story of Merlin" translated by Rupert T. Pickens in Lacy (1993: 1, 231, 233).

[8] = "Histoire de Merlin" translated by Rupert T. Pickens in Lacy (1993: 1, 230-31, 233).

References

Editions

Asher, Martha (trans.)
1993 "The post-Vulgate, part I: The Merlin continuation", in: Lacy (gen. ed.), vol. 4: 167-277.

Hamel, Mary (ed.)
1984 *Morte Arthure: A critical edition*. (Garland medieval texts 9.) New York: Garland.

Lacy, Norris J. (gen. ed.)
1993 *Lancelot-Grail: The Old French Arthurian Vulgate and post-Vulgate in translation.* 5 vols. (Garland reference library to the humanities.) New York: Garland.

Malory, Sir Thomas
1969 *Le Morte D'Arthur*. Janet Cowen and John Lawlor (eds.). 2 vols. Harmondsworth: Penguin.

1973 *Works*. 3 vols. (2nd edition.) Eugene Vinaver (ed.). Oxford: Clarendon.

Pickens, Rupert T. (trans.)
1993 "The story of Merlin", in: Lacy (gen. ed.), vol. 1: 164-424.

Spenser, Edmund
1977 *The Faerie Queene*. A.C. Hamilton (ed.). (Annotated English Poets.) London: Longman.

Studies

Hanks, Dorrel Thomas (ed.)
2000 *The social and literary contexts of Malory's Morte Darthur*. (Arthurian studies 42.) Cambridge: Brewer.

Kaeuper, Richard,
2000 "Chivalry and the civilizing process", in: Kaeuper (ed.), 21-35.

Kaeuper, Richard (ed.)
2000 *Violence in medieval society*. Woodbridge: Boydell Press.

Kennedy, Edward Donald
2003 "*Malory's Morte Darthur*: A politically neutral English adaptation of the Arthurian story", *Arthurian Literature* 20: 145-69.

Matthews, William
1966 *The ill-framed knight: A skeptical inquiry into the identity of Sir Thomas Malory*. Berkeley: University of California Press.

Lynch, Andrew
1997 *Malory's book of arms: The narrative of combat in* Le Morte Darthur. (Arthurian studies 39.) Cambridge: Brewer.

2000 "'Thou woll never have done': Ideology, context, and excess in Malory's War", in: Hanks, 24-41.

Saunders, Corinne -- Franciose Le Saux -- Neil Thomas (eds.)
2004 *Writing war: Medieval literary responses to warfare*. Rochester: Brewer.

Whetter, Kevin
2004 "Warfare and combat in *Le Morte Darthur*", in: Saunders -- Le Saux -- Thomas (eds.), 169-83.

Observations on the loss of final plosive consonants in late Middle English rhyme-words

Saara Nevanlinna (Helsinki, Finland)

1. Introduction

1.1. Aim of this study

This pilot study is just a series of observations trying to illustrate under what conditions plosives (stops) in final position could be lost in manuscripts of late Middle English verse, and to find out if dialectal or colloquial deletion of final stops could ever be regarded as a regional phenomenon. The terms *loss* and *deletion* are taken in a wider sense, so that this study will also include instances where a final stop is not completely 'lost' but only modified in one way or another.

The period examined covers the years 1350-1500, divided into ME3 (1350-1420) and ME4 (1420-1500). My material consists of fifty-seven late Middle English verse texts collected by scanning a large number of texts that were easily available. Three texts written in contemporary Older Scots were used as comparison material. The data represents the following *prototypical text categories* containing different text types (genres) after the nomenclature used in Kytö (1995).

(i) *religious instruction* (*IR*)15: homily 4, religious treatise 11;
(ii) *non-imaginative narration* (*NN*)11: history 3, biography: saint's life 8;
(iii) *imaginative narration* (*NI*)16: travelogue 1, fiction 3, romance 12;
(iv) *text type not defined* (*XX*)15 : drama, i.e. mystery play and morality play 5, lyric, including carol 7, dialogue 1, Bible paraphrase 2.

1.2. Middle English rhymes

1.2.1. Non-standard pronunciation

Middle English rhyming verse was primarily meant to be presented orally. Differently from vowels, irregularity of consonants in rhyme has rarely been touched upon. Deletion of sounds in words that form good rhymes with forms of the standard language, may be generally regarded as evidence of the poet's dialect. Anyone who has studied early Middle English verse must have observed that absolute consistency in rhyme was not the case at that time. Stanley (1988:

53) points out that especially assonance and impure rhymes were very common in early Middle English. Late Middle English rhymes again seem to have been predominantly pure, and scansion, mostly regular. Penzl (1970: 19) postulates that only poetry with predominantly pure rhymes can reveal phonemic changes when they occur in rhyme position.

Milroy (1992a: 66) points out that "language in use is always observed within a social context of some kind". He seems to imply that non-standard pronunciation is style-bound. We must remember that what is non-standard from the point of the standard language today may have been the "consensus form" in the community to which the speaker belonged. Not all the rhymes in a given text may go back to the poet or versifier. During the late Middle English period, there was no common standard language as yet. Thus, a variety of regional Englishes was used in writing. The evidence of rhyming words is especially useful when studying a period when many extant literary texts were versified (Milroy 1992b: 169).

1.2.2. Scribal translation

If a scribe's or reviser's dialect was different from the original poet's, a certain amount of translation was likely to take place. Where several people speaking different dialects tackled a text successively, impure and corrupt rhymes could easily be produced. With the spread of the developing standard towards the end of the fifteenth century dialectal differences became less frequent in written texts.

Occasional spellings reflecting the loss of a stop cannot be considered to be conclusive evidence on their own, but if consonants omitted reflect change in pronunciation, that implies simplification in colloquial register. Informal spoken language always aims at easy articulation. It follows the "principle of least effort", which is a prime source of variation (Samuels 1972: 17). Milroy (1992b: 197) argues that a number of present-day non-standard speech-forms may be traced back to certain variants in ME spelling. Penzl (1970: 18-22) advocates the important view that evidence through contact between languages can be valuable for phonetic identifications, and that occasional spellings may reveal a dialectal change that is not reflected by the established spelling.

1.3. Technicalities

The regional provenance of each example is given in square brackets by an abbreviation used in the county map of *LALME* (1986, 1: 569; 2: 381; 4: 333). Since many of the MSS included in the data were copied by a succession of different scribes, the language could be mixed, even corrupt. That is probably one of the reasons why their linguistic profiles are not to be found in *LALME*. An asterisk is added to suggested regional references which are not based on a thorough linguistic analysis by the editors of *LALME*.[1] The item reference numbers in *IMEV* (1943) are given for identification of the individual MSS examined.

To create a rough picture of how the data were dispersed, the examples will be presented within the frame of larger ME dialect areas, i.e. Northern, West Midland, East Midland, Southern, and Kent (no examples found), according to the map in Jordan (1974: 5), where the lines are drawn along county boundaries. That will serve the present purpose, though some modern scholars, such as Lass (1992: 34), seem to present more accurately drawn maps.[2]

2. The examples

The late ME evidence that I have collected is for the most part based on rhyming couplets (which metre is not specifically indicated in the examples). Verse texts written in stanzaic form, as lyrics and medieval mystery plays or romances, where two or more lines share the same rhyme, are also included. Since this study does not aim at a literary analysis of the verse, I venture to present some of the longer examples in a fragmentary way in order to save space. Longer passages omitted are marked with three dots. Single lines that have been left out between lines written in full are marked by hyphens between two slashes.

The rhyme-words under discussion have been written in italics, except for the final symbols of sounds that should not be pronounced. I have also tried to provide the reader with some translation of the parts of the text that are to be seen in the examples.

2.1. Loss of final plosive consonants

According to Milroy (1992a: 136), final stop deletion is very common in many varieties of English today. Colloquial loss of final stops, especially in clusters, has been discussed by several twentieth-century linguists, e.g. Dobson (1968: § 398), Milroy (1992b: 197), Romaine (1983), Wyld (1956: 303-304).

2.1.1. Loss of final stops after other stops

Loss of /t/ after voiceless stops is sometimes realised in spelling.

(1) Als to record in Goddes *wirschip*
How *þ*ai war broght out of *Egipt*.
(*The northern homily cycle* (3) 4631)[3]
['Also to record in God's worship how they [the Israelites] were brought out of Egypt.']
[NME] *IMEV* 3166.2. (*IR*)

(2) Of stedfast man *þ*e wittes *frek,*
And eke of wise corage *effec*
(Castleford, *Chronicle of England* 21678)
['The bold will of a steadfast man, and also the effect of wise courage']
[NME*] *IMEV* 1559.1. (*NN*)

Loss of /d, t/ was seen in weak preterites and past participles of French verbs where the stem ends in *d* or *t*.[4]

(3) þei dyd als he *commawnd*,
and sone was Amon slayn.
so for fowle luf *in land*
ar men oft put to payn.
(*Middle English Old Testament* 8421) (*XX*)
['They did as he commanded, and soon was Amnon killed. So are men often put to pain because of sinful love in the world.']
[WRY] *IMEV* 944.1. (12-line stz., a b a b a b a b C d C d)

(4) Thys holy mane of God was *accept*
For whatsoeuer that he ded prayd
Vs frome the daunger conseruyd and *kepte*
Of the ranson we Xuld haue payd.
(*As storys wryght and specyfy*, a carol, stz. 3) (*XX*)
['This holy man was accepted by God for whatever he made accessible to Him, saved and kept us from danger by the ransom that we should have paid.']
[Nfk] *IMEV* 405.1. (A b A b).

In one native verb (*to end*), the assimilated final stop of the stem, representing the weak past participle, rhymes with a French word in *–ent*.

(5) When Agamenoun his tale hath *ent*
Be-fore the lordes that were *present*
(*The 'Laud' Troy book* 15561)
['When Agamemnon had ended his story in front of the lords who were present']
Cf. ibid. 13231:
Vn-to that pes that wolde *assent*
For the batayle was as good as *ent*
['who would assent to the peace, for the battle was almost ended']
[EM*] *IMEV* 249. (*NI*)

2.1.2. Loss of final stops after fricatives

Loss of /t/ could occur after the reflex of the Old English palatal fricative (the *ich*-sound). In the example, the final <t> is seen in writing.

(6) For he was Kyng of Kynges *heghe* / *Rex primus aurum optulit*
And allso Lorde and Kyng ful *ryght* / *Secundus rex thus pertulit.*
(*As holy kyrke makys*, a macaronic carol of the Nativity, stz. 8)
['For he was King of Kings high / The first king offered gold
And also Lord and King in full / The second king thus persevered to the end.']
[WRY] *IMEV* 340.2. (A b A b) (*XX*)

Where /t/ is lost after the reflex of the OE velar fricative (the *ach*-sound) there may occur reverse spelling to produce an eye-rhyme.

(7) As *þ*ey seyd *þ*ey dyd *þ*at *wogh*te
*þ*e whyche dede ful soure *þ*ey *bogh*te
(Mannyng, *Handlyng synne* 4089)
['As they said, they did that harm (*wough*), for which deed they paid dearly']
[Bck] *IMEV* 778.3. (*IR*)

Final /t/ may be lost even after other fricatives.[5] The writer of the following revised version of Mirk's *Instructions for parish priests* is not very literate, judged by his spelling.

(8) And what *þ*u art gylty *of*
Boldely say it [b]othe styll and *soft*
(Mirk, *Instructions for parish priests* 789)[6]
['What you are guilty of, say it boldly, both still and softly']
[Li] *IMEV* 961.7 (*IR*)
Cf. Mirk, *Instructions for parish priests* [Stf] *IMEV* 961.6.:
... gulty *of* / ... make no *scof*

['...guilty of...do not mock']

Final /k/ may be lost after /s/ in the infinitive *ask*. The form *as(s)* has risen either through assimilation from the metathesised stem *ax*, or it is an analogical form after assimilation of medial /k/ in *askte* (Luick 1964, 2: 916).

(9) O pees I bidde *þ*at no man *passe* / - /
And takes gud hede to hym *þ*at *hasse* / - /
Kyng Pharo my fadir *was* / - /
I am his hayre as elde will *asse*/
(*York cycle, Moses and pharaoh,* XI.1)
['O peace, I tell no man to pass and pay good heed to him that has. King Pharaoh was my father. I am his heir as age will require']
[south of Yk] *IMEV* 1273.1. (*XX*) (A b A b A b A b c d c d)

2.1.3. Loss of final stops after nasals

Loss of /d/ was found in Northern present participles and verbal nouns ending in *-and.*

(10) And yf so be that sche be power
And haue no lame to offer, *than*
Two tyrtle-doves to Godes honoure
To bring with her for her *offran*d.
(*York cycle, The Purification,* XVII. 49)
['And if she be poor and have no lamb to offer, then she should bring two turtle doves with her as her offering in God's honour']
[south of Yk] *IMEV* 1273.1. (*XX*) (quatrains: a B a B)

Final /d/ may be lost in other words ending in vowel plus *-nd.*

(11) *þ*at schal be clepud god of *lon*d
He schal awreke al *þy fon*
(*Kyng Alisaunder* 311) [Sal] *IMEV* 683.3. (*NI*)
['... [a son] who shall be called god of the earth. He shall condemn all your enemies']
Cf. an EME variant *Kyng Alisaunder* 313:
*þ*at shal be cleped god of *londe.*
He shal awreke al *þ*i *shonde.*
['... who will be called god of the earth. He will avenge all your shame.']
[Ex] *IMEV* 683.1.

Loss of /d/ was also seen in participial adjectives and weak past participles after postvocalic *n* when the final vowel before *d* was elided.

(12) / - / on a day byfore *þe none*
/ - / To pley as *þey* were *ywon*yd.
/ - / Anone he made hyt stonde *sone*
/ - / & vndede *þ*at Jhesu had *done*/
(*The apocryphal history of the Infancy* 149)
['on a day before the noon ... to play as they were used to ... Immediately he made it [the water] stand still ... and [Judas] undid what Jesus had done.']
[Cnw] *IMEV* 250.1. (*NI*) (a B a B a B a B c d c d)

(13) Yea, God give me *pyne*
and that shalbe *thine,*
for thou art euer *inclin*d
to drawe towards thee.
(*Chester play,* XVI A., *The Passion,* 77)
['Truly, God, give me pain, and it will be yours, for you are always inclined to draw [men] towards you.']
[Chs] *IMEV* 716.1. (*XX*) (a quatrain: A A A b)

Sometimes an excrescent /d/ developed after homorganic *n* (Luick 1964, 2: 1038). In some words, loss of the final dental came to survive in Standard English, e.g. *lawn* (sb.) from OF *lande*. Texts may contain duplicate forms.

(14) *þ*at *þ*ou rise vp hale and *sounde*
And tell vs what man es *Symounde*.
(*The northern homily cycle* (1), *Peter & Paul* 179)
['that thou may rise up whole and sound and tell us what kind of man Simon is.']
[NME] *IMEV* 3560.1. (*IR*)
Cf. ibid. 90:
His first name es callid *Symone*/ *þ*e to*þ*er Petir, wi*þ* *resoune*
['His first name is Simon, the second, Peter, with reason']

From the fourteenth century on, final /g/ could be lost after *n*. This began in Norfolk and Scotland (Luick 1964, 2: 1044), then moved southwards; *g*-less forms were seen in writing in northern and north-eastern texts and in Scotland. The West Midland forms of the verbal noun ended in *-inge*/ *-ynge* (*LALME* 1986, 4: 106-108).

Skautrup (1944: 217) maintains that vowels were nasalised before *n* and *m* in early Danish, though this was not seen in the Latin alphabet. Nasalisation in early Middle English rhymes has mostly been ascribed to French influence. See Einhorn (1974: 9).

(15) Behold what lyfe that we ryne *ine*
Frayl to fale and euer lyke to *syne*
Thorow our enmys *entysyng*
Therfor we syng and cry to the
(*Behold what lyfe*, a carol of Candlemas, stz.1)
['Behold what life we run, being prone to fail, and always likely to sin through our enemy's enticing. Therefore we sing and call to thee']
[Nfk] *IMEV* 508.1. (*XX*) (A A A b + burden)

(16) Thane, fra Sanct Colme had *persawing* (*IR*)
Hou clerly godis grace cane *shyne*
(*The Scottish legendary, The life of St. Machor* 375).
['Then, from the time that Saint Columba became aware of how clearly God's mercy shone [in Machar]']
[Older Scots*] *IMEV* 842.1.

(17) His heritage if he wyll *wynne*
He behouys to do anoþer *thyn*ge
(*Creation* 199)
['If he wants to win his heritage he needs to do another thing']
[Lei] *IMEV* 1677.1. (*IR*)

Loss of final /k/ after *n* was already seen in early Middle English rhymes. There are parallel rhymes with final *k* either pronounced, or not.[7]

(18) That þey receyueth for to *dryn*ke
After that holy *hoselynge*
(Mirk, *Instructions for parish priests* 252)
['[Wine and water] that they receive to drink after Holy Communion'] Cf. ibid. 1233:
Hast þou I-stole mete or *drynke,*
For þou woldest not þerfore *swynke*?
['Have you stolen food or drink, because you did not want to labour for them?']
[Stf] *IMEV* 961.6. (*IR*)

In the final cluster /mb/, /b/ was assimilated in early Middle English c.1300, but more sophisticated writers, like Chaucer, retained the <b> in writing.

(19) And set þi luf so sad *in him*
þat þou may euer vpward *clim*
(Rolle, *Forme of living* 495) (*IR*)
['And fasten your love so firmly in him that you are always able to climb upwards']
[NME] *IMEV* 1442.1.

(20) And I griffed her
right vp in her *home*
And by that day twenty wokes
It was quik in her *wom*b.
(*I haue a newe gardyn*, a carol, stz. 17)
['I grafted her a shoot right in her home. And twenty weeks later it Was alive in her womb']
[Nfk] *IMEV* 1302.1. (*XX*) (a B c B)

2.1.4. Loss of final stops after vowels

Loss of /k/ after /a/ in the infinitives *take* and *make* was seen in rhymes written in the Northern dialect area (including Scotland). There also occurred variants with *k*. Loss of final /k/ in *take* has a parallel in the Scandinavian dialects. Both in Danish and Norwegian the infinitive has lost its *k*. See Skautrup (1944: 229) and Seip (1955: 134). The Northern second and third person present tense forms *tas(e* and *mas(e* were found as rhyme-words in neighbouring North Midland texts.[8]

(21) / weddid wyffes wolde he *ta* /
Maydyns, maryage *alswa*/
(*The wicked knight and the friar* 16) (*IR*)
['wedded wives would he [the wicked knight] take, maidens and wives also [would he spoil]']
[NME*] *IMEV* 1722.1. (12-line stz., a a b C C b d d b e e b)

Where final /k/ was lost in the infinitive *make*, the form *ma* may have risen analogically from a contracted form such as *made* from *makede* (Jespersen 1965: § 250). Jespersen is of the opinion that *ta* was formed on the analogy of *ma*. In MSS written by Southumbrian scribes we may come across the variants *to* and *mo* with the vowel rounded. Skautrup (1944: 276) postulates that in early Danish, long *a* could be rounded in labial neighbourhood. According to Gordon (1981: 322), a rounded long *a* was spelt with <a, aa, o> in Danish by c.1300. In Old Norwegian, long *a* had become identical with long open *o* through lip-rounding by 1250, but the spelling with *a* was retained and stood for both sounds (Gordon 1981: 267).

(22) agaynes hym to *goo* / - / - / - /
And strake hym *thro* / - / - / - /
He strykes the body *fra* / - / - / - /
Mirthe may scho *ma*!
(*Perceval* 1724) (*NI*)
['to go against him ... and struck him fiercely ... He strikes [the sultan's head] from the body ... May she rejoice!']
There is a more corrupt passage, cf. ibid.1891:
*þ*at will vs bothe *sle*! ... Ne wirke me no *wo*? ... His maistrys to *mo* ... Er *þ*at I hethen *go*!
['Who will kill us both ... Nor do me any harm? ... To behave outrageously ... Before I go from here.']
[NME*] *IMEV* 1853.1. (a a a B c c c B d d d B e e e B)

2.2. Modification of final stops in assonating rhymes

The majority of the types of assonating rhymes to be discussed below seem to be late Middle English copies of older texts from the early Middle English period when that kind of impure rhymes were acceptable.

2.2.1. Glottal replacement of /k/, /p/, and /t/ ?

Where final /k p t/ came to occur in rhyme-words, sometimes after the loss of final *schwa*, words ending in any two of the three voiceless stops would first occur in rhyme with each other in some copies of older texts written by late Middle English scribes. I suggest that such rhymes, which had been legitimate in early Middle English (cf. Einhorn 1974: 5-6), might possibly have become acceptable in oral presentation even after late ME standards. Gimson (1969: 170) postulates that replacement of final /k/ and /t/, and more rarely of /p/, by glottal stop is typical of several kinds of regional speech today. If these final stops had already been replaced by glottal stops in late Middle English casual speech, such rhymes might have sounded 'good' to contemporary audiences when a verse text was spoken or recited.

(23) / - / Vnblemyst I am, wythouten *bl*o*t* / - / Bot "makelez quene" þenne sade I *n*o*t* / - /A hondred and forty þowsande *fl*o*t* / - / Saint John hem syȝ al in a *kn*o*t* / On þe hyl of Syon, þat semly *cl*o*t* / - / Arayed to þe weddyng in þat *hyl-c*o*ppe* / þe nwe cyte o Jerusalem.
(*Pearl* 781) (*NI*)
['Unblemished I am, without a stain ... But then I did not say " peerless queen" ... A company of a hundred and forty thousand ... Saint John saw them all in a group on the hill of Syon, that fine mountain ... Dressed for the wedding on that hilltop, the new city of Jerusalem.']
[Chs] *IMEV* 2744.1. (12-line stz., a B a B a B a B B c B c)

(24) Whan Parfory harde *tha*t
Hym thought hys herte *bra*ke.
(*St. Katherine* (4) 247)
['When Porphyry heard that he thought that his heart broke']
[Lei] *IMEV* 227.2. (*NN*)

(25) And lewde men þan þer eyȝene *we*pe
That teres fell vndere þer *fe*te.
(*The stasyons of Ierusalem*, a travelogue, stz. 113)
['And then lay people cried their eyes out, so that tears fell down to their feet.']
Cf. ibid. 687:
And than sche praysyd hym all *abou*te
And with hyre pappes gane hym *sow*ke
['And then she praised him [baby Jesus] throughout and fed him from the breast.']
[Lei] *IMEV* 986.1. (*NI*)

(26) And anon after, as seynt Wylfride ley in his bed vpone a nyȝt –
Bot he nas not fulliche ȝet *a-sle*pe:
Hym þouȝt þat he sey an angel fulle bryȝt
Stondynge at his beddus *fe*te.
(*St. Editha* (Ethelreda) 621)
['And soon afterwards, as Saint Wilfrid lay in his bed one night - but he was not yet fully asleep: it seemed to him that he saw a very bright angel standing at the foot of his bed.']
[Wlt*] *IMEV* 3090.1. (*NN*) (quatrains: a B a B)

2.2.2. Assimilation of final stops in the clusters *-nd*, *-ng*, and *-mb*

Any two words ending in the above clusters could rhyme with each other in early Middle English, apparently after the model of frenchified nasalised pronunciation (cf. Einhorn 1974: 9). Some of these rhymes survived in late

Middle English. They were found both south, east, and north. Colloquial loss of final *d* and *g* after *n*, and that of *b* after *m* has been attested above (see 2.1.3.). The combination of vowel and nasal in these rhymes must have resulted in a nasalised vowel and a velar type of nasal consonant sound. Since all the rhyme-words involved in this assimilation in late Middle English texts were of native origin, we must bear in mind that vowels had been nasalised before *m* and *n* in early Danish (Skautrup 1944: 217).

(27) Wiþ hys ffoot he wolde nouȝt *won*de /
He slowȝ þe child ryȝt in here *wom*be
(*Athelston* 273)
['With his foot he would not hesitate. He slew the child right in her womb.']
[Li] *IMEV* 1973.1. (*NI*) (12-line stz., a a b c c b d d b E E b)

(28) They fare in chyrche as a lyone *strong*
And meke in feld as any *lom*b
(*God of hewine* 174)[9]
['They move about in church like a strong lion, and, humbly in field like any lamb.']
[EM*] *IMEV* 957.1. (*IR*)

2.2.3. De-voicing of final /d/

Wright (1968: 233) argues that de-voicing of final /d/ after /r, l, n/ has often taken place in modern dialects in words of more than one syllable, from Scotland to the South, but not in the eastern and south-eastern counties. The examples in my data are all from the West, where they also apply to mono-syllabics. Eye-rhymes (see no. 31 below) may occur even here.

(29) And euer haue pete on þe pore
And part with him þat God þe *send*
þou hast no noþer tresoure
Aȝayns þe day of *iugement*
I cownsel þe:
(Audelay, *ffede þe hungere*, a carol, stz. 3)
['And have ever pity on the poor one and share with him whatever God may send you. You have no other spiritual goods against the Judgement Day. I advise you:']
[Stf] *IMEV* 792.1. (*XX*) (a B a B c + burden)

(30) An angel drofe hym yn-to *desert*
Wyth a bryȝth brennyng *swerde*.
(*The legend of Ipotis* 233)[10]
['An angel drove him [Adam] into the desert with a brightly burning sword']
[EM*] *IMEV* 220.9. (*XX*)

(31) *þ*us alle men He do*þ* *cumford*
And cowncelis ȝou pur charite
Settis noȝt be *þ*e ioy of *þ*is *word*
Hit is bot vayn and vanete/
(Audelay, *Saynt ancelyne* 'St. Anselm', lines 27-39) (*IR*)
['Thus he comforts all people and advises you through love. Don't value the joy of this world, it is but vainglory and vanity.']
[Stf] *IMEV* 2853.1. (13-line stz., A b A b b c b c d e e e d)

De-voicing of final /d/ after vowels was found in northerly and eastern texts. Phillipson -- Lauridsen (1982: 12, 24) maintain that those speaking with a Danish 'accent' are not able to make a distinction between voiced and voiceless stops in final position. Before a pause only /p t k/ occurs.

(32) Hast *þ*ow any tyme with herte prowd
A-no*þ*eres synne I-spoken owt
(Mirk, *Instructions for parish priests* 1025)
['Have you ever, with a proud heart, made public another man's sin']
[Stf] *IMEV* 961.6.
The rhyme is retained in the Lincolnshire revision (*IMEV* 961.7.) (*IR*).

2.2.4. Final /d/ in rhyme with dental fricative

These rhymes were only found in Scandinavian-influenced areas. Gimson (1969: 162ff.) argues that the English alveolar /d/ is pronounced voiceless in final position. In the Danelaw, final *d* could occur in rhyme with the dental fricative. Skautrup (1944: 222) attests that the fricative could be written <d> in the oldest sources in Middle Danish. Both sounds appear to have been allophones of the same sound. Reverse spelling will occur in the examples.

(33) Kyng Edwarde *þ*an soght aflie *Davide*
He suffred hem haf no*þ*er pes ne *gride*.[11]
(Castleford, *Chronicle of England* 38076)
['Then King Edward tried to put David to flight. He allowed him to have neither peace nor security.']
[WRY*] *IMEV* 1559.1. (*NN*)

(34) 'Osanna' *þei* sange '*þe* sone of *Dauid*' / - /
And poure folke fecched floures of *þe frith*
(*York cycle*, XXX. 343.)
['Hosanna', they sang, 'Son of David' ... And poor people brought flowers of the meadow']
[south of Yk] *IMEV* 1273.1. (*XX*) (A b A b c d d d c)

(35) Of *þe* shall be sore *aferd*
When *þey* come yn-to myddul *erþe*.[12]
(*The legend of Ipotis* 311)
['[And all those who see] you [Satan] will be very frightened when they come to mid-earth.']
[EM*] *IMEV* 220.9. (*XX*)

(36) He wente forth yn *þat tyde*
Walkynge by *þe see-syþel*
(*Emare* 685.) (*NI*)
['He went along at that time, walking by the sea-side']
[EM*] *IMEV* 1766.1. (12-line stz., a a b C C b d d b e e b)

(37) No thynge that of hym *sterde*
/ - / - / Hymselff was the *fovrthe*[13]
/ - / - / And euery man drew his *swerd*
/ - / - / And bare them to the *erthe*.
(*Ipomadon* (1) 8418)
['[there was] nothing that moved him off ... he himself was the fourth ... And every man pulled his sword ... and struck them [Cabanus' men] down']
[EM*] *IMEV* 2635.1. (*NI*) (12-line stz., a a B c c B d d B e e B)

3. The Findings

The editors of *LALME* must have had their reasons for making a distinction between MSS written in the mixed dialect of the West Riding of Yorkshire (WRY) and the more or less mixed language of a number of other texts written elsewhere in Yorkshire which are referred to by the general term NME (Northern Middle English) but not entered on maps. A map presented by Skautrup (1944: 97) shows that the North was first occupied by East Norse (Danish) invaders at the time the Vikings settled down in Britain, but that West Norse (Norwegian) settlements spread from the north-western counties sporadically all over the West Riding (cf. the maps in Gilbert 1985: 11-14).

Table 1: Temporal and regional distribution of the manuscripts

Subperiod	NME	WRY	EM	WM	South	Totals
ME 3	12	2	11	5	4	34
ME 4	5	3	10	5	---	23
Totals	17	5	21	10	4	57

Table 1 shows that the MSS assigned to ME3 take up nearly 61 per cent of the data. The ratio of Northern Middle English texts to East Midland and West Midland texts is 12: 11: 5. The four Southern, and the two West Riding MSS seem to exhibit later copies of early Middle English texts. In ME4, the East Midland MSS outnumber the others. The NME and WM texts amount to half of their number. There were only three MSS assigned to WRY, and none to the South.

Table 2: Distribution of prototypical text categories among the regions

Dialect region	IR	NN	NI	XX	Totals
NME	8	3	5	2	18
WRY	-	2	---	3	5
EM	3	4	7	6	20
WM	3	---	3	4	10
South	1	2	1	---	4
Totals	15	11	16	15	57

As seen in Table 2, all the four prototypical text categories represented in the data were found in Northern and East Midland manuscripts. In West Midland and Southern texts, three text categories were represented, and in texts written in the West Riding, only two.

4. Conclusion

Narrative Middle English rhyming verse was meant to be read aloud. Late Middle English parish priests and friars addressed believers with verse homilies and saints' lives. The dialogue of mystery plays was in rhyming verse. Romances were recited to appreciative audiences. Lyrics and carols were sung to music. In texts that were meant to be recited or sung, final stop deletion was introduced as a concession to the needs of rhyme. Modification of final stops in rhyme-words was adjusted to regional or colloquial conditions.

The bulk of the texts were either translated from Latin or French models or modified after such models. The language of most of the manuscripts was no longer a pure dialect because they could be several times removed from the originals. That must be one of the reasons why the Linguistic Profiles of so many of them are not analysed in *LALME*. The texts included in the data differ greatly in length, some are even incomplete. Therefore no attempt was made to count any relative frequencies. Considering the fact that this is only a pilot study with the examples picked out at random, it is not possible to present any conclusive evidence. The findings can only be suggestive.

Different types of deletion of final stops appear to have varied region-wise. The colloquial pronunciation reflected in non-standard rhymes was not entirely region-bound. An established poet like Chaucer would use contemporary prestige forms. Non-standard forms which were not prestige forms in the original poet's community must have occurred in manuscripts copied by less literate anonymous scribes, or by scribes coming from a different dialect area.

A few of the types had apparently spread all over the country. Loss of stops in final position after other stops was probably a universal phenomenon. That also applies to loss of final dentals in inflexional weak endings of French verbs in which the stem ends in a dental consonant.

Some types of final stop deletion occurred in more than one regional area. Final *d* after post-vocalic *n* in weak endings of participial adjectives and ast participles was sporadically lost in southern, eastern and western texts. Devoicing of final stops after long vowels in *d* : *t* rhymes was only found in Midland texts, both East and West.

Some types seem to have been predominantly region-bound. Devoicing of final *d* after *r*, *l*, or *n*, to occur in rhyme with final *t*, was only manifested in Western texts. Words in which final *k* was deleted after a nasalised *n* in rhyme with words ending in *-ng* were mainly found in MSS written in the West.

The contracted *k*-less forms *ta* and *ma* of the infinitives *take* and *make* occurred in texts to which the dialect reference WRY or NME was assigned by the editors of *LALME*. They could occasionally be seen in MSS written in some neighbouring county.

There are more types of loss of final plosives in manuscripts written within the boundaries of ancient Danelaw than in any of the other regions. Final *t* is dropped after other fricatives (*s*, *f*) only in MSS written in Yorkshire and the East Midlands. Final *d* was lost in the Northern present participles ending in *-and*. Words in which final *d* followed after a vowel or *r* could occur in rhyme with words ending in a dental fricative. Rhymes of this type were only found in texts written in the North and East Midlands.

Some of the types of loss of final stops in early Middle English assonating rhymes that had been legitimate in the early Middle English subperiod survived in late Middle English. Firstly, rhymes in which the rhyme-words ended in assonating clusters of nasals and final voiced stops could probably be regarded as 'good' rhymes in late Middle English after the final clusters had undergone assimilation when presented orally. Secondly, rhymes consisting of two or more words ending in voiceless final stops in assonance seem to have become acceptable if the stops were suppressed through replacement by glottal stops when the verse was recited or spoken in colloquial, i.e. casual or vulgar style.

To sum up, it appears that deletion (as well as modification) of final stops in rhyme-words occurred most frequently in regions which had earlier been subjected to Scandinavian influence, and their neighbouring counties. The central regions in this respect were Yorkshire and East Anglia. In the fourteenth and fifteenth centuries, those areas were not yet well within the reach of the growing standard language. It can only be conjectured that the rise of final stop-deletion so conclusively attested by rhymes in northerly and easterly MSS of the period must be traceable back to poets or scribes who were inheritors of ancient Scandinavian settlers in the Danelaw. In their language, the "economy of expression" must have been fairly strong, judging by the important role that assimilation has always played in the development of the Danish and Norwegian languages.

Notes

[1] The estimates marked with an asterisk were found in text editions, manuals, grammars and histories of English, or scholarly articles.

[2] Lass's map is fairly similar to the "Map of dialect boundaries" drawn by Moore -- Meech -- Whitehall in 1935, which is reproduced in *MED. Plan and bibliography* (1954: 8).

[3] *The northern homily cycle: The expanded version in MSS Harley 4196 and Cotton Tiberius E vii.*, cf. Nevanlinna (1972-84).

[4] But through this loss, a correct rhyme is achieved in (3) and (4), see also (5), (8) etc. – if the correct form had been preserved, there would be an impure rhyme.

[5] In (8) *soft*, the *t* is preserved in spelling; see also (10), (11) etc.

[6] The MS was edited by Gillis Kristensson (cf. Mirk 1974: 177-224). In line 790 the edition reads *þothe* for *bothe*. The emendation is mine.

[7] See e.g. "Maiden in the mor lay" (*IMEV* 3891.1.), a carol written down in the South in the early fourteenth century, but inserted in a late Middle English MS. The latest (expanded) edition of the text is by J. A. Burrow -- Thorlac Turville-Petre (1997: 236-237). Here, lines 18-21 read: "þe chelde water of the – / Welle was hire dryng, / Wat was hire dryng? / þe chelde water of the welle-spring." ['The cold water of the – / spring was her drink, / What was her drink? The cold water of the spring.'] According to *LALME* (1986, 4: 321), *ng* is found for *nk*, and reversely, in MSS written in the South and Midlands. Norfolk and Salop are the northernmost counties where this is seen.

[8] The contracted past participle *tane* had already appeared in early Middle English texts written further south, but not the infinitive *ta*.

[9] This religious poem in rhyming couplets entitled "Merita Misse" ['Merits of the mass'] was wrongly ascribed to Lydgate in the MS. It contains several early Middle English assonating rhymes. I found none in Lydgate's long poem "Interpretacio misse" ['Interpretation of the mass'] in 8-line stanzas rhyming ababbcbc (*IMEV* 4246.6.). The editor Henry Noble MacCracken (1911: 86-115) maintains that assonance was very rare in Lydgate, not more than six instances to 150.000 lines. The only assonating rhyme (*th* : *d* of the East Midland type) was to be seen in a spurious couplet inserted in the poem (lines 15-16): "Ne that day shall he dy soden dethe / The sacrament to se in forme of brede." ['Nor is he to die a sudden death on that day to see the sacrament in the form of bread.'] (Not included in the data.)

[10] Cf. G *Schwert* 'sword'. This rhyme is a relict from a western MS. The oldest extant MS of the text [cf. *IMEV* 220.1.] contains this rhyme.

[11] *Grid* in the MS is Eastern dialectal spelling for *grith* 'peace, security'. *Peace and grith* is a common word-pair in Middle English verse.

[12] Instead of this regional rhyme, both *IMEV* 220.3. [Lei] and *IMEV* 220.8. [Li] have a good rhyme with *erde* for *erthe*. According to *ManualME* (1972: 3, 740), the original poem was composed at the beginning of the fourteenth century, and it has been suggested that the poem is East Midland or Southeastern (excluding Kent).

[13] *Fovrthe* in the MS is introduced by a Midland scribe for Northern dialectal *ferd(e* 'fourth'. There is a recent edition of the MS, cf. Purdie (2001).

References

Burrow, John Anthony -- Thorlac Turville-Petre (eds.)
1997 *A book of Middle English.* (2nd reprinted edition.) Oxford: Blackwell.

Dobson, Eric J.
1968 *English pronunciation 1500-1700.* 2 vols. (2nd edition.) Oxford: Clarendon Press.

Einhorn, E.
1974 *Old French: A concise handbook.* Cambridge: Cambridge University Press.

Gilbert, Martin (ed.)
1985 *Atlas of British history.* Cartography by Arthur Banks. (reprinted edition.) New York: Dorset Press.

Gimson, Alfred C.
1969 *An introduction to the pronunciation of English.* (2nd revised edition.) London: Arnold.

Gordon, E. V.
1981 *An introduction to Old Norse.* (2nd reprinted edition.) Oxford: Clarendon Press.
1957 Revised by A.R. Taylor.

Jespersen, Otto
1965 *A modern English grammar:* Part I: *Sounds and spellings* (Reprinted edition.) London: Allen and Unwin.

Jordan, Richard
1974 *Handbook of Middle English grammar: Phonology.* Translated and revised by Eugene Joseph Crook. (Janua Linguarum. Series Practica 218.) The Hague: Mouton.

Kennedy, Edward Donald -- Ronald Waldron -- J. S. Wittig (eds.)
1988 *Medieval English studies presented to George Kane.* Suffolk: Boydell and Brewer.

Mirk, John
1974 *John Mirk's instructions for parish priests.* Gillis Kristensson (ed.). (Lund Studies in English 49.) Lund: Gleerup.

Kytö, Merja (ed.)
1995 *Manual to the diachronic part of the Helsinki corpus of English texts: Coding conventions and lists of source texts.* (3rd edition.) Helsinki: Department of English, University of Helsinki.

Lass, Roger (ed.)
1970 *Approaches to English historical linguistics: An anthology.* New York: Holt, Rinehart and Winston.

1992 "Phonology and morphology", in: *CHEL* 2, 25-155.

Luick, Karl
1964 *Historische Grammatik der englischen Sprache.* 2 vols. Posthumously edited by Friedrich Wild and Herbert Koziol. Oxford: Blackwell.

MacCracken, Henry Noble (ed.)
1963 *John Lydgate.* (Reprinted edition.) (EETS e.s. 107.) Oxford: Oxford University Press.

Milroy, James
1992a *Linguistic variation and change.* (Language in Society 19.) Oxford: Blackwell.

1992b "Middle English dialectology", in: *CHEL* 2, 156-206.

Nevanlinna, Saara (ed.)
1972-1984 *The northern homily cycle: The expanded version in MSS Harley 4196 and Cotton Tiberius E vii.* (Mémoires de la Société Néophilologique de Helsinki 38, 41, 43.) 3 vols. Helsinki: Société Néophilologique.

Penzl, Herbert
1970 "The evidence for phonemic changes", in: Lass (ed.), 10-24.

Phillipson, Robert -- Hanne Lauridsen
1982 *Danish learning of English obstruents.* (Anglicana et Americana 16.) Copenhagen: Department of English, University of Copenhagen.

Purdie, Rhiannon (ed.)
2001 *Ipomadon.* (EETS o.s. 316.) Oxford: Oxford University Press.

Romaine, Suzanne
1983 "The sociolinguistic history of *t* / *d* deletion", *Folia Historica Linguistica* 5: 221-55.

Samuels, M. L.
1972 *Linguistic evolution with special reference to English.* (Cambridge Studies in Linguistics 5.) Cambridge: Cambridge University Press.

Seip, Didrik Arup
1955 *Norsk språkhistorie til omkring 1370.* (2nd edition.) Oslo: Aschehoug & Co.

Skautrup, Peter
1944 *Det danske sprogs historie.* Vol. 1. Copenhagen: Gyldendal.

Stanley, Eric G.
1988 "Rhymes in English medieval verse: From Old English to Middle English", in: Kennedy -- Waldron -- Wittig (eds.), 19-54.

Wright, Joseph
1905 *The English dialect grammar.* Oxford: Frowde.
1968 Reprinted edition. Oxford: Clarendon.

Wyld, Henry Cecil
1956 *A history of modern colloquial English*. (3rd reprinted edition.) Oxford: Oxford University Press.

Hyphens and hyper-hyphens in Middle English (corpus-based)

Manfred Markus (Innsbruck, Austria)

1. Introduction

Hyphens, and English punctuation marks in general, have been a minor, almost non-existent concern of English linguistics, whether synchronic or diachronic. Only a few, usually prescriptive rather than descriptive, studies are available at all.[1] This is not surprising in view of what McArthur's *Oxford companion to the English language*, in a substantial article on the hyphen, has to say: "The use of the hyphen to mark compound words ... and ... in words such as *to-day* and *with-out* ... has always been variable and unpredictable" (1992: 491).[2] In another article of the same source (s.v. 'Punctuation'), punctuation before the 17th century is generally called "haphazard and erratic, with little attention payed to syntax".

While the validity of this statement is non-disputable from a present-day point of view, one may well question whether our grammatical principles of today, and syntax in particular, are the proper tool for elucidating the rules of historical English punctuation. Moreover, most studies on hyphens in PDE have neglected derivations in favour of compounds.[3]

Two types of hyphens are usually distinguished: *link hyphens*, used within words, and *break hyphens*, used for breaking the line, i.e. for syllabification. The alleged inconsistency and "erratic" quality of the rules in PDE apply to both types alike.[4] But for lack of time and space, this paper will leave the bibliographical analysis of the break hyphens to another occasion and focus on aspects of word formation in connection with the link hyphen.

Traditional studies of Middle English word formation, such as those by Hans Sauer (cf. 1988 and 1992), have been onomasiological, starting from composition types and gleaning examples of the types from various texts without quantification. In this paper, I would like to try out a semasiological approach, taking the hyphens as used in ME manuscripts seriously and raising the question of their function.

The procedure is based on the hypothesis that the more we go back into the history of hyphens, the more will we be able to grasp the deeper reasons for what seems inconsistent. And the assumed marginal quality of hyphens as a merely allographic and negligible feature of language will turn out to be a misconception in view of the historical data that can now be retrieved from machine-readable sources such as the *OED* on CD-ROM and historical English corpora.

2. Rules for the usage of hyphens today

Link hyphens are generally used in PDE to mark two or more morphemes of compound words to be somewhat, yet not totally connected.[5] But in recent usage, there is a trend against the hyphenation of compounds, particularly in AmE. The reasons for or against hyphenation in these cases are manifold. According to McArthur, hyphenation is discouraged among other factors by:

(a) the monosyllabic structure of the elements (*birdsong*, not **bird-song*);
(b) the well-established association of a word's elements by usage, even with longer formations (*businesswoman*, *nationwide*);
(c) the first element of a word being a prefix that was formerly separated from the base by a hyphen, for example in the case of hiatus, as in former *co-ordinate* or *re-use*, now *coordinate*, *reuse*.

The use of the hyphen is, on the other hand, encouraged by:

(a) otherwise awkward collisions of letters (*breast-stroke*, *co-worker*);
(b) the need to mark syntactic connection in ambiguous constellations, for example in *Frénch-speaking vísitors* vs. *French spéaking vísitors*, or *twénty-odd péople* vs. *twenty ódd péople;*
(c) the need to connect the elements of combined words used attributively (*19th-century novel, Christmas-tree lights*).

McArthur also mentions the use of hyphenated derivations, such as *re-enact*, *re-form*, where the reason for the hyphen may be phonetic (*re-enact*), graphemic (*anti-Darwinian* vs. *antidote*) or semantic (*re-form* in its literal meaning, as opposed to *reform*). Two general thumb-rules can be articulated: AmE is less fond of using hyphens in border cases; and hyphenation very much depends on "how established and recognizable a formation is" (492).

All this may be confusingly indefinite to a learner. But the basic function of the link hyphen is what the term suggests: to link lexical elements half-way that otherwise, i.e. if spelt separately or in one word, would be subject to misinterpretation. The possible reasons for this misinterpretation are variable, but at any rate the basic motivation of language users to apply or avoid hyphens is to spell words in such a way that they appear clearer to the recipients, i.e. readers.

This pragmatic and historically conditioned motivation of hyphens is also to be found in Middle English. The hyphen marks the evolution of composition from the state of separateness to that of union.

3. Historical evidence from the *OED*

The *OED* on CD-ROM (2nd edition) is disappointingly limited in retrieving hyphens. Though a mode is available in the "Settings" menu for recognising hyphens as search characters,[6] there are different reasons in the various parts of the lexicon entries to prevent the user from identifying the hyphens. There is no way of scanning the quotation texts generally, i.e. with wildcards, and as regards the initial parts of the entries, i.e. the lemmas and the variant forms, hyphens are misleadingly used from a modern point of view and, what is worse, in a mixed mode, namely as object language, i.e. as proper parts of words, and also as meta-language, i.e. as an abbreviative substitute of left-out syllables. For example, hyphenated *-mite* and *-mett* are given as variants of the lemma *hermit*, for the reader to complement the first syllable *her*.

However, the *OED* software does allow quotation searches of hyphens and wildcards in combination with at least one character. The query *a-**, for example, provides a results file of 3953 quotation words with initial hyphenated *a-*, as in *a-bede*, *a-brod*, etc. This search mode also allows for combinations with other parameters, for example, the date parameter. Limiting the search period to 1000-1499, the computer provides 2235 samples of hyphenated words with the prefixoid *a-*.

Whether this *a-* is really a prefix or eventually a free morpheme, can, of course, not be decided by the computer; but the question is of secondary importance in the context of this paper. In any case, separation of morphemes by hyphens was obviously quite common in the Middle English period.[7] This impression is confirmed by the test on other prefixoids, such as *be-*, *ge-/ȝe-*, *i-*, *y-* and others (cf. Table 1):

Table 1: Hyphenated prefixes 1000-1499 (*OED*)

be-	780
ge-, ʒe-/i-/y-	3798
for-	1070
to-/te-	1313
un-	124
bi-/by-	1293
(a)gain(e)-/(a)gayn(e)-	18
in-	805
of-	188
ofer-/over-	71
on-	271
thurh-/thurgh-/thorugh-/thro(u)gh-	32
under-	48
up-	116
ut-	27
with-	807

A similar list can be provided for compounds with common pronominal adverbs as determinants, such as *here-, there-*, and *where-* (Table 2) or with common words such as *man-* and *God-/Gode-/Godd-* (Table 3):

Table 2: Common ME adverbs with hyphens

her(e)-	120
ther(e)-	774
wher(e)-	65

Table 3: Common ME content words with hyphens

man-/mon-/men-	69
God-/gode-/Godd-	26

The native quality of these words or morphemes arouses the suspicion that Romance words may be less concerned by hyphenation. To check this, I have selected those Latin and French prefixes that are less subject to variation caused by assimilation[8], such as *ante-*, *de-*, *per-/par-*, *post-*, *pro-*/OF *pour-*, *re-*, and *trans-*/OF *tres-*. Except for *de-* (30 cases) the output varies from zero to only five occurrences (cf. Table 4).

Table 4: Hyphens after Romance suffixes

	numbers of hyphens	numbers of no hyphens
ante- ('before')	0	162
de-	30	0
per-/par-	0/4	0
post-	2	209
prae-/pre-	0/2	5144
pro- (Lat)/*pour-/pur-* (Fr)	1/3	2040
re-	5	0
trans- (Lat)/*tres-* (Fr)	0/0	456/944

How can we interpret these data? All in all, the hyphens give evidence of attempted analyses of words, and sometimes re-analyses.

In terms of etymology, native words could naturally be analysed more easily than French or Latin words. The reason for the low figures with Romance words is not that the foreign prefixes were altogether less frequent than the native ones. *Ante*, for example, is used as an initial word element in 162 *OED*-quotations during the period at issue,[9] but not even once with a hyphen. As Table 4 shows, *post*, *prae/pre* and *trans* have even higher figures of word-initial occurrence, with hardly any evidence of hyphenation. The reason seems to be that these classical morphemes did not cause any problems of misunderstanding. But morphographemic support was needed in the case of the Old English prefixes that lost ground in the course of Middle English or even died out, such as *be-/bi-*, *for-* (in the sense of German 'ver-'), *ge-/i-*, *æt-* and *gain-* (as in PDE *to gainsay*).

In addition to this basic distinction between native and foreign words, the minor difference between French and Latin prefixes is striking. Thus, Latin *per-* is not once marked as a prefix by a hyphen, but its French equivalent *par-* is, if only in a few cases - as in *par-avnter* (Lydgate; 4 occurrences). Likewise, Latin *prae-*, according to the *OED*, never evoked a hyphen until 1499, but a query for its French equivalent *pre-* yielded two examples: *pre-supposyd* and *pre-elect*. Finally, I could find no example of Latin *pro* plus hyphen,[10] but three cases of its French equivalent, i.e. hyphenated *pour-* or *pur-*, namely *pur-dew*, *pur-poynt*, and *pur-sued*.

De-, according to Table 4, seems exceptionally prone to be hyphenated. But as the *OED*, in a special article on this prefix, points out, a large number of Latin verbs formed with *de-* lived on in French as popular words. The words that can be gleaned from the list of the 30 quotations provided by the *OED* are mostly first occurrences between 1290 and the 15th century. This means that they had not fully made their way into English yet, so that the hyphen was applied to mark the morphemic structure of such words and thus their foreignness – as in *de-bonerli* (= 'de+bon+aire+ly'), *de-clar*, *de-cre*, *de-foule*, *de-parte*, *de-gres* ('flight of stairs'), *de-fend*, *de-deyn* ('disdain') etc.

Comparing the role of hyphens with native words and with the French borrowings, we can conclude that hyphens were used in Middle English derivations in the case of morphemes that were either about to lose their productivity or, as in the case of new borrowings from French, on the point of being adapted to English. In either case did benevolent scribes try to add to the clearness of a word's meaning.

Given this motivation, the Middle English hyphens did not have a particular prime time. Their preference rather depends on the morpheme at issue. *ge-/ȝe-*, continuing the Old English verbal prefix *ge-*, was already on the decline in the 11th and 12th centuries; accordingly, hyphens were used for "supporting" this morpheme. *i-* and *y-*, as reduced forms of *ge-*, particularly in the South, were naturally used later. The more than 1000 quotations with *y-* are mostly from the 14th, some even from the 15th century. To get a clear temporal profile for a special case, I will select one of the more frequent prefixes, namely *a-*.

The number of occurrences provided by the *OED* must, of course, be seen in relation to the total number of quotations within the same period. This relationship is expressed in percentages in the following Table (5):

Table 5: Temporal distribution of *a-* in Middle English

	number of quotations	*a-*	%
1000-99	11810	5	0.04
1100-99	5944	15	0.25
1200-99	30946	395	1.28
1300-99	95718	990	1.03
1400-99	113792	830	0.73

It is clear from this survey that the tendency to mark *a-* as a prefix by a following hyphen was most striking in the 13th century, with a massive increase before and a gradual decrease afterwards. Why should there have been more of a need in the 13th century than before or after to make the morphological structure of words clear by spelling? It stands to reason that with the increasing influx of French words in the 13th century there was an extra source of confusion about what initial *a-* could etymologically and semantically stand for.

As the 20 examples of the 11th and 12th centuries (5+15) show, the morphological situation was then still fairly clear in that there were only three options: *a-* was either the OE prefix *a-*, corresponding to Gothic *uz-* and German *er-*, with the meaning 'away from' as in *a-rearan* and *a-streccan*. Or it was the reduced preposition *on/in*, as in *a-dun*, *a-bed*, or otherwise the reduced prefix *ȝe-*, mentioned above, as in *a-mong* (< *ȝe-mang*), *a-ware* (< OE *ȝe-wær*). It is not a coincidence that all the words of this group are native words.

The picture is different in the 13th century. With the large number of French words with initial *a-*, as in the many assimilated versions of Latin *ad-* and *ab-* (*adopt*, *acclaim*, *abuse*, etc.) there was an extra need to keep them apart from the native words and to mark these as morphologically transparent. Not that all scribes of the 13th century did this, but, as the statistics above shows, more felt the inclination at that time and during the 14th century than before or after.

Given that the basic motivation for abundant hyphenation in the 13th and 14th centuries was the tendency of marking native morphemes that were prone to be misinterpreted, other causal factors that were to play a role in Modern English have to be backgrounded, as the avoidance of hiatus (*pre-eminence, pre-exist*), the marking of nonce words (*pre-telegraph*) and (implicit) contrastive usage of different prefixes (*pre-* vs. *post-Romantic*).[11] The hyphens in Middle English are simply too frequent to be generally explained by such specific causes.

The hyphen seems to have been so fashionable that some scribes obviously forgot its original function and used it hypercorrectively. In a passage of the *South English Legendary* (c1290) we read "for-to bringe A-cord and loue ... bi-twene thomas and þe king". This scribe, according to the *OED*, was the first to hyphenate the French loanword *accord*, and a quick check on *for-to* in the *OED* reveals that he was about the only one from 1000 to 1499 to hyphenate it, with the 61 quotations provided by the *OED* almost all by this very scribe.[12]

What we have, then, is statistical evidence: hyphens were first used by medieval English scribes in reaction to the imminent etymological obscuration of the language, namely with the intention of marking native prefixes. This was quite a fashion – with the result that the habit well spread, particularly later, to French loanwords (as *a-cord*), and to the free morphemes of compounds or frequent syntactic groups mutating into compounds. Such hyper-hyphens, based on sometimes idiosyncratic exaggeration, paved the way for the partial inconsistency of hyphenation in PDE, particularly in compounds. But in Middle

English, when hyphens were mostly used for prefix-marking, hyper-hyphens are exceptional cases, typical of particular works and scribes.

In the following, we will have a closer look at hyphen-buffs and hyper-hyphens, on the basis not of selective samples from the *OED*, but of a full-text data-base.

4. Evidence from the Innsbruck Prose Corpus

The first few lines in Horstmann's MS Laud edition of the *South English Legendary* look as follows (ll. 1-14):

10 Sancta Crux

ÞE holie rode **i-founde** was : ase ich eov nouþe may telle.
Costantyn þe Aumperour : muche heþene folk gan **a-quelle**,
For huy ore louerd iesu crist : to strongue deþe brouȝte,
And alle þe heþene men þat neiȝ him were : sone he dude to nouȝte.
Eleyne, þat was is moder : to Ierusalem he sende
to sechen after þe holie rode : and heo gladliche forth **i-wende**.
þo heo cam þudere, heo liet crie : ase heo hire red hadde **i-nome**,
þat alle þe giwes of þe cite : before hire scholden come.
þo þe giwes **i-somoned** were : huy hadden grete fere;
gret conseil huy nomen **þare-of** : ȝwat þe enchesoun were.
þo seide on, þat hiet Iudas : 'Ich wene þat ich wot
ȝwat Þis somunce **a-mounti** schal : ȝif þat ich ou telle mot.
Ich wene þat þe quene enqueri wole : ase heo hadde **i-þouȝt**,
Aftur þe rode þat Iesu crist : to deþe was on **i-brouȝt**.'

The text shows that the scribe uses hyphenation to a still moderate extent and for transparent purposes. Table 6 presents the output of the total first page:

Table 6: Hyphenation at the beginning of *South English legendary*

i-founde ('found')	*a-quelle* ('kill')	*Þare-of* 3x
i-wende ('gone')	*a-mounti* ('amount')	*op-on*
i-nome ('taken')	*a-knowe* ('recognise') 3x	
i-somoned ('summoned')	*bi-tidez* ('happens')	
i-þouȝt ('thought')		
i-brouȝt ('brought')		
i-saiȝ ('seen')		

The scribe uses hyphens for the grammatical prefix *i-* (left column), for the derivational prefixes *a-* and *bi-* (middle column), and for compounding, as in *þare-of* and *op-on*. These findings are apt to confirm what we found in the *OED* earlier, namely that hyphens were preferably used for native morphemes, particularly the prefixes that were in the danger of getting lost.

But a more elaborate analysis of hyphens based on computer analysis unveils the less regular and therefore more interesting cases of Middle English hyphens. In line with the above information from the *OED* that 13th and 14th century scribes were particularly prone to hyphenate their words, I scanned texts of the Innsbruck Prose Corpus with the help of WordCruncher, paying special attention to 13th- and 14th-century manuscripts, and found a particular density of hyphens in the following texts (Table 7):

Table 7: 13-/14th-century texts with many hyphens

Title	date	number of words	number of hyphens	%
Ancrene riwle (Tit. MS)	1230	62,713	2206	3,5
Ayenbit of inwyt	1340	104,128	1564	1,5
Kentish sermons	c1220	3,996	165	4,1
OE homilies	c1200	42,394	192	0,5
St. Marherete (Roy)	1230	8,818	184	2,1
Vices and virtues	c1200	28,569	203	0,7
Wills	1387-1454	41,532	648	1,6

Looking at the first text, the *Ancrene Riwle* (Titus MS), in close-up, the use of hyphens is at first sight most erratic indeed. The words *again/against* are presented, apart from other spelling variation, in the following way:

Table 8: *again* hyphenated in *Ancrene riwle* (Titus MS)

1. *a-ȝain*	1
2. *aȝ-ain*	1
3. *aȝa-in*	1
4. *aȝai-nes*	1
5. *aȝain*	79

Obviously, the systematicity, if there is one, is both non-syllabic and non-morphological. But the editor (Frances Mack) makes clear in her introduction of

Ancrene Riwle (XIIf.) that the Titus MS does not have any link hyphens at all, but only end-of-line hyphens. Obviously, the lines were so economically used in the manuscript that lines and words were broken wherever necessary, irrespective of syllable or morpheme boundaries. In other words: the link hyphens in the editorial text are, in fact, break hyphens in the original manuscript.

In *Ayenbite of Inwyt*, the next example of Table 7, the general pattern for the use of hyphens is again based on the obvious intention of the scribe to mark the native morphemes, namely *a-* (*a-roos*), *all- (al-so)*, *an-* (*an-het* 'heat up'), *be- (be-fore)*, *bi-/by- (bi-leued)*, *where (huer-of)*, *i-/y- (i-write)*, *in- (in-to)*, *mis- (mis-do)*, *of- (of-acsed)*, *on-* (*on-lepi* 'single, sole'), *op-* (*op-nymynge* 'taking up'), *ouer-* (*ouer-al*), *out-* (*out-kestinge*), *to- (to-broke)*, *uor- (for-)*, and *with-* (*wy-oute* 'without'). There are also a few hyphenated compounds in the text (*bezide-zitteres, þi-zelue*), as can be expected. The only inconsistency is that there are two cases of hyphenated French words (*pre-ciouse*[13], *re-formeþ*) and one case of a pseudo-prefixation (*uor a-yer,* i.e. 'for a year') - such cases are examples of "hyper-hyphens", applied, perhaps thoughtlessly, by way of analogy. However, in more than 1500 samples altogether, these three exceptions are a negligible quantity.

The other inconsistency is that the hyphenated words are also spelt without hyphens, usually in the majority of cases. Thus, the adverb *again-*, i.e. the word of the title *Ayenbite*, is varied as regards the hyphen: 33 occurrences are hyphenated, 117 are not. The same ratio is provided by the word *away*: it is hyphenated in 2 cases, but non-hyphenated in 16. Such variants, as Middle English spelling variants in general, are apt to confuse modern minds. But while they are structurally inconsistent, they can be seen as didactic measures of scribes: the reader is occasionally, if not permanently and systematically, reminded of the literal composition of the old words that were still morphologically transparent.

In this didactic endeavour some scribes were prone to overdo things, occasionally motivated by lexical misanalysis to put in hyphens wrongly. Such misanalyses can also be found in the other texts of Table 7, and even more in later Middle English texts, i.e. in the 15th century, when the Old English prefixes had partly disappeared and hyphens were used, if at all, mainly for compounds.[14] Here is a small collection of hyper-hyphens, with tentative explanations of the hyphenated morphemes:

foreign or hybrid formations

an-vie < OF *envie* (Lat *invidia*): *an-* (= AN) perhaps affected by OE *an* 'on'[15];

an-amylyd ('enameled') (*Wills*) < OF *en+amayl*: *an-* = AN[16]

a-resunede: *a-* < OE *a-* (former *ar-* [cf. G *er-*] + *reason-ed* (< OF)

i-attred (OE *ge* + *a* + *try* + *ed*): *a-* is doubtful; *try* < OF *trier*

ante-quam (Lat) 'before-that' (*OE homilies*)

commissa-que

corpus-que/corpusque

de-faut (OF)

overe-plus (partial trans. of OF *surplus*)

hyphenation of suffixes

gylt-leas

senne-leas

nied-fulle[17]

rihtwis-nesse/riht-wisnesse

liht-inde (pres. part. 'lighting')

me-warde (< OE *-weard)*

hyphenation of non-morphemic syllables (often with de- or agglutination)

he-þen ('heathen')

a-loone (< *all* + *ane*)

a-noon ('anon') < *on* + *ane*)

a-noder (*an* + *oder*)

a-schappe ('escape'): < OF *es-capper* < Lat *ex* + *cappa*): deglutination

a-noynted: < OF *en-oint-*

syntactic groups

un-of-earned ~ *un-ofearned*: 'un + (earned of)'

ðin-hierte ('thine-heart') (Rolle1)[18]

warpest-me ('throw-me') (*OE homilies*)

Þer-a-fore ('there before'): < OE *þær+on+foran*

what-soeuer/whatso-euer/what-so-euer

my sone-is wyf ('my son his wife')

Thomas West-is soule

fulfille-wyth

a-bateile: a (art) +('battle') (context: *ther shal be a-bateile*)

in-esspeciall

now-of-dayes

neuer-þe-les

Hiatus

y-ered ('ploughed')
de-inde ('doing')
mou-oð ('mouth-oath')

5. Resume

The computer queries in the *OED* 2 do not allow a total wildcard search for hyphens, but only searches for hyphens after at least one character. Given this restriction, our results based on the *OED* were bound to be selective. Only the most striking prefixes were taken into consideration, and only the most common variants of these could be included in the investigations. For example, the prefix *ge-*, apart from *i-/y-* and *ȝe-* (with a yogh), also occurred in Middle English as *ȝi-*, *ȝœ*, *ȝie-*, *ȝy-*, *ie-*, *hi-*, *e-* and *a-* (*OED y*-prefix). All these variants, hyphenated or not, had to be ignored.

The tracing of hyphens in the Innsbruck Prose Corpus with the help of WordCruncher was, on the other hand, not restricted in the way of the *OED*; all the hyphens in a text could be found with one command. But then this search was limited by being work-specific.[19]

The combination of the two methods, however, provided a quantitatively sufficient basis for us to draw the following conclusions:

(1) The greatest proportion of hyphenated words in Middle English is found in the 13th and 14th centuries, amounting to more than 1 % of all word occurrences. This result seems to be connected with the confusion about word structures, caused by the influx of French loanwords in the 13th and 14th centuries.

(2) Until 1400, prefixes or prefixoids were far more affected by the trend of hyphenation than compounds. The 15th century initiated the later fashion of hyphenating compounds.

(3) Among the prefixes, both the native ones which were doomed to die and the all-purpose prefix *a-* were the best candidates for hyphenation, followed by the well-established French prefix *de-*. Other French prefixes and, above all, Latin ones remained almost untouched by hyphenation.

(4) Hyphenation in Middle English was a didactic measure of scribes to keep the structure of words, particularly of old native words, transparent. It can be seen as a reaction to the creolisation process that had had its impact on Early Middle English.

(5) The Middle English written documents give evidence of various types of a hypercorrective use of hyphens, particularly in the later Middle English period, when the original purpose of hyphens was no longer fully comprehended.

(6) Our present rather confusing system of hyphenation is a legacy of the late Middle English fashion of using hyphens in a more and more subjective and impressionistic way, particularly in compounds. In earlier Middle English, by contrast, hyphens were used with a surprising consistency.

Given the extreme spelling variation in Middle English texts, the high degree of consistency in hyphenation is apt to support the work of both readers and researchers of word formation. Seen thus, the study of Middle English hyphens is, as I hope to have shown, more than a historical linguist's trivial pursuit.

Notes

[1] A query in the *MLA* CD-ROM (last fourty-odd years) on ‘hyphen’ and ‘English’ provided no more than 25 hits. The only descriptive study on hyphens in historical English was Burchfield (1994), on line-end hyphens in the *Orrmulum* MS. – For hyphens in PDE, I consulted Partridge (1953: 134-151), Carey (1958: 80-83) and Friederich (1977: 52-57).

[2] Cf., in a similar vein, Friederich (1977: 52): “... kein Gebiet so uneinheitlich und umstritten wie das der Bindestrichsetzung”.

[3] Partridge (1953: 148-150) and Friederich (1977: 57) are two of the few who have provided rules for hyphens after prefixes.

[4] From my work with the Innsbruck Corpus, it has become known to me that lines in manuscripts are often broken in the middle of a word without any marker of syllabification.

[5] In this chapter, I very much draw on McArthur (1992: 491f.), Graustein -- Thiele (1987: 61-63) and Carey (1958: 80-84).

[6] The option ‘hyphens’ has to be unmarked in the menu ‘Settings’.

[7] It can be trusted that editors of ME texts, and accordingly the *OED* editors, have used hyphens in line with the manuscripts. To make sure, I checked the authenticity of the hyphens for the seven texts of Table 7 below. Apart from *Ancrene riwle*, the editor of which explicitly states that the hyphens used are those of the manuscript, we only have indirect hints: the distinction of hyphenated and non-hyphenated forms of a word; the role

of hyphens in the glossary; and the policy of pedantically abiding by the unique manuscript in other respects.

[8] By contrast, Latin *ab, ad, cum* and other prefixes were usually assimilated.

[9] Not always, it must be admitted, as a morpheme.

[10] The one output example has 'pro-' in brackets, where the hyphen is abbreviative usage of the *OED* editors.

[11] Cf. *OED* under *pre-prefix.*.

[12] *For to* (without a hyphen) is quoted by the *OED* no less than 3632 times for the same period.

[13] < OF *precios*, Lat *pretiosus* (< *pretium* 'price') (*OED*). There is no historical reason in English to put *pre-* apart.

[14] Cf., for example, *abbey* and *alphal*.

[15] To split *vie* from what is suggested to be a prefix does not make sense, not even in view of AN, since there is no semantic connection to *la vie*, but to Lat. *videre*.

[16] The word was first borrowed in its Central French version with *en-* (*OED*); the AN *an-* version (with and without the hyphen) first appears in 1420, i.e. some 100 years after its first occurrence (*OED*). There is no reason why AN should have been so influential in the 15th century.

[17] *-leas* and *-full* are rightly identified by the *OED* as suffixes for Middle English since they had already developed a specific suffixal meaning.

[18] The phrase is so frequent in Rolle's mystical text that he hyphenated it as if he meant to mark the single notion by using a single word.

[19] This article was written in 2001. From a present point of view (August 2006), WordCruncher should be replaced by a more modern concordance programme allowing the analysis of several texts at a time, such as WordSmith.

References

Burchfield, Robert
1994 "Line-end hyphens in the Ormulum Manuscript (MS Junius I)." Godden -- Gray -- Hoad (eds.), 182-87.

Carey, Gordon V.
1958 *Mind the stop: A brief guide to punctuation.* Harmondsworth: Penguin.

Connell, Tim
1998 "Is the end of the hyphen in sight?", *English today: The international review of the English language* 14: 2 (54): 15-20.

Falkner, Wolfgang -- Hans-Jörg Schmid (eds.)
1999 *Words, lexemes, concept: Approaches to the lexicon: Studies in Honour of Leonhard Lipka.* Tübingen: Narr.

Friederich, Wolf
1977 *Die Interpunktion im Englischen.* München: Hueber.

Godden, Malcolm -- Douglas Gray -- Terry Hoad (eds.)
1994 *From Anglo-Saxon to Early Middle English: Studies presented to E.G. Stanley.* Oxford: Clarendon.

Graustein, Gottfried -- Wolfgang Thiele
1987 *Englische Zeichensetzung.* (4th edition.) Leipzig: VEB Verlag Enzyklopädie.

Markus, Manfred
1999 "English historical lexicology in the age of electronic reproduction: Some suggestions", in: Falkner -- Schmid (eds.), 365-78.

Markus, Manfred (ed.)
1988 *Historical English: On the occasion of Karl Brunner's 100th Birthday.* Innsbruck: Institut für Anglistik.

McArthur, Tom
1992 s.v. 'Hyphen' and 'Punctuation', in: McArthur (ed.).

McArthur, Tom (ed.)
1992 *The Oxford companion to the English language.* Oxford: Oxford University Press.

McDermott, John
1990 *Punctuation for now*. London: MacMillan.

Partridge, Eric
1953 *You have a point there: A guide to punctuation and its allies.* London: Routledge & Kegan Paul.

Sauer, Hans
1988 "Compounds and compounding in Early Middle English: Problems, patterns, productivity", in: Markus (ed.), 186-209.

1992 *Nominalkomposita im Frühmittelenglischen: Mit Ausblicken auf die Geschichte der englischen Nominalkomposition.* Tübingen: Niemeyer.

Medieval English and German: A guide to modern similarities and dissimilarities

Horst Weinstock (Aachen, Germany)

1. Primaries

English-speaking visitors arriving at Austrian, German, or Swiss airports and railway stations can firmly trust in Otto Jespersen's logical and grammatical category of "primary words". In oral announcements and on written signboards (in competition with pictograms), primaries as substantial and substantival keywords help to satisfy present needs. Some two or three dozen English nouns (now internationalized or even globalized) draw attention to public services such as

> *arrivals buses car rental change city centre customs departures exit first aid gates hotel (left/lost) luggage minimarket passports police post office souvenirs taxi trains WC.*

Most of these predominantly Romance loanwords date back no earlier than to Middle English or Early Modern English. By the close of the first millennium, the continuity of Common Germanic had still been functioning homogeneously enough. For a long time, Anglo-Saxon missionaries to the Continent had more easily succeeded in winning the hearts and minds of their nonmonastic disciples by preferring West-Germanic vernacular speech to clerical Latin. In the *Battle of Maldon* in 991, the Anglo-Saxons needed no interpreter in order to communicate with the North-Germanic Vikings. Besides, Saxon English had not yet turned into Norman English with its Romance admixture above all among primaries.

Naturally, a "Guide to Modern Similarities and Dissimilarities" clearly asks for a presentation from documented evidence through cogent reasoning to tenable conclusions. At least for comparative and contrastive studies, both written and oral tradition can and do attest to similarities and dissimilarities.

2. Segmental description

Throughout the history of exegesis and pivotal ideas, Biblical, Classical, Medieval, Early Modern, and Modern approaches crystallized into a widely accepted canon of fundamentals. It starts with the small, simple, plain, easy, and minor units, with anything overt, obvious, literal, and partial, and it ends with the large, complicated, complex, difficult, and major, with the covert, hidden, figurative, and whole. For correct and complete description, it will be essential to combine universalistic with particularistic views.

As to the fundamentals of linguistic change and segmental description, the similiarities rest on various tempo patterns of instruction and penetration versus obsolescence and elimination respectively.

(1) Phonographically, the stability and continuity of letters normally outlives the variation and change of sounds.

(2) Morphologically, the surface structure depends upon contextual functions. Lexical word-composition varies more readily than syntactic inflexion does.

(3) Lexicologically, the basic vocabulary of inherited words of all classes except nouns remains fairly stable. Yet, nouns have undergone constant change or rearrangement in the face of cultural, scientific, and technological advance and competition.

(4) Syntactic structures resist change over long periods. Habits of word-order tend toward longevity.

3. Phonology

To start with phonology, Aristotle and Greek philosophers had already noticed the original and historical priority of sound over script. Roman thinking brought discontinuity, focusing on the documentary value of written evidence for the past, present, and future. The Roman tradition was still alive with Jacob Grimm at the time of the first edition of his grammar. It announced phonology as the chapter "Über die Buchstaben" ['On Letters'], judging living speech by the alphabet and the typographer's letter-case. Within the evolution and history of language, high frequency or ample distribution of typologically identical or similar features used to allow structurally systemic stability with slow and little change. By contrast, low frequency or rare distribution promoted fast and ample change. Thus, the quantity of sounds indirectly forms and determines their quality.

Striking similarities between English and German stem from the First or Common Germanic Consonant Shift about 500 or 400 BC. From then on, Indo-European labial, dental, and tectal plosives went on keeping their old places of articulation. With respect to the manner of their articulation however, they turned from voiced to voiceless and from plosives to fricatives. To demonstrate but one subcycle out of three on its way from West Indo-European to Common Germanic, West Indo-European voiced /b d g/ (for instance) remained stable in Latin, but shifted into Common Germanic voiceless /p t k/. Thus,

Latin	*se labi*	*edere*	*iugum*

stand against East, West, and North Germanic:

Common Germanic	**slapan*	**etan*	**jok*
Gothic (East)	*slepan*	*itan*	*juk*
English (West)	*sleep*	*eat*	*yoke*
Dutch (West)	*slapen*	*eten*	*juk*
(Old) Swedish (North)	(*slapa*)	*äta*	*ok*

North- and some West-Germanic dialects still stick to voiceless plosives. Yet among the West-Germanic languages and in contrast to Old English and Early Netherlandic, Old High German shifted the voiceless plosives /p t k/ into the initial voiceless affricates /pf ts kx/ and the medial or final fricatives /f s x/. Known by the name of the Second or Old High German Consonant Shift, a consecutive change occurred about 600 AD south of a line leading from Aachen via Düsseldorf, Kassel, Magdeburg to Frankfurt-on-the-Oder:

West Germanic	**slapan*	**etan*	**jok*
Old High German	*sla(p)fan*	*ezzan*	*jo(k)h*
Modern High German	*schlafen*	*essen*	*Joch*
Modern English	*sleep*	*eat*	*yoke*

Thus, Modern English unshifted *sleep*, *eat*, *yoke* stand against Modern German shifted *schlafen*, *essen*, *Joch*. Affrication and frication, no doubt, discontinued the English/German similarity and established dissimilarity or divergence instead.

From the 11th century onwards, another consonantal dissimilarity was creeping in throughout the Hohenstaufen Realm (East Switzerland, West Austria, South Germany). The clusters /sp st/ varied in allophonic coarticulation and phonemicized by standardized dissimilarity into Modern German /ʃp ʃt/. So, English /sp/ and /st/ in *spare* and *stone* differ from German /ʃp/ and /ʃt/ in German *sparen* and *Stein*. As an exception to the rule, the cluster /sk/ ended in total assimilation and dissimilarity. In words such as *Schule* or *Schottland* versus *school* or *Scotland*, /ʃ/ even lost its partial similarity with /sk/.

In the late 12th and early 13th centuries, Middle English triggered off a vowel lengthening in open syllables under the main word-stress. It ended in a dissimilarity of a fairly wide range. In disyllabic words, Middle English went far beyond German, particularly so in configurations before affricates and fricatives.

Thus, the Middle and post-Middle English vowels in *eat*, *ape*, *open* differ from Modern German *essen*, *Affe*, *offen* in both quantity and quality.

Linguistically and phonologically, by far the greatest change happened shortly after Chaucer, namely in the 15th century. Called the Great Vowel Shift (GVS) on Otto Jespersen's suggestion, the large-scale phenomenon touched late Middle and Early Modern English much more markedly than it did historical German. Long vowels under the main stress moved upwards by one tongue position in English. As for the highest vowels /i:/ and /u:/, the impulse ended in English as well as in German diphthongization. German *Zeit* and *Haus* follow the same pattern as English *tide* and *house*. Yet otherwise and in partial contrast to German with its 'Petty Vowel Shift' only, all late Middle and Early Modern English mid-high and low vowels rose to the tongue positions above. This makes Modern English long stressed vowels sound dissimilar from their Continental equivalents:

Modern English	Modern German
see /i:/	sehen /e:/
name /ei/	Name /a:/
loose /u:/	lose /o:/

4. Varro's conception

With all its extrinsic evidence, it should not be left unsaid that the Great Vowel Shift dealt phonography a serious blow. Among other acquisitions, the Roman and post-Roman impact on grammar and on letters as its smallest segments had helped to consolidate Early Medieval writing and spelling habits. Both Old English and Old High as well as Old Low German had come to adopt the Latin alphabet. On the whole, scholastic masters of the *Trivium* propagated the pansystem of the Latin alphabet in Varro's conception of the 1st century BC. He had subdivided, subsystematized, and more or less decreed it for shorter and easier memorization in the trinomial shape of vowels (V), consonants (Cē), and semivowels (ĕC). The subsystems yield three observations and conclusions:

(1) Long and stressed vowels in isolation had no chance to escape being raised from their lower to their higher tongue-positions. The Great Vowel Shift raised or diphthongized the original, natural, and unsystemic sound-values of A, E, I, O, U.

(2) For some five hundred years, English writers have spelt the letter-names of full consonants or plosives with double <ee> for spoken /i:/:

Bee Cee Dee Gee Pee Tee

German spelling has held on to Classical and Scholastic simple <e> for spoken /e:/:

Be Ce De Ge Pe Te

British boys and girls internalize their /ei bi: si:/; German pupils rather stick to Latin /a: be: tse:/. Yet even German gangsters shun the FBI /ef bi: ai/ and not an */ef be: i:/. The dissimilarities testify to the existence of certain exceptions to rules rather than to laws. The phonemic subsystems may vary from language to language. German carries on Latin *Ha* and Latinized Greek *Ypsilon*. English shifted to *Aitch* from French *Ache* and Latin contiguous consonantal *(H)A*, *Ka* and to *Wy* upon the contiguity of native *U* preceding foreign *I grec* within the vocalic subsystem *A E I O U Y*.

(3) None but semivowels within their subsystemic premodification in the shape of a short prop-vowel could stand a chance to survive the Great Vowel Shift as letter-names in unaltered similarity. Both English and German speakers spell the so-called *elementum* (*eLeMeNtum)* identically to this very day:

eF eL eM eN eS eX

5. Germanic initial word-stress

With regard to prosody and suprasegmentals, both English and German share initial word-stress on the stem or root syllable. The di- or trisyllabic names of the days of the week may serve as examples of similarity:

*Monday/*Montag *Tuesday/*Dienstag *Wednesday/*Mittwoch *Thursday/* Donnerstag *Friday/*Freitag *Saturday/*Samstag *Sunday/*Sonntag

Anglo-Saxon words of three or more syllables allow the same pattern of Germanic initial stress:

afternoon busybody caretaker doorkeeper everybody forefather grasshopper handwriting insider merry-go-round pickpocket runaway seafarer shortsighted sightseeing thanksgiving watertight

With the influence of Romance foreign words and components on their path to loanwords in Norman English, Germanic initial main stress attracted the Anglo-Norman final main stress. The two contrasting weight-principles changed their ranks and ends on the basis of the superior countertonic principle:

> *brevity carpenter chairperson comedy gentleman globetrotter, grandmother headquarters metrical noticeboard resident surgeon tragedy*

The results of the countertonic principle in Medieval Norman English have brought about another dissimilarity, namely the sharp contrast between Insular loanwords and Continental foreign words:

> *ágriculture*/Agrikultúr *áppetite*/Appetít *cóntinent*/Kontinént *élegy*/Elegíe *fántasy*/Phantasíe *hóspital*/Hospitál *líterature*/Literatúr *mánuscript*/Manuskrípt *médicine*/Medizín *mónument*/Monumént *quálity*/Qualität *quántity*/Quantität *sécondary*/sekundär *sýmbolism*/Symbolísmus *témperament*/Temperamént *tólerance* /Toleránz

A historical comparison of the similarities and dissimilarities between English and German yields two identifying sound-profiles:

(1) Phonically, the sound pattern of English differs from ancient West Germanic more strikingly than its German equivalent does.

(2) Prosodically, the dynamic pattern of word-stress in English resembles the ancient West Germanic more closely than its German equivalent does. English initial stress has never ceased to integrate the originally final stress of Romance borrowings.

Next in segmentation comes graphemic transcription. Historically, sound must have preceded script for ages. Speaking follows some natural, innate, spontaneous, and rather unreflected urge to communicate and interact. In contrast to this, writing originally needed invention and cultivation, and later on it depended on instruction, acquisition, and internalization.

6. Graphonemics

Roman minds at some stage started to hold writing in higher esteem than they did speaking: *Verba volant, scripta manent.* Indeed, words do fly and die away, while written documents live for centuries or for good. In the modern era, historical philologists have come to look back upon the same phenomenon both from identical and from different angles. Extant script can serve as the sole means to reconstruct bygone sound. In other words, the graphically living can revive the phonically dead. The optics of letters as visual communication witnesses to the acoustics of silent voices from the past. Spelling and writing, so to speak, function as unique keys to the history of language. Yet, the correlation between sound and letter needs cautious interpretation.

Much more so than speaking and hearing, writing and reading meet the expectations of a medieval *ars*. They impart a skill both teachable and learnable. The deaf and dumb excepted, all human beings could and would speak; but only a few experts or writing-masters knew how to write as well. With no more than two dozen letters as against some four or five dozen modes and places of articulation at human disposal, the uneasy task has ever consisted in proper disambiguation. A scribe or writer has had to hit the ideal or at least the canonized grapheme for the precise value or power (*potestas*) of the phoneme. Only the acoustic target would serve its proper semantic function. For lack of a one-to-one correspondence between sound and letter and in search of unattainable phonography, scribes and readers took refuge to audible thinking along or spelling aloud what they were going to write down. For this sort of activity, medieval observers coined the phrase "barking at books".

Since the introduction of the Latin alphabet to Germania, English and German have shared many similarities in the course of adopting an identical system and substance of transliteration. Both Otfrith of Weissenburg and Aelfric expressly stated a certain unevenness and some absurdities within the triad of *nomen*, *figura*, and *potestas* of letters.

After a period of ample variation as mirrored in allographic and idiographic writing, Late Medieval English and High German arranged and stabilized their own independent subsystems. From the 15th century onwards, Late Middle and Early Modern English scribal practice and spelling habits in the London area created a Chancery Standard. For graphonemic exemplification, Middle English vowel length can demonstrate one of the most intricate systems. Long vowels under the main stress and in closed syllables appear as digraphic duplications of the identification vowel:

<ii ee aa oo uu>

Long vowels under the main stress but in open syllables appear as digraphic combinations of identification vowel, hyphen for variant consonant, and final <-e> stemming from inflected forms:

<i-e (e-e) a-e (o-e) u-e>

The absence of digraphic combinations for the mid-low vowel values /ɛ:/ and /ɔ:/ reminds posterity of the circumstance that they correspond with the nonsystemic because nonduplicating digraphs <ea> and <oa>. Like many other languages, English has never regained its early medieval state of near-phonography. Middle English attempts at graphonemics or at least graphonetics stabilized before the initial stage of the Great Vowel Shift. Tudor and Early Modern English eventually led to completely (though still systematically) shifted long-vowel values.

By comparison and contrast, the Early Modern German Chancery Standard in the wake of Martin Luther's Reformation and Bible translation did not precede but rather followed a phase of sound-changes. Thus, the digraphs <ei> and <au> in German *Zeit* and *Haus* echo the diphthongization of high front /i:/ and high back /u:/. Besides, the late Middle High German 'Petty Vowel Shift' would not touch mid and low long vowels at all. Yet graphically, High German vowel-lengths have carried on as many as four more or less unfathomable subsystems: three for closed syllables and one for open syllables. As the German long and umlauted vowels *ä*, *ö*, *ü* had produced additional sound values and diacritic letters within the possible tongue positions and as mid-low open /ɛ:/ rendered dialectal variation or idiolectal modulation, the pansystem could work without the English oppositions of closed /e:/ and /o:/ versus open /ɛ:/ and /ɔ:/, leaving things more or less at neutral /E:/ and /O:/. Consequently, the three plus one subsystems have functioned in the following configurations:

(i) duplication of identification vowel;
(ii) simple identification vowel plus <h>;
(iii) simple identification vowel without diacritic letter <Ø>;
(iv) simple identification vowel plus heterosyllabic <-e>:

/e:/ <ee eh eØ e-e>
leer Schnee See Ehre Lehre sehr Keks stets wer geben lesen These

/a:/ <aa ah aØ a-e>
Haar Paar Saal Zahl zahm Zahn kam Rat Tal Hase Nase Phrase

/o:/ <oo oh oØ o-e>
Boot Moos Zoo hohl Kohl wohl groß Not Ton Hose Pole Rose

With all its irregularities, the graphonemic system of English as a compromise between custom and reason can pass for less complicated than the four practically haphazard subsystems of German. Even native writers of German obtain but little help from pondering on etymological origins. To the eyes of foreign readers, the four parallel subsystems must look like some chaotic "anything goes" (but not in any case).

To conclude the section on spelling in script and print, an old truism should be kept in mind: Whenever sound-changes have brought about a maximum difference between sound and script, experts will become active and try to reduce the growing discrepancies through a spelling-reform. German has for a couple of years been caught up in a very controversial spelling-reform. Meanwhile, some seventy per cent of the population are still hesitating or simply ignore the reform altogether. Advanced learners of German will best wait and see for another five years or so. Asking for orthographic help, information, or guidance will in all likelihood embarrass experts, nonexperts, and shirkers.

7. Morphology

The structural comparison continues with morphological findings. As a rule of thumb, philologists maintain that the farther two or more cognate languages date back, the more closely their morphologies will resemble each other. So, the two West-Germanic languages equally point towards time-honoured patterns. In retrospect, English and German carry at least as many dissimilarities as they show similarities. August Schleicher's "pedigree theory" cannot apply in its rigid form, as English (far more so than German) has evolved as a mixed composition of Germanic and Romance elements. Thus, English needs a corrective explanation based upon Hugo Schuchardt's "wave theory" for intersectional loans as well.

Among the English/German similarities, three phenomena deserve priority mention:

(1) initial word-stress with the consequence of reduced final syllables;
(2) the typological preservation of strong versus weak conjugation; and
(3) some centripetal force to regain uniformity or similarity by analogy.

First, initial word-stress could lead to the syncopation of the middle syllable and to a reduction of vowel-timbre in the final syllable. Latin *munisterium* survives as English *minster* and German *Münster* without medial *i* and without final *u*. In other configurations, the total reduction of final vowel-timbre in English converged in /e/ and /ə/. Ultimately, ə caduc ended in zero /Ø/ with loss of the final syllable. In German, the partial reduction stopped at indistinct but syllabic /ə/. So, word-lengths often diverge by one syllable less in English.

In late Indo-European and Common Germanic, an original and regular, so-called strong conjugation indicated the past tense and past participle by means of gradation or ablaut of the stem vowel. By and by, a sporadic but spreading, a so-called weak conjugation indicated the past tense and past participle by means of a dental suffix. The ablauted examples demonstrate the strong conjugation considered as irregular now:

begin	*began*	*begun*	beginnen	begann	begonnen
drink	*drank*	*drunk*	trinken	trank	getrunken
eat	*ate*	*eaten*	essen	aß	gegessen
sing	*sang*	*sung*	singen	sang	gesungen
speak	*spoke*	*spoken*	sprechen	sprach	gesprochen
steal	*stole*	*stolen*	stehlen	stahl	gestohlen

The examples with a dental suffix demonstrate the weak conjugation considered as regular now:

end	*ended*	*ended*	enden	endete	geendet
land	*landed*	*landed*	landen	landete	gelandet
mean	*meant*	*meant*	meinen	meinte	gemeint
plant	*planted*	*planted*	pflanzen	pflanzte	gepflanzt
say	*said*	*said*	sagen	sagte	gesagt

Present-day English and German use the dental suffix as the regular and functionally active formation. Ablaut no longer occurs outside a limited but old and high-frequency stock of verbs. Moreover, English and German have followed similar trends in restoring prior verbal roots by way of analogy or system constraint. For instance, Old English and Old High German gave up grammatical change through rhotacism in

freosan	*freas*	*fruren*	*gefroren*
freeze	*froze*	*frozen*	

and

frieren	fror(en)	gefroren

As a matter of fact, analogy seldom thrives to the full dominance of systematics. The grammatical change described by Karl Verner's Law allows exceptions such as *seethe/sodden* or *was/were*.

A survey of the dissimilarities between English and German morphology should certainly not skip two self-evident features of the surface structure, namely grammatical gender and plural formation. To English eyes and ears, it must seem rather strange that German native speakers should say:

der Kreis	**die** Kurve	**das** Dreieck

for what could more simply be:

the circle	**the** curve	**the** triangle

To Greek, Roman, and Germanic minds, gender-based niceties of the sort echo ancestral and aesthetic voices from afar. Yet for all that, educated native speakers of German should honour lapses of gender simplification as tokens justified or even superior otherness. As obedient teachers, however, native speakers should never cease to further linguistic correctness and human education by adding the proper solution in loving kindness.

Leaving aesthetic lapses and turning to the rational level of possible misunderstandings, Modern English excels in a higher degree of regularity by rule and grammaticalization. For instance, Modern German carries on the old and much more complicated system of variant forms which tolerates many idiomatic and thus tricky allomorphs. Plurals end either in vocalic *-e* or in consonantal *-n* or *-r*:

M(asculine)	Berg/Berge	Weg/Wege	Zug/Züge
F(eminine)	Dame/Damen	Katze/Katzen	Straße/Straßen
N(euter)	Buch/Bücher	Dorf/Dörfer	Haus/Häuser

Present-day English prefers graphemically uniform, but allophonic plurals in *-s* instead:

/s/	*books*	*cats*	*streets*
/z/	*ears*	*trains*	*ways*
/ɪz/	*houses*	*pages*	*villages*

In a commercialized world and a tendentiously 'pluralistic' society, careful speakers will mind the language universals and plural markers in order to avoid costly mistakes.

One of the most obvious dissimilarities of Modern English as against Modern German lies somewhere in between morphology, lexis, and syntax. For diachronic minds, Modern German numerals (cardinals as well as ordinals) from *twenty-one* to *ninety-nine* namely *ein-und-zwanzig* to *neun-und-neunzig*, cannot fail to be associated with Old, Middle and Early Modern English similarities of usage. Morphophonologically, the German compounds fall in with the Old Germanic sound pattern of initial stress. By contrast, English deviates from its normal pattern and echoes Romance final stress. Any deviation, of course, means markedness or special emphasis. Strange to say, both regular initial stress in German and irregular final stress in English suggest diverse methods of counting units. Indoor or abstract counting follows the Arabic abacus and the Romance metric system of registering from hundreds via tens to units, while outdoor or concrete tallying follows the Germanic sequence "*determinant*-and-*determinatum*". Dissimilarities and interferences of this kind do not disturb bilingual communication. For speakers of Educated English with a wide reading in historical documents, the Old Germanic word-order of "units-and-tens" as mirrored in *ein-und-zwanzig* or *neun-und-neunzig* makes Continentals appear older than their real age. "Unit-and-ten" numerals agree with the language of *Beowulf*, Chaucer, and some of the characters in Shakespeare.

To sum up the morphological findings, the loss of inflections in declension as well as in conjugation was almost total by the period of Early Modern English, whilst it has been only partial up till Present-Day German. With all consequences for globalization, the modern dissimilarities make the teaching and learning of English easier than a second-language acquisition of German. Yet unlike mere synchronics, a diachronic command of historical English can open up comparative aspects. It helps to overcome dissimilarities by finding or pointing out bygone similarities as the missing link.

8. Lexicology

Proceeding from smaller to larger units of segmentation, the survey comes to lexicology. Weighing statistics versus dynamics and constant versus variable factors, the stock and increase of lexis clearly form the most dynamic segment of all. Common origin, early evolution, and subsequent history make English and German share many inherent similarities. On the whole, a once almost pure, equal, and predominantly Germanic vocabulary in either language started to diverge over the centuries. By and by, English came to absorb an enormous number of French words compared with the modest pre-Enlightenment influx into Continental German.

With a modicum of reservation about anything too clear-cut, some seven waves of French influence can be discerned from century to century. A first wave between 1066 and 1250 brought a great many Anglo-Norman borrowings such as:

> *butler city count duke judge nephew niece parish reign servant tailor*

and the complete hierarchy of military ranks. Within two hundred years, they turned an originally homogeneous Germanic vocabulary of Saxon English into Norman English, into a heterogeneous mixture of Anglo-Saxon and Gallo-Romance. None of these early Gallicisms even entered into Middle High German.

In the same 11th and 12th centuries, a second wave of Northern French loanwords from chivalry and courtly culture described activities and instruments connected with armour, clothing, cuisine, festivals, games, hunting, jousting, society, and acquisitions such as:

armour bachelor blame chance dance danger dinner duty fashion feast gentle honour jest leisure manner mischief order supper table very virtue

A striking though quantitatively less marked similarity between English and German speaks from parallel loans. Lexemes such as

Blamage Chance Fest Manier Tournier

and morphemes such as English and German

des- dis- / Des- Dis- *-eer* / -ieren *-ery* / -erei

must have expanded from the Flemish or Lower Lotharingian Court at Ghent to the Cologne area.

A third wave occurred between 1130 and 1300 in the period of the Hanseatic League. The trading route from London via Calais, Bruges, and Antwerp to Cologne furnished English and German with French loanwords such as:

cable/Kabel *dozen*/Dutzend *fine*/fein *place*/Platz
price/Preis *profit*/Profit *sluice*/Schleuse

A fourth wave of Northern French influence between 1100 and 1400 may have reached Germany some decades in advance of England. In a complementary vein to the monastic canon of the *artes liberales* in Patristic and Scholastic days, the Talmud Torah academies founded and supervised by Rashi in the 11th and 12th centuries promoted a spiritual exchange along the eastern Moselle route from Troyes via Metz/Trier to Speyer/Worms/Main (SHUM) and vice versa. With the foundation and flourishing of universities in Western Europe, the southern Maas route from Paris and Reims via Liège or Stablo to Cologne spread thousands of French loanwords. In the 12th and 13th centuries, religious sources of inspiration radiated to Oxford and Cambridge. In Latinized or in vernacular shape, one dozen out of thousands of borrowings can demonstrate English and German equivalents such as:

> *cognition*/Kognition *definition*/Definition *essence*/Essenz *existence*/Existenz *figure*/Figur *hospital*/Hospital *justice*/Justiz *lesson*/Lektion *line*/Linie *medicine*/Medizin *session*/Session *study*/Studium *theology*/Theologie

A fifth wave in the 14th century concerned the knowledge of Central French among educated readers and speakers on insular as well as on Continental soil. The ideal of a medieval *poeta doctus* and his audience presupposed firm familiarity with French literary terms and standards:

> *cadence*/Kadenz *chronicle*/Chronik *comedy*/Komödie *elegy*/Elegie *epic* /Epik *epilogue*/Epilog *essay*/Essay *lyric*/Lyrik *miracle*/Mirakel *morality*/Moralität *mystery*/Mysterium *pause*/Pause *poet*/Poet *prologue* /Prolog *prose*/Prosa *style*/Stil *verse*/Vers

Even a fraction of evidence will suffice to demonstrate the similarity between English and German. And it does not militate against some dissimilarity either. Owing to its rather monolingual culture, Middle High German failed to bring forth three poetically polymath master poets comparable to Gower, Chaucer, and Langland.

A sixth wave in the late Tudor period 1570 to 1625, according to the recent state of research, appears to have formed the true summit of French influence. Other experts in lexicology, of course, argue that the impressions gathered stem from the growing number of publications in general as well as of dictionaries and handbooks in particular. In any case, the observation implies dissimilarity to German.

The seventh wave between 1650 and 1800 attained the highest degree of expansion, circularity, and internationality with English, French, and German original thinkers such as Descartes, Locke, Leibniz, Pope, Montesquieu, Chesterfield, Voltaire, Johnson, Hume, Frederick the Great, Kant, Lessing, Mendelssohn, and others. As a period of Rationalism and Enlightenment, it touched topics, ideas, and values of universal interest and trusted in the mediation of educated minds. In company with abstract nouns long familiar to Medieval and post-Medieval English ears, a sample catalogue reads:

autonomy compromise democracy equality federation fundamentals harmony humanity individual justice liberty literacy prejudice privilege progress realism society tolerance tyranny

With regard to surface structure, the Enlightenment or Authoritarian English wave was the first period to incorporate second-language acquisitions in their nonadapted forms, namely with foreign phonemes and accentuations as well as with foreign graphemes including diacritic marks and accents. In all similarity, English and German took over French foreign words from the fields of art, cuisine, fashion, life-style, and so forth with their originals unchanged:

beaux arts cliché comme il faut élan esprit genre œuvre on dit savoir-vivre tableau tête-à-tête vis-à-vis

Leaving the comparative aspect of French influence upon English and German, the section on vocabulary should not end without mentioning the direct exchange between the insular and the Continental Germanic sister languages. A wax-and-wane chart of English/German give-and-take shows rising/falling figures for the German influence on 18th- and 19th-century English. British dictionaries list Germanisms such as:

Abbildung Biedermeier Biergarten Bildungsroman Dankeschön Delikatessen Doppelgänger Ersatz Gemütlichkeit Gestalt Glockenspiel Götterdämmerung Heimweh Kindergarten Jugendstil Kulturkampf Lederhosen Rathaus Realpolitik Schadenfreude Sturm und Drang Umlaut Völkerwanderung Volkslied Weltanschauung Auf Wiedersehen Zeitgeist Zollverein

The low percentage of Anglicisms found in Johann Christoph Adelung's *Grammatisch-Kritisches Wörterbuch der Hochdeutschen Mundart* (1793–1801) suggests a more distanced attitude. Shortly before World War II, labels such as "Engländerei" or "Amerikafimmel" escalated into hostilities as harbingers of imminent war. After 1945, theory and practice went through prompt correction. Politics, the media, world trade, and the generation between eighteen and thirty have gained a mighty say in snatching new and foreign words.

Quite recently, the clipping-compound *Denglish* (obviously modelled on *Franglais*) as well as an ironical column of letters to the Editor of *DIE ZEIT* (March 2001, Number 11) under the title "Needen Sie Help?" leave no doubt about the latest vogue. Anglo-Americanisms in Modern German (including Austrian and Swiss German) tend to increase beyond what used to be customary.

Whosoever may really need help during her or his stay in Germany, should not hesitate to ask in English. Some aspects of the anglophile tendency do raise the question of quantity versus quality. Whilst English has acclimatized thousands of loanwords to the vernacular speech-habits, German carefully heeds the foreign surface-structures. Not seldom, it rather hatches them to the extent of its having been labelled "Imponiergehabe".

9. Syntax

Phonemes, graphemes, morphemes, and lexemes – all of them keep within the segmental structure of words. Only syntax transcends one single word for its arrangement with others. Indeed, sentences form units composed of all sorts of segments. In Indo-European and in Old Germanic verse, word-order continued to be comparatively variable. In the typological framework of Latin syntactic structures, the word-order "subject–object–predicate" or SOP had by and by reached dominant frequency. In the 2nd century AD, Apollonius Dyscolus shifted from the rhythmic pattern of poetic intonation to a rational basis of rhetorical syntax. To his mind, the word-order "subject–predicate–object" or acronymically SPO organizes things much more convincingly. The subject introduces the mental or logical foundation of a sentence. The predicate can (with or without an object) infer or deduce from it some partial aspect as a new message. So from around 400 AD onwards, medieval authors repeatedly and unanimously recommended an SP(O) word-order. A 10th-century Latin voice could still insist on the logical primacy of the substantival substance over the verb by formulating: "Omnis constructio ex substantia et actu fit". This overall formula holds good for any minimal nucleus.

In Merovingian and Carolingian days, the late Latin object-final word-order or the acronymic SPO developed into the regular Old French pattern. After the Anglo-Norman Conquest, the SPO order intruded from translations into early Middle English prose. From there, it gradually gained ground and entry to Middle English verse as a variant and ultimately as the dominant word-order as well. The transition from an etic choice between

SOP/SPO//PSO/POS//OSP/OPS

to the emic code

SPO

stands out as one of the rare dynamic changes in the history of English syntax with its normally stable and static structures. An interplay of morphological decay and syntactical restructuring must have initiated and completed the contact and influence of Anglo-Norman upon Saxon English. In contrast to Middle and Early Modern English, Middle High German, Early Modern High German, and even Modern High German have never ceased to hold on to flexible, idiomatically and stylistically conditioned subvariants. British, Irish, Scottish, American, Canadian, or Australian English visitors will soonest feel at home in Germany by recalling their university knowledge of Early Modern English with Shakespeare as a good guide. Tudor or Renaissance English still alternated between what was to remain Modern German usage and what was to become Modern English grammatical correctness. In a special liking for variety, diversity, and multiplicity, Tudor or Renaissance English tolerated a given spectrum of allosyntactic constructions. Aiming at neutrality, intersubjectivity, and interchangeability, Augustan or Authoritarian English preferred regularized and standardized patterns of utterance and language universals.

In Tudor or Renaissance English, affirmative sentences could either still vary considerably (as German syntactical patterns have done to the present day), or they could already have taken the way to stable and static structures similar to or identical with Modern English SPO:

I see him.	Ich sehe ihn.

In German, expanded structures with initial adverbs or modifying phrases will unleash an inverted word-order, which deviates from normal expectations and brings modern dissimilarity:

Yesterday, I saw him.	Gestern sah ich ihn.

In negative sentences, Early Modern English still allowed both alternative sequences, namely "predicate plus *not*" or "*do not* plus predicate". Authoritarian English decided in favour of *do not.* As another dissimilarity, Modern German has held on to "predicate plus *nicht*":

***I do not** see him.*	Ich sehe ihn **nicht**.

In questions, Elizabethan speakers could either use the simple inversion of the full verb or the periphrastic inversion with *do*. In spoken German, periphrastic *tun* 'do' does occur in children's simplifying patterns of the mother-tongue. By and by, Modern English and Modern German have ended up in total dissimilarity. English marks questions by introductory *do* in front of uninverted SPO; German marks questions by inverting the full verb patterned on the acronymic formula PSO:

Do you see him?	Siehst du ihn?

10. Synchronics via diachronics

The similarities and dissimilarities discussed in the tentative *tour d'horizon* were intended for the participants of the IAUPE Medieval Symposium in Munich on their way to the 18th IAUPE (Jubilee) Conference at Bamberg. This brief survey will (it is hoped) recall the fact that for the two Germanic sister languages a diachronic awareness can ease the cultural shock of synchronic communication, confrontation, and confusion. An academic knowledge and diachronic awareness of historical English may help as a 'simplistic' (though not quite unnatural) cure for synchronic problems. Shakespeare's Tudor or Early Modern English can be a safe guide. His similarities outweigh the present-day dissimilarities:

I doubt it not.	Ich bezweifle es nicht.
I saw him not.	Ich sah ihn nicht.
I wot not.	Ich weiß nicht.
Know you this woman?	Kennt ihr diese Frau?
What sayst thou?	Was sagst du?
What think you?	Was denkt ihr?

11. Farewell warning

This plea for historical English should certainly not close without a warning. At their return to the various destinations in English-speaking countries, the participants should forget in time about their Old, Middle, or Early Modern English. Otherwise, the Border Police or Customs Officer will suspect them of bringing in Medieval diseases or of not having set foot on their native soil since the days of *Beowulf*, Chaucer, or Shakespeare.[1]

Notes

[1] This article was also published in my collected writings, cf. Weinstock (2003: 253-59).

References

Baugh, Albert C. -- Thomas Cable
2002 *A history of the English language.* 5th edition. London: Routledge.

Böker, Uwe -- Christoph Houswitschka (eds.)
2000 *Einführung in die Anglistik und Amerikanistik.* München: Beck.

Crystal, David
1995 *The Cambridge encyclopedia of the English language.* Cambridge: Cambridge University Press.

Görlach, Manfred
2001 *Eighteenth-century English.* Sprachwissenschaftliche Studienbücher. Heidelberg: Winter.

Lehnert, Martin
1990 *Altenglisches Elementarbuch.* 10. Auflage. Sammlung Göschen 2210. Berlin: de Gruyter.

Markus, Manfred
1990 *Mittelenglisches Studienbuch.* Uni-Taschenbücher für Wissenschaft. Grosse Reihe. Tübingen: Francke.

Michael, Ian
1970 *English grammatical categories and the tradition to 1800.* Cambridge: Cambridge University Press.

Sauer, Hans
2000 "Sprachwissenschaft", in: Böker -- Houswitschka (eds.), 89–165.

Strang, Barbara M. H.
1979 *A history of English*. (2nd edition.) London: Methuen.

Weinstock, Horst
2003 *Kleine Schriften. Ausgewählte Studien zur alt-, mittel- und frühneuenglischen Sprache und Literatur*. Heidelberg: Winter.

Notes on contributors

Muhammad Abu Al-Fadl Badran, who hails from Upper Egypt, is a poet and scholar in Arabic literature with an international perspective and a comparatist outlook. He has especially strong connections with Germany, where he was a Fellow at Bonn University from 1988-1990, a Lecturer at Bochum University in 1991, and a Humboldt Fellow, once again at Bonn University, from 1994-1996. Since 1998, he has worked at the United Arab Emirates University in Al-Ain, where he was awarded the rank of Full Professor in 2005. His scholarly work covers both classical and recent Arabic writing; with regard to the latter, one of his main research interests is the appearance of the Faust motif in modern Arabic literature.

Alfred Bammesberger, born in Munich in 1938, studied English and French and Comparative Philology at the Universities of Munich and Oxford. He was a teacher in a secondary school, earned an M.A. at Yale University in 1964 and a Dr. phil. in Munich in 1965. He finished his habilitation in Freiburg in 1970. Since 1980, he has been Professor of English Linguistics at the Catholic University of Eichstätt. He is the author of many textbooks, has written a large number of learned articles, and is currently preparing an edition of Old English runic inscriptions.

Renate Bauer studied English and German at the Universities of Munich and York. She holds a PhD from the University of Munich (LMU) where she is a lecturer and teaches English linguistics, the history of the English language and medieval English literature. Her doctoral thesis *Adversus Judaeos: Juden und Judentum im Spiegel alt- und mittelenglischer Texte* was published in 2003. Articles include "Der antijüdische Diskurs im Mittelalter am Beispiel mittelenglischer Dramen und der *Prioress's Tale*"; "Opfer 'christlicher' Gewalt: Juden in Texten des englischen Mittelalters"; "'Lord Castlereagh moved ... Mr. Ponsonby objected': Parliamentary debates of the early 19th century".

Claire Fennell was awarded an MA in Romance Philology at Bologna University and a PhD in Comparative Medieval Literature at the Hebrew University of Jerusalem after she had graduated from Oxford (Italian and German). She has taught Old and Middle English at Bologna University. She has worked, first as assistant and then as director, in the Italian Cultural Institutes of Munich, Addis Ababa and Krakow. At present, she teaches Old English at Trieste University. She has edited and translated the Middle English debate poem *The owl and the nightingale* and the romance *Sir Tristrem*. Currently, she is working on an unpublished Middle English version of the so-called *Statuta angliae antiqua*. Articles include “Did the *anhaga* swim home? The case of Beowulf and the anonymous hero of Exeter Book, folios 76^{v}-78^{r}”; “A note on *The owl and the nightingale*, lines 427-8”; “Hodain and the love potion”; “‘Com natura libidinis perversitate polluitur:’ *The owl and the nightingale*, lines 1377-86”; “MSS Rm and SP of Eilhart von Oberge’s Tristrant, ll. 1672-3”; “A fifteenth century baker’s price-list: MS Douce Charters a 1, no. 62”.

Carol V. Kaske earned her PhD at the Johns Hopkins University. She is Professor of English Emerita at Cornell University, where she has taught since 1964 and continues to teach. She is the widow of Robert E. Kaske and has one child, Richard J. Kaske. She is the author of one book, *Spenser and biblical poetics*; has edited two, *Marsilio Ficino: Three books on life* (with John R. Clark, which she has also translated), and *Edmund Spenser, Faerie Queene, Book One*; published about 30 articles, mostly on Edmund Spenser, but also on medieval authors such as Dante and Chaucer. Articles include “Mount Sinai” and “Dante’s mount purgatory”; “The audiences of *The Faerie Queene*”; and “Spenser’s *Amoretti* and *Epithalamion*: A psalter of love.”

Ian Kirby has recently retired as Professor of Medieval English Language and Literature at the University of Lausanne, Switzerland, where he taught the whole range of Old and Middle English literature and the History of the English language. Prior to this, he taught at the University of Uppsala, and was the first Professor of English at the University of Iceland. His principal publications include books and articles on Bible quotation in, and translation into, Old Norse, but he has also published articles etc. on medieval English subjects, and on Shakespeare. He was President of IAUPE in the years 1986-89 and organised the 14th conference of the Association at the University of Lausanne in August 1989. Since 1995, he has been Secretary-General and Treasurer of the Association.

Patrizia Lendinara is Full Professor of Germanic Philology at the University of Palermo and Dean of her Faculty. She has published on Old English language and literature, particularly on the literary relationships and on the linguistic interferences between the Latin and the Germanic world. She has written several essays on Old Frisian, Gothic and Medieval Latin literature. She has also published on modern English literature, specifically on Hilda Doolittle, and on the history of English language. Part of her work on glosses, both in Latin and the vernacular, dating from the Anglo-Saxon period has been republished by the Variorum in *Anglo-Saxon glosses and glossaries* (1999). Her present research work focuses on literature and iconography of the Marvels of the East in Anglo-Saxon England and its sources. She is a member of the editorial board of *Anglo-Saxon England* (Cambridge) and *NOWELE* (Odense), and she was president of the Associazione Italiana di Filologia Germanica and the International Society of Anglo-Saxonists.

Conrad Lindberg, born 2 August 1924, PhD (Stockholm) 1959, docent (ibid.) 1961-67, lecturer (Linköping) 1967-74, professor (Trondheim) 1974-89, retired (Linköping) 1989-. Publications: *MS Bodley 959. Genesis-Baruch 3.20 in the earlier version of the Wycliffite Bible* (5 vols.); *MS Christ Church 145* (continuation in 3 vols.); *The Middle English Bible (Prefatory epistle of St. Jerome, The book of Baruch, The book of Judges)*; *English Wyclif tracts* (1-3 and 4-6); *King Henry's Bible: The revised version of the Wyclif Bible* (4 vols.).

Manfred Malzahn was born in the Federal Republic of Germany in 1955. He studied English and German Literature and Linguistics at the University of Bochum from 1974, and he obtained his PhD from the University of Wuppertal in 1983, presenting a thesis on aspects of identity in the contemporary Scottish novel. After national service with the Goethe Institute, he joined the Department of German at Edinburgh University in Scotland, and then went on to teach in English Departments in Tunisia, Algeria, Malawi, and Taiwan. He is currently Professor of English Literature at the United Arab Emirates University.

Manfred Markus is Full Professor of English linguistics and medieval English literature at the University of Innsbruck. With a strong background in the studies of English and American literature, he has, for the last twenty-five years, focused his academic interests on historical English, contrastive and corpus linguistics. His publications include a bilingual edition of *Sir Gawain and the Green Knight*, a *Mittelenglisches Studienbuch*, and a large number of articles on historical English linguistics. He is general co-editor of the book series *Austrian Studies* (formerly *Wiener Beiträge zur englischen Philologie*). As a corpus linguist, he has compiled the *Innsbruck Corpus of Middle English Prose*, the *Innsbruck Letter Corpus* and a corpus of 18th- and 19th-century German schoolbooks of English (HEDGEHOGS). In his present research, he is particularly interested in historical English phraseology and idioms.

Saara Nevanlinna was professor of English Philology at the University of Helsinki, from where she retired in 1984. Her fields of interest are the history of English, Middle English, and manuscript studies. Apart from a number of articles, she has published the following books: *The northern homily cycle: The* *expanded version in MSS Harley 4196 and Cotton Tiberius E vii* (1972-84), and, together with Irma Taavitsainen, *St. Katherine of Alexandria: The late ME prose legend in Southwell MS 7* (1993).

Michiko Ogura is Professor of English at Chiba University, Japan. Her field of interest lies in medieval English, especially in Old and Middle English syntax and word study. Her publications include *The syntactic and semantic rivalry of QUOTH, SAY and TELL in medieval English* (1981), *Old English 'impersonal' verbs and expressions* (1986), *Verbs with the reflexive pronoun and constructions with SELF in Old and early Middle English* (1989), *Verbs in medieval English: Differences in verb choice in verse and prose* (1995) and *Verbs of motion in medieval English* (2002).

Saburo Oka was born in 1929. He is Professor Emeritus of English and Comparative Literature at Aoyana-Gakuin University, Tokyo. He was vice-president (1993-94) and president (1995-96) of the Japan Society for Medieval English Language and Literature. He has published a number of books, e.g. a Japanese translation of Chaucer's *Troilus and Criseyde* (2005) as vol. 4 of The Trojan Story Series; *Studies in Sôseki-Natsumé*, 3 vols.; *An introduction to comparative narratology of medieval literature; Researches in English medieval and modern literature*; a Japanese translation with notes and introduction of Wordsworth's *Prelude*.

Hans Sauer is Full Professor of English Language and Medieval English Literature at the University of Munich. He has also taught at the universities of Eichstätt, Würzburg, Dresden and Innsbruck, as well as at Brno, Columbus (Ohio State University), Lodz, Palermo, and Venice. He was president of the International Society of Anglo-Saxonists. For IAUPE, he organized the Medieval Symposium in Munich in 2001 and the Middle English Section in Vancouver in 2004. His publications include *Theodulfi Capitula in England* [Latin and Old English] (1978), *The owl and the nightingale* [Middle English and German] (1983), *Nominalkomposita im Frühmittelenglischen* (1992) as well as numerous articles, entries in handbooks and dictionaries, and reviews. He was an author and co-editor of the *Lexikon des Mittelalters* (1977-1999), and he is co-editor of *Anglia* (1996-), *Middle English Texts* (MET; 2000-), and *Texte und Untersuchungen zur Englischen Philologie* (TUEPh; 2000-).

Liliana Sikorska, professor of English literature and head of the Department of English Literature and Literary Linguistics at the School of English, Adam Mickiewicz University, Poznań, Poland, is the author of several books and numerous articles on medieval English literature, primarily on drama and medieval mystical culture. Her books include among others *In a manner of morall playe: Social ideology(s) in English moralities and moral interludes* (2002), and *An outline history of English literature.* (2nd edition, 2002). She edited *Aspects of suffering: Classical motifs in the literature of English* (2003), *Ironies of Art/Tragedies of life: Essays in Irish literature* (2004), and *A universe of (hi)story: Essays on J.M. Coetzee* (2005). Besides, she is co-editor of the series Medieval English Mirror. Liliana Sikorska was a visiting scholar at the University of Florida (Gainesville), University of California at Los Angeles, Brown University (Providence), and the American University (Washington, DC).

Michael W. Twomey is Professor of English at Ithaca College. His most recent publications are: "Editing *De proprietatibus rerum*, Book XIV, from the sources" (2005); "Reading Chaucer's Latin aloud" (2005); "The *Gawain*-poet" (2005). Currently, he is producing a reception study of medieval encyclopedias in England and is part of an international collaboration, based in Münster and Orléans, to edit the *De proprietatibus rerum* of Bartholomeus Anglicus.

Horst Weinstock studied English, French, and Philosophy at the universities of Mainz and Munich from 1949 to 1954. He continued and completed his postgraduate and doctoral studies in Munich, receiving his PhD in 1957 and assisting at Munich University for a postdoctoral period. From 1961 until the habilitation in 1970, he lectured at the University of the Saar in Saarbrücken. He has since been teaching English Historical Linguistics and Medieval Literature as Professor (Emeritus 1996-) at Aachen University of Technology. His publications include *Die Funktion elisabethanischer Sprichwörter und Pseudosprichwörter bei Shakespeare* (1957/1966), *Mittelenglisches Elementarbuch* (1968), *Die englische Literatur in Text und Darstellung*, vol. 2: *16. Jahrhundert* (1984), *Kleine Schriften* (2003), and the editorship of *English and American Studies in German* (1983-2005).

Studies in English Medieval Language and Literature

Edited by Jacek Fisiak

- Vol. 1 Dieter Kastovsky / Arthur Mettinger (eds.): Language Contact in the History of English. 2nd, revised edition. 2003.
- Vol. 2 Studies in English Historical Linguistics and Philology. A Festschrift for Akio Oizumi. Edited by Jacek Fisiak. 2002.
- Vol. 3 Liliana Sikorska: *In a Manner Morall Playe*: Social Ideologies in English Moralities and Interludes (1350-1517). 2002.
- Vol. 4 Peter J. Lucas / Angela M. Lucas (eds.): Middle English from Tongue to Text. Selected Papers from the Third International Conference on Middle English: Language and Text, held at Dublin, Ireland, 1-4 July 1999. 2002.
- Vol. 5 Chaucer and the Challenges of Medievalism. Studies in Honor of H. A. Kelly. Edited by Donka Minkova and Theresa Tinkle. 2003.
- Vol. 6 Hanna Rutkowska: Graphemics and Morphosyntax in the *Cely Letters* (1472-88). 2003.
- Vol. 7 The *Ancrene Wisse.* A Four-Manuscript Parallel Text. Preface and Parts 1-4. Edited by Tadao Kubouchi and Keiko Ikegami with John Scahill, Shoko Ono, Harumi Tanabe, Yoshiko Ota, Ayako Kobayashi and Koichi Nakamura. 2003.
- Vol. 8 Joanna Bugaj: Middle Scots Inflectional System in the South-west of Scotland. 2004.
- Vol. 9 Rafal Boryslawski: The Old English Riddles and the Riddlic Elements of Old English Poetry. 2004.
- Vol. 10 Nikolaus Ritt / Herbert Schendl (eds.): Rethinking Middle English. Linguistic and Literary Approaches. 2005.
- Vol. 11 The *Ancrene Wisse.* A Four-Manuscript Parallel Text. Parts 5–8 with Wordlists. Edited by Tadao Kubouchi and Keiko Ikegami with John Scahill, Shoko Ono, Harumi Tanabe, Yoshiko Ota, Ayako Kobayashi, Koichi Nakamura. 2005.
- Vol. 12 Text and Language in Medieval English Prose. A Festschrift for Tadao Kubouchi. Edited by Akio Oizumi, Jacek Fisiak and John Scahill. 2005.
- Vol. 13 Michiko Ogura (ed.): Textual and Contextual Studies in Medieval English. Towards the Reunion of Linguistics and Philology. 2006.
- Vol. 14 Keiko Hamaguchi: Non-European Women in Chaucer. A Postcolonial Study. 2006.
- Vol. 15 Ursula Schaefer (ed.): The Beginnings of Standardization. Language and Culture in Fourteenth-Century England. 2006.
- Vol. 16 Nikolaus Ritt / Herbert Schendl / Christiane Dalton-Puffer / Dieter Kastovsky (eds): Medieval English and its Heritage. Structure, Meaning and Mechanisms of Change. 2006.
- Vol. 17 Matylda Włodarczyk: Pragmatic Aspects of Reported Speech. The Case of Early Modern English Courtroom Discourse. 2006.
- Vol. 18 Hans Sauer / Renate Bauer (eds.): *Beowulf* and Beyond. 2007.

Peter Lang · Europäischer Verlag der Wissenschaften

Keiko Hamaguchi

Non-European Women in Chaucer

A Postcolonial Study

Frankfurt am Main, Berlin, Bern, Bruxelles, New York, Oxford, Wien, 2006.
IX, 194 pp.
Studies in English medieval language and literature. Edited by Jacek Fisiak.
Vol. 14
ISBN 3-631-55057-X / US-ISBN 0-8204-9875-0 · pb. € 39.–*

Since Jeffrey Jerome Cohen edited *The Postcolonial Middle Ages* in 2000, some scholars have applied postcolonial criticism to the study of the Middle Ages. However, even in postcolonial studies of Chaucer, the role of non-European women in his work has not yet been fully discussed. Using postcolonial theory, the author explores how Chaucer represents non-European women, his Others both in gender and in culture. Her examination of non-European women in his work from a non-Westerner's point of view reveals that his representation is complicated and ambivalent, showing diverse views. The ambivalence in Chaucer reflects his own complicated position as courtier, soldier, minor diplomat, controller of customs and poet, and also the fourteenth century's historical background and attitude.

Aus dem Inhalt: The Resistance of the Syrian Mother-in-law in the *Man of the Law's Tale* · Canacee's Problematic Marriage in the *Squire's Tale* · The Colonization of Dido · Domesticating Amazons in the *Knight's Tale* · Transgressing the Borderline of Gender: Zenobia in the *Monk's Tale*

MLR Press Authors

Featuring a roll call of some of the best writers of gay erotica and mysteries today!

Derek Adams
Z. Allora
Maura Anderson
Simone Anderson
Victor J. Banis
Laura Baumbach
Helen Beattie
Ally Blue
J.P. Bowie
Barry Brennessel
Nowell Briscoe
Jade Buchanan
James Buchanan
TA Chase
Charlie Cochrane
Karenna Colcroft
Michael G. Cornelius
Jamie Craig
Ethan Day
Diana DeRicci
Vivien Dean
Taylor V. Donovan
Theo Fenraven
S.J. Frost
Kimberly Gardner
Michael Gouda
Kaje Harper
Alex Ironrod
AC Katt
Thomas Kearnes
Sasha Keegan
Kiernan Kelly
K-lee Klein
Geoffrey Knight
Christopher Koehler
Matthew Lang
J.L. Langley
Vincent Lardo
Cameron Lawton
Anna Lee
Elizabeth Lister
Clare London
William Maltese
Z.A. Maxfield
Timothy McGivney
Tere Michaels
AKM Miles
Robert Moore
Reiko Morgan
Jet Mykles
William Neale
N.J. Nielsen
Cherie Noel
Gregory L. Norris
Willa Okati
Erica Pike
Neil S. Plakcy
Rick R. Reed
A.M. Riley
AJ Rose
Rob Rosen
George Seaton
Riley Shane
Jardonn Smith
DH Starr
Richard Stevenson
Liz Strange
Marshall Thornton
Lex Valentine
Haley Walsh
Mia Watts
Missy Welsh
Ryal Woods
Stevie Woods
Lance Zarimba
Mark Zubro

Check out titles, both available and forthcoming, at
www.mlrpress.com

Ten years and many boyfriends later, Cassidy Winters finally returns to the ancestral home of his grandmother, Sadie Hart, despite the best efforts of his father to prevent it. Cassidy's plans of a quiet, seaside ceremony to wish a final farewell to Sadie quickly unravel as interruptions run roughshod beginning with Neil who walks out of the ocean and straight into Cassidy's bed. The dominos topple one by one when the little dog he rescues from the hounds of hell brings him to Ben, the hunky vet who rescues Cassidy right back. News of his arrival spreads faster than Cassidy's legs, bringing his boyhood friend and first love Nate Sommers to his doorstep – leaving Cassidy spiraling into a multi-layered love snafu. As if the island wasn't getting crowded enough for Cassidy's good taste and bad decisions, best friends Ollie and Spencer arrive in time to witness the uninvited return of Cassidy's most recent ex, Teddy, who's refusing to stay dumped.

Fists fly and all hell breaks loose amid mojitos and martinis as Cassidy finds himself planning a huge party to celebrate Sadie's life. Accusations are aimed as arguments and libidos boil over, but even through the chaos Cassidy knows exactly what he wants. While he's certainly willing, he isn't sure if he's ready or able for love and life...At Pipers Point.

At Piper's Point

Ethan Day

mlrpress
www.mlrpress.com

Published by
MLR Press, LLC
3052 Gaines Waterport Rd.
Albion, NY 14411

Visit ManLoveRomance Press, LLC on the Internet:
www.mlrpress.com

Cover Art by Deana Jamroz
Editing by Kris Jacen

Print ISBN# 978-1-60820-666-7
Issued 2012

For my Grams, who taught me everything I know about strength of character.

A very special Thank You to Cherie, Pati, Ro, & Maxwell for being my extra sets of eyes.

A more personal story for me - my heartfelt gratitude goes out to Kris, Laura, and everyone else at MLR Press for releasing the paperback edition of At Piper's Point.

Chapter One

Cassidy peered up out the windshield to discover he was parked in front of Sadie's shack. He sat there as if he'd fallen into a trance at some point over the five-hour road trip, unable to recall when it was he'd pulled off the road onto the private drive. He stared at the house, a combination of neoclassical and Colonial Revival architecture, and his heart sank as he noticed the olive green paint.

The house at Piper's Point, a two-and-a-half-story Foursquare, had been built in 1901 by Sadie's father. It had always been white, gleaming in the sunlight like a beacon. It wasn't even that he disliked the color. The house just wasn't the way he remembered it, and his memories were all that he'd had to hold on to for so long. A little sting ripped through his gut, and he wondered for a moment if someone had intentionally wanted to make him aware of how much time had passed—that life had gone on without him.

Most, if not all, of the really *good* memories Cassidy had growing up occurred during the summers he'd spent here in this house with his grandmother. Ever since the judge had declared Sadie's will valid, the pull of her home had tugged at him all the way from Chapel Hill. He'd waited until the end of the semester to make the trip, since he'd missed enough work over the past year due to his legal troubles.

Cassidy surveyed the exterior, the railings, and square tapered columns that framed the covered porch and supported the second-story open balcony. The only things missing were the large ferns Sadie always had hanging from the porch. He'd expected the place to be in much worse shape. He opened the door and listened to the familiar crunch of the gravel drive under his feet as he got out of the car.

While the wood lap siding and shutters were freshly painted, all the trim around the windows and the posts and beams was newly scraped, waiting for a fresh coat. A large dormer jutted out of the bell-cast hip roof that made up the attic. When he'd been little, the windows seemed like eyes to him. This place had felt alive to him back then, but now it seemed like another house altogether—a stranger.

He thought about Sadie for a moment, remembering he should go through that attic and see what, if anything, he might be able to turn over to the island historical society. He grinned, realizing he was totally hoping he might be able to buy his way back into the good graces of some of the elders that way. It was very pessimistic of him, a quality he'd come to cling to the way a toddler clutches his binky.

"Marianne must've had someone over to work on the exterior," Cassidy said, noticing the shrubs that surrounded the foundation on each side were trimmed and the sidewalk free of any debris. He shook his head, wondering why he was standing there talking to himself.

He could smell the freshly cut grass, and it dawned on him that had he arrived any earlier, his brilliant idea to stop in Corolla to buy supplies and groceries so he could hide out until his friends arrived at the end of the week would have all been for nothing. He took one last look at the house as he climbed back into the car.

The only person he'd spoken to since the court ruling had been Marianne Abbott. She was pretty much the only island Realtor and property manager, so she was who he'd called to get the house back in order. He'd definitely be having a word with her over this paint color. He had half a mind to insist she have the damned thing repainted. He closed the door and pulled around to the back side of the house, which was only visible from the beach.

He'd pull the car into one of the detached garage spaces later, ensuring he'd be able to fly under the radar and keep himself out of sight for the next five days. He unloaded his bags and provisions from the car and placed it all on the screened-in back porch next to the door. When he finished, he stood there, key in hand, but unable to make himself open it. As if being pulled back in time, Cassidy was once again like a teenager, dripping wet from the ocean, feet encrusted with sand, about to head inside for a large glass of Natalie's freshly brewed sweet tea.

Natalie had been like a second mother to him, as well as Sadie's best friend and housekeeper. He said them in that order, because to Sadie, that had been the order of their importance.

Cassidy took a deep breath, trying his best to blink back the burning in his eyes, desperately wishing he could once again bound through the door, listening to Sadie laugh as Natalie screamed, "*You boys get off my clean floor with your sandy feet!*" What he wouldn't give to find Sadie on the other side, her dyed dark red hair loosely bound with tendrils winding down her bare shoulder, one of the caftans she liked to wear having slipped down to expose it as she delicately held a lit cigarette in one hand and a glass of wine in the other.

Cassidy propped himself up against the back door for balance, losing the battle as a tear rolled down his cheek. He smiled, remembering her light rolling laughter, the joy it would always bring to those who were around to hear it, and that gave him the lift he required to continue.

He wiped his cheek on his shoulder as he pushed the key into the lock, feeling the notches grab slightly as it slid farther in. He took a deep breath and unlocked the door, pushing it open. For months, he'd been hoping to lay the last of his ghosts to rest once he arrived back at the Point. As he stood there, hovering in the doorway, he couldn't quite shake the feeling he risked waking up the ones he'd thought to have already rid himself of.

His mind flooded with memories as he breathed in the familiar light scent of jasmine from Sadie's favorite perfume, the mustiness that comes from old woodwork, pine-scented cleaner all mixed together with the salty sea air, telling him he was back, for better or worse.

Cassidy was back at Piper's Point.

§ § §

After Cassidy had finished unpacking the groceries, his clothes, and his toiletries, he went about the house, opening up all the windows not visible from the driveway. He'd noticed water sitting in the bottom of the large porcelain apron sink and wondered if Natalie had been coming to the house. He wasn't sure if Marianne had informed her he'd be arriving sometime this month, or if Natalie had kept a key and had been taking care of the place all these years—which was more than likely the case, considering Natalie wouldn't allow any old judge to scare her away.

Cassidy had been devastated when the judge ordered the property vacated until the legal matters had been settled. It had been an all-new low for him, as it had been her home for more years than it had Cassidy's. He thought it was wrong to force her to leave. Of course no one had believed it would take as long as it had to settle the will, and it shouldn't have.

Cassidy gave his father's lawyers credit for having strung things out for so many years. He suspected they were trying to wait him out, assuming he'd run out of money or tire of fighting Lionel and just give up. Lionel didn't have too high an opinion of Cassidy; that much was true. Fortunately, the feeling was mutual, so it was the one thing he wasn't losing any sleep over.

His mother didn't share her husband's opinion of their son but had never been much of an ally to him either. Lillian Winters seemed constantly irritated with her one and only son for whatever reason, as if it were all his fault for not playing along. It stung that she never had his back, as if what was good for the family should be good enough for Cassidy. He should just swallow whatever crap Lionel wanted to feed him and smile like an obedient little pod person.

The only room he'd avoided for the bulk of the day was Sadie's. But he finally ran out of chores, and when he couldn't procrastinate any longer, he walked up the stairs for the hundredth time that afternoon, this time stopping in front of the closed door to her bedroom.

He wrapped his fingers around the ornate polished-brass

doorknob and slowly pushed the door open. Sunlight poured into the room from the two large windows and the single French door that led out onto the second-story balcony and out over the front of the property. It appeared deceptively cheerful to the naked eye, but Cassidy could feel Sadie's absence acutely, as if someone had sucked all the oxygen out of the room.

The disturbingly cheerful yellow floral wallpaper had browned slightly from the flood of natural light it had been exposed to over the years. The deco-era bedroom set, specifically the vanity, appeared incredibly lonely, sitting there as if awaiting the return of their mistress. Dust floated through the light as he let his gaze wander around the room. Everything was laid out the way he imagined it had been since the last time Sadie had breezed through the room. Cassidy exhaled, realizing he'd been holding his breath, and he suddenly felt like Howard Carter opening Tutankhamen's tomb for the first time.

He cringed, remembering her vanity, and realized she'd be none too pleased over the mummy reference. *Sorry beautiful.*

Her vintage black velvet dressing gown lay draped across the upholstered chair that sat in the corner next to the closet door. The items on her vanity sat undisturbed, the sterling-silver comb and brush waiting as if she might come into the room any minute humming some song she couldn't fully remember despite having its melody stuck in her head.

The scent of jasmine hung a little heavier in the air in this room, and he closed his eyes for a moment, imagining he could hear her giggle as the gazillion gold bracelets she loved to pile on each wrist made that clinking sound that alerted anyone she was headed their direction.

He laughed a little, thinking about those bracelets, the way he'd loved the noise as a small child, only to despise it in his early teens—slightly embarrassed by the excess—eventually becoming grateful around the time he hit seventeen, as it signaled the alarm when he and Nate would be in his bedroom, tongues shoved into each other's mouth while they gave each other handjobs.

Cassidy had been too afraid to ask Marianne about Nate. Nate was not only a walking wet dream, like a young Robert Redford; as Natalie's son, he'd practically been like an older brother to Cassidy when they were little.

With his floppy blond hair blowing in the breeze, that dark, tanned skin, wide chest, and narrow hips Nate used to drive Cassidy to the brink of distraction. He'd spent hours mesmerized by the way the corners of Nate's bright blue eyes crinkled up when he smiled.

Cassidy walked over to her bed, sat down, and ran his fingertips over the little knobs of yarn that created the three-dimensional pattern on her bedspread. Nate was likely hell and gone from Hart's Island by now. He lay back on the bed and then rolled onto his side, pressing his face into the mattress, breathing in the scent.

"I fucking miss you, Sadie." He curled his legs up, wrapping his arms around them, going into a fetal position. There was no one else that would ever love him the way she had, which left him feeling empty and alone—like an orphan.

Cassidy rolled onto his back and stared up at the ceiling, wide-eyed, as it fully sank in that he was truly alone.

He recalled the delight he'd always experienced being here with Sadie and the dread that came over him every year as the summer came to a close, signifying he'd have to return home to his parents. He could practically hear the music as if it was straining to pierce through the passages of time, pulling him backward to when he was a child.

§ § §

"You'll never be truly alone as long as I'm around, kiddo," Sadie said, reaching over and ruffling his hair with her fingers.

Cassidy fell back onto her bed. The record player was spinning around as Doris Day belted out the lyrics of "Again," backed up by a big-band orchestra. He was miserable because the summer was almost over. "Why can't I just stay here with you, Grandma?"

"Because your father would never allow it, Cass." Sadie turned back, examining herself intently in the mirror. "And don't call me Grandma."

"Sorry." Cassidy moped as he watched her sweep up several chunky fistfuls of hair before shoving in a jeweled comb that miraculously held it all in place. "It's just not fair, damn it."

Sadie spun around to face him. "Listen here, kid. We'll have none of that kind of talk." She turned back to her reflection. "Christ Almighty, you go home speaking like that, and I'll never see hide nor hair of you again. I can hear your sanctimonious father already." Sadie picked up a tube of lipstick, then went about painting her lips a rich deep red. "He's eleven years old and cursing like a heathen. I knew allowing him to spend time with you would be a mistake."

Cassidy frowned, knowing full well his father was likely to say exactly that. "It's just…" Cassidy sat up, staring down at the floor feeling embarrassed. "I like it here better…than back home."

He didn't want to tell her that the other kids back in Charlotte didn't like him all that much. He was embarrassed enough admitting to himself that he had no real friends. At least none like Nate. The kids he went to school with were mean, to him and to one another. How could he admit to her, of all people, that being here on Hart's was the only time he didn't feel lonely? Everyone loved Sadie, and they all seemed to love him too because he was hers. He never had anything like that at home.

He rarely saw his parents, who were always traveling or going to stupid parties and charity events. He didn't understand why his own mother cared more about other people's kids than she did him. He didn't know how to make her love him more. He tried being good, doing everything he'd been told, but it had never been enough. He hated his father for always trying to keep him away from Sadie.

"I love having you here too, baby boy." Sadie watched him intently through the reflection in the mirror. "You're the kind of boy I always imagined I'd have."

Cassidy nodded, thinking she seemed a little sad as well. Nate stuck his head into the doorway.

"Quit your bellyaching, doofus." Nate grinned tauntingly. "Let's go outside and do something."

"Code for get into massive amounts of trouble," Sadie winked while attempting to appear disapproving.

Cassidy sneered. "Bite me, Floppy."

Nate smiled all toothy and then started gnashing his teeth as though he was ready to make good on his threat and cannibalize Cassidy.

Cassidy sprang up off the bed, taking off after Nate, who let out a whooping noise before tearing down the stairs.

Sadie laughed, cackling away as Natalie started screaming for the boys to stop making such a ruckus. Cassidy stopped just before exiting the room. He glanced over at Sadie, smiling sweetly. "You sure are pretty…Grandma."

She picked up a comb and chucked it at him as he ducked out of the room and down the stairs while she screamed, "Rotten boy!"

§ § §

Cassidy stepped out of the shower; the scalding-hot water had helped to loosen his tight, achy muscles from the stress of the long drive. He opened the small window to allow the steamed heat to escape.

He began to towel himself off as he went back to stand in front of the vanity, running his hands through his thick, black, damp hair, which had a slight wave as it cascaded down, feathering across the back of his neck.

Cassidy was tall and lean, with a naturally dark complexion that made his sharp, angled features more masculine, like those of a European fashion model. He slipped on the thick black-framed glasses, which gave him an air of approachability he might not have otherwise had.

Cassidy had been acutely aware he was more to his students than a mere teacher. It was well known all over campus that he was starring in every coed's erotic fantasy and erecting more wood than Habitat for Humanity with regard to the homo student body. It wasn't something he encouraged in any way; it merely was the way of things and had been every bit as much of a hindrance as it had been an asset to him. The other professors and grad students in his department constantly gave him shit about it, as if he could never really be taken seriously due to the reaction he tended to elicit.

He was aware from a very young age that others had a tendency to stare when he came into a room. It unnerved him as a child, and he'd been a late bloomer in terms of sexual development, lacking the sophistication to understand the nuances of lust and desire until his midteens. In the moneyed world of his parents, rife with jealousy and envy, he either inspired hatred from some or festered false adoration from others who only wanted whatever they perceived he could give them.

He'd learned trust wasn't something to be offered with abandon, not to friends, colleagues, and especially not lovers.

He did his best not to dwell on those years and was thankful he'd had his summers on Hart's, as they provided him with solid examples of what friendship was truly meant to be. It made all the posers that much easier to spot, standing out much like plastic pink flamingos would on the well-manicured grounds of his father's estate.

He was a little on the thin side, with a wide, square chest and a long torso. His long legs and arms held a grace of fluidity about them that made one unable to imagine he'd ever gone through an awkward prepubescent phase. His hands were well manicured, with long fingers that might have been considered delicate had it not been for the knobbiness of the joints.

People were drawn to him in much the same way they had been to Sadie. She'd possessed an energy or electricity that subconsciously drew others to her. People often said they were energized, if not altogether excited, by her presence.

He exited the bathroom and strolled into the bedroom, grabbing the black briefs he'd tossed on the bed when unpacking his clothes earlier. Pausing for a moment, he stared at them curiously as he started to put them on, then glanced around the room. He shrugged and tossed them back onto the bed, wondering who the hell he was covering up for, before turning to exit the room.

Naked, Cassidy came down the stairs, passed the living room and the formal dining room, listening to the wood floors creaking under his feet. Almost strange, walking around the shack in the buff, and he enjoyed the wickedness, feeling as if he was doing something illicit.

He shook his head, irritated by the cluster fuck of different styles of furniture and periods of antiques. The living areas looked more like antique stores than cohesive rooms that flowed from any sort of design scheme. Sadie gave a whole new meaning to the word *eclectic*. She was a clutter bug, and despite the fact there were a lot of beautiful pieces of furniture within these walls, Cassidy had never believed that just because something was an antique meant it needed to be crammed in somewhere to be displayed.

He made his way down the center hall toward the kitchen. The house already seemed less stifling, thanks to the windows he'd opened, bringing in the light breeze coming off the Atlantic and invigorating the interior. The fresh air chilled his bare skin slightly as the mid-May temperature outside still sat in the low seventies.

He entered the kitchen—oddly, the largest room in the entire house. He thought it humorous, considering Sadie could barely boil water. He laughed, remembering her telling him not to be a little smart-ass whenever he reminded her of that fact.

"*I didn't build the place. My father did*," she would always say. "*My mother wanted it this way.*"

A package sat on the huge island that Sadie had had installed back in the midnineties when she renovated the entire kitchen. Cassidy stood there, inspecting the white cabinets, thinking they were already a little dated. His gaze landed back on the package, and he let out a long sigh before walking past it and around the far side of the island.

He passed the small table and chairs that sat nestled up to the upholstered bench tucked into the small breakfast nook in the corner. He and Nate had eaten most of their meals there, with Sadie and Natalie yapping away as they stood around the island.

Removing the bottle of Stoli he'd shoved in the freezer earlier, he emptied a liberal amount into the glass, listening to the ice make crackling sounds. Placing the bottle back into the icy depths that now sat nearly empty compared to the days when Natalie ruled the roost, he kicked the door shut before picking up his drink. Cassidy took a sip from the glass and closed his eyes momentarily, enjoying the burn trickling down his chest. Eyeing the package again, he then turned to glance out the back door toward the empty beach below. He took another drink, concentrating on the blue water that appeared to endlessly stretch out across the horizon, bringing with it a sense of his own insignificance in the world. Strangely enough, he found comfort from that realization.

He set the glass down, removed a knife from the butcher block, took hold of the box, and sliced through the tape before pausing to take another sip from the glass. He let out an appreciative grunt and proceeded to unfold the top of the box. He removed a few fistfuls of shredded paper before reaching down into the box and removing a shiny silver urn.

He stood there, silently holding it for a few moments before tucking the urn under an arm, yelping when the cold metal made contact with his sensitive skin. He cursed under his breath from the shock as he grabbed the glass and headed for the back door.

Coming out onto the screened-in porch, Cassidy paused for a moment before opening the cabinet next to the door and removing a beach towel, thankful they hadn't been packed away. He sniffed it, deciding it didn't smell the least bit musty, as he pushed the screen door open with his foot. He crossed the paved courtyard and made his way down the slight hill, bare feet padding across the stone steps until he reached the sand.

The beach stretched out toward the west, the rolling dunes

covered in sea oats and American beach grass forming a barrier between the ocean and the tree line. The woods and the natural curve of the shoreline created the private oasis that was Piper's Point. Once he decided on a worthy spot, Cassidy leaned over, placing the urn into the sand, then spread out the towel before squatting down, taking care not to spill any of his drink. He shook his head, thinking he was getting old after hearing his knees pop.

The sun felt incredible, warming his naked skin, though he began to wish he'd had the foresight to bring sunglasses. He scanned the horizon, seeing a few boats off in the distance as he lifted his glass and chugged the remaining vodka. The ice cubes poked into his lips as they tried to escape the glass.

He placed a hand on the urn, patting it as he laid back, stretching out onto the towel on his back. Cassidy smiled at the urn and then squinted up at the sky before shutting his eyes. "Welcome home, Sadie."

Chapter Two

Cassidy groaned as something wet and cold dripped onto his stomach. His eyes jerked open as a man spoke.

"I said hello," the man repeated as Cassidy squinted, holding a hand up in an attempt to ascertain who was speaking.

He forced a grin, not unimpressed by the hunky guy standing over him in a wet suit that was rolled down to his waist. He was holding goggles and a snorkel in one hand and a set of flippers in the other. His dark brown hair was wet, and water rolled down his neck and chest. He looked a little like Josh Hartnett, on the more slender side, but his arms and shoulders were well muscled. Cassidy realized the stranger was leering at him in a most familiar way.

"What you got in the container?" he asked with a cheeky smile and overt come-hither expression.

"My granny," Cassidy said in a slightly sarcastic tone, and propped himself up by his elbows. He laughed, imagining he could hear Sadie yelling at him to stop calling her Granny. "This is a private beach, you know."

"I did indeed know that." He grinned wider, nudging as if to draw Cassidy's attention toward his feet. "Though I must say you don't *seem* unhappy to see me."

Cassidy was a bit confused for a moment, feeling his eyes widen as he peeked down to see his hard cock, pointing up at him like a long spear over his belly.

"Jesus," he said, flinging sand into the air as he tried to cover himself with his hands.

The sexy interloper laughed as Cassidy sat up, grabbing the urn and placing it between his legs.

"Hardly an appropriate place to put Granny," he said.

Cassidy climbed to his feet, scowling at him as he snatched

the towel up out of the sand and wrapped it around his waist while juggling the urn.

"Who the hell are you?" he asked, using the urn to once again camouflage his rapidly softening dick.

"Neil Mason." He held out a hand, only to laugh and take it back when Cassidy shot him a look that said he wasn't going to fall for that one. "Right, sorry."

They stared at one another for a few minutes. He wasn't quite sure what the hell to say at this point, considering Neil hadn't done the polite thing and turned to vacate.

"Would it be too much trouble…" Neil started, holding out his snorkeling gear. "I sorta got a little distracted and wound up a ways off course. I hate to bother, but I could really use some water."

The irritation was already dissolving as Cassidy noticed the guy was a little winded and worn, slightly hunched over as if he'd swum himself silly. "Sure, no problem." Cassidy nudged his head toward the house before heading that direction. "Where are you staying?"

"That obvious I'm a tourist, huh?" Neil grinned as Cassidy shrugged an apology. "On the western half of the island right on the beach—Bishop's Place, I think it's called."

Cassidy nodded, knowing exactly where that was as they crossed the courtyard to the screened porch. "You are a ways off course."

"Sorry I disrupted your nap."

Cassidy grinned, peering back. "It's getting a little late in the day anyway." He pulled on the screen door, listening to the squeak of the hinges as he held it open for Neil.

"This is a beautiful spot," Neil said, following Cassidy into the kitchen. "I'd been wondering who was lucky enough to live here."

Cassidy set Sadie on the island and opened the fridge. He pulled out a couple of bottles of water. "You should be careful snorkeling alone." He twisted off a cap and passed a water to Neil, who immediately downed half of it. "The currents around the island can be brutal."

Neil wiped his mouth with the back of his hand and then smiled. "Like I said, wasn't really my intention. I apologize for the inconvenience, but—grateful for the hospitality."

Cassidy smiled as Neil took another quick swig. He held up his bottle in an apologetic cheerslike gesture before taking a drink out of his own bottle. "Sorry if I came off like a prick before."

Neil laughed, his gaze once again trailing down Cassidy's body. "No pun intended, right?"

Cassidy followed suit, feeling his face flush a little. "No extra charge for the peep show."

"That's good." Neil finished off the last of his water. "I left my wallet back at the house."

"Another one?" Cassidy asked, wiggling his bottle in the air. He grabbed another out of the fridge after Neil nodded. "Are you new to the island or just on a holiday?"

"Working vacation of sorts. I was supposed to be here for the summer, but I've decided to pack it in and head home at the end of the week."

"Too beautiful here for you to take on a daily basis, huh?" Cassidy said, immediately chastising himself for the flirty tone.

Neil laughed again. "No, I just don't really know anyone here. I was supposed to be renting the place with some friends—a couple. They decided to break up last week instead of vacationing with me." Neil glanced down at the floor, backing up a bit. "I didn't want to waste the deposit. Sorry I kinda got sand all over the place."

Cassidy took note of the kitchen floor, instantly feeling as if he were in trouble. He laughed, wishing Natalie were there to yell at him, and followed Neil back out onto the sun porch. That sudden stab of loneliness rumbled through his gut, and he became grateful for the company.

"Let me help you out of that wet suit," Cassidy said, placing his water bottle down on a table. "There's an outdoor shower across the courtyard you can use to rinse off."

"Thanks," Neil said, smiling as he began to push the wet suit farther down.

Cassidy placed a hand on Neil's shoulder to keep him from losing his balance and falling over. He was more than amply rewarded by the sight of Neil in skintight turquoise blue trunks that hugged the man's ass and narrow hips like a second skin and nicely contrasted with his tanned skin. He'd forced himself to look away when the wet suit pulled Neil's trunks down just enough to see the lighter skin from his tan line hiding underneath. Cassidy swallowed hard, doing his best to keep himself from losing it and sprouting another boner.

Hanging the wet suit up on a hook, Neil then followed as Cassidy led the way toward the outdoor shower, which consisted of a spigot attached to a pipe running up one side of the exterior wall of the detached garage.

"The water's probably pretty cold, but it'll get the sand and salt off of you," Cassidy said as he reached over and turned the faucet on.

"You look a little sandy too," Neil said with a sly smile as Cassidy yanked on the pull chain. Water hissed out of the showerhead, spattering onto the stone pavers that directed the excess water off into the grass.

Cassidy grinned, trying to look cool and not gawk as his guest stood under the spigot. Neil readied himself as he pulled the chain, cursing under his breath as he went about rinsing off as quickly as humanly possible.

Cassidy tried concentrating on the ocean, disturbingly distracted by his guest's nipples, which had gone rock hard under the cool water. He couldn't manage to exorcise the mental image of Neil's tan line from his mind, turning back with a smile as the water shut off and a dripping Neil walked over to where he stood.

"Towel?" Cassidy offered, holding up the one that had been tucked around his waist.

Neil blinked a few times, taking the towel as Cassidy took his turn rinsing off. He noticed that Neil didn't bother busying himself by doing anything other than ogling Cassidy as he stood under the steady stream of icy water.

Cassidy stood there, gaze locked with Neil's, both standing perfectly still as if in a man-trance. Cassidy finally released the pull chain, and both men moved silently toward each other, Neil letting out a moan as their mouths came together. Their tongues intertwined in a slow dance for control as they snaked their arms around each other.

It was the last thing Cassidy had imagined happening today. As Neil's hand moved over his bare ass, roughly squeezing, he decided he really needed to start imagining days like this. While Cassidy slipped his fingers down into the front of those turquoise swim trunks, fondling the head of Neil's rapidly swelling dick, he let out a low groan of his own. His brain buzzed with sex, and he was suddenly thankful to be single.

§ § §

Cassidy lay back across the twin bed, smiling as he took in a sharp breath. The ceiling fan was spinning, almost whispering above his head as his body softly twitched while Neil's tongue worked up and down his cock. They'd fondled and fumbled their way through the house, backing each other up the flight of stairs and into Cassidy's childhood bedroom. He had slowly and proficiently sucked Neil off, and now the favor was most delightfully being returned.

He wove his fingers through Neil's hair, arching his back as he let out a long, deep moan of approval. He glanced down, not sure he enjoyed anything more than seeing his cock buried deep inside another man's mouth. His eyes rolled back in his head as Neil pulled back, running the tip of his tongue over the head before taking him all the way into the back of his throat again.

Cassidy panted heavily, desperately trying to catch his breath.

The hair around his face was wet and sticking to his forehead. "Christ, Neil… Close… Gonna fucking blow."

Cassidy completely lost it when Neil moaned deeply, pushing him over the edge as he expelled hushed curses, holding Neil's face firmly between his legs, lightly thrusting until every last drop had been sucked out of him.

Cassidy's body fell limp, all tension evaporating out his muscles in an instant. "That was…"

Neil slid up Cassidy's body, licking and sucking his way back up to his mouth. Cassidy opened for him, tasting the salty tang of his orgasm on Neil's tongue. Their sweat-soaked bodies rubbed together, and Neil's third erection of the afternoon pressed into Cassidy's upper thigh.

Tearing his mouth away, Cassidy pushed him by the shoulders, as if holding him back. "Seriously, dude?"

"What?" Neil asked as he ground his cock into Cassidy's leg.

"You're like a cyborg or a Cylon—the Cockinator or something."

Neil laughed. "I can't seem to control myself. Getting you off is kind of addictive."

"So I'm like Neil-nip?"

"Apparently." Neil smiled as he leaned in and started sucking on Cassidy's neck.

Cassidy groaned as the nibbling and sucking shot sensations straight down between his legs. He tried to roll over onto his stomach, and Neil lifted his body slightly yet somehow managed not to remove his lips from Cassidy's neck.

Cassidy began clawing his way across the bed, dramatically inching his way toward the nightstand. "Must have water," he gasped.

Neil laughed and Cassidy grinned, feeling those hands seductively pressing into his back as he pulled his body farther away. He finally got close enough to snag one of the plastic bottles and wasted no time chugging it down.

"What the hell do you do for a living?" Cassidy asked, wheezing. "Porn?"

"I actually just sold my bed-and-breakfast back in Richmond, Virginia, to a conglomerate who buys up small but successful inns." Neil slowly ran his hand down the center of Cassidy's back. "They add spa facilities, turning them into more of a resort."

Cassidy grinned as Neil massaged his ass cheeks. "You just sold it? Were you tired of running an inn?"

"No, I loved it." His thumbs were pressing dangerously close to Cassidy's glory hole. "It was a lot of money. Part of the reason I came to Hart's was to see if this place might make a good location for a new inn."

Cassidy felt his eyes fluttering as Neil lightly ran a finger over his hole. "Jeez, man, you're insatiable." Cassidy grabbed the second bottle of water with the intention of passing it back to Neil. "Holy fuck!" Cassidy fumbled, dropping the water. He fisted handfuls of blanket as Neil's tongue pressed into his ass.

His mouth fell open, and he began pushing his ass back into Neil's face. "Fuck. Me."

Chapter Three

Cassidy opened his eyes, immediately squinting from the morning sunlight filtering into his bedroom through the open windows. The temperature in the room was on the cool side, as he'd passed out soon after the trisexathon. He could tell he was alone, but was unsure if Neil had left altogether or was simply downstairs somewhere. Part of him hoped Neil was still around, feeling the throbby ache coming from between his legs.

He let out a faint whispery sigh and then smiled, not daring to move an inch. He lay spread-eagle on his stomach. A slight dewiness in the air left a dampness clinging to the bedding. He knew he'd fallen asleep with his feet sticking out the bottom of the blankets, because they were freezing like two blocks of ice.

The sound of the waves drifted up the beach to the house, and a pang of nostalgia swept over Cassidy as he allowed his gaze to drift over the bedroom he'd stayed in every summer. The red-and-black-plaid wallpaper that ran around the bottom of the wall below the chair-rail molding was the slightest bit faded.

The seaside theme was on the masculine side, the matching brass portals that hung on the wall were in need of a good polish, and the painting that depicted the schooner crashing through the violent waves. He noticed the large black pirate flag with the skull and bones, and laughed at the poster of Heather Locklear in a bikini hanging next to the one for *Party of Five*. At the time, he'd convinced everyone he liked Neve Campbell, when in reality he'd had the hots for Matthew Fox.

The entire room was a giant time capsule. The sets of Judy Blume and Hardy Boys books were still lined up intermittently on the bookshelf with the random *Transformers* and *Star Wars* action figures.

"Jesus, Sadie, did you never throw *anything* away?"

Stupid question, he thought, wondering about his comics for a moment. He made a mental note to check the trunk at the foot of the bed later, since that's where he used to keep them. He chuckled thinking back to the books, wondering if his preteen doppelgänger had subconsciously mixed the Hardys in with good ole Judy, thinking it would butch things up a bit.

"A misguided attempt that would've been," he said, pondering whether anything was gayer than the Hardy Boys.

His chest began to ache at the realization that had he bothered to come back that last summer, this room would likely hold other artifacts of the boy he used to be. And *that* boy wouldn't have been quite the asshole either.

Not liking the direction his thoughts were heading, Cassidy quickly shifted his gaze toward the window while concentrating on his body. He winced suddenly, feeling his back protesting the lumpy twin-size boyhood bed. Cassidy made a mental note to crack open his laptop long enough to get online and order a new bed. Damn the shipping costs, he thought, knowing his body couldn't take the abuse.

Cassidy let out a light sigh as he grinned, feeling like a greedy little kid. Neil was perfect—exactly what he needed to fill the next few days before Ollie and Spence showed up. He wouldn't feel so alone in this house all by himself. Neil could keep him occupied and away from all the memories that permeated the air he now breathed.

Best of all, he'd be leaving the island and headed back to wherever he came from. No emotional entanglements with mutually beneficial, orgasmic good times. It was all he could handle in his current emotional state. He'd only shed himself of his last boyfriend a few months ago, not soon after the trial was finished.

"Teddy," he mumbled under his breath. He was a great guy—hot, sweet, great in bed—there just hadn't been anything deeper than what lay just below the surface. It had sucked all the way around, as Teddy seemed like the first guy in a long while who was genuinely saddened by the breakup, even though it had been a mutual decision. They'd both been aware there was a time limit on their relationship from the beginning, since Teddy was graduating and moving back to Kansas. It was a little sad to admit, but Cassidy found it refreshing going into a relationship that came with a preexisting expiration date. For once he didn't have to be the grim reaper. He'd been able to sit back and enjoy what they had for as long as they had it.

And Teddy had it—that pretty-boy-jock appeal. Very masculine and sporty looking, yet not the type you'd expect to find shoving the nerdy guy into a locker. Teddy had a sweetness about him. At twenty-four, he wasn't *that* much younger than Cassidy, but the maturity level wasn't there. It was almost as if Teddy hadn't ever had to deal with anything unpleasant, like he'd led a charmed life up until that point. It was the quality that had initially drawn Cassidy to him. Not innocent so much as uncomplicated, he thought. Considering how proficient Teddy was in the sack, he was under no delusions as to his sexual experience. Unfortunately, he just wasn't in love with Teddy. Cassidy was beginning to feel he wasn't actually capable of falling in love…or maybe he was simply afraid he couldn't stay that way.

"Dead inside," he mumbled, then laughed at the maudlin and melodramatic thought.

Cassidy pushed himself up onto his knees and crawled out of bed. He twisted from side to side, listening to his spine pop and crack like a bowl of Rice Krispies. He scampered around the corner into the bathroom off the hall, heading directly to the toilet to relieve himself. His entire body trembled and he let out a loud groan as his eyes rolled back into his head a tiny bit.

"Fuck yes," he mumbled once his bladder was finally empty. He grabbed a tissue from the fuzzy dispenser on the back of the toilet and did the obligatory shake before wiping himself dry.

Cassidy fumbled with the handle, flushing the toilet before stumbling over to the vanity. He flipped on the overhead light and squinted, taking a few steps back so he could fully take in his reflection. He started laughing, mildly grossed out by the dried semen on his chin. Cassidy shook his head as he snagged his specs off the counter. He put them on, enabling him to see close-up as he scratched at the crustiness with his fingernail.

"Cum slut," he said, giving his reflection a curt, take-that head nod.

A long shower and thorough brushing of his teeth and tongue had him feeling almost shiny and new again—well, fresh at the very least. He ran an electric razor over his stubble and massaged a tiny bit of lotion into his chin and neck.

He decided not to tempt fate by running around nude again. He pulled on a yellow pair of baggy cotton shorts, a formfitting V-necked undershirt, and added a thick pair of tube socks since he couldn't get his feet to stay warm. He smushed the elastic down around his ankles just before he headed downstairs.

After he entered the kitchen, he immediately busied himself gathering yogurt, an apple, and then slicing an English muffin that he proceeded to toss in the toaster.

"Good morning, Sadie," he said as he walked past the urn. "I apologize for leaving you alone your first night back, but I did things last night I'd prefer you never see, beautiful."

He winked at the urn and smiled, imagining her spouting off how she could probably teach him a thing or two, while arching her eyebrows.

His smile faded, as he began to feel cheated—not having her in his life now that he was all grown up. He knew it was silly to be talking to the urn as if it were some magical vessel directly linked to her spirit. But lame or not, it kept the more depressing feelings of guilt and abandonment at bay now that he was once again alone in the big, empty house.

He jumped, startled by the toaster, announcing the English muffin was good to go. He placed everything on one of the handled trays that he'd removed from the wall above the nook and carried his breakfast out onto the screened-in porch. He ran back inside, grabbing Sadie and his cell phone before finally taking a seat, grinning as he flinched, receiving a reminder of his shenanigans from the night before.

"The gift that keeps on giving," he mumbled, feeling his dick swell as he reached down and adjusted himself.

Cassidy bit a big chunk out of the apple as he picked up his phone, praying it wasn't completely dead. He'd not bothered to plug it into its charger the night before. He nodded, happy to see it still had a few bars left on the tiny battery symbol. He had three missed calls, all from Ollie.

Oliver Elliot could be best described as blond and bendy, only one of which was a naturally God-given attribute. An art major in college, he now made jewelry from home and sold it on eBay to pay his bills. The rest of his spare time was spent doing sculpture…and Spencer. Ollie had that Michael J. Fox syndrome, where despite the fact that his birth certificate attested to his twenty-nine years, he still looked like he was sixteen.

Cassidy punched in the appropriate codes to get into his voice mail while continuing to shovel food into his mouth. He gazed out over the beach below at the bright blue water, waves gently rolling up the sand as he squinted from the morning sun. He placed the phone to his ear, hearing the beep, followed by Ollie's singsong voice saying, "Hey, Cass, just checking in to see if you'd made it. Call me."

Cassidy deleted it and listened to the next beep. "Hey, Cass, it's just me again. Starting to worry a bit. You should've made it there by now. Call me so I know you're okay, okay?"

Cassidy grinned, shoving a spoonful of yogurt into his mouth as he punched buttons with his thumb, then placed the phone between his ear and shoulder in time to hear the last message, which concluded, "I suppose you're just not going to bother calling. Thanks for making me worry all goddamn night, by the way." Cassidy laughed hearing Spencer saying, "Someone kill me—" in the background. He heard Ollie telling Spencer to shut up as the message abruptly cut off.

He knew he was in deep shit as he let out a frustrated sigh. He snarled at the phone, contemplating whether or not he should postpone the guilt trip or make like a Band-Aid and get it over with now.

Finishing off the last bit of the yogurt before shoving the tray across the table, Cassidy then punched the numbers on the phone. He mentally prepared for the verbal onslaught and leaned back, relaxing into the seat as he waited while the phone continued to ring.

"You're alive?"

"Yeah, I'm so sor—Hello?" Cassidy inspected the display on his cell to see Ollie had hung up on him midsentence. "Son of a bitch." He punched the green Call button, resending the call.

"Hello, Oliver here."

"Was it really necessary to—Ollie?" Cassidy rolled his eyes, tossing the phone into his lap after seeing he'd done it again. "One more time, you little…" he mumbled as he snatched up the phone and tried again.

"Hello, this is Oliver, who's like the single best friend you've ever had, bitch."

Cassidy laughed, his irritation already dissipating. "Don't bitch me, bitch. What's with all the hang-ups?"

"What a loaded question that could be." Ollie sighed. "You should have called to let me know you were okay."

"I'm sorry, sugar bean." Cassidy grinned, knowing Ollie loved it when he called him that. It was usually foolproof when followed up with a rib tickle and a pat on the ass, but considering the long distance, he'd have to work with what he had. "You placed your phone number in every single compartment of my car with *emergency contact* scribbled over it. It wasn't likely you'd not be the first to know had there been an accident."

"That wasn't what I meant by *okay*, and you know it."

"I know, Ollie. It wasn't an intentional slight. I just…got distracted, I guess."

"You're depressed. I can hear it in your voice."

Cassidy felt a grimace pass over his face as he rooted around in the wicker chair. As much as he adored Ollie, he didn't love the fact he seemed incapable of getting anything past him.

Using his told-you-so tone, Ollie sang, "Your silence says it all."

"Oh shut it." He chewed on his lower lip. "Know-it-all."

"I told you to wait for us to come with you, and stop chewing your lip."

Cassidy sat up, trying to pinpoint the hidden camera. "I really hate it when you do that." He settled back into the chair, listening to Ollie laugh. "And you know why I needed a few days up here alone. I didn't want to cry with company. It's tacky."

"Nice. Like we're complete strangers." There was a pause followed by a huff. "Hear that, Spencer?" Oliver yelled. "*We're* not cryworthy!"

"You know how I feel about feelings."

"Yes, yes…so anti-emo! You and your yucky-love phobia. God forbid you allow a crack to form in that facade you call your life."

"Um, judgey much? Besides, cracks lead to…"

"Yes?"

"Bigger cracks?"

"You've had the emotional shit kicked out of you for years, courtesy of your twisted Ps. Honestly, Cass, we all get it—you have the inner strength of any character ever played by Sally Field. You've made your point, and I promise no one's going to judge you for having a bit of a meltdown, so just let go."

Cassidy scowled at the double standard. "Just judge me for *not* having one, apparently."

"It's okay, Cass. Just close your eyes and imagine I'm taking your hand. You're perfectly safe. You can let go. I won't let anything happen to you."

"Dude, that was like totally beautiful, man."

"Prick."

Cassidy was trying to hold back his laughter. "No, seriously, I'm writing this entire conversation down and e-mailing it to Lifetime Television this instant."

"You can go straight to hell, you…you pussy. It's not like I enjoy all this touchy-feely crap."

"Ew!" Cassidy squealed like a little girl. "Was it necessary to go *there*?"

He lost it, placing his hand on the table for balance, laughing his ass off as he heard a click followed by complete silence on the other end of the line.

"Ah…goodness." He settled back into the chair, laughing a bit more as he set his cell on the table. The burning behind his eyes stung as the pressure built up in his chest. "Shit," he whispered as a tear rolled down his cheek.

Cassidy knew full well he didn't want to be alone, but his desire not to be seen in this state was strong and far outweighed any discomfort he might suffer at the hands of loneliness. It wasn't that he really had anything against people becoming emotional. He was fine with it—hell, even good to have around in a crisis—as long as it wasn't *his* crisis.

He enjoyed being that voice of reason friends or students could come to when they felt their lives were spinning out of control. He loved being able to help, to make them feel better, to rescue them, for lack of a better word. He just wasn't all that good when it came to needing to be rescued.

He sat up, resting his elbows on his knees and placing the palms of his hands over his eyes. Instead of fighting it, he decided to let go after all, praying behind his eyes that he could get it all out if he did. The rational part of him knew with *every* fiber of his being that he had done *everything* humanly possible to help Sadie after the stroke. He'd tried to convince Lionel to let him take her, begged him to at least allow her to come back to Piper's Point and let Natalie care for her.

He'd even taken legal action when nothing else had worked, but he didn't have any rights since Sadie had never bothered to make a living will. It wasn't as if Lionel had abused her in any way a court would have been able to see, despite the fact he had indeed been abusing her. It had been pure spite on Lionel's end, like he'd been waiting for the earliest opportunity he could find to control her or at the very least have control over her.

Cassidy wiped his eyes, the sunlight and ocean view blurred by his tears. It had been the first time she'd *really* needed him, and he'd failed her. Cassidy couldn't rescue the one person he'd like to have saved more than anybody else, and he wasn't entirely sure he'd ever be able to reconcile himself to that truth. He observed the urn sitting next to him on the table, his own distorted reflection glaring back at him. Despite knowing there'd been nothing he could've done to return her to this place back when it would have mattered, it did make him feel the tiniest bit better knowing he was able to bring her home now.

§ § §

Cassidy surveyed the kitchen, contemplating what the hell he was supposed to do with himself. He'd already come to the conclusion that heading into town would be a crapshoot. There was a strong possibility that the locals might not be all that happy to see him. That they might feel he'd abandoned Sadie when she needed him most. He couldn't exactly blame them, considering he felt that with regard to himself.

He could hide out for a good week if he needed to. By then his friends would arrive and he'd have a buffer knowing most of the Hart's Island inhabitants wouldn't confront him while surrounded by outsiders

"Know your limitations," he said, figuring it best to keep himself busied with anything menial. "And gird your loins, for the natives are quite possibly restless—and out for blood."

He hadn't been down to the dock and boathouse yet, so he decided that might be as good a place as any to start. He ran up the stairs, stopping momentarily to rip off the socks as he went. He grabbed up a pair of sandals, then hopped down the hall on one foot while sliding one on, stopping at the top of the steps to tend to the second one.

He tromped down the stairs, making an awful commotion and smiling as he imagined Natalie yelling at the top of her lungs for him and Nate to quit stomping through the house like a herd of elephants.

He came busting out onto the front porch and down the front steps toward the trail that led into the trees to the small half-moon-shaped beach on the eastern edge of the property. It was very secluded, with a small dock and boathouse where they stored the *Tempest*, Sadie's modest sailboat, during the off-season. Cassidy wasn't quite sure why Sadie even had a sailboat, considering she never went on the water.

He'd never really taken to sailing—that was Nate's thing—though in truth he didn't mind it as long as he didn't have to do any of the actual work. That's what it always felt like to Cassidy. "Pull this jib. Grab that jab." Cassidy laughed, certain he wasn't using the correct terminology. "Bunch of jib-jab if you ask me."

He'd secretly thought Nate just enjoyed bossing him around. He was only a little over a year older than Cassidy, but man, to hear Nate tell it, you'd have thought the earth had been created in that one year. Cassidy sighed, stepping out of the tree line at the tiny beach. He grinned, walking toward the boathouse, remembering the way he used to try getting Nate mad enough to shove on him or wrestle him to the ground.

Cassidy hopped up onto the wood plank walkway and strolled over to the side door of the boathouse. "Anything I could think of to get you to touch me."

Cassidy laid a hand on the doorknob, closing his eyes, momentarily remembering the summer he'd turned sixteen. He'd expected to be relaxed, having yet another happy summer away from his parents, who deposited him on Hart's before leaving on their two-month annual vacation to wherever it was they'd decided to go to that year. The longer that summer wore on, however, the more frustrated Cassidy got.

It had been the last day of his next-to-last summer on the island. Lillian, his mother, had called, letting Sadie know the car they'd sent to pick him up would be there anytime. He'd come down to the boathouse to say good-bye to Nate. Part of him was glad to be going for once. Cassidy had been like a raw nerve, irritated and exposed the entire summer. He'd become so infatuated with Nate that he could barely stand to be around him. At the same time he'd practically snapped anyone's head off who'd dared insert themselves between them.

Nate's best friend on the island, Jimmy Dobbs, had been at some baseball scouting camp for eight weeks of the summer. Cassidy had always liked Jimmy in the past, yet he found himself wanting to strangle the life out of him once he got back. He hated having to share his time with Nate.

Cassidy had begun to feel like a crazy person and had come to the conclusion that leaving might not be such a bad thing after all. He knew what he wanted from Nate, even though he couldn't bring himself to admit it. He'd also come to believe that Nate didn't share those feelings, but he discovered how wrong he'd been on the last day of what turned out to be the best summer he'd spent on Hart's Island at that point in his very young life.

§ § §

Cassidy yanked the boathouse door open and laughed as Nate jumped, practically tripping over his own feet.

"Asshole," Nate said. His muscles relaxed as he halted his attempt to cover up the bag of pot, lighter, and the thin pack of papers. He was wearing nothing but a faded pair of short khaki golf shorts and worn deck shoes. "Shut the door, dweeb."

Cassidy nodded as he stepped in and closed the door behind him. He maneuvered around the coils of rope and the pile of canvas sacks they sometimes used to fill with sand during the stormy season to prevent the boathouse from flooding.

He'd always liked it here, as it was one of the few places he could come to be alone with Nate. He walked around the canoe that was turned upside down and hanging from the posts. Cassidy watched briefly as Nate sprinkled the dried leaves onto the paper before he found it impossible to keep his gaze from wandering over Nate's wide shoulders and muscled back.

He was amazed that something so firm could still appear to be soft as silk as he watched the planes of tanned skin over flexing muscles while Nate fiddled with rolling the joint. Cassidy let his gaze wander down the slow curve of Nate's back and the tiny beads of perspiration forming there. He swallowed hard, imagining the way the skin disappearing down the top of those shorts might feel.

Cassidy rubbed his hand over his mouth, feeling the heat for the first time as he wondered whether Nate was wearing underwear. He could feel himself getting a boner yet couldn't manage to make himself stop ogling Nate as if he were a piece of meat. He'd been doing that all summer long and, despite his best efforts, couldn't stop now.

He practically shot off a load in his briefs watching Nate's tongue slide over the edge of the paper.

"You okay?" Nate asked with a slight grin.

Cassidy locked eyes with Nate, feeling his face heat up, fairly certain he'd just moaned out loud.

"Totally. Just came to say good-bye," Cassidy said, staring at the floor, humiliated yet still unable to not notice the way the sunlight was causing the blond hair on Nate's legs to glisten. "Where'd you get the pot?"

"Swiped off some tourist camping out on the beach." Nate turned, holding up the perfectly rolled joint as if were the finest achievement in his long and illustrious soon-to-be seventeen-year-old life. Cassidy shook his head at him.

"You ever?" Nate asked, holding out the joint.

"Sure," Cassidy said, not too impressed by pot, yet still taking a toke when Nate passed it over to him. He sucked the smoke into his lungs and held it in as he handed the doobie back.

Cassidy exhaled the smoke, and they passed the joint back and forth, neither one saying much of anything, just smiling as they watched each other take hits off it.

Cassidy was trying to maintain his cool despite his frustrations, which were now reaching a heightened state of desperation. Over the course of the summer, Nate had become the root of any and all things sexual as far as Cassidy was concerned. Despite being willing to give his left nut for five naked minutes with Nate, he no longer held on to any hopes he'd ever get the opportunity.

"Come here." Nate pulled Cassidy closer. "There's not much left, so we'll have to hot-box the rest."

Cassidy stared blankly into Nate's face.

"You don't know how to hot-box?" Nate shook his head. "What the fuck do they teach you ivy-bound prep-school kids anyway?"

Cassidy grinned, noticing Nate's gaze drop to his lips.

"I'll inhale and then blow the smoke into your mouth from mine."

Sweet Jesus, Cassidy thought. I have got to be the luckiest son of a bitch to ever walk the planet. "Cool." He nodded, trying to keep his cool, despite the fact his cock went instahard the second Nate explained hot-boxing to him.

Nate carefully held on to the little bit of joint that was left as he inhaled, causing the cherry to momentarily burn bright orange. Cassidy watched in anticipation as Nate smiled, closing his eyes while he held in his breath. Then, as if in slow motion, Nate leaned forward and pressed his soft lips to Cassidy's and blew the smoke into his mouth. Cassidy reciprocated by taking the smoke into his lungs, not daring to so much as move a muscle.

Cassidy exhaled as Nate was sucking in the last bit that was left, then dropped the tiny butt to the floor. He ground it into the plank with the bottom of his shoe as he leaned in, pressing his lips over Cassidy's once more.

Cassidy thought it was the drugs for a second, that he was merely hallucinating that Nate had indeed slipped his tongue into his mouth. He then remembered pot made him hungry, not delusional. He opened his eyes momentarily, seeing the tiny bits of smoke escaping from between their lips as Nate forced his tongue in farther. Cassidy thought for sure both his head and his cock were about to explode as he opened up his mouth for Nate, who seemed to take that as a sign of encouragement, considering his hands were making their way around Cassidy's waist.

Cassidy concentrated on the sensations of Nate's tongue intertwining with his while Nate pulled him closer. The flavor and the light-headed effects of the pot mixed with their kiss and the heat from Nate's mouth set Cassidy's body on fire. He moaned as Nate pressed into him, grinding his pelvis into his erection, nearly making him shoot.

Nate pushed Cassidy away, glancing down between the two of them. "Already hard as a rock."

Cassidy was confused for a second, unsure if there had been a question in there or if Nate had simply decided this would be a great time to pause and state the obvious. He started to open his mouth in response, only to have Nate cut him off with another kiss. He finally allowed himself to touch Nate. He'd been holding off, afraid whatever spell had come over Nate would be broken should he make the slightest movement. Cassidy lightly slid the tips of his fingers over Nate's chest, feeling Nate react as he ran his pinkie over a hard nipple. Nate pressed his upper body into it, and as if instinctual on some level, Cassidy began massaging the warm, moist skin.

Cassidy moaned when the palm of Nate's hand pressed into his hard-on. He gently thrust into it, wanting more. He could feel Nate smiling through the kiss just before they heard the door swing open. They separated like two cats that'd just been doused with a bucket of water.

Sadie was standing at the doorway, mouth hanging open as both Nate and Cassidy froze in place. She let out an indecipherable little squeak before pulling the door closed, leaving them alone once again. Cassidy couldn't bring himself to look at Nate, and he could tell Nate had turned away from him as well.

Cassidy was mortified, yet half ready to kill Sadie for opening that damned door when she had. He knew he should care more about what Sadie might think about all this, but the only thing that was important to him at that moment was whether he'd ever get another chance with Nate.

He cocked his head to the side, wondering if he'd heard correctly, then peered over at Nate, who was now staring at the door as well. It sounded odd, like laughter, only not, or perhaps muffled? He caught Nate shooting a quick glance in his direction before they each began to walk toward the door. They froze again, each standing up straight as they watched each other, listening to Sadie really lose it on the other side of the door.

Nate shrugged, and Cassidy started to giggle, then placed his hand over his mouth. He knew it was probably the pot, but he too started to laugh. Nate watched him with this quirky half smile, shaking his head as he started to laugh also.

Cassidy pushed the door open to see Sadie doubled over, her long red hair cascading toward the ground as she held her belly. "I'm"—she tried to get out between laughs—"so sorry."

"I take it you're not upset?" Cassidy asked, giggling.

"My grandson, the homosexual!" Sadie yelled at the top of her lungs, beginning to lose it again.

Nate was frowning a bit now, and Sadie reached over and placed a hand on his arm.

"Don't worry, dear," Sadie said, wiping her eyes with the backs of her index fingers. "I won't tell your mother, so long as you roll me a joint."

Nate started to laugh as Cassidy's mouth fell open. "Grandma!"

"Don't look so goddamned shocked." Sadie stood up straight and smoothed out her caftan, bracelets clinking. "I haven't had a decent buzz in a decade." An irritated expression took over her face. "And don't call me Grandma."

§ § §

Cassidy stood in the doorway to the boathouse, still holding the door open, but unable to make himself go in. He could feel her presence enveloping him as he stared into the shadows. Shutting the door, he then turned slowly and made his way back up to the house, unsure he could ever be happy like that again at Piper's Point. He was beginning to think there might be too many ghosts here for that to ever be a reality.

Chapter Four

Cassidy stared at the door off the upstairs hall that opened to a cramped flight of stairs leading to the attic. Folded arms and a plethora of excuses currently stood in his way. He knew it needed to be done. Sadie had been the pack rat to end all others, and he could only imagine the mess that lay at the top of the stairs just on the other side of that door.

For as long as he could remember, any time Natalie had suggested Sadie get rid of something she no longer needed or had any use for, her first and only response had been, "*To the attic!*"

Cassidy opened the door and stood back, staring up the stairwell. He'd always made fun of her, he thought, as he flipped the switch on the wall, turning on the overhead light.

"*That's why attics were invented,*" Sadie had always blasted back should there be any objections. "*You'll thank me one day when I'm gone*"—pointing up at the attic, she'd add—"*for leaving you a treasure trove of goodies up there.*"

As Cassidy came to the top of the stairs, he took in a deep breath of stale, dusty air. He stumbled around, turning in a circle, and practically shit his pants. It was floor-to-ceiling, cobweb-covered, mountainous piles of God only knew what.

"You are such a fucking liar, Sadie." Cassidy mumbled, thinking what he needed was a match. "Treasure trove, my ass."

The enormous attic had so much stuff piled up that he wouldn't even begin to know where to start. Building a bridge over the Grand Canyon seemed less intimidating than this.

"Not to mention the dust."

His nose crinkled up just before he sneezed. His eyes widened, seeing all the dust he'd disturbed now floating through the air searching for a new home. A high-pitched squeal cut through the silence, and he stared down the stairs, hearing barking and growling coming from somewhere outside.

He took off, thankful for any excuse to vacate the attic. Reaching the foyer, he could hear multiple dogs growling and went over to the bay window, catching a glimpse of two large dogs trying to get at something next to the foundation of the house. He cursed under his breath and ran outside to investigate.

As he rounded the side of the house, he could see there were actually three large dogs, all of which looked a bit rough, according to his standards. Granted, he'd never been allowed so much as a goldfish by his parents, so he wasn't the best judge. They appeared to be frothing at the mouth, trying to get at whatever was wedged behind the air-conditioning unit. He wasn't taking any chances since the hair on the back of his neck was standing on end.

He ran back toward the front yard and grabbed the coiled hose at the foot of the spigot sticking up out of the ground. He twisted the faucet handle on as far as it could go. When he turned around, the German shepherd-type dog stood about fifteen yards away growling at him.

"The fucking hounds from hell are now nipping at my heels," Cassidy mumbled as he quickly adjusted the water gun screwed onto the end of the hose to the Jet setting. He tried to keep his cool and not panic as the dog inched closer. He prayed his plan would work as he turned the hose on the dog, slightly relieved when it yelped and ran away.

He wasn't relieved for long, as it turned and started barking again. Cassidy squeezed the handle and advanced toward it, hoping he could force it farther away from the house. The dog turned tail and ran when he pelted it with a second blast of water, stopping once it reached the tree line, where it turned and continued to bark and snarl at Cassidy.

He moved toward the two still growling and scratching at the air conditioner, both of which yelped and ran once they were greeted by the sting from the jet of ice-cold water. Once reunited, the three-pack disappeared into the woods. Cassidy backed up toward the house, afraid to turn around since he could still hear them barking off in the distance somewhere.

He finally turned, exhaling. He'd been scared shitless. He laughed, shaking his head as he dropped the hose and bent over, placing his hands on his knees.

He heard a whimper and craned his head to peek around the corner of the air conditioner, half-afraid to discover what in the name of hell he'd just risked life and limb for. He squinted, trying to make out what the tiny matted mound of hair was.

"Please don't be a rat," he muttered as he inched closer, peering over the top of the unit, seeing whatever it was shaking in the corner, large glassed-over eyes gazing back up at him. "What the hell is it?" he asked, only to roll his eyes, realizing there was no one around to answer him.

It hobbled a little way out of the corner, and Cassidy could see that it was bleeding. He placed a hand on his tummy, feeling a wave of nausea come over him.

He pushed back his glasses that had slid forward a bit as he got down on all fours. "I really don't like blood, little…thing."

It hobbled a bit closer, sticking its head out into the light, laying its ears back.

"You look like a rat, dog," Cassidy said, speaking softly, which seemed to coax it farther out. He could see it was holding its back leg up.

"Shit," Cassidy said, immediately regretting it as the dog started to retreat. He didn't want to touch it, because it was bleeding, but he knew he couldn't just leave the little thing there to bleed to death. "You are a dog…right?"

He sat up and pulled off his shirt, then spread it out on the grass. He spoke softly again, gently patting the fabric. The runt inspected Cassidy for a moment, then glanced at the shirt. Finally, as if sensing Cassidy was probably its best shot at survival, it hobbled onto the shirt. The poor scrub was on the thin side, and it licked one of his fingers before settling onto its side.

"Smart little thing, aren't you?" Cassidy asked, wrapping it up in his shirt, being as careful as he could to avoid the injured leg. He took in a sharp breath when it yelped as he placed it in his arms. "Sorry, dude."

He went around toward the back of the house, walking as quickly as he dared while doing his best not to jostle the runt. Once inside the kitchen, he grabbed his keys and phone and snagged a few beach towels on his way to the car.

Gently placing it in the passenger seat, he then softly closed the door before hurrying around to the driver's side and getting in. Without much thought, he backed out of the garage and tooled down the driveway. He sat at the end of the drive, arguing with himself, knowing it would be faster to go right, but he'd have to drive right down the main drag and past the harbor, greatly increasing his chances of being seen. If he went left, it would take longer, but he could take mostly back roads, cutting through a residential area to get to the veterinarian's.

He watched his little passenger, who lifted its head on cue and peered up at Cassidy as if to say, "I gotta die because you've got a big name around here?"

He caught a glimpse of the blood and pulled his car out onto the road, making a right, doing his damnedest to think of anything that might keep his mind off hurling. He sank down in his seat once he reached town, keeping his face plastered to the road ahead in an attempt to avoid any faces that might recognize his.

The business section of town was relegated to twelve blocks surrounding the small harbor, consisting of mostly two- and three-story brick or stone-front buildings. The town hall was located on one end, and the world's tiniest hospital on the opposite side. There were several restaurants, all independently owned, a two-screen movie theater, one grocery store, and even a small eight-lane bowling alley. The harbor held a mix of pleasure and fishing boats along with a small ferry that used to be the only way to and from the island back in the day before they built the causeway back in the sixties. Now it took tourists around the island on a water tour.

The local newspaper, the *Hart's Gazette*, only came out twice a week, and in addition to the legal records maintained by the town hall and the historical society, was a good source for island history, as it had been around since the early eighteen hundreds.

There was pretty much one, maybe two of anything else such as lawyers, Realtors, judges, etc. The island had just over twelve thousand inhabitants, but that number could grow to well over fifty thousand during the summer when the mainlanders came over for holiday.

Cassidy had actually loved it when he was a kid. Everything used to seem so much simpler here—uncomplicated people living uncomplicated lives. He'd been envious of Nate, who got to live here year-round, going to school with all the same people. Nate couldn't quite see the big bonus, but different strokes.

Now here he was, hunkered down in his car, terrified everyone held him responsible or at the very least thought he was weak or an unfit grandson for the great Sadie Hart.

"Not so uncomplicated now, huh?" Cassidy asked, looking down at the tiny brown fur ball that was probably bleeding all over his leather upholstery.

He managed to hold down another wave of nausea, scolding himself for thinking about the blood and feeling bad for worrying about his leather seats at a time like this.

"I won't hold it against you till you're better," he said, finally turning into the small parking lot.

He cut the engine, trying to decide the best tack to take once he got inside. Cassidy knew Dr. Downey. He pretty much knew most of the people on the island one way or another, but most of the residents knew Cassidy from the Founders' Day party Sadie had thrown once a year at Piper's Point. Dr. Downey had always seemed like a kind man, so Cassidy was just going to beg, prey on his sympathies, and pray he'd keep his mouth shut about his arrival on the island.

Once inside, Cassidy paused for a moment as he steadied his stomach from the antiseptic odor in the air. Luckily the waiting room was empty except for the girl who smiled up at him from the other side of the counter. Cassidy smiled back, not recognizing her and hoping she wasn't a native. She smiled, innocent as could be, even though Cassidy could tell she'd been sizing him up, much the same way he did any time a good-looking guy crossed his line of sight. She'd pushed back her pin-straight blonde hair with one of those white plastic headbands you'd expect to see on a tween. The pixieish Lolita wore a gray T-shirt that had *Downey Veterinary Clinic* written on the chest, and she quietly chewed her gum.

"Is Dr. Downey in?" Cassidy asked, bending over so she could see he had a wounded animal on his hands. "If you could hurry, I'm really…not good with blood."

She bolted up and out of her chair in a split second.

Cassidy decided she'd already pegged him as gay and not worth wasting what he assumed could be her considerable charms, as it was obvious to him she'd disabled her sex radar.

Written off for being gay, Cassidy thought, disappointed. Do the girls these days have no gumption?

"Do you need me to take the—"

"Dog?" Cassidy finished. He shook his head, not sure why, but feeling an odd sense of protectiveness come over him. "It's some kind of little dog. Was attacked by several mean-ass big dogs, and no, I'm okay so long as I don't look at it."

She nodded and picked up the handle of the seventies-era manila-colored phone and punched in a couple of buttons, smiling as she waited.

Cassidy surveyed the waiting room, the white walls, and plastic chairs, thinking the place had gotten stuck in a crack in time. He noticed the *People* magazine on the table with Brad and Angelina on the cover, thinking that was the only thing that ruined the seventies vibe. He glanced down into his arms, feeling the dog rummaging around as it let out a squeak.

"Hey, boss, we got an emergency out here. Yeah. Sounds like another victim of that pack of feral dogs. Sure thing." She nodded and placed the handle back on its cradle.

"What's the dog's name?" she asked, taking a seat and pulling out a form.

"I don't know," Cassidy said, as a man he didn't recognize stepped out of a door, pulling on a white coat. Cassidy took note of the short, wavy light brown hair and thick, full lips as the man came up behind the receptionist. He smiled at Cassidy, who guessed him to be somewhere in his mid to late thirties, maybe even early forties. He was not at all unattractive but not necessarily the type you'd notice right away if you passed him on the street. He had kind eyes and slightly bushy eyebrows that projected a sense of trustworthiness. It was something he took note of, thinking the vet might also be a mainlander import. It suddenly occurred to him that Dr. Downey was probably getting up there in years.

"Right," she said, shaking her head and nodding. "Well, what's your name, then?"

"Let's worry about the paperwork later, Sarah." He patted her on the shoulder while smiling at Cassidy. He reached over, swinging open a gatelike half door. "Come on back."

Cassidy did as instructed, then followed the man back to an examination room. He kept his eyes open just in case he was wrong about the vet's retirement and the old man was roaming around somewhere after all.

"I'm Dr. Downey," the man said as Cassidy followed him into a room, before gently setting his bundle down onto the table.

Cassidy gasped slightly, feeling the cool stainless-steel tabletop against his stomach, and for the first time realized he didn't have a shirt on. He glanced down, a little embarrassed to see he was wearing nothing but the sandals and the yellow sweat shorts he'd put on that morning.

"Cassidy Winters, right?" the vet asked as he unwrapped the bundle. "Sadie's grandson?"

Cassidy noticed the doc take a second long, lusty gander over his naked upper body. *He's a big ole Mo.* Cassidy vaguely remembered some talk of Dr. Downey having a son, yet he wasn't able to place the face.

"Yeah." Apparently he should know the guy, he thought, wishing he hadn't just peeked down at the table, seeing his white bloodstained shirt. "I'm sorry, I guess we've met?"

"Not really," the doc said as the dog licked his finger, causing him to smile. "Seen you around once or twice with Nate when you were younger. Years ago, back when I was off at college and would come home for summer break. Name's Ben."

Cassidy tried to concentrate on Ben's kind smile and did his best to avoid watching the man carefully pull, prod, and poke around on the dog. He placed a hand on the table, feeling an odd sense of sickening euphoria sweep over him. A cold sweat crept up his spine, and he tried to concentrate on what was happening to the dog. "Is it…going to be all right?"

"You don't look so good."

Rude much?

Cassidy was suddenly light-headed, and he blinked. He had just come to the conclusion he might need to take a seat in the chair behind him as the lights in the room dimmed.

§ § §

Cassidy opened his eyes, confused as he stared up at the fluorescent lights and foam drop-ceiling tiles. His stomach roiled, and his entire body was cold and damp. He glanced to his right seeing the underside of the chair he last remembered attempting to sit down in. Cassidy realized he was on floor. His forehead throbbed a little, and he jerked, startled by Sarah, who thrust a cool pack wrapped in a washcloth at him.

"I've got a soda and some chocolate here for you," she said. "It'll help to get your sugar up. You totally passed out, by the way."

Cassidy took the cool pack from her and placed it to his forehead, wincing a bit.

"Dr. D. managed to get to you before you cracked your head open on the floor, but you nicked your forehead on the table."

Cassidy could feel a bit of a cold sweat clinging to his body that lay stretched out over the cool tile. All he could see from his vantage point as Dr. D. came back into the room were his legs.

"How you doing down there?"

"Just…great, really." Cassidy was completely mortified. All he'd been lacking was a good fainting spell, placing the final nail in the coffin of his reputation as a spineless girlie-man.

"I told him what happened," Sarah said with a smile as she stared at Ben innocently. "And that you saved him."

Cassidy wasn't positive, considering he wasn't quite himself at the moment, but he could have sworn Sarah was trying to pimp the two of them out to each other.

"Sorry I forgot to tell you about that whole queasiness-around-blood thing he mentioned," she added.

Ben walked around the table and glanced down at Cassidy. "That would be useful information to have in the future, Sarah."

Cassidy realized she was likely in trouble. "Don't go blaming her." He tried to lift his upper body off the floor and sit up. "You should know better—telling a half-naked gay man he doesn't look very good."

Sarah laughed until Ben frowned his disapproval. He reached down and helped to pull Cassidy up and into a chair. Sarah placed the can of soda and a few Hershey's Kisses onto the stainless-steel exam table.

"Seriously," Cassidy said, with a half smile, "the shock of it almost killed me."

Ben grinned a little, and Sarah grinned a lot, obviously thinking she might not get fired after all.

Ben shook his head at her and shooed her out of the room. "I'm very sorry about all this."

"No biggie," Cassidy said, feeling slightly relieved Sarah might not lose her job simply because he was a big squeam-queen.

"So what gave me away?" Ben asked, placing the back of his

hand over Cassidy's cheek.

Cassidy smiled, watching Ben's gaze drift down to his upper body again. "That."

Ben's gaze met Cassidy's, and his cheeks burned a light pink as he removed his hand and sat down in the chair next to Cassidy.

"Sorry, rude of me. Not used to sexy shirtless men stopping by the office with rescued…"

Cassidy stood up, surveying the room in a sudden panic, and quickly placed a hand on the wall for balance as he became a bit dizzy. "Whoa…shit."

"Okay?" Ben asked, already at his side, placing an arm around his waist.

"Where is the little guy?" Cassidy asked, fearing the worst.

"Fine!" Ben helped him back down into the chair. "She's fine, or will be. She's a little dehydrated and malnourished, in desperate need of some TLC and a good scrubbing, but other than that she'll be fine."

"So all the…blood?" He could sense his cheeks had gone ashen as he thought about the bloody shirt.

"Surprisingly little blood, actually. Probably the white shirt made it seem worse than it really was. She had a good-sized gash and a few scratches but only needed some stitches. She was lucky you found her when you did, though." Ben stood back up. "I'm going to keep her overnight, make sure all her tests come back okay, and get her rehydrated. You can probably take her home tomorrow."

"She's not really mine," Cassidy said with a little boy-like shrug.

"Right." Ben laughed. "I forgot in all the commotion."

"I wouldn't mind taking her, though." Cassidy looked down at the tile. "I mean, you know…until the owners could be located."

"Hmmm." Ben nodded, very serious all of a sudden. "Well, what happens if we're not able to find the owners? No one's reported a missing Yorkie, and from the condition she was in, I'd say she's been out there fending for herself for at least a week. Kinda surprised she lasted so long, actually. She's more than likely been dumped."

"That's okay." Cassidy tried on a blank stare, trying not to show he cared one way or the other. "She's welcome to stay with me as long as she wants." Cassidy shook his head, talking about a dog as if it were a houseguest popping down for a visit. It made him furious anyone could abandon an animal like that.

"It's been happening quite a bit," Ben said, as if reading his last thought. "The crummy economy, I guess. People drive over from the mainland and just let 'em loose. We believe that's how that pack of wild dogs got here in the first place, although they could have crossed the causeway on their own."

"Someone needs to find them before they corner a little kid off on their own," Cassidy said.

"We caught two of them, and they have yet to attack any people."

Cassidy shrugged. "That big German shepherd one sure tried coming after me this afternoon."

"I'll need to alert the sheriff to that," Ben said, watching as Cassidy nodded unhappily. "I take it you were hoping to hide out for a bit?" When Cassidy agreed he said, "I won't mention to anyone else you're back on the island, but I have a feeling Sheriff Larson will want to talk to you about the incident."

"Of course he will," Cassidy said. *Great, now I'm involved in Doggy-gate. So much for keeping a low profile.*

"Sorry." Ben frowned. "Now, back to you being ready to watch over our little furry friend back there…"

"He already gave it the shirt off his back, Dr. D.," Sarah said, peeking around the corner.

Cassidy pointed in her direction. "Exactly. What she said."

Ben nodded, showing he was in agreement.

"It was designer too. Prada or Dolce, I think," Cassidy added, as if that made the sacrifice all the greater despite it being a plain white undershirt.

§ § §

When he got back to the shack, Cassidy found a note that said: *Neil was here. Where were you?* scribbled on the back of a deposit slip for a bank he'd never heard of.

A phone number was scribbled below it, and Cassidy couldn't help but wonder what kind of a moron left a note on something that had their checking-account information on it in this age of identity theft.

Okay, so I'm obviously irritable, he decided as he let himself into the house, realizing he hadn't bothered to lock the door.

What kind of an idiot runs off and leaves their house unlocked? he thought, locking the door behind him. It was already dusk, and his stomach was still a bit queasy. Since Cassidy wouldn't let Ben call anyone to give him a ride, he'd been made to lie down on the small couch in the vet's office until the dizziness had completely subsided.

Cassidy had never passed out before and was a little surprised by the effect it had on his body. His entire day had been pretty much shot, and he was completely drained. *So not like it looks in the movies.*

He wasn't really hungry but forced himself to eat a couple of pieces of toast anyway. He didn't call Neil, as he was quite certain he wouldn't be up for another night of power fucking. He did try calling Ollie, thankful when Spencer picked up the phone, as it made for a much shorter conversation.

He was absolutely exhausted, and for the first time, happy to be in this house. Despite all the memories it held, which saddened him more than they comforted him, he realized that he was home. He sneered at the staircase, opting instead for the fluffy chaise lounge in the parlor. Cassidy lay down, tossing his glasses on the coffee table while yanking a throw over him with his free hand. He kicked off his sandals, snuggled into the cushions as he shut his eyes, and whispered, "Thank you, Sadie."

CHAPTER FIVE

Cassidy sat up, eyes still half-closed as he tried to figure out what that noise had been. He relaxed a little, stretching as he yawned, and then curled up his lips, having caught a whiff of his underarms.

"Man stink."

He turned toward the front window, hearing the crackling noise again. He tried to focus through the haze, already craving coffee as he attempted to suss it out. It was a crunchy noise, and it was getting louder. Recognition swept over his face as he shot off the couch and sneaked over to the window, peeking out across the front porch.

He zeroed in on the pickup slowly crawling up the gravel drive, and he pressed his fingers into his eye sockets, attempting to rub the sleep out of them. He blinked rapidly as he focused in on the driver. "Fuck. Me. Shit."

He quickly ducked back behind the wall, already panicking before catching a glimpse of his reflection in the mirror hanging over the wood-carved fireplace mantel. A whimpered curse escaped from between his lips, after Cassidy saw his hair standing up on end.

He reached up and tried smushing it down, but it stood right back up whenever he removed his hand. He tried two more times, to no avail. Each time the hair sprang back up like morning wood. He then took note of his morning wood pitching a tent in yesterday's yellow shorts.

The crunching of tires on gravel stopped and he panicked, unwilling to allow this heinous vision to be Nate's new first impression of him. He ran toward the door that led into the foyer, cursing obscenities under his breath as he hopped on one foot, holding the other in his hands after stubbing a toe on the ottoman.

His eyes watered, but he continued to hop toward the doorway, refusing to give up. He heard the truck engine cut off and spun around, hopping backward as he peered out the window. He dropped his foot, knowing he'd need it to start running if he was to prevent this catastrophe. He turned just in time to walk into the doorjamb.

"Son of a cocksucker," he hissed, hand on his forehead as he took off running toward the kitchen, his free arm extended out in front of him to prevent yet another collision.

He came to the back door and turned the handle, trying to yank the door open with no success.

"What kind of an idiot locks their damn doors at night?" he mumbled as he frantically fumbled with the lock.

He froze as it suddenly occurred to him he should have run upstairs to the actual bathroom. He cursed under his breath, able to see the outdoor shower through the window. He never had been known for his precoffee cool head and clear thinking. Exhaling as he flung the door open, deciding it was too late to turn back now, Cassidy shot onto the back porch and ran out the screen door, practically tearing it off its hinges. He stopped suddenly, going back to the porch and shimmying out of his shorts as he grabbed a rolled-up beach towel out of the cabinet. He kicked the shorts off and ran like mad, sprinting across the courtyard.

He turned on the outdoor shower and whimpered as he dropped the towel, knowing how cold the water was going to be. He held his breath and jumped under the spray, furiously rubbing his body as he allowed it to completely soak his hair. He didn't have any soap, so he scrubbed his crotch and underarms as best he could while praying he wouldn't smell like day-old stale male. Taking full advantage of his now-decidedly genius idea of alfresco bathing, he aimed for the planting bed where all the runoff from the shower was headed and let out a deep groan as he took a piss.

He finally shut off the water and snatched up the towel, running back toward the house. Between his adrenaline and the cold water, he felt like he'd just downed half a dozen shots of espresso as he manically dried himself. He took long strides across the porch and back up into the kitchen.

Tossing the towel over his shoulder, he slicked his damp hair back off his forehead. He was trying to think of something for his morning breath while attempting to regulate his breathing, a result of his panicked antics. He took the towel and wrapped it tightly around, low on his hips. Opening the fridge, Cassidy heard what he hoped was the first knock on the door. He grabbed the OJ and quickly opened the carton before taking a big swig. He was swishing the juice around his mouth and gargling with it as he heard another knock.

He swallowed and closed his eyes, taking a deep cleansing breath before slowly making his way through the house toward the front door. He smiled, seeing Nate's outline through the glass. He was staring out toward his truck, as if contemplating leaving. Cassidy paused, feeling a lump forming in his chest. The angst began creeping up on him until Nate turned back to face the door. Cassidy watched Nate's head bobbing as though he'd caught a glimpse of him. He felt the smile stretching across his face, and he quickly walked to the front door before yanking it open.

For several moments they just stood there smiling, all goofy, like they'd been transported back in time and were once again two awkward high school boys. Cassidy shook his head, realizing Nate was most definitely no longer a high school boy.

He was thicker, wider through the shoulders, and pretty much larger muscled all the way around. The crinkles around his eyes and mouth from smiling were deeper set, but the blue eyes and floppy blond hair parted to the side were exactly the same. Cassidy noticed Nate's gaze trailing up and down his body, and tingles ran over his skin as Nate finally spoke.

"Hi."

Cassidy smiled as if he'd said *I love you.* "Hi."

Nate laughed, nodding as he started chewing on his lip. He

turned away for a moment, squinting as he looked across the porch, and when he turned back, Cassidy felt like someone had belted him.

"Wow," he mumbled under his breath.

Nate shook his head. "Been a while."

"Ya-huh." Cassidy nodded.

"Gonna invite me in?"

"Course."

Nate moved to come inside but stopped, watching curiously until Cassidy realized he needed to move out of the way so the man could get through the door.

"Sorry." Cassidy's cheeks flushed as he jerked his head, making room for Nate to pass.

Nate placed his hand on Cassidy's waist, leading him into the house. It was just like him, ever trying to take the lead. It should have bugged Cassidy, as it had been a very long time since he'd needed that from a guy. Instead he was entirely too caught up in the sensation created from the palm of Nate's hand on his bare skin to care about anything else.

"You look great," Nate said, pulling Cassidy into his arms and squeezing him up in a hug. "So sorry about Sadie."

"Thanks, Nate."

Cassidy relaxed into the hug for a moment, thinking it had come to an end too soon as they separated. They continued to stare at each other in silence. Cassidy wasn't sure what to say.

"You look great too, Nate," Nate finally said in a mocking tone.

Cassidy scrunched his face all up, feeling like a moron. "You do. Amazing, actually." He could feel his eyes rolling as he laughed a little. "Gee, buddy, you look like you work out," Cassidy added in a cheesy pick-up-line-like way.

Nate grinned, mildly sexed up, eyes practically glittering like sunlight on the rippled surface of the ocean. "Gonna bother even buying me a drink, or skip right to the fucking?"

Christ, is that an option? "I was just about to put on some coffee." Cassidy motioned toward the kitchen.

Nate nodded, half a grin lingering on his face as if he was still considering the possibility of sidestepping any and all formalities. "What happened to your forehead?"

"Huh?" Cassidy asked, slightly clueless as he reached up feeling the stinging sensation. "Oh…nothing…early-morning Pilates incident."

Cassidy led the way through the house as a chill ran down his back. He turned back and caught Nate admiring his ass out of the corner of his eye, confirming that, if nothing else, his instincts were still dead-on.

They entered the kitchen, and Cassidy smiled as Nate automatically snatched up the coffeepot and made his way to the sink while Cassidy grabbed the bag of fresh ground he'd picked up at the market in Corolla the day he arrived. A tinge of guilt sped through him as he remembered this had been Nate's home too. He'd grown up here, spent more time in this house than Cassidy had. He and Natalie belonged at Piper's Point every bit as much as Cassidy did.

He knew he should've already called Natalie and asked her to move back in, but planned on waiting until Ollie and Spence got there for emotional backup in case she was angry with him. He'd been counting on Natalie staying here while he was away during the school year anyway. He wondered if perhaps too much time had passed, or maybe there were too many painful memories here for her now? Cassidy knew he could board the place up, but this house was meant to be lived in. It made him sad to think of it being empty. It had always been so full of life.

Cassidy glanced at the urn on the table of the breakfast nook and thought how happy Sadie would be, having so many people staying over the summer. She always loved a houseful of people and all the parties—practically the whole island would show up. He'd wondered at times if she just couldn't stand being alone.

Perhaps loneliness had been the only thing that really scared her. He could practically hear Ollie saying, *Hi, Apple, meet Tree.*

It cut at his gut a little, thinking about the way she'd been forced to spend her final years. He could feel his fists clenching. Yes, it had been a five-star-resort nursing home, but it wasn't Piper's Point, and Cassidy knew this was the only place Sadie had wanted to be. Lionel had known it too. At the heart of it lay some sick, twisted thrill Lionel received out of finally being able to control his mother. The son of bitch was a multimillionaire; he could have easily set her up here with Natalie and a nurse. He'd done it out of spite, which made Cassidy sick to his stomach.

Cassidy jumped slightly, feeling Nate's hand on his shoulder. "You okay, Cass?"

Cassidy smiled away the bitterness, forcing his body to relax. "Fine. How 'bout that coffee?"

Nate smiled yet maintained an air of concern as he pointed to the bag of coffee in Cassidy's hand. "You're sorta…um, holding things up on that front."

"Right!"

Nate jerked, obviously startled, and they both burst out laughing.

"Shit, I didn't mean to yell that so loudly."

"Give it." Nate held out his hand, and Cassidy passed him the bag, then watched as Nate scooped out the appropriate amount of grounds. "So where'd you go before?"

"Nothing really. I mean, nowhere." Cassidy shook his head, trying to shake loose the cobwebs. "I was thinking that I needed to call Natalie. This place belongs to the two of you as much as it does me. It's probably time you both came home."

Nate finished pouring the water in the coffeemaker and stood as if frozen in time for a moment. "Thank you for that."

Cassidy could see that he was getting a bit worked up when Nate placed his hands on his hips and turned away for a moment, softly nodding his appreciation.

"It's been…off, being back on the island and not living at the Point. Mom and I have done our best to keep the place up."

Cassidy smiled. "So you're the one who painted the new color?"

"Shit, you don't like it?"

"It's not that. It was just a bit of a shock—expecting one thing after all that time away and finally coming back to find another."

Nate cringed before grabbing two coffee mugs out of the cabinet behind him. "I'm sorry, Cass. I wish I'd taken that into consideration."

"I like it, though, Nate. Thank you for keeping her in such amazing shape." Cassidy leaned over, resting his arms on top of the island. "It's a beautiful color, and maybe it's a good thing—the same yet slightly different."

"Fresh start?"

"Yeah." Cassidy smiled, feeling his skin tingle as the aroma from the brew filtered in through his nose, filling his senses. "I hope you'll both move back in." Cassidy glanced over to the urn. "Sadie would've wanted that."

"Is that…"

"Yeah."

"So sorry, man."

Cassidy took in a sharp breath, then smiled as Nate handed him a steaming cup of joe. "She's back home where she belongs now."

Nate motioned toward the back door. "Maybe we could go outside and have a seat?"

"Sure. Please, after you."

Cassidy followed Nate out to the screened-in back porch, completely lost in how incredible his ass looked in denim. He cursed, nearly spilling his coffee as he bumped into Nate, who had stopped abruptly.

Eyes forward, asshole. "Sorry," Cassidy said. He looked up to see

Nate staring at his yellow gym shorts, which were dangling from one of the ceiling-fan blades. *Shit.*

"Should I even ask?" Nate asked, appearing highly amused and taking a drink as he watched Cassidy snatch them off the blade.

"Please don't." Cassidy fidgeted, momentarily unsure what to do with the shorts, before tossing them across the porch and into the towel hamper. He laughed nervously.

"I think you'd be hard-pressed to get Mom to move back in." Nate took a seat at the table, which had been made out of salvaged planks of wood from old boats. "But if you're serious, I certainly wouldn't say no."

Cassidy sat across from Nate and watched as the guy he'd lost his virginity to stare out over the courtyard, seeming relieved at the thought of being back. Nate was at home here, like a fixture or part of the architecture, but Cassidy hadn't considered the possible weirdness of living here, just the two of them. Of course, Ollie and Spencer would be here by the weekend. But he couldn't guarantee they'd both want to spend every vacation they ever had for the rest of their lives on Hart's Island in order to keep Cassidy from dealing with any weirdness.

"Natalie doesn't feel at home here anymore?"

Nate grinned and leaned back into the wooden chair, stretching his long legs out in front of him. "It took getting thrown out by court order for Max to finally ask her to move in with him."

Cassidy nodded. "Of course." Maxwell Barnes owned the local hardware store and had been courting Natalie since the dawn of civilization. Natalie had been trying to get Max to propose for decades. *Hear that, Sadie. Natalie finally got her man.*

"If that changes things and you don't want just me…"

"This is your home, Nate." Cassidy shrugged, thinking it did change things, despite the fact he wasn't sure how or why. "You don't require anyone's permission to be here. I'll put you and Natalie on the deed if that's what it takes to make you believe it. Probably not a bad idea anyway. That way Lionel can't ever get his grubby hands on Sadie's shack."

Nate sat up and leaned across the table, placing a hand on Cassidy's arm. "Thanks for that, but it's not necessary."

"I'm glad Natalie's happy, though. That's a relief. I was never able to muster up the guts to call and face her after the judge ordered a mandatory evacuation of the property until ownership could be determined. It's nice something good came from it."

"Oh, Cass, she never… Tell me you don't think Mom ever blamed you for one second."

Cassidy remembered he had coffee and took a big sip, intensely enjoying the burn as much as he did having something to camouflage his face. "Either way, all under the bridge now, I hope. I've invited a couple of friends down for the summer from Chapel Hill. They won't be here till the weekend, so as long as you won't mind the extra company?"

"Your house, your rules." Nate smiled but seemed to be fidgeting a little. "Boyfriend?"

Cassidy nodded, only half listening. "Well, they're boyfriends—to each other. I introduced them in a roundabout way."

"Sadie would love that." Nate chuckled. "A house full of men."

Cassidy laughed a bit in agreement. "She and I had that in common."

"I remember."

Cassidy knew exactly what had changed, seeing the nasty-dog way Nate was now watching him. *Dog?* He needed to go get the dog. Thank God for that little runt of a dog. "Well, welcome home, Nate." Cassidy stood up. "I assume you still have your key?"

"I do," Nate said, getting up as well, seeming not to know how to react to whatever was now happening.

"Great!" Cassidy nodded, then gave Nate a quick hug, trying not to think about how wonderful it was to have Nate's hand resting on the small of his back, just above his ass. "Well, I've got some errands to run, so…"

"I can come with." Nate was noticeably confused as Cassidy pulled away. "We've got eight years to catch up on, you know."

"We're roomies now." Cassidy slapped him on the arm, again trying not to think about how incredibly smokin' hot his body must be naked. "I'll grab some wine and a couple of steaks when I'm in town, and we can get drunk, swap stories, and braid each other's hair tonight."

"Are you sure? 'Cause…"

"Honestly, Nate, it's fine," Cassidy said. "You go get some, or all of your things, and I'll help you unload it later. I just have to pop over to Dr. Downey's to pick up my…this little dog I saved from becoming kibble to a pack of wild dogs yesterday."

"Okay, then," Nate suddenly agreed, finally letting it go. "You have a dog. That's great. I love dogs."

"Off to the showers I go," Cassidy said, heading back into the house. "Till tonight, then, roomie."

"'Kay," Nate managed to toss out before Cassidy hopped up the steps and disappeared into the kitchen.

He smacked himself in the head as he set his coffee cup in the sink, whimpering as he managed to hit the bruised spot from his case of the vapors the day before at the vet's. *Roomie?* Cassidy wasn't sure what had happened to his whole "lying low" plan, but it had been officially blown out of the water. He weaved around the island and through the house, finally ascending the stairs. On top of everything else, he'd managed to somehow wind up living alone in this house with Nate?

"You suck at flying under the radar." He chastised himself under his breath. He ripped the towel off as he walked into the bathroom, closing the door behind him. He shook his head and glared at himself in the mirror, knowing that legally, he might have the right to keep Nate from moving back in, but morally, he didn't have a leg to stand on. "Don't be an asshole, Cassidy."

He reached into the shower and turned the faucet on, realizing he actually liked the thought of Nate being here, and that really had him freaked. "Apparently quite a lot." Cassidy dropped his gaze down between his legs and eyed his rapidly swelling cock. "Sorry, dude, but we can't be going there. Nate isn't someone we can just break up with when things don't work out."

Cassidy sighed, rolling his eyes as he hopped into the shower, feeling his dick growing thicker as it continued on its destructive rise to power. *Damn you and your wicked ways.* He took the head of it in his hand and began to massage himself as the water ricocheted off his body. He let out a low groan, shutting his eyes and allowing himself to get lost in the waves of lust and pleasure as he whispered Nate's name.

Chapter Six

"You have got to get here el pronto, damn it!" Cassidy yelled out while steering his car around a sharp curve, tires squealing. "I mean it, Spencer. I'm at DEFCON five or something!"

Spencer Reynolds had been one of the very first people Cassidy met when he arrived at UNC at Chapel Hill to begin his freshman year. He was the son of a Washington lobbyist and a work-from-home event-planning diva, who now referred to Ollie as *That Boy*. Spencer and Cassidy had bonded over growing up with cold, distant parents who held unrealistically high expectations no ordinary human could ever live up to.

"I thought you said it was as much Nate's home as it is yours?" Spencer asked, his voice coming over the car speakers.

"It is, damn it…but that really isn't the point here," Cassidy said while trying to keep his panicked, bugged-out eyes peeled on the road ahead of him.

"Well, what is the damn point?" Ollie asked, joining in the audio three-way.

"That I want to do slutty, desperately lustful, and debasing… *things* to him!"

"I'm not seeing the problem." Spencer laughed. "Have at it."

"With our blessing," Ollie added.

"Guys, this is Nate. Not some random guy I met at a coffeehouse or while jogging through the park. There are no take-backs or do-overs…"

"We get it." Oliver sighed, sounding bored. "Someone you can't fake it with for six to nine months."

"Lasting just long enough to get you through the school year," Spencer added.

Oliver laughed. "Before being unceremoniously dumped."

Cassidy scowled. "That's not fair."

"That's your MO to a tee," Spencer accused. "You did it all through college as a student and have continued the same destructive pattern now that you're teaching."

"I'm sorry, Cass, but we can't come early. We're having some much-needed alone time, *couple-only* alone time," Oliver said.

"This is not negotiable! I cannot stay in that house with him for another second by myself."

"You have got to calm down," Spencer commanded.

"You bitches owe me! You'd never have met if it weren't for me!"

"Oh puh-lease!" Ollie said. "You're seriously going to try using that!"

"When did you become such a drama queen, Cassidy?" Spencer asked, causing Cassidy's mouth to fall open as he glared at the console.

"Don't be lookin' at my man like that, Cassidy Winters," Ollie snapped. "And close your mouth."

"I hate it when you do that!" Cassidy searched over his console, then under the visors while attempting to keep his car on the road. There simply had to be a hidden camera.

"We aren't coming, not even one day earlier, damn it," Spencer said in an authoritative voice.

"But you're my best friends," Cassidy said, stunned as he steered the car around another tight corner and onto the main drag. "You're supposed to be there for me."

Cassidy listened as Ollie said to Spencer, "Baby, that was so butch."

He rolled his eyes, irritated that he was now being ignored by Ollie completely.

"Well, this is just silly." Spencer blew a disgusted puff of breath into the phone. "Surely even you can manage to keep your legs closed for a few fucking days."

Cassidy decided to ignore the snarky "don't count on it" that came from Ollie.

"When did you get so mean, Spencer?" Cassidy asked, cocking his head to the side as he heard what sounded suspiciously like lip smacking coming through the speakers.

"Sorry, Cass, but you've had hair on your balls for a long time now. Man up and stop whining like a little pussy."

Cassidy heard Oliver moaning softly followed by the sound of a zipper. He decided to ignore it until Spencer whispered, "Shit."

"I can't believe I've become part of your foreplay!"

It got dead quiet for about a half a second. "Don't be ridiculous," Ollie snapped.

"Screw it," Cassidy snapped back. "Just suck each other off already. I'll handle this all by myself."

"Okay," Spencer said.

"You'll be fine," Ollie added.

"We have the utmost—oh…fuck yeah—faith in you, buddy," Spencer managed to get out just before the click, followed by the car switching automatically back to music from the stereo.

"Rancid sluts." Cassidy punched the Off button for the stereo as he pulled into the parking lot of Hammond's Grocery. He found a parking spot, cut the engine, and then took a moment to massage his temples while taking several deep breaths, exhaling slowly.

"You can do this, Cassidy. The empire struck back, and you kicked its ass. Surely you can control your…light saber."

He laughed out loud at how ludicrous he sounded as he sat back in the seat. He noticed the sheriff's car parked behind him through the rearview mirror. "Shit." *Why not just hold up a neon sign, Larson? Cassidy Winters is here!*

Cassidy removed the keys from the ignition and opened the car door, realizing it didn't matter at this point how conspicuous the sheriff was. Obviously Ben hadn't kept his word, having turned into the town crier. Otherwise Nate wouldn't have shown up on his doorstep first thing that morning.

"Good morning, Sheriff Larson."

"Cassidy," Larson said, giving a curt nod in that professional procedural way. "Good to have you back at the Point. Everyone was very sorry to hear about Sadie's passing."

"Thank you." Cassidy nodded, feeling the instaguilt returning.

"We kinda expected to have you back a lot sooner, though."

Here it comes, Cassidy thought.

"Guess the whole legal mess with your father took its toll."

Cassidy leaned against the car, wondering if the sheriff was giving him an out. "It wasn't a pleasant experience."

"We're all relieved you came out on top."

Cassidy smiled, happy to hear that.

"So Ben Downey tells me you had a run-in with those damn dogs."

Cassidy nodded and went through the entire story again for the sheriff. He kept nodding and waving as other islanders would pass by, telling him hello. Two even interrupted the sheriff's interview to tell him how sorry they'd been to hear about Sadie. Cassidy tried to decide if they were being friendly on the outside while secretly judging him for not protecting her behind the smiles. It had been almost four years since Sadie died, yet it seemed to be as fresh in their minds as it was in Cassidy's. Like time had stopped and no one had been able to move on. Had they all been waiting to say good-bye too?

He liked to died when Mrs. Nichols told him he was too thin and that he wouldn't be fainting all the time if he'd put some meat on his bones. He'd passed out one time, and all of a sudden it was an affliction. "Thank you, Mrs. Nichols; I'm sure you're right."

Sheriff Larson closed his little notebook. "I guess that's enough for now, Cassidy. You call the station and let us know if you see those dogs again."

"You got it, Sheriff."

Using the exact same curt nod he'd used upon greeting Cassidy, the sheriff got back into his squad car, gave a little two-fingered salute, and drove off. As Cassidy headed toward the automatic doors of the store, he made a mental note to get some of those big green olives to go with the vodka. Something told him he'd most definitely need them before the week was out.

Hammond's Grocery had been built in the early sixties, and it looked it. Not that it wasn't well cared for, mind you, but the architecture and design of the building screamed Kennedy era. It had this screwy white roof that looked like a rolling wave. The entire front of the building consisted of glass panes, up to two stories high in the middle where the roofline curved up.

Cassidy waited for the doors to swing open, greeted by that familiar scent of aged linoleum, floor wax, and produce. The floors had that yellowed hue, yet they shined like new due to the high-gloss buff. Mr. Hammond insisted the employees get that beast of a machine out every couple of hours to polish them. Cassidy grabbed one of the minicarts, which were about half the size of the ones you'd expect to find at your local grocer's. People on the island usually stopped by the store two or three times a week as opposed to two or three times a month.

Of course, he'd probably have graduated high school never having seen the inside of a grocery store at all, if he hadn't spent his summers with Sadie. His parents paid other people to do those kinds of things for them.

Hammond's had always been more than an errand; it was a social outing. An hour in the grocery store could get you caught up on a month's worth of news across the island, which was why he'd stopped and purchased food before hitting the causeway. Cassidy thought it was neat when he was a kid. He actually still might think it was neat if he didn't feel as though he'd be the main topic of conversation over the coming weeks.

As he made his way through the aisles, Cassidy decided on one of those prepackaged salads that came with everything, including the dressing. He noticed that people kept stopping him. He'd thought it was sweet at first, hoping that maybe no one blamed him after all. But after fifteen minutes in the grocery store to pick up a handful of items, he was beginning to wonder. It seemed as if they were actually trying to prevent him from leaving—even Mrs. Taylor, who always smelled like Cheez Whiz and kept her gray hair tied up into a tight bun, was being nice. And everyone knew she didn't like anyone apart from her cats.

He'd finally managed to make it to the checkout, fumbling with the cash he pulled out of his pocket. He was counting it, hoping he actually had enough with him when something out of the corner of his eye grabbed his attention. Cassidy turned, and his stomach dropped, seeing Natalie's tan wood-paneled station wagon screeching into a parking spot. He watched as she flew out of the car, only to turn back remembering she forgot to grab her purse.

Natalie had always appeared small to Cassidy with regards to her physicality, with her pixie-cut dark red hair, and fingers like little sausages. She even had a "welcome to Munchkinland" chipmunklike giggle. But what she lacked in height she made up for in exuberance, possessing all things motherly in spades. Natalie was the antithesis of Cassidy's mother, who should have never had children. It would have been a true crime against humanity had Natalie not been a mom. If not for the fact they had the exact same eyes, one would never pick her out of a lineup as Nate's mom. He was like the Jolly Green Giant in comparison.

When she finally made it into the store, pushing on the automatic doors instead of waiting for them to open on their own, she paused for a moment, scanning the store as if to decide which way to go. Once their eyes met, that immediate rush of warmth that came off Natalie in waves slammed into him. It was one of the qualities that drew people to her.

"You, young man," Natalie said, pointing at Cassidy, tears already running down her rosy cheeks. "You get over here this instant and give me a hug."

Cassidy exhaled, allowing a short laugh of relief to escape as he slowly went to her. His eyes burned when she fell into him, burying her tiny face into his chest. Cassidy squeezed her tight, trying not to cry, considering everyone in the store was surely watching.

"I should be so angry with you for not calling me the instant you got back." Natalie sniffled, her voice muffled. She pulled away slightly, allowing her to fully inspect Cassidy.

Cassidy shook his head, taking a deep breath. "I'm sorry for a great many things, Natalie."

"Oh, you. Stop that nonsense right now. I won't hear any of it." Natalie reached up and pinched his cheek. "Such a dashing young man you've turned into, Cassidy Winters." She giggled as if embarrassed and turned to Mrs. Taylor, who was shuffling toward the exit. "Isn't he just so handsome? Like Tyrone Power."

"You're the slowest woman I've ever had the displeasure of assisting with intrigue, Sommers," Mrs. Taylor snapped, finally allowing her true colors to shine through as she gave Cassidy a once-over. "Looks a little thin if you ask me."

"Such a lovely ray of sunshine you are, Mrs. Taylor." Natalie giggled, seeming to know that would irritate the old woman more than returning the same grumpiness back at her. "You have a super day!"

Cassidy shook his head at Natalie as Mrs. Taylor mumbled something under her breath he was sure would make a sailor blush. "You're a mean little lady, Nat." Cassidy teased her once he believed the elderly woman was out of earshot.

Natalie examined him as if checking for any marks or bruises, making sure he was in the same condition he had been ten years before. She scowled a little at the bruise on his forehead and then wiped her cheeks, being careful not to completely ruin her makeup. "You are a sight for sore eyes." She nodded toward the cashier. "Go get your groceries. You're coming with me."

"Actually, I need to get to Dr.…"

"No excuses, Cassidy." Natalie put on her serious face, which didn't come off as very intimidating yet was something anyone who knew her didn't say no to. "I'm not letting you out of my sight until we sit down and have a long talk."

Cassidy nodded in agreement, unable to deny her peaches-and-creaminess. He smiled when she giggled while softly clapping her hands. Being around Natalie had always been a little like being on antidepressants. No matter how foul your mood, you inevitably wound up getting a bit of a contact high, a quality that Sadie liked to call proximital bliss.

As Cassidy paid for his food and gathered up his bags, he could already feel a slight shift in his little corner of the universe. There was a little more love for him to grab hold of should he need it. He was thankful to have it, as Natalie was the closest thing he had left to a parent.

His mother had never been very warm, too caught up with the societal expectations of being married to Lionel Winters. That's what he liked to tell himself, anyway. It just seemed to sit better than admitting she might simply be cold and unfeeling or that there might be something wrong with him, that he was unlovable.

"Come on, Peanut." Natalie beamed, grabbing Cassidy by the arm as if able to detect the slight sadness that had come over him. "Let's see if we can't put a little meat on those bones."

Cassidy grinned, liking the fact that someone found fault with his appearance.

§ § §

Cassidy sat at the small table, completely mesmerized by all the tchotchkes in the tiny kitchen of Max's little house on Ocean Boulevard. Everywhere his gaze landed, a glossy pink ceramic piggy was staring back at him. The lime green paint and wallpaper only made them stand out that much more as Cassidy surveyed the terrain, which he guessed hadn't been updated since the day Max moved into it. Cassidy had never been in Max's house before, so it was odd being there in the first place, but even stranger was the knowledge that Max was a ceramic-pig collector.

The house was what was referred to architecturally as a honeymoon bungalow, built around the end of the Second World War; well built but simple in design, with arched doorways, oak floors, and oversize double-hung windows. The wood-sided house had two bedrooms, a small formal dining room, and a cozy living room with dark-stained built-in bookshelves and a wood-burning fireplace. It was nothing like Piper's Point in terms of either scale or amenities, but Cassidy couldn't ever remember seeing Natalie as happy as she trotted around the tiny kitchen.

When she came from the mainland thirty-odd years ago, running away from an abusive husband, she was broke and eight months pregnant. She arrived on Sadie's doorstep searching for a job. Sadie's fourth marriage had ended only weeks before, and they wound up putting each other back together again.

His mouth watered as she set one of her large, fresh-out-of-the-oven homemade cinnamon rolls in front of him, along with a steaming cup of coffee. She was famous all over the island for her cinnamon rolls. The dob of icing she'd placed on the top was slowly melting and oozing down the sides.

Cassidy could feel his entire body having a physical reaction from the smell of it as he grinned at Natalie. "You're the devil, woman." He wouldn't exactly call it an aphrodisiac, though it did have that kind of effect on him.

She giggled and plopped down next to him at the breakfast table off the kitchen. "Mrs. Taylor was right about one thing—you could use a little fattening up."

Cassidy picked up the fork and helped himself to a large bite of the molten gooeyness, feeling like he might cream in his jeans as his eyes rolled back into his head. "So good," he managed to get out between bites.

"Those cinnamon rolls were about the only thing that could ever get you boys to sit still when you were little." She took a sip from her coffee cup. "At least some things haven't changed."

"Now I feel like I'm home," Cassidy mumbled between chews as he pointed at the pastry with his fork.

Natalie shook her head at him, beaming. "I'm so proud of you. Sadie would be so proud of you—an English professor." She got a little teary-eyed. "Both my boys turned out to be such fine men."

"Don't, Natalie." He set his fork down. "I don't deserve it."

"I'm only going to say this once more, Cassidy Winters. I know how difficult it was for you, not being able to do anything to help her. I know exactly how you feel, because it broke my heart not being able to put a stop to Lionel. After everything Sadie had done for me, taking me in and giving me a safe home to raise my child in. I had nothing, Cassidy—nowhere to go and no money to get there even if I had. She gave me a second chance at a life that led to far more happiness than I'd ever dreamed possible, and the one time she really needed my help, I wasn't able to."

Cassidy took another bite. He'd spent so much time fearing Natalie would be angry or blame him. It never occurred to him that she might have been experiencing the same desperation and guilt he had.

"It's like this weight pressing down on me, Natalie." Cassidy could feel his resolve slipping, and his shoulders slumped. "Any free time I had I'd drive down to spend with her."

"The nurses said you were there nearly every weekend sitting with her, squeezing in your homework while she slept and talking to her about school and classes when she was awake."

"I just wanted to try keeping her distracted. She wasn't able to communicate very well, but I could see it in her eyes—pleading for me to get her out of that place." Cassidy's vision blurred as the tears ran down his cheeks.

"That's how I know how strong you are, Cassidy," Natalie said, brushing her fingertips over his arm. "You still showed up week after week, knowing you'd have to witness that. A lot of people wouldn't have been able to do that."

"I was so close to graduating…"

"You got your degree in four years, didn't you?"

"My undergrad, yes." Cassidy nodded. "I was a wreck, but I kept pushing. Lionel had used my age and the fact that he didn't want me to quit my studies to convince the judge I wasn't in a position to care for Sadie. He actually used my dream of being a teacher to convince the judge not to allow me to halt my education. The sick bastard practically had an aneurysm when I told him that I wanted to be a teacher."

"You told the judge you'd drop out of college to care for her?"

"In retrospect, it probably made me sound naive and immature, but I could tell the judge respected the fact that I was willing to do it. I just knew I could get her out of that place once I graduated. I kept telling Sadie to hold on a little longer and I'd get her back home."

"I believe you'd have done it too, Cassidy."

"Four days, Natalie." Cassidy's jaw set, as he felt himself getting angry. "I'd already petitioned the court for a new hearing. If only she'd held on for a little longer. I'll never forgive myself. I should have worked harder…been faster…"

"Oh, my sweet boy." Natalie got out of her chair and took Cassidy into her arms, holding him tight as he let it all out. "You can't save everyone. Sometimes you have to find a way to be content with the knowledge that you had the best of intentions. Wherever Sadie is, she knows how hard you fought for her."

Cassidy's muscles went limp as Natalie brushed the hair back off his forehead. She began to softly shush him as she rocked back and forth. He was embarrassed at the outburst, as it had been unintentional. Yet he also felt as if another tiny piece of the weight he'd been carrying had been chipped away. He wasn't so alone after all, and for the first time in a long time, Cassidy experienced a calming sense of relief wash over him.

The sadness was still there hanging over him, but perhaps a little more bearable. He explained to Natalie that he didn't have his PhD yet, so he wasn't actually a professor, even though he was able to teach. He still needed to complete his dissertation and go through the whole process of defending it, which had begun to feel like some insurmountable summit he'd never be able to reach.

A great many things began to make sense to him as Natalie talked about life on her end of the world. He'd always assumed Natalie had visited Sadie during the week because she wanted to avoid seeing him on the weekends. In reality, she had done it so Sadie spent less time by herself. She also admitted that she'd been distracted that first summer after Sadie's stroke. Nate had come home from school after his sophomore year and wasn't himself.

"He was very withdrawn and somber." Natalie's forehead scrunched up. "I still to this day don't know why exactly. I assumed a bad relationship, but you know Nate—never one to open up."

Cassidy smiled, wondering what this mystery man who'd broken Nate's heart had been like. Whoever the guy was, Cassidy hated him. It was beyond strange to suddenly feel like such a stranger to the guy he'd practically grown up with. He honestly knew nothing about the man Nate was today. It was as if Nate had been locked away in a time capsule for ten years and just released back into Cassidy's world.

"You know"—Natalie grinned—"he still to this day has never actually told me he's gay."

Cassidy laughed, feeling his cheeks flush with heat. "Considering you walked in on us in my bedroom that last summer…"

Natalie let her chipmunk giggle fly loose as she too turned as red as her hair. "Oh my. I suppose so. That was certainly a doozy of an eye-opener. I never again opened a closed door without knocking, let me tell you. Oh my, and Sadie was so damn calm about it."

"That's 'cause she'd known since the previous summer," Cassidy said. "She walked in on us kissing in the boathouse."

"No!" Natalie's face froze in shock. "That little floozy never said a word!"

"She said she'd keep our secret if Nate rolled her a joint."

Natalie squealed, slamming her arm onto the table. "Damn that woman—she knew I suspected Nate was smokin' the reefer, and told me I was being paranoid. Blackmailing high school boys. I could wring her neck."

Cassidy smiled at the way Natalie called it *the reefer*. "The woman could keep a secret like no other."

"She was a deviant—some sorta mobster."

"The way you two used to argue." Cassidy leaned back into his chair.

"We were so different, like sisters, on each other's last nerve one minute…"

"And laughing your fool heads off the next."

"I do miss her terribly." Natalie sighed. "She was my very best friend, you know."

"Mine too." Cassidy smiled.

Natalie nodded, not needing to say another word for Cassidy to understand exactly how much less their lives were, not having Sadie in them. Natalie forced another cinnamon roll on him, and he didn't have the heart to say no—or the willpower.

"I'm so excited to have my other boy back." She sat back down next to him, patting his arm. "I've been happy here, living with Max, but I must say I felt a little useless after Sadie and Nate were gone. You know I need someone to take care of."

"It is your way," he added with a wink.

"I never felt lonelier than I did when there was no one left to fuss over." Her brow furrowed as she thought back.

Cassidy reached over and squeezed her hand until she smiled. She shook her head at him and nudged for him to finish eating. He laughed, realizing she was probably itching to get the plate cleaned up and put away.

As Cassidy left Max's bungalow to pick up his new ward, Natalie promised to drop by in a day or two to check on them, and he asked her to bring Max over for dinner in the next few weeks.

"I'm happier than I can remember being in a very long time." They hugged for what seemed an eternity as Natalie teared up again, apologizing, though not meaning it. "You know, of course, the council elders are anxious to meet with you."

Cassidy groaned his disapproval at the thought of dealing with that mess.

"They want to discuss your role with regard to island politics and taking Sadie's place on the council."

Cassidy cringed at the realization he'd have to deal with it at some point. "Thanks for the warning." He didn't have the heart to mention to her that he wasn't planning on staying year-round and therefore probably shouldn't have a role in any of Hart's affairs.

As he got back into his car and backed it out of the skinny one-lane driveway, he waved once more at Natalie. He could see her beaming from the street, and once again, he exhaled his relief and whispered one more thank-you to Sadie.

Chapter Seven

Cassidy looked down at his new ward, unable to believe it was the same little creature. Dr. D. had insisted she stay in the crate while traveling. Cassidy continued calling her Dog, for lack of deciding what to name the poor thing. Ben had instructed him to keep her from chewing and licking the stitches; otherwise she'd pull them out too soon. They were supposed to dissolve on their own, but he warned it would be itchy and to make sure to keep a close eye on her.

Cassidy had snidely hinted to Ben that he appreciated the fact he'd kept his word about not blabbing his arrival all over the island. He called Sarah into the exam room, and she confessed that she'd told her mother all about *the fainting*.

Of course she would have to be the daughter of Marianne Abbott, island Realtor, and gossip extraordinaire. He was wondering what he'd even been paying her for, considering it was Nate and Natalie who'd been taking care of the property.

He wanted to be pissed, but Cassidy assumed the poor child came by it honestly. Despite being irritated, he couldn't blame the girl, considering neither Ben nor he had bothered asking her to keep mum about the incident.

Cassidy reached over and slid his fingers through the grate, wiggling them. He was relieved the little thing was okay. Ben dosed her for fleas, worms, and rabies. They cleaned her up, and her matted brown, black, and silver hair had been buzzed short. She looked like Gizmo from *Gremlins* when her ears stood straight up. He smiled, feeling her cold, wet nose on his fingertips, followed quickly by her pink tongue, which curled up on the end as she licked away.

He'd been gone a lot longer than he'd meant to be and wound up having to go back to Natalie's since he'd managed to forget to grab the steaks and salad out of her fridge. Natalie had been delirious when Cassidy told her Nate was moving back to Piper's

Point. She'd just about knocked him out of his chair, hugging him.

Cassidy had been equally astounded by Nate's infiltration of the island old-timers. Nate had set up a Web site that allowed all the vacation rental properties to be listed on one site. People could check out pictures, and he linked it to Google Maps. You could also book each individual property by day or week and pay for it all online in advance. He'd singlehandedly revolutionized the holiday and summer vacation industry for the island, which was now booked out three years in advance with a waiting list.

Each homeowner had the option of maintaining their own rental pages, or they could pay extra and let Nate do it all for them. It was amazingly intricate and had bled over into a companion site that listed all the landmarks, historical sites, restaurants, and other businesses, which all paid a nominal fee to be included.

Nate had even been given a seat on Hart's city council. It was a little surprising, considering very few outside the families who originally settled the island had ever been given such an honor. Natalie had beamed talking about her boy, but Cassidy couldn't help but feel like she was the tiniest bit worried about Nate, though she never came out and said as much. Since Natalie was somewhat prone to worry, Cassidy decided to let it go without comment on his part. He'd seen Nate that morning, and the man seemed fine to him—damned fine at that.

Cassidy pulled his hand away from the crate to help steer the car around the long curve that went past the lighthouse and recreation area on the east side of the island. He cleared his throat and shifted slightly in the driver's seat as he tried to purge the memory of Nate's ass in Levi's that had somehow become newly burned into his brain. He remembered jacking off in the shower that morning. Imagining what it might feel like to once again have Nate's naked body pressing into his as the hot water rained down over him.

He wondered what that might feel like now, as opposed to the way it had when he was seventeen. Would it be familiar to him at all, or every bit as foreign and exciting as it had been the first time? Cassidy had no clue what he was doing back then. His sexual experience consisted of little more than the bit of gay porn he'd been able to download from the Internet. Well, that and the bit of experimentation he'd attempted on his own, locked away in his bedroom at night.

Cassidy's face burned slightly. He was a little embarrassed, despite being alone in the car with only his thoughts and a strange dog. He glanced out the window of the car, seeing the trees whipping by and let his mind wander back to the first time he'd ever been behind the wheel of a moving vehicle. It wound up not being the only lesson he'd had that day.

§ § §

It was late afternoon and unseasonably warm for early June along the coast of North Carolina. Nate had been giving Cassidy shit for being seventeen and still unable to drive. It hadn't seemed that strange to Cassidy, who was driven anywhere he wanted to go back in Charlotte. But considering the cow Nate was having over it, Cassidy finally told him to either teach him how to drive or shut up about it.

Nate agreed, but only after making a huge production over the fact that Cassidy would once again owe him for dragging him out of his pathetically pampered existence. Nate drove them inland in his old white pickup to the back roads in the forested part of the island where there was little to no traffic aside from the rare hiker or camper. Most of the vacation traffic on Hart's revolved along the coastline—the beaches, town, and harbor, and the campgrounds around the lighthouse. The only people who really ever came out to this part of the woods were local kids who wanted to screw, drink, and party.

Cassidy carefully steered the pickup down the one-lane dirt road. The radio was blaring Shania Twain's "You're Still the One," and they had the windows rolled down, leaving a cloud of dust kicking up behind them. Nate was drinking a beer he'd pulled out of a cooler tied down in the bed of his pickup and was laughing his ass off as Cassidy white-knuckled the steering wheel in a panic he would do something wrong.

Nate loved making fun of him, and the fact that Cassidy had spouted off, sounding like a PSA on teen drinking and driving, had given him plenty to work with. Cassidy never knew where Nate got the beer, but he somehow managed to occasionally come up with the stray six-pack. It wasn't that Cassidy was uptight, as he'd normally be drinking right along with him, but he did have a tendency to react badly under stress. Since Nate had all but threatened him with bodily harm should he so much as scratch his Caddy, as he liked to refer to his truck, Cassidy was anything but comfortable.

As the sun began to go down, Nate had him turn off the main drag, parking down a wooded lane that came to a dead end. They each got out of the truck, and Nate put the tailgate down. Cassidy was popping his knuckles and attempting to stretch his fingers, which were sore from gripping the hell out of the steering wheel for so long.

Nate pulled off his sweat-soaked *Friends* T-shirt and tossed it over the side of the truck. He hopped up and bent over the cooler, fishing out two beers. Cassidy's dick was reacting to the stimulus of Nate's tight-muscled upper body. As he stood back up and turned around, Cassidy all but drooled over the perfect V shape that led from his chest down into the front of his jeans. His skin glistened slightly, catching the light coming from inside the cab of the truck. Cassidy's head swam from the heat, and seeing Nate like that didn't help.

Cassidy had been back at Piper's Point for over a week now, and neither one of them had talked about their pot-induced kiss the summer before in the boathouse, which had been cut short by Sadie and her shitty timing. He'd come to the sad conclusion that Nate was going to simply pretend it never happened. It had merely been some awesomely weird combination of pot and the heat that made Nate kiss him the day he left the island all those months ago.

My kingdom for a doobie!

"Christ, it's hot out, Cass," Nate said, handing a beer over to Cassidy. "Aren't you hot?"

"Yeah." Cassidy opened the beer can and took a sip. He shook his head a little from the taste. He'd had it several times before but still didn't love the bitterness. He set the can down and pulled off his shirt as Nate jumped down next to him and leaned back into the truck. Cassidy wiped his face with his shirt and noticed that Nate was looking over his chest. Nate glanced back up at Cassidy and smiled, turning his head to stare out into the trees.

"You should come to the gym with me," Nate finally said, taking another sip of beer. "You've got a nice body. Bet we could get you cut like me in no time. Combined with that mug of yours, you'd be practically unstoppable."

"Really?" Cassidy asked, picking up his beer can and taking another drink. His cock swelled as images of Nate and him hitting the showers flashed through his mind. "That would be great, Nate. Thanks."

"It's quiet out here," Nate said.

Cassidy was staring up at the darkening sky but could feel Nate's eyes on him. Strange, he could always tell when Nate watched him. Cassidy reached up, slowly running a hand down his own stomach.

"I like it. It's nice," Cassidy said, turning around and bending over, resting his elbows on the tailgate as he sucked down more beer. "Peaceful."

"You do like it quiet, book boy," Nate said, stretching his back out. "We should get going."

"Oh please, Nate"—Cassidy hopped up and sat on the truck bed—"can't we stay awhile? We can lie back and watch the stars."

"Fine, for a bit," Nate said, peering over his shoulder as Cassidy scooted back.

Nate laughed when Cassidy made little cooing noises as he lay back in the truck bed. "The metal's still warm from the sun. Feels good."

Cassidy watched as Nate walked along the side of the truck and reached over to grab another beer out of the cooler. He pulled out an extra and walked to the back, then hopped up next to Cassidy. He set the cold beer on Cassidy's stomach, laughing as Cassidy jumped, grabbing for the beer.

"Fucker!" Cassidy punched him in the side.

A deviously sexy expression came over Nate's face as he lay down next to him. Cassidy's dick went rock hard as Nate put an arm behind his head. The faint light coming through the back window of the cab illuminated the muscles in Nate's chest and stomach as he stretched out next to Cassidy. He imagined himself reaching over to touch Nate, getting a little light-headed.

Cassidy closed his eyes, trying to control his own excitement, which was about to boil over. He bit his lip and begged the erection pushing up against his jeans to go the fuck away already. Cassidy slyly slid a hand down the front of his jeans, trying to adjust himself, in an attempt to conceal the erection. He could already feel the wet spot on his briefs from the precum.

Cassidy opened his eyes and ripped his hand out of his pants, seeing Nate sitting up watching him. His entire body flushed with heat, and he sat up. He scrambled across the bed of the truck and hopped down. He was completely embarrassed as he drank the last of his first beer. His hands were shaking, and beads of sweat began to collect under his arms.

Nate hopped down and stood in front of Cassidy, facing him. He grabbed Cassidy's face and pressed his mouth over Cassidy's, forcing his tongue inside. Nate pressed into his body, pushing Cassidy's ass against the gate.

Cassidy was a little stunned when Nate's tongue entered his mouth. He began to reciprocate, feeling Nate's erection grinding into his. He reached up, hands still shaking as he ran his fingertips over Nate's chest and nipples, amazed he was actually being allowed to do it.

He'd fantasized so many times over the past few years. He'd gotten his hopes up after the boathouse, only to feel them crushed after being back for a week and having nothing happen. Now here he was, chest about to explode as he tried to decide whether he was going to shoot in his pants or puke due to the nerves and butterflies that were wreaking havoc on his insides.

Nate pulled back, wide-eyed and breathing heavily as Cassidy examined his face. It took every bit of courage he could muster when Cassidy reached down, rubbing the palm over Nate's hard-on, which lay just on the other side of the denim. Nate licked his lips as he watched it happening. Cassidy pushed him back a little and dropped to his knees. Wasting no time, fearing Nate might snap out it at any given moment, he unbuttoned Nate's jeans and slowly pulled the zipper down, exposing the head of his cock sticking up out of his briefs.

Nate moaned, as Cassidy licked the head. He pulled the jeans and briefs down, freeing Nate's dick, listening to him take in a sharp breath as he slid his mouth over the head, slowly working his lips and tongue up and down the shaft like he'd seen the guys in the video clips doing it.

Cassidy was getting more excited, listening to Nate's moans, the way his entire body tensed when Cassidy did something he liked. He sucked and licked slowly, wanting to savor the taste of his precum in the back of his throat, the musky smell that made him hungrier and hornier than he had ever imagined he could be. He began lightly tugging on Nate's balls. He'd read about guys doing that in some of the erotic stories he'd found online. Cassidy was beyond pleased, considering it seemed to be doing the trick, as Nate became more vocal.

Nate ran his hands through Cassidy's hair, and he choked a little as Nate forced himself deeper inside Cassidy's mouth. He kept sucking, refusing to let anything stop him now. Nate's balls pulled up, and he could feel the head of his cock swell as Nate yelled out, shooting his load into the back of Cassidy's throat. Cassidy coughed, and his eyes watered. He hadn't been prepared for the orgasm and he tried to swallow while breathing through his nose.

After Nate finally stopped bucking, Cassidy fell back a little, sitting on his feet as he tried to catch his breath. He looked up at Nate, afraid he was going to start freaking out that he'd just let a guy suck him off. Cassidy could feel a little cum running down the side of his chin, so he wiped the corner of his mouth with the back of his hand. Nate was watching him with wide eyes, still breathing heavily. He knew Nate's fist was probably going to make contact with his face any second. He didn't care. It was fucking worth it if that's the way this was going to end. He could live off this night for decades.

Nate reached out with his hand and pulled Cassidy up onto his feet. He stood in the near darkness with his pants around his ankles and a still-hard cock.

"Where did you learn to do that?" Nate asked in shock.

"Internet porn and…bananas," Cassidy said, leaning back into the truck, feeling his cock throbbing in his jeans. He was already wigging out over the banana admission, thinking it would have been sexier had he lied and said he'd sucked lots of dick.

"Christ," Nate said, staring at his dick in amazement. He looked back up at Cassidy, who was adjusting himself. "Take off your pants."

Cassidy was frozen for a moment as his eyes widened. Nate moved closer with an expression on his face that told Cassidy to do what he said and be quick about it. Cassidy kicked off his sneakers while undoing his jeans, then yanked them down around his ankles along with his briefs.

Nate reached over and took Cassidy's cock in his hand while he stepped out of the pants. Nate ran his hands over Cassidy's chest before he leaned in and kissed him, thrusting his tongue into his mouth. He slid his hands down to Cassidy's hips and back over his ass, squeezing. Holding on to Cassidy's hips, Nate pulled away. Cassidy could make out the smile spreading over his face right about the time Nate turned him around.

Cassidy breathed heavily as Nate rubbed and squeezed his ass cheeks. He knew exactly where this was headed. His breathing became irregular as he remembered he'd tried out more than just a banana before, and it had hurt like hell.

He told Cassidy to spread his legs, and once he complied,

he opened his mouth to protest just as the head of Nate's dick made contact with his hole. The head was slick, and Cassidy's knees buckled slightly as Nate massaged the sensitive skin. Cassidy moaned, surprised by the sensation and how much he was enjoying it. He was in sensory overload, beginning to smile as he listened to Nate spit. He could feel the warm saliva running down his ass, and Cassidy bit his lip to keep from making a sound as Nate repeated the action. He was just about to start praising Nate's efforts when he suddenly hissed in pain as Nate forced the head inside.

"Fuck, that hurts, Nate." Cassidy dug his fingers into the metal as the intense pressure increased. He wanted to push Nate off him as his ass was invaded.

"Shit, Cassidy, just…give it a sec. Ah, fuck, you feel so good." Nate continued to force himself deeper.

Cassidy's arms were shaking as he tried to breathe, doing his best to relax into it as Nate kept inching farther in. He exhaled as Nate let out a deep groan, feeling his pelvis pressing into his backside.

"Fuck," Nate said as he placed his hands on Cassidy's hips and pulled him back, bending him over more. "Are you okay?"

"Yeah," Cassidy lied, clenching his eyes shut as Nate started to fuck him. It hurt, which it never had when he'd imagined Nate doing it. He bit his lip, trying not to make any noise, for fear Nate would realize he wasn't enjoying it all that much.

"Fucking hell, Cassidy." Nate took one of his hands off Cassidy's hips and slowly slid it up the center of his back. Nate worked his cock in and out, moaning and saying Cassidy's name over and over again.

Cassidy loved hearing it. The more worked up Nate got, the more into it Cassidy began to get. Nate thrust all the way in as he tugged on Cassidy's shoulder, standing him up straight. Nate slid his arm around Cassidy's waist, trying to force his cock in deeper.

Cassidy twisted his upper body, throwing an arm around Nate's neck. They kissed. Nate smothered Cassidy's soft moans with his mouth. Cassidy's dick began to stiffen again as Nate pulled his mouth away. He was breathing heavily as he shoved his face into Cassidy's armpit.

"Fuck, you smell incredible," Nate groaned, then inhaled deeply.

All Cassidy could smell was the fact that his deodorant had stopped working, but Nate's reaction filled him with a renewed sense of lust. He found himself wanting Nate to fuck him harder, though he couldn't quite bring himself to say the words.

Nate bent Cassidy back over after he reached down, feeling Cassidy was hard. He picked up the pace, rubbing and massaging Cassidy's ass.

Cassidy reached down and started jerking himself off as Nate became faster and rougher. Cassidy's skin tingled, and his nipples went hard as something changed in him, like a switch being flipped.

"Fuck, Nate." Cassidy became more vocal, his breath now ragged. He held on to the tailgate for dear life as Nate continued to pummel him. His eyes rolled back into his head, and Cassidy knew he was getting dangerously close.

"You feel so good, Cass," Nate said, digging his fingers into his hips. "Do you like it?"

"Yes," Cassidy muttered, feeling his balls rise up. "Don't stop."

Cassidy pressed his forehead into the tailgate and groaned uncontrollably. He yelled out Nate's name, shooting hard, coming a little more each time Nate slammed into him. His ass clenched tight around Nate's cock as Nate let out a loud moan, unloading into Cassidy, who let out a whimper as the pain returned. Nate forced himself in with one last thrust, and Cassidy's legs gave out. Nate managed to keep him from crumpling into the dirt, propping him up on the tailgate.

"You okay, Cass?" Nate asked, trying to catch his breath as he pulled out. He went back to rubbing Cassidy's back as he tried to reach down with his free hand and pull up his pants.

"That hurt like a motherfucker," Cassidy managed to get out through a wheeze, still unable to move as if all the life had just been sucked out of his body.

"Shit, Cass…it sounded like you really got into it."

Cassidy lifted his sweat-soaked head, the hair stuck to the skin around his face. "It was the most incredibly intense…" He stopped to take a breath. "I've *never* shot a load like that before, and if I ever regain the strength and feeling in my legs…we're totally doing it again."

Nate laughed out loud, placing a hand over his chest. "You had me worried for a sec."

"Have you ever done that before?"

"No, man." Nate grinned as he reached down and rubbed his dick. "I've had a girl suck me once, and after you left last summer, I let a tourist suck me in the men's room at the campground."

"Help me get my pants on." Cassidy pushed his upper body up off the truck bed. "I feel like an idiot lying here with my ass blowing in the breeze."

Nate reached over, squeezing a cheek. "I'll help you get your pants on, Cass, but believe me when I say, as long as I live, I'll never forget how hot your ass looks bent over the back of my truck. "

Chapter Eight

Slowing his car around the final curve before reaching the private drive that led to Piper's Point, Cassidy groaned, feeling his erection throbbing between his legs. The desire he had to indulge in an encore was palpable as he cracked a window, hoping some fresh air might clear the sex-induced haziness out of his head.

"Christ, I'm in trouble," Cassidy whispered, somewhat thankful Nate no longer had that beat-up white truck. He heard the door to the crate clatter and turned to inspect Dog. "I saved your furry little ass, and now I think you're gonna need to help save mine." Cassidy shook his head as Dog cocked her head, perking her ears up. "Don't let Daddy do anything he's going to regret tonight."

Dog whimpered and lay back down in her crate, as if Cassidy had just asked the impossible. He turned off the road onto the gravel drive that cut a path into the trees. He immediately tensed, taking note of Nate's truck backed up to the front porch. He didn't have much time to fret over the consequences of Nate moving back in, wondering instead whom the pimped-out monster SUV belonged to.

Cassidy considered the possibility that Nate had a boyfriend who was helping him move his stuff back. *Why hadn't Natalie mentioned that?* "A boyfriend suffering from obvious inadequacies with serious insecurity issues," he said to Dog as he ogled the gaudy electric blue SUV with shiny chrome trim. He chastised himself for taking pleasure at the thought and continued to pull around to the back of the house. *Like I really care.*

Beginning to wish he could crawl into a hole, Cassidy cringed and his stomach dropped once he spotted Nate sitting on the screened-in back porch with Neil. He'd inconveniently forgotten all about Neil since coming home to find his note the night before. As he braked to a slow stop, Cassidy began to wax nostalgic, ready to trade in the pro-gay-marriage rights of his present for the good ole free-lovin' days of the past, when gay men could supposedly have anonymous sex and never have to see each other again.

Okay…awkward. He glanced down at Dog. "My life is rapidly spiraling out of control, little one."

Cassidy quickly went through all the ways he could possibly play this as he got out of the car and waved at the two men. The rotten smile on Nate's face had most definitely not gone unnoticed. He settled on the classic "*que sera*" approach, pulling Dog's crate out of the passenger seat. *This only has to be as uncomfortable as I make it.*

Plastering on a smile, Cassidy reached through the window, removing the canvas grocery bags from the backseat of the car with his free hand, and he made his way up toward the house. "Hello, boys."

Nate got up and held the screen door open for Cassidy. "How was your day, dear?"

Cassidy stopped smiling and shook his head. "Don't be an ass." He smiled once again as he turned to Neil. "I got your note last night. Sorry I didn't call. I had a day."

"Where do you find them?" Nate asked under his breath, smirking.

Cassidy brushed past him, setting the crate onto the table. *Like it's my fault I'm a hot-man magnet?*

"Not a problem," Neil said, peering into the crate and jumping slightly as Dog barked at him. "I didn't realize you had a dog."

"I do," Cassidy said as Nate sat back down at the table. "Well, I didn't…but now I do." Pointing at Neil, he added, "And this one found me—came right up out of the ocean like a present from Poseidon."

"You always did like getting gifts," Nate said, taking a swig from his beer bottle and turning to Neil. "He tore right into 'em, never bothering to read the card."

Neil grinned. "Hopefully I'm the gift that keeps on giving."

"How *cute* is that?" Nate asked, using a tone that only Cassidy could read as annoyed.

Cassidy tossed the bag into Nate's lap a little harder than necessary, and he coughed from the impact. "Make yourself useful, and put those away."

Nate got up from the table, smiling in a way that made Cassidy want to clobber him. He took Neil by the arm, pulling him gently up from the table. "This isn't the best night for us to…hang out." Cassidy tensed, listening to Nate laugh from inside the house. "It's Nate's first night back home, and I've had two really long and very stressful days. You understand, don't you?" Cassidy led Neil to the screen door.

"Well, sure. I mean, yes, of course I do."

"Call or stop by tomorrow?" Cassidy held the door open for a now-scowling Neil.

"Okay," Neil said, turning to face Cassidy. He started to slowly move in for a kiss.

Cassidy leaned in and reciprocated, lips softly pressed together. He quite enjoyed the taste of Neil's mouth, which had a slight hint of the beer he'd been drinking. The kiss was soft and sweet, and Cassidy only pulled away after Neil started to get a little more aggressive than he was comfortable with.

"You are a good kisser." Neil grinned. His cheeks were slightly flushed. "But I never saw my night ending with a cold shower."

"Try a nice swim in the ocean," Nate offered from behind them, making enough noise with the chair to let Cassidy know he had no intention of offering them any privacy. "But you probably already knew that, being pals with Poseidon and all."

Smart-ass.

Neil glanced back at Nate for a moment. "I haven't stepped into something here, have I?" He reached up and ran his hands over Cassidy's shoulders as if straightening out his shirt. "Are you two…?"

"It's complicated," Cassidy said, laughing nervously as

he resumed nudging Neil out the door. He wasn't sure it was complicated, but it was the best noncommittally vague answer he could come up with spur of the moment. "Sorry to blow you off like this last minute."

Neil shrugged as Cassidy watched him head toward the side of the house before stopping. His forehead crinkled up. "We didn't actually have plans, so…no big thing."

Cassidy raised his hands up. "Oh…you're right. Yay! I'm not a jerk!"

Neil laughed, but Cassidy could tell it wasn't genuine, as he appeared to be more interested in staring down Nate, who was staring back, before Neil disappeared around the side of the house.

Cassidy slowly spun around to find Nate holding Dog in his arms, chuckling as she licked his chin.

"Who's a sweet little baby girl?" Nate mumbled, baby-talking Dog, who obviously loved it, considering her little nub of a tail was going a mile a minute.

"What was all that about?" Cassidy asked, walking over to the table. He reached down and snatched Nate's beer off the table and took a swig.

Nate stared innocently at Cassidy and shrugged like he couldn't possibly understand to what Cassidy was referring. He returned his attention to Dog and scratched her chin and behind her ears. "I never thought I'd be a little-dog kinda guy, but she's a slice of irresistible."

Dog looked at Cassidy with what appeared to be a smile, along with what Cassidy assumed was a "can we keep him?" pleading in her eyes. Cassidy took another swig of beer, feeling a smile forming as Nate continued to baby-talk Dog before finally praising her for "barking at the mean old man."

Cassidy rolled his eyes as he turned and went into the house. He reminded himself that Nate used to intensely enjoy teasing and taunting him when they were kids, which was the best explanation he could come up with for that reaction. *Of course he'd take any awkward situation and do his best to make it worse.* "Shit head," he mumbled while searching through the kitchen cabinets until he found a bowl he thought would be small enough for Dog's water.

Nate walked in holding Dog, who seemed quite content, as if she'd been held by Nate all her life. "Well, he seemed…nice."

Cassidy sneered, placing the water bowl on the floor, realizing he had no clue whether Dog had been fed. "You're an asshole, and you and I are not going to discuss Neil." Cassidy squinted, wondering where he'd left his glasses. "Do you think she's hungry?"

"Your glasses are hanging from your shirt there." Nate held up the dog and laughed when she got him in the nose with her tongue. "It's cool. Neil already told me all about how amazing the other night was. He went on and on about it… And on… And on…"

Cassidy sighed, putting on his glasses. "I think I get it."

Nate shot a sideways glance at Cassidy. "It probably wouldn't hurt to give her a little something to eat." He leaned over and set her down, and she seemed peeved at having been relegated to the floor.

Crossing the room to the back counter, Cassidy then reached up and took a saucer from the cabinet and opened one of the small cans of dog food. Dog immediately went ape-shit, running around in circles as her claws clicked against the tile.

"I'd say she's hungry," Nate said, taking a teaspoon out of a drawer and handing it to Cassidy.

Their eyes met momentarily as their fingers brushed when Cassidy took the spoon. He scooped some food out, carefully inspecting her for a moment, trying to determine how much to give such a tiny dog. He shrugged and scooped out one more spoonful before passing the saucer to Nate.

Awkwardness settled between the two of them before Cassidy remembered he needed to marinate the steaks. He mentioned running into Natalie, as he went about busying himself with food prep, and their conversation eased back into a familiar rhythm. Nate jumped in, anticipating whatever Cassidy might need next. Like Johnny-on-the-spot, he'd show up at Cassidy's side to hand over whatever the item happened to be. Cassidy found it a little freaky but also enjoyed the familiarity of it, not to mention the convenience.

Sharing the same oxygen with Nate set off alarms and warning bells left and right. Every fiber of Cassidy's being cautioned him to tread carefully and to please not go grabbing for Nate's big… stick.

When Nate offered to do the grilling, Cassidy told him tomorrow night could be his turn to do dinner, to which Nate commented, "Deal."

Cassidy was still a tad anxious as the realization they were once again residing under the same roof began to sink further in.

"Is this weird to you? You know… Us…here?" Cassidy asked as they walked out the screen door and into the courtyard.

Nate handed over a cold beer after Cassidy set the plate with the steaks down. "Yeah…but due more to the fact that it feels so…"

"Not awkward." Cassidy nodded, fiddling with the controls on the large gas grill until the flames ignited.

"But at the same time…awkward?" Nate laughed, appearing to be as confused by it all as Cassidy was. "Should we hug it out?"

Yes, please. Cassidy laughed, liking any suggestion, no matter how cheesy, that included touching Nate in any way. "But if you call me bro, I'll have to kick your ass."

"Right, because *roomie* is way more nondescript," Nate reminded, causing Cassidy's cheeks to flush with heat.

"That was totally lame. Sorry." Cassidy cringed, remembering that morning.

They both smiled at each other awkwardly, and then Nate reached over, taking Cassidy into his arms. As they embraced, Cassidy's resolve began to slip due to the heat traveling between their bodies. Nate's felt incredible, and they still fit together perfectly, shoulders at just the right height for each of them to rest their chin on.

He did his best to convince himself that he was just becoming more acclimated to being around Nate, but he knew that was a lie. He was really becoming more acclimated to the idea that he wanted to have sex with Nate—badly.

§ § §

Cassidy was feeling good. He was a little intoxicated from the vodka and beer—not drunk, but filled with the warmth that accompanies alcohol. His face warmed, as he watched Nate's silhouette, lit in hues of gray from the moonlight as he stacked the pieces of firewood on the beach. Dinner had flown by as they started to scratch the surface of the things they no longer knew about each other. They left Dog closed up on the screened porch, and she'd barked several times, letting them both know she wasn't altogether happy about it.

Cassidy stared up into the night sky at the same canopy of velvety black and brightly lit stars he had been under so many times before as a boy. He smiled, momentarily shutting his eyes, allowing the familiar sounds of the waves to flood his senses. The wind whistled through the trees behind him, and Cassidy dug his fingers into the sand. He could feel the hard granules between his fingertips exfoliating the skin.

He had an undeniable connection to the bit of earth on which he now sat. It was deep in him, ingrained into each and every pore in an almost past-life kind of way—as if he'd been here many times before and would continue to find himself back here again and again.

Cassidy opened his eyes when he heard the artificial clicking of the lighter Nate used to start the fire. The noise sounded out of place, in much the same way Cassidy had been afraid he might be, coming back to Piper's Point. He no longer feared that anymore. He belonged here, despite not being convinced everyone else on Hart's would feel the same. Nate walked across the sand on his knees, taking a seat next him on the blanket they'd pulled from the cabinet on the back porch.

As the fire grew, Cassidy resented the intrusion of the light, which cut into his very own starry night. At the same time he enjoyed the heat it produced, warming the bare skin of his arms. A chill swept over him as he wiggled his toes into the cool, damp sand.

Dinner had been a success, Cassidy decided as he handed Nate his beer. Ease had been the overall feeling between them as the evening rolled along. Examining Nate further, he was once again taken aback by how handsome the man was. Even with the shadows cast from the golden-hued firelight, which could have made the chiseled features of his face come off as menacing, they couldn't mask the overwhelmingly good-natured spirit that was housed inside the muscled, masculine frame occupying the space next to him.

A smile spread across Nate's face. "I look good, huh."

Cassidy laughed, noticing Nate said it more like a statement than an actual question. He was also embarrassed, having gotten so lost in his own thoughts that he neglected to realize he'd been staring. Good-natured and massively egotistical.

"So good," Cassidy moaned, gently stroking his beer bottle as he lightly licked the cool glass rim before taking a quick drink. "I can barely control myself."

Nate laughed, shaking his head disapprovingly as he shoved Cassidy, nearly knocking the bottle out of his hand.

"So not cool, dude," Cassidy said in a mocking tone, cradling the bottle as if it were filled with precious nectar.

Nate smiled in a way that let Cassidy know he wasn't the least bit sorry.

"So, what happened to you? You're like Hart's very own golden boy. Businessman of the year or some such nonsense."

Nate choked a little as he tried to swallow. "Oh, nice… Nonsense, is it?"

"The Nate I remember couldn't wait to get the hell off this rock."

"Ah. That Nate, yes. Well, he got his wish." Nate stared into the flames of the fire, seeming a little more serious. "He drove west across the causeway, vowing never to look back."

"So what gives?"

Nate smiled slightly, starting to chew on his lip. "I suppose he made the mistake of looking back."

Cassidy turned away, thoughts of sucking on and nibbling Nate's lips arousing him. "To be honest, I didn't actually expect to find you here. I figured you'd be in a penthouse somewhere with a string of hot guys coming in and out of the revolving front door. You always talked about going to New York, conquering the world…"

"Christ, you make me sound so Gordon Gecko, or God forbid, like your father. How was it that I ever managed to get into your pants?"

"Wow." Cassidy glanced down at his wrist as if he were wearing a watch. "Only took us how many hours to work our way around to sex? And I don't have a father, by the way." He stared off into the night, wishing Lionel hadn't been brought up, as it instantly irritated him. "I knew you'd use your powers for good—lift people up, not shove them down. That's what got you into my pants. Well…that and the fact that I wanted to get into your pants."

Nate laughed. "And you teach English to a bunch of freshmen? I certainly don't recall any of my college professors looking like you."

"I'm not actually a professor just yet. Still have that tiny detail of a dissertation to finish."

Nate moaned an acknowledgment, seeming to remember the way that worked. "What's this dissertation about, anyway?"

Cassidy took a sip of beer, taking a glimpse at Nate's face as he said, "American masculinities, secret identities, and hero worship in the twentieth-century superhero genre."

"Of course it is." Nate grinned, losing the battle as he finally burst into full-on laughter. "You and your comic books, you big geek."

Cassidy felt his cheeks burning as he took another sip out of his bottle. "Fuck off."

"So damn sexy when you're pissed." Nate settled himself as he reached over, and clinked his beer bottle against Cassidy's. "Do any of your students actually pass your classes, or are they as distracted as I surely would've been?"

"Ha! Don't start trying to sweet-talk your way back into my pants now, Nate Sommers." *Unless you just can't seem to help yourself.*

"That always was my least favorite thing about you, Cass."

Cassidy was confused. "What's that?"

"You always knew how gorgeous you were." Nate looked over at Cassidy. "Put the rest of us at a disadvantage."

"You weren't exactly beaten by the ugly stick, Nate."

"No, I know I'm a hottie."

Cassidy laughed. "And so modest."

"You've always been on this whole other level, though." Nate continued to stare. "You're the type that inspires, inflames, and then engulfs the rest of us mere mortals."

Cassidy could feel the words as if they'd pricked his skin. He lifted the glasses that had been sitting on top of his head and slipped them back on. He went back to the ocean view, trying to concentrate on the moonlight reflecting off the surface of the water.

"That doesn't actually work, you know."

"Huh?" Cassidy asked, clearing his throat. "What are going on about?"

"Those specs you still wear, like Clark Kent. They're not any better of a disguise on you than they were for Superman."

"Don't be ridiculous. I need them to see."

"You need them to read, Cassidy. You wear them like a mask whenever you feel embarrassed by how beautiful you are. The funny part is they never did prevent the whole world from turning to look whenever you'd walk by."

Cassidy took a big sip from his bottle, refusing to look at Nate, as he knew he might not be able to ever stop if he did. "It's getting late, huh?"

"I apologize if I spoke out of turn. Perhaps it's just the beer and moonlight making for a little nostalgia."

Cassidy tried a smile, but even he knew it wasn't very convincing. He wasn't ready or maybe just not willing to go down the road Nate attempted to lay out in front of him. Sex he could handle and welcome with open arms…and legs. But the yucky love stuff he was fairly certain he wouldn't be able to deal with.

"So why'd you really come back to Piper's Point, Nate?" Cassidy wondered again about the mystery man who broke his heart during college. For some reason he had trouble picturing what the guy might have looked like.

"It's my home. I guess it took leaving to make me recognize how much I loved it. What's really kept you away from Piper's Point, Cass?"

Cassidy knew he had a lot of good excuses, but he wasn't sure any of them were the real one. He'd never allowed himself to delve too far into that minefield, and he wasn't about to let Nate push him into it either. "What hasn't?"

Nate seemed to accept that answer, at least for the time being, and Cassidy experienced a tiny sense of relief over that fact, which he took as further proof there was more there, lying under the surface. He made a mental note not to go scratching at it.

"I'm glad you're here, Nate." Cassidy reached over and took his hand, giving it a squeeze. "You make it feel like being home again."

"Funny—I was just sitting here thinking the same thing about you."

They sat for a few minutes, never making eye contact. Cassidy could feel that theoretical cord he liked to imagine kept him tethered to Piper's Point, reeling him in a little closer to the ground below.

Nate yanked on his arm, a signal to move closer. Cassidy obliged by scooting over and leaned back into Nate, who wrapped him up in his arms and legs. Nate's body was warm, and Cassidy could feel the tension literally evaporating from his. He didn't know if or for how long he could keep Nate at arm's length, but he began to secretly not care. As much as the thought of free-falling into that reality scared the hell out of him, he couldn't deny it also excited him to the point of distraction.

Chapter Nine

Cassidy stood next to the coffeemaker, impatiently waiting for it to finish spitting out the steamy black liquid. He yawned and smiled at Dog, who was snarfing down the food he'd laid out for her. He knew he shouldn't have, but he'd let her sleep in the bed with him last night. He reminded himself that Dr. Downey had cautioned to keep a close eye on her, and used that to justify it. She'd curled up and fallen right to sleep in the curve of his lower back.

Cassidy hadn't been quite as fortunate, lying awake for nearly an hour, despite the alcohol, which would have normally aided him in sleep. He had way too much going on inside his head to drift off, and he slept restlessly once he finally did pass out. His foot tapped in time with Keith Urban's "Sweet Thing" playing in the background from a small radio on the far counter.

He turned, hearing Nate walk into the kitchen, and his eyes were suddenly wide open. He swallowed and tried clearing his throat as Nate walked toward the fridge wearing nothing but a loose-fitting pair of gym shorts.

"Good morning," Nate said, pulling a carton of cream out of the refrigerator door.

"Is it?" Cassidy asked, absentmindedly watching Nate move around the kitchen gathering up mugs and the ceramic sugar container. His body was every bit as hot as Cassidy had imagined, and he had to resist his natural instinct to reach out and touch.

Nate was obviously puzzled as he reached for the coffeepot. "Isn't it?"

"Huh?" Cassidy asked, wondering what Nate's views were on friends with benefits. He shook his head, reminding himself it was Thursday. He just needed to retain control over himself for another day and a half. After that, Ollie and Spencer would be here to chaperone. "It is. Of course it's a good morning."

Nate grinned, so sexy yet slightly evil, as he filled a cup and passed it to Cassidy. He took a step closer, invading Cassidy's personal space, making him both uncomfortable and exhilarated at the same time.

"Would you prefer it if I put on a shirt?" Nate asked, exhibiting an air of heated sexuality while appearing as innocent as the day he was born, an art Cassidy had never perfected.

Cassidy blew out a puff of air. "Get over yourself." He'd done an excellent job sounding unaffected, despite becoming the slightest bit unhinged as Nate moved close enough to fog up his glasses with his breath.

"You let me know should you change your mind," Nate whispered, his lips inches away from Cassidy's.

Cassidy couldn't quite focus. "Change my mind?"

The corners of Nate's lips curled up as he leaned forward, milliseconds away from kissing Cassidy. The two men jumped, startled by Dog's single bark. Cassidy turned away, taking a drink from his cup and cursing under his breath as he scalded his mouth. He could see Nate turning away out of the corner of his eye as well and wasn't sure if he should be thankful or pissed at Dog. He then reminded himself to pick out a goddamned name already so he could stop calling her Dog as if he were some kind of twisted, homo Holly Golightly.

Cassidy glanced over at the urn, then mentally rolled his eyes imagining Sadie asking him what the hell he was waiting for—*jump the man already*. She never was one for asking too many questions, Cassidy thought. *Leap first and worry about the consequences later*. But Cassidy knew that wasn't the smartest thing to do. Especially considering how badly he wanted it. He'd not had this many spontaneous hard-ons since his teens, and Cassidy was fairly sure that to err with caution was the only way to go.

He'd never made any decisions about his love life without having seriously considered all the possible outcomes. He'd been lucky so far, in that no one had ever gotten hurt. And it most certainly never ended well for Sadie, who always jumped in headfirst, although she never complained either.

Cassidy became entranced by Nate, who slid his fingers just below the waistband of his gym shorts, scratching at an itch. He grinned as he held back the urge to ask if he needed any help.

They both froze, hearing a knock at the front door. They glanced at each other, and both made a move toward answering it as Cassidy followed Nate out of the kitchen. Cassidy could hear Dog's nails clicking on the hardwoods as she followed them. He caught a glimpse of Natalie through the glass on the front door, standing on the porch with several others. As he got closer, Cassidy was able to make out that the tall, lean gentleman was Jacob Pringle, and realized the council heads had made good on their threat to stop by.

Cassidy was instantly uncomfortable for one reason alone. Both Natalie and Nate were about to discover that his arrival on Hart's wasn't going to be permanent, at least in a full-time sense. He was already dreading the universal expressions of disappointment as he smiled when Nate opened the door.

The four council elders followed Natalie into the foyer as she hugged Nate, then made a beeline for Cassidy. His heart sank as she once again all but fell into him, squeezing and jiggling him about until he started laughing.

"So glad to have you home again," Natalie said as she pulled away.

His smile wasn't quite up to par as he avoided eye contact with Natalie. Jacob, whose prickly demeanor was standoffish yet never intentionally so, briskly shook Cassidy's hand.

"Cassidy," Jacob said with a quick nod and a smile that Cassidy knew from experience only appeared forced.

He was a bit shocked by how much older Jacob looked as Henry Abbott, the Hardy to his Laurel pushed past, grabbing Cassidy by the arms and shaking him excitedly.

"So good to have you back, Cassidy. So good indeed." Henry, shorter and quite round, had a full head of thick hair that Cassidy remembered as more peppered, but now was stark white.

Henry was a loud individual, much like his daughter, Marianne. They each had a laugh that could be heard from a block away.

Richard Hammond offered his hand along with a warm smile once Henry released Cassidy from his death grip. "Welcome back to Hart's, Cassidy."

As the reigning Hammond in control of the Hart's Island grocery-store dynasty, he was younger than his counterparts, having taken over the post along with the business back in the late eighties when his father retired.

The only remaining female member of the council heads was Edie Taylor. She was the Glinda the Good Witch counterpart to her cantankerous Cheez Whiz-scented twin sister with all the cats. They were like night and day, as Edie was very neighborly, unless you tweaked her nose. Cassidy remembered getting into big trouble once when, as kids, he and Nate stole one of her garden gnomes. They wound up having to pull the weeds in her flower gardens for a month as punishment, and Edie had a lot of flowers.

She'd no doubt taken note that each one of the men had pushed themselves in front of her as she gracefully took Cassidy's hand in hers. "Very glad to have you back, dear," she said quite genuinely, considering Cassidy had always believed she'd permanently tagged him as a ne'er-do-well ever since the gnome incident.

"Welcome back to Piper's Point," Cassidy said to all of them. "Can I get anyone coffee?"

They all erupted in pleases and thank-yous as Natalie pushed Cassidy to stay and chat while she went to take care of the coffee. Nate asked them all into the dining room before excusing himself to go put on a shirt. Cassidy was a little peeved when he came down fully dressed, leaving only him in less formal attire.

"I'm very sorry. I would have been a little more prepared—better dressed, at least—had I known you were all coming."

Edie smacked Henry in the arm. "I told you we should have called first." She trailed off, muttering something about the manners of a mule.

"Be glad you'll never have to suffer the ill temper of a woman," Henry said, scowling at Edie. "I envy you boys that."

It was all Cassidy could do to keep a straight face at Henry's attempt to bring up Cassidy and Nate's homosexuality. He could see Jacob was none too comfortable, as his eyes were slightly bugged out. Nate was full-on laughing, while Hammond was shaking his head in disbelief.

"I hope you'll forgive us. We're all just excited to have you back and for Piper's Point to once again have a caretaker." Jacob eyed the room in a manner that some would presume as taking stock of something he coveted, though Cassidy knew him well enough to understand he was merely impressed by the condition of the property.

"I think Nate and Natalie should really be credited with keeping her in such phenomenal shape." Cassidy smiled.

"I apologize for the indelicate way Henry attempted to broach the subject of…er, um, well… Nate of course knows we fully accept him and his…um…" Edie stumbled, her forehead crinkling as she attempted to find the words she appeared to have lost.

"I think I understand, and thank you. I appreciate your… support." Cassidy desperately tried not to imagine them all sitting around, arguing over the right way to bring this all up. He wondered if Nate had gotten the same awkward speech.

"We're very progressive." Henry nodded with a wide politician's smile.

The foursome all sighed as they eyed one another as if to say, *Thank God that's over*, obviously hoping they'd never need to discuss it again.

"My wife surely did like that *Will and Grace* program back when it was on the television," Jacob said, turning a little red. "God rest her soul."

Cassidy noticed Edie rolling her eyes.

Nate turned red as well, doing his best to not burst out in laughter. "That was an awesome program."

"I think it really raised awareness about your people," Henry said seriously.

"I'm going to go check on that coffee, folks." Cassidy smiled, doing his best to act natural.

Nate stood up. "Let me—"

"No, no," Cassidy jumped in, cutting Nate off. "You just have a seat there, buddy. You've been doing most of the heavy lifting around here for a while now."

Nate shot him a quick, you'll-pay expression as he sat back down at the table, scooping up Dog, who was already scratching at his legs for attention. Cassidy rounded the corner into the hall, mouthing, *Oh my God*, as he walked into the kitchen. Natalie was standing at the island, her hand on the urn as tears ran down her cheeks.

Cassidy cringed, wishing he'd left the urn upstairs this once.

"Still can't believe she's really gone." Natalie sniffled. "It's like it just happened, you know? Still so fresh in my mind."

Cassidy walked over and gave her a quick squeeze, refusing to allow her to drag him along with her today. He needed to keep his wits about him while he had a house full of people who were undoubtedly about to be very unhappy with him.

"I don't know how you've handled all you have and managed to stay sane, Cassidy."

"I did it for Sadie," he said matter-of-factly as she nodded, beginning to regain a little control over her faculties.

"Let's get that coffee so we can get on with this. I'm sure you have other things you'd like to be doing with your day."

"Yes, I do, in fact," Cassidy said seriously. "Setting fire to the attic being the first on my to-do list."

Natalie giggled, dabbing her eyes with a paper towel she dampened with cool water. "I haven't been up there since the nineties. The good Lord only knows how many skeletons are buried up there."

Cassidy laughed, remembering the way Natalie always teased Sadie about hiding the bodies of her husbands and boyfriends up there, calling her the black widow. Sadie always acted offended, but they all knew she secretly liked the idea of being a man-eater. Perhaps because, despite all her bravado, she had a soft heart hiding under all the makeup, too much jewelry, and brightly colored caftans.

Joining the rest of the council back out in the dining room, Cassidy realized they were all patiently waiting for everyone to be served and settled before wanting to dive in. The pressure built, and Cassidy wished they'd just get on with it already. He looked around the dining-room table at all the smiling faces and couldn't take it any longer.

"I'm not going to be staying on the island year-round," Cassidy blurted out in one long string of word vomit. He sighed, seeing everyone's expressions immediately change. Natalie looked as if he'd struck her, and Nate stared forward stoically, all traces of humor evaporated from his face.

"But Sadie assured us you'd take your place on the council when the time came," Jacob sputtered out. "She swore you'd do the right thing."

"I'm so sorry, guys," Cassidy said, finally taking a seat. Even Dog stared, wide-eyed, as if judging him. "I have a job at the university. I just can't walk away and leave them in the lurch."

"So it's just temporary," Henry said, a smile starting to return. "Just until they can replace you?"

"Not exactly." Cassidy started to fidget, squirming slightly in his chair. "What I mean to say is, I really love teaching. I don't want to give that up."

"Of course not," Hammond said, as if understanding in some way, like he too had given up something in order to take his father's place. "It's not really as if Cassidy's a true islander."

Cassidy knew he meant it more as an excuse than an

indictment, but it stung and stuck in Cassidy's chest all the same. Natalie shook her head, as if thanking goodness Sadie wasn't here to witness him turning his back on his birthright.

"Guys, I'll do whatever I can to make myself available to you when I'm back in Chapel Hill, and I'd really like it if the Founders' Day parties could be held here at the Point again, the way Sadie always did them." Cassidy glanced around the table, realizing he wasn't appeasing any of them. "And Edie, I was really hoping the historical society might help me go through the attic. I wanted to donate most of Sadie's things, maybe set up an exhibit dedicated to her at the museum?"

Edie suddenly appeared like she might spring out of her chair after hearing that suggestion. The historical society had been after Sadie for decades to hand over some of the Hart family heirlooms. Sadie had always scoffed, saying she wasn't about to let them rummage through the family archives, her other term of endearment for the attic. "*All they want to do is dig up scandals and gossip.*"

"That's very generous of you, Cassidy." Edie cocked her head and licked her lips. "Are you sure about that?"

"There are things I'll want to keep, of course," Cassidy said.

"Of course." Edie nodded, a little glassy-eyed.

"Obviously, everything will need my approval before leaving the property. But in exchange for your help, I'd like to do something, and I think it would be nice for there to be an exhibit—a sort of tribute to her. I would of course assist financially with the project as well."

"I do think that's a very nice gesture," Henry said, though still not nearly as excited by the prospect as Edie was.

Cassidy sank back into the dining chair, feeling every bit as crappy as he had suspected he would. They each slowly got out of their seats, thanking Cassidy for his time and begging him to please really think things over. The seat vacated by Sadie was his, should he decide to stay on Hart's where he belonged, and all Sadie ever wanted was for Cassidy to take her place. They turned to leave after saddling him with more guilt and regret, as if he didn't have enough of that already.

Nate stayed seated as Cassidy showed everyone else to the door. Natalie gave him a hug before leaving, reaching up and taking his face in her hands. "Baby boy." A term of endearment Sadie had had for him. "I hope you really think this over, because it sure doesn't feel right to me."

Cassidy nodded. "I will, Nat." He felt small and selfish all of a sudden, even though he didn't believe he was wrong. He shut the front door and watched them all file into their cars before driving away. He could practically feel Sadie's disappointment slamming into his back as he turned around to find Nate standing there instead, still holding Dog.

"So you're just going to turn around and leave again?"

"I'll be back, Nate." Cassidy was sick to his stomach now, desperate for someone to see things from his perspective. "Summer and winter break, all the holidays."

Nate nodded, though somehow didn't appear convinced as he handed Dog over before grabbing his keys off the table by the front door. "I'm going to go in to the office. Got some work left unfinished from yesterday."

"Come on, Nate." Cassidy reached out to grab him. "I will be back."

"You know, I distinctly recall you saying something along those lines the last time you graced us all with your presence, and that was what, nine…ten years ago?"

Nate didn't turn around, glancing down at Cassidy's hand on his shoulder instead. "All this time I thought maybe…" He shook his head and shrugged off Cassidy's hand before walking out the front door.

Cassidy watched as he climbed into his shiny black pickup and drove off. He snuggled with the dog for comfort, who licked at his chin as if she could sense how horrible he felt. Cassidy lived with the guilt of choosing not to come back to the Point that last summer. Had he known Sadie would've had her stroke during his freshman year at college, he would've made a different decision. He'd give anything to go back and do that particular summer over.

Nate didn't even know the real reason behind that decision. He'd told Sadie that Lionel was forcing him to intern at the company, but that wasn't the truth. He knew that as mad as she'd be about it, she'd never call Lionel to confront him, as they'd ceased all communication years before. It was true that he'd interned for his father that summer, but he'd asked Lionel, not the other way around. Cassidy feared the truth behind that selfish decision would drive a wedge between Nate and him that time itself might not be able to erode.

He meandered back into the dining room and leaned over to place Dog back on the floor. He started to gather up the cups and saucers of barely touched coffee. "That went well," he said sarcastically, then let out a long sigh. He hoped the whole lovefest for the prodigal son wasn't over before it started, considering he was mentally flogging himself enough as it was. Most importantly, though, was whether Nate would ever look at him the way he had in the kitchen that morning—half-naked and intensely interested.

§ § §

"What the hell is the big friggin' deal?" Ollie asked as Cassidy walked barefoot in the grass. He watched Dog sniff around searching for the right spot to distribute her poo, while holding the cell phone to his ear.

"This place is beginning to sound a little too Waco to me. Honey!" Ollie yelled. "This island might be kinda culty!"

Cassidy could feel the corners of his lips curling up as he heard Spencer off in the background yelling back, "We'll stop and get a few cases of bottled water on our way, then. Just don't drink anything you haven't opened yourself, and it'll all be okay!"

"Ah, so just like a circuit party, then," Ollie said.

Cassidy burst into laughter. "There's a long history here, which goes back to a time when the Fourth of July was just another meaningless date on the calendar." Cassidy made little kissing noises once Dog finished her business, still keeping an eye on the tree line for the devil dogs as he walked back toward the house. "There hasn't been a time in over two hundred years when there wasn't a Hart on the council. It's kind of a big deal here."

"And you just threw it back in their faces. I get it."

Cassidy heard a clicking noise and held up the phone to view the screen. He shook his head and placed it back to his ear.

"I didn't throw it in their faces. I tried to offer a compromise, but they want all or nothing. I want to fix things. I just don't how."

"You'll figure it out, Cassidy. It may not happen today or even next week, but you will figure out the right thing, and then you'll do whatever that turns out to be, because that's who you are."

"That was a really nice thing to say." Cassidy grinned.

"Well, you don't have to act like it's something that never happens. Sheesh. You make me sound like a shrew and a half."

Cassidy opened the screen door and let Dog scamper in, making a shushing noise at her when she started licking at her stitches. "What do you think a half a shrew would actually look like?" Cassidy shushed Dog for once again trying to lick her stitches.

"Um, someone who makes irritating shushy noises into the phone?"

"Really?" Cassidy laughed as he took a seat on one of the wooden chairs and leaned over to pick up the dog, who he'd neglected to mention thus far to his friends. "Not a short bitch?"

"Short as in tempered or vertically challenged?"

Cassidy leaned back in his chair, contemplating. "I'd have to say vertically challenged, as *bitch* already lends itself toward the indication of an individual's temperament."

"You two have the strangest conversations," Spencer cut in, startling Cassidy, who now realized what that clicking noise had been.

"Eavesdropping is way rude, dude," Cassidy snapped, shaking his head.

"I'm going with short, as in tempered," Spencer added, suddenly having an opinion now that Cassidy sounded pissy. "The short could merely be a descriptor as to how quickly said individual becomes bitchy."

"All right, you two," Ollie said in a holier-than-thou tone, as if he wasn't normally the instigator of all the drama. "We'll be there tomorrow before dark, sweet cheeks. So just hang on a little longer. I wanna be there in time to watch them strap you into the pillory in the town square."

"Oliver," Spencer said in a disapproving tone.

"Oh come on, honey. You've got a good arm, and despite being visitors, they may let us take part in the stoning."

"I'm hanging up now, asshole."

"Love you too," Ollie got out before Cassidy was able to disconnect.

"Sick," Cassidy said, shaking his head as he sneered at the phone. Dog jumped up, propping her front paws on his chest as she attempted to lick his face. Cassidy laughed as he tried to keep her from slathering him down.

"At least you still like me." Cassidy grabbed her and held her up in the air. "How 'bout a treat?"

Dog began wiggling furiously and panting in excitement as she tried to run a mile a minute despite being suspended in the air.

"You sure are a smart little thing." Cassidy grinned, impressed she already understood the meaning of the word *treat* in such a short amount of time. "Maybe Nate would like me again if I held him up in the air and offered him a treat?"

Dog again went ape-shit after hearing the *T* word, and Cassidy pulled himself out of the chair, laughing. "Okay, little one. Okay."

Chapter Ten

Cassidy yawned, standing in the kitchen, coffee cup in hand, waiting for the brew to finish percolating. He scratched under the waistband of his black boxer briefs, not having bothered to finish getting dressed after his shower. Nate hadn't come home at all last night, and Cassidy hadn't slept for shit. He wasn't too happy about the fact he obviously cared more than he should as to what the great Nate Sommers's opinion of him happened to be.

He'd been so pissed by the time evening had rolled around that he called Neil and asked him over for dinner. Of course, by the time they made it through dinner and an old noir classic called *Laura*, which they had to watch on Sadie's tiny-ass thirty-two-inch television, Cassidy wasn't pissed anymore so much as angst ridden. He'd been secretly hoping Nate would come home and get pissed that Neil was there. At least then, Cassidy would have known whether the man gave a shit one way or the other.

They made out a little, but Cassidy's heart wasn't in it, and Neil wound up leaving after a bit of a row. He'd accused Cassidy of thinking about *him* all night, referring to Nate. When Cassidy tried to apologize, making an attempt to inform Neil things weren't likely to go anywhere between them, Neil stormed out of the house as if in some freaky jealous rage. He wound up calling Cassidy a little later and apologizing for the way he behaved, which Cassidy hadn't considered so bad, possibly since he knew his own motives hadn't been on the up-and-up. All poor Neil wanted was some lovin', while asshole that he was, he'd tried using the guy as jealousy bait.

Cassidy filled his coffee cup, then gently blew across the surface before taking a tiny sip. It wasn't like Cassidy to use people, at least not intentionally and with no regard for anyone else's feelings. He'd have to sit Neil down the next time they met up and make sure he understood they couldn't be anything more than friends.

He didn't know what the hell was wrong with him. He was acting weird, being all clumsy and awkward, and his behavior was beyond abnormal. He nodded to himself, figuring it had to be the stress of being back here. Confronting his failures in regard to Sadie and dealing with the pressure of expectations he hadn't seen coming his way.

Cassidy stood up straight, hearing the front door open and close. He started to fidget a bit, listening to Nate toss his car keys on the tiny table next to the front door. Running a hand through his damp hair, Cassidy leaned back against the counter in an attempt to come off casual. He cursed a little under his breath after taking another sip, forgetting how hot the coffee was.

Nate sauntered into the kitchen, carrying some papers and a laptop case along with a pan covered with aluminum foil. Cassidy caught a whiff of that familiar scent and smiled, knowing Natalie had baked cinnamon rolls for them. He hoped that meant she wasn't upset with him any longer. Nate smiled while allowing his gaze to wander up and down Cassidy's frame.

"Hey there, girl," Nate said to Dog, who was running around in circles at his feet.

"Good morning," Cassidy said, wishing it hadn't come out sounding so much like a damned question.

"Not a bad sight to come home to." Nate set the pan down on the island and tossed the rest of his things onto one of the bar stools. He grinned playfully, back to his usual self as he walked over and stood right in front of Cassidy. Nate leaned in, smiling seductively as he placed a hand on the countertop next to Cassidy's hip.

Cassidy was frozen to his spot. When Nate's hand lightly brushed against his side, his heart beat at a slightly faster pace. Nate's gaze locked with Cassidy's, holding him there as if in a trance. Cassidy tried to regulate his breathing, thinking for sure Nate was about to lay one on him.

He was now close enough for Cassidy to feel his breath lightly brushing across his face. He noticed Nate's eyes dart down toward his lips, and Cassidy took in a sharp breath when Nate lightly licked his own lips. As Nate reached up with his free hand, reaching behind Cassidy's head, he knew this was it, the first time their lips would meet in almost a decade.

"Ow," Cassidy said, hearing a bonk as the cabinet door made contact with the back of his head.

"So sorry." Nate grinned, retrieving a coffee cup from inside the cabinet Cassidy was standing in front of. "You're kinda in the way, though." Nate pushed away and spun around to pour himself a cup.

Cock-teasing, motherfucking asshole! Cassidy rubbed the back of his head while scowling as he took another sip from his own cup. "I would have moved."

"I thought I could grab one without needing to disturb you." Nate's eyebrows arched as the man glanced down, checking out Cassidy's crotch.

Cassidy peeked down to see the front of his briefs was a little more swollen than it had been moments before. His face burned hot as Nate's intense gaze was averted thanks to Dog's scratching at his leg, demanding some attention. Nate took a quick sip before placing his mug down and bending over to pick her up. He scratched behind the pup's ears, and Cassidy watched as Nate eyed his dick a second time.

Nate laughed when Dog got a lick in, right on the lips, and Cassidy smirked, a little jealous. Nate wiped his mouth on the arm of his shirt while trying to love on the dog.

"Aw, I missed you too." Nate fired a gaze right into Cassidy's eyes after saying that.

"Decide to bring your work home with you?" Cassidy asked as Nate set the dog back on the floor.

"I've actually taken the day off." Nate picked up his coffee cup. "Was planning to get some of that trim painted on the exterior today."

"Oh," Cassidy said, watching as Nate reached across the

island for the aluminum-wrapped cinnamon goodies. "Can I help with the painting?"

"If you like." Nate peeled the foil back, and the entire kitchen smelled like heaven.

Cassidy's tummy grumbled, and Nate turned, wide-eyed, having heard it as well. "Sorry."

"Grab some plates, will you?" Nate asked. "I don't want to risk giving you a concussion."

"Sure." Cassidy turned, shaking his head while trying to ignore the snark. *You could at least pretend you didn't enjoy whacking me upside the head.*

"You know, it really wouldn't take much to get this place ready in time for Founders' Day." Nate grabbed a knife out the drawer, cutting into the rolls.

"It's like a week away," Cassidy said.

"I know," Nate said, dipping his finger into the icing and sucking on his fingertip, "but you have to admit the house and grounds are in great shape."

Cassidy nodded, setting the plates down so Nate could place the still-warm rolls on them. "I was thinking." Cassidy leaned against the cabinet. "It seems like no one on the island has had a chance to really say good-bye to Sadie, me included."

Nate nodded, pulling out two forks and handing one to Cassidy. "You could combine them."

"Make the Founders' Day party a wake?"

"Why not, though I'd probably say tribute, not wake." Nate took a bite, making that same little moan he always used to after the first bite of Natalie's cinnamon rolls. "I think it would be fitting to have the first Founders' party back at the Point also be a tribute to the woman who actually started them in the first place."

"You don't think it's a little selfish?"

Nate smiled, swallowing another bite. "I think everyone will appreciate the gesture and the fact that we're focusing on her life. Funeral services always have an air of sadness. Don't you think Sadie would prefer having a party with everyone drunk as a skunk and dancing?"

Cassidy knew she would. "I guess the next day I could spread her ashes at the lighthouse."

"And let anyone who wants to show up for that as well."

Cassidy took a big bite of the dough bomb and nodded in agreement. "Will you come with me to spread her ashes?"

"Of course." Nate reached up, ruffling his fingers over the top of Cassidy's head, messing up his hair. "Don't be such a dweeb."

Cassidy shoveled in another forkful. He liked the idea and knew it would be something Sadie would approve. Nate patted the side of his leg, and Cassidy was relieved he wasn't mad at him any longer. Dog made a little snort, distracting them both as she politely sat there as if expecting to be given a bite. Cassidy could tell Nate wanted to give in, but he made sure with one look to nip that instinct in the bud. He rolled his eyes and reached over, snagging the bag of vet-approved jerky treats. He tossed it to Nate, who grinned and, for just a moment, resembled the carefree, high-jinks-fueled high school boy he used to be.

Nate set his plate down and opened the bag. He tore off a chunk, dropping it to the floor for the dog. He sighed, tossing the bag back onto the counter, and finished off the last of his coffee. He grinned all evil-like before reaching over and giving Cassidy a titty twister.

"Son of a…" Cassidy said, rubbing his now-bright red nipple. "That fucking hurt, asshole."

Nate dodged the fist Cassidy aimed in his direction and took off running when Cassidy tossed his plate on the counter and lunged at him. Dog started to bark, startled by the ruckus. Cassidy chased Nate out of the kitchen and up the stairs, barely missing him as Nate ran into his bedroom, slamming the door shut in his face. Cassidy tried pushing it open, but Nate was blocking it, laughing his fool head off.

"Fucktard!" Cassidy yelled, kicking the door with his foot, half pissed and half turned on due to his now burning nipple.

"Go put on some clothes, you cock-tease!" Nate yelled back. "We got chores to do."

Cassidy mumbled a few more obscenities under his breath as he turned, and made his way toward his bedroom.

Cassidy listened as Nate cracked his door open, whistling in a taunting manner. Cassidy refused to turn around, giving him the satisfaction. He reached back and tugged at the elastic waistband of his briefs, offering Nate a glimpse of his bare ass instead.

"Me so horny," Cassidy said, grinning from ear to ear as he heard Nate groan slightly before slamming his door shut again.

§ § §

Nate let out a sickening moan as he stood back, stretching while he watched Cassidy finish up the last little bit of trim around the French door that led into Sadie's bedroom. Cassidy turned just in time to see Nate wipe his brow with his arm. A tiny bead of sweat ran down from Nate's belly button, disappearing under the waistband of his paint-encrusted cutoffs.

"Man, it's hot up here today," Nate said, jarring Cassidy out of his own drool-fest.

Cassidy stood back, facing the door to check out his work. He'd been more than a little nervous about the khaki-mushroom color Nate picked out for the trim at first, but seeing the contrast against the olive green paint on the siding, he decided he was very impressed with it.

"I'd never have picked these colors," Cassidy said, sounding genuinely astounded.

"Please tell me there's a but coming?"

"I like it!" Thinking Nate wasn't too convinced, he added, "Seriously, Nate. I'm shocked, but I actually love it."

"Thank goodness for that," Nate said, obviously relieved.

"Otherwise I'd have tossed your ass over the side of the balcony for waiting until we got half the damn house painted before mentioning it."

Cassidy laughed, squinting a bit from the afternoon sun. "That actually sounds more like something I'd do."

"Don't I know it. If I had a dime for every time we'd get halfway into something as kids only to have you start whining, saying you didn't want to do it anymore—"

"Oh sure," Cassidy interrupted. "Never mind that it was usually something that would've gotten us into big-time trouble!"

Nate laughed, a saucy smugness taking over his demeanor as if getting into trouble had been the ultimate goal back in the day. "I want a beer."

Cassidy scoffed. "Quitter! There are two other sides to this beast."

"Calm down there, Skippy." Nate winked, working a half smile. "No one said the whole thing had to be done today."

"Okay," Cassidy said, immediately caving after putting on a good show by initially protesting. His arm was about to fall off, and he was roasting under the full glare of the sun.

"You little shit." Nate poked him in the side, causing Cassidy to wiggle away. "You wanted to stop hours ago, didn't you?"

"No!" Cassidy opened the French door so they could go back inside, while trying to maintain a straight face.

Nate shook his head and went into the house. Cassidy followed, momentarily losing himself in Sadie's bedroom, feeling a slight stab of that same loneliness he'd experienced that first day back. He quickly went to close the door, leaving it cracked just enough to allow the wet paint to dry. He ran to catch up with Nate, who had already headed down the stairs. He marveled over Nate's sweaty, glistening skin, and all Cassidy could think about was licking the man from head to foot. The muscles in Nate's back flexed and undulated as he took one step at a time. His T-shirt, tucked into the waistband, drew Cassidy's attention to the small of Nate's back and tight waist.

Every fiber of his being told him to reach out and touch, and Cassidy discovered that the temperature inside the house was no cooler than it had been outside. He swallowed, feeling how dry his throat actually was.

"That beer's not sounding so bad."

"That's the spirit," Nate said as they made their way down the hall toward the kitchen.

Dog was already on their heels, clicking along behind them as they each placed the paint buckets and brushes into the sink. Cassidy grabbed a beer and walked the dog out to the yard to do her business while Nate worked on cleaning out the brushes. He pulled his T-shirt off, using it to wipe his brow and the back of his neck. It was cooler in the shade from the trees, and his temperature had regulated by the time he went back inside.

Nate watched Cassidy from the sink, staring a little longer than necessary with his mouth hanging slightly open. Cassidy was feeling a little vindicated, not being the only one who was practically in heat from the sex haze hanging over each of them.

He made his way over to the pantry and scooped out some kibble, which he deposited into the dog bowl as Nate finished rinsing out the sink and shut the water off. He finished off his beer, tossing it in the garbage, and turned to find Cassidy standing behind him.

Cassidy handed his empty over. "You want another?"

Nate nodded, somewhat more serious than he had been before, when they were joking around. "What time are your friends supposed to get here?"

"Close to dinnertime," Cassidy said, opening the fridge and pulling out two more cold ones.

He turned around to find Nate standing behind him this time. Cassidy handed him a beer before twisting the lid off his. He turned the bottle up, taking a long swig, catching a whiff of his underarm. He lowered the bottle, smiling when he realized Nate had taken a step closer.

"I forgot you sorta get off on that, huh?" Cassidy asked, raising his arm again.

Nate shut his eyes, chewing on his lip as he inhaled deeply. Cassidy grinned, feeling a slight sense of power until Nate took yet another step, practically shoving his nose into Cassidy's armpit. His smile faded away when Nate opened his eyes. Cassidy saw the pure lust staring back at him, and found himself relieved when Nate removed the open beer from Cassidy's hand and turned away, setting both bottles down on the counter. A sudden awkwardness swept over him as he slowly lowered his arm.

The energy in the room shifted into something almost animalistic as Nate spun back around. Neither of them was smiling anymore as Nate came back and stood in front of Cassidy.

"Can you lift your arm again, please?"

Cassidy did as Nate asked, somehow feeling that despite his saying please, Nate would have attempted to force him had he not complied willingly. Nate rested his forehead on Cassidy's arm as he inhaled. His hand was sliding up Cassidy's other side, pushing his other arm up into the air. Cassidy's breath went a little ragged as Nate slowly made a move for the opposite armpit. Nate groaned so softly Cassidy almost thought he'd imagined it.

Cassidy's head was becoming a bit fuzzy as the heat pouring off Nate began to radiate into him. When the back of Nate's hand bumped Cassidy's cock, Nate took note of the physical reaction it caused. Within seconds, Nate's hand was shoved down the front of Cassidy's shorts. Cassidy's head rolled back as Nate took him into his hand, massaging the head. When Cassidy moaned, Nate once again took advantage by placing his open mouth over Cassidy's, thrusting his tongue inside.

Cassidy finally fully gave in when he lowered his arms, snaking one around Nate's neck and finding a nipple with the other. They were both full on, all systems go as the kiss deepened while they pawed at each other.

Dog let out a bark, but this time neither of them so much as flinched. Cassidy massaged Nate through the front of his shorts as his slid down his legs and came to rest around his ankles. Cassidy stepped out of his briefs as Nate roughly squeezed his ass.

Cassidy moaned through their kiss, and Nate reached down, grabbing the backs of his legs, lifting Cassidy off the floor. Nate turned and sat him on top of the island, and Cassidy sucked in a sharp breath as his ass made contact with the cool countertop.

Nate pulled away for a moment, and they sized each other up while trying to catch their breath. Cassidy reached over, running his hand over Nate's cheek. He glided his fingertips over an eyebrow before allowing his thumb to slide over Nate's bottom lip. Nate took Cassidy's thumb into his mouth, sucking it momentarily as his gaze drifted down Cassidy's naked body.

Cassidy removed his hand from Nate's face, propping himself up as Nate massaged his hard-on. Nate kissed, licked, and sucked his way down, starting at Cassidy's neck, then finding a nipple. Cassidy allowed his head to fall back, knowing he'd shoot for sure if he allowed himself to watch his cock sliding into Nate's mouth.

As Nate slowly worked his way down Cassidy's abs, the tiny hint of stubble dug into his skin. Cassidy held his breath, his entire body going taut as Nate's hot mouth took him all the way in.

"Fuck," Cassidy whispered, placing a hand on the back of Nate's head, urging him back down.

Nate growled as he sucked Cassidy, who wasn't quite sure whether this was a good idea, then decided he didn't care as Nate's tongue worked over the head of his dick.

Cassidy's eyes popped open, and he jerked his head back up, hearing a gasp and a thud. Natalie was standing in the kitchen one hand over her eyes, the other over her mouth with a basket of bread turned on its side at her feet.

"Holy shit!" Cassidy screamed, which triggered Nate's enthusiasm, and had him sucking more intensely, obviously misinterpreting the exclamation. Cassidy could feel his eyes rolling back into his head due to Nate's renewed vigor, so he kicked Nate hard in the gut, yelling out in pain as Nate uncontrollably clamped down a little too hard with his teeth.

Nate choked on Cassidy as Natalie squealed, "I'm sooo sorry!"

Nate stood straight up at his mother's voice, and Cassidy bumped one of the beer bottles while trying to hop down off the counter. Fumbling to grab the beer, he lost his balance and rolled off the far side of the island. Dog barked as Cassidy hit the floor with a thud while somehow managing to not spill a drop.

"Oh my goodness… I," Natalie mumbled as Cassidy poked his head up over the top of the island just in time to see her flailing about, eyes shut tight.

She slammed into the door, letting out a squeak as she spun around in a circle.

"Christ, Mom, be careful!" Nate said, scrambling to zip up his shorts while trying to kick Cassidy his clothes.

"Don't you mind me," Natalie said, finding the doorway. "Go back to doing… Oh goodness me."

"Shit," Nate whispered as Natalie tore down the steps, disappearing from view.

Cassidy was on all fours and naked as a jaybird, staring up at Nate while gathering up his undies and gym shorts. He was beyond mortified, and his entire body was already slightly stiff. His dick throbbed for all the wrong reasons as Nate helped him up off the floor. Cassidy covered his bits with the clothes in his hands but peeked down to make sure his johnson was still attached, relieved that, despite the teeth marks, he didn't appear to be bleeding.

"Christ, Cassidy," Nate said, taking a step forward. "I'm so sorry. Let me see it?"

Cassidy stepped back, holding up his hand up for Nate to stay back. "I'm fine." He twisted his body, listening to his spine crack a few times as he attempted to compose himself. "It's fine as well." He checked out his dick. "Slightly traumatized…and hopefully not scarred for life, but still attached."

"Oh God, I'm really… I mean, you kicked me so hard that…"

Cassidy smiled weakly while walking backward toward the hallway. "Right, exactly… I should…go."

"Let me help…"

"No!" Cassidy said, holding up his hands, inadvertently exposing himself. Realizing his error, he whipped his hands back, covering his business. "I'm fine… All good. Just going to go ice my crotch."

He turned and hobbled out of the kitchen, not realizing his ass was exposed, as all his attention was currently placed on his dick. He silently gave thanks that he wasn't currently strapped down, being medevaced to a hospital with his dick sitting in a beer cooler packed in dry ice.

As he slowly climbed the stairs, he looked upward and vowed in Scarlett O'Hara-like fashion, "As God is my witness, I shall never kick a man who's got my dick in his mouth again."

Chapter Eleven

Cassidy pulled on a clean T-shirt when he turned around to find Nate leaning against the doorjamb, watching him.

"Come to finish the job?" Cassidy asked, gently tucking in his shirt.

"That question could be taken more than one way," Nate said, cocking an eyebrow.

Cassidy laughed as he shook his head. "It most certainly cannot."

Nate smiled, letting Cassidy know the message had come in loud and clear. "Feeling any better?"

"Well, I have a sinking feeling I'm going to be really sore come tomorrow morning."

"And for all the wrong reasons," Nate said, nodding with another please-forgive-me-for-almost-biting-your-dick-off expression.

There just really isn't a decent card out there for that one. Cassidy headed toward the door, patting Nate on the shoulder. "Look, Nate—"

"I get it," he interrupted. "The whole thing was a mistake. We shouldn't have been…"

"Fucking around?"

Nate sighed. "Something like that. I apologize for attacking you…in the multitude of ways I wound up doing so."

Cassidy brushed the backs of his fingers over Nate's cheek. "It's not all your fault, pit boy."

Nate burst out laughing, backing out of the doorway so Cassidy could pass. "Your friends showed up while you were soaking in the tub, by the way. They seem nice."

"They seem early," Cassidy said, praying Nate hadn't

mentioned any of the events from earlier that afternoon as he suddenly remembered Spencer making some comment about only needing to keep his legs together for two days.

"Don't worry. I didn't say anything about—"

"About what?" Ollie yelled up from the bottom of the stairs. "Can you speak up a little? I'm finding it terribly difficult to eavesdrop from down here."

Ollie's naturally light brown hair was a little long on top, and the chunky cut had been streaked with various shades of blond. He had that California beach-boy look, which was only betrayed by his Midwestern accent.

He had a thing for vintage concert tees from the eighties and low-rise jeans, a combination he wore so often it had begun to feel like a uniform. Currently, he sported his newest find, a graphic Monkees twentieth-anniversary world-tour T-shirt. Cassidy never knew for sure which ones he bought because of the music versus the ones he thought were colorful, fashionable, or merely topical.

Cassidy started to laugh as Nate cocked his head to the side and said, "Now that one's trouble."

"You have no idea," Cassidy warned.

"I heard that!" Ollie yelled back.

§ § §

Cassidy turned on the radio that sat on the counter. The Dixie Chicks belted out the chorus to "Cowboy Take Me Away," and he turned the volume down so it was more background noise, should the conversation take an unimaginable turn and come to a screeching halt.

Nearly unimaginable, considering Ollie is in the room.

Cassidy scooted behind Nate, going to the far side of the island, once again turning his attention toward prepping dinner.

Spencer came walking in from the back door, nodding. "It's beautiful out there."

He wore designer jeans, sandals, and a blue and white rugby

shirt unbuttoned at the neck to show off one of Ollie's beaded amber necklaces.

Spencer looked like the perpetual frat boy from a well-to-do family, but he seldom behaved like one. He actually enjoyed playing sports and going to the gym, as opposed to Cassidy, who viewed it more as maintenance and Ollie, who viewed it more as a social outing. He'd taken the money he'd managed to pry away from his family and opened a small chain of coffeehouses called the Mo-Joe. Like Cassidy, he wasn't intent on world domination so much as being comfortable and attaining a certain quality of life.

The only time Spencer and Ollie argued was whenever Mr. Business Major attempted to help Mr. Art Major by butting into his jewelry-making business. The problem was the help was never solicited, and Spencer couldn't wrap his brain around the fact that his ideas weren't the only ideas. He always appeared to mean well, which was probably the only reason Ollie hadn't strangled Spencer in his sleep.

It had been no easy feat convincing Spencer to come to Hart's for the entire summer. He didn't like the thought of being so far away from his business, but Ollie had begged and pleaded, reminding Spencer that he did the bulk of his work at home now anyway. That, combined with the fact he could make it back within five hours in case of an emergency, wound up swaying him.

"So did you guys all meet in college?" Nate asked, setting his beer down as he inspected the head of lettuce on the cutting board.

"You could say that." Spencer smiled at Ollie, who was grinning like he'd been waiting for this topic to come up.

Cassidy rolled his eyes. "Yes, we all met in college." He was hoping the topic could die there as he watched Ollie lean down and give Dog a tiny piece of bread. "Will you stop feeding her people food?"

Ollie scowled. "I can't help it. She keeps staring at me with those big eyes."

"She found an easy mark." Cassidy shook his head.

"Which is why we don't have a dog," Spencer said with a pointed gaze at Ollie. "You cave entirely too easily. You need to learn how to say no."

"I thought you liked that about him." Cassidy grinned, licking a little marinade off his finger.

Nate laughed under his breath as Spencer's face flushed slightly. "That's different."

"Hypocrite," Ollie said, taking a sip from his bottle. "And to fully answer your question, Nate, Spence and I are both Cassidy cast-offs."

Cassidy dropped his spoon into the bowl he mixed the marinade in, and dramatically rolled his eyes.

"Spencer had been freshman year's model, and I was the sophomore edition. We were each voted off the island after our six-month contracts were up."

"Do you really have to say it like that?" Cassidy shook his head. "You make it sound so calculated."

"Truth hurts, huh?" Ollie grinned like he'd won something. "At the time, I was devastated, sitting alone at a bar and drowning my sorrows, in a total state of shock."

Cassidy let out a puff of air as he turned his attention to Nate. "He's so melodramatic. He was more than likely planning and plotting, indulging in some elaborate revenge fantasy."

"Then suddenly, I started laughing," Ollie said, raising his voice to let Cassidy know he didn't appreciate the interruptions, "realizing how much I resembled one of the ridiculously corny country-music songs I'd been forced to listen to for months on end. All of which I'd made fun of, mind you."

Cassidy shrugged. "And he wonders why I dumped his skinny ass?"

"As I was saying, I was sitting at the bar," Ollie continued, firing off another hateful look, which now had Nate amused, "when this hunky guy comes over." Ollie winked at Spence, who smiled back with obvious lust in his eyes. "He offered me a bottle of beer and his condolences."

"And we never looked back," Spencer added, reaching down to allow Dog to lick his fingers. "I was jealous as hell when they started dating, but it didn't take long for me to figure out I was jealous of Cassidy, not the other way around."

Cassidy set the platter of marinated tuna steaks on the counter next to the fridge. "That makes me feel all warm inside."

"My rebound boy turned out to be the real deal." Ollie reached over and squeezed Spencer's knee.

"And you all wound up being friends…how?" Nate asked, freezing when he turned, almost bumping into Cassidy, who jumped as if he'd been stung by a bee.

"We were sitting in the library together junior year, and the asshole"—Spencer pointed to Cassidy, who was awkwardly scooting past Nate—"comes up and plops down and starts chatting away."

"As if we'd all been BFFs since growing up in short pants together," Ollie interrupted. "Didn't even have the decency to pretend he was bothered by the fact his last two boyfriends were dating one another."

"Friggin' sociopath." Spencer held up his beer bottle in a cheerslike fashion, shooting Cassidy a faux-infuriated glare.

"Walked all over our fragile egos." Ollie picked Dog up off the floor after she scratched at his ankle.

"We'd both been waiting for the day he'd see us together and rue the day he'd let either of us go." Spencer nodded as he and Ollie grinned.

Nate laughed as he rinsed the freshly chopped lettuce, shaking the colander. "He was probably too busy taking all the credit for getting the two of you together."

"Nice!" Cassidy grabbed a chunk of carrot and chucked it at

Nate's head, who managed to deflect it with his arm.

"He still does!" Ollie said. "Just the other day, he was calling us from his car, all in a panic after—"

"And we've been best friends ever since," Cassidy said, cutting Ollie off. "The end."

Nate directed a gaze toward Cassidy, as if slightly worried for his sanity. "He's always had a major hero complex—big-time comic-book geek back in the day."

"I do not!" Cassidy sneered at Nate.

"He's all blushy." Nate pointed at Cassidy. "He totally thinks of himself as the radioactive love bite that brought you into one another's lives."

"That makes complete and total sense." Ollie nodded.

"Complete load of crap," Cassidy mumbled. "So how do you explain all the other poor, unfortunate souls I've dated and dumped who didn't wind up dating each other?"

Ollie looked around the room, lifting Spencer's arm as if searching for something. "Will they be coming for dinner? Because I don't see any of them around."

"Ha…busted!" Spencer pointed at Cassidy.

"You're awfully pointy with that thing," Cassidy said, nodding toward his finger, which Spencer quickly made into a gun while making a clicking noise as if firing off a few rounds.

"All the others?" Nate asked, raising a brow as he tossed the salad.

"There weren't that many," Ollie said.

"One a year," Spencer blurted out, then laughed a little nervously as if having said too much. "But they last longer than six months now that he doesn't spend his summers sitting with Sadie."

The room got quiet, and Cassidy winked at Spencer, who appeared to be struggling to decide whether he should continue talking, digging yet a larger hole in which to bury Cassidy. He smiled, letting Spence know he wasn't upset by that last comment.

"So I keep trying people on to see if they fit?" Cassidy shrugged, hoping to keep the conversation away from the subject of Sadie. "And there were two guys that one year," he added, realizing that actually wouldn't be considered a bonus in this particular argument.

"At the same time?" Nate asked, wide-eyed.

"No…Jesus!" Cassidy leered at Nate as he reached for the bread. "So, fine. I'm not so good at being alone?"

"Poor Cass." Ollie pooched out his lower lip in an exaggerated pout.

Nate patted Cassidy's behind as he walked behind him, causing Cassidy to flinch a little, as he was still a little freaked out from nearly having his nub gnawed off. Nate sighed, looking guilty as he placed the bowl of salad in the refrigerator. Cassidy winked, offering a weak smile, letting Nate know he appreciated the comfort intended by the tiny act and went back to thinly slicing the baguette for bruschetta.

"So, Nate," Ollie said, turning his attention away from Cassidy. "What's your story? You been a big ole whore too?"

Cassidy tried not to laugh as Nate placed his hand over his mouth, attempting not to spew the beer he'd just drunk as he stumbled over to the sink. It was running down his chin as Ollie and Spencer made fun of him.

Dog let out a short bark as they all turned toward the front of the house, hearing someone knocking at the front door.

"I'll go," Nate quickly volunteered, turning off the sink. He wiped his chin with a paper towel as he rounded the corner of the island.

"Seriously?" Cassidy whispered after Nate disappeared from the room. He picked up the baguette that hadn't been sliced yet, and whacked Ollie upside the head with it.

"Ouch!"

"Shhhh!" Cassidy and Spencer simultaneously said as they

each started chuckling.

"You want to know, don't you?" Ollie asked.

Cassidy scoffed. "Why would I care?"

"Oh puh-lease!" Ollie said, ripping the baguette out of Cassidy's hand and whacking him in the side with it.

"Ouch!"

"Shhh!" Ollie and Spencer said this time as they all started laughing again.

Ollie nudged Spencer with the bread, as if asking for backup. "Don't think for one second you can…"

The threesome turned, hearing Nate yelling Cassidy's name from the front of the house.

"Christ, what now?" Cassidy asked as he followed Spencer out of the kitchen with Ollie and Dog in tow.

§ § §

Cassidy froze as he walked into the parlor. He heard Ollie gasp before letting out a little laugh. Cassidy knew the blood had drained from his face, along with the smile that was once there. He glanced at Nate, who was standing somewhat defensively to the side with his hands on his hips.

"Hi, baby!"

Cassidy jerked his head toward Teddy, realizing he wasn't suffering from the delusions he'd been hoping for. "Wha—Um…hi?"

He listened to Ollie whisper, "Holy shit, this is gonna be good," behind him and began to long for the baguette.

Teddy sauntered over, grinning like he'd just discovered the cure for cancer before planting his lips on Cassidy's, thrusting his tongue right on in as if it still belonged there.

Cassidy made a noise that landed somewhere between an eek and a moan as he pulled away, smiling nervously. He held Teddy at arm's length. "What are you doing here, Teddy?"

Teddy shrugged, reaching over as he ran a finger down Cassidy's torso. "I was back home in Kansas, hating my life, not knowing what the hell I was going to do now that I graduated. I was missing you desperately, when it hit me."

"Who hit you?" Cassidy holstered the urge to reenact the scenario. *Maybe he has a concussion—amnesia—and he forgot we broke up months ago?*

"No, ding-ass, it hit me."

Semantics? Really! Cassidy fired a gaze at Teddy that he seemed to understand all too well. *Please let his next words have something to do with falling space debris or having been beaned by a rogue baseball.*

"I love you!" Teddy said in a eureka-like tone.

Kill me now. Cassidy laughed out of nervousness and a newly discovered *Fatal Attraction*-esque fear building inside him.

"And I've decided I'm not going to allow you to follow the same tired patterns of your past." Teddy shook his head. "No, sir. I'm not going to fade away into the background like all the guys before me."

Cassidy threw his hands into the air as he stormed into the living room. "There have not been that many guys!"

"Focus, dear," Ollie said, coming up behind Cassidy and patting him on the shoulder.

Nate let out a puffing noise and shook his head while walking over to the fireplace. His arms were folded and eyebrows arched as he paced back and forth in the background.

"I'm not letting you break up with me," Teddy said matter-of-factly as he dropped his bag and followed Cassidy.

"You already did let me," Cassidy said, becoming frustrated as his voice cracked. He cleared his throat and glanced around the room like he'd fallen into some sick, twisted episode of the *Twilight Zone.* "There are no take-backs in boyfriends!"

"Ex-boyfriends," Nate tossed out.

"Who's he?" Teddy asked, glaring at Nate, who was smiling in a taunting manner.

"That's Nate, Teddy." Cassidy took Teddy by the arms and shook him slightly. He raised an eyebrow as he allowed his hands to roam over Teddy's biceps. "Wow…you've really been working out."

"Yeah." Teddy grinned, getting that cocky smirk that always turned Cassidy on.

Cassidy continued, sliding his hands over his upper arms and shoulders. "It really shows. You…"

"Fo-cus," Ollie muttered under his breath.

Cassidy ripped his hands away. "Right, Teddy…you really need to focus. You can't just come back three months later and demand we get back together."

"Why not?"

"Not real bright, this one," Nate mumbled.

"Suck it, dude," Teddy said.

Cassidy glanced up at the ceiling. "For the love of all that is gay and holy."

"I know my rights," Teddy blurted out, only to realize himself that his statement didn't actually make sense. "Spencer and I talked a few weeks back, and it revealed this whole twisted pattern you've had."

Cassidy slowly turned, glaring at Spencer, who leaned against one of the columns separating the living room from the entryway. He quickly turned away from Cassidy, cringing slightly.

"Really?" Cassidy asked as if begging for mercy as he stared down Spencer.

Ollie burst out laughing, the only one in the room who appeared to be enjoying himself. "This is like the best vacation ever, honey." Ollie's greedy smile melted away as Cassidy cast a nasty smirk his way.

"Listen," Teddy said, forcing Cassidy back around to face him. "I realize now you've just been waiting for someone to fight for you. A guy with enough balls to stand up to you and say, 'No, I'm not going to let you push me away.'"

"Oh dear God," Nate said.

All five men jumped as the front door burst open from behind them.

"What the hell?" Cassidy asked, turning to see Neil standing in the foyer. He closed his eyes as a whole new level of dread swept over him. He whispered in a prayer, "Pretty please, let him just be out of gas."

"You listen up, Cassidy… Uh." Neil's forehead scrunched up as if he were searching for the right name. "Um, shoot."

"Jesus," Nate said, throwing his hands in the air as he stared Neil down. "You don't even know his last name!" Nate turned to Cassidy. "Is this Piper's Point or *Dante's Cove*?"

"Mel-ho's Place!" Ollie yelled, his smile fading as Nate glared, letting him know this might not be the best time to play Who's the Queen of Pop Culture?

"I want you to know that the other night was the most incredible evening I've ever spent with a guy."

Oh God.

"Who's this guy?" Teddy asked, his voice going up an octave as he made an attempt to sort of puff himself up.

"Teddy, please," Cassidy said, pressing his fingers into his temples.

"Who the hell are you?" Neil asked defensively.

"I'm the boyfriend."

"You have a fucking boyfriend?"

"Ex, damn it, ex-boyfriend," Cassidy mumbled.

"You fucked this guy?" Teddy asked, motioning toward Neil.

"This is way better than *Real Housewives*," Ollie said greedily before Spencer smacked him in the arm.

Cassidy sighed. "I'll take that aneurysm any time now."

Teddy's arms flew up into the air as if to say, *What gives*? "I turn my back for like a minute, and you fuck some other dude?"

"Hey, pal, it was more than just a fuck," Neil said, stomping past Spencer as he walked into the room and vehemently pointed his finger at Teddy. "It was transcendent!"

Oh. My. Lord. Cassidy couldn't help himself, despite trying to hold back a smile.

"Oh please, you're nothing but a stupid trick," Teddy said, shoving Cassidy out of the way and lunging at Neil.

"Screw you!" Neil locked arms with Teddy, and they began to wrestle. "You're yesterday's fucking garbage."

Spencer jumped in, trying to pull Neil off Teddy as Cassidy steadied himself. He stood there, mouth hanging slightly open, completely in shock.

"Careful, honey," Ollie said, climbing up into a wingback chair and standing over them with Dog under his arm, who was now barking her fool head off.

"You're all fucking nuts." Nate shook his head as he crossed the room. "You wanna try helping here?" he asked Cassidy as he tried getting between the two. "I think you each need to go back to wherever the hell you came from."

"You piece of shit!" Teddy screamed, taking a swing at Neil.

Cassidy came to, out of the haze he was in. "Cut it out, guys. This is stupid."

Neil shook Spencer off and reared back as Teddy's eyes widened. Nate managed to get his arm around Teddy's waist, pulling him away. Spencer grabbed Neil's arm as he turned back around, attempting to free himself.

Ollie stood on the seat of the chair, bouncing up and down with a bloodlusty expression on his face as he growled in a guttural tone. "Break his arm, honey!"

Cassidy, Spencer, and Nate all turned to stare at Ollie, somewhat astonished, while Neil and Teddy still struggled to get loose. Cassidy glanced back as Neil wiggled loose from Spencer.

Teddy ducked, seeing Neil's fist coming his way, which instead made contact with Nate's chin, causing his body to spin around slightly.

"Nate?" Cassidy said, as all the commotion in the room came to a halt.

Cassidy watched as if in slow motion while a sort of drunken half smile spread across Nate's lips. His eyes rolled back, fluttering, just before he crumpled to the floor.

"Son of a bitch!" Cassidy yelled.

§ § §

"Ouch, damn it," Nate said.

"Sorry." Cassidy cringed and nervously fidgeted with the baggie of ice as he sat on the edge of Nate's bed.

"Just give it to me," Nate grumbled. He sat up, propping up a couple of pillows behind him. He sighed as he leaned back, inspecting his shirt, which had been ripped open and now missed a few buttons. "Ridiculous."

"I am so sorry," Cassidy offered again, handing over the ice pack while doing his best not to ogle the bit of naked chest exposed to him.

Nate snatched the ice from him. "Your friends are a pack of nutters, you know."

"A little difficult to argue at this point," Cassidy said, smiling with a shrug.

"Maybe if you had some friends you hadn't fucked?" Nate asked, acting superior.

Cassidy gave him a look that let him know he was unimpressed. "Hypocrite much?"

Nate blushed, as if just now remembering that they too were once an item. He rooted around a bit on the bed. "I'm gonna break that Neil guy's face the next time I see him." Nate pressed the ice against his chin. "What the hell, Cass? Is your lube laced with heroin?"

Cassidy laughed. "I can honestly say nothing like this has ever happened before."

"Great, so just in time for my face." Nate shook his head, hissing a little from the pain as he attempted to work out his jaw.

"You have been tweaking Neil's nose since you met him," Cassidy said.

Nate glared at him.

"Not really the right time to bring that up. I see that now."

Nate grinned, and Cassidy relaxed, thinking he might not be as pissed off as he was sure to have been were the situation reversed. They stared at each other for what felt like an eternity to Cassidy, who was no longer sure what to say. He finally broke their gaze and surveyed the room. It wasn't frozen in time the way Cassidy's old bedroom was.

Nate's was a grown-up's bedroom. It was nothing like he remembered, now painted in shades of mocha with a grayish French blue accent wall. Being a longer, rectangular-shaped space on the back side of the house, Nate's room had French doors that opened onto a small balcony that barely had enough room for two chairs and a table. But you could see the ocean through the tree line. Cassidy came to the realization that Nate had to have been living here with Natalie back before the judge ordered the property be vacated.

He wondered why Nate had never returned any of his phone calls as he admired the Stickley-style head and footboards that were well cared for, though obviously antique. Granted, he hadn't called but a few times over the years, but if Nate hadn't been truly angry with him, then why not call him back? Was it because of the mystery guy Natalie had mentioned? Nate must have really been in love with the guy if that were the case. Cassidy suffered a sting of jealousy at that thought.

The warm glow created by the amber-hued glass mission-style lamp shades had an oddly calming effect, and he pushed away the bad, angst-ridden thoughts. Cassidy wiggled his toes into the plush pile of the shag area rug, enjoying the feel and texture.

The artwork consisted of black-and-white framed photographs of sand dunes, the lighthouse, and a smattering of miscellaneous architectural elements.

A thirty-two-inch plasma sat on top of the highboy on the opposite wall next to a framed picture of Cassidy and Nate posing on the beach when they were just kids. Cassidy sighed, longing for a life that was once again…simple. The TV had been muted, but the light in the room flickered as the pictures on the screen changed.

Cassidy wished he could lie down on the other side of Nate and go to sleep. He was exhausted from the day's antics and felt as if he'd been in a constant state of tension for days—like a hunted animal ready to bolt at the slightest hint of danger. A wave of loneliness swept over him, and Cassidy found himself dreading the thought of sleeping alone in his bed.

"Can I ask you a question?" Nate asked, pulling Cassidy back out of his thoughts.

"Sure." Cassidy lay back, stretching his body out. He caught a whiff of the suede duvet cover when he turned toward Nate. The scent of leather drifted up through his nostrils, traveling straight down his spine, and headed directly between his legs. He could feel his goose-pimply skin and exhaled slowly in an attempt to gain control over his senses. "Anything you want."

Nate raised an eyebrow as he attempted to hold back a grin, making Cassidy realize how leading that last comment was. The playfulness faded suddenly as he pulled the ice away from his jaw. "What is it really…bionic cock?"

Cassidy started laughing.

"'Cause that was totally fucked-up, Cass," Nate said with a shit-eating grin. "I know you're gorgeous, but now you're inciting riots?"

Cassidy shook his head while letting out a belly laugh. He was thankful deep down that Nate was already joking around about it.

"Come on," Nate said, nudging his head toward Cassidy's crotch. "Whip it out already. If it lights up or something, I'll understand."

"You had it your mouth this afternoon," Cassidy said, feeling his face flush with heat. "You nearly bit it off, remember?"

"I do not recall any such thing." Nate shrugged. "Perhaps I have a concussion, a little amnesia or something?"

"I probably still have the teeth marks to prove it."

"You think?" Nate smirked, checking out Cassidy's package. "I should probably take a look, if that's the case. You could be making it all up, trying to take advantage of me in my fragile condition."

"Fragile, my ass." Cassidy squinted at Nate, unable to believe the nonsense that was flying out from between those very enticing lips. "Considering you never even got your clothes all the way off, if anyone was having trouble remembering the other's equipment correctly, it would be me."

"You damn well better remember it correctly," Nate said, puffing his chest out. "I'm the one who tapped that ass…back when it was still virgin territory."

Cassidy moaned deeply as he slowly ran his hand down his stomach toward his package. He started breathing heavily as his fingertips wiggled under the waistband of his jeans. "And you fucked me sooooo good…Tate."

Cassidy laughed as the rolled neck pillow beaned him in the face, ricocheting off onto the floor.

"Asshole," Nate said, flopping back down into the pillows like he'd been mortally wounded.

Cassidy sat up on the bed after hearing a light knock on the door.

"Come in," Nate yelled, nudging Cassidy playfully in the hip with the pad of his foot.

Spencer opened the door, allowing Dog to scamper into the bedroom. "I just let her out. I'm heading to bed and dragging my bloodthirsty little husband with me."

"Ashamed to show his face, I see." Cassidy smirked.

"I should hope so," Nate added.

"We wrapped up two plates and put 'em in the fridge, if you guys get hungry, and Ollie's set Teddy up in your room, Cass."

Nate squirmed a bit. "Why the hell is he still here?"

"Don't be an ass," Cassidy said.

Nate's mouth fell open, and Cassidy rolled his eyes, apologizing as he remembered Nate had been unconscious during that revelation. "He just came out to his parents, who were less than happy about it, and then used what little money he had taking a bus to get here."

"Of course he did." Nate nodded as he laughed at the ludicrousness of it all. "So we're now a homo halfway house."

"We assumed you wouldn't want anyone in Sadie's room other than yourself?" Spencer questioned with a shrug as he chuckled over Nate's objections.

"That's fine. Thanks, Spencer." Cassidy leaned over to pick up Dog. "We can sleep downstairs on the pull-out tonight, can't we, girl?" He laughed as Dog licked his chin, her nubby tail going a mile a minute.

"Night, guys," Spencer said, starting to close the door. He popped his head back in. "Sorry again for my totally innocent role in tonight's festivities. I figured Teddy would call, not show up on your doorstep. He seemed like he needed closure or…"

"It's all good, Spencer." Cassidy nodded. "You're a good friend for him to have right now."

"Oh yes… Thank goodness he has you," Nate growled as Cassidy punched him in the leg.

"And hey, since Nate has this big bed, you should just bunk in here if you don't want to stay in Sadie's room," Spencer said, turning to leave.

"G'night, Spencer," Nate called out as the door pulled shut. He smiled in an ornery manner at Cassidy as he rubbed his leg where he'd been punched. "That's probably not a bad idea, by the way. Lord knows that prepubescent 'roid-rabbit will be trying to sneak into your bed in the middle of the night otherwise."

Cassidy momentarily got lost in erotic flashes of his pretty-boy jock of an ex, who, while having had good-guy written all over him, became amazingly nasty in the sack once the lights went out. "He's really not a bad guy, you know."

"If you say so." Nate gave Cassidy a suspicious sidelong glance as if having just read his thoughts. "I'm just a little wary of your judgment at the moment."

Cassidy smirked, turning his attention to Dog, who sat politely on his lap as he scratched behind her ear. "Thinks he knows it all."

Cassidy laughed as Nate pushed him with his foot again. Dog jumped up, placing her paws on Cassidy's chest, and went about licking his chin.

Chapter Twelve

Cassidy smiled, stretching as his eyes fluttered open. He smacked his lips as he gazed sleepily around the room, waiting for his eyes to come into focus. Remembering he'd slept in Nate's bed, he turned, smile fading slightly as he realized he was alone. He rolled onto his side and reached over, snagging one of the pillows Nate had slept on.

Shoving his face into the pillow, he inhaled deeply as he hugged it, taking renewed notice of the hard-on between his legs. He moaned, breathing in Nate's scent once more, intensely enjoying the feel of his erection straining against the warm, cottony fabric of his briefs. He acknowledged the fact he wanted Nate, and for once embraced the notion as opposed to chastising himself over it. Feeling a tiny bit of precum leaking out as he thrust his pelvis into the mattress, he decided there would be no more hiding behind his fears and objections. He was going to man up and own it.

Cassidy yelped, tossing the pillow when he heard the door clicking like someone was coming into the room. He sat up in the bed, breathing heavily as he stared, wide-eyed, at the bedroom door. Cassidy placed a hand over his chest, realizing the door wasn't actually shut and a breeze from the open windows caused the latch to click against the plate.

He started laughing once he noticed he'd chucked the pillow halfway across the room. Staring disappointedly down at his now-softening cock, he sarcastically said, "And you were going to man up and own it."

Cassidy's eyes widened as he kicked and tossed the blankets off, suddenly taking note that his dick was working. He yanked down his briefs, wiggling his hips, and thoroughly inspected the skin around the base. "My precious, precious." He smiled, falling back into the mattress, relieved his engines were once again firing on all cylinders. "Not so much as a bruise."

He shimmied back into his undies and got out of bed, stretching while adjusting himself in his briefs. The sunlight filtered in through the light sheers softly blowing in the breeze. He stumbled over to the highboy and patted Sadie's urn, which he'd placed there the night before. Cassidy hoped some of her fearlessness might somehow rub off on him. He squinted, trying to focus on the photograph of Nate and him as kids, then turned back toward the nightstand, spotting his glasses.

Crossing the room, he became aware of the fact he was oddly at home in Nate's bedroom. Putting on his glasses, he chewed on his lip, thinking maybe he should just come clean with Nate and lay it all out on the line. He had feelings for him, and even though he wasn't sure how deep those feelings ran or whether Nate felt the same, was it really that big of a deal? Perhaps holding it all in was lending more weight to it than there should be.

"So what if we went out and it didn't work?" Cassidy asked, staring out the French doors across the beach below. Nate was family in a sense, and nothing could ever change that. "And if it did work?"

Cassidy started to imagine what it would be like to have Nate back in Chapel Hill with him when he heard the screen door snap from down below. He sighed, watching Teddy head across the courtyard toward the beach.

He turned and walked past the highboy, winking at Sadie, who he decided to leave right where she was. He spotted the photo with crystal clarity this time as he pulled on the jeans he'd tossed over the footboard last night. He slid the belt out of the loops and set it on the foot of the bed, deciding he would forgo his shirt as well. He had the oddest desire to leave something of his in Nate's bedroom, marking his territory in some weird way.

Aware of how badly he needed to pee, he headed for the door, prioritizing his needs. Pee, brush the teeth, and then find Nate so they could have a little talk, Cassidy thought.

Maybe some coffee first and then the talk?

Cassidy reached for the doorknob, feeling positive about the possibilities of his summer for the first time.

§ § §

Coming down the stairs, Cassidy cornered on the small landing and froze, noticing Dr. Downey and Nate in the living room talking. Whispering, to be exact, Cassidy thought, unable to tell what they were saying, yet aware of the obvious tension between the two. Ben was holding Dog, and the two were barely a foot apart.

Cassidy could feel a sickening sense of dread creeping into his gut as he quietly took another step down, freezing again the instant he heard the creak of the wood. Ben and Nate practically sprang apart, like kids caught doing something they knew they weren't supposed to be. That sense of hopefulness he'd woken up with faded to black as his chest began to ache.

He smiled, making an extra effort to hide his disappointment at realizing Nate and Ben were most definitely seeing each other. He even flashed back to the day he took Dog to the vet's, distinctly remembering not only the fact that Ben had mentioned Nate's name, but that his voice had been laced with a very distinct tone. It hadn't been mere idle curiosity as he'd imagined at the time. Ben had been pumping Cassidy for information.

"Hello, Doc," Cassidy said in his most convincing jovial tone. He reached out to take Dog from him. *You can't have Dog too, asshole.*

"Just came to check on our little patient," Ben said, smiling cheerfully as he passed the dog to Cassidy while doing a horrible job at trying to mask the obvious tension in the room.

"She's doing great, by the way," Nate said with a nod.

Cassidy snuggled her up in his arms as Dog did what she did best by giving his chin a tongue bath. He eyed them both suspiciously as they stood in place smiling back at him. He resisted the urge to tell them to cut the crap already. "Wow, do I ever need coffee."

Ben and Nate laughed, obviously overcompensating by faking

amusement, considering he hadn't said anything even remotely funny.

Nate's gaze flitted nervously from Cassidy to Ben and back again. "I think Ollie and Spencer are in the kitchen."

I get it. You want me to vamoose. "I slept great, by the way."

"I'm glad," Nate said, absentmindedly rubbing his bruised chin.

"Nate has the most comfy bed," Cassidy said, instantly feeling like an asshole as Ben appeared to shrink a little, despite keeping up the facade with his facial expression. He made his way out of the living room and down the hall toward the kitchen, hearing the whispers resume from behind him.

You didn't have to be such a jerk, asshole. Like it's Ben's fault you crawled out of the woodwork after all these years, wanting Nate back.

As if sensing Cassidy was beating himself up, Dog reached up and gave the underside of his chin one more lick.

Cassidy kissed the top of her head. "Thanks for the sugar."

He let out a disgruntled groan and spun back around, trying not to take it personally as the whispers ceased the instant he rounded the column. "We're all planning to make a day of it on the beach, Ben. There's plenty of food and drink to go around, if you'd like to join us."

Ben glanced at Nate, folding his arms as he turned to Cassidy. "Would there happen to be any liquor in those drinks?"

"Oh yeah!" Cassidy said, adding a very sarcastic laugh as he turned.

"I'd love to stay, thanks."

"Grrrreat!" Cassidy called back as he walked away, trying to purge the images he had in his head of drowning Ben in the ocean and feeding him to the sharks.

§ § §

Entering the kitchen, Cassidy found Ollie and Spencer standing around the island. He could tell by the expressions on their faces they'd come to the same conclusions regarding Ben.

"Tough break, dude," Spencer said, leaning on the top of the island with his elbows, coffee mug in hand.

Cassidy wandered over to the island, feeling deflated. "I did not see that one coming."

Ollie's eyes widened as he grabbed the coffeepot. "He's not even making an attempt to deny it. This can't be good… Oh wait, we aren't talking about me, so it's okay." He filled an empty mug that had been sitting on the countertop.

"We'd better never be talking about you," Spencer said to Ollie.

"It's a sign." Cassidy shrugged. "It's not meant to be."

Spencer shook his head. "If you aren't willing to go after him, you don't deserve to have him."

"I'm not a home wrecker," Cassidy said, leaning over to place Dog on the floor. He watched as she went about sniffing the floor for any hidden morsels of food. "I can't believe he'd blow me while having a boyfriend."

"Sweet!" Ollie pointed at Spencer, who had a grimace on his face. "You lose. I told you he couldn't keep it in his pants!"

"Damn it, Cass!" Spencer said, shaking his head in disappointment.

Ollie passed a cup to Cassidy. "If it makes any difference, while I couldn't really hear anything when I tried to eavesdrop, it did appear as if all wasn't well between them."

"Well, I'm not going to be the reason either of them use to jump ship." Cassidy took a sip of coffee, feeling the burn slowly make its way down into his chest.

"I realize you're not exactly used to needing to chase after a guy," Spencer said, standing up straight, "but I seriously think now would be the time to start."

"Thank you! That's it!" Cassidy said, a sense of relief washing over him.

"What's it?" Ollie asked, looking around the room with a "who farted?" expression.

"Spencer's right. I don't know how to chase after a guy because I've never had to." Cassidy took another drink, feeling a new clarity sweep over him, like his eyes were finally open. "That's why I suck at this. God, I feel so much better about myself."

"Really not the thing to be bragging about at the moment," Spencer said, straddling a bar stool.

"Yeah," Ollie said with a snort, "a little hard to empathize with you when you point out how easy you've always had it."

"I can't help it," Cassidy said, grinning. "I'm not an asshole. I'm just clueless."

Ollie sneered. "Can't you be both?"

"Quit trying to bitch-bait me. I'm having a revelation here."

"It's so not in my nature," Ollie sighed, "but I'll try."

"So neither of you would have a problem coming in between two other guys?" Cassidy asked.

"No regrets, baby." Spencer shrugged.

"Is this the same speech that Teddy got?" Cassidy asked, causing Spencer to snarl up his lip.

"Let me just say," Ollie piped in, his head bobbing as he placed a hand on his hip. He pointedly locked eyes with Cassidy, "that if two people really love each other, ain't nobody gonna come between 'em."

"All of a sudden he thinks he's Madea," Cassidy said to Spencer as Ollie rolled his eyes. "No more *Housewives of Atlanta* for you." Cassidy cocked an eyebrow, mocking Ollie's 'tude. "You're getting a little too sassy for your own good."

Spencer laughed at Ollie. "You really are, gurrrl."

Cassidy laughed at Spencer, who always looked ridiculous whenever he tried to channel the sistas.

Ollie put up a hand and turned away. "Fuck you both… bitches."

Cassidy went to the back door, seeing Teddy sitting out on the beach by himself. He sighed as his mind went right back to thoughts of Nate, wishing he could turn back time and not have seen what he had when coming down the stairs that morning.

It wasn't going to be easy, trying to put this particular genie back into the bottle, but he knew he needed to try. Hart's Island wasn't like other places. It was a very close-knit community. There were consequences to a person's actions here, and Cassidy knew he couldn't play fast and loose with whatever was going on between Ben and Nate.

Considering he wasn't even going to be living here full-time, he also didn't feel he had the right to step in and muck up the water. He needed to make sure he left everything the way he'd found it, and not mess around with the natural order of things. Cassidy saw Spencer playfully kissing on Ollie and wanted to be all, *Aw…how sweet.* But considering he had a strong urge to hurl something at their heads, he decided he could make better use of his time by going out and making an attempt to figure out what the hell had gotten into Teddy.

§ § §

Kicking off his sandals, Cassidy bent over and picked up Dog before walking down the stone-paved steps and into the sand. The ocean was a little more active today, the waves rushing up the sandy beach a little farther and faster than they had been. The sun was breaking through the clouds as they rolled by, and Teddy seemed slightly mesmerized by the Mother Nature of it all.

Cassidy cleared his throat, alerting Teddy to his presence. "Whatcha doin'?"

"Hey." Teddy glanced back, as if he was particularly down in the dumps. "Just sitting here, thinking how beautiful this all is."

Cassidy sat down in the sand next to him, letting loose of Dog, who was slightly alarmed by the sand and the fact that her feet sank into it. Cassidy and Teddy both chuckled as she took a step, carefully lifting her paw and sniffing about before moving forward.

Cassidy crossed his arms, resting them on his knees. "Like she thinks each step might be her last."

Teddy nodded. "I get that."

"Your parents?" Cassidy asked.

Teddy nodded again. Cassidy wondered if he'd be able to get to the bottom of things, if all he was going to get out of him was a series of nods and grunts.

"Can you tell me what happened?"

"They didn't throw me out or anything," Teddy said, pushing his sunglasses up onto the top of his head and squinting at Cassidy. "They sure as hell let me know they'd never accept it, though."

"I'm sorry." Cassidy sighed, putting his arm around Teddy.

"You should be, according to them," Teddy said. "They totally blame you."

Cassidy's mouth fell open. *No way in hell was I his first trip to the rodeo.*

"They kept saying I'd never be happy, never be able to fall in love or have a family of my own, and I guess I finally lost it. Yelling at them like a crazy person about how wrong they were. That I'd already fallen in love and that the only reason we broke up was because I graduated and had to move back home."

Cassidy began to understand how Teddy wound up on his doorstep.

"I know that when we met I said all that stuff about not wanting anything serious, that I'd be leaving at the end of the school year and we could only be together if you were cool with it being a casual thing." Teddy shrugged, reaching over to caress Cassidy's ankle. "But I really did fall for you, Cass."

They both started laughing when Dog pounced on Teddy's fingers, wanting to play. She barked until Teddy began to play along, running his fingers across the sand while she chased after them.

"And you don't think that this flood of feelings for me might have more to do with what's comfortable to you…"

Teddy started to puff himself up for his defense. "Just because I might be a little scared at the moment doesn't give you the right to tell me how I feel, Cass."

"You're right, Teddy, but I'm not telling. I'm just throwing some things out there to see if anything makes sense to you."

Teddy settled back down, though he didn't appear all that happy about doing so as he turned his attention back down at the sand. He continued to taunt Dog, who was never quite fast enough to catch his fingers.

"But I do want you to really consider that you might only be drawn to me now because you're craving the familiar. The ground under your feet has completely shifted on you, and your whole world has changed overnight. That would scare the shit out of anyone. Believe me, I know." Cassidy wondered if he wasn't also speaking about himself in regard to Nate. Maybe being back here, feeling as alone in the world as he did, he'd manufactured feelings that weren't really there.

"Perhaps having your parents say those horrible things to you might have also played a tiny part in that you really wanted to prove them wrong?"

"I don't know. Maybe." Teddy reached down and scooped up the dog, loving on her.

"And they are wrong, Teddy." Cassidy reached over, gently forcing Teddy to face him. "You may have to work a little harder to get it, but you can have everything a straight couple has."

"Just not with you." Teddy jerked his chin free, milking the drama. "I'll see about getting a job so I can earn enough for the bus ride back to Kansas. I'll get out of your hair as soon as I can."

Cassidy smacked him in the side. "I don't want you to leave, asshole. I actually think it would be great if you stayed for the summer."

Teddy got that glint of hope in his eye.

"As a friend, Teddy." Cassidy gave him the no-bullshit face. "Nothing else."

Teddy scowled, turning his attention back to the pup. "I don't know, maybe. I still need a job, though. I can't just live off you."

Cassidy slung an arm over Teddy's shoulder as he looked out over the ocean. "I'd like it if you could think of Piper's Point as your home. It's always been like magic for me. Maybe it could wind up becoming the same for you."

"Can it mend a broken heart?" Teddy asked, trying to guilt Cassidy a little.

"I don't think it's broken, babe." Cassidy winked as he stood up. "Bruised, perhaps, but not broken."

Teddy laughed a little after Dog managed to get in a couple of surprise licks.

"You want me to take her back in with me?"

"Nah, it's okay. I got her."

Cassidy turned to head back to the house, and Teddy called back, "Thanks, Cass."

"You're welcome, Teddy."

Cassidy slowly made his way back up the stone steps, meandering across the courtyard as he thought about all the things he'd just said to Teddy. A shudder crawled across his skin. The thought that his feelings for Nate might not be genuine frightened him. He paused for a moment before opening the screen door, listening to Ollie and Spencer laughing and flirting with each other inside the house. Cassidy was intensely grateful to have them here, despite having the constant reminder of how happy they were together shoved in his face. He hated himself for thinking that, yet there was truth behind it. It was one of those revelations he wasn't too happy to discover. It may have been part of who he was as an individual, but it certainly wasn't the best part.

§ § §

Cassidy came back up the stairs to dig out his bathing

suit, having left Ollie in charge of the blender, making a poor man's version of frozen sangria. The poor man's version being microwaved store-bought fruit concentrate as opposed to hovering over the stove boiling real fruit and sugar. Spencer was assembling kebabs to marinate in the fridge for later that afternoon, and the entire house vibrated and hummed from the blaring club music provided by Ollie.

It's like living in a Janet Jackson video, Cassidy thought, half expecting backup dancers to come flying out of the bedrooms as he cleared the last step. He caught a glimpse of some movement through Nate's bedroom door, which wasn't closed all the way. He froze, feeling as if he'd been gutted like a fish while taking a step back. He felt as if his eyes might bug right out of skull, seeing Nate and Ben hugging each other as they stood at the foot of the bed in nothing but swim trunks. Cassidy quickly averted his eyes as Nate noticed him standing there. He wasted no time crossing the landing, shutting his bedroom door behind him.

Cassidy placed his hand over his chest as he leaned back against the door. If these feelings were manufactured as a result of his loneliness, they certainly packed quite the punch. He took a few deep breaths before finally pushing himself off the door. Momentarily forgetting what the hell he'd come upstairs for, Cassidy stood clueless, in the middle of the room attempting to recall the ill-fated reason.

Total recall kicked in, and he started to unbutton his jeans, kicking them across the floor after they fell to his ankles. Inviting Ben to stay was supposed to be torturing to Nate, not him. He shimmied out of his briefs, trying to purge the image of them hugging each other from his brain. Cassidy walked over to the kid-sized bureau and rifled through the drawers until he found the black formfitting trunks.

Lots of liquor, he thought as he headed back out into the hall on his way to the bathroom to make a quick run through the shower. He didn't particularly care whether anyone happened to catch him in the buff. He wasn't going to tiptoe around all day worrying about what everyone else thought. *I'm having fun today, so help me—even if it winds up killing me.*

§ § §

Cassidy opened the bathroom door, still adjusting the goods in the snug brief-cut suit. He found Nate leaning against the wall next to the staircase waiting for him. A little smile formed as he watched Cassidy rearranging his bits.

"I don't particularly want to talk to you right now," Cassidy said, crossing his arms and taking a stance as if claiming one-half of the landing to be his territory.

Nate pushed his body away from the wall. "What did I do?"

"Don't play coy with me. You've got some nerve."

Nate stood there, arms wide open, as if he was genuinely confused.

"You really think I'm too stupid to figure out what was going on between you and Ben earlier?"

Nate's arms fell to his sides as his face pinked up. He fidgeted as if trying to buy a little time to figure out what excuse to go with.

Cassidy lowered his voice to a whisper, despite being doubtful anyone downstairs would be able to overhear, as the bass from the boom box in the kitchen vibrated the floor under his feet. "I can't believe you tried to have sex with me!"

Nate's mouth fell open. "You actually think…" He stopped and took in a deep breath. "Of course you would. You brought your harem with you!"

"Oh, that's rich!" Cassidy tossed an arm into the air.

"I mean really, Cass, exactly where was I going to fit in?" Nate practically hissed he was so pissed. "Going to pencil me in on Thursdays and every third Saturday? Maybe before you go accusing me of two-timing, you might consider shedding a few of the three guys you're currently juggling."

Cassidy was shaking, and he folded his arms in an attempt to prevent himself from reaching out to strangle Nate. He hadn't exactly planned the Neil thing, which could hardly be considered a relationship at this point, and he certainly hadn't encouraged Teddy to travel across the country for a reunite-ment. But the fact that Nate had the gall to start throwing out ultimatums when he himself was dating the local dog whisperer infuriated Cassidy. "You know what, Nate? You can't just insert yourself back into my life ten years later and start making all these demands on me."

"Demands? What fucking demands have I made? Suggesting you might want to chose one of us already and stop stringing the rest along?"

"Ha! You mean hurry up and pick you." Cassidy fumed, realizing on some level he wasn't even making sense any longer as they'd both supposedly agreed that they shouldn't be anything other than friends. "And you aren't even free to be picked!"

"Fuck you, Cassidy. Stop acting like you're starring in some foreign-language film—a French farce where you're cast in the lead as the ardent and steadfast boy-next-door who goes home for a visit to find himself in quite the pickle as three hotties vie for his attentions."

Cassidy wasn't able to hold back the smile forming, despite chewing on his lip in an attempt to squelch it. "Why a foreign film?"

Nate thrust his arms through the air like a madman. "Like Hollywood would ever make that movie!"

Cassidy laughed, feeling a tug or maybe some type of old connection, realizing he'd known exactly what Nate had meant by it. "I just can't handle you putting all this pressure on me right now."

"Jesus, Cass, is your reality really that skewed, or is this some type of twisted game at playing hard to get?"

"That's not fair!"

"Well, you of all people should know life isn't fair. I need some air." Nate turned and headed for the staircase.

"I'm not the one playing games, Mr. Cock-tease one minute

and Mr. Freeze the next." Cassidy smiled, watching Nate stop at the top of the stairs. "I mean, really…why now, Nate?"

Nate turned, shaking his head as if disgusted by the insinuation, although Cassidy thought he could spot a tiny glimmer of guilt peeking out from behind the mask.

"You really aren't very smart, huh." Nate strode across the landing until they were practically face-to-face.

Cassidy reached out, grabbing Nate's shoulder to keep him from advancing farther. He didn't know what the right thing to say was, and he was convinced that regardless, he was sure to say the wrong thing. He wasn't even sure what the fuck they were arguing about anymore. The only thing he did know was that he wanted Nate. Cassidy knew what he wanted to say, but he could feel the words sticking there in the back of his throat.

Nate reached up with both hands, and took Cassidy's face in them. He leaned in, pressed his lips to Cassidy's, and slowly slid his tongue inside. The kiss was soft and warm, practically inviting Cassidy in for more. It wasn't forceful, and there was no desperation behind it. To Cassidy, it was simply Nate giving a little piece of himself in perhaps the only way he knew how at that particular moment.

And just as quickly as it had been given, it was taken away as Nate pulled back, meeting Cassidy's eyes for a flicker of a moment before turning away and heading down the stairs without another word.

Cassidy stood there, mouth hanging slightly open as he reached up, and ran his fingertips softly over his lips. He really hated it when Nate did shit like that. "Emotional terrorist," he mumbled under his breath, half expecting to see an actual film crew of burly French men standing about wearing berets and smoking cigarettes. He found himself wishing he were seventeen again, figuring that back then, after a kiss like that, Nate would've had him naked and bent over something by now. He curled up his lips, overly aroused and agitated as he reached down, and readjusted himself in his trunks once again.

"*Merde*!" he yelled, starting for the stairs while moaning his disapproval.

Chapter Thirteen

Neil came walking into the kitchen, towel and T-shirt slung over his shoulder as he held up both hands, declaring that he came in peace—this time. Nate was none too pleased to see him, and Dog barked exactly one time before laying her head back down on Nate's leg. Teddy didn't exactly jump through hoops either, while everyone else welcomed him heartily as they all tossed back another shot of vodka. They made an enticing little man-buffet, all circled around the island in nothing but swim trunks like they might be the hors d'oeuvres.

Cassidy smiled, thinking how much Sadie would love this. He could practically picture it—her breezing into the kitchen in one of those peacock-colored silk caftans, eyes widening as she brushed her hair back behind her ear, saying something like, "All this beefcake…for me? Cassidy, you really shouldn't have."

Ollie and Nate were sitting on stools while everyone else stood, waiting patiently for Spencer to pour another shot.

"What gives?" Neil asked as he took a spot next to Spencer. "It's gorgeous out. Why the hell are you all inside?"

"'Cause we can't leave till the bottle is empty," Cassidy said, pointing at the vodka while holding back a smile as he briefly allowed his gaze to run over Neil's torso. He had a few mental flashbacks of their sexcapades a few evenings ago, and he quickly averted his eyes, fearing everyone might suddenly be able to read his thoughts. Damn Nate for getting him all worked up and walking away.

"And everyone must do their part." Ollie tapped the countertop.

"Yeah." Nate looked Neil over in a not-too-friendly way. "Pour Douchey here two of those bad boys."

"Why the hell is my nickname Douchey?" Neil asked.

"Because you sucker punched me." Nate nodded. "Which

was a douchey thing to do."

Dog's head popped up, and she barked once more as if to say, *Yeah!*

"Quite the tough little wingman you got there." Neil downed his first shot and eyed Dog as he picked up his second shot. "I'll get you, my pretty."

Dog's ears perked straight up, and her head cocked to the side as Neil drank the second one, then slammed the shot glass down onto the counter.

Neil hunched over the top of the island toward her. "And your little dog too."

Dog's eyes widened a little, and she whimpered, spinning around in a circle before lying back down on Nate's lap.

"You scared her!" Cassidy chucked a lemon wedge at Neil, who snickered all evil-like.

"Way to go, shit head," Nate said as everyone else joined in giving Neil a hard time for frightening the poor, defenseless puppy.

"Okay, I'm sorry!" Neil yelled while trying to stop laughing.

"He has to take an extra shot for being such a jerk," Ollie insisted as everyone began to quiet back down.

"Fine," Neil said with a smug shrug. "I can handle it."

Nate chucked another lemon wedge at him, which smacked him right in the forehead.

Neil pushed a shot glass toward Spencer in a fill-'er-up manner as he eyed Nate. "Not cool, dude."

"No more fruit tossing allowed," Spencer yelled out, as if he were the official rule maker.

Everyone started to chuckle under their breath right before pelting Spencer with lemon wedges.

Spencer seemed less than amused as Cassidy tried to stop laughing, patting him on the shoulder in an attempt to console him.

"Whose bright idea was it to do vodka shooters, anyway?" Cassidy shook his head as Neil swallowed his last shot. He smirked, realizing no one was going to come out and take responsibility. "This has to be the single worst idea ever."

"I know!" Ollie grinned, doing everything but laughing maniacally while rubbing his hands together. "It's gonna be a wickedly interesting day."

"As I suspected," Cassidy said. "Any and all blame for what happens here today will be left lying on your doorstep, you little imp."

"Why do I feel like I've missed something?" Teddy asked, dipping a lemon wedge into the bowl of sugar. He squished up his face as he clamped down on the piece of fruit and sucked.

"Because you have, as usual," Ollie added.

"You're not alone," Neil said, doing a little dance as he too sucked on a sugared wedge.

Teddy frowned, tossing the rind onto the countertop. "Great, I'm stuck in the dark with Douchey?"

"If it makes any difference, I believe I'm out of the loop as well," Ben said with a quick wink.

"Thanks," Teddy said, standing there like an obedient golden retriever, as if awaiting praise from his master.

Amazing how quickly that one's feelings can be mended. Cassidy caught Nate watching him. He'd tried a couple of times to pull Cassidy aside after the little accusapalooza that went on earlier that morning, but Cassidy wasn't ready to listen. He wanted to feel good, not like shit, and was under the distinct impression that whatever Nate wanted to tell him would likely have the latter effect.

Spencer emptied the last of the bottle, doing his best to divvy up the remaining vodka equally between all of them. Cassidy was certain they'd all be completely hosed before the sun went down. There was a fridge full of beer, and Ollie and Spencer had made a vat of frozen sangria, which now sat in two large containers in the freezer. He'd already collected everyone's keys except Neil's, something he remedied immediately after finishing off his last shooter.

As everyone finally began to head outside, Cassidy held back, grabbing the mop out of the pantry.

"Come on, Cassidy," Spencer called back. "Leave that for later."

Cassidy laughed, imagining that later would produce zero cleaning, considering he already had a decent buzz going. "I'll be right out. I need to clean this up. I don't wanna come in later and find the dog hungover and passed out in the middle of the kitchen floor."

"Gotcha!" Spencer said, hopping down the step onto the back porch, pushing Neil out in front of him.

"You want me to take her out?" Nate asked, thumbing toward the west lawn. "To do her business."

"If you don't mind," Cassidy said, holding the sponge mop under the faucet as Nate spirited the dog outside.

"Come on, Ben-vet." The only way Ollie now referred to him. "You can fill me in on all the juicy island dirt." The volume in the room dropped dramatically as Ollie yanked the enormous boom box off the counter and exited the door with it.

"So you're like a vet, huh?" Teddy asked, following them. "What war did you fight in?"

Cassidy bit his lip to keep from laughing. *Thank God he's pretty.* He could actually form a coherent thought again, now that the decibel level had dropped. He circled the kitchen island, picking up all the fruit wedges. Upon further consideration, he decided it best not to attempt thinking, as it couldn't lead anywhere good. He mopped up the little bit of spilled vodka he found and rerinsed the mop, wringing it out before placing it back into the pantry.

Nate brought the dog back in, immediately ripped open the bag of pepperoni-flavored dog treats, and tossed a chunk down on the floor for her. "She loves those things."

Cassidy nodded, wondering if it was good for her to have so many as he pulled the footstool across the floor and stepped up to open the cabinet above the fridge. He peered in, letting out an *aha* as he reached toward the back, fumbling for the cheesy plastic coconut cups he'd always admired when he was little.

"Christ, I haven't seen those in ages," Nate said, taking them one by one from Cassidy as he pulled them out.

"Sweet!" Cassidy snagged a box of neon bendy straws before climbing back down.

Nate rinsed out the coconuts, setting them to the side of the sink as Cassidy took one of the sangria containers out of the freezer.

"We broke up months ago," Nate finally said, taking the ice-cream scoop from the drawer and passing it to Cassidy.

Cassidy stood there watching him for a moment, licking the sangria off his fingers after removing the lid. He was wondering if this convenient breakup had happened around the same time he won his lawsuit, alerting everyone on the island that he'd most likely be coming back home.

"And no," Nate suddenly added, "it happened several months before I knew you'd be coming back."

Cassidy grinned as he started to scoop out the now-half-frozen concoction, unsure whether he liked the fact Nate appeared able to read his thoughts like that. "It doesn't really matter does it?"

Nate watched Cassidy suspiciously while Cassidy held back the urge to ask why things hadn't worked out between them.

"I thought we were both of the same opinion—that it would be a mistake for anything to happen between us."

Nate shut the water off, setting the last coconut on the cabinet for Cassidy to fill. "I guess—I mean, you're right. No reason to risk it."

Other than the fact I wanna lick all your boy bits. "Glad we agree. Now pop some straws in those coconuts. I need to maintain a certain level of intoxication if I have any hope of surviving this train wreck of a day."

Nate nodded, exhaling dramatically. "True dat."

§ § §

The sunlight was amazing, soaking into his skin as Cassidy and Nate joined everyone else on the beach. The warmth from the sand squishing up between his toes allowed some of the tension to drain out of his shoulders. A dance remix of Santana's "Smooth" was blaring out of the enormous boom box, sitting in the shade back along the tree line.

Huge blue-and-white-striped beach towels were spread out across the beach as Ollie came running like mad from the ocean. Spencer and Neil were catcalling at him from the water, where they were trying to splash each other.

Ollie screamed back in a shivering, shrill tone of voice, "Shrinkage!" He swiped one of the frozen cocktails from the tray Cassidy was holding. "That cold-ass water completely obliterated my buzz."

Note to self—steer clear of the water.

Teddy, who'd been huddled up with Ben after spreading out the last of the towels, came running up to Nate and Cassidy. "I got a job! A job! Ben just hired me to do…something!" Teddy grabbed a coconut cup and began slurping, not seeming to care that he had no clue what sorts of duties this job would entail.

Nate mumbled something under his breath as Teddy took off after Ollie, who'd gone to the designated sunbathing area. Cassidy smiled at Ben, who came over shaking his head, obviously feeling pretty decent considering he'd just made Teddy's day.

"He's really excited," Ben said, scratching his head. He was obviously a little confused by Teddy's reaction and slightly embarrassed by it.

"That was really good of you." Cassidy handed Ben a coconut. "He needed some good news." Cassidy was irritated Ben had done it, as it made hating the guy somewhat slippery in terms of his conscience. The man also filled out the pair of trunks Nate had lent him quite nicely. Cassidy caught Nate admiring Ben and his package as well. Two-timing ogler. Cassidy sighed, not appreciating it so much when he wasn't the one being ogled. He was doubly irritated realizing he'd have to be ridiculously friendly to Ben; otherwise everyone would be able to tell how intensely jealous he was of the man. "Thanks for doing that, Ben."

Nate took a drink off the tray and walked away, not saying anything. Cassidy wondered whom Nate was jealous of—Ben, who'd now be spending his days with Teddy, or Cassidy, who'd invited Teddy to live at the shack in the first place. He started to play Connect the Jealousy Dots in his head, until he realized too many of them led back to him. He smiled as if able to hear Sadie calling out to him, *No sense stewing over the bad stuff, baby boy.*

Cassidy's entire body jerked, and he fumbled, trying not to drop the tray as Ollie let out a bloodcurdling shriek, pointing at the water, screaming, "Shark!" He immediately doubled over, laughing his ass off as he watched Neil and Spencer stumbling over each other as they panicked in an attempt to get out of the water. They yelled a multitude of obscenities once they figured out Ollie had just paid them back for calling him a wuss.

"It wasn't a big deal," Ben said, watching with a half smile as Teddy jumped around Ollie, who was less than enthused by his antics. "He's kind of helping me out of a tight spot. I had to fire my receptionist."

"You didn't!" Cassidy accused, wondering when Marianne would darken his door and point her finger, as it was sure to be Cassidy's fault.

"No—well, not only because of you." Ben took a sip and coughed a little, staring at his drink. "Jesus Christ." He wiped his eyes, which were watering slightly. "Sarah—wow, that's strong stuff—she sent a pet home with the wrong family. It was a mess."

"Didn't the person notice they had the wrong…?"

"Cat."

"Yeah…they didn't bother double-checking before they got

it home?"

"Apparently not." Ben took another cautious sip. "She was a fucking nightmare. Honestly, Cassidy, I'd have fired her after the fainting if I hadn't feared you might suffer the blame."

Great…Ben's a saint, and I'm an evil, cock-mongering man-whore. And please don't tell me the entire island's referring to it as the fainting. *Sounds like a goddamned M. Night Shyamalan film.*

He squinted, laughing as Teddy attempted to pull Ollie up off his towel to dance. Nate was laughing as well, now standing over by them as Ollie hurled one slur after another at Teddy.

"Teddy's a sweet guy." Cassidy gave Ben a sideways glance. "There's not a disingenuous bone in his body. He'll bust his ass to be the best damned receptionist you've ever had."

"Lucky for him I'm not the kind to take advantage." Ben started to walk away and then stopped without turning around. "I'm actually not too bad of a friend to have around either."

Cassidy sighed, snarling up his lip slightly as he followed Ben toward the others. His arms began to shake from holding the tray of drinks all that time. And Cassidy wondered how good of a friend Ben could actually be, considering he felt the need to go around advertising the fact.

Passing the tray to Nate, who placed it on the sand, Cassidy dropped to his knees on the towel next to him. Nate passed him a cocktail, which he quickly began to suck down, stirring the now-melting concoction with the straw.

"Puh-lease call off your ex-minion from hell," Ollie said as Teddy finally gave up and spun about, running toward the water. "Thank God. Peace at last!"

Cassidy sat down, nodding as Nate waved the sunscreen at him. "He wouldn't keep harassing you if you didn't insist on letting him know how annoyed you were by it."

"He's an idiot," Nate said, flicking the lid open and squirting some lotion into his hands.

"Overgrown freak of a man-child," Ollie said disapprovingly.

"Honestly, Cass, I never could figure out what you saw in him."

"Wait, so you dated him too?" Ben asked, confused. "I thought that Neil guy was the one who punched Nate."

Cassidy took another big sip before smushing his coconut into the sand so it wouldn't topple over. "Well, Ben, I'm apparently the man-whore of Babylon, having fucked every man along the eastern seaboard."

Ollie burst out laughing as Ben turned red, obviously not having meant his question in the finger-pointy way in which Cassidy had taken it.

"Please pardon his sarcasm, Ben," Nate said, rubbing suntan lotion between his hands.

Ben shrugged, then lay back on his towel, propping himself up on his elbows. "I didn't mean it—"

"I realize that…now," Cassidy interrupted, forcing a smile. "Sorry. And Teddy's a good guy, very loyal. Not a mean bone in his body, unlike some people." Cassidy fired a nasty glare at Ollie, who stared back, mouth agape, all wide-eyed and innocent.

Cassidy jumped slightly, feeling Nate's hands land on his shoulders. "What are you doing?"

"I thought you wanted some sunscreen."

"Oh…right." Cassidy laughed, nervously eyeing Ben, who either wasn't paying attention or was doing a great job at pretending so as he stared out over the water.

Cassidy relaxed slightly, shutting his eyes as Nate began massaging the lotion into his skin. His fingers worked their way into the muscles of Cassidy's back, and as Nate's hands slowly slid down over the small of his back, his eyes popped back open. There was a definite reaction taking place.

"That's good, thanks," Cassidy said, wiggling away as Nate's fingers started to run just under the fabric of the drawstring waistline of the trunks.

"Would you mind doing me?" Nate asked.

No, sir, I mean, yes, sir… Oh hell, just bend me over and stick it in already. Cassidy slowly glanced over, half tempted to kiss him, half ready to kill the man. "Sure, just…um. I need a minute."

Nate smirked, obviously not disappointed by the prowess of his magic sex fingers. Cassidy shot Ollie the evil eye after hearing him laughing under his breath.

Ben's knees popped as he stood up off the towel. "Think I'll give the water a try."

Fuck…son of a mother, Cassidy thought. The last thing he wanted to do was make Ben uncomfortable. Why was it so damned difficult to convince his body to do the right thing?

"Should I just come over there?" Nate asked with a sigh, trying to act as though he was put out by it all. "I could just wiggle my way back between your legs—"

"Fuck off and die, asshole," Cassidy said, cutting him off. He growled at them both as Nate and Ollie burst out laughing. Rolling his eyes, he peeked down between his legs, thinking that uncontrollable boners weren't quite what he had in mind earlier when he'd wished he could be seventeen again.

§ § §

It was quickly approaching dusk as Cassidy caught a whiff of the kebabs that Nate and Ben were overseeing on the grill. His stomach grumbled, and he realized how hungry he was. The sun had fallen down below the trees, and the sky had a hazy orange tint, which reminded Cassidy of orange sherbet. He enjoyed the tingling sensation on his lips and skin from the alcohol. He'd managed to drink just enough to maintain a nice buzz for most of the day, never getting full-on drunk and sloppy yet holding on to a yummy giddiness. Basically he loved everybody, and the world was full of nothing but sunshine and happy, half-naked men.

Teddy rinsed the salt water and sand off under the spigot, making shivering noises as he cursed under his breath. Neil set the table on the back porch with Ollie and Spencer, who were doing more kissing and giggling than they were anything else.

Cassidy set Dog on the ground and waited until Neil stopped long enough to take a drink of beer and check out his surroundings.

Cassidy waved him over once he caught his eye. Neil grinned and Cassidy groaned, thinking the man was a little slice of man-heaven. He wasn't relishing the conversation he was about to have. He continued to walk with Dog over to the grassy knoll, which had become her designated poopie spot.

"What's up, sexy?" Neil asked, finally catching up to Cassidy.

"I thought that maybe, well, that we should probably have a little talk."

"That's never good." Neil cringed before taking a swig of beer. "I'm not usually a violent guy…"

Cassidy laughed. "It has nothing to do with that, though you really shouldn't go around knocking people out." Cassidy shook his head, wondering why the hell he was getting all big brother on him. "That's…not the point. Wow, this is harder than I imagined."

"Then don't do it," Neil said, all adorably pleading.

Cassidy placed a hand on his shoulder. "I'm afraid I have to. As much as I'd love to keep you off to the side, waiting in the wings in case certain…things don't work out, it's not the right thing to do. I'm trying not to be selfish here."

"So you really think he's the guy for you?" Neil asked, glancing back at Nate, who Cassidy noticed was watching the two of them.

"I don't know. I think…could be? There's a lot of history there, and we might end up just being friends for all I know. But I'm pretty sure it's not fair for me to string you along while I figure that out."

Cassidy watched as Neil sorted things out in his head. He was staring at the ground, squinting a little before taking another swig from the beer bottle. Finally he nodded, and his gaze met back up with Cassidy's.

"I get where you're coming from, Cassidy, and I appreciate you considering my feelings and all. But if it's all the same to you, I think I'll stick around. Wait things out, see if you don't go changing your mind or anything."

"Obviously you're welcome here—as a friend, Neil." Cassidy gave Neil his most serious face so he knew this wasn't a joking matter. "I've made my decision, and it's highly doubtful I'll change my mind."

"I get it." Neil nodded, throwing in a little grin and a wink. "And I believe you truly mean everything you just said, but that asshole's bound to fuck things up."

Cassidy laughed, throwing his hands in the air. "I tried."

Neil gently poked Cassidy in the chest, smiling wickedly. "You did indeed. But you don't get anywhere in life throwing in the towel before the final bell rings."

Cassidy groaned, putting his arm around Neil, watching Dog continue to sniff around. "No more boxing metaphors, please."

Neil offered him his beer while reciprocating by placing his arm around Cassidy, who shrugged and took a swig from the bottle.

"Damn," Neil said, watching Dog take a shit. "I can't believe a turd that size could come out of such a tiny dog."

And just like that, Cassidy was laughing again. At the very least, he'd placed Neil on notice. If the guy happened to find him too irresistible to give up the hope that things might fall in his favor, there wasn't anything Cassidy could do about it.

Chapter Fourteen

Spencer let out a groan as he leaned back in his chair, placing his hands over his stomach. It was now dark out, minus the light from the moon and the two white pillar candles burning on the table. A shaft of light cut across the slate floor of the back porch from the open door that led into the house. A light breeze passed over them as the sound of the waves from the beach below mixed with Carrie Underwood singing about smashing up her boyfriend's pickup, which drifted outside from the small transistor radio in the kitchen.

Cassidy was feeling no pain as a shiver came over him. He jiggled in his seat and agreed with the sentiments behind Spencer's groan. His feet were freezing cold, and he wished he'd had the foresight to grab socks when he'd run upstairs earlier to throw on a pair of jeans and a thin black cotton turtleneck. Teddy and Spencer were still shirtless but had pulled on jeans like everyone else. It still got a little cool at night despite almost being June. And the wind coming off the ocean had most islanders in sweaters or long sleeves come nightfall.

The entire table erupted in laughter after Ollie let out a loud heinous belch.

"Whoever thought up meat on a stick was a genius," Ollie said with a sigh.

Spencer laughed and then groaned again, rubbing his full tummy. "And my man sure does love a good stick o' meat."

"Who's sticking their meat where?" Teddy asked, grinning as he licked the rim of his beer bottle.

"The first person to mention hiding the sausage has to leave," Cassidy said, knowing all too well where the conversation was headed.

Ollie pointed across the table at Cassidy. "That would be you, dumb-ass."

Cassidy smiled. "The first next person, be-hotch."

"Pretty talk coming from the wannabe English professor," Spencer said.

"Of literature, not grammar." Cassidy picked his beer up off the table. "And Shakespeare used made-up words and phrases all the time, or at least received all the credit for having first used them in print." Cassidy stared down at his belly, which appeared slightly swollen. "*Obscene* was one, like the amount of food we just ate. He also penned *dishearten*, which describes my sentiment over seeing all these dirty dishes on the table." Cassidy leered across the table at Ollie. "And of course who could forget *flaming youth*?"

Ollie laughed and then chucked a half-eaten piece of bread across the table at Cassidy.

Nate pushed his chair away from the table and stood up. In a pathetic excuse for a British accent, he added, "'Tis a miracle the great bard never latched on to *be-hotch*."

"*Devil incarnate*!" Cassidy lifted his foot, shoving Nate in the hip with it as he attempted to stack and balance dirty dishes. "*Puking* was another one, smart-ass. They weren't all laced with *pomp and circumstance*, you know."

Nate looked down at him lustfully as he intentionally bumped into Cassidy's chair on his way into the house. Ben got up and yawned as he followed Nate's lead by collecting some of the dirty dishes.

"Oh here," Spencer said with a drunken smirk. "Let me help clear the table." He stayed seated, not moving an inch until Ben stopped, glancing over at him. "No, really, I don't mind at all," Spencer added, still not moving a muscle as Cassidy laughed. "Well, okay, if you're sure you can handle it without me."

"Jerk," Teddy said, shaking his head as he and Cassidy got up to help.

An evil smile spread over Spencer's face. "Sorry, single fucks, but I need to conserve my energy for the bedroom later."

"You got that right, lover," Ollie added, turning to Neil, who appeared to have already passed out.

"You can get off your ass and help me get Neil to a couch," Cassidy said, chucking a napkin at Spencer, who frowned, obviously unhappy with his new assignment.

"This is the suckiest vacation ever," Spencer mumbled, still not moving. "Guests shouldn't be forced into labor."

"It's not a bed-and-breakfast, asshole."

"Somebody turn off that ceiling fan," Neil mumbled, staring up at the ceiling as he attempted to root around in his chair. "It's freezing."

They all glanced up, checking to make sure the fan was indeed off as they thought, then glanced back down at Neil.

"Dude's totally wasted." Teddy snickered as he walked around the table to grab Neil by the arm. "I'll get him to bed." He lifted Neil and slung him over his shoulder like a sack of potatoes. As Teddy strode toward the door, he stopped in front of Cassidy. "If he pukes down my back, I'm killing him."

Cassidy nodded in agreement, thinking that seemed fair while hoping it wouldn't come to that. "It's on you if the man winds up dead, Spence."

"I'm good with that." Spencer stretched, winking at Ollie while puckering up his lips and kissing his biceps.

"My hero." Ollie laughed, reaching over and pinching Spencer's nipple, causing his entire body to twitch.

Everyone but Spencer got up and helped finish clearing the dishes from the table. Teddy eventually rejoined them, stating he placed Neil in his room with an empty trash can to snuggle with. Not exactly the sexiest of mental pictures to be left with, Cassidy thought, thankful the man was still alive if nothing else.

Nate had started a pot of coffee, which he was now pouring into a thermal carafe. Ben and Teddy gathered up the mugs and headed back out to the screened-in porch. Cassidy had waited his turn for the tiny half bath off the kitchen, too lazy to attempt going all the way upstairs. He came back out to find Ollie was the only one left in the kitchen.

"'Bout time," he said, dancing a little pee-pee jig before shoving Cassidy out of the way to get to the toilet.

"Damn it," Cassidy muttered, going back outside. "This place is still a wreck."

"Tomorrow, babe," Nate said as Cassidy sat back down. "I'm feeling good we managed to get the dishes to the sink."

"Looky what I found!" Ollie said in a happy singsong voice, hopping down the steps with a half-empty bottle of vodka.

Nate and Ben groaned as if in pain as Cassidy covered his eyes. "Well, for the love of all that is gay and holy, go put it back."

"Oh come on, you pussies." Ollie slammed the bottle onto the table with one hand, setting three shot glasses down with the other. He rummaged three more out the pockets of his jeans, smiling like a greedy child. "We can do shots and play Truth or Dare."

Cassidy's eyes widened. "Hell, no!"

"Okay, fine, you wussy… I Never?"

"No!" Nate chimed in, protesting right along with Cassidy.

"Well, how else are we supposed to get to know our new friends?" Ollie asked, unscrewing the bottle and sniffing the vodka.

"God only knows how old that is." Cassidy waved his arm toward the bottle.

"Exactly." Nate nodded as Ollie started filling the shot glasses. "Surely vodka goes bad?"

"Only when you drink it." Ben's head drooped down as Ollie slid one of the shots in front of him.

"Very good, Ben," Ollie cooed as he passed the remainder of the shot glasses around the table. "See there, it's already working. I like you way more than I did five seconds ago."

"He's pure grade-A evil." Spencer sat up, scooting his chair closer to the table before leaning over and planting a soft kiss on Ollie's lips. "But he's mine, all mine."

Ollie laughed when Spencer poked him in the side, tickling him. He lifted his own shot glass into the air and surveyed the faces around the table. "Down the cum hatch."

Cassidy rolled his eyes as Ollie, Spencer, and Teddy all knocked one back. Ben shrugged, following suit, and Nate smirked at Cassidy.

Nate picked up his shot. "You've got some really fucked-up friends."

Ollie winked at Cassidy, who knew on some level he was trying to get Nate and him so drunk that they'd uncontrollably maul each other the instant they got behind closed doors. That was Ollie's idea of a resolution to any problem. Highly inappropriate sex with the man you loved. As Cassidy drank the warm vodka, feeling it burn as it made its way down, he wasn't sure if sex with Nate would actually fix anything, but it sure would be fun finding out.

§ § §

Cassidy stood on the far side of the bed smiling, obviously lit as he watched Nate pull off his shirt and toss it onto the floor in front of the closet door. He turned away, trying to concentrate on the pictures on the wall. *Do not sprout a boner, Horny McGee.* His entire body was amazingly tingly, but he wasn't so drunk that he felt out of control or unable to communicate. He was a little sleepy and a whole lot turned on. But he knew that if he concentrated, he could keep control over his wanton, slutty libido.

Cassidy undid the buttons on his jeans, then pushed them down over his hips. Wriggling his legs in an attempt to get his pants off, he lifted the black turtleneck over his head, getting his hands tangled in the elastic wristbands as he attempted to pull them free. He started to laugh, realizing his head was stuck in the neck as well, trapping him. "Who turned out the lights?"

"You're drunk off your ass," he listened to Nate say while

laughing at him. "Just hold still while I finish getting my pants off."

"Ah…the phrase every little intoxicated homo *dreams* of hearing."

"I'd prefer to not know how many times *you've* heard it, if it's all the same to you."

Cassidy laughed, liking it when Nate got jealous. He began turning his head around frantically in an attempt to get his bearings. He decided there was no need to wait for Nate, feeling he could free himself as he continued to wriggle around.

He was just beginning to feel hopeless, like he was caught in one of those Chinese finger traps where the more you struggled, the more hopeless your chances of getting loose became. He managed to pull one hand free with a grunt, then stopped moving altogether as he listened to Dog's nails clicking furiously across the wood floor.

"I feel like I'm falling," Cassidy got out just before he hit the floor with a thud. He started to belly laugh, hearing Nate lose it. "Dude, that fucking hurt."

"You idiot."

His pants were pulled loose from around his ankles.

"I told you to wait and I'd help you."

"I didn't need any help," Cassidy said as Nate's hand closed around his free wrist. "I almost got free."

"Difficult to believe, coming from the doofus lying on the floor." Nate helped him up onto his feet.

Cassidy decided not to struggle, holding his trapped wrist out for Nate, who jerked it loose. *Perhaps I'm worse off than I thought.* His head bobbed around a little as Nate yanked the turtleneck from around his neck. Nate stood directly in front of him in nothing but a pair of dark gray spandexlike boxer briefs, and Cassidy was feeling particularly good about it.

Cassidy enjoyed the seductive sense of security having Nate's hands around his waist, holding him up. His skin was still warm from lying out in the sun all afternoon, and for some reason that made him feel all sexy. He knew he was drunk, but as he stared into Nate's eyes, he struggled to remember why they'd come to the conclusion that having sex with each other was a bad idea.

Nate blinked, turning away momentarily, breaking the dreamy spell Cassidy had been under.

"Where's Dog?" Cassidy asked, trying to push away the thoughts that maybe Nate didn't want to fuck him because he wasn't interested.

Nate shoved Cassidy back onto the bed. "She shot under the bed when you started to fall."

Cassidy laughed again, feeling slightly dizzy as he hit the mattress, bouncing up and down a little.

"Take those trunks off," Nate said, turning to the dresser. "If you can even get 'em off."

Cassidy fumbled with the drawstrings until he got them untied, then lifted his hips and peeled them down. "You didn't mind them so much earlier today," Cassidy said, sitting up so he could take them the rest of the way off. "Considering the way you were checking me out."

Cassidy smirked, pleased with himself as a pair of jersey boxers hit him in the face. They fell down onto his lap just in time for Cassidy to watch a very naked Nate bending over to slip on a pair of the same.

Cassidy's eyes went immediately forward as he took a deep breath and stood, slipping on the undies Nate gave him. "There you be," Cassidy said, seeing Dog poke her head out from underneath the bed.

Dog scampered the rest of the way out, and Cassidy sat back down on the bed, bending over to pick her up. He could feel Nate crawling into bed behind him, letting the dog get a few licks on the chin in before he, too, scooted back.

"What do you think you're doing?" Nate asked, leaning back against the headboard with a smile as his gaze flitted back and forth between Cassidy and Dog.

Cassidy pretended to be unaware of what Nate was referring to while unable to tear his attention away from Nate's pecs and those mouthwatering hard nipples.

"Last night you said she'd be too lonely and scared to sleep in her own bed, being in a strange room," Nate said.

"And you caved faster than a politician in a public men's room." Cassidy snorted, laughing at his own joke.

Nate's eyebrows both arched as he pointed across the room to the fluffy dog bed he'd gone out and purchased for her. "You said it would just be that one night."

Cassidy scoffed as he started to root himself down under the blankets while still holding on to the dog. "Like you actually believed that nonsense."

Nate's expression said he wasn't going to budge, and Cassidy frowned. He looked down at Dog. "You know what to do."

Holding her up under his chin so Nate would be forced to see her face, Cassidy said in a cartoonish little-kid voice, "Please, Daddy Nate…don't make me sleep all alone on the cold hard floor."

"Please tell me you're kidding with this." Nate said, trying not to laugh.

"I promise to be good and sooooo quiet you'll forget I'm even here."

Cassidy nodded like she was telling the God's honest truth.

"This is the single most pathetic attempt—"

"Please, Daddy Nate…I'm just a poor little orphalan that some mean ole people dumped off at the side of the road—unwanted, unloved."

"You're an asshole, Cass." Nate folded his arms, trying to avoid the dog's big brown eyes.

"And when you wake up with morning wood and start thinking about how much you'd like to stick it into Daddy Cass's butt, I'll be right there to stop you."

Nate laughed, shaking his head as he reached over and patted her head. "I'm not sure that last one's much of a selling feature." He rolled his eyes. "This is a bad idea, letting her get used to sleeping in bed with us."

Cassidy smiled, watching Nate's face turn bloodred as he realized the way that had come out.

"I didn't mean it like that, so you can wipe that cocky grin off your face." Nate punched a few pillows and settled into the bed.

"Ha-ha! Way to go, Dog." Cassidy held up his hand for a high five, but Dog leaned forward and licked his palm instead.

"And you need to pick out a name for the poor little orphalan," Nate scolded. "Might as well be calling her Generic or Acme."

Cassidy let her loose to go find her own little spot to root into. "You don't think it's kinda cute—a little Holly Golightly-ish?"

Nate turned back, having started to reach over to turn off the bedside lamp. "Seriously, you've slept with practically every guy currently under this roof, and you're *seriously* going to make comparisons to a literary hooker?"

Cassidy rolled his head back, laughing as he placed his hands over his belly. "I can't help it, Nate. I keep thinking of names, but nothing feels right."

"Name her Sadie," Nate said, shaking his head like *duh…don't be stupid.* "There's been a Sadie in this house for as long as I can remember."

"I know. It just feels not quite right."

"How about Dasie?" Nate nodded, spelling it out for him. "That's Sadie, but sort of rearranged a little."

"And a little queer," Cassidy said, examining Nate as if seeing a whole new side of him.

"Well, I hate to state the obvious, but we are in fact homosexuals."

"I think we established that fact years ago, when you bent

me over the gate of your pickup and redefined the term *tailgating* for each of us." Cassidy mushed the pillow with the back of his head, trying to get comfy and forget the fact he was still buzzed and still horny. "I'll think about it."

Nate sat up and peered down the bed at Dog. "What do you think, girl?"

Cassidy opened one eye and watched as Dog lifted her head, taking notice that Nate was talking to her.

"Do you wanna be my Dasie?"

She immediately ran up the bed, hopping onto Nate's stomach as she tried to lick his chin.

"That settles it," Nate said. "Her name is Dasie."

"Oh brother," Cassidy said, trying not to grin at the cheesiness of it. He could already hear Nate, spelling it out for everyone whenever people asked what her name was. He rolled over onto his side, turning away from the lovefest. "Get the light, you big queen."

He listened as Nate scoffed, muttering something to the dog. Cool air rushed over his back as the blankets fluttered right about the time the palm of Nate's hand made contact with his ass.

"Son of a…" Cassidy shot across the bed, rubbing his ass as he laughed. "You shit head."

The lights went out with a click, and Cassidy rolled over, now facing Nate, who settled back down into the bed. His ass cheek was on fire, and he could feel the reaction his dick had to the sensation. He was now really aching to have at it, smiling as he got an idea. Cassidy lifted an arm, taking a sniff, then pouting as he cursed his stupidity for having taken that shower before dinner.

He let out a grumble and reached up, snagging one of the longer king-size pillows, and dragged it under the sheets, wrapping his legs around it. He had a full-on erection straining against the fabric of the boxers and was doing his level best not to pounce on Nate.

"Let that be a lesson to you," Nate said, breaking the deafening silence.

Christ, you son of a bitch, if you wanna teach me a lesson, don't half ass it. A little follow through wouldn't kill you.

"What the hell…" Nate said.

Cassidy could see he'd lifted his head off the pillow as his eyes began to adjust to the dark. His mouth fell open because he heard it now as well. He gasped, as a very distinct long, low muffled moan came through the wall.

"Holy hell," Nate whispered.

They both burst out laughing, listening to a muffled voice followed by another long, deep moan.

Nate sat up. "There's some serious fucking going on in this house."

And it sure ain't us. The muffled voice started again, and Cassidy chuckled, saying in a deep gruff tone, "You like that dick, boy?"

He and Nate both lost it, as Nate tried shushing Cassidy, who added, "Oh yeah, daddy…you fuck my ass *good*."

They were both rolling as another moan vibrated through the wall. Cassidy started to keep pretty good time, adding his own dialogue whenever he heard voices. "Fuck my hot hole, daddy."

"Stop…" Nate was now sitting up, laughing so hard the bed jerked as he convulsed.

"Take it all, ass-bitch," Cassidy squeaked out, trying to keep from laughing long enough as he added, "I'm gonna ream that ass."

"Fuck." Nate fell back, racked with convulsions. He rolled up into a ball and fell onto his side. "Can't breathe." He punched Cassidy in the arm in an attempt to get him to stop, and finally grabbed him in a headlock.

"Oh yeah, fuck-stud…" Cassidy managed to get out before Nate silenced him by covering his mouth with his hand.

Nate continued to shush him as he tried to say stuff, despite being muffled. They each eventually began to calm down once Ollie and Spencer's big climax came to pass on the other side of the wall. Cassidy sighed, enjoying Nate's body pressing against his own. Nate's hand fell away from Cassidy's mouth, and the headlock morphed into an embrace as he snaked his arm across Cassidy's chest. Cassidy's stomach fluttered when Nate kissed the back of his neck as they spooned. Nate pulled him closer, tightening his grip. Cassidy could feel Nate's erection against his ass, and despite the fact his was aching for release, he didn't dare move. He wanted so much more, but as the sleepiness once again came over him, Cassidy decided he didn't mind waiting to get it. Closing his eyes, he knew he could wait an eternity as long as he could do it like that—wrapped up in Nate's arms.

Chapter Fifteen

Cassidy came slowly down the stairs, rubbing his crotch, which was more than a little pissed at him for not having had the decency to rub one off the night before. He yawned, feeling his throbbing head fighting back as well—punishment for all the alcohol. Dog, tucked under his arm, wiggled a little, reminding him of her presence. He stopped as he got to the landing and looked down at her.

"Shit, that's right. You're named Dasie now," Cassidy mumbled, smiling briefly as her nubby tail began to wiggle.

His head started in with the throbbing again as he continued down the remaining stairs. Cassidy glanced into the living room at the sofa bed briefly before heading toward the kitchen, where he could get coffee and Ibuprofen. He stopped suddenly, as if something finally registered. He cocked his head to the side, taking two steps back for a second look. He could feel his eyes widening, which made him curse as it caused his head to hurt more.

Teddy was completely naked minus the hand resting on his ass. He was lying on his stomach, partially draped over Ben, who was not, as evident from his hard-on which had pitched a tent under the sheets.

I hate all men…who had sex last night, he thought to himself as he made his way down the hall. He took note of the answering machine and its pushy little blinking red light but decided he was in no condition to deal with whoever had the audacity to call before… He suddenly realized he had no idea what time it was. He shrugged and then noticed that the drawer he'd hidden everyone's keys in was open. He got a bit paranoid as he watched the blinking light and reached over and opened the drawer, trying to focus enough to count.

When he finally came to the conclusion that Neil's keys were missing, he punched the Play button on the machine, assuming the worst. He listened impatiently as the antiquated device from the dark ages of technology rewound the minitape. He caught movement coming from the drive as it clicked over, and he breathed a sigh of relief watching Neil's blue SUV slowly pulling away.

Asshole scared the shit out of me. He glanced back down listening to the beep. "Hi, Cassidy, this is Edie, and I was just calling to let you know that Cecelia Hodes and the rest of the historical society, along with a whole slew of volunteers, will be around bright and early tomorrow morning to get started on clearing out that attic of yours."

Fuck me!

"Since you mentioned having the Founders' Day party at Piper's Point again, which as you know, is coming up quickly, I figured it best to not waste a single day…"

Cassidy whimpered, pressing the Stop button. "No more, you wretched, evil woman."

Do—Dasie wiggled again, as if trying to tell Cassidy that she really needed to go. He nodded and continued toward the kitchen.

He stumbled through the door to find Ollie sitting at the island in a plain white T-shirt and oversize boxer shorts. He was wearing sunglasses and staring at the coffeemaker, which was just starting to drip, while pressing his fingers into his temples. It was as if he was attempting to psychically connect to the coffeepot. One foot was sitting on the rung of the stool, the other dangling as it hovered above the tile.

All he's missing is the turban. Cassidy kept walking, pausing momentarily when he reached Ollie. He pointed back toward the front of the house and opened his mouth to speak.

"Uh-uh," Ollie mumbled, holding up a hand.

Cassidy shrugged, in too much misery to care as he made his way outside, wishing the sheriff would catch those devil dogs already. He was too paranoid to let Dasie out by herself, but the fact that the sunlight was causing his skull to feel like it might implode had him tempted to leave her to her own fate.

He came back in after letting the dog do her business, to find that nothing had changed other than the level of coffee in the pot, which was still spitting out steamy black liquid. It was going to be a bitter, long-ass day, considering he now needed to get the house pulled back together because the stupid historical society would be showing up first thing in the morning. He could practically hear Sadie laughing her ass off while telling him that's what he deserved for letting Edie nose into the Hart family archives.

Cassidy went to the pantry with Dasie's bowl and filled it to the brim for fear he'd say fuck it all and go back to bed, forgetting to feed her later. He came back out to fill her water bowl and found Ollie still in his chair, but with a cup of coffee in his hand. A second steaming cup sat on the island waiting for him. He heard Dasie crunching her food and watched Ollie staring down at her as if she was killing him with all the noise. Cassidy opened his mouth to ask a question.

"Nuh-uh." Ollie held up his other hand this time while timidly taking another sip.

Ten more minutes passed as Cassidy chose one tiny chore at a time to accomplish. Picking up the paper towel lying on the floor next to the trash can was the first thing, and the pressure in his skull as he bent over almost killed him. Then he went through collecting the stray bottle caps. It felt like hundreds, though he was fairly certain there had only been five or six. He briefly considered gathering up the beer bottles that seemed to be everywhere, but decided against it. All the clanking of glass might give him leave to crawl the mile or so to the lighthouse and hurl himself off the cliff like his great-great-granny Piper Hart was rumored to have done. Thus the name, Piper's Point.

It was assumed she either fell or jumped to her death after her disappearance, though her body was never discovered. Cassidy rubbed at his temple, momentarily wishing he were dead or at the very least smart enough to have not gotten quite so inebriated.

He thought about Sadie and Piper, about the stories of the Hart family legacy as they'd been told to him over the years.

He absentmindedly picked up a warm, half-drunk beer bottle and made the mistake of emptying it into the sink. His eyes watered as his stomach soured from the smell, and he forced his thoughts back to Sadie as distraction. She had told him Piper had suffered from depression and would disappear from town only to be found at the Point, sitting on the rocks at the foot of the lighthouse, staring out across the ocean. He reached down and rubbed at his crotch, feeling slightly depressed himself; carefully attempting to massage the sore rocks between his legs.

Ollie sat back in his bar stool, shifting in the seat, and Cassidy glanced over at Dasie, who continued to chow down. He wondered why Sadie felt such a kinship with a woman she'd never met—to the point she wanted her ashes spread at the very spot Piper had supposedly died. Was it merely that she'd been the reason the Hart family wound up with this particular parcel of land since it was Jeremiah's father who'd purchased it in order to build her a house closer to the Point?

The locals say that on the right night her ghost could still be seen standing at the edge of the cliffs, hair gently blowing in the breeze. Some kid had fallen and drowned back in the twenties, and an urban legend was born that Piper Hart lured people to the edge, only to push them to their deaths.

Sadie thought all the ghost stories were a load of bunk, and liked to say her granny probably faked the whole depression angle to get her hands on the prime piece of real estate. But maybe that was Sadie's way of trying to romanticize Piper, turning her weakness into the kind of strength the family was known for.

Ollie belched loudly, scaring the dog, which had her barking in terror. Both men winced, and Cassidy felt his headache ratchet back up a few notches as he surveyed the prime piece of filthy, dirty kitchen. He struggled for a moment to recall the train of thought, which left him with the impression he'd been on to… something. He shrugged, realizing it was gone, and decided a scalding-hot shower might be just the thing. He downed the last of his coffee and set the cup next to the sink, which, thanks to him, was not only overflowing with dirty dishes, but now stank of stale beer. He reached back down and rubbed at his crotch again. "My fucking nuts are killing me."

Ollie's eyebrows rose, poking up over the rim of his sunglasses. Cassidy nodded, deciding that was indeed all he really had to offer. He stumbled back out into the hall, leaving Dasie to her food bowl and Ollie to his coffee and meditation.

§ § §

The rest of the day went by in a haze. Cassidy tried calling Neil once, making an attempt at checking in on him, but had been forced to leave a message.

Ben vanished before Cassidy made it out of the shower, which he'd apparently stayed in too long, considering all the dirty looks he received over the next hour. It did actually help, making him feel a little better. Cassidy snuck back into Nate's bedroom, once Nate vacated it in lieu of a shower. He laid the man's pillow over his face while he beat off, which did more good than anything. His nuts still ached, but the rest of his body was a little more at ease.

As much as he was loath to admit it, Ben showing back up with jumbo-sized coffees and several boxes of sugary starched goodness was what really pulled everyone out of their funk. Ollie all but sucked him off when he spotted the to-go cups. A stranger would have assumed they'd known each other for years. Which jealous Spencer didn't even notice, as he was too busy snarfing down three doughnuts without appearing to have actually chewed.

Cassidy watched as Spencer constantly shifted around in his seat. All day long he'd get Nate's attention and mouth, *Ass-bitch*, while pointing at Spencer, causing them both to lose it. Their laughter never lasted long, as it inevitably brought about the return of the pounding inside their skulls.

It took at least three times longer than it should have, but by dinnertime the house was back in order and they were all slouched around the table on the back porch. Even Dasie seemed spent as she lay passed out on the slate tile next to the screen door. Nate and Teddy came out with a beer for each of them, which caused a series of groans all the way around.

Spencer hissed like a vampire as he backed away from the bottle. "Take it away, cocksucker."

"Don't be that way, Spence," Nate said, a playful expression taking over his face as he lowered his voice a little deeper. "C'mon, take it like a man."

Ollie choked on his beer, coughing as Spencer reached over to pat him on the back. Cassidy laughed so hard he nearly fell out of his chair. Ben shrugged as he and Teddy realized they had likely missed something yet again.

"Damn it, Nate," Cassidy said, beginning to settle back down and pressing a hand to his head as the latent throbbing started up again.

Nate took a seat next between Cassidy and Spencer, smiling like the cat that ate the canary.

"I think we need to eat again," Ollie said, forcing more beer down.

"And then a nap would be nice," Cassidy added, rubbing his eyes.

"The kind that lasts until tomorrow," Spencer agreed.

"Pizza?" Ben asked.

"And paper plates," Ollie suggested, watching Spencer's face contort as he choked a mouthful of beer down.

Teddy placed his now-empty bottle of beer onto the table and licked his lips. "I'm ready for another." He glanced around the table, the smile fading as if he could sense the older guys he was surrounded by were less than happy by the resilience of his twenty-four-year-old existence. "And now might be a good time to go get it."

As Teddy vacated his seat, Ben whipped out his cell phone. "Any particular toppings?"

"You're not getting dinner too," Cassidy said. "You already

saved the day with breakfast."

Ollie smiled as if fondly remembering some far-off memory from his childhood. "For which I'm still eternally grateful."

"I'd love anchovies," Teddy offered, coming back outside, fresh beer in hand.

Spencer placed a hand on his stomach and belched as a slightly soured look came over his face. "I'm going to murder you in your sleep, Teddy, so help me."

Teddy got a "what'd I do now?" expression as he slumped down into his seat. Cassidy patted his shoulder.

Ben winked at Teddy as he punched keys on his phone. "I like anchovies too."

Teddy smiled again, perking right back up like an insta-inflatable blow-up doll.

"Tell Ricky to put it on my tab," Nate whispered as Ben nodded and said hello to whoever answered on the other end. "You remember Ricky, right?"

Cassidy nodded while wondering how many times Nate and Ben had ordered takeout together in the past. He then laughed at himself for getting jealous over takeout while remembering he didn't have any room to bitch about Nate's one ex when he currently had four sitting around the same table.

But should I really be penalized for being not only uncontrollably handsome, but the sweet, loving type of guy who just happens to maintain friendships with all his ex-boyfriends?

"Yeah," Nate said, as if on cue. "Of course you remember him. We kinda trade food for my services on the Web site."

"You have a Web site?" Teddy asked, starting to smile.

Cassidy smacked him upside the head. "Not that kind of Web site, you pervert."

Ollie and Spencer laughed as Nate shook his head.

Ben tossed his phone onto the table. "Forty to forty-five minutes."

"Enough time for a nap," Spencer said, getting up from the table.

Ollie hopped up, following suit. "Come wake us when it gets here."

"Um, sure." Cassidy wasn't relishing the thought of being saddled with Ben in such limited numbers.

"Say, Ben," Teddy said as if suddenly gifted with good timing. "Want to take a walk on the beach, and tell me a little more about my new job?"

Cassidy watched Nate's face, noticing the man either didn't care or had no clue that was probably code for *hey, Ben, want to go make out on the beach*? He noticed Ben quickly glancing at Nate before turning back to Teddy.

"Sure." Ben nodded, getting up and grabbing his beer off the table.

Cassidy watched as they left, pointing at Dasie as they cautiously stepped over her. She was unable to muster up enough strength to do more than crack open one eye. Ben kept the screen door from slamming, then followed Teddy across the courtyard toward the beach.

Nate was semi-stretched out, leaning back in his chair with his legs extended. He smiled at Cassidy and seemed to be in pretty good spirits. Considering how badly Cassidy was handling Nate's one ex, he was beginning to fear Nate wasn't harboring the same feelings. He left the impression he was cool and in complete control. Perhaps Nate's obvious physical attraction was nothing more than skin-deep?

"What's going on in that twisted, sexy head of yours?"

Cassidy shrugged, realizing he was chewing on his lip. He instantly made himself stop. "I'm sorry I didn't keep in touch." Cassidy leaned on the table, watching Nate for any clues he might reveal through the expressions on his face. "I know I called a couple of times, but I shouldn't have just let our friendship, relationship, or whatever the hell it was just fade into the background. We practically grew up together, for Christ's sake."

Nate took another drink as sadness seemed to sweep over him. "I missed you too, Cass. I really did, but…"

"It's something I regret, one of the many things." Cassidy picked at the label on his beer bottle. "I never realized how much I missed you until I saw you standing on the porch the other morning."

Nate placed his beer on the table and he sat up. "Hell, Cass, I'm the asshole."

Cassidy was a little confused by that statement.

"You had so much going on. You were *exactly* where you were supposed to be, doing exactly what you should have been doing. Taking care of Sadie, trying to get her out of that home, and doing it all while going to school. It should've been me…" Nate trailed off, staring out over the yard as if trying to figure out the right thing to say. "I wasn't there for you, Cass. So don't you have any regrets where I'm concerned."

Nate finally turned toward Cassidy but didn't speak. Their gazes locked, and they stared intently at each other until Cassidy stood up. Nate appeared slightly stunned as Cassidy came around the corner of the table.

Cassidy placed his arms on Nate's shoulders and nudged him to lean back in the chair. He straddled Nate, who opened his mouth to speak.

"Whatever it is you want to say right now"—Cassidy placed his hands on either side of Nate's face, turning his head slightly before moving in for a kiss—"don't."

Cassidy stared into Nate's eyes for what felt like hours as opposed to the reality of mere seconds. He'd gotten lost in them, bewitched as he covered Nate's lips with his. It took everything he had not to let out a moan from the sensation of Nate's mouth opening up for his tongue. There was a tentativeness behind the kiss, as if they were both a little afraid of letting go. The heat from their breath, the wetness of their mouths created an almost electric familiarity that shot through Cassidy's gut. It transported him back in time—he was once again that seventeen-year-old kid who'd walked into the boathouse that summer day. The taste of Nate, the smell of his skin were both foreign and familiar at the same time.

Just as Cassidy began to really lose himself, Nate pushed him away. Cassidy moaned in protest as Nate gently pushed him back. Nate swallowed hard, obviously every bit as affected as Cassidy had been. Cassidy searched his face for some sort of clue as to what was going through Nate's mind.

"I can't, Cassidy," Nate said, his voice cracking as he lifted Cassidy off his lap so he could get out of the chair. He walked toward the house and stopped just in front of the steps. "Damn it." He placed his hands on his hips, staring out over the east side of the property. He took in a deep breath and exhaled, shoulders slumping slightly. "I'm sorry, but I can't do this right now."

With that he disappeared into the house, leaving Cassidy alone on the back porch. He slowly sat down in the chair, wishing he hadn't just done any of that. He was confused about why Nate had stopped, but the more he thought back over it, the more he realized that he'd wanted that kiss every bit as much as Cassidy had. You can't fake that kind of reaction, and Nate had definitely been affected. Now all he needed was the why.

Cassidy relaxed into the chair. His lips still tingled, and the taste of Nate continued to linger in his mouth. The sun began to set, signaling the day was coming to a close, and despite having been shot down, he was oddly confident in one thing—Nate Sommers wanted him as much as he wanted Nate Sommers.

Cassidy smiled, getting up from the table to head inside the house. "I can work with that."

Chapter Sixteen

Cassidy stood staring out the kitchen door off the back of the house as the white tent was being erected. He'd gotten a glimpse of the similar scene happening on the west side of the house as he was coming downstairs from his shower. The detached garage was also being utilized as an unloading area for the contents of the attic, and Cassidy appreciated the precautions the historical society took in case of a sudden change in the weather.

Cecelia Hodes masterfully directed the action as people scurried around in all directions. Cassidy watched the scene unfolding before his eyes, continuing to flip-flop back and forth, deciding between elegant ballet or DeMille-like spectacle.

"This is providence, people!" Cecelia called out to her minions while clapping her hands. "We're embarking on a journey, standing on the precipice, ready to rewrite the history of Hart's Island with the treasures that lay just beyond that door." She spun around, motioning with melodramatic flair toward the door where Cassidy stood.

Cassidy waved and smiled while resisting the urge to deflate her moment by reminding them all there was probably nothing up there other than knickknacks, old throw pillows, and dust mites.

"Good morning, Mr. Winters!" Cecelia called out with way too much enthusiasm as Cassidy stepped out onto back porch.

"I told you to call me Cassidy, Cecelia." He shook his head as he leaned against the table, holding his coffee cup. "You used to babysit me, for Christ's sake."

"Leading by example, Mr. Winters," Cecelia said with a smile. "I want to make sure everyone treats you respectfully."

"Well, please cut it out." Cassidy cringed as he placed a hand over his stomach. "Every time I hear 'Mr. Winters,' I get sick to my stomach, half expecting to see my asshole father."

"Point taken," Cecelia said, obviously feeling uncomfortable. "Perhaps you might consider a change of name, then? You are also a Hart, after all." She swiveled back around on a spiked heel and yelled into the crowd, "Please address Mr. Winters as Cassidy!"

Cassidy rolled his eyes as she continued around the side of the house screaming it over and over again. He laughed to himself, wondering how the teenager who wore black nail polish, caked on smudgy eyeliner, and claimed to be a Wiccan had turned into Polly Prissy Pants. She used to refer to herself as Cee Cee, the demon goddess of smite, for crying out loud.

Cassidy would probably have been more frightened as a child when she threatened to smite him had he had any understanding of the meaning of the word at the time. As it was, he thought it was just some type of citrusy soda like Sprite, and he could imagine worse things than having soda dumped on his head.

Cassidy watched as the white tent was slowly raised, creating the familiar canopy that accompanied Sadie's Founders' Day parties. The islanders would all dress up in period clothing of some sort and descend upon Piper's Point en masse to drink and dance to the live music until the sun came up. Staring off in to space he thought about the remark Cecelia had made about being a Hart, and before he knew it, Cassidy was drifting back in time recalling the eve of the Founders' Day party just before his sixteenth birthday.

§ § §

Ornate multicolored Japanese paper lanterns blew softly in the breeze as the light emanating from them cast a warm glow across the courtyard covered by the white tent. Cassidy stood just under the center of it, directly below the highest point in the canopy, and giggled while spinning in circles, making himself dizzy.

He stopped, hearing Natalie shrieking at Nate like a banshee from inside the house. Nate was mad as hell that he was being forced into the "queer white tux" as he'd been referring to it for days. He laughed as Natalie threatened to smack Nate if he used that word one more time, followed by a door being slammed.

Cassidy tugged on the lapels, straightening out the jacket, rather liking his own costume, with the long black tails that hung down from the back. He felt like that Fred Astaire guy from the black-and-white musicals Sadie always liked to watch. There was something about the way it fit, forcing him to stand up straight—it made him feel more grown-up and classy.

Sadie whistled as she glided across the courtyard in a shiny silver and black flapper dress. Her dark auburn hair was all bundled up under the bone-straight, bobbed black wig, and her lips were painted bloodred. "My, you are quite dapper, Mr. Winters."

Cassidy laughed, slightly embarrassed as he bowed toward Sadie. "Why, thank you, madame."

"I'm no madame, youngster," Sadie said wickedly. "I'm a broad through and through. A flapper is a woman of ill repute."

Cassidy shook his head, amazed that his granny somehow managed to pull off ravishing at her age. "I sure hope I take after you, lady."

Sadie was instantly irritated. "You, my boy, are a Hart through and through, you understand me?"

"Yes, Gran—" Cassidy cut himself off midword and smiled wickedly right back at her. "I mean, Sadie."

"Land sakes alive, boy, you sure are a sight to behold. Another year and you'll be breaking hearts left and right, if you aren't already. The girls'll be fainting at your feet as you walk by."

"I know. It's almost sinful." Cassidy rolled his eyes at her, feeling awkward in his skin at the thought of girls behaving that way. It was bad enough Jennie Jones had been following him around since he'd arrived, never leaving Nate and him alone.

"You little smart-ass." Sadie grabbed him by the arm. "And be nice to that Jennie Jones girl tonight."

Cassidy groaned.

"She's cute. What's the problem?"

"Nothing, she's just annoying."

"I can't ever tell if you're just putting on a good front for me while ruthlessly chasing skirt when I'm not paying attention."

Cassidy fidgeted, pulling away from her, not knowing how to say the one thing he wanted to yet somehow never could.

"Don't go getting all teenagerish," Sadie said, grabbing his arm again. "You're fifteen years old, and this is probably the last summer I'll have with you before you turn into an asshole."

"You say that every summer," Cassidy said.

"The older you get, the more you'll discover the need to begin preparing yourself for the worst in advance." Sadie grinned, facing Cassidy as she reached up, cupping his face in her hands. "You're the only family I have that I actually like, kid. You keep that in mind, because you're the only one of the lot of them I'd be pained to lose."

"I love you too, Sadie." Cassidy smiled.

"You listen to me, baby boy—you're a Hart, regardless of the name on your birth certificate, and this place…" Sadie got behind him and hugged him as she turned him around in a circle. "Piper's Point and everything that you see before you—it's in your blood, dark red, pulsing through your heart and into those veins."

"Gross," Cassidy said, feeling nauseated from the image she planted in his head.

"Don't be such a girlie-man." She squeezed him tight. "You will go through that phase when I'm going to be the last person you want to be around. I'm a little surprised, but thankful you haven't managed to get there already."

Like right now, Cassidy thought as he rolled his eyes. He was thankful she couldn't see him doing it. Sadie always got so weird before the party. Like clockwork every year as he tried to squirm free. "I'm not a girlie-man either!"

She squeezed him tighter until he gave in and stopped fighting her, which was when she finally let him go. He'd figured that part out years ago. She never let go until he gave in, so he now struggled just enough to make it believable.

"You and Nate try not to drink too much tonight," Sadie said matter-of-factly, as if resigned to the fact she knew they'd find a way to get into the rum. "And for God's sake, don't go and get that Jones girl knocked up."

Cassidy's face went bloodred as he stared at her, mouth agape.

"Don't act so damn surprised," she said, placing a hand on her hip. "I was fifteen once, and I sincerely doubt boys have gotten more respectful since my day."

Cassidy felt a little naked, despite standing there in his tux, all the while hoping she was right. He'd been fantasizing about Nate since he'd arrived that summer and secretly hoped something would happen tonight once they got drunk. He wasn't altogether sure what he wanted that something to be, but he sprang a woody whenever he pondered the possibilities for very long.

Cassidy and Sadie turned toward the bandstand as the orchestra started tuning up their instruments. He chewed nervously on his lip and noticed she watched him intently. Sadie leaned in, kissing him on the cheek. She began rubbing at his face with her thumb, and he grinned, realizing she'd gotten lipstick all over him.

"I love you, baby boy," Sadie said, eyes sparkling like the strands of beads that hung down from all over her dress. "You know there's nothing you could ever do or say to change that, right?"

Cassidy nodded, feeling an ache in his chest, wondering how true that was. He was desperate to talk to someone, anyone about the things he was feeling, the thoughts he'd been unable to stop. He knew the way people acted about stuff like that, but no matter how many times he tried to convince himself that what he was feeling was wrong, something deep inside told him otherwise. It went right down to the bone, as Sadie liked to say. It felt too right to be wrong, yet every time he opened his mouth to speak the words, they seemed to get stuck down in his gut.

"Now don't go using that as a license to kill a hooker or

anything," Sadie demanded with a sarcastic smile. "I don't want you becoming one of those rich, entitled white men who think life holds no repercussions for them."

Cassidy smiled. "I'm pretty sure you aren't supposed to talk about hookers in front of me."

"You're probably right," Sadie said as Natalie came barreling out of the house in a tizzy. "My goodness, woman, you have got to calm yourself down. Have a martini!"

§ § §

Cassidy was startled by a voice coming from behind him.

"What are you doing out here all by yourself?" Nate asked, standing in the doorway at the back of the house. He was dressed in faded khaki cargos and an untucked, short-sleeved blue plaid button-up. Cassidy was delighted to see it was only halfway buttoned up.

He reached up, wiping at his eyes as he turned around, suddenly embarrassed to be standing on the back porch crying.

"What's wrong?" Nate asked, quickly coming down the steps and crossing the porch.

"Just got a little lost for a minute." Cassidy started laughing, feeling his face really begin to heat up as he sniffled.

Nate carefully inspected his condition before that half grin began to form. "Lucky for you, I came along and found you, then, huh?" Nate placed his hands onto Cassidy's shoulders, giving them a little squeeze. "The guys are ready and waiting, if you still want us to help you go through Sadie's bedroom."

"I don't wanna do that by myself," Cassidy said, a little panicked.

"All right, calm down," Nate said, pulling Cassidy into his arms. "You don't ever have to do anything else alone if you don't want to. You're home now, remember—where you belong."

Cassidy rolled his eyes, feeling a smidge too emotional for this kind of talk as his eyes started to burn again. It wasn't lost on him either, the way Nate slid in that little dig about where it was he belonged. He squeezed Nate, to let him know he wasn't uncomfortable with the hugging, and then pushed himself away. "I'm okay, just got a little nostalgic seeing the tents going up."

"The Founders' Day parties." Nate cringed at the tents and nodded. "I hadn't thought of that."

Cassidy turned back around, taking in the scenery of the courtyard. "I was remembering the knock-down, drag-out you and Natalie had over that tux with the white jacket."

Nate started laughing. "I forgot about that."

"You really didn't want to wear that thing." Cassidy squinted as he faced Nate. "You were fucking hot in it too."

"Was I, now?" Nate asked, raising one eyebrow slightly.

"Most definitely droolworthy." Cassidy shook his head as he reprimanded himself for flirting. "Sadie in her flapper dress, telling me not to kill any hookers and not to get Jennie Jones preggers."

"What?" Nate asked.

"You had to be there," Cassidy said with a shrug.

"If you say so." Nate led Cassidy toward the house. "Like there was any chance your gay ass would get Jennie Jones pregnant."

"Hey." Cassidy shoved him as they walked into the kitchen. "She totally wanted my boner!"

Nate started laughing as Cecelia spun around, heading back in the direction she'd come from.

"Shit," Cassidy said, cringing as he watched her scurrying down the hall and out the front door.

"Considering you wanted my boner, I still stand behind my original statement."

"You wanted mine too!" Cassidy laughed, like that somehow made any difference. "I did have this whole plan that night involving you, a whole lot of rum, and the boathouse."

"So did I," Nate said.

"You did?"

"Oh yeah." Nate placed his hand on the small of Cassidy's back as they started climbing the stairs. "Unfortunately, the rum managed to be the only thing that had its way with either of us."

Cassidy scowled, thinking about what he missed out on that night. "Damn demon liquor."

Chapter Seventeen

Cassidy sat on the stool at Sadie's dressing table, staring at the perfume bottles, beaded hair combs, and the infamous collection of gold bracelets dangling from the wooden pegs on her jewelry tree, that littered the top of the desk. He reached over and ran a finger over the gold hoops, taking the tiniest bit of comfort in the clinking sound they made as they bounced off each other.

He traced the wood grain with his fingertips before cracking open the long, skinny middle drawer. Immediately catching that unique scent of makeup when he inhaled, Cassidy closed his eyes briefly, remembering Sadie singing "*Don't sit under the apple tree, with anyone else but me*," to Nate and him while they rolled around on her bed as kids. He smiled at the umpteen tubes of lipstick, certain that were he to open each one, he'd find only the color red in varying shades—as if Sadie feared running out due to some apocalyptic event, hence her need to squirrel it away. God forbid she not be wearing lipstick.

He glanced up, watching Spencer, Ollie, and Nate laughing as they taped together boxes, and stacked them outside on the balcony. Teddy had already departed for his first day of work with Ben, and Cassidy still hadn't heard back from poor Neil. Cassidy picked up one of the tubes of lipstick and removed the lid. He held it up to his nose and breathed in that waxed-lotion scent. He wished he wasn't the one doing this. It depressed him to no end, being surrounded by all her things. Made him want to cry, wishing she'd walk through the fucking door already and say something highly inappropriate.

He watched the volunteers traipsing back and forth through the hall in the process of unloading the attic. He exhaled, feeling guilty for allowing any of her stuff to be removed. He knew on some level Sadie wouldn't have expected the door of her bedroom to be hermetically sealed, never to be of any use to anyone. But somehow that knowledge didn't make him feel any better about clearing out her things. He laughed, realizing she'd have expected him to put it all in the very attic he was currently allowing Cecelia and Edie to empty out.

A stab of sadness hit Cassidy again as his gaze made its way around the room. Not even the dusty yellow floral wallpaper could mask the loss of energy, as if even the air surrounding him was slightly stale. He hadn't experienced that since his first day back on the island. Even that had changed in the sense that he no longer believed himself as alone in the world as he had a week ago. Cassidy glanced over at Nate, knowing he was the biggest reason he no longer felt that way. He smiled slightly when their gazes met for a flicker of a moment before Nate went back to taping up boxes.

Cassidy absently fiddled through the contents of the drawer, knowing his biggest problem was that he didn't want to say good-bye to Sadie. But he was quickly running out of things he'd be able to do for her and coming to that realization carried with it a growing sense of uselessness. He'd been fighting for her for so long now that he could barely remember a time when he wasn't. It had given him a purpose and drive he wouldn't have had otherwise.

It had also been a key component in his insane drive to get through grad school. He'd pushed himself to get farther, faster. Now his PhD was all he had left to fight for, which he found a little ironic. He was officially finished, minus his dissertation, but now feared that alone would no longer be enough.

There was also something about being back at Piper's Point that made him keenly aware of the fact that all those years of struggle had provided him with an ironclad curtain he'd been able to hide himself behind. He wouldn't be able to keep people at arm's length anymore and still be able to convince himself it was because he had more important things to fight for than his own happiness. For the first time, it really hit him that his entire world was about to change—drastically.

"Cassidy, I feel a little weird going through Granny's pantie drawer," Ollie said, peering into the open drawer of silky undergarments as he played with the hem of his black T-shirt that had *Blondie is a Band* written in hot pink letters.

"Don't call her Granny," Nate and Cassidy said simultaneously.

"That's a little creepy, you two." Spencer eyed them both suspiciously, looking very Abercrombie in his cargos and ribbed tee.

"We had it drilled into our heads," Nate said.

"She was the vainest woman I've ever met," Natalie said, standing in the doorway. "I put a pan of cinnamon rolls in the oven, dear." She stuck her cheek out so Nate could give her a peck. "This place is a madhouse."

Cassidy got up off the stool and went to her, giving her a long squeeze. "Please tell me you can stay, because I don't know what the hell to do with all her…this stuff."

"Of course I can stay," Natalie said, sliding her purse off her shoulder. "I almost did this myself on several occasions over the last few months. I just wasn't sure if I should. I didn't know if you'd be angry or upset with me. I was already terrified you'd freak out over the new paint color."

"That was a bit of a shock."

"I already said I was sorry," Nate reminded, holding his hands up like he was conceding the battle before it began.

Ollie not so subtly cleared his throat as Spencer muttered something about being none too happy he'd have to help finish painting the trim on the remaining two sides before the Founders' Day party that weekend.

"This is Ollie." Cassidy waved his hand at him and then scowled, motioning toward Spencer. "And this is Shrek."

Spencer snarled his lip up at Cassidy as he and Ollie crossed the room. Natalie of course swatted their hands away, giving them each a hug.

"Welcome to Piper's Point." Natalie grinned from ear to ear as she sized them up. "Oh my goodness, many handsome men have found their way into this bedroom over the years, but never so many all at once."

Cassidy laughed as Ollie practically preened as if she'd been referring to him alone.

"We're a little at a loss, Mom." Nate placed his hands on his hips, shaking his head at all the boxes they'd put together.

"I see that."

Cassidy helplessly surveyed the terrain. "I honestly don't know what to save. If there's anything you want, Natalie…by all means."

"Thank you, dear. I appreciate that."

"I want the historical society to take all the vintage clothes and hats, but I think most of that is up in the attic." Cassidy crossed the room and opened the wardrobe. "Would you think it bad to donate most of her clothes to a women's shelter?"

Natalie nodded, tearing up a little. "I think she'd approve."

"Please don't do that, Nat." Cassidy sighed as Nate went to her and hugged her. "I'm barely holding it together as it is today."

"Oh shoot, I'm sorry, it's just…" Natalie rubbed her eyes, letting loose her little chipmunk giggle. "I'm so happy to have you home, kiddo. You've always had such a kind heart, and I've worried that all the time you spent fighting with that man would somehow change you."

Cassidy smiled, seeing Nate wink at him before he nudged his head toward Spencer and Ollie. "I've had a few friends around who've helped keep my head above water."

Natalie smiled, all rosy cheeked. "Well, you both have a home here on Hart's. We owe you a debt of gratitude."

"Be careful telling Ollie things like that, Nat." Cassidy winked at her. "He's sure to collect—when you least expect it."

Ollie blew out a puff of air. "Stop that. She won't know you're joking."

"I certainly hope he's not." Natalie blushed a little. "I might not mind if he did collect."

Ollie gasped, trying to act shocked, despite sporting a huge toothy smile. "Saucy woman!"

"Mother, please," Nate scolded, placing a hand on his stomach. "I'm never going to be old enough to listen to you talk like that."

Natalie laughed, clapping her hands and doing a little dance at having embarrassed her little baby. Cassidy was beyond happy she'd shown up today of all days. He wondered if Nate had made a call, alerting her to the fact they'd be doing this today. That would be just like him, quietly trying to anticipate everyone else's needs while standing in the background, never attempting to claim any of the credit.

"Well, dear child of mine," Natalie said, helping Ollie empty one of the drawers, "if I can survive witnessing what you boys were up to in the kitchen Friday afternoon…"

Cassidy knew his eyes were wide as saucers as both he and Nate awkwardly averted their gazes. Cassidy was mortified once again as Ollie and Spencer were dying from laughter.

"I certainly hope you boys gave that countertop a good scrubbing."

"Kill me now," Cassidy mumbled, his face fully flushed with heat.

"Mother, really," Nate said, shaking his head as Spencer passed him a box.

"Oh my," Ollie said, wiping the tears out of his eyes. "I love this lady."

Natalie laughed, obviously enjoying herself as well as the effect she was having on Ollie. "I doubt that's what Sadie had in mind when she had that island installed."

I wouldn't count on it.

"On second thought, I wouldn't be all that surprised if that *was* what she had in mind," Natalie said, closing the top drawer of the bureau.

Thank you!

Nate walked into the closet and grabbed an armful of clothes still on their hangers and carried them out onto the bed.

Ollie sort of frowned. "I hate that I never got to meet her."

Cassidy nodded in agreement. "She would've gotten a kick out of you."

"What about me?" Spencer asked, removing a blouse from a hanger and folding it before placing it into a box.

Cassidy and Natalie looked at each other and giggled.

"She would have hit on you," Cassidy said.

"Nice," Spencer said, wiggling his eyebrows as if nothing else in life were more important than that.

Natalie subjected Spencer and Ollie to a barrage of questions about their lives together, what they each did for a living. She quickly commented on how lovely it would be to have one of Spencer's cafés on Hart's, as there was nothing else like it here. Not missing a beat, she brought up the fact that Hart's averaged around fifty thousand tourists a day. Cassidy could practically see Spencer's eyes glazing over as he imagined the revenue. She was also quick to remind Cassidy that the loft above the garage would make a wonderful studio for Ollie to work on his sculpture.

Cassidy nodded in agreement, sorting through a stack of papers and old bills he'd pulled out of the bottom drawer of one of the nightstands. He'd completely forgotten about the loft, as it hadn't been used for anything other than storage for as far back as he could remember. It really did get fantastic light from the large windows on all four sides. It had nice high ceilings and was large enough that he could have Internet installed so Spencer could sit up there and conduct his business while watching Ollie work, something Spencer loved to do.

"So why is it we've never heard anything about your grandfather?" Spencer asked, helping Nate unload another large armful of clothes from the closet.

"I don't really know much. He died back in the forties. I think Lionel was only like one or two at the time."

Natalie started to wring her hands a little. "She never told you much, did she?"

Cassidy was surprised by the question. "No, she didn't, actually. Whenever I asked, she'd offer up something vague like 'he was a good man' or 'you'd have really liked him.'"

"You're going to be so vexed with me. I just know it," Natalie said, fidgeting a little more as she crossed the room, heading toward the closet. "I meant to get it for you the day I stopped by with the council heads, but I sort of forgot after the news you weren't planning to stay. Then on Friday…and I think we all vividly remember what happened that time."

Ollie clicked his teeth together, making biting noises, and Cassidy shot him the evil eye, wishing he'd never told the little shit.

"What are you talking about, Mother?" Nate asked suspiciously as he stopped folding clothes.

Natalie vanished into the closet and began rummaging around. "Just promise you won't be angry with me."

"About what?" Cassidy asked, his ass slipping off the stool as he craned his upper body, trying catch a glimpse of what she was after. He hit the floor with a thud, scrambling to get himself off the floor as Ollie and Spencer snickered.

Natalie came out of the closet carrying a black lacquer box with art deco and Japanese-influenced detail. It had red wooden handles on the side and a silver medallion in the center of the lid. Natalie wiped the dust off with the sleeve of her shirt as she carried it over to Cassidy and held it out for him.

"She rarely ever spoke to me about your grandfather. I think it pained her to talk about him, even all those years later. His name was Samuel." Natalie sighed, turning to Spencer and Ollie. "But she called him Sam. We'd been drinking quite heavily one night after she split with her last boyfriend. That's when she showed me this box."

"Which boyfriend was that?" Cassidy strained to remember as he took the box from her and sat back down on the stool.

Ollie scoffed as if Cassidy was being insensitive.

"There were a lot of boyfriends," Cassidy snapped back. "It's a little difficult to keep them all straight."

"William," Natalie said. "But Ollie's correct. That's kind of beside the point, dear. She told me if anything happened to her that I was to get this to you. She didn't want Lionel to have it."

"What's in it?" Cassidy asked, half-afraid to open it.

"The things she kept of your grandfather's." Natalie took a few steps back as Cassidy ran his fingertips over the lid. "He was quite the hunk. She told me he was devastatingly handsome, with a swagger and a cocky grin. A charisma that rivaled her own, which both frightened and exhilarated her at the same time." Natalie walked over to the bed and sat down, gently brushing some dust off her slacks. "She said he was the only man she'd ever really loved. Straight down to the bone, she'd say."

"I don't understand," Cassidy said, cracking open the lid and peeking in. "If she loved him so much, then why never speak of him?"

"I think she missed him terribly. He died so young, so unexpectedly. She said he'd been taken from her before they'd ever had the chance to really begin. They never found his body, just the boat."

"The *Tempest*?" Nate asked.

Natalie nodded. "He bought that boat for the two of them. It's where they spent their honeymoon, sailing up and down the East Coast."

"But Sadie hated sailing," Cassidy said, surveying the contents—some letters and photographs bound in yellowed white ribbon, a red velvet-covered jewelry box, and an ancient gum wrapper, the inside of which was marked with Sadie's red lip print. Cassidy held it up for Natalie to see.

"From what I've been told, she used to love sailing."

"That's so sad." Cassidy picked up the pocket-size leather-bound book, running his fingers over the gold lettering. Cassidy turned it around so everyone could see it was a copy of William Shakespeare's the *Tempest*. "He must've really loved the play."

"He gave that to her. It was his pet name for her, always calling her his tempest. I've never read it, but she said it had something to do with Hart's Island and the way she fought so vehemently to protect it from outside influence or control. Sam's father, the original Lionel Winters, your great-grandfather, had made several attempts before the war to buy up land on Hart's. He wanted to turn the island into the East Coast vacation destination for the wealthy and privileged. Fancied himself the William Randolph Hearst of North Carolina, that one."

"At least I know my father comes by it honestly."

"And she wound up married to his son?" Nate asked, obviously confused.

"I bet Great-Granddaddy Hart loved that," Cassidy said, pulling a small bit of dried jasmine out from beneath the pages of the book.

"He most certainly did not like it," Edie said from the doorway, where she was eavesdropping. She had that glint in her eye everyone on Hart's got just before the gossiping began. "He threatened to cut Sadie out of the will after they got married. Old Jeremiah thought Lionel Senior was attempting to get Piper's Point by having Samuel seduce his baby girl. Of course your great grandparents on the Winters side were none too happy that their one and only heir had gone and married so far beneath his station."

"Like anyone would be able to seduce Sadie," Cassidy scoffed.

"If anyone ever had a shot in hell, it would have been Samuel Winters," Edie corrected.

"So they married on the sly?" Ollie asked.

"Got in a boat on a Wednesday, went to the mainland, and drove to Virginia, then came back on Thursday married." Edie smiled as if remembering it like it happened last week. "The news rocked the entire island, even for Sadie, who'd always done exactly as she liked, regardless of the consequences." Edie shook her head, trying to cover up her obvious jealously with self-righteousness. "But marrying that Winters boy—at the time it was scandalous, and Sadie going around saying things like she hadn't the strength to refuse him. That he'd promised she'd never again have to wear the same pair of nylons for as long as she lived, and how could any red-blooded American girl resist such temptation."

Cassidy could tell Edie had loved the drama of it all intensely. "Sounds pretty romantic."

"Oh, it was," Edie said, then straightened herself, "later, that is, after everyone got used to the idea—not that Sadie gave anyone much choice in the matter."

"I don't mean to sound simple," Ollie asked, raising his hand in the air like Edie was his schoolteacher. "Nylons?"

"They were in short supply during the war. We used do anything we could to make them last." She laughed, shaking her head. "Sewing up the runs with matching thread. It was a pain in the ass." Edie smiled, looking Cassidy up and down. "You remind me of him, you know—Samuel. He was a stunning specimen, truly made you weak in the knees when he walked by. He'd been a pilot in the war. Something else his father had forbidden him to do that he'd gone and done anyway. He was magnificent—a real hero."

Cassidy watched Edie with a raised brow, as it was painfully obvious she'd been in love with his grandfather. She took note of the accusation written all over Cassidy's face and quickly cleared her throat, excusing herself before disappearing into the hall.

"Stalker!" Ollie called out in a high-pitched shrill voice, accompanied by a *Psycho*-esque, squeaky sound effect to go along with his hand thrusting through the air like a knife.

Everyone laughed while Cassidy glanced back down into the box.

Natalie pulled herself up off the bed and walked behind Cassidy, squeezing his shoulder. "They only had a few years together, some of which they spent apart fighting over where they were going to live. A battle of wills that Sadie somehow managed to win. She was genuinely surprised by that fact. Samuel gave up trying to lure her away from her island and sort of succumbed to it…to her, she liked to think. She said that he saw past the girl who refused to put on an apron and couldn't make a decent cup of coffee had her life depended on it. That he'd fallen in love with her spirited nature and she worshipped him for never trying to break it."

There were several pencil sketches of Sadie's face lying underneath all the odd little mementos such as the Coca-Cola bottle cap and a random seashell. Cassidy carefully pulled them out; they'd yellowed and appeared to have become brittle. He passed them to Ollie.

"They're very well executed. Lovely composition," Ollie said, delicately holding one up by the corner of the paper. "Sadie was quite the babe."

There was an old record underneath everything else. Cassidy lifted it out of the box and smiled, reading the song title "You'd Be So Nice to Come Home To" by Dinah Shore.

"She told me she gave that to him," Natalie said. "She laughed and laughed, as he was anything but amused by the insinuation."

Cassidy untied the ribbon that bound the square black-and-white photographs together. He smiled, surprised by the resemblance between himself and Samuel Winters. It made him a little sad, seeing Sadie all decked out in a long gown, so young, and beaming as if she were the happiest woman in the world wrapped up in his grandfather's tuxedo-clad arms, dancing. He wished he could have known her then.

"She told me she'd been too happy," Natalie said, tearing up. "That he'd been taken from her because she loved him too deeply, as if that in itself was a sin." Natalie sighed as she shook her head. "That he'd given up his other life in order to make her happy, and it had cost him his."

"God, Nat, surely she didn't truly blame herself?"

"I don't know, but I do think she'd have given him up had it meant he'd have a long, happy life otherwise."

"That's the saddest story I've ever heard," Spencer said, sitting on the bed holding the same blouse he'd folded and refolded God only knew how many times now.

Cassidy finished flipping through the photographs before passing them over to Nate. He untied the letters, then dropped them back down into the box and picked up the red jewelry box. It creaked as he opened it. He lifted the cottony padding to find a simple gold band and a tasteful diamond engagement ring tied together with a perfect little bow of ribbon. They were tasteful, unassuming. Cassidy replaced the cotton and shut the box, going back to the letters.

The envelopes had been addressed to Sadie. Cassidy noticed how precise the handwriting was as he carefully opened the one on top, sliding out the folded piece of paper. Cassidy cleared his throat as he unfolded it, examining the handwriting. His grandfather began to feel like more than just a story as he could now imagine him sitting down to write it. He was becoming real, a man who loved Sadie enough to give up the wealth and influence of his family to be with her. Cassidy smiled, feeling a new connection to his grandfather since he too had turned away from the Winters legacy without a second thought. He began reading the letter aloud.

My dearest Tempest,

It has been over a week since I left you standing alone on our beach, and I have yet to hear from you. My father continues in his attempt to lure me back with excessive blustering and threats of disinheritance. It has become almost amusing in that it has had the opposite effect. I find myself daydreaming of a sleepy, simple life on the beaches of Hart's Island with you. How I wish we hadn't quarreled before I left, and yet I find myself still infuriated with you for not coming back to Charlotte with me. My mind retreats to darkness when I think you could love anything more than you love me. It's a sad occasion when a man must admit he is envious of the sand under your feet. I cannot hide my disappointment in the belief you are not as lost without me as I seem to be away from you.

I am driven to distraction, unable to think of anything other than the fullness of your red lips. How I long to have you back in my arms. This meager flesh that covers my bones burns red-hot, yearning to once again experience the way in which you give yourself over to me. The way you whisper my name haunts me. The long cascading curls of your dark red hair brushing against my cheek. I ache for you, Tempest. You've bewitched me, and I now believe myself to be ruined for any life that does not include you. I lay awake at night and like a siren's song piercing through the darkness, I imagine you standing on our beach calling up into the heavens above, Come back to me…come back to me.

Cassidy quietly refolded the letter, noticing the edges appeared worn beyond the typical wear and tear, as if it had been taken out and reread every so often. A warmth passed over him, and he found himself drawn to Nate in particular, who was staring at him. Cassidy couldn't move or even breathe as he was suddenly able to imagine the way Sadie must have felt whenever his granddaddy looked at her.

"That was—" Cassidy began, shaking his head, still unable to tear his gaze away from Nate's.

"Beautiful," Nate interrupted.

"I may need a cold shower," Ollie said, fanning his face with his hand. "Is it wrong that I'm so turned on right now?"

"Yes," Cassidy said with a grimace.

Natalie burst out laughing. She wiped her eyes as she headed over to Ollie, giving him a big hug. "I think you might be my new favorite person in the whole wide world."

Ollie smiled, giving Natalie the evil eye. "Don't go trying to drag me down that tearstained road, lady. I don't do puffy."

Natalie giggled again, as if she was as innocent as the day she was born. Cassidy knew exactly what she'd meant, as Ollie had been gifted with the ability to say just the right thing at the right moment, keeping the mood from spiraling too far down into the dumps.

Everyone got back to the job at hand, bantering back and forth, trying to keep things light. Cassidy tied the letters back together, though not with quite the same precision Sadie had. He replaced all the contents and closed the lid. Removing his glasses, Cassidy glanced at his reflection in the mirror, thinking he appeared a little worn around the edges. He pressed his fingers into his eye sockets in hopes of relieving some of the strain building up.

Cassidy wondered what losing Sam like that must have done to her. It had to have altered who she was, damaged her deeply. He thought about his relationship with his own father and what that change in her could've meant for Lionel at such a young age. Considering Cassidy's relationship with his father mirrored that of Lionel and Sadie's, it felt as if the forces of history were punishing them. That this horrible family curse had them stuck on some twisted loop, dooming them to repeat the same mistakes.

Cassidy didn't believe Lionel had ever liked his mother, and to some degree, Cassidy understood why. As much as Cassidy loved Sadie for her eccentric ways, her loud, boisterous spirit that overwhelmed nearly anyone else, he also knew it had embarrassed his father as a child. And it would have been an understatement to say she didn't exactly hide any disappointment she had in Lionel, who represented an elitist standard for which she had nothing but contempt. He became everything she'd been raised to despise, and he loathed her for keeping him from the Winters legacy his entire childhood. The fact that she'd been married so many times, not to mention all the lovers she'd taken up with after Sam passed away, didn't exactly help things.

Maybe his father would have turned out differently had Sam been there to shape him as Lionel grew up and developed into a man. Perhaps it would've made no difference and he'd have just wound up hating Samuel as much as he had Sadie. He sighed, realizing there was no point in sitting around all day playing what-if. He was happy knowing that at least for a little while Sadie had been loved. A tiny bit jealous, even.

Putting his glasses back on, he then went back to sorting

through the papers he'd laid out on the desk, placing them into keep and shred piles. Every so often he'd feel the back of his neck becoming warm. He'd peer up into the mirror to find Nate watching him. A week ago he would have been unnerved by it. But in that particular moment Cassidy took comfort from it, even found himself missing it whenever Nate would turn away. As he went back to sifting through the stack, he wondered if there'd ever be a next time with Nate. And if there was, would he somehow screw it up?

§ § §

The next few days wound up being more of a madhouse than Cassidy thought possible. He'd met with the council elders Monday evening, and both he and Edie assured them they'd be finished no later than Wednesday, ensuring Piper's Point would be ready in time for the Founders' Day party that weekend. Cassidy went over Nate's idea of inviting everyone who wished to attend to the lighthouse on Saturday when he'd be spreading Sadie's ashes. They all agreed it was an appropriate gesture, and while no one actually did, he couldn't help but imagine they all wanted to press him as to whether he'd changed his mind about leaving at the end of the summer.

The house had been crawling with a couple of dozen people for days working from early morning and well into the night as the contents of the attic were unloaded and displayed for Cassidy, Cecelia, and Edie to assess their importance. Cassidy had also asked Natalie to hang around, as she was the closest thing to an expert they had in regard to what had transpired over the last thirty years.

The goal at this point was merely to separate the items that might have any historical relevance from those that didn't. From there, what was left was divided into three separate areas—things that might have monetary value and could be sold to help fund Sadie's exhibit were taken directly to the historical society. The items that weren't of any notable value but might still be useful were packed up to be shipped to the shelter for battered women along with most of Sadie's clothes. The third and final area was trash. Cassidy was actually fairly impressed that precious little wound up in the trash pile, somewhat redeeming Sadie's pack-rat existence.

By Wednesday evening, both the attic and Sadie's bedroom had been emptied and sifted through, along with the loft above the garage, which Natalie had reminded him of on Monday. Any documents and photographs had been taken back to the attic. As part of the deal, Cassidy would have to sort through each shred of paper in order to approve what was acceptable to release to the historical society. The letters from his grandfather and anything else so personal in nature would never see the light of day outside the walls of the house in which they now resided.

Most of the heavy items, the furniture, and knickknacks had all been loaded up, including a few pieces from the house that Cassidy and the others agreed might hold interest, such as Jeremiah's Victorian claw-foot desk from the formal parlor, and Piper Hart's tiny pianoforte that had been sitting in the living room as far back as he could remember.

Cassidy knew Sadie wouldn't be happy he'd handed over her daddy's desk, but it was so bulky, almost intimidating, and he'd always disliked it intensely. He kept a few things from the attic—a carved oak desk from France, which had fat barley twist legs, that Cassidy wanted to use in the parlor to replace Jeremiah's desk, a full-size Victorian sleigh bed that he planned to put in his old bedroom after doing a little redecorating. He fell completely in love with a set of midcentury modern iron patio furniture discovered above the garage, which he was determined to have restored.

He kept a small Egyptian-influenced, art-deco bronze lamp of a woman sitting on her legs and holding up a basket that held a frosted-glass globe. It needed to be rewired, and he doubted it would bring as much money as a result. They found a vintage portable Royal typewriter from the thirties that appeared practically brand-new. It had been kept stored in its original case, and he couldn't part with it, along with three Bakelite telephones, two black and one cream colored. None of them worked, but they were just like the ones you'd see in an old black-and-white noir film.

The pièce de résistance had been three wooden crates filled with leather-bound books. Cassidy had nearly wet himself, unable to imagine why anyone would have locked them away, yet quite grateful for their stupidity. His hand had been shaking as he reached into the first crate, as if afraid the books might turn to dust and crumble before his very eyes, were he to physically disturb them.

Cassidy nearly broke down after cracking open the first book and seeing the name *Samuel Winters* scribbled on the inside cover. Instantly sad for Sadie, Cassidy realized she must have put them away because they reminded her of him. He dug through the crate, seeing the names Hemingway and Melville, Twain and Poe, along with Virgil and Dickens. And that was in the first crate alone. It was like the Holy Literature Grail had fallen into his lap.

What had been more priceless to Cassidy was the knowledge that his grandfather had loved to read, the same way he always had. For the first time, Cassidy truly connected to the Winters side of his family. He was angry, feeling cheated for not having had the opportunity to meet his grandfather.

Cassidy had stood there looking over the books, thinking that as short as his life had been, Sam had loved and been loved in the way all people dreamed possible before life and ruined expectations caused them to give up and settle for what was easy and available. At no other point in his life had it been true, yet Cassidy was a little pissed at Sadie for not having shared any of this with him.

Despite all the personal discoveries he'd made, and perhaps because of them, Cassidy was relieved to have all the heavy lifting completed as the endless parade of people tromping through Sadie's shack mercifully came to a halt. Teddy had barely been around since starting his new job with Ben. Something told Cassidy they were likely doing much more intense training than Ben had ever done with any of his previous employees.

Nate had spent the bulk of Tuesday and Wednesday at his

office, trying to catch up on some of his neglected work, and Spencer, Ollie, and Neil had been doing some island sightseeing during the day, while Cassidy had been kept busy, being pulled in one direction or another. Cassidy was a little bummed, as he'd been hoping to take Ollie and Spencer around himself, but it gave them something to do and kept them out of the vortex of chaos that the Point had become.

As he crumpled into Nate's bed Wednesday night, more exhausted than he could ever remember being, he wondered if perhaps his age and the ruthless tempo he'd set for himself for the bulk of the last decade were finally catching up with him. Nate slipped his arm around his waist as he dragged Cassidy across the bed to where he lay somewhere between wake and sleep. Cassidy offered no resistance yet couldn't be bothered to help, more like a rag doll than an actual human being.

The heat from Nate's body burned into his back, relaxing him further, something he hadn't realized possible until that moment. As sleep came over him, now safely tucked away in Nate's arms as if nothing or no one could possibly get to him, Cassidy hoped there truly was a heaven. He wanted to believe that somewhere Sadie was also safely tucked away. That Samuel had his Tempest again. That only seemed fair, he thought, drifting deeper into sleep. It would almost make losing her bearable if it were true.

Chapter Eighteen

Cassidy opened his eyes, still exhausted and feeling as if he'd just come to bed and lay down only minutes before. His mind immediately went to the amount of work still left, getting through all the Hart family documents, and he began to secretly hope it wasn't a complete history, taking into account the length of time his family had been on the island.

Neither Cecelia nor Edie had been too happy when they realized Cassidy wasn't planning on allowing them to go through the family documents, but Cassidy knew Sadie would expect a certain amount of discretion to be taken into account. It was somewhat laughable, considering Sadie's sordid history with men had been the talk of the island for the past fifty or sixty years.

He let out a long groan as he rolled onto his stomach, seeing Nate was once again already up and nowhere to be found. He smiled, feeling Dasie crawling up the mattress behind him, and he rolled over, giggling as she went to town trying to give his face a tongue bath. He noticed the top of the white tent out the open French doors, irritated that his view of the ocean from Nate's bed was still obstructed.

Cassidy quickly shoved all the Hart family history aside in his mind in order to make room for the full day's worth of party planning he had ahead of him. Despite Jacob and Henry assuring him that it was all planned, he somehow knew relocating everything to Piper's Point from the lighthouse grounds wasn't going to be as easy as they made it sound.

All Cassidy wanted to do was stay in bed. The past few days had emotionally drained him. He was even willing to ignore his own bladder to do so, if not for the fact he knew he didn't have a choice in the matter. He listened to the loud motor coming from somewhere outside the house, along with the occasional muffled voices yelling back and forth. Dasie hopped up onto his stomach and plopped down, sitting like the sphinx with her front paws stretched out across his chest. She then laid her head down, resting her chin on her paws as she stared at Cassidy, her big, pleading eyes saying, *I need to pee, and I'm hungry, Daddy.*

"Not you too?" Cassidy tried pouching his lower lip out to see if that would have any effect on the dog. He whimpered when she didn't so much as flinch. "Okay, you win. I'll get up."

She sprang up off his chest, bouncing across the bed in circles as he slowly pulled himself out of it. He once again cursed under his breath, able to hear the ocean but not see it as he slipped on his jeans.

§ § §

Cassidy followed the scent of Natalie's cinnamon rolls all the way into the kitchen, just in time to see Nate going out the door. Ollie sat in the breakfast nook with Spencer, Teddy, Natalie, and Neil.

"This evil, wicked woman continues to seduce me with dough and icing," Ollie said, rubbing his full belly while Natalie munchkin-giggled away.

"Want me to take her out?" Teddy asked, getting up from the table.

Cassidy handed the dog over. "Shouldn't you be at work?"

"Nope." Teddy winked as he headed out the door. "Ben let me off to help out here."

They all jumped slightly, hearing a loud bang coming from outside.

"What the hell…" Cassidy rushed out the back door, freezing in his tracks as he surveyed the courtyard.

Tables and chairs were being unloaded into the garage along with plastic-wrapped white tablecloths and racks upon racks of glassware in green plastic dividers. White paper lanterns were being strung throughout all the tents and Christmas-tree lights slung over anything else that would stand still long enough to be caught up in its web of green wires. Cassidy turned to his right to see the large stepped bandstand going up on the east lawn. The torches were being installed down the path to the beach as four men carefully carried half of the long bar down the steps. To his left, he noticed the first bar was already set up and ready to be stocked with booze.

"Nate thought you might be in need of a little break from tedium after dealing with Cee Cee and the historical society." Natalie placed her arm around his waist. "He and the council have taken over the party organizing. You can do as much or as little as you like, but they all wanted to do this for you and Sadie."

"Wow." Cassidy waved at Henry and Edie as they walked by arguing about exactly where the dance floor should be placed. Teddy weaved his way back through the maze of people with Dasie tucked under his arm like a football as Cecelia came chasing after them.

"Can we please pick up the poo until after the Founders' party?" Cecelia shrieked.

Cassidy and Natalie laughed as Teddy and Dasie both ran, wide-eyed and panicked, having been chased down by a fist-shaking Cecelia.

"I'll make sure it doesn't happen again," Cassidy yelled out as Teddy disappeared into the house.

"That woman is a menace," Natalie scolded. "Frightening that sweet little Teddy."

Cassidy did his best to keep a straight face, considering Teddy was anything but tiny. He'd immensely enjoyed seeing the big, muscle-bound hunk running like a little girl from the vicious demon goddess of smite. "She does have a tiny bit of a point, though."

"Nonsense. A little poo on the shoe never killed anyone." Natalie nodded curtly as she spun around to head back into the house. "Come in and eat some breakfast. You boys all need to go pick out your tuxedos today so Mrs. Tate and her quilting circle can make any necessary alterations."

"Isn't Nate coming with us?" Cassidy asked, following Natalie back into the house.

"No dear. He already has one—make that two. Why he went and exchanged tuxedos at the last minute is beyond me." Natalie seemed slightly peeved by that. "Spencer appears to be about the same size as Nate, so perhaps all is not lost. I better go call Mrs. Tate."

Natalie darted out into the hall, and Cassidy blinked, startled by how quickly she'd moved. He padded softly toward the island, noticing someone had already fed Dasie. He poured himself a cup of coffee and tried rubbing the sleep out of his eyes. He wanted to go back to bed and found himself somewhat irritable toward Nate as well. He didn't like waking up to find him gone, considering they'd barely had any time to talk the past few days.

He shook those thoughts out of his head, chalking it up to exhaustion and a lack of caffeine. He was certainly ready to spend some time with his friends away from this circus where his biggest decision could be made by pointing to a suit on a rack while uttering four simple words…

§ § §

"I'll take that one," Cassidy said as Mrs. Tate removed the tuxedo from the rack, rescuing it from the remaining unwanted, which were slightly sad in their appearance, hanging there all lifeless.

The older woman in her late fifties shoved the rack, sending it hurtling toward the back wall with no regard for where it might happen to stop. Neil was already finished, putting his street clothes back on behind one of the old cardboard set paintings from *Guys and Dolls*, now being repurposed as changing screens. Ollie, Teddy, and Spencer were all standing up on wooden boxes, as minions from Mrs. Tate's quilting bee fussed with hems, pinned crotches, and pleated jackets.

All this activity occurred on the stage in the high school auditorium behind the drawn red velvet curtain, which had definitely seen better days. Cassidy stepped behind one of the partitions and started removing his clothes. He watched over the screen as Ollie stepped down and went to stand in front of a mirror, so he and his seamstress could take a peek at her progress.

Cassidy pulled his pants up and buttoned them turning in time to catch Neil watching him. He cast a gaze at the man only to receive a shrug and a wink as if to say, *Don't blame me for looking.*

Cassidy tucked in his formfitting T-shirt and came back out as Ollie stepped back up on his box. Pulling on his own jacket, Cassidy walked over to the mirror as he and Mrs. Tate both nodded, realizing there wouldn't be much alteration required.

"Lady," Ollie said, snapping his fingers until the woman who was working with Spencer finally turned around. "I apologize as I don't think I ever got your name, and please forgive me for being rude, but could you please take care and watch where you're pointing those shears?"

Everyone turned, including the seamstress, who went bright red when she realized her hand rested on Spencer's thigh, and the tip of the intimidatingly long and sharp-ass shears were mere centimeters away from the jewels.

"Oh my," she said, ripping her hand away in a bit of a panic as Spencer watched with the slightest bit of fear in his eyes.

"Thank you," Ollie said, placing a hand over his chest, obviously relieved. "I apologize once again, but I've grown quite attached to the goods, and I'd certainly hate to go home with anything less than what I arrived with."

All the women started giggling away, turning as red as the velvet curtains while Cassidy stepped up on his box.

"As would I," Spencer muttered, breaking out in a cold sweat.

"Thank you for squeezing us all in last minute, by the way," Cassidy said. "Please excuse my friends' lack of a filter."

"Not a problem, Cassidy," Mrs. Tate offered, pinning up the hem of his pant leg. "We're all just so happy you're back home where you belong."

"No offense taken," said the girl working on Spencer as she smiled up at him with a gleam of lust in her eye. "That would indeed be quite a shame."

Spencer winked, obviously enjoying being flirted with, since the corners of his mouth turned up slightly.

Cassidy rolled his eyes and laughed as Ollie took note of said flirting as well.

"Not that I wouldn't be opposed to a little snip, snip for the man with a wandering eye," Ollie reminded as Spencer pursed his lips and laughed.

"Could you two be any more crude?" Teddy asked, shaking his head. "I doubt these ladies care to hear such things."

The women all laughed as the one working with Teddy, who looked like Aunt Bea from Mayberry, patted him on the ass. "If you had any idea the things we ladies talk about when you men aren't around."

"Well, still, ma'am," Teddy said, glancing down and watching curiously as she decided to cop another feel. "It's not very polite."

"It's Sir Gala-dud to the rescue," Ollie said.

"Please, boys." Cassidy shut his eyes, praying for mercy. "I'm begging you—can we please have a pleasant and peaceful afternoon?"

"Well, why invite us along if you wanted that?" Ollie quipped, winking at Cassidy.

"Sorry, Cass," Teddy said, scowling at the ground like a little freshly scolded kid. "It's just, I really like it here. Everyone's so nice and friendly." He glanced pointedly over at Ollie. "And I'd prefer not to have the entire island praying for my departure."

"Just me, then?" Ollie asked, cracking himself up until he realized Cassidy wasn't enjoying his snark. "Kidding!"

"I'm glad to hear you're enjoying Hart's, Teddy. That makes me happy."

"Not nearly as happy as Ben-vet," Ollie muttered through his teeth.

Neil, who sat on the floor, leaned back against the wall and burst out laughing. Cassidy assumed Neil must have gotten the same eyeful he and Ollie had Sunday morning after sneaking out of the house, hungover.

Teddy lifted his arms in a "what gives?" manner. "Now why even bring that up?"

"You're all done, my dear," Mrs. Tate said, standing up and taking Cassidy by the hand and gently shaking it.

"Because he just can't help himself, Teddy." Cassidy hopped down from the box. "He's like a monkey with an uncontrollable compulsion to fondle himself."

Spencer laughed, shoulders bouncing up and down until Ollie eyed him as a traitor.

"I need more coffee." Cassidy sighed. "Or a cocktail."

"If I were your boyfriend, I'd already be on my way to finding you one or the other," Neil reminded, as an orneriness took over his face.

Cassidy placed a hand on his hip, letting him know by the expression on his face that he didn't appreciate the insinuation.

Neil shrugged, mumbling, "I'm just saying."

Cassidy itched to get to his phone, as if he needed to prove Nate was willing to drop everything to come meet him. He chastised himself for allowing Neil to almost bait him into it. Nate was helping set up for the party in an attempt to give Cassidy some time away from the madness. The only problem with that scenario was Cassidy couldn't help thinking he wouldn't mind the madhouse so much, if it meant being with Nate.

Maybe he could take a break and come meet us for lunch?

Mrs. Tate winked at Cassidy before leading him over to the mirror. "You are a sight to behold, son."

Cassidy smiled back at her through the reflection in the mirror, and she reached up, fussing with his bangs. He was unsure why he'd been so tense all morning, but that one simple act somehow reset his entire internal temperament, and all the frustration sort of bled out him.

"So handsome," Mrs. Tate added. "Sadie would be so proud of the man you've grown into."

"Thank you for saying that, Mrs. Tate." Cassidy turned and reached out to give her a hug, cringing in pain, feeling several pins prick him in the sides and arms.

"Careful, dear," she said, helping him remove the jacket. "Now go take off your pants."

Cassidy looked her up and down. "Mrs. Tate, I'm shocked."

The women all started to laugh as the one working on Teddy said, "Stop flirting, Josephine Tate, and come help me finish up with this young man."

"Don't get fresh with me, young man." Mrs. Tate reached over and pinched Cassidy in the arm, turning a little red in the face. Cassidy yelped dutifully, making sure she was satisfied he'd suffered enough for his cheeky behavior.

She shoved him playfully toward the changing area as Ollie hopped down from his box to go change as well. As Cassidy removed his trousers, handing them to Mrs. Tate over the makeshift screen, he heard his cell ring. He grabbed his jeans by a belt loop and pulled the phone out of the pocket. Scowling, he realized he'd forgotten his glasses. He held it out, squinting to see who was calling.

Perfect timing. Practically elated, he punched the green button and placed the phone between his shoulder and ear. "Hi, babe, what's up?"

"Did you order a bed?" Nate asked.

"Um, yeah…I did." Cassidy started to slide on his jeans, wondering why the hell Nate sounded so cranky.

"Well, it's here, and they want to know where the hell to put it."

"Oh, okay. Calm down, Nate." Cassidy zipped and buttoned.

"I don't want to calm down," Nate snapped. "I have enough to deal with today, you know."

"All right, I'm sorry. I'm finished here so, just tell them to wait, and I'll be there in ten." Cassidy scoffed, hearing the click on the other end of the line. "Jesus, overreact much?"

"What's the problem?" Ollie asked, putting on his last sneaker.

"The bed I ordered arrived today, and it's apparently the straw breaking the camel's back."

Ollie raised an eyebrow, getting up out of the chair. "When did you order a bed?"

"Last week—that next morning after I arrived. That old twin bed I slept on in my room did a number on my back."

"I hope it wasn't only the twin bed?" Neil said, smiling wickedly.

"No, you fuckfest freak of nature," Cassidy said under his breath to ensure the ladies couldn't over hear him. "You helped plenty."

Cassidy watched as Ollie eyed Neil as if seeing him from a whole new perspective. He shook whatever illicit thoughts he had out of his head and turned to Spencer, obviously relieved his husband had been too busy yapping away with Teddy and the women to have caught any of that.

"Does Nate know that's when you ordered the bed?" Ollie finally asked.

"What the hell difference would…" Cassidy's eyes widened with recognition. "So he probably thinks…"

"Yeah." Ollie nodded.

"Shit." Cassidy began patting his pockets for his keys, before remembering he hadn't driven.

"Need a lift?" Neil asked, grinning.

"I'll be coming with," Ollie said to Neil, like he no longer trusted the man could behave himself.

"What about them?" Cassidy asked, pointing to Spencer and Teddy.

"Gotta go, boys!" Ollie yelled back as he pushed Cassidy

toward the exit. "Call my cell when you're done, and I'll come back to get you."

Chapter Nineteen

Neil slowly pulled his SUV up the drive, inching toward the front of the house. All the other delivery trucks were gone except the one with the new bed and a flatbed that was cram-packed with a wide variety of tropical plants and flowers in a multitude of sizes, all the way up to potted palm trees nearly fifteen feet tall. As they parked and got out of the monster truck, Cassidy noticed four guys unloading plants while waiting to be directed by Natalie and Cecelia. The men were standing there with armloads of foliage as the two women argued about what was to go where.

When he walked through the front door, Cassidy peered down the hall into the kitchen and spied Nate talking to someone Cassidy couldn't see. Nate turned, obviously none too happy to see Cassidy, which pissed him off. *The least he could do is wait for a goddamned explanation before writing me off.*

Ollie mumbled something about the delivery guys and Sadie's room, and Cassidy nodded, despite not really paying any attention. A somewhat nastier expression took over Nate's face, and Neil stood beside Cassidy and smiled at Nate as if he hadn't a care in the world. It appeared innocent, but Cassidy knew Neil was baiting Nate, and was half tempted to deck Neil right then and there for enjoying this a little too much.

"You wait right here," Cassidy ordered, as Neil held up his hands in an "I surrender" fashion.

Cassidy started toward the kitchen, then stopped as he came to the stairs, seeing Ben place a hand on Nate's chest as he leaned forward and peeked down the hall at him. Cassidy was instantly furious, seeing nothing but red. *You've got to be kidding me with this shit!*

Nate stared at Cassidy as if daring him to go ahead and say something about it. Cassidy smirked, even more furious when he saw Dasie dangling from Ben's other arm. Cassidy turned, shooting Nate a glare that said he'd best be following his ass if he knew what was good for him; then he stormed up the stairs thinking, Get your hand off my guy and keep the fuck away from my dog!

§ § §

Cassidy paced back forth, cursing himself as he surveyed the room for the location of his fucking glasses. Spotting them on the nightstand, he went over and snatched them up, before putting them on as Nate came into the bedroom.

"Shut that damn door," Cassidy said under his breath.

Nate stared blankly as he took it by the hand and shoved it, causing it to slam and vibrate the walls. "Anything else you need?"

"Yeah," Cassidy said, rounding the bed. "I *need* to know what the fuck has crawled up your ass."

Nate started to speak and then closed his mouth. Cassidy was sporting a cocky grin. He knew Nate didn't want to actually admit what was bugging him. They had each agreed they shouldn't risk being together, despite the fact all either of them had been thinking about over the past week was, in fact, being together.

"You fucking know why," Nate snapped.

"I want to hear you say it."

"Fine, you fucking asshole." Nate took a step forward, muttering between clenched teeth. "It hurt my little girlie feelings to realize you've been sleeping in the same bed with me out of convenience, not because you wanted to be there."

"I ordered that damn bed before I'd even laid eyes on you, you big, dumb ox," Cassidy fired back. "I've been sleeping in the same bed with you because I like being close to you—would very much like to have you a whole helluva lot closer, not that I haven't given you plenty of indication." Cassidy saw the tension draining out of Nate's face as they each took a few steps closer to each other. "What I can't figure out is why you'd give a damn whether or not I'm in your bed, if you don't want to be with me."

Nate reached out, taking Cassidy by the hand and pulling

him into his arms. Cassidy sighed, feeling the heat coming off Nate's body. The man smelled so damn good, and the scent went directly from his nose to his dick. No one else had ever had that kind of a physical effect on Cassidy. The mere fact of Nate's being sent Cassidy spiraling into lust, triggering thoughts and desires he'd definitely experienced with other men in the past, but never so intensely.

He'd forgotten it was like this between them after being apart for so damn long. Cassidy couldn't hold on to a clear thought whenever they were close. It was as if something visceral, something deeply ingrained in his DNA, only surfaced with the smell and touch of this one man.

Nate started to rock back and forth while they stood locked in each other's arms. Cassidy couldn't think of anything other than being completely naked in the kitchen with Nate the other day. The way he took in Cassidy's body, like a man who'd been wandering through the desert for days and had suddenly found water.

The smell of sweat and paint mixed with excitement and lust, along with that new first kiss, searing the sensation of Nate's lips into his consciousness. Having Nate's hands on his skin and his cock inside the man's mouth—it was all there, instantly, whenever either of their planets became caught within the other's gravitational pull.

Cassidy could feel Nate's heart beating faster, knew he was affected as well, as the man breathed deeper and more frequently. He slid his hands down to Nate's hips, pulling their bodies closer and lightly grinding into him. He could feel Nate's erection pressing into his own, and he lost it. Damn everything else to hell and back again, Cassidy thought as he once again decided to make the first move.

Cassidy cocked his head slightly, leaning in only to pull away, never allowing their lips to fully come together. It was the most difficult thing he'd ever done—denying himself by pulling away. He needed Nate to meet him halfway. As Cassidy moved in a third time, deciding it would be the last if Nate didn't make a move, he closed the gap, ferociously covering Cassidy's lips with his. It was pure desperation for the release they'd each been aching for. Cassidy ran a hand into Nate's hair as they continued to grind into each other. Nate's hands were on Cassidy's ass, pulling him tighter, as if he was unable to get close enough.

A white heat flashed through Cassidy as he lifted Nate's shirt. All he could think about was getting his hands on Nate's bare skin. More, wanting more, half-terrified he'd never be able to get enough.

Nate tore his lips away, shoving Cassidy back as he bent over, placing a hand on his knee for support. His other hand covered his mouth as if he was trying to hide the lust that was pouring off his body in waves. "We can't do this."

Cassidy felt the words as if having been physically struck by them. "What the fuck?"

"I'm sorry, Cassidy, but…"

"This is a goddamned joke, right?" Cassidy begged, so turned on that every pore in his body was screaming for release. "We're doing this now, damn it." Cassidy stomped his foot as he pulled off his T-shirt. "You can get naked the easy way or the hard way"—he could barely catch his breath as he started on his belt buckle—"but we're not leaving this room till we've fucked!"

"Please stop, Cassidy. I'm begging you." Nate was doing his level best to avoid seeing Cassidy's shirtless body by speaking to the floor. He held out a hand as if asking for mercy, as if knowing he wouldn't be able to hold out if Cassidy were to take off his pants.

"For Christ's sake, Nate." Cassidy tossed his hands into the air. "What the hell is your problem? Because frankly, the story coming from your body contradicts the one coming out of your mouth. And I'm beginning to get whiplash as you shift back and forth between the two speeds available to me at the moment."

"I can't settle for half of you—" Nate started.

"I'm here, Nate," Cassidy interrupted, patting his hands on chest, "desperate to give you all of me, every inch—to pleasure you in every way possible."

"Fuck, don't say that," Nate said, a pained expression taking over his face.

"The things I'd be willing to do to you—for you, at this precise moment…"

"I just can't, Cassidy, so let it go."

"That's not going to cut it, Nate! You're gonna have to muster up a little more than that if you expect me to back off."

"You're leaving at the end of the summer, so what's the point?"

Cassidy paused for a moment until a renewed determination came over him. He shook his head. "No, Nate. That's just geography. So unless you have something better," Cassidy said going back to his belt.

"I don't deserve you!" Nate screamed, his body beginning to shake.

Cassidy was completely confused. "I don't understand you."

Nate sighed, peeking over before going back to staring at the floor as if it physically hurt to see Cassidy like that and not touch him. "I came to see you in Chapel Hill, you know. Thanksgiving break of my sophomore year. It had been the first chance I'd had to get to you after Sadie had her stroke back in September." Nate rubbed at his crotch as he stood back up. "I'd been worried sick about you, knowing how devastated you'd be, especially considering you weren't able to come to Hart's the previous summer. I figured that alone was probably eating at you. It had been hell waiting, but Mom kept saying you were okay. I guess at the time you still thought you could convince Lionel to let her come back to the Point."

Nate straightened out his shirt and ran a hand through his hair. "As soon as my last class was finished, I jumped in that beat-up old pickup truck I used to have…"

Cassidy smiled, remembering that truck. He missed that truck.

"I was praying the damn thing would actually make the trip,

and I drove practically nonstop."

"I don't understand. If you came then…"

"Mom had told me you were going to spend your break with Sadie in that elder-care facility. I was going to surprise you, drive you up there and stay with you both. I told Mom I'd be with you, that she should spend the weekend with Max." Nate's jaw clenched a little, and he still refused to meet Cassidy's gaze. "There I was, striding up the steps to the house you were living in at the time. Your front door—it had that large oval pane of glass, just like the one here at Piper's Point."

Cassidy remembered it well, having been one of the reasons he picked that house. Every time he walked up to that door, for a split second he was able to imagine himself back at Sadie's shack. Of course, at a certain point it became a constant reminder of his failure to get Sadie back home. It was the very thing that drove him to move and eventually buy the house he now owned, naively thinking Lionel would consent to allowing Sadie to come live with him at least. Back before he realized the extent of Lionel's loathing for her.

"I remember how nervous I was at the time, standing there on the front porch. I was surprised by that as I walked up to the door and raised my hand to knock." Nate repeated the action, lifting his arm as if to knock, his expression going blank, unreadable to Cassidy. "That's when I saw you."

Cassidy watched as Nate's gaze finally met with his. Cassidy grew the tiniest bit uneasy watching the change in Nate's demeanor.

Disappointment washed over Nate's face.

"You were on the sofa, straddling some other guy, kissing him." Nate swallowed and turned away. "I was in shock. I couldn't believe what I'd just seen. It dawned on me what a dumb-ass I'd been, assuming you wouldn't have someone. At first I only felt stupid, driving all night like some ridiculous knight in a white pickup, come to rescue the dude in distress."

Cassidy felt instantly guilty for having caused Nate pain.

He was aware he'd not actually done anything wrong, but that wasn't the point. He remembered that first Thanksgiving alone with Sadie. Trying to keep the constant smile on his face, despite wishing he could curl up in the bed with her and cry. Wanting to apologize to her for not having visited that summer and for lying to her about it. Thinking he'd give anything to go back in time and make a different decision.

"It would have been nice to have had you there," Cassidy said, not intending to hurt Nate by saying it, though that was the effect his words had.

"And that's really it, Cass." Nate's shoulders slumped, and he seemed defeated. "More than any other time in your life, you needed a friend. People to help support you, help hold you up. And I ran away like some punk. Seeing you with that guy, who I assume was Spencer?"

Cassidy nodded blankly, not really remembering anything other than spending that lonely weekend with her, but knowing it was who he'd been dating at the time.

"I realized for the first time I was crazy in love with you. The contempt I felt for him…you, even as I got back in my truck and headed back to Hart's. I told Mom you'd wanted to be alone with Sadie, because I was too ashamed to admit the truth to her. I could've handled being around you and not being able to be with you, Cassidy. But having to stand on the sidelines, forced to watch you with someone else? That thought drove me insane. It made me sick to even think about it."

"Jesus, Nate," Cassidy said, nervously crossing his arms. "You should have said something. Things might have been different had you—"

"I couldn't handle the repercussions of what it would mean if I laid it all out there, only to have you not feel the same. Doing nothing seemed less final, since the possibility of an *us* still remained." Nate exhaled as if he'd unloaded a huge burden. He stumbled to the bed and plopped down. "It was selfish and cowardly, all those wasted years… I've not been able to *really* look myself in the eye ever since."

"You can't—shouldn't carry that around with you," Cassidy said. "You were what, twenty years old at the time? One stupid decision doesn't make the man."

"Even one stupid decision that I made over and over again, day after day, year after year?"

Cassidy knew he was right, but he also understood all too well the power that fear and denial could hold over a man, dooming him to repeat the same mistakes until he found himself in a rut so deep it seemed impossible to claw his way back out. "Do you think you're the only one with regrets?"

"Of course not. I just…"

"You want to know the real reason I didn't come to Hart's that summer before freshman year?" Cassidy asked, walking over and kneeling down at Nate's feet. "I lied to Sadie and to you. I told you Lionel was forcing me to intern with his company that summer. While I did do that, it was all me. I asked Lionel, made him think I was interested in the business, but I was even lying to him." Cassidy took a deep breath and placed his hands on Nate's knees. "I was screwing his VP. The guy was the father of one of my classmates."

Nate's mouth fell open slightly as he stared back at Cassidy in shock.

"I told myself that I was in love with him, in some lame attempt to justify what I was doing. But it had nothing to do with love. Deep down, I knew how much it would kill my father to know his son—someone of the Winters' caliber and breeding—was taking it up the ass. From a subordinate and one of his most trusted employees, no less." Cassidy sensed that same intense hatred crawling into his gut. "I hadn't realized how much I disliked Lionel until I finally accepted that fact."

"Jesus, Cassidy," Nate said, obviously shocked, as if seeing him for the first time.

Cassidy stood and sat next to Nate on the bed, not particularly caring for the change in Nate's demeanor. "I knew that would be the one thing that would hurt Lionel. Not because he cared about me, mind you, but the tainting of his reputation. What it would say to the world to have the fruit of his loins bent over his very own desk, begging to be fucked."

"I never knew you felt that way about your dad," Nate said. "All those summers growing up, you barely mentioned him."

"Is that so odd? Do most boys enjoy admitting that their father doesn't love them?"

"Hey." Nate held up his hands as if surrendering. "Mine was a monster, so it wasn't like I could've rubbed your nose in it. Not that I ever would've."

"Have you ever tried—"

"Nope," Nate interrupted, instantly pissed. "That sick fuck beat up on my mom—while she was pregnant with me. If I ever found him, I'd probably kill him."

Cassidy stared back down at the floor, nodding.

"I can't believe you of all people would've had sex with someone just to punish your dad." Nate appeared genuinely shocked. "It's not you."

"I went through this fucked-up *Cruel Intentions* phase during my senior year." Cassidy placed his hands on his lap to keep from fidgeting. "It made me feel powerful all on my own. Something I usually only felt when I was here with you. Not really my finest moment, I know."

"It's funny, because when I think back, I don't believe I ever truly bought that whole internship excuse. I honestly thought it was me," Nate said. "The sex had been so intense between us. I was afraid we'd pushed things too far the summer before and you just didn't want to see me."

"That summer with you freed something in me," Cassidy said. "I felt liberated. All the things I'd been hiding away deep inside for so long were loose. We broke the dam, and the subsequent flood of my sexual awakening was intoxicating. It was as if overnight I became this person that people noticed."

"People always noticed you," Nate said.

Cassidy shook his head. "Maybe so, but up until that point, I didn't fully understand what it meant—that I could use another person's desire for me to my own end."

Nate was obviously irritated when he got up off the bed. "I don't think I want to hear anymore."

"Nate, please, I've never told anyone else this stuff before."

"Maybe you should keep it that way." Nate paced back and forth now, obviously pissed off. "All this time I've had this image of the sweet guy I fell in love with who I turned my back on."

Cassidy shot up off the bed. "Well, I'm very sorry I'm not the right kind of pathetic for you."

"Don't put this off on me," Nate snapped back. "You're just pissed because I won't fuck you. You come back here, and I'm supposed to drop everything, including my pants, sprout a hard-on, and gratefully perform my duties?"

"This is insane! I'm being penalized for being attracted to you."

"Seems to me like I'm just convenient once again," Nate said, cocking an eyebrow.

"We can't keep having this same argument, Nate." Cassidy scooped his shirt up off the floor. "I'm sorry you fell so hard for me that summer. I'm sorry I've had a little too much sex in the past to be considered worthy of your apparently sainted cock." Cassidy wrestled his shirt back over his head, then pressed his hands together prayer-style, and bowed down as if worshipping Nate's dick. "Unlike you, Mr. Perfect, I'm a bit of a work in progress. My father has all the warmth of a serial killer, and my mother, for all intents and purposes, is a fembot. Christ! How long did Max keep Natalie at arm's length, for fuck's sake? And my grandmother was basically Hugh Hefner with a vagina! So it's not as if I've had a solid example of what love is supposed to look like!"

"It's supposed to look like me!" Nate screamed back. "You… asshole!"

"Oh, really! Well, next time, you might try mentioning that *before* an entire decade comes and goes!"

"Fuck you!" Nate wildly flung his arms through the air before storming out of the bedroom.

Cassidy chased after him as Nate started to stomp down the stairs.

"Yeah…well…I'd like that!" Cassidy yelled. "Since I'm nothing but a big *whore*!"

Luckily, Neil stood halfway up the staircase on the small landing, as if offering proof of Cassidy's sluttiness.

"I told you he'd do something to screw it up," Neil said smugly as Nate passed him.

Cassidy let out a squeak as Nate hauled off and punched him, knocking Neil back into the railing, where he seemed to hang momentarily before slowly sliding down onto his ass.

Cassidy jumped, catching movement out of the corner of his eye as the front door slammed shut downstairs. He turned, feeling the blood draining from his face as Ollie and two delivery guys huddled in the doorway of Sadie's bedroom.

The larger of the two pointed with his thumb. "Got your bed all set up."

Shit, fuck me now. Cassidy tried to force a smile.

"Should be, uh…good to go," the shorter, stockier one said, holding out a clipboard.

"Just sign the paper, and you can get back to all your whoring," Ollie added.

The two delivery guys nodded in agreement.

Cassidy refrained from strangling Ollie, considering there'd be witnesses. *I'm not doing time over that bitch, despite all the pleasure it would give me to choke the life out of him.* He took the clipboard, scribbled a signature, and passed it back. Ollie announced he'd show the nice men the way out, and they rushed past Cassidy as if unable to exit the premises fast enough.

They stopped to help Neil to his feet before scrambling out the door. Ollie shook his head at Neil, grabbed him by the arm, and yanked him down the steps, muttering something about getting some ice for his face.

Cassidy placed a hand over his eyes, rubbing them before walking into Sadie's bedroom. Despite the fact that her things were no longer in it, Cassidy couldn't shake the feeling that it was still her room. They'd scrubbed the entire room from floor to ceiling, but Cassidy could still make out the faint scent of jasmine that permanently clung to the plaster walls.

He went over to the bed, all set up on the modern platform with the leather headboard, and sat down. He'd forgotten he even ordered the damned thing. He covered his face with hands as he slouched over, resting his elbows on his knees. *Showed up just in the nick of time.*

That wounded Cassidy, made him feel betrayed to a certain degree. The way Nate reacted stung at his chest, which was tightening, making it difficult to breathe. He'd tried opening up, tried explaining what he was so afraid of, and found the thing he feared most staring back at him. Rejection and judgment from the one person he'd always imagined he could count on in the back of his mind, the one guy who was supposed to always be there for him. It wasn't right.

You can't pick and choose which parts of another person to love. It's all or nothing.

The giant black hole churning away inside his gut told Cassidy something he was no longer sure he wanted to hear.

"Hey there, whore," Ollie said.

Cassidy shrugged at Ollie, desperately trying to hold it together, despite feeling his eyes begin to well up. "I don't just want him for the sex. It's not fair that he accused me of that."

"I know, sweetie," Ollie said. "But try taking it a little easy on the boy. He's the only one of your exes who seems not to understand you're only able to communicate your feelings through your dick."

Cassidy started to laugh and then cringed as he rubbed his chest. He stood up and wriggled his upper body as if he'd just caught a chill. He shook his head and pushed past Ollie back out into the hall. Cassidy stopped in the middle of the second-floor landing, not sure where to go, yet feeling the distinct urge to vacate the area. He resigned himself to the fact there was nowhere to run that the feelings he was experiencing wouldn't be able to follow.

"You okay, Cass?" Ollie asked as Cassidy stumbled forward a few steps.

"Son of a bitch, I forgot I could feel like this." Cassidy placed a hand on the wall for balance. "It hurts to breathe, Ollie."

"You've kept everything bottled up for so long, it's a miracle you're able to function at all."

Cassidy continued to rub his chest and groaned at Ollie pleadingly. "I don't like it. Make it stop."

"It's just love, sweetie. It won't kill you. I promise."

"Love *totally* sucks ass!"

Ollie shrugged nonchalantly. "Perhaps I'm wrong. Maybe you're having a heart attack."

Cassidy glanced back up, hopeful. "You think?"

Ollie shook his head. "You're one sick bitch."

"I *know*," Cassidy said, smacking himself upside the head as he spun around and fell back against the wall. "I can't help myself, damn it." He sighed and slowly slid down until he was sitting on the floor, legs jutting out and hands lying limp and lifeless at his sides. "Tell me what to do?"

Ollie sat on the floor and placed his arm around Cassidy's shoulders. "I can't, babe. This is all on you."

"Damn it!" Cassidy chewed his lip for a moment. "Then go find Spencer and tell him to tell me what to do."

Ollie laughed as little Dasie came hopping up the steps, taking one at a time. Her nails clicked across the hardwoods as she scampered over to Cassidy. She gave his hand a lick before hopping onto his lap and curling up into a little ball, snuggling in.

Cassidy lightly massaged the scruff of her neck, she let out a tiny sigh, and the two men snickered.

"If only life were that simple." Cassidy smirked before resting his head on Ollie's shoulder.

"If only," Ollie said, squeezing Cassidy. "I doubt it helps, but I like you much better this way."

"Miserable and confused?"

Ollie laughed, despite being a bit more serious. "Human and fallible, as opposed to some shiny white beacon of strength and determination."

"But I really like being white 'n' shiny."

"Do you really?" Ollie asked. "Or have you just become so accustomed to needing to be that guy—all hard and full of determination—that you've forgotten there's any other way to be?"

Cassidy moaned, not sure how to answer the question. "I really hate you sometimes, but thanks for love-hating me. You're a good friend, Ollie—mostly."

"Stop with the excessive praise before I swoon." Ollie laughed, ruffling Cassidy's hair a little as they settled into each other. "I really do want you to be happy, which is why I call you on all your shit."

"I know that," Cassidy said. "But you do appear to enjoy it an awful lot."

"It's my free gift with purchase." Ollie winked. "Don't begrudge a bitch for taking pleasure from it."

Cassidy grinned when Ollie squeezed him again. "I'm scared, Ollie."

"I know," he said, patting Cassidy's head.

"I think he might be the only guy I can totally be myself with." Cassidy chewed on his lip and finally looked over at Ollie when he neglected to comment. "Tell me it'll all be okay?"

Ollie sighed. "But it—"

Cassidy frowned, cutting him off. "Just lie, damn it."

"Oh, in that case." Ollie cleared his throat. "Everything's going to work out, and you'll be happier than you ever knew possible."

It was quiet for a moment with only the random noise from downstairs and muffled voices coming from somewhere outside.

"Wow," Cassidy said, lifting his head to see Ollie was trying not to laugh. "You totally blew that line."

"Really badly," Ollie agreed.

"Pathetic." Cassidy placed his head back on Ollie's shoulder.

§ § §

Cassidy lay on the new bed in Sadie's room, trying to fall asleep as Dasie sniffed around the mattress. It was dark outside, and the chain from the ceiling fan above his head clanked as the blades furiously spun in an attempt to cool off the room. He wasn't sure if it was the outside temperature or merely his stressed-out, overly angst-ridden body, but Cassidy was hot, unable to handle having more than a sheet for a cover. It was finally quiet outside, and the house was in a state of silent bliss.

Dasie continued to roam, lying down for a few minutes before getting up again and checking out the other side of the bed, as if to tell Cassidy they'd forgotten something.

"I'm sorry, baby girl." Cassidy reached out, wiggling his fingers, tempting her over to his hand. "It's just you and me again. He's not going to be joining us."

She went about giving the palm of his hand a tongue bath while he scratched behind her ear with his other. He'd heard Nate come back home about an hour ago. It was a guess, since there wasn't a clock in the room anymore and he'd been too lazy to reach down and pick up his phone off the floor to check the time. But it had to have been around ten thirty, as he hadn't been in bed for very long when he heard Nate's truck pulling in the drive.

Once again, the son of a bitch had pulled an all-day disappearance, something Cassidy was quickly discovering to be particularly frustrating. *How the fuck are you supposed to work shit out if the other person pulls a vanishing act?* His eyes burned from lack of sleep; he just needed to shut down his mind, which had been on a nonstop Indy 500-style loop of their stupid argument that afternoon. He was absolutely exhausted and resentful of the gnawing in the pit of his stomach from the knowledge that Nate was pissed at him.

Finally, Dasie settled for a spot near his feet, letting out a tiny sigh as she curled up in a ball. Cassidy smiled, thankful the runt had decided to wander into his yard that morning, even if she had made him faint. Each time Dasie produced one of her sweet little sighs, she reminded him that none of this crap was the end of his world.

Cassidy rolled onto his back and lifted his head, hearing the doorknob squeak as it turned. He laid his head back down on the pillow and watched as the door was carefully opened and closed. Nate tried shushing Dasie after she sprang up, frantically running in circles at the foot of the bed. Cassidy wanted to judge her for being so obviously happy to see the prick, but he couldn't quite manage it, considering his stomach was doing flip-flops, fluttering full of butterflies.

"Shit, I woke you, didn't I?" Nate whispered.

"No," Cassidy said, watching him hover at the edge of the bed, petting the dog. "I'm regrettably too upset to fall the fuck asleep. I hate feeling like you're mad at me, and I hate myself for being the kind of guy who can't sleep because you're mad at me."

"I'm really sorry, Cass," Nate said, crawling onto the mattress. He flopped down next to him. "You just said some things that took me by surprise. I guess I've had all these memories of you and me—ideas in my head of this romanticized version of who you are. Apparently I don't do so well when my imaginary world is contradicted."

Cassidy sighed, reaching up and rubbing his tired eyes. "I can't pretend to be something I'm not."

"I know that, and I'm sorry I took my own crap out on you. That wasn't fair." Nate sighed. "That's all I wanted to say. I didn't come in here to start a fight or get you all worked up again."

"Did you come in here to blow me?" Cassidy asked in a flirty tone.

"No," Nate said, laughing under his breath.

"Then blow me," Cassidy said, in a faux-huffy tone as he rolled over to his side.

"Asshole." Nate smacked him on the back as he got up off the bed.

Cassidy watched as he gave Dasie some loving. "Where you going?"

Nate pointed toward the door. "Back to my room, I guess."

"Well, get back in bed," Cassidy said, not wanting him to go but doing his best to play it all nonchalant. "The least you could do after being such a prick is not making me sleep in here all by myself."

Nate hemmed and hawed for a moment.

"And the dog can't settle into one spot. She keeps getting up and sniffing your side of the bed." Cassidy refused to look at Dasie, for fear she'd be staring back at him all judgey for using her in such a pathetic attempt to guilt the man into staying.

Cassidy grinned as Nate got back in the bed. The sheet ruffled about as cool air rushed down his backside. Nate rearranged some pillows, punching them. Cassidy lifted his arm so Nate could slide his through, backing into Nate's body as he pulled Cassidy toward him. They settled into each other, and Cassidy was beginning to relax for the first time all day. He'd barely seen the fucker in days, and when he finally did, they wound up in a screaming match.

Nate cleared his throat. "Are you naked?"

"Well, I wasn't exactly expecting company when I got into bed."

Nate took in a deep breath and held it before exhaling. "Okay."

Cassidy smiled as he wiggled back, trying to get closer. Nate pulled him tighter. "Don't worry; I'm too damn tired to attempt tempting you. You're quite safe."

Nate let out a low rumble of a laugh. "That's good to know. Not sure I can say the same for you, though."

"Don't tease the animals, you shit."

Nate squeezed him again, kissing the back of his neck. "Sorry, beautiful."

Cassidy shimmied onto his back and stared into Nate's shadowy face, able to make out a glint in his eyes from the diffused light in the room. Cassidy gave him a soft peck on the lips. "Thanks for staying." Cassidy went back on his side and settled into Nate's body once again. Their breathing began to slow and regulate, each falling into sync with the other. Cassidy could feel that haziness filtering into his brain, right before he drifted off to sleep, feeling content.

Chapter Twenty

Cassidy hung his tux on the hook protruding from the back of the closet door. The small walk-in closet was huge now that Sadie's forty years' worth of clothes had been removed. Cassidy had hung up a few of the things he'd brought with him that actually required a hanger. Being able to dress down had always been one of the things he'd enjoyed about island life as a child. No more neckties or blazers emblazoned with private-school crests; summers on Hart's meant loose-fitting cargos and strolling shirtless on the beach with sand between his toes.

He should have been getting dressed for the party instead of standing in the middle of the room wearing black socks and gym shorts. He could hear the musicians warming up their instruments, the clinking of glassware, and the yelling of the caterer, who'd been less than happy about the last-minute change of venue. The temperature was a little cooler today, and he was very much enjoying slumming it. Everything was more relaxed here; it was a low-key and less pretentious way of living. The tuxedo was a little out of place, despite the fact he was excited to wear it.

Thus far, the entire day had gone off without a hitch, beginning with the tiny parade that kicked off the traditional Founders' Day ceremony, including the usual impassioned speech delivered by Henry Abbott. The carnival had been much larger than Cassidy remembered, stretching from the town square all the way down to the harbor. Jacob Pringle seemed particularly proud, as ringmaster and organizer extraordinaire. Cassidy was inclined to agree with him.

Teddy in particular had a really great time. All day long he had practically bounced around like an excited kid, all bug-eyed and pointy. Cassidy had tried to tell him that this was one day, that the island, while having several festivals throughout the year, wasn't normally this exciting. But it landed on deaf ears. It had become painfully clear Teddy had fallen in love with Hart's. Cassidy was happy to see that Hart's was falling for Teddy as well. He wasn't sure how much Ben had to do with Teddy's enthusiasm, but it was obvious he was a contributing factor.

Ollie and Spencer had been equally impressed, though not quite as exuberant in expressing it. They'd been at their best with one another throughout the day's events. Each of them relaxed, laughing and flirting with one another. They were like a live-action commercial for Match.com, rife with opportunity for movie-montage-worthy photo ops. It had been about midafternoon before Cassidy realized that Ollie hadn't uttered a single catty remark. He wasn't positive, but he was fairly certain it was a new record for him.

He and Nate, while avoiding any serious subject matter, had slipped back into an ease with each other evocative of the history they shared. It was like old times to Cassidy, who was nearly intoxicated by the nostalgia of it all. Neil's presence was very much an open wound on the day, which everyone tried to ignore. Cassidy refused to cut the guy off, though, as it conflicted with his harmonious nature. It just wasn't in him to do, and the poor guy hadn't really done anything other than make the mistake of having sex with Cassidy. In addition, he didn't have any other friends on the island.

Cassidy continued to be racked with thoughts of sex and lust, while fearing the unknown of what would be were he and Nate to consummate again—and again and again. That was the one thing Cassidy knew for certain. If he and Nate started anything, it would burn so hot it might not even matter whether they wound up staying together. They'd likely neither one survive the explosion. Of course, the feasibility of this scenario was beginning to feel less likely to Cassidy. A weird cloudy funk settled over him, refusing to budge and leaving an ominous trace of energy behind. It made him feel like things that only days before had felt probable were no longer possible.

After hearing a grunting noise coming from the stairwell, he ventured out to the landing. Natalie was attempting to hoist a huge-ass potted fern up by herself.

"What the hell are you doing?" Cassidy asked as he quickly hopped down to relieve her of her armload.

"I want this to sit up here in the hall," she said, gasping for air.

Cassidy carried it up the remaining steps, seeing the wooden plant stand in the corner. "Why is it going up here?"

"This hallway needs some life. It's too drab." Natalie pointed as if ordering him to stop asking questions and do as she asked already. "That Cecelia all but ruined the entire party with her Castro-like need for autonomous control. I had to sneak back over early and rearrange the entire layout."

"Oh, Natalie, I'm sure it's all spectacular out there." Cassidy placed the fern on the plant stand.

"Now!" she made sure to remind him. "I've fixed it all. It was near disaster."

Cassidy wondered how long it would take for him to murder the poor plant. He glanced around at the windowless square that made up the large landing, and decided it wouldn't be long.

"Don't worry; it's not going to stay. It's just for the party," Natalie said.

You've been given a reprieve, Cassidy thought as he reached over and brushed his hand over the leaves. "Surely there won't be anyone straggling up here?"

Natalie shrugged. "It's doubtful, but either way it feels more homey."

The bathroom door swung open, and Ollie and Spencer came stumbling out clad in nothing but matching towels and smiles. They straightened up seeing Natalie, politely crossing in front of her and Cassidy on their way to their bedroom.

"Boys," Natalie said, cocking an eyebrow at them.

"Hi, Mrs. Sommers," Spencer said.

Ollie pointed at the fern. "That looks lovely there."

They scampered into the guest room that used to be Natalie's bedroom, and shut the door behind them.

Natalie shook her head, appearing somewhat jealous. "I bet that bedroom's seen more action in the past week that it did the entire thirty-odd years that I lived in it."

Cassidy's mouth fell open as he slowly turned to look at her.

"What?" she asked, all innocent.

Cassidy laughed nervously as he headed back into Sadie's bedroom. "I think you're channeling Sadie, and please don't ever use the word *action* like that again."

Natalie followed Cassidy into the bedroom. "You gay boys are all so squeamish whenever it comes to the lady parts."

Cassidy began to feel like his brain was hemorrhaging as he placed his fingers into his ears. "Ya-ya, la-la!" He was wondering when Natalie had become such an expert on homos, then decided he might not want to know after all.

Natalie giggled in delight as Cassidy shot her a dirty look. She flopped down on the bed, and Cassidy wondered how the hell he was supposed to get his pants on with her in the room.

"Oh goodness me, it's not like I've never seen you in your undies before." Natalie shooed at him with a hand. "Just go in the closet."

Cassidy rolled his eyes as he strolled into the closet. He pulled the door to before removing his shorts and slipping on his pants. He slipped his shirt off the hanger and pushed the door open with his foot as he slid it on.

"Are you boys going to be able to work things out?" Natalie asked.

Cassidy shrugged. "Maybe there's nothing to work out."

Natalie made no attempt to hide her disappointment with his attitude.

"Don't look at me like that." Cassidy frowned back at her. "He's your son! Why am I the only one in trouble?"

"Because, Lord help us all"—Natalie stared up at the ceiling as if saying a quick prayer—"between the two of you, you're better at getting things out into the open."

"Well, how the hell am I supposed to do that?" Cassidy shook the stress out of his hands before making an attempt at putting on his bow tie. "He storms out of the room midargument before we ever have the chance to get anything settled."

"You know why he does that, don't you?" Natalie asked, walking over and pushing his hands away so she could get at the tie.

"Because he doesn't like whatever it is he's hearing."

"It's more than that, Cassidy. He's always worried that there's a tiny piece of his father hiding deep down inside." Natalie sighed as she fussed with the tie, getting it just the way she wanted it.

"That's just crazy. Nate would never intentionally hurt anyone."

"You and I know that, but when he feels himself getting too angry, I think he runs for fear of losing control. I really hate that. He's never even met the man, and the bastard is still messing with my boy's head. It makes me so mad I could spit."

Cassidy smiled. "That's the Sadie in you."

"She made everyone a little stronger than they probably would've been otherwise."

Cassidy thanked her as he checked out her handiwork in the mirror. He glanced down at the floor for a moment, shoving his hands in his pockets. "But what if I'm not the long-haul kind of a guy? I mean, regardless of whether or not I love him…what if I'm not *for keeps*? I'll wind up losing him for good."

"I think you'll lose him anyway, my dear. He loves you too deeply, not that he'd ever admit it. I swear, you boys are so silly and pigheaded." Natalie walked over and sat down on the bed. "There's no magical combination that will guarantee a happily ever after, you know. You have to want it, work for it, and then nourish and cherish it once you get it."

Cassidy nodded as he chewed on everything she'd just said.

He slipped on his shoes, before bending over and tying each one. He wanted to believe what he was hearing, but thought it sounded too good to be true.

"All I'm asking is that you talk to him," Natalie said, picking a piece of lint off her dress. "Once the party is over, and after you're done spreading Sadie's ashes at the lighthouse, sit my boy down and talk things over…*please*."

"I'll try, Natalie," Cassidy said, taking his tuxedo jacket off the hanger. "I don't know that it's gonna do any good, but I'll try."

Natalie beamed, clapping her hands. "That's all I can ask."

"Why the hell couldn't I have gotten a mother like you?"

"Don't be so hard on Lillian. She did what she thought was best for you. Lionel never wanted you to come here at all, you know. It was Lillian who insisted."

"Why does that not surprise me? He's a fucking sociopath."

"You're quite right, dear, but language."

"Sorry." Cassidy tried to hold back a grin, amused at being chastised by Natalie.

"I think your mother was very aware of her limitations. She sent you here because she wasn't capable of providing the home environment Sadie could. Lillian knew it was important for you to have that. From what Sadie told me, Lillian never was the motherly type, yet she wouldn't let Lionel send you off to boarding school. I think she did the best she was capable of doing for you, and made sure that there was someone like Sadie to pick up the slack."

"That's a nice fairy tale, Natalie, and as much as it warms me to think she loved me—in her own way—I would've preferred she actually loved me the way mothers are meant to."

Natalie held out her hand, and she pulled Cassidy down, sitting him next to her. "You'll always have me for that."

Cassidy nodded, hugging her and thinking how she might be the last bit of unconditional warmth left in his life. He wondered why he'd allowed all that time to pass, depriving himself of her company. As she squeezed him, Natalie let out a little grunt, and Cassidy promised he'd never again exile himself. From this point forward, he'd cherish it, protect it with as much determination as he had his relationship with Sadie, but this time around, nothing was going to keep him at bay.

§ § §

Cassidy walked out the back door of the house, smiling from ear to ear. It was lovely, he thought. Like something out of a movie. The entire courtyard and even the beach below glowed from the hazy light of the white paper lanterns, elegant torches, and the gazillion white Christmas lights. There were huge ornate chandeliers with white pillar candles hanging from the center of each tent. Tone-on-tone white floral arrangements on the tables, mixed with thick, glossy green leaves and sprigs of jasmine, scented the air. And the large potted palm trees added an exotic *Casablanca*-like atmosphere.

Cassidy hadn't even realized he'd stumbled out into the middle of the courtyard until Nate took him by the arm. His heart stopped beating as he stared at Nate. Cassidy was completely dumbfounded and near-drooling. Nate wore that same white-jacket variation of black-tie dress that he'd fought so vehemently to avoid all those years ago. He was even more the picture of swagger and knee-weakening manly goodness at age thirty. Cassidy discovered it required a man to fully pull off the look.

Nate grinned, exhibiting even more brashness than usual seeing the way Cassidy ogled him. "I remember you mentioning you liked this tux on me."

This man is the devil. Cassidy swallowed, feeling very dry in the mouth. "And you just couldn't resist torturing me with it again, I see."

"Something I learned from Sadie." Nate cocked an eyebrow, killing Cassidy a little more with a cockiness that, while warranted, was somewhat punishing to the nerves. "Give them time to catch their breath, and you've lost them."

He smiled, feeling very much like he couldn't get his wind

back. Deciding on distraction as the most sensible and ego-preserving retreat, he went back to surveying the terrain. He was amazed that so many people had given up their time to make this all happen, and he felt instantly rotten for not having done a lick of the work. Nate and a few of the other guys from town, including Nate's best friend from high school, Jimmy Dobbs, had come over and helped finish painting the trim, something Spencer for one was quite pleased to discover.

"It's beautiful, Nate." Cassidy spun around in a circle as the orchestra began to play and the first few partygoers rounded the corner of the house. "Thank you, everyone!"

He'd screamed it way too loud, but he didn't give a damn. He was moved beyond words. He hadn't seen many of them in years, yet they all still came to his aid, and it was like…magic. *This is all for you, Sadie.*

"It's the most beautiful thing I've ever seen." Cassidy glanced around at all the folks standing about who'd helped over the past two days. "You've really outdone yourselves. Sadie would truly be honored. As for myself, I'm not sure I'll ever be able to properly thank you for all your help."

Nate grabbed him up in a hug, and once they separated, Natalie led Max over. Cassidy shook Max's hand, a little surprised when the man yanked him into a big bear hug. Max had always been a friendly sort but never offered much in the way of physical affection. He was frostier on top, his dark hair now peppered with gray and looked rather dapper in his tux. But he still had those bushy eyebrows, like fuzzy caterpillars, that used to mesmerize Cassidy as a child.

"You look fine, son," Max offered with a nod.

"I'm feeling pretty damn fine too." Cassidy shook his head, taking in all the sights and sounds. "Thank you for helping with all this, Max. I'm so grateful to—"

"Nonsense, son. We're family." Max interrupted, nudging his head toward Natalie. "Besides that, the drill sergeant here would be after me if I didn't help out."

Cassidy and Nate both laughed as irritation swept over Natalie's face. She muttered something as she reached over and pinched him in the arm. Max always loved teasing her, and he made a much bigger deal of it, hopping around as he rubbed his arm like it might fall off. She shook her head at him before walking away in a huff.

Max wiggled those caterpillar eyebrows. "Guess I better go make up and get myself a little smoochie."

Nate groaned as Cassidy yanked on his arm, insisting Nate take him around to each and every person who had given their time, so he could personally thank them. Cassidy was very happy to meet the lovely Mrs. Dobbs, who was young, pretty, and blonde. Jimmy had a Johnny Knoxville-type thing going on—even dressed up he appeared slightly disheveled. He knew it was ludicrous since Jimmy was and always had been straight as a pin, but Cassidy had long harbored a minute amount of jealousy over him. Jimmy had been a sight to behold in his baseball uniform. Well. Cassidy hadn't thought he was all that great, but he always noticed that Nate seemed to.

"Holy shit!" she squealed while incessantly clapping her hands. "I'm soooo excited to meet you!"

Cassidy chuckled under his breath and marveled at how quickly words spilled from her mouth, contradicting the cool blonde exterior that would have made her perfect for the lead in an Alfred Hitchcock film.

She placed a hand on Cassidy's stomach. "I am Mrs. Dobbs," she said, rolling her eyes, "or Virgie, duh! I teach first grade, so I forget I'm talking to adults sometimes."

"Hello—"

"It's short for Virginia—I was named after my gran!"

She fanned her face, taking a breath, and Cassidy wondered if it was safe to once again attempt some sort of response.

"Well, it's—"

She gasped, placing her hand over her chest, cutting Cassidy off once again. "I'm genuinely touched at the way the entire island has rallied around you like this. It's so damn sweet, it makes my heart hurt."

Cassidy looked at Nate, who was biting his lip, obviously enjoying the fact Cassidy couldn't get a word in edgewise, while pretending to listen to Jimmy by nodding his head at regular intervals.

Cassidy patted her hand, which was still on his stomach, and she ripped it away, turning bright red as she threw her head back and laughed.

She pointed at herself. "So embarrassed. Didn't intend to fondle you!" More laughing as she took to fanning herself again.

"Not a prob—"

"Thanks for understanding," she cut in. "I'm just so delighted to meet you, as there are no *fun* gays on this island—at least none that I've found thus far." She wiggled her eyebrows as if to insinuate something. "I desperately miss my gays back in Cali!"

"She had a lot of gays in Cali," Jimmy tossed out, as if no one would believe her otherwise.

Cassidy assumed *Cali* stood for California, as she finally took a breath to grab a shot, clink glasses with her hubby, and swallow it down in one gulp. She slammed it on the bar and pointed tauntingly at her husband for beating him.

She turned her attention back to Cassidy. "Nate, as you well know, is gay, but he's the yucky boring kind—way too much like my husband, and let's face it, I didn't marry the man for his conversational skills and good shopping sense." Virgie leaned over, running her hand up Jimmy's inner thigh as if Cassidy might need the clarification.

Cassidy found himself amused by her as she continued for another five minutes like a rambling freight train. He liked her instantly, though he feared he might not be able to handle her in long intervals. *She sure as fuck isn't dull.* Nate eventually pulled Cassidy away, informing him that while Virgie was always chatty, that was somewhat of an extreme.

Cassidy wondered if perhaps she'd been holding out, waiting for the first random *fun gay* to come along, so she could purge herself like a newly unclogged drain. As Nate pulled him away so they could thank everyone else, he pondered what qualities might constitute being a fun gay. He wondered if he actually was one, while secretly realizing she was probably hoping for someone like Ollie. He glanced back to the bar, watching her suck face with Jimmy, and knew exactly why he'd married her. He was beginning to get a little jealous, wishing he were somewhere sucking face like that with Nate when a light breeze brushed across his cheek. He caught a whiff of the jasmine, and he thought of Sadie.

You'd love this, lady.

The jasmine made him feel like she might come walking around the corner at any moment. And he loved that they'd placed Sadie on one end of the bar next to a full martini glass completely surrounded by flowers.

Nate was obviously irritated when Neil showed up at Cassidy's side with a martini. Neil became equally miffed when Nate took the second martini out of Neil's hand without offering so much as a thank-you. Cassidy suspected it wasn't really meant for Nate when Neil frowned, turning to head back to the bar. He prayed they wouldn't come to blows during the middle of the party, despite realizing how much Sadie would have approved of such a thing.

You always did love a good fight.

"I think she'd approve, yes?" Edie asked as she and Jacob Pringle strolled over.

Cassidy nodded his agreement. "I believe Sadie would have been as speechless as I was, when I walked out and saw it all pulled together. It's truly elegant. Thank you both for everything."

"When Henry comes along, attempting to use this to guilt you into staying—" Jacob glanced around as if suspecting Henry might overhear. "Well, I just want you to know we didn't all have ulterior motives."

Of course Henry would do that, the louse. "Thanks for that, Jacob.

I'll never forget your kindness."

Edie rolled her eyes dramatically, hearing Marianne Abbott's ludicrously loud laughter rolling over the crowd, which had quadrupled over the last thirty minutes. "That woman!"

Cassidy laughed, seeing Jacob cringe over the social faux pas hanging on his arm. "Edie, dear, let's not allow things to get ugly."

"At least not quite so early," Nate interjected, coming back up behind Cassidy with a martini refill.

Cassidy smiled, happy at least that the Neil/Nate rivalry had been keeping his glass from becoming empty. "Thanks, Nate, but you don't have to keep—"

"Yes, I do," Nate interrupted, his expression letting Cassidy know that he didn't appreciate being forced into a competition.

Cassidy took the glass and shrugged, refusing to feel guilty over something he hadn't encouraged in either of them. *That's right, folks. Boys are dumb.*

"Cassidy! Sweetheart!" Marianne called from behind him.

Edie muttered something under her breath that Cassidy desperately wished he'd been able hear.

"Have a lovely evening, dear," Edie said, yanking Jacob away with her.

"Are they dating?" Cassidy asked Nate as Edie pulled Jacob off into the crowd.

"I honest to God have no idea," Nate whispered. "But the entire island's buzzing to find out."

I bet they are. "Marianne!" Cassidy said, turning to face her. *With any luck it'll take some of the attention off me.*

"I swear, you are even more handsome, you sly devil!"

If any one individual should've ever come equipped with volume control, it was Marianne. She had one level, and it was loud. She was the world's biggest, as Sadie used to say. Any adjective you could think of to describe Marianne could almost always be preceded by *the world's biggest*, as she didn't do anything in a small way—the world's biggest gossip or the world's biggest flirt.

"Well, not half as fabulous as you, beautiful."

Her hair had been bleached nearly white. She was full figured and knew how to use it. She came off sweet as syrup, and for the most part, she was. But everyone knew to avoid being on her shit list, if possible, because she'd annoy the fuck out of you. She was the type to continue beating the dead horse till it was nothing but dust, and it made life simpler to avoid the drama.

"Can you believe Edie Taylor and Jacob Pringle are doing the nasty?" Marianne shook her head, making that tsk-tsk sound with her tongue. "Viva Viagra!"

Cassidy did his best not to laugh, while Nate just let loose. "Marianne, you are wicked." Cassidy smacked Nate.

"I can't help it, darling. I keep having this nightmare." She paused for dramatic flair. "It's like *Night of Living Dead* meets *Cocoon*." She pursed her lips up at Cassidy before doing the same to Nate. "Such a pity."

With that, she turned and headed over toward the next group of people, singling out someone else and squealing their name. *All she's lacking is the fake microphone and some ABBA to lip-synch to.* Cassidy couldn't believe the biggest drag queen he'd ever met in his thirty years had been born with an actual vagina.

"Is it just me, or is she a live-action, Technicolor dream sequence filmed in Cinemascope?" Ollie asked, sneaking up behind Cassidy.

"It's not just you." Nate exchanged his empty martini for a glass of champagne as a server passed by with a tray.

Ollie sighed, eyes widening in relief. "Thank goodness. I thought I was hallucinating, and it's a little early to be cutting myself off."

With that, Cassidy finished off the last of his martini. The orchestra began playing the old standard from the late forties "Again." Cassidy had always loved it, as it had been one of Sadie's favorites, and she'd break into the lyrics at a moment's notice. He surveyed the empty dance floor installed on the east lawn under the largest of the three tents next to the band. He was half tempted to ask Nate to dance but thought better of it, as he'd made spectacle enough of himself.

In many ways, he was like Sadie, not really caring what other people thought of him. Unlike her, though, he didn't necessarily go out of his way to garner attention. And considering his antics over the past week and a half, all Cassidy wanted of this evening was to fly under the radar—way, way under the radar.

As if the fulfilling of a prophecy, Henry Abbott did descend on Cassidy, making good on Jacob's threat of jabbing at him with guilt worthy of a devout Catholic mother. He took it all in stride, smiling like the wife of a politician and trying not to be distracted by the fact Nate had hooked a finger into the right pocket of his pants. It was such an odd, minute act—almost possessive, yet it stung at Cassidy's chest, making him feel like he belonged with Nate.

He didn't think he'd have the strength to hold out much longer, giving in to whatever demands Nate might make on him just so they could be together. Cassidy didn't relish coming to that realization, but at the same time another part of him was already making the necessary excuses, ready to provide any justifications that may be required to secure a successful follow-through. Cassidy was hooked and he knew it. He didn't know what the final push might be, enabling him to freely fall into Nate's arms, but he hoped it would come soon. Something held him back. He just couldn't figure out what.

Nate continued to lead Cassidy through the crowd, shaking hands and welcoming all his guests back to the Point. It felt as if everyone on the island was there, and as happy as he was to see them all, Cassidy missed the friendly faces of his friends. He'd barely spoken to Ollie and Spencer, and he'd seen only the backs of Teddy and Ben as they went down to the beach. Nate and Neil continued to annoy each other, which was starting to annoy Cassidy, but he was aware that Natalie had been making an effort to always be within earshot, as if knowing he might become overwhelmed at some point and need her to help him make a quick exit.

He was standing with a group of people, making small talk while Nate excused himself to run to the bar. Cassidy decided he had to be hallucinating, having stopped midsentence, and slowly made his way around the mob of people that had closed in on him. He slowly but assuredly moved around his guests, making a beeline for his parents, who stood just off the courtyard area at the corner of the house. He was impressed by the set of balls his father had, showing up at all, let alone managing to pull off the air of stoic entitlement that oozed off the man who'd acted as though the world were meant to bow at his evil feet.

Lionel with his airs was enough to have Cassidy seeing red. That distinguished salt-and-pepper hair and the enticingly unassuming way in which he carefully examined his enemy—so relaxed, almost charming, putting them at ease just before cutting their legs out from under them. And his mother, Lillian, hanging off Lionel's arm like an expensive accessory. She was flawless, with her black hair and olive skin, perfectly made up—almost doll-like. Unlike Lionel, however, Lillian wasn't able to or simply didn't care to mask the cool nature with which she viewed the world. Cassidy respected her for that. For some reason, being a bitch and owning it was less of an offense to him.

Cassidy hadn't been aware that the entire party had come to a standstill until Sheriff Larson took him by the arm, stopping him in his tracks.

"Take it easy, Cass," he said, with that stern we-don't-want-any-trouble expression all cops somehow managed to patent.

He wondered briefly if there was a class they all had to take while at the police academy—Intimidation 101? Cassidy plastered on a smile, glaring past the sheriff at his parents as he managed to pry Jake's hand off his arm. "Butt out, Sheriff."

Jake sighed and stepped aside, allowing Cassidy to pass as people began to move to one side or another, as if parting the Red Sea to allow him access to Lionel.

"What the hell do you think you're doing here?" Cassidy said, stopping just in front of Lionel.

"It would seem there's been some sort of gross negligence in that the announcement of my mother's wake has been misplaced."

"It was no oversight, you—"

"Who do you think you are?" Lionel interrupted, staring down his nose at Cassidy with an air of self-importance. "I have more of a right to be here than you ever could."

"Not according to the judge, asshole." Cassidy smiled tauntingly as he folded his arms.

"Cassidy, please, darling," his mother said, smiling flatly at the faces standing behind him. "You're making a scene."

"Amazing. It's amazing to me that despite everything you know about this man"—Cassidy looked Lionel up and down with complete contempt—"you *still* stand by him. I suppose money can buy obedience after all." Despite feeling it was true, he wished he hadn't said it, noticing the stung expression that washed over her face before magically vanishing again as the mask of indifference returned. "But allow me to be perfectly clear by informing you that the only thing in poor taste here is his presence. Please leave at once."

Lionel laughed slightly. "You actually believe you can keep me away from my own mother's—"

"Don't give me that shit." Cassidy laughed back, mocking, the way Lionel had just done it. "Like anyone believes you actually give a damn."

"You seem to have lost yourself, Son." Lionel visibly stiffened as if his patience had worn thin. "I am your father, and you will treat me accordingly."

Cassidy stood completely straight, making sure he conveyed once and for all through his body language that he wasn't going to be backing down from this fight any more than he had when it had come to ensuring Sadie's final wishes were honored.

"Eight years ago, you were arguably a father to me." Cassidy took a step forward, standing close enough to feel Lionel's breath on his face. "Today, you're just some *prick* who had my grandmother locked up."

Cassidy heard a slight gasp come from somewhere behind him along with the quick rustle of fabric and a few whispers before it went quiet once again. He could tell Lionel was seething underneath the surface. That he'd like nothing better than to backhand Cassidy for having had the impudence to speak to him in such a manner. Cassidy smiled, letting Lionel know he knew the man's every thought, practically daring him to go ahead and try it.

Lionel began to turn slowly, that coldness in eyes. "You'll regret this, Cassidy."

"A threat—how original." Cassidy took Lillian by the arm as she too began to turn away. He gave her a brief hug and quick peck on the cheek. "Good-bye, Mother. *You're* welcome here anytime."

As their eyes met for that brief flicker in time, Cassidy knew she understood that there was an alternative out there, if she ever decided to take it. Realistically, he knew his mother could hold her own, should she ever decide to leave Lionel. He just needed to make sure she understood she wouldn't be alone if it ever came down to it.

After they disappeared back around the side of the house, Cassidy turned, and a few people began to clap. The applause grew as it bled through the crowd, growing more vigorous. Hearing the yelping and whistling, Cassidy grinned, knowing Lionel likely hadn't made it to his limo just yet. He didn't believe it would actually affect the man other than possibly the embarrassment. But perhaps if nothing else, it would twist the verbal knife Cassidy had just plunged into his chest.

Henry Abbott slapped him on the back. "I think you just might turn out okay, after all, son." He let out a huge belly laugh as he and Jacob Pringle headed toward the bar.

Cassidy murmured a thank-you. His shoulder stung where Henry had slapped him, snapping him back into reality. He noticed Ollie and Nate heading his direction as Natalie scooted in, taking him by the arm.

"Are you okay?" She whispered the inquiry.

Cassidy nodded, despite feeling a growing sense of body backlash creeping up from his feet. He was startled by how angry he'd actually been.

"Good." Natalie glanced down. "You may want to unclench your fists, then."

Cassidy forced open his fingers, rubbing his palms over his hips. That feeling slowly continued up over his shins, creeping toward his knees.

"You might be a teensy bit pale," Natalie said, using her eyes to signal toward the back of the house.

Cassidy forced on a smile. "Perhaps I should take a minute or two?"

"Lovely idea, dear. Truly inspired."

Cassidy turned, realizing he must have appeared slightly mechanical in his movements as he briskly headed to the house. The feeling of darkness had made it all the way to his stomach, and the dread growing there as his body's reaction to all the rage threatened to take him over.

Chapter Twenty-one

Cassidy stopped once he reached the upstairs landing. He needed to be alone, even if only for a moment, so he could get his head back on straight. He tried to make himself breathe regularly and stifle the sense of panic that gurgled up inside of him.

It had taken every ounce of control he could muster to keep from connecting fist to face during the entire altercation with Lionel. The images that had been flashing through his mind had been shockingly exhilarating as well as the stuff of nightmares. He'd never been a violent person, and the strong desire he'd felt—hell, could still feel—to pummel Lionel's face into a bloody mess was foreign to him.

Cassidy didn't like feeling out of control, and he stared at his hands, wide-eyed, as he held them out in front of his face. They shook uncontrollably. Worse yet was the fact that it was now bleeding up from his fingertips into his arms and slowly over his shoulders, as if the shaking might take over his entire body. He was becoming genuinely freaked-out when he heard the creak of the stairs.

Nate quietly stepped into the shadows, taking Cassidy's hands in his. He pressed his lips against Cassidy's knuckles, exhaling a long, warm breath of air over them before pressing his cheek into them. Cassidy was a bit taken aback by the gesture, but more than a little relieved, as it calmed him.

"Nate, I—"

"Shhh," Nate interrupted.

Cassidy gasped when Nate's fingers brushed across his cheek and into his hair. Cassidy leaned into the touch, and Nate placed his forehead against Cassidy's. He guided Cassidy's hands down, pressing them to his chest. Cassidy could feel Nate's heart beating, his whispered breath across his face.

Without thinking on it too long, Cassidy cocked his head

slightly and kissed Nate, whose lips were warm and so soft. He immediately opened for Cassidy's tongue. Nate tasted like vodka and olives, and Cassidy's cock went hard when Nate reciprocated by kissing him back.

Within seconds, a heated urgency came over them as their kiss deepened. Cassidy imagined himself like an addict, falling off the wagon after a long sobriety. Hands fumbled as they clumsily groped at each other. It was like the earth spun under his feet. When his back made contact with one of the closed bedroom doors, he realized it wasn't the earth moving after all. Nate ground into Cassidy's erection, groaning as he pulled on Cassidy's lip with his teeth.

Nate pinned him against the door until Cassidy pushed his body away, forcing Nate backward. They rolled along the wall, fighting for control as they continued to assault each other with their mouths. Cassidy's hip bumped into something that moved, and they separated at the loud crash.

"Shit," Cassidy whispered, attempting to catch his breath as Nate turned the overhead light on.

Dasie was barking her fool head off inside one of the closed off bedrooms. They each stared down at the shattered ceramic pot. Dirt and roots splayed across the wood floor from the plant, now lying on its side along with the wooden plant stand. Panic rose inside Cassidy, the way it did when they had been boys and he knew they'd be in trouble for roughhousing. He could tell by the expression on Nate's face that he was experiencing the same sense of dread.

Nate started to grin. "You're in trouble."

"Asshole." Cassidy shook his head as they both began laughing. "You always did blame me for everything."

Nate placed a hand over his stomach. "'Cause you *never* got into any trouble. And it still wound up being my fault for not watching you more closely."

Cassidy chewed his lip as he wondered how to segue way back into the kissing and fondling. *Damn it, Natalie, why'd you have to go and put a stupid fern there in the first place?*

"Grab a sheet out of the closet, and we'll cover it up," Nate said.

"Like she's not going to just lift the sheet?"

"What was that noise?" Natalie called up the staircase.

They both jumped, startled as they shoved on each other to answer her already.

"Nothing," Cassidy yelled, punching Nate back.

"That's it," Natalie said. "I'm coming up."

They both panicked, staring wide-eyed as Nate called out, "Don't come up. We're coming down."

They pointed at each other, whispering frantically as they tried to tuck in their clothes and pull themselves back together. Nate hit the overhead light when they noticed her shadow hovering across the steps below. They shoved each other, fighting over who'd have to go first.

"What about the sheet?" Nate whispered as Cassidy pushed him forward.

"Fuck the sheet, moron. Get down there and quit stalling," Cassidy whispered back as Nate attempted to force Cassidy down first by tickling him.

"Are you boys coming?" Natalie yelled. "It's not as if half of Hart's isn't out on the lawn waiting or anything."

"Stop being a pussy and get down there and face her," Nate whispered as Cassidy shoved him down the first two steps.

"I just took on my evil father!" Cassidy pointed out in a hushed tone.

Nate stopped wrestling with him for a second as if mulling over that fact. He started to shake his head as their arms started flailing again. "I'm way more afraid of my mother."

"What in the heck?" Natalie asked, shaking her head at them as she stood on the little landing. "You two stop that roughhousing this instant." She turned, muttering something about them being grown men.

"Way to go, doofus," Nate said, shaking his head as if it had all been his fault. He turned to make his way down the stairs as Cassidy stood there, mouth agape.

§ § §

Cassidy glanced down, quickly fastening a button he'd missed as he stepped out onto the back porch. He hummed along to "As Time Goes By," which the band played while he smoothed out the shirt. He grinned, hearing Marianne Abbott's loud-ass laugh somewhere off in the distance. He walked out into the courtyard, happy to see the party was once again full steam ahead. Everyone seemed to be having a good time, and Cassidy headed for the bar, thinking he had quite a bit of catching up to do.

He was desperate for another cocktail as he smiled and helloed his way through the crowd. Spencer and Ollie were at the buffet talking to Neil, who was nibbling off a plate. Natalie tapped Ollie on the shoulder, and he smiled at her as they gave each other a quick hug. Cassidy ordered a martini from the bartender. He couldn't spot Teddy or Ben, but assumed they were still down on the beach somewhere.

He thanked the bartender and took a sip from his martini. He turned to face the crowd and froze, seeing Nate standing about six feet away staring at him. Cassidy lowered his arm, smiling nervously. He'd become aware of the fact that for the second time now, the crowd had separated, leaving nothing standing between the two of them. He wanted to be irritated that they weren't a more selfish and motley crew of stubborn assholes who budged for no man. But he assumed they could all ascertain what he had—that whatever the hell Nate was up to, he meant business.

"Wha…what are you doing?" Cassidy whispered, feeling more uncomfortable than he had seeing Lionel standing back on the soil of Piper's Point.

"I know the timing here sucks, Cass," Nate began, nervously checking out all the people standing around watching. "But after seeing you take on Lionel like that, I don't think I can wait any longer."

"Try?" Cassidy asked, laughing until Nate gave him an unappreciative look. *Christ Almighty. So much for flying under the radar! Sadie would be so proud.*

Cassidy's face flushed with heat, and he twisted his neck slightly, feeling like his collar was choking him. "What can't wait, Nate? You're kinda freaking me out here."

"I need to prove to you that I'm not afraid, that I'm doing this in front of God and everyone, because"—Nate paused, as if searching for the right words—"you're worth risking my pride."

Cassidy's chest tightened as he realized where Nate was headed. He raised his martini glass, held the tooth-picked olives in place with a single finger, and downed the rest of its contents in one gulp. Absently, he reached back, attempting to find the top of the bar so he could rid himself of the glass.

"Aren't you *tired* of being on your own, Cassidy? Because I am."

Cassidy had been helpless, as if unable to turn away. *Or are you just too chicken?*

Nate placed his hands on his hips, and he glanced down at the ground, as if momentarily lost in his thoughts. "Hell, I don't even have the strength to fake being okay without you anymore. Do you?"

Cassidy opened his mouth to speak as someone removed the glass from his hand.

"How many years are we going to let pass us by before we get it right?" Nate asked, now looking him dead in the eyes as if attempting to discover the truth hiding behind them.

His persistent glare nearly stopped Cassidy's heart from beating.

"I've loved you since the time I understood what that actually meant."

Cassidy rubbed at his chest and shook his head, wishing Nate would stop.

"And I know you love me, damn it. It's written all over your face every time you look at me. It's as real as anything I've ever known before, and I've come to depend on seeing it." Nate took a few steps closer. "I've tried going it alone, tried being with others. But not being with you is the same as being alone. All there is for me is you, Cassidy."

"Wow, I…" Cassidy chewed on his lip, not really able to speak. No one other than Sadie had ever loved him like that—so strongly that it felt as though an eternity could pass and that love would still be there, waiting for him.

"I don't…know what else I can say. All I can do is promise to love you—be a hand to hold when things are good and a shoulder to lean on when life sucks. What else could you possibly want from another person? I'm *right* here, and I'm tired of patiently waiting for my moment to come along. I want it now. I want you now."

Cassidy could hear the whispering coming at him from all sides. Feeling a little conspicuous, he began to fidget, as even the music had lowered, playing softly in the background like the friggin' soundtrack in a movie. It was like roots had sprung up out of the dirt and wrapped around his feet and ankles, holding him to that spot, and the pleading in Nate's eyes was about to break him in two.

"Well, fuck!" Neil said, standing by the buffet as he glanced back and forth at the people standing next to him. "How the hell is anyone supposed to compete with that?"

Nate forced a smile, shaking his head as he mumbled something about really hating that guy. Cassidy started to laugh when he saw Spencer smacking Neil upside the head out of the corner of his eye.

Cassidy finally peeked over at Ollie, who'd been staring so intently throughout the entire speech he'd practically bored a hole into him, silently pleading for Cassidy to jump already. Natalie stood next to Ollie, watching and doing her best to show no emotion. But the clenched fists and the fact she was muttering the word *please* over and over were a bit of a giveaway.

"I fully admit it, here in front of all the good people of Hart's, that I've been practically paralyzed with fear. But the thought of you saying no has held me back for far too long." Nate took a few steps closer, drawing Cassidy's attention back to the man standing before him. "So you tell me, Cassidy Winters, what are you waiting for?"

Cassidy could feel his brow furrowing, and he forced himself to stop chewing on his lip, as he could now taste a tiny bit of blood. "I guess…I'm waiting for it to all mean something."

Nate took the final few steps required to close the distance between them. "It already *means* something. You can run from it, even hide yourself away from me if you decide to, but it won't change the fact that I love you—I have always loved you and most likely always will. That's what it means, Cass, and that's supposed to be enough."

"It is, huh?" Cassidy reached over, taking Nate's hand in his, examining it as he turned it around in his own hand. He ran the pad of his index finger over the tiny blond hairs along the side and peppering the fingers just above the knuckles. Examining the lines and wrinkles etched into the palm.

"Damn right," Nate said, the corners of his mouth beginning to curl up. "So what do you say?"

Cassidy felt it, that electricity crackling between the two of them. Standing there under Nate's persistent glare, it was as if he were naked and out on display, skin almost raw. "I'd say my world just got a little clearer."

Cassidy leaned in, pressing his lips to Nate's. He quietly sighed as Nate cocked his head slightly and they kissed. He could feel his entire body filling up with relief, love, happiness, and any other good thing he could possibly think of. Nate's other hand slid up his arm as he heard Henry Abbott gruffly declaring in a half-relieved, half-disgusted tone, "I never thought I'd ever be so goddamned happy to see two men kissing."

"Just go with it, Grandpa." Ollie sighed, grabbing on to Spencer's arm. "Embrace the homo lovin'."

Both Cassidy and Nate started laughing, holding on to each other, foreheads pressed together as their eyes met.

"How does it feel?" Nate asked.

"Like I'm back where I belong?"

Nate reached up, and ran the back of his hand over Cassidy's cheek before placing it on his shoulder. "Was that an answer or a question?"

Cassidy cringed slightly. "No…sorry, just…guess I'm not used to *being* rescued."

"I think maybe we rescued each other."

Cassidy grinned as that last tiny piece of the puzzle finally fell into place. "I really love the way you think."

§ § §

"Wow," Nate said.

Cassidy grinned as he kissed and sucked his way down Nate's neck and over his collarbone.

"I still can't believe you said yes."

Cassidy slid his hands under the white tuxedo shirt, sliding it over Nate's shoulders and allowing it to take its rightful place on the floor next to the jacket and bowtie. He let his hands glide over the soft skin and hard-muscled terrain that made up Nate's chest and torso. His brain practically buzzed from the sights and scent of the man standing before him. It was already after three in the morning, and despite being completely exhausted, Cassidy wasn't going to let another night pass without having his way with Nate. He'd waited as long as he could.

"You did say yes, right?" Nate asked, grabbing Cassidy by the arms and pushing him away. "I didn't misunderstand you?" Nate searched Cassidy's face, waiting for confirmation. He grinned, sighing with relief when Cassidy nodded.

Cassidy leaned back in, lightly kissing and sucking on Nate's chin. The newly grown stubble prickled across his tongue, and he moaned in frustration as Nate repeated his actions by pushing him away once again.

"You didn't say yes just so we could do it, right?" Nate asked, finally having processed the obvious lust on Cassidy's face.

Cassidy sighed, frustrated as his cock painfully pressed against the fabric of his shorts and trousers. "Apparently not, considering you still aren't allowing us to *do it*."

"Oh, right. Sorry, babe." Nate pulled Cassidy's head back down to his chest, to the spot where Cassidy assumed was Nate's rough estimate of where he'd left off before the last interruption.

Cassidy went right for a nipple, ready to toss aside his original plan, which included the slow and methodical suckling of every inch of Nate's body, for a more direct and hopefully lust-inducing "take me now, sailor" approach.

Nate groaned in a husky voice as Cassidy clamped down with his lips, licking and playfully pulling on the nipple with his teeth. Nate's hand went into Cassidy's hair, pressing his face firmly into his chest. "Fuck, that feels good."

Cassidy moaned his approval, grateful he finally had Nate's full attention. Cassidy pressed his palm over the obvious protrusion in Nate's pants. He slowly massaged him while getting more excited as he considered all the places Nate was going to put it.

"Shit, Cassidy," Nate said, taking in a deep breath.

Cassidy smiled and made his way over to Nate's other nipple.

"We haven't even talked about where we're going to live." Nate's arms flew up into the air before falling down to his sides. "How is this all going to work?"

Cassidy stood, seriously biting his lip, not wanting to say anything he might regret. "I don't know, Nate. And right now I really don't give a good goddamn."

Nate cringed, obviously realizing he'd done it again.

Cassidy took Nate's hand and placed it over his hard-on. "Right now, this is the only thing I care about, honey."

Nate grinned as he took over massaging Cassidy through the fabric.

"Seriously, babe," Cassidy warned. "If you're unable to control what comes out of your mouth, I'll be forced to put something in it that will."

"You're right," Nate said, nodding as he undid Cassidy's pants. "My bad. Very sorry."

Cassidy groaned up at the ceiling as if begging for divine intervention. "I can't believe I have to beg my new boyfriend to fuck me."

"I wouldn't say *have* to." Nate shoved his hand inside Cassidy's briefs and wrapped those thick fingers around his cock. "But a little begging would certainly be a turn-on."

Cassidy's eyes rolled back, and his knees quaked as Nate squeezed the head, smearing precum down the shaft. "Shut up and kiss me, Nate."

Nate covered Cassidy's mouth with his, and Cassidy grabbed on to his shoulder for balance. He was seriously beginning to lose control over his limbs while Nate continued to slow-jack him. Cassidy closed his eyes, feeling that electricity begin to build from the persistent assault of Nate's tongue in his mouth. He moaned in protest when Nate pulled his lips away, but was unable to articulate his frustration. His head fell back, mouth agape as Nate sped up the tempo and pressure with his hand.

"Boy, I just don't think I can keep all the questions I have at bay," Nate said.

"Baby, please." Cassidy whimpered, feeling as if his sanity was slipping away. He opened his eyes, momentarily confused until he glanced farther down to find Nate on his knees. He almost shot right there, watching Nate jack him off while staring up at him from the floor.

"Guess you'll have to make good on that threat"—Nate shrugged—"and think of something you can use to shut me up."

Cassidy grabbed Nate by the back of the head, forcing his

cock into Nate's mouth. As the wet heat enveloped his shaft, a smile slowly stretched across his face. "That'll do it."

§ § §

Cassidy could tell by the amount of light in the sky that the sun would be coming up soon. He lay on his stomach, propped up on his elbows, while biting down on his lip. Nate's hands pressed into the small of his back, pinning him to the bed. He slowly thrust his dick in and out of Cassidy, who took in a sharp breath each time Nate's pelvis pressed into his ass.

"Fuck, Cassidy," Nate said in a breathy whisper and gyrated his hips as if attempting to go deeper.

Cassidy watched a bead of sweat drip off the tip of his nose and onto the mattress. "Fuck yes, Nate…just like that." Nate grabbed a handful of Cassidy's hair and pulled his head back while he continued to pump into him. "So close, baby. I'm gonna come."

Nate smothered the sounds of Cassidy's orgasm with his mouth. Cassidy could feel the wet heat shooting out between his body and the damp sheet as Nate forced his tongue farther down Cassidy's throat. Once Cassidy's moans subsided, Nate released his mouth and let go of his head.

Nate spread Cassidy's ass farther apart as he picked up the pace. His fingers dug into the flesh of Cassidy's rounded cheeks as he slammed into him with renewed abandon. Cassidy's entire body jerked from the force. His face clenched from the slight discomfort. He knew he was going to be feeling the effects of having his ass reamed like this all day long, and he smiled.

Nate let out throaty groans. Cassidy looked back at him over his shoulder, chewing his lip and screwing up his face to make sure Nate could see the effect his cock had on him. That was pretty much all it took to push Nate over the edge as he whispered, "Cassidy," in between moans and curses. He collapsed on top of Cassidy, gasping for air as his body continued to twitch. They were both drenched, and Nate's skin was slick and slippery against his. Nate slipped his arms under Cassidy, sliding his hands across his chest and squeezing him from behind.

"That was amazing," Nate said between breaths.

"I may not be able to walk straight for a week."

Nate laughed a little. "I didn't hurt you, did I?"

"Not in any way I didn't thoroughly enjoy," Cassidy said, feeling immensely satisfied at having been fucked senseless, for lack of a better phrase. Every square inch of skin was on fire. Nate softened inside him, and Cassidy started to miss the sensation created by having that thick hardness invading his body.

Nate softly kissed his back between his shoulder blades. The warm air from his breath tickled Cassidy's skin. "Christ, Cassidy, I'm not sure I'll ever get enough of your body."

Cassidy grinned while stretching out his arms, which shook from the strain of holding up his torso while Nate had gloriously pummeled his ass. Nate ran his palm over Cassidy's side, gently kneading the skin. "You keep that up, and I'm going to get hard again."

"I don't give a shit." Nate laughed. "I'm willing to suffer the consequences."

"We've got to be at the lighthouse at eleven. Will we be forgoing sleep altogether?"

Nate sighed dramatically. Cassidy listened to the wet, sticky sound of their sweat-soaked bodies pulling apart as the cool rush of air moved over his back. He jiggled as a chill ran down his body while Nate rummaged around the room. He didn't want to move, knowing full well the sticky mess that lay in wait underneath him.

The bedroom door opened, and he finally groaned, getting up on his hands and knees. He cringed, then nodded, impressed by the amount he had blown, considering it hadn't been his first load.

"Damn, baby, now that's sexy," Nate said, coming back into the room.

Cassidy laughed, arching his back a little more. He glanced back as Nate closed the bedroom door and headed toward him with a damp washcloth.

"Fuck me, you little demon," Nate said, biting his fist. "You're an evil man."

Cassidy got up on his knees, pointing at the mattress. "Just look what you made me do, young man."

Nate covered Cassidy's mouth with his own as he absently went about cleaning him up. Cassidy moaned when Nate got a little too attentive wiping off his dick. "There I go again."

Cassidy grinned, feeling slutty in the best sense as he watched Nate trying to wipe off the sheet the best he could. Nate shoved him, knocking him over onto the bed.

"Hey," Cassidy said, rolling out of the bed. "At least no one has to lie in the wet spot."

"Where you going?" Nate asked, appearing to be all torn up.

"To take a piss." Cassidy held up a hand. "Toss me that cum rag, asshole."

Nate shook his head pretending to be disgusted as he chucked the rolled-up washcloth at him. "You're a class act, Winters."

Cassidy snagged the wet rag out of the air and went for the door. "I'm classy where it counts, stud."

"And *so* trashy where it counts," Nate mumbled.

Cassidy decided to let that one go as he sprinted naked across the landing toward the bathroom. He cleaned up a little bit more, since Nate managed to get distracted during his attempt. He was so exhausted that he decided to play it safe by sitting down to pee. His muscles were already achy, and he groaned while relieving himself, thinking the piss was nearly as incredible as the orgasms.

When he yanked open the bathroom door, he froze. Ollie stood in the doorway of the guest room. Cassidy quickly covered his bits and then felt silly, considering Ollie had seen them plenty in the past. Deciding to go with his instincts, he kept himself covered.

"Please tell me Fuckfest 2010 is coming to a close?" Ollie

asked, eyelids at half-mast.

"That loud, huh?" Cassidy tried a smile, but that only irritated Ollie more. "We're going to sleep now, yes."

Ollie spun dramatically, growling under his breath as he shut the door behind him.

Cassidy ran back into Nate's bedroom, thinking how nice a bedroom with a private bath would be. He walked to the bed, gazing at Nate's long naked body stretched out before his eyes. One would assume he'd already fallen asleep had it not been for the goofy grin plastered on his face. Nothing else about the man was goofy, though.

Nate reached out as if to say, *Get in bed already*, and Cassidy's cheeks flushed as he realized Nate was well aware he'd been staring. He quickly grabbed Dasie up off her little bed on the floor, despite her groans of protest. He climbed into bed, feeling slightly guilty for forcing Nate to move as they got under the covers. They went directly into spoon mode, Nate wrapping Cassidy up into his arms. Dasie stumbled like a little drunkard, still half-asleep as she waited patiently for them to settle before curling up into a ball against Cassidy's chest.

"Ollie read my ass in the hall for being too loud."

"Serves the little bastard right for last weekend," Nate said, reminding Cassidy, who instantly wished he'd thought of that before when it would have been useful.

Cassidy's eyes burned when he closed them from want of sleep. "Love you."

Nate nuzzled the back of his neck with his nose and chin, groaning a little. "Say that again, please."

All the muscles in Cassidy's body relaxed, like a slowly deflating tire. "I love you, Nate Sommers."

"Love you too," Nate whispered back.

Thank you, Sadie. Cassidy sighed, exhaling one last time before falling into the haze of sleep.

Chapter Twenty-two

As they drove up to the lighthouse, Cassidy was a little taken aback by the number of people who were already there. The lighthouse had undergone a renovation about five years ago, right around the time Sadie had passed, and it gleamed in the sunlight, stretching 117 feet up into the sky. It had been repainted in thick horizontal black-and-white stripes, and someone had taken the liberty of setting up a podium and microphone next to the base.

Cassidy hadn't really planned on saying much, but as they got out of the car, he heard people already talking about Sadie, reminiscing over one experience with her or another. It struck Cassidy, who'd spent so much of his adult life up until that point concentrating on school and his course load, as strangely comforting that one person had touched so many in such a tangible yet personal way. One of the things Cassidy loved about being a teacher was that concept. Helping to shape or influence all those lives in some small way. Something Sadie had managed in a big way, but on a smaller scale.

Cassidy imagined exactly how satisfying that must have been, to mean so much to so many. *Not bad at all, Sadie Hart. Not bad at all.*

Cassidy winked at Ben and Teddy, who squeezed his shoulder as they passed by, making their way into the crowd. Ollie and Spencer each gave him a quick hug, as did Neil, who hung on a little too long for Nate's taste.

"That'll do, pal," Nate said.

"Behave yourselves, boys," Natalie whispered as she took Cassidy by the arm and led him up to the front, where Max was waiting. The sun sat high up in the sky, and for once the usually strong breeze at the cliffs had dialed back and become almost tranquil. Cassidy could spot the old ferry making its way round the Point, packed with tourists as usual. There were larger ships off in the horizon, along with a stray sailboat or two. He breathed in the salty sea air, remembering the way Sadie used to, stepping outside with her cup of coffee every morning.

"That's rich Carolina air, baby boy. You breathe air like that for very long, and it becomes a part of you, makes you invincible like Mother Nature herself."

Cassidy shut his eyes tight for a moment, thinking she wasn't invincible after all, which still felt like a bit of a shock to him and everyone else on Hart's.

As different folks got up to speak, some brought up her outrageous and often shocking behavior, especially when taking into account the moral compass of the world during the first half of her life. They referred to her as a trailblazer, even though no one on the island ever acted as if they held that against her. Mainlanders would have wanted to crucify her, but the inhabitants of Hart's never did. One of the more elderly citizens got up, stating that her father, Jeremiah, often joked that Sadie was the son he never knew he had.

Sadie liked to say people were simply desensitized to it all, that she'd come out of the womb doing exactly what she liked regardless of who might have disapproved, and they just expected it of her.

Others spoke of her commitment to the island, saying Hart's had been the great love of her life. She had taken up the mantle of her father where the wealthier mainlanders were concerned. As they came in, trying to buy up property on the beach side of the island, wanting to build themselves lavish vacation homes, it had been Sadie's idea to change the city's building and zoning requirements, placing limitations on the size of homes allowed and creating an architectural and historical society that had to approve any new construction.

She made sure the locals maintained control over who and what moved into their neck of the woods. She didn't want any so-called blue-blooded robber barons moving in and taking control over her home, which was somewhat amusing considering her first choice of husband.

Cassidy finally decided to make his way up to the podium after everyone had finished and people began to look his way. He stumbled a little going up the carved stone steps, grateful he didn't drop Sadie, whom he'd been clinging to for dear life. He set the urn on the podium for safekeeping, as he no longer trusted his limbs to do their job.

He knew he hadn't her public-speaking skills, despite all the practice he'd received in the classroom. He wouldn't be talking about books in this instance, something he was painfully aware of as he bumbled once or twice as he tried to get started. Finally, he found the familiar faces of his friends and relaxed a little, despite noticing the crowd was much larger from his new vantage point.

He took a deep breath and reached into his jacket pocket, pulling out the little leather-bound, pocket-size copy of *The Tempest*—the one Samuel had given to Sadie. He clutched it in his hand, feeling the soothing texture of the soft leather.

"I know I've been away from Hart's and Piper's Point for a very long time—too long." Cassidy stopped, surveying the faces before him. "I kept telling myself you'd all be upset with me for being unable to free Sadie from my asshole of a father. That any grandson of the great Sadie Hart who couldn't manage to bring her back home probably wasn't much of a grandson after all—not one worthy of the name Hart, in any case. I certainly wouldn't have blamed you, since it was something that was constantly running through the back of my own mind."

Cassidy leaned into the podium a little for balance, resting his arms on the top as he stared down at the book in his hands for a moment.

"I can say that after having been back on the island for such a short amount of time, it's become glaringly obvious that I really stayed away because I couldn't bear to come back here without her. I didn't deserve to come back without Sadie, and I honestly doubt I could have taken any pleasure in being here when she could not."

Cassidy noticed the nodding heads that appeared to offer

their understanding, then glanced at the urn. "I finally did it, Sadie. I hope you can forgive me for having taken so long." He turned, staring out over the water, doing his level best to keep his wits about him.

"She loved this place and all of you so fiercely. I have no doubt she would have been capable of just about anything when it came to protecting her home. And for Sadie, Hart's was her home. Not just the Point or the shack, but the entire island. This place was part of her, like DNA—ingrained so deeply that I don't believe Lionel was truly ever able to separate the two. You could take her to the ends of the earth, and she'd still feel part of *this* place. I continue to feel her here—in the very air I breathe. Like her father before her, Sadie was Hart's."

Cassidy glanced over to Natalie, who clung to Nate on one side and Max on the other. "We all know she loved…a lot." Cassidy smiled, hearing a low, rolling laughter move over the crowd. "But it's this place where she met my grandfather, strolling down the beach one late summer's eve, that she loved most. I think he might be the only thing that ever came close to competing for her affection."

Cassidy's steely resolve was slipping a little, so he took a deep breath. Nate was squinting from the sun with that sexy half smile, and Cassidy managed to get hold of his senses. Natalie nodded and winked when their gazes met, as she stood arm in arm with Max.

"It makes losing her sting a little less to realize how much she meant to all of you. It was her wish to have her ashes spread here at Piper's Point. She would've been proud that so many of you came today." Cassidy grinned, doing his best to avoid direct eye contact by settling on foreheads, as he feared all it would take was one sad face to push him over the edge.

"She'd have gone on about making such a fuss. Lord knows she loved being the center of attention, but she'd have been proud. And I for one will never be able to thank you all enough for sharing this with me. I'm indebted to you and so grateful for your unconditional love and support. I don't think I could ever put into words what it means to me, but take it from someone who's lived only half his life on Hart's—cherish what you have here, for it's *everything* there is. If anyone out there doubts that for one second, all you have to do is leave it for a little while. You'll be surprised by how quickly it calls you back home."

Cassidy nodded, deciding he was finished, and slipped the little book back into his jacket pocket. He picked up the urn and smiled out over the crowd before heading back down the steps. As he made his way around the base of the lighthouse, he could hear the footsteps following.

Cassidy walked out to the edge of the cliff and unscrewed the lid on the urn. He dropped it onto the ground and took the base of the urn in both hands. He turned, twisting his body before spinning his torso, flinging his arms, and forcing the ashes to fly out, and shoot through the air.

He watched as the wind picked up, spinning and twisting the ashes as if giving form to them momentarily before they slowly drifted down the side of the cliff.

The tears were coming, and he didn't want to turn back and have anyone see him crying. The inhabitants of Hart's had seen enough of Cassidy Winters since he had returned to Piper's Point, and he didn't want to give any more of himself than he already had.

Nate came up from behind and wrapped his arms around Cassidy. "You okay?"

Cassidy nodded, sniffling a little, somewhat embarrassed for even Nate to see him that way. "I don't have anything left I can do for her."

"And what, you think you have to say good-bye?" Nate asked.

"Well, yeah, sort of. I mean, don't I?"

Nate laughed a little. "Hell no, Cass. She's going to live on inside you, certainly inside me. She brought you back to me. I don't ever intend to say my good-byes to Sadie Hart. I owe her entirely too much to ever do that."

Cassidy reached up, wiping his eyes as he smiled. Nate was right. He allowed his body to relax into his lover's, resting his head against Nate's shoulder. Cassidy stared into the sky. "I think we owe her everything."

Epilogue

Cassidy craned his neck out as Nate turned his black pickup onto the newly paved drive leading to Sadie's shack. The large moving truck had backed up to the front porch as the movers carried items across the metal ramp that stretched like a bridge from the back of the semi to the porch. Cassidy hadn't been back since Christmas, as he and Nate had spent their spring break in a little hut on a private beach in Acapulco. He hadn't seen the finished product now that the eight-month remodel of Piper's Point was near completion.

"I know the office is done, minus you putting your stamp on it by moving your own stuff in there," Nate said.

Dasie, who had been curled up on Cassidy's lap, sat up and stretched her legs. She yawned before hopping up and placing her paws on the window. Her nubby tail began to wiggle.

"She always remembers it," Nate said, patting Cassidy on the thigh.

"She's a smart little bug," Cassidy said as they got out of the truck.

Cassidy placed her on the grass so she could go about doing her business. He could see the side of the new two-story porch they'd had built on to the back of the house, and he began to get excited. It appeared to be already painted, and even though it took up some of the courtyard, he'd been willing to sacrifice it. He loved the ocean view from the back and had wanted to add a porch that rivaled the one on the front of the house in size and scale, taking full advantage of the Atlantic Ocean scenery.

"Come on," Nate said, holding out a hand, having scooped Dasie back up into his other arm. "Let's go take a look at our new home."

Cassidy chewed his lip, shaking out his hands, nervous about seeing it now that it was done. He'd been having weird-ass dreams of his ancestors coming after him for disturbing the property. It wasn't too big of a mystery as to why, considering he and Nate were still sifting through all the family documents. But they had stumbled across one or two things. Discovering that Jeremiah had an older brother, Caleb, who'd drowned when Jeremiah was just a baby had been the biggest revelation. It explained why Piper Hart had withdrawn from reality and retreated to the Point. Cassidy now wondered whether Sadie had been aware of it. Considering his own grandfather had been lost to the sea as well, it would reveal the connection Sadie had to the woman she'd never met.

But on top of the fear of raising any family demons, he was also a little scared they'd risked changing the place so much that it wouldn't feel like home anymore.

Nate rolled his eyes and grabbed Cassidy's hand, yanking him back out of his head while pulling Cassidy along behind him. He knew Nate was happy to be back full-time and was grateful to him for traveling as much as he had over the past nine months of Cassidy's final semester at UNC. It was important for him to honor the commitment he'd made to the university and complete the last two semesters teaching entry-level English courses.

Considering all he really needed to complete his PhD was to finish his dissertation, which in theory, he could do anywhere, they'd made a deal that Nate would come back to Chapel Hill with him for the school year, after which Cassidy would return to Hart's for good. He knew he'd have to go back and forth a few times a year to meet with his faculty advisors and to make use of the library, but other than that, he was free as a bird.

They hopped up the front steps, then paused as the movers came back out to the truck to get another load. Cassidy followed Nate inside, a little sick to his stomach seeing all the disorganization—boxes stacked up and miscellaneous pieces of furniture crammed into the largest living area. It felt like an impossible task—putting the shack back together again. They'd taken full opportunity of having the place empty to have the entire inside repainted and the wood floors redone. He did get a little excited, seeing the freshly painted walls and the bright white trim, and the floors were amazing—all shiny like new.

"Come see your office," Nate said, pulling Cassidy out of the doorway so the movers could get past.

They'd turned the formal parlor into an office for Cassidy and set it up with state-of-the-art camera and mixing equipment so Cassidy could teach contemporary fiction as part of the university's online courses. He was excited he'd still be able to teach, and depending on how well it worked out, he'd possibly be able to add another course or two in the future. He knew he'd never be tenured doing things this way, but that wasn't what was most important to him, at least not anymore.

"Hey, guys!" Teddy said, a little lost, all tangled up in wires.

Cassidy tried not to laugh as he walked over and gave Teddy a hug. "Helping Max out, I see."

"I'm doing the wiring myself!" Teddy nodded as if he'd tasked himself with this one thing, and nothing and no one was going to get in his way.

"Hey, boys," Max said, climbing down from the stepladder. "How do you like your bookshelves?"

"Max made them all by his lonesome for Samuel's books," Nate said, grinning like a proud son, as Max had been somewhat of a father figure to him over the years.

"They won't get any direct sunlight here." Max opened one of the framed glass doors. "And I installed gauges on the side here to measure temperature and humidity on the inside of the case."

"They're beautiful, Max. Thank you."

"Not very fancy, I know." Max shrugged. "But they'll be somewhat protected, and you'll be able to see them and take them out whenever you want."

"They're perfect," Cassidy said.

"Ben here?" Nate asked.

"Later." Teddy tied a clump of wires together. "He's going to try closing up early, if he can."

"Where's Mom?" Nate asked Max.

"Should be back any minute. She just ran home to clean up a bit and grab some sandwiches for us."

"And I'm starving too," Teddy added. "Oh, and Neil called."

Nate growled under his breath, muttering something.

Cassidy shook his head, wishing Nate would get over it already.

"I don't have to like everyone just because you do," Nate reminded him.

Cassidy rolled his eyes. "You're quite right."

Teddy dropped the cords and reached over, taking Dasie, who went about licking his chin. "Neil said to tell you *both* welcome home and that he'd be down for the fourth."

"That's great news," Nate said with a fake ass-smile that had Max rolling.

Teddy pointed up toward the ceiling. "Ollie sent you a package, Cass. I set it up in Sadie's room for now. Figured it'd be safe in there."

"What is it?" Cassidy asked as Nate shrugged.

"Go find out," Teddy said.

Cassidy shoved past Nate and made a run for the stairs. He knew it was slightly childish in nature, but he did love gifts, possibly even more now than he ever had when he was a kid.

"Slow down, you cracker," Nate called after him as Cassidy clomped up the steps, taking them two at a time.

Cassidy laughed like a fool, enjoying Nate getting on to him as much as the thrill of the unknown surprise that awaited him. "I win!" He jumped up and down when he reached the second-floor landing, and pointed at Nate, who calmly strode up the stairs. "Loser!"

Nate wrapped an arm around Cassidy's waist as he topped the last step. He leaned in and kissed Cassidy, who made several groans of approval as their tongues teased each other. Cassidy let out a low, lusty laugh when Nate's palm pressed into the front of his jeans, massaging his dick, which was quickly reacting to all the stimuli.

Nate smiled, breaking off the kiss. He was obviously pleased by the effect he was having on Cassidy as he forced him back into Sadie's bedroom. "I'm glad we're finally home. Feels like you are as well."

Cassidy started thrusting against Nate's hand. "Home is where I hump your hand."

Nate laughed. "That's lovely. I'll ask Mom to needlepoint that on some throw pillows for us."

Cassidy leaned in for soft peck, then glanced across the room. His mouth fell open as he let go of Nate. "Wow, it's…"

He crossed the room, amazed by the construction of the metal sculpture stretching up from the floor. A base shaped like a tree trunk with roots that splayed out for feet supported six long, winding metal arms snaking up into the air. Smaller branches came off those, and it appeared to be made of bronze. Cassidy gasped when a breeze swept through the room, setting into motion the round hoops that dangled from the metal arms, causing them to spin.

He almost cried when he realized the hoops were Sadie's gold bracelets. They made soft clinking noises as they bounced off one another until the breeze dissipated, and the spinning ceased.

"That's seriously cool," Nate said, hugging Cassidy from behind.

Cassidy shook his head. "I can't believe he…never let on in the least."

Nate reached out and ripped off a card hanging by a string. He read the card aloud. "Family tree."

They both noticed the contractor's pickup pulling in the drive.

Nate stepped out onto the balcony and waved down, making sure he saw them. "We need to go find out when that jackass is going to be done."

Cassidy frowned when Nate took him by the arm and led him away from his tree.

§ § §

They came out the back door and crossed the courtyard. Cassidy's mouth fell open after he turned to take in the new addition to the back of the house. The porch was beautifully constructed, and if it weren't for the men in the process of painting it, he'd have thought it had always been there. It was an exact replica of the front with the exception of being two stories tall with a balcony accessible from the attic, which they'd turned into a master suite with their very own private bath.

The contractor, Tom Bailey, walked up, folded his arms, and smiled up at the porch. "She's a beaut, isn't she?"

Cassidy squinted as he examined the unpainted wood, and Natalie ran out the back door with Max trailing behind her. Cassidy pointed up at the sections of wood that were noticeably brand-new. "I thought you were using salvaged wood to build the porch."

Nate started laughing. "I told you to have it painted before he saw it, Tom."

Cassidy smirked, not appreciating Nate's comment. He'd have laid into him but good, had Natalie not saved his ass by strangling him in a hug.

"We did the best we could, Cassidy," Tom said, tossing his arms into the air as if he were being persecuted. "You wanted an *exact match* to the front. Do you have any idea how difficult it is to find spindles to match a hundred-year-old house?"

"Looks to me like you found some," Cassidy said, causing Tom to cover his face in his hands.

"Lord deliver me," Tom said.

Nate and Max held back laughs as Natalie ignored all the drama by hugging and kissing on Cassidy now that she'd finished with Nate.

"You boys stop this arguing at once," Natalie said, beaming, which did little to aid the severity of her threat. "I'm so happy you're back home where you belong."

"I'd be happier if you and your pack of thugs were finished and gone, Tom," Nate said, winking at Cassidy.

Tom rolled his eyes. "You can't rush perfection, guys. And I'll not have Sadie Hart coming back from the grave to haunt my ass for cutting corners on Piper's Point."

Max mumbled something about bullshit under his breath, which garnered him a smack from Natalie for the foul language.

"So how long are we talking here, Tom?" Nate asked.

"A few days at the most," Tom answered, nodding confidently.

Nate shot an unmistakable expression that screamed bullshit, which somehow managed to slide past Natalie's crass-o-meter. "You said that two weeks ago when I was here."

"I don't know what to tell you, Nate." Obviously the least of Tom's worries. "You know how things are on Hart's. It takes everything longer to complete here. Always has, always will."

Cassidy nodded. "I understand, Tom. I really do. I just hope you're done by the weekend."

Nate shook his head, obviously confused.

"I'll do my best, Cassidy, and thanks for being more understanding than your, uh… Well, than Nate here." Tom shifted back and forth from one foot to the other having inadvertently stumbled into a topic he obviously wasn't too comfy with.

"Not a problem in the least," Cassidy said, folding his arms. His gaze went from the men on ladders painting away back down to Tom. "I'm sure none of our houseguests this weekend will mind either."

Tom glanced at Nate. "You never mentioned having guests so soon."

"Well, they're friends of mine, Tom, so not really guests, per se. Maybe ten to twelve gay men, running around all oiled up in their little short-shorts." Cassidy started wiggling his hips and shaking his shoulders, gyrating in place as he did his impersonation of the thumpin' bass track of the club music. "Dancing around to the techno music…and getting all excited by you and your guys. They do love big, beefy eye candy. I can see them all now." Cassidy pointed out to the courtyard. "Lounging in chairs, sipping cocktails while whistling and catcalling things like, *Oh yeah, daddy, stroke that.*"

"All right, all right," Tom said, holding up his hands and scrunching up his face, appearing to get a little queasy. "You don't need to go getting all graphic. I catch your meaning. We'll be done before the weekend. I swear it."

Cassidy laughed as one of the older guys up on the ladder, who'd obviously been able to overhear, dropped his paintbrush and scrambled down to get it. He also took note of the younger guy on the second level of the porch who stared off into space as he chewed seductively on his lip, as if not minding that whole scenario all that much.

Tom walked back toward the garage, and Nate nodded, more than a little impressed. "I'm beginning to think I should have let you handle the remodel, babe."

"Ten bucks says the guy up on the porch finds an excuse to stop by this weekend," Cassidy said out the side of mouth.

"Cassidy Winters!" Natalie scolded as Nate started to snicker. "Idle gossip will not be tolerated, young man." She smacked Nate's hand away from Cassidy's ass. "Neither are idle hands, dear."

Nate turned three shades of red as Cassidy lost it. His ass had become the favorite resting place for Nate's hand over the past months, to the point neither one of them took much notice anymore whenever it found its way there.

"Maybe Mr. Painter Boy would make a nice new friend for Neil?" Cassidy whispered excitedly.

Max laughed as Natalie threw her hands up in the air in disbelief while Nate snarled up his lip at the mention of Neil's name.

"One could only hope," Nate muttered, glancing back up the porch to take a closer look.

Cassidy noticed Tom leaning against the garage door laughing and yakking away on his cell phone. Cassidy started doing the club music and dancing in place again. Tom got all frazzled, unable to decide which direction to run in order to escape Cassidy's version of evil charades.

Max chuckled as he turned to head back into the house. "You remind me more and more of your grandma every time I see you, Cassidy. A wicked lady, that one."

Nate, Cassidy, and Natalie all simultaneously said, "Don't call her Grandma!"

About the Author

ETHAN DAY lives in Missouri. He is currently single but always looking for that special someone that makes his heart skip a beat. He was the youngest of four children and the only boy.

After a few stints in college, he eventually signed up for a Creative Writing course. He took the class because there were no tests. For once his scholastic laziness paid off, and he found an outlet for all the fantasies running amuck in his head. It was love at first write, and he's been doing it off and on ever since.

Visit Ethan on the internet at:

http://www.ethanday.com

http://groups.yahoo.com/group/EthanDay/

CPSIA information can be obtained at www.ICGtesting.com
Printed in the USA
LVOW062154090413

328373LV00001B/11/P

9 781608 206667